SHIRTALOON

HE WHO FIGHTS
~ WITH ~
MONSTERS
BOOK TEN

www.aethonbooks.com

HE WHO FIGHTS WITH MONSTERS TEN
©2023 SHIRTALOON

Aethon Books
www.aethonbooks.com

Print and eBook design and formatting by Josh Hayes. Cover art by Harry Bui.

Published by Aethon Books LLC.

Aethon Books is not responsible for websites (or their content) that are not owned by the publisher.

This book is a work of fiction. Names, characters, places, and incidents are the product of the author's imagination or are used fictitiously. Any resemblance to actual events, locales, or persons, living or dead is coincidental.

ALSO IN SERIES

HE WHO FIGHTS WITH MONSTERS

Check out the entire series! (tap or scan)

Want to discuss our books with other readers and even the authors like Shirtaloon, Zogarth, Cale Plamann, Noret Flood (Puddles4263) and so many more?

Join our Discord server today and be a part of the Aethon community.

AUTHOR'S NOTE

Ten books in, Jason's magical abilities have reached levels of complexity that I really should have thought through better when I was first devising the magic system. To help those looking to figure out what some specific power or affliction does, there are two appendices following the final chapter offering a list of Jason's essence abilities. Note that the list was written for brevity and lacks or consolidates many specific details. It is intended as a reminder that people can reference, not a comprehensive or thorough record of the magic system.

BOOK NINE SUMMARY

The monster surge and the Builder invasion both came to an end, with Jason Asano negotiating the departure of the Builder and his forces. The Storm Kingdom suffered, Jason and his companions just a few of the many who helped weather the tribulations. The world began the process of recovery as the old threats departed, leaving devastation in their wake, but new threats had already arisen. Angel-like beings of arrogance and power, the messengers used the distraction of old enemies to stage an invasion of their own.

After recovering from his adventures in the Storm Kingdom, Jason Asano and his team formed a convoy planning to slowly span the globe. At the same time, Jason was looking to complete his long-unfinished task of forging a link between his new world and his old one, saving the Earth in the process.

With the intention of stealing messenger magic that would help him reach his goal, Jason's convoy of adventurers travelled to the elf city of Yaresh. The city was in conflict with messengers in the area and Jason quickly came in conflict with the angelic imperialists and their agents. Jason and the messengers were confronted with their similarities, which didn't sit well with either side.

Conflict with the messengers escalated as they bred horrifying worms that killed people from the inside and puppeteered their corpses. When an infestation was found in the local towns and villages, the conflict escalated into a massive invasion of Yaresh by the messengers and an army of monsters. Jason and his team participated, standing with the defenders.

Over the course of the battle, Jason drew the negative attention of both sides. He incited the messengers, most of which tried to kill him in a frenzy, yet some surrendered to him for mysterious reasons. The most powerful messenger moved to strike him down yet fell dead at the adventurer's feet, confusing Jason as much as anyone, including the diamond-rank adventurers who wanted answers he didn't have.

At the climax, several of Jason's companions were caught up in deadly duels, including Jason himself. Faced with a young messenger, he realised he was fighting what amounted to an indoctrinated teenager and took drastic measures to capture, rather than kill her. The cruelty of what that required left him wondering if the greater mercy would have been letting her die.

The messengers were ultimately driven back, but while most of the population was saved, the city itself was left in ruins. The messengers were beaten back but not eliminated while the adventurers and the people of Yaresh were left with the fallout of the catastrophic battle. Politically, logistically and militarily, the days ahead would be filled with challenges.

1

AFTERMATH

MESSENGERS DIDN'T DREAM. THEY UNDERSTOOD THE CONCEPT, BUT IT wasn't something they experienced for themselves. Dreaming was a trait of lesser beings. Of the weak. This was what the messenger Tera Jun Casta had been told her entire life, which left her confused when she roused from dreams of her own. She didn't remember them as they skittered away like spectres in the night, but it felt like she had been living them for an extremely long time.

She opened her eyes to an unfamiliar ceiling. It was dark crystal containing swirling sparks of gold, silver and blue, as if filled with viscous fluid and expensive glitter. She was in a bed made of fluffy white cloud-material, which was comfortable with her wings. Her armour, torn to shreds last she had seen it, was now whole.

There was no sign at all, in fact, of the fight that was the last thing she remembered. Her armour had been repaired and the injuries were gone, as was the blood they had painted her with. What remained was the bitter sense of defeat. It was not that she lost to Asano that troubled her but that she had accepted the loss before the fight was over. Her thoughts had turned, in desperation, to using the people in the bunker as hostages. The soul barriers around her and Asano would have killed any normal-rankers they touched.

Thinking of the power she had used on Asano spiked her confusion.

Once enacted, either one or both of them should have died; both surviving was impossible. Yet here she was, and the fact of Asano's survival was obvious. She could sense his singular will dominating her surroundings, feel the aura that pervaded every scrap of matter. She was in an astral kingdom; his astral kingdom. This was only her second time being inside one; there was no mistaking it, or who it belonged to.

Jason Asano. Her instincts screamed his name, her certainty going beyond just recognising the aura. She remembered surrendering not just the fight but her very soul; an infinite and eternal defeat. She felt an unsettlingly intimate familiarity with him that she could not explain. Mercy, shame, indignation and rage all stormed within her, a mess that would take time to untangle.

She had no idea how the fight had ended. She had flashes that didn't make any sense, as fleeting as the remnants of her newfound dreams. She needed more information and sat up, shifting her legs off the bed. The cloud she was lying on accommodated her, transforming into a chair in response to her desire. She remained seated for the moment and looked around.

The room she was in was large, more a luxurious suite than the cell she would have expected. The furniture an eclectic mishmash of elegant wood, stone, crystal and plush cloud-material. There was a low set of drawers against the wall, atop which was what looked to be an array of baked goods on plates under glass display domes. The windows showed gardens outside, sunlight shining on blood-red flowers on thorny green stems.

There were two ways out: doorways with no doors, only veils of mist. One was in the wall directly in front of her while the other was a circle in the ceiling in the style of messenger architecture. It was odd to see in the realm of her enemy.

The room did not seem at all designed to keep her contained, but she realised it didn't need to. There was no escaping an astral kingdom; you stayed until the king allowed you to leave. Perhaps there was some leeway, given that Asano was only silver rank, but she doubted it. Even a gold-rank fish was not mightier than the silver-rank ocean in which it swam.

How she ended up in an astral kingdom without consenting to pass through the portal she did not know. She had an unsettling feeling that it was related to her surrendering her soul to Asano. She felt different, unsure how long she had been unconscious. She was about to assess herself with her magical senses when a voice came down through the door in the ceiling.

"Tera Jun Casta," the male voice called out. "I am told that you are awake."

It wasn't Asano's voice, but she thought she recognised it. Her senses failed to escape the walls to probe further.

"Who are you?" she called out.

"Marek Nior Vargas."

The commander. Tera was only a loose addition to the forces Marek commanded in the raid on Yaresh, and not one that would garner the commander's individual attention. Messengers unable to advance beyond silver were to be pitied, with only everything in the cosmos other than messengers being more lowly.

Tera realised that she was caught up in her thoughts and had not responded.

"Commander," she said, looking up at the misty ceiling. Through it, she could only see a winged silhouette. "I do not know how to let you in. Or if I can get out."

"Do I have permission to enter?" he asked, startling her.

"You don't have to ask, Commander."

He descended through the veil slowly as she stood up, hovering just off the floor. She noted that he didn't remain floating, his feet settling on the floor. He was wearing light armour like her and stood slightly shorter, especially as she was floating in the air. His wings with their subdued plumage folded tight on his back as he looked at her with eyes as sharp as his handsome features.

She knew him only by reputation and what she had seen in battle herself. In both cases, protectiveness was his most well-known trait, followed by careful tactics and conservative strategies, contrasted with moments of bold action. Many counted him as an ideal messenger, while others considered him fearful and weak. Potentially, even an Unorthodoxy sympathiser.

During the raid, Tera had seen for herself as Marek prioritised keeping not just his own troop safe but all the messengers under his command as well. She felt the sting of shame as she remembered throwing away his efforts and charging after Asano in a reckless fervour. If he was here with her, he most likely had placed himself in danger to protect the many who, like her, had disobeyed his orders.

"You were captured as well," she said sadly. To her surprise, an awkward smile crossed his face that shattered the image of stern commander to show the man behind it.

"It's complicated," he said. "A lot has happened, and I imagine your memories of the battle's end are scattered at best."

Tera nodded.

"I have many questions, Commander, but there is no need for you to —"

"Waking up in this place must be disorienting, and there is much you have yet to understand. Even about yourself, I see. Come fly with me, Tera Jun Casta."

Without waiting for a response, he floated up through the misty door. As she pushed more strength into her aura to lift herself, she realised her aura had undergone a permanent change. Startled, she dropped back to the floor.

"Do not rush," Marek's voice came from outside. "You have only just awoken from a lengthy slumber to find everything is different. Everything. We have an abundance of time, so take as much of it as you need."

"I cannot make you wait on me, Commander."

"Yes, you can. Look inward before you look out, Tera Jun Casta. That's an order. I will be here for your questions when you are done."

"Jason," Humphrey said, "the longer you refuse to meet with the diamond-rankers and the Adventure Society, the worse they are going to make things for you once you do finally leave your soul realm."

They were in the gardens of Jason's soul realm, watching Rufus and Sophie spar with a half-dozen copies of Jason. More copies of Jason were duelling one another, floating in cross-legged meditation, reading or going through dance-like weapon forms.

Jason could have easily conjured luxurious cloud chairs, but they were using cheap Earth-style folding camp seats. It was an odd match with Humphrey's well-tailored attire but fit perfectly with Jason's loud shirt and tan shorts. They had drinks on the table between them, colourful concoctions of juice and alcohol in tall glasses.

"Humphrey, the diamond-rankers broke into my cloud palace. Our home. They rummaged about for the things they wanted and left. They may have only taken Taika's imprisoned messenger, but if any of us had been there instead of in here, they would have taken us as well. Most likely Sophie's mother too, if it had come to that. And the cloud palace is a hospital right now. They were highly disruptive."

"I'm not denying that they were in the wrong, Jason," Humphrey told him. "I'm saying they have the power. They're diamond-rankers."

"You know I've faced down a lot worse than that. With you right beside me for some of it."

"I know. They should never have barged into the cloud palace, and I know how you react to authority figures forcing you into things. But I'm asking you to think back on what that approach has gotten you over the years, and what it will get us in the years to come. Yes, there will come a time when we're powerful enough to make the Adventure Society leave us alone, but I don't want them giving us problems every day until then. They might be an annoying ally, but they would be a terrible enemy. They're like you in that way."

Jason nodded.

"I still let my pride get the better of me, don't I?" he asked. "But I'm going back out today. It would appear the Adventure Society here have taken the same approach as the Rimaros branch did to my seclusion. They found an ambassador."

"They used Rick in Rimaros," Humphrey said. "Who are they sending to talk to you here?"

Jason's eyes sparkled.

"Rick again. The locals lack imagination, it would seem."

"Rick went north after the monster surge."

"And I sensed them portal him in less than an hour ago."

Humphrey let out a sigh.

Marek waited in the shadow of the massive dome containing the cocoon that loomed taller than most of the buildings in Asano's astral kingdom. In the weeks he had been present, the cocoon building had, like much of the territory, undergone large changes. Sometimes he noticed them and others he didn't perceive them at all, as if time had skipped, and suddenly, a building was gone. Asano's realm was in a constant state of flux, with only a handful of places remaining static. The pagoda tower at the centre was one, as was the forge where the leonid, Gary, practised his weapon-smithing.

Marek had given the lion man a wide berth, as he was not friendly to the messengers. He had killed no small number of Marek's kind during the raid and seen them kill civilians in turn. One of Marek's people had let pride rule his head and accosted the leonid; he only survived because Asano all but rebuilt the messenger's body from scratch.

Marek's most unruly subordinate was Mari Gah Rahnd, and Marek tried to find her before she went after the leonid for fun. Asano, inevitably, found her first, delivering her to Marek to look after. A few days later, Asano gave her mouth, arms, legs and wings back to her.

Asano seemed to have an astral king's instinctive understanding of how messengers worked. The punishment he delivered was exactly what Marek would expect from any astral king. Asano could remould their bodies despite not being one of them, or even a complete astral king. He lacked the third part of the astral throne, astral gate and soul forge trifecta, an absence that got Marek thinking.

The astral king Marek had served until recently was Vesta Carmis Zell. Marek did not know her exact agenda, but he could make certain guesses. Zell was known for her fascination with soul engineering. It was an uncommon practice, as tools were almost impossible to find and raw materials even more so. She and her chief agent, Jes Fin Kaal, were after something deep underground, and a soul forge would explain the absurd resources expended to obtain it. Marek was no soul engineer himself, but he knew that a second forge was deeply coveted by astral kings who indulged in soul engineering.

Marek shook his head, clearing out his latest postulation. With little to do for weeks, his mind was running through one possibility after another. Without the power to leave, he neither had nor could obtain the evidence to confirm or disconfirm his suspicions. He was better off planning what he and his people would do once Asano let them go. If he let them go. He was confident now that Asano wouldn't just hand them over to the Adventure Society, although that wasn't the same as releasing them.

Marek watched as the cocoon dome rose from the ground, revealing itself as a giant sphere that floated away through the sky. He wondered how much the shifting nature of the space was due to Asano's proclivities and how much was instability from his lack of a soul forge.

He was still watching it when Tera rose through the misty door, her expression a mix of concern, confusion and rage.

Rick and his team were sobered by the aftermath of the Battle of Yaresh as they flew over the city. They were riding in an open-top flying carriage as blackened flatland passed under them. Magic could rebuild destroyed infrastructure with startling speed, so the city being little more than rubble two full weeks after the battle told a bleak story. Only tiny pockets of reconstruction were scattered across the city, the beginnings of what would come next. Given that Yaresh had been a city where most of the buildings had been made through the shaping of living trees, it would be a lengthy process of recovery. A few trees were already starting to grow in the bleak landscape, but there was such a long way to go.

In most places, recovery meant clearing enough room for whole districts of temporary housing, be it tents or rough buildings shaped with hasty magic. It was simple survival in the wasteland that had once been their homes. The idea of rebuilding was still a distant dream.

"Most of the population is still living in the bunkers," Vidal Ladiv explained. He was the Adventure Society's official liaison with Team Biscuit, Jason's team, although he always seemed to find himself conveniently forgotten. Attached to the team in Rimaros, he had been 'accidentally' left behind in no fewer than three towns on the journey to Yaresh.

During the raid, Vidal had not been fighting with Jason and the others but evacuating people from the riverside districts. His water essence and expertise in administration and logistics had made him a valuable asset there, although he couldn't help but feel fobbed-off again.

The local Adventure Society had not been happy with Vidal's inability to get Jason to fall in line, although the letter he showed the local branch director had helped. Signed by both the Rimaros branch director and Soramir Rimaros himself, it detailed some of the difficulties in dealing with Jason Asano and suggestions against provoking him.

It didn't entirely surprise Vidal when the diamond-rankers ignored this and smashed their way into Asano's cloud palace, coming out with only one messenger and a raft of complaints. With the church of the Healer and other organisations using the building as a hospital at the time, this inevitably led to formal protests to the Adventure Society about diamond-rankers causing chaos.

Rick and his team rode through the air in silence, as they looked out in dismay. The area that had once been a giant parking lot for adventurers' vehicles was one of the more intact zones in the city, behind only key infrastructure that had secondary defence systems. Those additional defences were how the Adventure Society and Magic Society campuses, along with the ducal palace, all remained essentially intact.

The area with the adventurer vehicles did have one bombed-out area, where the original refugee camp had been. People evacuated from towns to the south overrun by world-taker worms had stayed there until the attack on the city, at which point they had bunkered down in Jason and Emir's cloud palaces. Now that area was once again covered in tents. As for the vehicles themselves, many showed scars from the messenger raids, but the district had held out, fending off the messengers.

"We're confident that the diamond-rankers won't go barging into the cloud palace again, the moment you leave your soul realm?" Neil asked Jason.

They were standing in a courtyard near the central pagoda of Jason's soul realm. Along with Humphrey and Sophie, the four were the greeting party for Rick and his team.

"They won't," Humphrey said. "Even if diamond-rankers don't need to care what people think of them, they still do. They operate in this city, and while they can endure a bad reputation, it would complicate things for them. Not only is going after a silver-ranker a second time heavy-handed, it tells people they didn't get what they wanted the first time. They can't afford to have people think I got the better of them."

"Do they really care what people think?"

"They choose to be more public figures than most diamond-rankers, so they have to. Going in again makes them look tyrannical and weak at the same time."

Jason opened a portal to the world outside and they stepped through.

Jason's cloud palace was buzzing with activity as the carriage set down on the roof. The roof itself was clear but looking over the roof's edge, they saw people filing in and out of the building. Once the group took the elevating platform inside, they found a hubbub of chaos. It was barely kept in order by a panoply of clergy and Asano's spooky one-eyed avatars that looked like alien creatures draped in void cloaks.

"Asano's cloud palace was used as a hospital after the attack and still is," Vidal explained to Rick's party as they shouldered their way through a crowded hallway. "But now it serves more as a processing centre. We make sure that everyone gets a hot shower and a hot meal before going to their assigned accommodation, which is usually just a tent or a stone-shaped building or the like. We also make sure that no unpleasant surprises have been left behind inside people. We were in the midst of dealing with body-controlling parasites when the attack began."

Vidal led them to a lounge room that was small for their group, but they had seen the premium on space in the building. Shortly after they arrived, a portal opened in the corner to admit Jason, Humphrey, Sophie and Neil.

Greetings were made all around. Neil and Dustin from Rick's team were childhood friends. Phoebe had been instrumental in Sophie's initial training back in Greenstone, both of them being pugilists. She hadn't seen Jason since Greenstone, as she'd been occupied when Rick's team travelled to Rimaros. As for Rick himself, he was looking around as if something was missing.

"What's wrong?" Jason asked him.

"Where's the small army of beautiful women?"

"What are you talking about?" Jason asked as Rick's team member and girlfriend Hannah thumped him on the bicep.

"It's a little strange not seeing you surrounded by gorgeous women."

"Well, there's Sophie, Phoebe and the lovely Adeah twins," Jason said. "Is that not enough for you?"

"Yes, Rickard," asked Rick's girlfriend, Hannah Adeah. "Is that not enough?"

"I'm just saying that there's usually a gaggle of women I've never seen before when I see you."

Jason shook his head.

"Rick, you need to get over this. I'm not always…"

Jason trailed off, turning to frown at the door.

"Yeah, I have to pop out real quick," he said as Shade rose from his shadow for Jason to step into and vanish.

"The diamond-rankers again?" Humphrey guessed.

"No," Neil said, walking over to the door. "He'd have gone back to his soul realm if it was that."

There was a knock at the door and Neil opened it. On the other side was a priestess in the full robes of the Church of Fertility, with a cluster of young female acolytes behind her.

"Sorry," she said. "My god told me that Jason Asano was in here."

2

HARDER THAN THEY HAVE TO BE

"HE SAID NO," TAIKA TOLD THE FERTILITY PRIESTESS FIRMLY.

"Mr Asano represents an unusual confluence of factors that could potentially be used to produce powerful forces that can be deployed against messengers and similar threats."

"I'm pretty sure you shouldn't be trying to breed super-soldier armies. That sounds like some creepy eugenics stuff."

The priestess gave Taika's mountainous body an assessing look up and down.

"You're an outworlder as well, aren't you?"

"I have to go," Taika said and vanished through a mist door, leaving the priestess alone with her acolytes.

"Uh, Priestess Hennith?"

"Yes, Acolyte Fennick?"

"I thought we were just here to deliver food."

"These are difficult and busy times, acolyte. It pays to grab any opportunity you can get."

"Is adding this man Asano to the breeding program really an opportunity worth chasing?"

"While the goddess does want samples, it's not of any great importance, no. But the goddess wants the man's goodwill, which we apparently fostered by arriving exactly when and where we did. I have no idea how that works, but that's why we have faith, Fennick dear."

"Why would the goddess want the goodwill of some mortal?" another acolyte asked. "And even if she does, why not just show him even the barest favour? What mortal would not be honoured by that?"

"I think we may need to get you out of the temple more often, Acolyte Cassa."

The image of Marek and Tera sitting on the roof of a building was not the standard to which messengers typically held themselves. Messengers conceived themselves as higher beings, their tendency to float over the ground instead of walking on it a message that the ground-dwellers were both literally and figuratively below them.

Messengers also favoured diaphanous clothing that lent them an ethereal air, while Marek and Tera wore what looked like simple leather armour. In reality, it was a magical synthetic with the physical integrity to endure through most battles of the material's rank. Only after an extended battle with Jason had Tera's armour turned ragged, although she found it repaired when she awoke. Asano could easily do so here, and her cloud bed had kept her clean during what she now knew to be weeks of sleep.

Tera's senses were still exploring her body and soul, coming to grips with the changes. Asano had reached into her soul and changed things, and had not done so expertly. His most egregious had been removing the brand of her astral king master, Vesta Carmis Zell. Marek Nior Vargas might call it freedom, but Asano had literally ripped the faith from her soul.

Marek, sitting beside her, looked on with concern while not knowing what to say. Freedom from astral kings was what he had always hoped for and never believed possible. He had spent far longer than Tera's entire life working his way free of the conditioning every messenger was put through. He'd risked everything on the chance that Asano could give him that freedom.

He knew that Tera viewed the same thing very differently. If nothing else, Asano had forced it on her in an act of spiritual violence Marek struggled to even imagine. The indoctrination new messengers went through not only still had a hold on Tera but was the foundation of her identity. She had always lived with the understanding that she could never aspire to be more than the silver-ranker she was born as. At most, she could have hoped to find an astral king that would let her become a Voice of the Will, becoming a puppet in return for power.

Now, that limit was gone. The soul mark of the astral king that held her loyalty was gone too. For Marek, those absences were everything he ever wanted, not just for himself but for his people. But what he saw as freedom, she saw as everything she knew and everything she was being taken away. Added to the lingering trauma of how Asano forced her to open her soul, she was helplessly adrift.

It was Marek's intention to bring that same freedom to all the messengers, but Tera had shown him that it was even more complicated than he had imagined. He hoped that, with time and care, she would realise how rare and precious freedom was for their kind. But he recognised that the indoctrination was strong. Left to their own devices, many messengers given freedom would immediately surrender it.

It wasn't a simple path that Marek had ahead of him, even assuming that Asano let them go. He had a good sense of the man, having lived inside his soul for weeks, but what he had learned left him uncertain. While Asano was clearly trying to step back into the light, many dark corners remained in his astral kingdom. His thoughts were disturbed when Tera finally spoke.

"What…"

Her voice was hesitant after sitting in silence for so long.

"What do I do?" she asked, as much of the cosmos as of Marek. "Who even am I, now?"

"That's for you to decide," Marek told her. "I know that's going to be hard when you've spent your entire life having other people tell you exactly who and what you are."

She turned to look at him, her eyes hollow and lost.

"He did to you what he did to me, didn't he?"

"Yes."

"Why aren't you as lost as I am?"

"Because I long ago came to desire what Asano has given us. I just didn't realise it was possible. You were forced into this, but I came looking for it."

Her eyes narrowed, her deference replaced with suspicion.

"You're part of the Unorthodoxy, aren't you?"

"Yes," he admitted.

"Traitor," she accused.

"Yes," he admitted freely. "And you will be marked the same, should the astral kings find out what we are."

"And what are we?"

"Free. Free of their influence and free of their limitations. They cannot tolerate even the possibility of that or everything about our society will crumble. You were not restricted to silver rank by some inherent defect, Tera Jun Casta. Vesta Carmis Zell was using you as a power source, sapping away your potential."

"You think I haven't been warned about Unorthodoxy lies?"

"I'm quite certain you have, but you don't have to take my word for it. The truth is inside your own soul, and all you have to do is look. However much you might deny it, you are the proof."

"Asano forced me to let him into my soul."

"Yes."

"He poisoned me. His very existence is heresy."

"Look at your word choice, Tera Jun Casta. That is a word of the gods, and we both know what you have been taught about them. Yet, our people speak of faith in our astral kings. One of the many contradictions that led me to a path that, like it or not, you and I now walk together."

Tera floated off the roof, hovering in the air as she looked down at Marek.

"You can try all the verbal tricks you want, traitor. Once I find my way out of here, I'll return to the astral king and reveal your betrayal."

There was no way out and they both knew it. Marek sighed as Tera flew off into the air.

Rick and Jason's teams were crowded into a lounge room.

"The Adventure Society has instructed me—again—to request your cooperation," Rick said to Jason.

"Which is exactly what we're doing," Humphrey responded in Jason's place. "Beyond providing some facilities, however, there is little we have to contribute. We could take normal contracts. The monsters don't stop coming just because we've gone to war with the messengers. But there are diamond-rankers out there, hunting Jason down. As team leader, I cannot, in good conscience, advocate that he expose himself to that."

"The society has assured me that it won't happen again."

"The society can't control the diamond-rankers any more than it can me," Jason said. "If someone that powerful wants something, who can stop them?"

"You, apparently," Phoebe told him. "They are extremely eager to know where you sent those messengers."

"Which is where they are going to squeeze you," Rick added. "They have countless witnesses to what happened in that bunker at the end of the battle, Jason. They saw what looked like you portalling a bunch of messengers, including multiple gold-rankers, to safety."

"And how do they explain my ability to portal one gold-ranker, let alone multiples?"

"They don't," Rick said. "And they don't have to. They just have to accuse you of aiding the enemy in battle and they can drag you out by the hair. Your connection to Soramir Rimaros is the only reason they haven't."

"No," Jason said. "Their inability to go where I've been hiding is the reason they haven't."

"Is that place where you've been hiding the messengers?" Rick asked. "Because it looks from the outside like you're hiding them."

"I'm not hiding them," Jason said. "I'm holding them."

"For what?"

Jason sighed.

"I don't have to tell you that, Rick. I don't answer to you."

"Yes, Jason, you do. I'm representing the Adventure Society and I'm doing my best to not have them strike your membership and haul you in as a traitor."

Jason ran his hands over his face in a weary gesture.

"I knew this was going to be trouble. Alright, Rick, you tell whoever that if they want the messengers, I'll open up that portal you mentioned and let them through. The messengers are there."

"They said they want the location that portal leads to."

"That's a question with a complicated answer. Suffice to say, there is no other way in, only the portal."

"They won't believe you."

"I'll try not to cry myself to sleep over it."

"Jason, you're a silver-ranker and you need to accept that. Why are you making things harder than they have to be?"

The atmosphere in the room grew heavy. Jason and the building around them became difficult to distinguish from one another, merging into a single, overbearing power.

"Because the easy way involves giving up all my secrets and all my control, Rick. If these people understood who and what I am, they would try to take me and control me, and that is something" **I will not allow to happen.**

Jason finished the sentence not by speaking but by reverberating the words through his aura. It left the room physically and spiritually trembling, the air thrumming with power. In the long silence that followed, Rick and his team looked at Jason with discomfort. Jason was not a large man, but in that moment, his presence suffocated the room.

"I'm sorry you were dragged into this, Rick," Jason said softly. "You've been placed in an awkward position. You're thinking of me as a silver-ranker, and that's fair because I am one. But that's not all I am, and they know that. They're trying to make me think of myself as only a silver-ranker, so that I'll capitulate to their demands, let them take control of my actions and rummage through my secrets. They want to know why gods and great astral beings listen to what I have to say. They want to take my knowledge and excise me, claiming my place for themselves. Do you think they desire what is mine so they can use it for altruistic purposes?"

"Are your reasons altruistic, Jason?" Rick asked. To his surprise, this drew a wide smile from Jason.

"It's a good question, isn't it? There are things I have to do, but is that altruism or just responsibility? Survival? I'm hoping there isn't a difference and, when all is said and done, I come out the other side as an intact person."

Jason sighed and stood up.

"Here's the bottom line, Rick: if anyone from the Adventure Society or the diamond-rankers want to see the messengers, they can. They just have to go through the same portal."

"Can't the messengers come out?"

"Not until I let them."

"So let them."

"No. I'm sorry, Rick, but I don't just think of myself as a silver-ranker anymore, whatever the Adventure Society might want. My rank isn't who or what I am; it's a deficit I need to correct before I can handle all the other things I have going on. Arrogant, I know, but there's only so many times you can save the world before you admit to yourself that you really are special."

Rick stood up as well.

"They won't like hearing what you have to say," he told Jason. "And I don't think they'll be too happy with me as the messenger, but maybe now they'll stop calling me every time you freeze them out. I don't want my adventuring career to be defined as the guy to send after you every time you're being a pain."

Jason grinned and shook Rick's hand.

"You can take them back now, Vidal," Jason told the Adventure Society liaison standing in the corner. Soon Rick and his team were gone, leaving Jason and his team behind.

Jason let out another weary sigh.

"Rick stood his ground well," Jason said. "Good for him, even if the circumstances are not. Like all of you, he's been dragged into a mess on my account. I'm sorry I've done that to you. Again."

"You don't have to apologise for that," Sophie told him. "I don't know where I'd be if you didn't stick your head places no sane person would, but it's somewhere very bad."

"Hey," Neil said. "If getting in trouble with diamond-rankers from time to time is what it takes to sleep in a cloud bed and wake up to quality breakfast every day, then those diamond-rankers can sod right off."

"We're all with you, Jason," Humphrey said. "No regrets. But we do need to have some sense of where this is going."

"For now, I'm stalling," Jason told him. "I think the woman in charge of the local messengers is going to make a move, and we need to see what it is before we can decide what our next one should be."

3

DEVELOPING ANY SKILL TAKES PRACTISE

"No," Amos said, looking at the portal to Jason's soul realm atop the roof of the cloud palace.

"No?" Jason asked lightly.

"No," his aura teacher confirmed. "I am not going in there."

Amos Pensinata was a gold-ranker from Rimaros travelling with Jason, instructing Jason in aura use. Amos had an unusual qualification in this regard, having an experience of extreme spiritual trauma early in his adventuring career that mirrored Jason's. As a result, they shared a significantly above-average aura strength and sensitivity. Amos was able to instruct Jason on how to leverage that, using aura manipulation techniques developed over his long career.

Amos was not able to instruct Jason in every method of leveraging his aura manipulation, however. Jason's unusual nature, hewing closer to a messenger than a normal essence user, allowed him to manipulate his aura in ways that normally only messengers could. Most notably, Jason could wield his aura as a physical force in addition to a spiritual one, outside of what even Amos could accomplish. This left Jason learning what he could in this aspect from observing messengers.

As an aura-use pioneer, Amos was interested in the potential of Jason's aura. He had already been studying messengers, whose aura manipulation skills outstripped those of adventurers. While many aspects were unavailable to him, he could still use what he learned to refine his own techniques. Jason represented not just a way to advance the study of aura manipulation but also to combat the aura advantage messengers held over adventurers.

Messengers were more advanced in how they employed their auras than the adventurers of Pallimustus. Only exceptions like Amos and Jason were able to overpower their messenger counterparts, and even then, it was often with brute force rather than skilful employment of aura suppression. If Jason was to fulfil his potential, he would need to master the aura techniques of the messengers.

When Jason informed Amos he had a line on how to do that, Amos was appropriately interested. It was common knowledge now that Jason was holding messenger prisoners and refusing to turn them over to the Adventure Society. Amos suspected that Jason had managed to torture some secrets out of them.

Jason had little to do in the weeks since the Battle of Yaresh. Hiding out in his soul realm from the diamond-rankers, he mostly emerged to check on his cloud palace, which was currently serving as a hospital. Specifically, he was making sure that the Healer priestess running the place didn't serve inedible slop in the cafeteria kitchen.

Most of Jason's time had been split between training and coming to terms with his messenger prisoners. Throughout the weeks since the raid, Jason had been having lengthy daily discussions with the gold-rank leader of the messengers, Marek.

Marek was a window into the messengers and their knowledge that Jason very much needed. He did not have access to the kind of dimensional knowledge Jason needed, but he was an authority on messenger aura combat. This was what led Amos and Jason to the rooftop of Jason's cloud palace. Marek had insights that both adventurers would welcome, and Jason wanted to double-check something else. He wanted to know if Amos would enter his soul realm—and was hoping he would refuse.

"I cannot sense what is on the other side of that portal," Amos said. "But I can sense that it is a danger to me, if whoever controls it wants it to be."

"Yep," Jason said happily, and Amos frowned at him. Jason noted that getting to know Amos was essentially a matter of studying frown variants.

"You are satisfied with my refusal?" Amos asked.

"I was pretty sure you'd have a sense of what's through the portal, but I wanted to double-check."

"Why?"

"The diamond-rankers. I offered to let them in, but if they actually take me up on it, there's a solid chance they'd kill me the moment I let them back out."

"It would pose a threat to even them?"

"Yes."

"Then you are likely right. Whatever responsibilities they feel to this city and adventurers as a whole, a silver-ranker that could pose an actual threat to them is something they would be unable to tolerate. I would be wary of allowing even gold-rankers you do not trust implicitly inside. More importantly, they should be ones that trust *you* implicitly."

Jason took heed, not just because he valued his mentor's opinion, but because he spoke for so long on it. Amos Pensinata did not use two words when one would do, or use one word when he could get away with ignoring you. Given his power and prestige, he could get away with ignoring most people.

Jason was further interested in Amos' warning because of the nature of his soul realm itself. Before he acquired his astral throne, the portal itself had a restriction that only those who trusted Jason completely were able to enter. He'd often wondered about that restriction, especially since it had been lifted. He now suspected that it was a defensive mechanism that prevented those with the power to harm him into his soul. That such a restriction was no longer necessary set Jason's mind to gaming-out the ramifications.

Amos looked sternly at Jason while he stood in thought, eyes unfocused as he stared into the middle distance. Before them, the city of Yaresh was showing scant signs of reconstruction.

"Why would diamond-rankers want to go through your portal?" a female voice asked as an elf walked up the stairs to join them on the roof.

"Politics," Amos grumbled unhappily.

"Hmm?" Jason said, looking up at the newcomer. "Oh, yes. Lord Pensinata is right. Politics. Which I always feel I should be better at than I ever turn out to be, sadly. Still, developing any skill takes practise."

The elf was Hana Shavar, High Priestess of the Healer and the person in charge of operations using Jason's cloud palace as a base. Those operations had gradually moved the cloud palace from a triage hospital in the wake of the messenger attack to a processing and support centre. It was now mostly oriented around reuniting separated families, arranging temporary housing and making sure everyone had regular access to food and clean water.

At the same time, it was filtering the population for anyone trying to sneak in any unpleasant surprises, like world-taker worms. The parasitic apocalypse beasts were still being dealt with to the south and their appearance in Yaresh in its current state would be a disaster.

"What can I do for you, Priestess Shavar?" Jason asked.

"Before we get to that," the priestess said, "I want to hear about these diamond-rankers. I assume we are talking about the same ones that came tromping through my hospital operations?"

"We are," Jason told her.

"Can I expect further disruptions, then?"

"I'm hoping not," Jason said. "I've played the hard line with the Adventure Society representatives, so now I need to show that I can make a concession. I've offered to let the diamond-rankers into the place I'm keeping the messengers, but since I don't want to make an actual concession, I'm hoping they will decline when presented with the offer."

"Hoping?"

"I was very confident in my political predictions early in my adventuring career, and other people paid the price of my foolishness. These days, I keep my options open, even when some options fall precipitously short of being ideal ones. There are acceptable outcomes even if the diamond-rankers choose to go through this portal."

Hana focused her attention on the portal for a moment.

"I don't think they will go through," she said. "I think it will make them uneasy, and they will take that unease out on you."

"I do hope so," Jason said. "Things will get awkward if they think they are unable to keep me in line."

"They can keep you in line," Amos said with certainty.

"Of course they can," Jason agreed.

"You're looking to be brought to heel," the priestess realised.

"Yep. I've gotten used to making bigger splashes than is warranted by my rank, and I don't always have accommodating authority figures to bail me out. If I can at least make a show of conceding to the diamond-rankers, they're more likely to leave bringing me into line to the Adventure Society."

"Which would come down to lumping you with the least desirable contracts they can muster," Hana said. "But you're playing a dangerous game, Asano. Every adventurer trained by a guild or an adventuring family has heard stories of diamond-rankers making bad decisions when confronted with power they can neither understand nor overcome."

"Your privilege is showing, Priestess. I was trained in a place where diamond-rankers are practically mythical."

"Then that is your loss, Mr Asano. The fact that the diamond-rankers forced their way into the cloud palace demonstrates that the stories I mentioned are accurate. The simple fact is that diamond-rankers become accustomed to doing whatever they want. Denying them that goes badly."

"I have to acknowledge the point," Jason said. "And they ransacked the palace when they thought I was refusing to accept their power over me. I hate to think what they'll do when they realise how much power I really have."

"And how much power is that exactly?" Hana asked. "I watched the gold-rank messengers that invaded this building during the raid desperately fight their way back out without accomplishing anything."

Jason nodded at the portal.

"Step through and find out."

"No, thank you. Be careful provoking these diamond-rankers, Asano. They won't want to be seen bullying a silver-ranker, but an unrepentantly defiant one is a different matter. It won't hurt their reputation to chastise an idiot who doesn't know when to back down."

"Thus, the concession of letting them go see where I'm keeping the messengers," Jason said. "If they turn it down, that's on them. It's not like they're going to go around explaining to people that it's okay to beat on a silver-ranker because he has a scary portal. That just makes them look even weaker."

"Unless they go into that portal and realise how much power you have over them there," Amos pointed out. "They may just kill you outright, whatever it does to their reputation."

"Yeah," Jason acknowledged with a sigh. "I hope that's not the way it goes, but I'll deal with it if it is."

"You'll deal with dying?" Hana asked.

"It's kind of my thing," Jason told her. "Ask your boss."

"I am the High Priestess. I do not have a boss."

"You're a high priestess," Jason told her. "Your whole job is having a boss."

"You mean...? You should not speak so casually of the gods, Asano."

"So people keep telling me. You're a busy woman, Priestess; what brought you up here in the first place?"

"I would like you to convert dormitory room four into a second cafeteria and expand the kitchen."

"Now?"

"Late afternoon, during the shift change and before the dinner service."

"Okay," Jason said. "Anything else?"

"A warning if any diamond-rankers will be going on a rampage."

"I'll do my best. No promises."

Hana gave Jason a look up and down, her expression showing dissatisfaction, and then headed back downstairs.

"Now," Amos said. "Why am I here, if you never expected me to go through the portal?"

"Just a sec," Jason said as cloud-substance rose up from the roof to swiftly encase them in a dome. The stairwell was also sealed off. Direct sunlight was blocked by the cloudy barrier and instead filtered diffusely through the dome. Jason's aura flooded the area inside, making it a part of his spirit domain.

Jason's spirit domains were locations where he had extreme control over the spiritual forces within and even an amount of control over the physical reality. Along with his permanent domains on Earth, he could take any or all of his cloud constructs into his domain, although he had been leaving the hospital mostly free of his influence. Amos frowned as his senses were cut off, no longer extending beyond the new roof.

"Can't have anyone peeking," Jason told him apologetically, then gestured casually at the portal. Through it stepped a gold-rank messenger.

4

WAR GUILT CLAUSE

MAREK NIOR VARGAS STOOD BEFORE THE PORTAL LEADING OUT OF Asano's astral kingdom. In the weeks since he first entered, his life and future had been entirely transformed, but he found himself nervous as he looked at the way out. The world outside held immense potential now. It held a hope that he had never felt before, but with hope came the chance for that hope to be crushed. Given Marek's ambitions, being crushed was the more likely outcome.

"This isn't me letting you run loose," Asano reiterated. "I just want you, me and a man I know to have a talk about auras."

The Jason Asano standing next to Marek was one of countless copies, lesser avatars running around Asano's astral kingdom. He would not have a prime avatar until he was complete as an astral king. Even so, he had no trouble holding a conversation with Marek while his true body was talking with whoever was on the other side of the portal.

"I know," Marek said. "I won't run."

Not only did Asano still have all of Marek's people, but there was no telling who or what was waiting through the portal. For all Marek knew, Asano could be handing him over to the Adventure Society or an unscrupulous researcher eager to dissect a powerful messenger.

He didn't believe that to be the case. Marek had been living inside Asano's soul for weeks, which had given him an unusually intimate perspective on the man, although that in itself could be deceiving. Time and again, Marek had seen people work against their own interests and core beliefs for reasons that he could scarcely comprehend.

He had spoken at length with Asano, largely about the messengers. Marek had a sense that Asano was looking for reasons not to kill them, and perhaps even let them go. It made little sense to Marek as messengers did not show mercy. He couldn't help but wonder if that was an aspect of his indoctrination that he had yet to dig out and examine. Perhaps his incarceration in Asano's astral kingdom was a chance to do that. It was something to discuss with Payan, who was as close as he had to a brother.

"There's a slight delay," Asano said. "I'm talking with a high priestess. I don't think bringing you out while she's there will be a good move."

"I'm not sure bringing me out while anyone is there is a wise choice."

"Yes, but the man I want you to meet is not foolish enough to come in and meet you here."

"He doesn't trust you?"

"Not that much. You came in here and opened up your soul, but would you have done that just to save your life?"

"No. I wanted an astral king that was not like the others. If I had known you would free us, I would have rushed in."

"Tera would not," Jason said. "Have you made any headway with her?"

"There is nothing you do not see and hear in this place," Marek pointed out. "You have been privy to our every interaction."

"I know what you and she have said, yes, but not how you think. Ascribing my sensibilities to messenger mentality will only lead me to false assumptions."

"She is still fragile. You gave her and me the same thing, but the way you gave it was very different. For me, it is a chance at a future for my entire people. From her, you have taken everything. Who she is, what she is. Her identity as a messenger. You've poisoned her to other messengers, taking even her right to offer loyalty. She hates you from the depths of her being, and doesn't like me much better. Everything she despises, I see as a gift greater than I can ever reciprocate."

"Assuming I give you the chance to go out and do something with that gift."

"I believe you will, sooner or later. I still don't understand what you get out of mercy, but I believe you do get something."

Asano gave Marek a long, assessing look before speaking.

"The greatest martial arts trainer my world ever produced was asked by one of his students why he showed mercy to an enemy. He said that for a person with no forgiveness in their heart, living is a worse punishment than death."

"Mercy is leaving the roots of trouble to grow back stronger."

"Mercy can seem like foolishness, and perhaps it is. But it's also the hope for tomorrow. Ruthlessness will never turn an enemy into a friend. It leaves only barren ground, in the world and in your soul. I've seen that in a half-dozen years of having power, so you must have seen it over and over."

"I have," Marek confirmed. "Barren worlds and barren souls are how messengers operate."

"Well, if you're going to stage a revolution anyway, maybe consider revisiting that policy. There's a term in my world: 'Carthaginian peace.' It means to set terms of peace, following a military victory, that cripple the defeated so they cannot recover and rebuild. To take those who have been put down and keep them down."

"A sensible policy, although I imagine you are about to argue the opposite."

"There was a war in my world. The Great War. A tangled mess of political alliances turned one incident into a globe-spanning conflict. The war to end all wars, they called it."

"There is never an end to wars."

"No," Asano agreed. "No, there isn't. When the Great War was done, there was a peace treaty into which the victors placed what became known as the war guilt clause. It lay all blame at the feet of the vanquished. It stripped them of power, of dignity. Of the ability to rebuild in the face of the greatest conflict my world had ever seen."

"The seed of a new war?" Marek asked. He had seen many worlds and Asano's tale was a familiar one.

"Yes. From the ashes of a fallen nation rose a monster. He raised that country from the ashes using pride and hate, fed on the bitterness of a people who had been spat on and ground into the dirt. The next war was worse, worse than anyone imagined was possible. There are few cases where war has truly right and wrong sides, but there was an evil spreading across the world. Even then, those who were supposed to be on the right side used weapons that annihilated entire cities. Much as your people tried to in Yaresh. Oddly enough, your people cannot match mine for bending the power of creation to unconscionable ends. Our weapons of mass destruction proved more effective than your apocalypse beast."

"What came of the garuda that stopped the naga genesis egg?"

"If anyone knows, they haven't told me. He vanished while you and I were underground. But the battle we fought in Yaresh was nothing compared to the war I'm talking about. Of the nations that were the primary instigators, one was in the east and the other in the west. In the east, it was a nation called Japan. One of the many countries opposing them was Australia. My country, although I would not be born for another half-century."

Asano smiled and gestured at his face.

"My mother's people come from Australia and my father's from Japan. As ugly and brutal as that war became, as much as millions suffered and died, and for all the depravities carried out by both sides, the day came when those nations were not enemies but allies. That change came about in your lifetime; probably only a fragment of it. There is always a future, Marek. You could say I'm the living embodiment of that. You have told me over and over that you want to build a new future for your people. Mercy is the only way to build a future worth bothering with."

"Ideals are all well and good, but I face an enemy unlike anything your world has ever seen. A level of control it has never known."

"Yeah," Jason agreed. "But you have to consider that you've already recognised mercy, and seen that sometimes it's the only way forward."

"How so?"

"If you didn't think I'd show you mercy, and know what it could lead to, would you have brought your people to me and surrendered yourselves?"

"I knew that you would use us."

"Shielding you from my people is more trouble than you're worth to me, and you're too smart not to have known that. Think about it, Marek. You seem to have trouble admitting it to yourself, but you know the value of mercy. That being said, I will use you, since you're here. It's time to pop out, chief."

———

Jason warily kept his senses locked on both Amos and Marek as the latter emerged from the portal. They both tensed up on spotting one another, auras sharp as weapons, but neither opened hostilities. They were inside a dome atop the roof of Jason's cloud palace. Jason's presence flooded the area, which he had made a part of his spirit domain. His domain had neither the power nor the influence of his soul realm, through the still-active portal, but it still allowed him to command considerable power.

"Be civil," Jason told them. "This is a conversation, not a war."

"He and his kind brought war to this city," Amos pointed out. The intensity of his gaze fell just short of boring through the messenger's head.

"I was merely doing as commanded," Marek said.

"Okay," Jason said, pointing a finger at Marek's face. "I get that you were a slave, but you and I are going to have a long talk about the 'just following orders' defence. In the meantime, no more war talk. From either of you."

Jason's gaze moved from Marek to Amos.

"Marek, here," Jason told Amos, "has agreed to give up the goods on how messengers use their auras. In return, I've told him that you won't crush his skull to paste in your bare hands, okay?"

Marek and Jason both looked at Amos' hands. They remained at his sides, but his fingers were flexing as if aching to do exactly what Jason had just described.

"Why would you betray your own kind?" Amos asked Marek.

"I won't," Marek told him. "I betray the astral kings who enslaved their own kind long before I emerged from the birthing tree."

"The birthing tree?" Amos asked.

"Messengers are born from trees," Jason said. "I think that means they're technically plants, but we shouldn't get side-tracked. We're here for Marek to teach us about messenger auras."

"I ask again," Amos said, his glare still locked on Marek's face. "Why would he do that?"

"I have long wished to undermine the astral kings," Marek said. "Not for your people, but for mine. We are slaves, indoctrinated to think our bondage is glory, our servitude superiority. In freeing me from that bondage, Jason Asano has done something I did not think possible: left me free to act. If he ever releases me to do so."

"That doesn't answer the question," Amos growled.

"Doesn't it?" Jason asked. "You don't know gratitude when you hear it?"

"From a messenger?"

"I am as surprised as you," Marek told Amos, who turned back to face the messenger.

"You're saying that you serve Asano now?"

"No. He could have made me and mine his slaves. Instead, he gave me the freedom to serve no one and nothing but my own ideals."

Marek glanced at Jason, then back to Amos.

"He showed me mercy."

"I won't," Amos said. "If you serve your own messenger ideals, I should put you down before you get the chance to spread them."

"That's enough," Jason said sharply, drawing on the power of his spirit domain. Although a foot shorter than Amos and two shorter than Marek, his presence loomed over them. Both Marek and Amos had supreme aura senses, but they didn't need them to know exactly who owned the ground on which they stood.

"I know what Marek is offering sounds too good to be true," Jason told Amos. "All the techniques messengers use for aura combat, freely offered up. Mostly freely. Kind of freely. I mean, yes, he's my prisoner and I told him that it was a condition of me ever letting him out. One condition of many. So, not freely at all. But still, offered up."

Jason resisted smiling as Amos and Marek looked at him with the exact same mix of exasperation, wariness and disbelief.

"It's hard to believe, I know," Jason told Amos. "I bring out a messenger commander who claims that I've done something mysterious and now he wants to go off and fight the astral kings instead of continuing the invasion of this world."

"I am decades, if not centuries, from taking any fight to the astral kings," Marek said. "What I seek is the chance to plant a seed. A seed that may, in time, grow into a tree of revolution."

"You realise that plants don't revolt, right?" Jason asked him. "Are you just big on plant metaphors? You know, because you're a plant?"

"I am not a plant."

"Bloke, you fell off a tree like an apple. Is dimensional scrumping a major impediment to your reproductive process?"

"Please be serious, Jason Asano."

Jason laughed.

"Mate, you picked the wrong astral king to hitch your wagon to if you don't want jokes. No promises on the quality of said jokes, mind you, and they may just be me talking about old episodes of Monkey Magic."

Amos and Marek looked at him with a mix of disapproval and confusion.

"Yeah, I know," Jason conceded. "It's just called *Monkey*, not Monkey

Magic, but everyone calls it Monkey Magic. Because of the theme song."

He started patting the pockets of his tan shorts.

"I have a recording crystal with the theme song, actually. Let me find it and you'll see what I'm talking abou—"

"The messenger is right, Asano," Amos cut him off. "This is not the time for your childishness."

The amusement fell off Jason's face instantly, as if he'd been waiting for the interruption. He tapped into his spiritual domain again, using the space around them to lightly pressure Amos' aura.

"Lord Pensinata," Jason said. "You need to learn from my team and pay attention to what I do, not what I say. Does it feel like I'm not taking this seriously? We both know how strong your aura is. Try throwing it around and see how far it gets you."

Amos turned a glare on Jason which would have left most Rimaros adventurers trembling. Jason stared up at the taller man, uncowed.

"I'm not your nephew or some mewling guild member, Lord Pensinata; don't bother with the death stare. I've had a lot worse than you give me the evil eye."

"You should not treat these situations with flippancy," Amos told him.

"I've tried being grim and grave when things get heavy. It doesn't work out. I don't know if it's an overdeveloped sense of melodrama, but I don't like who it turns me into. Marek and I were just talking about mercy, and when I start spiralling down, I don't have any. If the price of me not killing a bunch of people is you putting up with the occasional *A-Team* reference—series, not film—then I suggest you suck it up. You can just ignore that while we otherwise talk things through like sensible adults. If that's too much for you to handle, Lord Pensinata, I suggest you run off and tell on me to the Adventure Society."

Amos pushed back hard against Jason's aura. Jason was startled at its full strength, yet it was not enough. They were in the cloud palace, one of Jason's spirit domains, and the very magic around them answered to him. Jason held Amos to a stalemate as Marek shielded himself without interfering. The floor beneath them and the dome over them started trembling with power. Amos' eyes went wide and he slowly withdrew his aura. Jason matched him in backing off.

"How many secrets do you have, Asano?" Amos asked.

"Enough that I'm starting to regret sharing some of them with you, Lord Pensinata. Marek, go back inside. We won't be having any aura discussions today."

When the messenger was gone, the portal closed. The archway remained, but the screen of light within disappeared.

"For a being that claims to be free, he does what you tell him readily enough," Amos said.

"We're done for the day, Lord Pensinata. I think we both need to think about how we each want to move forward from here."

"You engineered this confrontation," Amos accused. "You knew what my reaction would be to you bringing out a gold-rank messenger who is personally responsible for untold death and destruction, and you did so in a place where you have the power."

"Yes," Jason admitted. "That's exactly what I did."

"Are you looking to put me in my place somehow? That will end very badly for you."

"I'm aware, but I'm not trying to put you in your place, Lord Pensinata. I'm showing you that you're wrong about *my* place. You and the diamond-rankers and the Adventure Society all think you know who and what I am. All you see are the essence abilities that have barely nudged forward since I came back this world. But make no mistake, my power has grown to a level you can't understand until you step through that portal. The one you refuse to, because of the danger."

Jason took a long breath and let it out slowly.

"My place is not what you think, Lord Pensinata, and I'm tired of playing upstart. I will bend when bending is the best choice because yes: I am, for now, a silver-ranker. But I'm not *just* a silver-ranker. The messengers understand that; Soramir Rimaros understands that. The gods understand that. The day is coming, Lord Pensinata, when you will need to grow a Tom Selleck moustache or get out of my way."

Amos frowned, not in anger but in thoughtfulness. Jason waited while the man stared at him for a long time in silence. Jason knew him well enough to keep his mouth shut for once and, finally, Amos spoke.

"If you were anyone else, I would say you are a child shouting into the void. But you told the Builder to leave and he did."

"It was more like making a deal than—"

"Learn when to stop talking, Asano; I have no doubt your mouth gets you in twice as much trouble as it gets you out of. But I am forced to acknowledge that your claims of power beyond your essence abilities are not without merit. If you say that you can stand up to diamond-rankers and suborn messengers, then I will accept it. Until such time as you prove you cannot."

5

PRIMARY PURPOSE

Jason and Gary were standing outside the forge Jason had conjured up in his soul space for Gary to practise his craft. In this space, Jason could conjure countless materials, including exceedingly rare ones, for Gary to consume. Gary had even secured samples of the materials he wanted to work with so that Jason could accurately reproduce their nature and properties.

It was a level of resource even massive crafting guilds could not offer. Attempts had been made to create specialised mirage chambers for simulated crafting, but the results had never been worth the expenditure.

Gary's forge was a modest building of light-coloured stone. He and Jason leaned against the outside wall, holding fruit drinks that Jason had conjured up. From a magical perspective, they were identical to spirit coins, simply in the shape of delicious tropical beverages in coconut shells with colourful straws and tiny umbrellas. Gary's was significantly larger than Jason's.

"I know you're not happy I have them here," Jason said as they watched a trio of messengers flying through the air in the distance. "Most of the team has been giving me the stink-eye over it. I've fortunately not had to run into Carlos while I'm hiding out in here. For a healer, that guy carries an astounding amount of hate for messengers."

"I'm not a vindictive person," Gary said, "but I can see his point. I saw what they came to this city to do. I saw them doing it; there was only so much I could stop. I don't see how they deserve to live. What do we get from keeping them alive beyond more cruelty and death?"

"I'm trying to figure that out. Can you tolerate it if I forgive them?"

"They don't deserve forgiveness."

"Probably not. But what if I do it anyway?"

Gary sighed, then took a long, loud slurp of his drink. Jason didn't push for an answer, waiting until the lion man was ready to talk.

"When two sides hate each other," Gary said, "there's never going to be peace until someone lets go of that hate. There will always be reasons to hold on to it—good reasons—but then nothing changes. But it can't be one-sided, or it won't work. It can start with one side, but the other still has to meet them halfway. Are these winged bastards going to meet you halfway, Jason?"

"These ones just might. Maybe. And if we're really, really lucky, they may get more of their kind to do the same."

"In time to make them to leave my world?"

"Definitely not. It's more of a planting seeds situation. Ugh, now I'm making plant metaphors. Did you know the messengers are plants?"

"They don't look like plants."

"I know, right? But they grow on trees. They're basically evil fruit. Like broccoli."

"Broccoli is not a fruit," Gary pointed out.

"Exactly," Jason said. "Imagine delicious chunks of pineapple, dusted with cinnamon and salt, and then roasted until they're caramelised and tender before having a little bit of lime squeezed over them. Now imagine what you get instead is broccoli. That's what messengers are."

"Please tell me that pineapple thing is what you're making for lunch."

"No, I'm cooking broccoli."

"What?"

"See? They're the worst."

Jason rubbed his temples as Shade set a cup of tea on the wrought-metal picnic table where he sat. They were in a small clearing in a garden that had a natural and wild feel to it, inside Jason's soul realm. To get some peace and quiet, no one else in the soul realm could detect it, to the point that the realm would change to lead off anyone that approached. Only Jason and his familiars had access, although Colin was still in a cocoon and Gordon was busy with some of Jason's avatars in his soul realm's library.

"Thank you," Jason said. It had been a long day of mostly minor frustrations, from adjusting the cloud palace to dealing with politics. Now that he had decided to start resolving his issues with the Adventure Society and the diamond-rankers, Vidal Ladiv was shuttling between the cloud palace and the society campus with messages.

There had been bright moments, however. Acquiring magical materials for personal use was still almost impossible in Yaresh, with everything being commandeered for the reconstruction. It had taken weeks for Clive to collect the materials to resummon Onslow, whose body had been destroyed during the Battle of Yaresh. Jason left the reunited pair happily sharing a salad.

Another positive was the Adventure Society branch director throwing his support behind Jason in the face of the diamond-rankers. Jason suspected it was some local power play, but he wouldn't turn down the assistance. Vidal Ladiv insisted that the director's motive was genuine gratitude for Jason's role in getting the Builder to depart early. Jason found his inability to believe in simple gratitude a little saddening.

Jason's plan for the diamond-rankers worked best if their back and forth came out in rumours rather than a public display where things could go wrong. His 'concession' to the diamond-rankers proved enough to save face and keep them off his back, at least for the moment. If he failed to generate any actionable intelligence from the messengers, their patience would not last. But for now, the branch director would make sure the right rumours started spreading.

The Yaresh diamond-rankers were not the only ones Jason had to deal with. He had sensed the periodic attempts to interfere with his cloud palace and discovered a third diamond-ranker using some manner of device. Jason quickly realised she was the person who had created his cloud flask in the first place, having arrived in the city and now living with Emir.

"I find myself in a strange state of mind," Jason said to his familiar. "I don't have trouble filling my days, yet it also feels like I'm just waiting around. Waiting for diamond-rankers and/or the Voice of the Will to make a move. Waiting for a genius idea on how to deal with the messengers I've got stashed away. Waiting for Colin to emerge as a pretty, pretty butterfly."

"Even so, Mr Asano, you have had at least some time to stop and contemplate some of the issues surrounding you."

"Yeah. The gap between my spiritual development and my essence abilities is increasingly a problem. I almost want to go back to Earth and drain vampires until I'm gold rank."

"Perhaps you should. I imagine the vampires have gone to war by now. If you prioritise stealing messenger dimension magic, you will likely be able to ride the link back to your homeworld."

"You think this Jes Fin Kaal will hand over what I need?"

"I suspect that it is less important to her than to you, Mr Asano. Exactly the kind of bait to get you to participate in whatever scheme she has planned."

"Yeah, well, we'll need to stop whatever that plan is before we even think about Earth."

"There is one thing we should discuss, Mr Asano. We spoke on it briefly when things were more chaotic, and now we have time to talk it through properly."

"Oh?" Jason asked, taking some leftover roasted pineapple from his inventory. He set the plate in front of him, next to his cup of tea.

"Do you recall our talk about your former ability, the quest system?"

"I do," Jason said. "We were talking about how my own ability managed to know things that I didn't."

"I have a suspicion as to the magical sense at the heart of that ability, and what may have happened to that sense when the ability evolved."

Jason leaned back in his chair.

"Do tell."

"There is a rare phenomenon that, so far as I am aware, I have not witnessed myself until meeting you. It would be easy to miss as it is something that does not show itself overtly. Most have not heard of it, and many that have do not believe it to be real."

"And what is this mysterious phenomenon?"

"It has many names. Eyes of the crucible. Destiny magic. Fate senses. Way of the crossroads. Whatever it is called, the effect is the same. At least in the beginning. It allows any who possess it to unconsciously sense events of importance. Then, they make a choice without realising it, whether to seek those events out or avoid them. Think of it like hearing a gunshot, and your instincts telling you to run toward or away from the sound. It is rarely so overt, however, with the person often not realising they are even making a choice."

"You're talking about a fight-or-flight response for destiny?"

"A not entirely inaccurate description."

"Okay," Jason said, brow creasing as his mind went over what Shade had just told him. "I have about a million questions. I'm going to start with the idea that I've been running around, guided by my unconscious mind this whole time. If that's true, have I made any real choices, or has this thing been leading me by the nose from the beginning?"

"It has not, Mr Asano. It is not a controlling force but a sense of where important events could potentially take place. For you, it was a quest system. It could have led you safely out of that maze in which you found yourself upon arriving in this world. Instead, it sent you directly to a Builder cultist and his cannibal family. It also sent you to Mr Remore, Mr Xandier and Miss Farrah. It set you on a path that, step by step, led you to the place you are now."

"But it could have gone the other way. Kept me out of all the trouble I keep landing in, over and over."

"Yes. You didn't realise it in your conscious mind, but you were choosing, over and over, whether to place yourself in safety or a crucible. And I think we know which way you chose, every time."

"Why?" Jason asked. "What is this destiny sense for? How does it even work, mechanically? I mean, do potentially important events let off fate waves or something? And how did I end up with this power or sense or whatever it is?"

"I do not know how it works," Shade said. "It is rare enough that I do not know of it ever being studied."

"So, don't tell Clive is what you're saying."

"That may be best," Shade agreed. "I could only guess at the mechanism, but I would imagine that it measures probabilities in some manner. As for how you came to possess it, that is something I can reliably guess at. So far as I am aware, the conditions for developing fate senses are both specific and unusual. First, it requires a soul at a near-inert stage."

"Near inert?"

"Normal or iron rank. Perhaps bronze. Surely, by your level of development, you have realised that your soul is not growing stronger as you advance in rank, but unlocking more of the potential that has always been there. That was how you had the strength to fend off the Builder when he came for your soul."

"Is that why I wasn't harmed as badly as before when I overcharged my aura with Gordon's ritual? I've been tapping into my soul so much, outside of my essence abilities, that I can take the strain now? My soul and my body are the same thing, after all."

"It is as valid a hypothesis as any I can formulate with the information I have. But to return to the topic at hand, the first requirement of fate senses is a near-inert soul, meaning low rank. It also needs to be in an unusually malleable state."

"Such as when it's been yanked through the astral by a magical phenomenon, destroying the body it was attached to, and it's reworking itself from a human into an outworlder."

"Just so, Mr Asano. And the third requirement is that it needs to have an extremely close encounter with a maximally powerful force. A god or a great astral being. Certain astral phenomena that you are not allowed to know about would also qualify."

"A great astral being like the World-Phoenix. If it was to, say, pay close enough attention to the soul that it gave them something to take with it. A portion of the World-Phoenix's power in the form of a token."

"Yes. The soul, being in a state of flux and coming into contact with that level of power, may develop fate senses as a reflexive defence mechanism. In your case, it manifested in the quest system."

"And it's programmed to prompt either fight or flight," Jason realised. "Depending on whether your instincts are to run from that power or to match it."

"Yes," Shade said.

"And that's why I always treat authority figures like they don't matter. It's my fate senses."

"No, Mr Asano. Fate senses are just that: senses. You are responsible for your own behaviour. You cannot blame fate senses for your behaviour any more than you can blame your hearing or sense of taste. Even when they seem to guide you in a certain direction, it is you who unconsciously chooses the direction. The senses themselves only present you with the option. Fight or flight, as you put it."

"Alright," Jason said, sipping at his tea as he processed all the new information. "So, it isn't some inherent destiny pushing me around. It's just me choosing to be in all the situations I've complained about being in for the last half-decade."

"To a degree. I believe that these senses still guide you, but remember that the ability through which they manifested, the quest system, evolved. It stopped pushing you."

"Why would it stop?" Jason asked.

"Think of when it evolved, Mr Asano. When you were iron rank and you chose to fight a silver-rank monster you could not possibly defeat yet could have easily fled. Instead, you chose to fight. You never got another quest after that."

"The waterfall village," Jason said. "When I had to stall out the elemental tyrant while the villagers evacuated."

"You didn't have to, Mr Asano, and that is the point: you made the choice. And you received what is, to this day, your largest soul scar in the process. Then, shortly thereafter, you encountered another maximally powerful being. This time, you defied it, and your power evolved. Your soul was once again in flux, but you no longer needed the defensive mechanism of the fate senses. What you needed was power on a level of the Builder. Which, of course, you couldn't muster at iron rank."

"Then what did the fate sense turn into? The ability that replaced the quest system rewards chasing danger, but doesn't guide me to it."

"I believe it is largely dormant. It may be guiding you in more subtle ways, but I think it was waiting. You had Gordon, at that stage, and I suspect your fate senses evolved into a different kind of perception: the ability to sense Gordon's potential for the magic he can tap into. You couldn't use it immediately because Gordon still couldn't use it. His vessel was too low-ranked. But then, he bound himself permanently to you, and did so after his vessel was two ranks higher. He still was not high enough rank to use that magic normally, but you could sense it, allowing him to tap into his own potential through you."

"And what is this magic?"

"I did not recognise it, at first. He has only used it at the absolute lowest level and it shouldn't be possible for him to use it at all yet, to the point that the possibility didn't occur to me."

"Why is this what my fate sense turned into?"

"I suspect that it is a natural evolution of the fate senses to move from guiding behaviour to granting access to higher-order power when the opportunity presents. You proved that not only were you resolved to confront a force on the level of the Builder, but you had potential access to at least one power that operates on the same scale he does: intrinsic-mandate magic."

"That's what it's called, Gordon's magic?"

"Yes."

"And it operates on the same scale as a great astral being?"

"It is a form of magic they use themselves, often involving the expenditure of authority. It lacks the versatility of the magic you are familiar with, and is meant for shaping physical reality, not being used within it. This is the magic the Builder uses to forge worlds. That the World-Phoenix used to harden the dimensional barrier of Earth. If you think of all intrinsic-mandate magic as different kinds of guns, the power Gordon has used thus far—"

"Is a water pistol?"

"No, Mr Asano. It is a piece of paper with the word 'bang' written on it. This magic is typically employed by transcendent entities and sometimes their diamond-rank agents. Miss Dawn used it when she annihilated the Builder city fortress."

"She used authority for that?"

"No, Mr Asano. She used her star seed to tap into the most meagre trickle of the World-Phoenix's power. If she had used actual authority, the results would not have been so modest."

"Modest? She glassed an area the size of a state."

"Which is why the great astral beings would not allow you to possess loose authority, Mr Asano."

"Yeah, well… fair enough. Can astral kings use this magic?"

"Yes, as can their diamond-ranked Voices of the Will, if their kings allow it. If you can complete your transformation into an astral king, you may have an easier time tapping into Gordon's magic potential, even before you surpass diamond rank."

"Why does Gordon even have that potential?"

"I do not know. Perhaps it is the connection of his kind to the Sundered Throne or the All-Devouring Eye. But those are topics that I will not expound upon. Not until you are stronger."

"You think I can't handle it?"

"I think the wider cosmos has etiquette, and that etiquette exists for a reason. I will not violate it to introduce you to things you have no power to influence. Unless you order me to do so."

"No," Jason said. "If you say that's for when I'm a big boy, I trust you. I know that if ignorance will blindside me, you'll warn me ahead of time."

"Thank you, Mr Asano."

Once again, Jason paused, eating pineapple and drinking tea as he pondered the ramifications of what Shade had told him.

"The World-Phoenix," he said. "She had to know what she was doing to me."

"Yes, Mr Asano. In fact, I imagine that instilling you with fate senses was the primary purpose of giving you the token, not a side effect. She wanted you drawn into events, and if her contact with you left you a gibbering wreck, she could always explore other avenues. Dawn made it clear enough that you were simply one path the World-Phoenix was exploring."

"Hold on," Jason said. "What's this gibbering wreck business?"

"The conditions that generate fate senses are quite extreme, Mr Asano. I mentioned how souls develop those senses as a defence mechanism. This is the same process that alters a soul in the wake of spirit trauma. And like spirit trauma, not everyone comes back stronger. Some are ruined, their own souls poisoning their minds, rendering them insensible."

"Oh, that's great. Remind me to tell the World-Phoenix to bog off."

"No, Mr Asano."

6

EVERYONE HAS A PRICE

"WHATEVER YOU MAY BE THINKING, MR ASANO," VIDAL SAID, "THE diamond-rankers aren't spending their days plotting ways to snatch away your secrets."

Vidal Ladiv was not enjoying his job. He had always imagined people with real power to be sober and serious, dedicated to carrying out the duties that came with the power and influence they possessed. Sadly, they turned out to have the same pride, biases and vested interests as everyone else.

"I definitely wasn't thinking that," Jason said unconvincingly.

"The diamond-rankers have largely concerned themselves with monitoring messenger activity in the wake of the attack on Yaresh," Vidal continued.

Part of his job as liaison between the Adventure Society and Jason was giving Jason regular reports on the broad activities of the Adventure Society. It wasn't what Vidal had been directed to do, but Jason would freeze him out if he didn't. And if that happened, the Adventure Society would deem Vidal's assignment a failure.

Falling short on one assignment would not torpedo Vidal's career, but such an important job came with extra attention. If the Adventure Society was happy with his work, it would mean not just more important jobs but some flexibility in choosing them. Vidal was very much looking forward to a diplomatic or administrative job, far away from anyone as volatile as Jason Asano.

"The best assessments we have suggest that the messengers lost more people in the attack than intended," Vidal continued. "Once their numbers were sent into a frenzy, they were less effective at using their summoned monsters as a shield. Then, when our diamond-rankers were freed up, they inflicted a lot of messenger casualties, especially during the withdrawal. As a result, the messengers have abandoned one of their five fortresses to consolidate in the others."

"And they don't have a diamond-ranker anymore," Jason said.

"No," Vidal said. "But we also don't have the forces to stage counter-attacks. Many adventurers are still working to purge the world-taker worms in the towns and villages to the south. There was talk of our diamond-rankers attacking the messenger fortresses alone, but the defence infrastructure of those fortresses is formidable. While our diamond-rankers are tangled up in the defences of one fortress, the others could mount punitive attacks."

"For all the messengers took a hit," Jason said, "we took a worse one. Diamond-ranker aside."

"That is the current assessment," Vidal said.

He looked around the rooftop garden in which they sat, atop Asano's cloud palace. Days earlier, it had been a domed area that sent the diamond-ranker, Charist, into a fresh rage. His inability to penetrate some areas of Jason's building with his magical senses was what had prompted him to invade the palace in the first place. The other diamond-ranker, Allayeth, mostly kept him in check, but Charist's patience had run dry. He was not to be stopped when he had burst into Jason's cloud palace and, even as she disagreed with the move, Allayeth had gone along to present a unified front.

While the two Yaresh diamond-rankers worked together, they were very different. Charist embraced the power and authority that came with his rank, using it to bull through any situation, be it combative, diplomatic or social. Allayeth was more subtle, working within societal strictures instead of lording over them as her power would allow. If not for the need to be a moderating force on Charist, people might not have even known her name.

The reason Vidal had so much insight into the pair was due to an unlikely friendship formed between himself and Allayeth. He knew that she had only approached him to be a lever on Asano, doubtless one of many she was cultivating. Even so, Vidal genuinely enjoyed her company. She had a knack for turning the normally imposing presence of a diamond-ranker into something compelling instead. He didn't know if she cared at all about him, but she had certainly given him access to information he otherwise would never have encountered.

Part of that information was Allayeth's thoughts and plans around certain topics. One example was that Allayeth had respect for Asano making the appearance of concession, even as it frustrated her. Having looked into Asano's background and connections, she now realised that pushing him as much as Charist advocated could have greater repercussions than they had originally realised.

"I think you should sit down with one of the diamond-rankers," Vidal suggested to Jason.

"One of them?" Jason asked pointedly. "That implies that most of the friction is coming from the more confrontational of the pair."

"With respect, Mr Asano, most of the friction is coming from you. You disrespect their rank. You take an entire force of messengers prisoner and refuse to reveal where they are being held. You hide away for weeks from attempts by the Adventure Society to debrief you."

Vidal couldn't sense Jason's aura. He knew that, even if he could, he would not have been able to read his emotions through it. It was unnecessary, as it turned out, as Jason's anger was plain to see in his expression.

"I have larger concerns than one battle in one city, Mr Ladiv."

He was using Vidal's surname, which was not a good sign.

"Larger concerns than a city all but razed to the ground?" Vidal asked.

"Yes. You know the kinds of forces I deal with. It's the whole reason the Adventure Society attached you to me, but I find myself increasingly regretting my acceptance of that. The reason we came to this city was to fight messengers, and I don't like the fact that my integrity seems to be in constant question."

"You are keeping a lot of secrets, Mr Asano."

"As is every other adventurer. But my secrets are a sin because powerful people want to know them? Go back to your diamond-rankers, Mr Ladiv, and tell them to come here and tell me *their* secrets. Does my wanting to know them make them traitors if they refuse?"

"Of course not. That doesn't make any sense."

"I agree, Mr Ladiv. Yet, here you are, calling me to account for not handing over mine."

Jason's smile sent a chill down Vidal's spine. He had some experience

—certainly more than he wanted—dealing with diamond-rankers of late. They always restrained their formidable presence around him, and he got an unnervingly similar feeling from Jason. Such experience, however, had made him very good at holding his nerve.

"There is one other thing, Mr Asano."

"Go on."

"I have been asked to request that you stop projecting your senses across the entire city. It's not strictly prohibited, but it is considered extremely rude and several gold-rankers have made complaints."

"Not to me. Any gold-rankers wishing to complain," Jason continued, "are welcome to come here and do so in person."

They both knew that there was little chance of that happening. Gold-rankers had the survival instincts to not get caught up in diamond-rank conflicts, even if that conflict was with a silver-ranker. Perhaps especially with a silver-ranker, if the silver-ranker in question was anything but immediately crushed.

"I will convey your response to the Adventure Society," Vidal said and stood up.

"That's it?" Jason asked him. His voice sounded casual but had a dangerous undertone Vidal was certain did not slip in by mistake.

"What else would there be, Mr Asano?"

"The messengers made contact with the city authorities yesterday. Were you not going to share that information?"

"Mr Asano, I—"

"If you're thinking about lying to me, Mr Ladiv, I would suggest you revise that idea."

Ladiv felt Asano's aura pressuring him heavily, to the point that he took a staggering step.

"Did I do something to anger you, Mr Asano?"

Jason frowned and shook his head. The aura pressure vanished.

"No, Mr Ladiv. You just have the unfortunate role of being the messenger. I'm getting very tired of authority groups telling me what to do while trying to take what I have. It was something I put up with a lot in my old world, and it's dredging up bad memories. I need to get to a higher rank, and to stop involving myself in major events until I do."

"I believe it is far too late for that, Mr Asano."

"Yes," Jason said wearily, "but I can at least try. It may be time to relinquish my membership in the Adventure Society, removing that as a lever for people to pull on. Now, Mr Ladiv, tell me what the messengers discussed with the city authorities. As much as the society let you know."

"Which is very little, Mr Asano. Genuinely. They know that you will get answers out of me if you wish, so they restrict the information they give me. The messengers sent one of their suborned locals as an envoy, knowing that a messenger wouldn't be allowed to leave again. They've made contact with the government, not the Adventure Society. The messenger approached the ducal manor where I have no information sources on the inside."

Jason raised his eyebrows, his expression offering Vidal a chance to correct himself.

"No high-level information sources," Vidal revised. "I've made inroads with some of the low-level bureaucrats, but the duke's office is being careful with this information. I was lucky to find out the messengers had made contact at all. I'm curious as to how you even heard about it."

"You just asked me to stop spreading my senses across the city, Mr Ladiv. I learn much simply by watching and listening."

"Yes, but it's not like a messenger came flapping their way into the city. It was an elf taking care to be discreet. You would need to pay diligent and near-constant attention to numerous places around the city simultaneously to catch information like that."

"Or be very lucky."

"Are you a lucky man, Mr Asano?"

"I would say yes, on the whole. I've also developed a knack for splitting my attention without diminishing focus."

"Superior multi-tasking is something every essence user shares, Mr Asano. It is a function of the spirit attribute. Monitoring this entire city, however, would require something far more developed. Your shadowy familiar is no secret, Mr Asano, and it's alright to admit having spies. We all do, and we all assume that everyone else's are listening."

"Fair enough. We are done here, Mr Ladiv. Find out more about what the messengers want."

"Mr Asano, I agreed to give you a broad overview of Adventure Society news, not to become your investigator. I'm just a liaison and you're taking liberties. I don't work for you."

"Then perhaps it is time that our arrangement comes to an end."

Jason stood up and plucked a folder from his dimensional space, holding it out for Vidal.

"All the identity documents for John Miller," Jason said. "If I'm going to revoke my Adventure Society membership, I can hardly run around with the false identity they provided for me. I never did a great job of maintaining it anyway."

"You're seriously considering separating from the Adventure Society?"

"The point of being an adventurer is that the Adventure Society facilitates me helping people. If all they are going to do is make demands and get in my way, then what is the point?"

"And the rest of your team?"

"That is up to them."

***

Jason ran a hand over his face as his senses tracked the departure of a troubled Vidal Ladiv.

"I'm cranky today," Jason observed. "I didn't mean to be that confrontational. I don't like it when the Adventure Society starts reminding me of the Network, though."

"You don't truly intend to void your Adventure Society membership, do you?" Shade asked from Jason's shadow.

"No, that would escalate tensions. But I want to see how they react. It's an option, albeit one I'm unlikely to take up."

"Do you think they will take more care to avoid or block your senses?"

"No, they'll be watching for you, not me. They know you're my real best source of information."

"I can only learn so much," Shade said. "Only the weaker gold-rankers fail to notice my presence, and only when they are inattentive. Like you, Mr Asano, I need to grow stronger to handle the events in which we always seem to find ourselves."

"But we don't just find ourselves in them, do we? This fate sense. It means I'm seeking them out subconsciously. I need to take myself off the board. The idea of returning to Earth and hunting vampires until I'm gold rank was a frivolous idea, yet it increasingly appeals."

"You have things to do here."

"Yes," Jason said, then let out a small sigh. "Now that I've prodded, it will be interesting to see if the ducal government and the Adventure Society seek to include or exclude me from what the messengers are after."

"What are you expecting?"

"The Voice of the Will has a problem. She wants something from the underground array, and she needs essence users to get it. But even if she's in command, the rank and file won't accept the help of what they see as their lessers. The indoctrination that controls the messenger masses cuts both ways. Marek seems sure the voice will use me as an excuse to make the messengers accept some kind of alliance. I may be an enemy to them, but after what happened in the Battle of Yaresh, they may accept me as an equal."

"An equal that needs to be eradicated."

"That's probably part of how the voice is selling it."

"Will the city be willing to entertain anything the messengers want after the attack? They may refuse any cooperation out of hand."

"Everyone has a price, Shade."

"And what is yours, Mr Asano?"

"Really well-pickled capsicum, tender and sweet. I think I'm going to go make a sandwich."

7

TRUST

JASON DIDN'T NOTICE THE DIAMOND-RANKER UNTIL SHE SET FOOT IN HIS cloud palace and blended in with a stream of civilians making their way to the cafeteria. Even then, he almost missed her as that section was not a part of the cloud palace currently within his spirit domain. Rather than react to her presence, he observed how she was using her aura to completely blend in.

Jason's own aura control was beyond masterful for his level, but the diamond ranker demonstrated just how far he had to go. The chance to watch one in action was not to be missed. He observed as she filed in with the others, waited in line and then sat down to eat her food. It wasn't until she was almost done that Jason approached her himself.

Jason had his own technique for blending into crowds. He had first developed it by studying the aura of his vampire friend, Craig, back on Earth. From there, he had refined it over time, learning to let his aura bleed into that of the world around him until they were all but indistinguishable from one another. The base concept he had taken from the first diamond-ranker he had ever encountered, the Mirror King.

The Mirror King's aura had not been overbearing, instead seeming to merge with the world around it. That had been a revelation for Jason, whose aura and aura senses at the time were still at the most basic levels. For that reason, it was hard to tell how the diamond-ranker in his cafeteria, Allayeth, compared.

Jason was curious as to how long it would take Allayeth to notice him approaching, but his best guess was that she sensed him the moment he emerged from the part of the palace covered by his spirit domain. For all of his impressive aura strength and refined technique, she was still a diamond-ranker. Each rank represented an exponential leap in power, and for all the power that gold-rankers possessed, diamond-rankers were on another level entirely. Comparing one to Jason's silver rank was all but pointless.

"That's an impressive technique," Allayeth said as he sat opposite her.

The cafeteria was a series of long tables with benches in front of them that Jason definitely hadn't modelled after the great hall from Hogwarts. People were sitting close to both Allayeth and Jason on either side, but a nuanced aura trick from Allayeth prevented them from paying attention to her words.

"Impressive for my rank, perhaps," Jason said, mimicking Allayeth's trick. It was surprisingly easy, being very much like his own technique for crowd blending.

"You're frustrated that your rank isn't higher," Allayeth said. "That puts you in the same position as every adventurer ever. Even I get frustrated when comparing myself to the likes of Soramir Rimaros. And even he falls short compared to Dawn."

"You know Dawn?"

"She travelled to many places to warn them of the Builder invasion. I was surprised to hear that you and she were so... close."

"You know how it is. When work takes up all your time, everyone you know ends up being from work."

"You worked together?"

"There's no Adventure Society in my home world, and the local equivalents aren't up to facing cosmic threats."

"And you are?"

Jason burst out laughing.

"No," he said. "No, I am not."

"I find that hard to believe. I've sensed the power on the other side of that portal. I don't know what it is exactly, but I'm certainly not accepting your offer to go through."

"That's your choice. The offer is still there."

"I can't imagine you fail to understand our concerns, Jason. Can I call you Jason? I heard that you used to prefer more casual forms of address before you returned to our world."

Jason leaned back a little on the bench, looking at Allayeth thought-fully. The elf's immaculate diamond-rank beauty would have arrested attention if she was not using her aura to shunt that attention away. Her eyes were a soft green, her skin was the light brown of a fawn's fur, and she had wavy, wood-brown hair. Overall, she looked like a dryad of myth —the kind of beautiful, ethereal creature that led men to their demise in folklore.

"You're a little too well-informed for the kind of actions you've been taking thus far," Jason observed. "Is Charist really so much to handle that you've made this many missteps?"

Allayeth's laugh sounded like a merrily trickling stream.

"He is," she said. "You have no idea how hard it is to deal with an obstreperous diamond-ranker."

Jason looked at her from under raised eyebrows and she laughed again.

"I suppose you do," she acknowledged. "Charist is like a dog or a child. You have to let him run around or he starts taking it out on the furniture."

"So you let him take it out on my furniture?"

"Yes. If I couldn't stop him anyway, I could at least see how you reacted."

"I can respect that. I don't like it, but I can respect it. Is he all tuckered out now?"

"He's come to recognise that forcing you to capitulate isn't going to happen. He's agreed to step back and see if my approach works any better. He has an enviable ability to let go of things that he can't change, especially given his enthusiasm about checking if he can change them first."

"The ability to let go is something I'm trying to cultivate in myself."

"How is that working out?"

"Mixed results. Why are you here, Allayeth?"

"I was hoping that you and I could get a fresh start. Perhaps both let go of some things."

"I'm open to that. But can you really accept not knowing the secrets you've been trying to dig out?"

"No," she admitted. "If we're going to move forward, at least some of our concerns will need to be put to rest. I'm hoping that you're open to talking it through and seeing if we can find a place where everyone is comfortable."

Jason let out a slow breath, an unhappy expression on his face.

"And here we are," he said sadly, and tapped the table with his finger. "I've been here, right here, more times than I'd like. Someone wants something from me. Someone, or maybe some group, with enough power that they're used to getting their own way. They come at me hard, at first. Pressure is what they think of as the nice way to do it. Telling me how impossible they are to go against, maybe some thinly veiled threats against the people I care about. Sometimes they don't go the nice way, or they don't like that the nice way doesn't work. I've been kidnapped. People have tried to kill me. One guy killed my lover, brother and friend all at once. I got talked into letting him die way too easy."

Jason stopped and looked at the people around them and stood up.

"Walk with me, Allayeth. Is that your given name or your family name?"

"Family. But I'm the only one left to carry it. I also know what it's like for people to go after you through the people you love."

They made their way through the crowded cafeteria, people instinctively moving out of their path. Jason led them to a door that no one else seemed to notice and through it into a narrow but empty hallway.

"After they come at me hard," Jason continued, "and they realise that isn't going to work, that's when they start talking about compromise. When they can't just take what they want, then it's suddenly time to talk it through and see if we can find a place where everyone is comfortable."

Jason gave Allayeth a side glance as they reached an elevating platform.

"Do you think I've ever been comfortable in those situations?" he asked her as they stepped onto the platform.

"No."

"No," Jason agreed. "It's always the other people who deserve to be comfortable, for some reason. But I worked with them anyway, because some things need to be done. Even if you have to hold your nose to do them. But I don't have to do anything here. This world isn't on the line—not in any way that I can do something about. As such, I don't see any reason why I should compromise with people just because they failed to strongarm me."

"Sometimes you have to bend to political realities, Jason."

"I'm not so sure I do. You pushed, and I didn't budge. Now you're telling me to move because you don't want to push harder while threatening that you will if you have to."

"I wouldn't put it so crudely."

"I would. I've seen this meal picked down to the bones. Have you ever considered that I might not want to push back, but will if I have to?"

"Is that a threat?"

"Yes."

"You would stand against the entire Adventure Society? Diamond-rankers and all?"

"I stood against the Builder. More than once. And every time I did, I got what I wanted and he went away frustrated. Will you be the next to test my resolve?"

The elevating platform reached a rooftop garden. Jason sat down in a padded wrought-iron picnic chair and Allayeth did the same, a round outdoor table between them.

"I don't doubt your resolve, Jason. Or the threat you can pose. There is no question that you have dangerous secrets and powerful allies. I suspect that should you and the Adventure Society come into conflict, you can do more damage than anyone realises. But I don't think you want to do that. Not unless you're truly pushed to the brink."

"Says the person doing the pushing. You think I'll roll over?"

"I think you have more power than anyone realises. But I also think that you won't be able to truly change things until the more orthodox elements of your power have grown considerably. You understand that as well, and that you have to bide your time. It's why you made a show of concession with your offer to let us go to where you're keeping the messengers."

"Just because I won't go berserk doesn't mean I won't walk away. I have no responsibilities here."

"Nor did you in the Battle of Yaresh. Or the underwater mine rescue in the Storm Kingdom. Or when people who are now your team members were just thieves at the mercy of powerful political forces. You have a pattern, Jason Asano, and that pattern is that you'll put everything on the line to help people for no more reason than they need you to."

"Then why am I the one who needs to prove my good faith? Why do you need anything from me but my word? I got the Builder to walk away from this entire planet, and that's not enough? You question my trustworthiness when all I've seen you do is break into my home."

"I would have liked to have done things differently."

"But you didn't. Don't come into my house to tell me that I have to do things your way, then complain that you had to do things someone else's."

"I apologise. But however much you dance around it, Jason, you have to put people's minds at ease if you want to operate without harassment from the civic powers."

"And how would I do that?"

"At the very least, let us know who is backing you. Whoever controls the other side of that portal is powerful at a level I can't measure, and that's who you've handed the messengers over to."

Jason sat up straight, confusion on his face.

"*That's* the problem? You're afraid of some powerful unknown player messing around with the messengers I handed over?"

"I would have thought that was obvious."

Jason laughed, shaking his head.

"Jason, I am willing to trust you, as is the director of the Adventure Society. But at least when Dawn was standing behind you, we had some understanding of who was taking an interest in events. I've met Dawn, and whatever is on the other side of that portal isn't her."

Jason rubbed his temples with one hand.

"No," he said. "You pushed me and it didn't work, so now you want me to compromise. If you want the answers that lie on the other side of that portal, you'll need to step through it."

She didn't respond for a long time. She sat back in her chair, staring at him as her mind ticked over. Jason stared back, all but seeing the cogs turning in her head. Finally, she spoke, her voice quiet and soft.

"Alright."

"Alright?"

"I'll go through."

"You'll go through the portal?"

"That's what I just said."

"What about the danger? You said that you definitely wouldn't go through. You said that just minutes ago."

"It's possible I misrepresented myself a little in order to understand you better. My investigation into you, Jason Asano, has been swift but thorough. I've heard time and again that you're hard to understand, but you're not. You're a good man, desperately scrambling to survive events you aren't ready for. And every time you're forced to choose between doing the right thing and staying alive, you make the sacrifice."

"I don't always do the right thing."

"You do when it matters. Enough that it should have earned the trust of people like me. So, I'm going to trust you and go through that portal."

"Uh…"

She laughed.

"You really weren't expecting us to accept your offer, were you?"

"No," he admitted. "I'm a little worried about how you'll react. And by a little worried, I mean I'm worried that you'll kill me."

Allayeth sighed.

"It's starting to sound like the real gesture of trust is not to go through that portal but to accept your word that it isn't a threat to us."

Jason narrowed his eyes.

"Which you knew before coming here," he said. "You've seen through me like a window."

"I'd like to make a different proposal, Jason. I'll offer you two things, and in return, we clear the slate. No more concessions, no compromises. Just cooperation. You tell us as much as you are willing about the messengers and what you've learned from them, and we don't push for more. And we work together for what comes next, which I think you would do anyway."

Jason continued to give Allayeth an assessing stare.

"So, that's why you're here," he said. "Jes Fin Kaal doesn't want to talk to you. She only wants to talk to me."

Allayeth smiled in spite of herself.

"I think you and I can do good things together, Jason."

"You said you'd offer me two things."

"I did. Two things you very much want."

"And they are?"

"One is trust. Trust that your intentions are good and that you are capable enough to carry them out, however unlikely that might seem. No conditions, just acceptance."

"And the other thing?"

She plucked a plate with a large sandwich out of the air and set it on the table between them.

"A delicious sandwich," she said.

"Do you really think that *this* will get me to come around?"

"Yes."

"You think I'm that easy?"

"Yes."

"It's going to take more than some conversation with a smart and stupidly gorgeous woman to win me over. Also a sandwich."

"A *delicious* sandwich. And no, it won't."

"That's absurd."

"Yes. But you like absurd, don't you?"

"No. Yes."

He ran a hand over his face.

"Oh, bloody hell," he muttered as he reached for the sandwich.

8

ORIGINAL DESIGN PARAMETERS

WHILE JASON'S CLOUD PALACE WAS STILL LARGELY OCCUPIED WITH servicing the displaced population of Yaresh, Jason maintained an area for himself and his companions. Part of it was a living area, with Sophie and Belinda in one room and the boys in a bunk dorm to save space. Sophie's mother, Melody, was in a secure room adjacent to her daughter, while other members of the convoy were stashed elsewhere. Amos Pensinata was staying with his nephew's team in their vehicle, and Rufus' mother, Arabelle, was staying with Emir, her old team member. Emir's cloud palace was being used much like Jason's, and he had even more room that he could put to use.

The open space between the two cloud palaces had been a refugee camp until the battle pounded it into a mud pit, but earth shapers had already established a new series of crude but functional stone buildings. One part of it had been left clear, a flat stone area that served as an arrival destination for portals. The towns to the south were still being cleared of world-taker worms, with the cloud palaces serving as processing centres for surviving townsfolk.

Rain fell heavily as a portal opened that did not come from the southern towns but from a city half a continent to the north. Three people stepped through, and Jason, inside his cloud palace, immediately sensed their presence. He stepped through a Shade body to shadow jump to them, rising from Travis Noble's shadow like he was riding an elevator.

Travis stumbled back, startled. He was an outworlder from Earth, a specialist in magical technology. His precise specialisation was large-scale weaponry but, like Clive, he was an enthusiastic researcher whose expertise bled into a variety of adjacent fields.

Farrah laughed as Jason appeared and the rain stopped falling straight down, curving around them as Jason's aura pushed it out of the way. Jason grinned as he clasped her in a hug.

"You paid a gold-ranker to portal you here?"

"The Church of Knowledge did," the third new arrival informed him. It was Gabrielle Pellin, priestess of the Church of Knowledge and Humphrey's ex-girlfriend.

Jason spared Gabrielle a glance as he stepped back from Farrah. He and Gabrielle did not get along very well, which had been a factor in ending her relationship with Humphrey. She was now attached to Farrah and Travis' current project to combine Earth technology with Pallimustus magic to create a new communication network.

"Let's go inside," Jason said, nodding in the direction of his cloud palace. "More people are portalling in on the regular, so we should avoid clogging up the arrival site."

The cloud palace was, at the moment, a blank slab that looked like a Soviet Bloc construction. Compared to the adventurer vehicles around it that were all exotic mobile fortresses, the starkness and size of it stood out. Arrayed in front of its four storeys were stone-shaped buildings that matched the bleakness of the current cloud palace with boxy designs and hard edges. The wide pathways in between were simple, just large flagstones set into the dirt. The value of this was evident as the rain turned that dirt into mud, saving the many people around from needing to trudge through it.

Even with the rain, there was no shortage of people around them as Jason led the trio in the direction of his cloud palace. Some people were ignoring the rain while others hustled to move through it quickly. More than a few had water-repelling umbrellas, much like one Jason used to have. The expensive umbrellas had water slide off smoothly, much as Jason's aura did. The cheap ones sent water spraying off violently, annoying anyone who lacked their own water repulsion. This included other users of cheap umbrellas, which often didn't shield from the sides.

They came across a pair of men with cheap umbrellas that had managed to splash each other. On the verge of getting into a fight, Jason used his aura to introduce a subtle but pervasive sense of calm. The men exchanged more insults but didn't come to blows, storming off in different directions.

"Did you...?" Farrah asked, giving Jason a side glance as they moved on.

"A little bit," he admitted.

"You're directly influencing people now?"

He chuckled.

"No, it's not influencing people as such. It's more like tweaking the feel of a room. Have you ever been around a bunch of people, having a good time, and then someone comes in and announces that something bad has happened?"

"Sure."

"The atmosphere of the room goes from fun to tense or unhappy straight away, right?"

"I've felt that, yeah," Travis said.

"What I did was something like that," Jason explained.

"I wouldn't even know how to even attempt that kind of aura control," Farrah said.

"It's a messenger trick," Jason said. "They use it to make impressive entrances or cow their slaves. It's like background music in a film; the people involved can't hear it, but it impacts the mood."

"Where did you learn to use your aura like a messenger?" Gabrielle asked, her tone accusatory.

"Your boss didn't tell you where I learned it?" Jason teased her. He noticed unease in Travis' aura at the hostility between himself and Gabrielle.

"My lady delights in her followers seeking knowledge for themselves."

"I can respect that," Jason conceded. "I learned that messenger trick from a messenger."

"You would traffic with the enemy?"

"The enemy in question is my prisoner, and he has a lot of free time."

The teleport arrival area where they had started out was midway between Jason and Emir's cloud palaces. As they were the destinations for most of the people out in the rain, Jason and the trio of new arrivals were part of a flow heading for Jason's palace. Farrah looked up at it as they drew closer to the plain building.

"Why did you make it look so bland?" Farrah asked. "Just looking at it makes me feel forlorn."

"It does look like an insane asylum from an eighties movie," Travis agreed.

"It just came out that way," Jason said. "I may have been influenced by the priestess in charge."

"They put a priestess of the god of desolation in charge of managing all these homeless people?" Farrah asked. "That's not a good choice."

"It's a priestess of Fertility running things now. There was a Healer priestess, but she moved central operations to Emir's palace yesterday. They're focused on filtering out anyone who's worm-infested, while my place is pretty much doing food now. I tore the whole building down overnight and put it back up as a multi-storey food court. The Fertility church is supplying all the food, so their priestess is running the show."

Farrah stopped and looked up at the building again. The others stopped with her.

"A priestess of Fertility," Farrah said.

"Yep," Jason confirmed.

"The Church of Fertility where their temples are all covered in murals of people... being fertile."

"That's the one."

She gestured at the blank, grey walls of the building.

"How does a priestess of Fertility inspire this?"

"I think it's because I *really* don't want her thinking about fertility-related things. But honestly, the Healer priestess was just as bad, but for different reasons. I'll give you a sample of what she was serving in the cafeteria before I fixed it and you'll understand. Speaking of churches, though, what is Humphrey's fundamentalist ex-girlfriend doing with you?"

Gabrielle glowered but didn't rise to the bait. Instead, Travis explained the Church of Knowledge's role in his and Farrah's project. The church wanted input into what they— especially Travis—were doing, making sure that any otherworldly knowledge introduced wouldn't be false or damaging. This was not proving an issue; Travis actually knew what he was talking about, compared to Jason's fumbling efforts to explain scientific concepts. In return for being allowed to observe, the Church of Knowledge was providing resources and contacts.

"After all," Travis pointed out, "greatly improved mass communication would be a boon for the dissemination of knowledge."

"I can't say that I'd be up for letting the gods dip a finger into my porridge," Jason said, "but it's your project. If you're happy, that's what matters."

He glanced at Gabrielle.

"Just make sure you aren't letting them participate for the wrong reasons," he added.

Gabrielle had already been astoundingly beautiful at seventeen when Jason first met her. Now that she was out of her teens and into silver rank, she was basically Helen of Troy.

"I, unfortunately, had the opportunity to test out the weapons you designed for the cloud palace," Jason said, changing the subject. "I was a little surprised with the end result, to be honest. I was expecting something more like Gatling lasers than techno-eyebeam things."

"I'm not sure that 'designed' is entirely the right word," Travis said. "Your cloud palace has such powerful adaptive properties that it was far more efficient to provide it tools it could use to its own ends. Trying to force a specific result would be inefficient. Not to mention fruitless, unless I knew a lot more about how cloud flasks work."

"That's all well and good," Jason said, "and the results were excellent, don't get me wrong. But I really would have liked something with spinning barrels."

"Of course you would," Travis agreed. "Spinning barrels are awesome. I put them on the latest version of the Compensator."

Jason recalled Travis' unfortunately named personal firearm, a wildly impractical, belt-fed pistol. Travis was not a combat-oriented essence user, despite possessing the gun essence. The Compensator was designed to make up for his lack of skill by allowing him to unload a surplus of ammunition. Sadly, the gun was as ill-conceived in design as in name. Not only was it unwieldy, even with an essence user's strength, but everyone assumed it was compensating for something else entirely.

"Are you still using that thing?" Jason asked him.

"Well, not using," Travis said. "I haven't been in combat since…"

He thought it over.

"…since you broke into my workplace to steal a weapon of mass destruction."

"I wouldn't exactly describe that as combat," Farrah said. "The only person who pointed a gun at you was on your own side. It was that girl you liked, which can't have been a great moment for you."

"Could you please not?" Travis asked her, his voice almost a squeak.

"What weapon of mass destruction?" Gabrielle asked. "Was it like the one that felled the Builder's flying fortress city?"

"Yep," Jason said cheerfully. "Some people wanted me to do a thing, and I thought why not blow it all up with a weapon that can flatten a city?"

"You are a reckless maniac."

Jason gave Gabrielle a look that she couldn't quite read but made her flinch despite his not enhancing it with aura.

"As a priestess of Knowledge, you shouldn't have such strong opinions on things you know very little about," he told her in a flat tone. He gave no indication of having recognised the wild hypocrisy in his statement.

"You know," Jason said, turning back to Travis as the joviality returned to his voice. "There's someone floating around who knows about cloud flask mechanics, if you're interested in learning more about integrating weapons into them. She made the flasks that Emir and I use, and she's staying with Emir. She's been poking around at my building for a little while now. I think she installed some back doors she's trying to get to work."

"And you just let her try that?" Travis asked.

"She's diamond rank; what am I going to do? She doesn't seem to be getting anywhere, though. I've modified the flask beyond its original design parameters."

"You know how to do that?" Travis asked.

"No," Jason said with a laugh. "No, I do not."

They approached the main doors where people were filtering in under the guidance of clergy and other staff. Jason ignored the main doors and moved around the side, lifting his feet off the ground to float along as the stone pathways gave way to mud around the parts of the building that didn't lead to doors.

"You move like a messenger," Gabrielle accused.

"I tried walking like an Egyptian," Jason told her, "but it was slower, gunked up my boots and left these little troughs in the mud for other people to navigate."

"I see you are still a fool," Gabrielle said.

"Actually, I dabbled in edgelord for quite a while there. It didn't work out. I've been working on myself, trying to get back to fool, and I'm pretty happy with how it's going. And how is your project going, Farrah?

I'm assuming you're not here for a social visit or you wouldn't have brought Little Miss Grumpy."

"We need to borrow your soul space," Travis explained. "We need to do a bunch of tests on a bunch of materials, all of which are quite expensive. It'll be a lot cheaper if we can just replicate them over and over. We brought samples, obviously, so you can reproduce the material accurately."

"You realise I'm not just a laboratory for you to run experiments in, right?" Jason asked.

"Where's Gary right now?" Farrah asked casually. "And, I'm guessing, Clive?"

"In my soul space," Jason grumbled. "Running experiments."

They reached the back portion of the palace that Jason had for the use of himself and his team. Rufus came out to pull Farrah into a hug and Travis held out his hand for Taika to shake. Taika ignored Travis' hand and pulled the skinny, alarmed-looking man into a giant chocolate hug. Aside from Jason, they had been the only two people from Earth in Rimaros, two strangers in a strange land.

They moved inside, out of the rain, the cloud floor cleaning boots while people were still wearing them. Gabrielle looked like she'd bitten into a lemon as Jason's spirit domain cut her off from her goddess.

9
UNSTABLE

Jason and his team, including new member Taika, headed to Emir's palace for a meeting. With them were Farrah, Gary and Travis; Gabrielle had long gone off to find members of her own clergy. She would arrive at the meeting with them.

Using Emir's palace as the venue made sense purely from a space perspective, as Jason's smaller palace lacked the room. Emir had also dedicated most of his home's space to facilities aiding the displaced population of Yaresh, but his larger palace could spare the space to accommodate a large meeting.

It was worth breaking down and rebuilding Jason's palace when the main purpose became hosting a massive food court. It wasn't worth doing the same with Emir's in the middle of the day just to hold a meeting. Emir lacked Jason's ability to remake whole rooms on a structural level without returning the cloud construct to the flask and remaking the entire building. This meant that, instead of a dedicated meeting room, they had to make do with the space he already had available.

"A bouncy house?" Taika asked as they walked in. "Bro, this is awesome."

He immediately made a superhuman leap into the middle of the room, spilling head over heels through the air as he skipped like a stone. This drew raised eyebrows from the people already present who were leaning against the walls.

"It was Jason's idea," Emir said. He arrived right behind Jason's team, having come from elsewhere in the palace. "Too many children have been through too much unpleasantness, so it's nice to give them some silly fun for a little while."

Emir entered and set cloud furniture rising from the floor. The chairs and couches all faced one side of the room that remained empty aside from Taika bouncing around, ignoring the disapproving glares. The chairs and couches were plush cloud material but nothing like the bounce-inducing floor. The people present immediately occupied the furniture, Arabelle and Rufus claiming a couch, as did Emir and Constance, Emir's wife. While it was Emir's cloud palace, Constance ran it. That had been true when she was Emir's chief of staff, and nothing had changed on becoming his spouse.

There was also a significant number of clergy. The Healer was represented by Arabelle and Neil, as well as Carlos Quilido and Hana Shavar, who grabbed another couch near the front. The rest of the clergy were in two contingents of silver-rankers, each led by a gold. One group were priests and priestesses of Knowledge, including Gabrielle, while the other was from the Church of War.

The attire of the Knowledge clergy marked them as warrior scholars. This was not a surprise; the goddess Knowledge had been quietly militarising her forces for years. This had caused consternation amongst the other churches as the scale of it was revealed, particularly with the Church of War. They had matched the Church of Knowledge's unexplained build-up, often in the same areas. When the messengers subsequently invaded those areas, Knowledge's motives had been revealed, with the Church of War in place to respond.

The attire of the War priests and priestesses was a lot less scholar and a lot more warrior. Gabrielle and her companions wore robes not unlike the ones Jason preferred, albeit in lighter colours than he used. They looked like Jedi to Jason's Sith in outfits that were free-flowing and loose without obstructing movement. The clergy of War were dressed in armour ranging from flexible leather to heavily plated outfits, even though they were here for a meeting. Jason wondered how they were ever comfortable without cloud furniture to sink into.

More people arrived after Jason and his friends, starting with Rick Geller and his team. Next came the team led by Korinne Pescos, Rimaros adventurers travelling with Jason. This included their latest team member, Zara Nareen, formerly Zara Rimaros, Hurricane Princess of the Storm

Kingdom. She had been adopted into her mother's family so she could roam around without quite as much stink of royalty on her. Also on that team was Orin Pensinata, whose uncle, Amos, arrived with them.

The final arrivals were officials from both the Adventure Society and the Ducal Palace, the government of the Yaresh city-state. The director of the local Adventure Society branch led their contingent, while the ducal delegation was led by a blank-faced bureaucrat. Both men were gold rank, their status achieved through monster core use, rather than through battle. This was standard for high-ranking bureaucrats, as their silver-rank flunkies also had auras thick with monster-core energy.

Each group had a pair of gold-rankers with them, not adventurers but also not core users. These were personal guards, ex-adventurers lured by offers of slightly less money but significantly less monster fighting. The Adventure Society maintained a force of such personnel outside of their normal membership, as did many high-end branches. The Ducal Palace had something similar, with even the Duke of Greenstone maintaining a similar practice.

Vidal Ladiv was amongst the Adventure Society contingent, standing out with the absence of monster residue in his aura.

Jason found the social dynamics fascinating as the people in the room shuffled for chairs in a political game simultaneously played out in aura interactions. Jason glanced at Farrah, reminded of their first lesson in aura manipulation. She had told him how adventurers and other powerful essence users used their auras like handshakes, which was explanation enough for a guy no one had heard of learning to meditate in a park. In high society, it was a subtle and complex game of supremacy.

While the silver-rankers were shuffled to the back, gold-rankers fought over seating positions without looking like they were, shuffling awkwardly between the furniture. There was an aura game being played as well, not reliant on power but nuance, at which the monster-core using bureaucrats were surprisingly good. The goal was to align with the more prominent people in the room, namely the famous gold-rank adventurers, rather than being stuck at the back with the silver-rankers.

There were exceptions to pure rank amongst the odd social dynamic. Zara Nareen, as daughter to the Storm King, held a prominence above her rank. Jason also held an odd position, and one that most of the gold-rankers didn't know what to do with. In a fairly crude manner, the government bureaucrat and his gold-rank guards tried to influence Jason, but his sleek aura defence deflected it easily.

In Pallimustus, personal power trumped political influence. This made Emir, Amos and Arabelle, all renowned adventurers, the islands around which the rest of the room drifted. Amongst the silver-rankers, this was reflected as well, with the officials playing second-fiddle to Jason, Rick and Korinne's teams. The clergy were somewhere in the middle, commanding respect as the servants of the gods, but lacking the personal achievements of battle-hardened adventurers.

Things had almost settled down when the arrival of the diamond-rank Allayeth threw the room into a subtextual frenzy of politely claiming chairs. She could have tamped her aura down to avoid unnerving the group, especially the silver-rankers. But there was an expectation of an imposing presence from a diamond-ranker. Violating that to make people comfortable was more a breach of etiquette than leaving them unsettled.

Jason was the only completely unfazed silver-ranker, although Zara, Rufus and Humphrey faked it very well. The gold-rankers had mixed results when masking the discomfort of their auras. Emir had spent more time with diamond-rankers than anyone in the room who wasn't one. His wife was fairly new to gold rank but maintained the perfect equanimity of a hostess. Amos Pensinata was bold enough to forcibly shrug off the aura, having the gall to use it as training.

The two gold-rank priests also showed admirable resolve, being used to the presence of their gods. Even a diamond-ranker on the level of Dawn could not outshine that. It was the gold-rankers who had arrived with the various officials who were most visibly ill at ease, but there was no shame in that. If anything, it was ruder not to show the effects of being in a diamond-ranker's presence. The priests were particularly good at displaying just the right level of being impacted.

Most of the silver-rankers looked sweaty, as if Allayeth was a box of hot rocks in a sauna. Jason's team had encountered Dawn enough times that they weren't too off-kilter, but the other teams and the officials were looking queasy as they took their seats at the rear.

Finally, everyone was seated, with gold-rankers at the front and silver-rankers at the back. Up front was Emir, the host, with his wife next to him as they shared a couch. Allayeth, as the most powerful, was front and centre. Jason ignored glares backed by gold-rank auras as he sat next to her. If she was happy to make small talk with him, no one was stupid enough to try and send him to the back with the other silver-rankers.

"Jason," Allayeth said. "I know I agreed to refrain from probing you with questions, but can you at least share what happened to the messengers' diamond-ranker?"

Although her tone was casual, it arrested every ear in the room. One of the greatest mysteries of the Battle of Yaresh was what had happened to the most powerful combatant on the messenger side.

"Honestly, I have no idea," Jason said, with only Allayeth able to read his aura well enough to know he was telling the truth. "I'd never heard of the guy until he rocked up dead at my feet. It was probably a god or something."

"Is a god's intervention something you'd consider likely?" Allayeth asked.

"Something swatted a diamond-ranker like a fly, and the only mortals I know that could do that are off transcending or in prison."

"Prison?"

"Space prison. I'm not clear on the details."

"Did you know that there was a strong residual magic of time manipulation in the area?" she asked.

"So I've heard. I also heard that the Adventure Society was hoping to keep the details of the investigation as secret as they are able."

"Ah," Allayeth said before looking to the Adventure Society director, standing in front of all the chairs. "My apologies, Director Heath."

"Thank you, Lady Allayeth."

The director of the Adventure Society and the gold-rank priest of Knowledge were the only ones who remained standing, positioning themselves at the side of the room all the chairs were facing. Like most Yaresh locals, the two men were elves.

"Thank you all for coming," the director began. "For those of you I have yet to meet, I am Musin Heath, director of the Adventure Society's Yaresh branch. As most of you are aware, this meeting is to discuss the latest moves by the messengers and what our response will be. I will start by making sure that everyone present knows the situation as it currently stands."

An illusion lit up behind him showing a map of the Yaresh region. It was zoomed well out, clearly marking the city of Yaresh, the towns to the south infested with world-taker worms and the projected area in which the worms were suspected to have spread. The director pointed out the messenger fortresses, including the one that had been abandoned.

"The messenger strongholds, and now our city, have been the focal points of the battles between our forces and those of the messengers,"

Musin explained. "Neither of these are the true crux of this conflict, however."

The map panned to a location some distance away, where a range of mountainous plateaus rose out of the jungle.

"The true objective of the messengers lies beneath this mountain range: a natural array, unnoticed for centuries, deep in the ground below us. For those of you unaware, a natural array is a location where magical manifestations, taking place over centuries, have slowly formed a cluster of objects that generate unanticipated magical effects. A natural array is an exciting resource, but not to the point of justifying the effort and attention the invading messengers have put into controlling it. Which leads to the question of what they truly want."

Musin pointed out a mark on one of the plateaus.

"This is the location of the shaft the messengers had their slaves dig to the natural array. We do not know what they want, but we do have information about their activities. Priest Jillet, I invite you to share what you have managed to put together."

The Knowledge priest stepped forward as Musin stepped back.

"My name is Ebson Jillet. I am a priest of Knowledge and chief information officer of the combined holy forces in this region. Before anyone asks, the goddess of Knowledge cannot give us all the information about the disposition of the enemy. That would not only violate her purview but also encroach upon that of the god of war."

He gestured at the map.

"My goddess guided us to this region, from which point it became our divine mandate to learn why. What we found was that as soon as the messengers arrived, they began excavating all but right under our noses, using the suborned labour of this world's natives. We naturally sought the reason why, but it still eludes us. Even the slaves, traitors and messengers we've captured and interrogated gave us conflicting information. We believe that the leadership of the messenger forces has been lying even to her own people."

"By leadership, you mean Jes Fin Kaal," Allayeth said. "The Voice of the Will."

"I do," Jillet said. "This messenger is a direct servant of a transcendent entity called an astral king, whose agenda we assume her to be carrying out. We believe that she is telling conflicting stories to even her own people, to contain whatever the truth is. Despite this, we have managed to put together a basic idea of events. The messengers arrived in the region and secretly initiated an excavation program far from where the holy army was camped. This was inefficient but successfully kept their activities from us for some time. They sought the natural array we did not know existed. Then they found it and were no longer able to hide their activities. Instead of a magic array, buried in solid ground or encased in magma, they found something else entirely: A sub-species of the smoulder people in a centuries-old underground civilisation."

"What do you mean by sub-species?" one of the government officials asked.

"Typical smoulders," the director stepped forward to say, "are a people that, like elves, humans, celestines or leonids, have a sufficiently low inherent magic level that they can absorb essences. If a sufficient population is exposed to sufficient magic over a sufficient number of generations, that population may become a magical variant, as has occurred here. You may have heard of the Blood Song Leonids or the Sky Eater Elves. I'm oversimplifying, but, in short, the smoulders down there have their own inherent magic instead of essences."

"What's more," Jillet continued, "these people were at war with the Builder cult, just like the rest of us. Unbeknownst to anyone on the surface, the cult had discovered this hidden civilisation, along with a large astral space. We believe the space was either created or altered by the natural array, and the Builder sent a powerful force to claim it. Not only did the cult have an array of gold-rankers leading an army of silvers, but also burrowing machines to approach the city unnoticed by us on the surface. They were still waging war on the smoulder population until the messengers arrived, turning it into a three-way conflict. This was the point where we discovered the magical emanations of this subterranean war."

Jillet nodded in the direction of the gold-rank War priest.

"At this point, we joined the battle, but we were still trying to understand what was happening. We know that the messengers attempted to alter the natural array somehow, and that whatever they did went wrong. The astral space was warped and the messengers started to be negatively affected. They fled, leaving the cult, the smoulder and what seems to be a large number of mindless, altered messengers to their conflict underground.

"The messengers realised that the holy forces knew about them and have been fighting over control of the underground excavation access ever since. Yaresh was supplying the holy forces for months, along with a steady stream of adventurer reinforcements. The messengers had their own massive reinforcement at this time, however, right at the time the Builder was withdrawing from our world. The new messengers bolstered the existing ones and established the strongholds we've been besieging ever since."

"What about the Builder cult members underground?" Arabelle asked. "Were they withdrawn along with the Builder's other forces?"

"No," Musin answered. "Builder cult groups around the world had their resources revoked and any non-native forces withdrawn. The Pallimustus natives who signed on with the cult were left behind and we've been cleaning them up ever since. You wouldn't have seen it in the Storm Kingdom, where the Builder had already withdrawn, but Adventure Society branches around the world have been mopping them up."

"What we know," Jillet said, "is that Builder cult members remain underground. What we don't is whether they are a remnant native force that poses little threat or a powerful army prevented from extraction by the now-unstable natural array."

"Which brings us to the main issue," the director said. "Whatever the messengers did, the natural array is no longer stable. Some kind of magic is building up down there, and we need to either stabilise or destroy the source before it escalates beyond our ability to handle. Assuming it hasn't already."

"And how do we do that?" Emir asked.

"Someone has proposed an alliance for the purpose of putting a stop to it. They claim to have the expertise but are unable to send their own people, who have proven vulnerable to the magical forces at play. I think most of you in this room are well-informed enough to realise that I'm talking about the messengers. Jes Fin Kaal has made us an offer."

10

DARK BARGAIN

AURAS ERUPTED IN CONSTERNATION AFTER MUSIN HEATH, THE Adventure Society director, announced a potential alliance with the messenger leader. The gold-rankers kept their equanimity, but many of the silver-rankers were spiritually up in arms. It was here that the director demonstrated his expertise, spreading his aura out to gently chide the silver-rankers, forcibly imposing calm through deft aura suppression. The director might not be an expert at handling monsters, but the veteran administrator was the Amos Pensinata of controlling an unruly meeting.

"Yes," the director said. "Obviously, the idea of an alliance with the woman responsible for levelling the city is unpalatable. And make no mistake: she is responsible. We know the plan to attack the city was hers and we all have every reason to be angry. Most of you aren't from this city and even you're furious. I am from this city. This is my home and this woman ground it under her boot. I lost people in the attack. Every friend I have lost people in the attack. If I can muster up the resolve to look at things the way they are and not the way I wish they were, so can all of you."

He panned his gaze across the room as the people in the meeting settled down. Ebson Jillet, priest of Knowledge, stepped forward.

"The simple fact is," he stated, "that there is a greater threat to this city than the messengers, although they are ultimately the source of that danger as well. We have explained the instability that has affected the natural array. The equilibrium that is the most intrinsic property of such an array is out of balance. Breaking that balance would normally cause the magic of the array to dissipate. Whatever the messengers did to it, that is very much not what happened. Instead of breaking down, the array has been growing in power, at the cost of stability."

"It took a long time for us to notice the change," Musin said, picking up the narrative. "The array is feeding on ambient mana that has picked up earth and fire affinities, the purest strains of which come from deep underground. For this reason, it took a long time before we noticed what was happening from the surface. Only once the array started reaching dangerous power levels did we start investigating. The best assessment the Magic Society has is that the power will continue to build to a tipping point where the array can no longer maintain stability. All that power will then be unleashed in catastrophic fashion. Our best estimates place that happening sometime in the next three to five months."

"How catastrophic?" Emir asked.

"The Magic Society has been using the term 'supervolcano'," Jillet said. "I'm assured it means extremely catastrophic."

"We should probably stop that, then," Emir said.

"That was also the conclusion we reached, Mr Bahadir," Musin said. "Unfortunately, the Magic Society has been coming up short in terms of solutions."

"We lack the knowledge base," Clive called out from the back. "The Magic Society—"

"Shut your mouth, silver," one of the gold-rankers guarding the government contingent growled. "The adults are talking."

A silver-rank aura settled over the room. The strength of it approached gold rank and there were unsettling elements that were hard to read, like silhouettes in a fog. Then it withdrew and all eyes were on Jason. He showed no indication of having just let his aura blanket the room like a poison cloud and leaned towards Allayeth. They held a whispered conversation as if they couldn't be heard by everyone in the room.

"I don't like people talking to my friends like that," he mentioned offhandedly. "I'm trying to be less imperious, though. I don't suppose you could be imperious for me?"

"You'll owe me one," Allayeth said lightly.

"I can live with that."

"I wouldn't go making assumptions, Jason," she teased and he flashed her a grin.

Allayeth reached into her pocket and took out a seed the size of a golf ball and tossed it into the lap of the offending gold-ranker. The seed burst, a plant tentacle monster rapidly growing and wrapping itself around the man. It engulfed his head, limbs and torso, ignoring his struggling. Once it had grown larger than him, essentially a mass of tentacle vines, it dragged him away.

The people who had looked on, not willing to cross a diamond-ranker, scrambled out of its path as it hauled the man out of the room. They could hear the dragging sounds and muffled screams moving down the hall.

"Not exactly subtle," Jason said. "It's a bit messy to use inside someone else's cloud palace."

"I don't think he'll complain," Allayeth said.

"Being diamond-rank will be nice."

"You think you'll be a diamond-ranker?"

"For a while, sure," he said distractedly. "What were you saying, Clive? Something about a knowledge base?"

The room was silent and still for a long moment, all attention laser-focused on Jason and Allayeth. The diamond-ranker herself was giving Jason an assessing look as he watched Clive attentively.

"Uh…" Clive said.

Jason gave him an encouraging nod. Clive's eyes flickered over the diamond-ranker and he continued.

"Well, as I said," Clive explained, "we lack the knowledge base to do anything with natural arrays. And by 'we,' I mean the Magic Society and, by extension, the entire magical research community of Pallimustus. Partly, the problem is that natural arrays are rare. Mostly, the problem is internal Magic Society politics. Because of their rarity and lucrative research potential, the people who get the chance to study natural arrays have started hoarding the results of their research instead of disseminating it. Despite the dissemination of research being the entire point of the Magic Society."

"Why would they do that?" Humphrey asked.

"Because the next time a natural array comes up," Clive said, "the people permitted to research it will be those that know the most."

"Which leads," Knowledge Priest Jillet said with disapproval, "to a situation where too few people are participating in the research of a field of knowledge. On top of that, those who end up doing the research are the ones who were best at politics, not magical study."

"Exactly," Clive glowered, sharing an understanding grimace with the Knowledge priest.

"The result," Jillet told the room, "is that, as Mr Standish here said, we lack an understanding of how natural arrays work. The Magic Society attached researchers to the forces contesting the entrance to the underground excavation as soon as we realised what was down there, but they don't have any response to what's happening."

"In fairness," Musin said, "I don't know to what degree expertise would help. They never had direct access to study the array and were left trying to analyse the distant aura from the surface."

"The only thing that would accomplish is removing an easy excuse for their incapability," Clive muttered, with Jillet nodding his agreement.

"In short," Musin said, "no one from this world understands how to stop the array from annihilating Yaresh and all the towns and villages around it. Which brings us to the messengers. They have magical expertise that we do not."

"That should not be news to anyone familiar with the new magic that has been spreading over the last few years," Jillet said. "As to whether that expertise extends to resolving this situation or they are just lying remains an open question. Whatever insidious pact the messengers struck with the Builder cult and what we believed was the Church of Purity, it involved sharing magic not available on this world. A lot of that, we've managed to capture and add to our own store of magical knowledge. My church has been a large part of that, as has Mr Standish, here."

He gestured at a nervous Clive.

"If any of you have enjoyed the improved astral magic being spread over the last few years, you should thank Mr Standish."

Clive shook his head.

"All of that work was based on materials given to me by the Church of Knowledge," he said. "More precisely, they were given to Jason, and I kind of stole them all."

Clive's expression became awkward.

"Then he took them back to another universe and I was given my own copies," he admitted, his words coming out in a rush.

Jillet laughed.

"Yes, Mr Standish. Do you truly think you came into possession of that material by accident? A book is worthless if no one can read what is inside. You took what were worthless scribbles on a page and turned them into knowledge. Then—and this is important—you shared that knowledge."

"Eventually," Clive grumbled.

Clive had been lured into researching astral magic used by the Builder cult following Jason's seeming demise. This was when the enthusiastic researcher from a small Magic Society branch discovered how riddled the institution was with self-serving politics. He had thought the corruption of his local director to be an isolated incident, but the greed and lack of ethics proved to be an unfortunate standard.

With no influential background, Clive was kidnapped in all but name and exploited by a high-ranking official. It was only with the help of Belinda and a sympathetic fellow researcher that he made good his escape. His complaints lodged with the Adventure Society and Magic Society prompted little and no action respectively. He resigned from both his employment and membership in the Magic Society and publicly released all the work he had done while under the society's thumb.

It was only a matter of time before the Magic Society realised the treasure they had lost in Clive. They had been trying to lure him back ever since, but he hadn't come close to being tempted. He still pursued his research interests, using the Church of Knowledge to spread any fruit produced by his personal research. The clergy of Knowledge's church were *very* nice to Clive.

"The point is," Musin said, "that the messengers have magic that we do not. And they claim they can prevent the natural array from growing into a catastrophe that destroys what's left of our city."

"We can't trust them, obviously," Emir said. "The best you can hope for is to trust you know what they want and can predict them accordingly. That is a dangerous game."

"It is," Musin agreed. "But we're desperate and they know it. While we don't know exactly what they want, we know they can't get it for themselves and we can leverage that advantage. They need us. The next step is to learn more about what they want, or at least what they claim to want."

"If we help them get whatever they've been after this whole time," Carlos called out angrily, "then what was the point of fighting them in the first place? And how do we know that what they're after isn't even worse than the natural array exploding? What if they get us to turn the array into a volcano weapon they can take from city to city, wiping out our civilisation?"

"That's... one potential scenario, I suppose," Musin said. "I don't think any of us believe that we should let the messengers get what they want. But the reality is, they have a want and we have a need. If we fail to stop the array from going completely out of control, Yaresh is gone and the whole region will be uninhabitable. Even if we evacuate the whole region, the volcano will bring desolation, blotting out the sky. So soon after the monster surge, it may even damage the still-fragile dimensional membrane, causing additional monster manifestations. Elementals of fire, ash and magma in almost monster surge numbers, roaming out to spread the desolation even further."

"No one is suggesting we do nothing," Emir said. "But we're talking about a vicious and cruel enemy who will sacrifice her forces to hurt ours even worse. They lost a diamond-ranker attacking this city and I've seen no indication she even cares."

"Actually," Musin said, "we believe the diamond-ranker's death may have been one of Jes Fin Kaal's intentions. Given the unusual nature of his death, she may have even arranged his assassination using the battle to hide it. We would need to know more of the event in question to confirm anything, but not all parties involved have proven willing to share."

The room's occupants once again turned their eyes to Jason, who looked up from the drink he was mixing, ingredients held floating in front of him by his aura.

"What?" he asked innocently. The director shook his head and continued.

"Messengers have their own politics, and the absence of a local diamond-rank messenger has left the Voice of the Will as the solitary authority. It's possible that the entire attack was simply a messenger power play."

"And you want to make a deal with someone willing to wage war on a city full of innocent people for only that," Carlos said. "We have diamond-rankers and they don't anymore. We should plunder their strongholds and steal their magic before a new diamond-ranker arrives to reinforce them."

"An approach that has been discussed, certainly," Musin said. "Discussed and rejected. We could eliminate the remaining messenger strongholds, yes, but the cost in adventurer lives would be prohibitive. We've lost enough, and there were always compelling reasons to not throw away the lives required to overrun those fortresses. You are free to try and convince Lady Allayeth to change her mind, however. She would not be amongst the casualties."

Carlos looked at the diamond-ranker, bowed his head and sat back in his chair, done.

"If I read this situation correctly," Emir said to Musin, "your plan is to form an alliance with Jes Fin Kaal, who will absolutely betray us, and betray her better and first."

"It's not a good plan," Musin confessed, "but days are desperate. In the end, we must do what we have always done: trust in adventurers to keep us safe. The people in this room represent power and knowledge in many fields. You are the best we can muster."

"I can't help but notice," Jason said, "that natural array expertise is not one of those many fields. That strikes me as an odd omission, as does the absence of anyone from the Magic Society. The closest we have here are adventurers with Magic Society membership. No actual officials; no researchers. Not even a spokesperson functionary. Is there a problem with the Magic Society, Director Heath?"

It was not Musin but Jillet who answered.

"The natural array experts, as it turned out, were hiding the scope of the natural array problem. They told no one and continued their research until the city was attacked. After the attack, they warned us finally of the danger the array presents. In a final report left behind when they quietly departed the city."

"The director of the Magical Society claimed he had no authority to force their return," Musin said. "I requested new natural array experts, but that request is pending. Which I was told by the Magic Society's deputy director, due to the director's sudden sabbatical. I am, in short, not filled with confidence."

"Sounds about right," Clive grumbled.

"It comes down to this," Musin said. "Our options are to abandon and evacuate the entire region or make a dark bargain with the messengers and hope that we can outplay them when the time comes. We have the advantage of their inability to go anywhere near the array."

"And they have the advantage of having the first idea of what's actually happening," Emir said. "I'm hearing nothing but bad ideas built on guesswork, assumption and a level of optimism I can only describe as ill-founded. We have months before this disaster, yes? Yaresh is already little more than an ash heap and half the region's towns are infested with world-conquering parasites. Perhaps the time and resources currently earmarked for reconstruction would do more good preparing to contain the eruption of the natural array. Minimise the damage to this and the surrounding regions."

The room got extremely tense, with the Yaresh residents filled with hostility towards Emir. This included Allayeth, whose aura settled on Emir like concrete shoulder pads.

"This meeting," she said in a voice so cold, her breath almost fogged up, "is about saving this city. If you are unwilling to accept that as an absolute objective, Mr Bahadir, then we will thank you for the venue and thank you to leave the room while we continue discussing how to save our home."

Emir threw his hands up in surrender.

"Alright," he said. "I just think that any discussion should table every option, even if they're dismissed out of hand."

"Then consider your suggestion dismissed, Mr Bahadir," Musin said. He then took a dimensional satchel slung over his shoulder and opened it, removing a cube covered in glowing runes.

"A table if you please, Mr Bahadir."

A small cloud table rose in front of the director and he placed the cube down. He tapped at the runes in a complex sequence than involved turning the cube on its various sides. The glow faded, rune by rune, until they had all dimmed. Musin opened one side of the cube and removed a slightly smaller but otherwise identical cube and repeated the sequence.

"Constance," Jason said, "if there's another Rubik's babushka in there, I'm putting out a snack table. Is that okay?"

"Why are you asking her and not me?" Emir complained. Constance and Jason both looked at him and his expression wilted to a sulk.

There was no third cube but a blue sphere, twice the size of a fist.

"We've spoken about the messengers having magic more advanced than ours," Musin said. "This is a messenger communication stone through which we can contact Jes Fin Kaal. As we cannot be sure if she can spy on us through this device, we had it under as much restriction as was remotely practical. But there is one more element that I have not raised. The messenger leader is only willing to continue discussion if Jason Asano is involved."

"Is that because she wants a snack table as well?" Jason asked. "I need to find out about messenger cuisine, although I'm not optimistic. I'm picturing a lot of bran."

11

DECORUM

A LARGE GROUP OF MOSTLY VERY SERIOUS PEOPLE WERE HAVING A meeting in a room with a bouncy house floor. The attendees were looking at a blue orb sitting on a table.

"This device was delivered to us by a messenger," said Musin Heath. "Accordingly, we don't trust it at all."

The Adventure Society director was behind the table with the Knowledge priest, Ebson Jillet, who tapped the two boxes behind the orb. The smaller box had previously contained the orb, while the larger one had contained the first box.

"If the orb explodes or does anything unexpected," Jillet said, "this box will absorb and contain it. It can even draw in poison gas, explosive force or a variety of other magical threats."

"Using the orb is very simple," Musin explained.

"Is it?" Jason asked. "I don't think you've got it the right way up."

Musin rocked the orb back and forth with his finger.

"I don't think there's any way to tell. I don't think there is a right way up."

"If you say so," Jason said, sceptical but not pushing the issue. Musin continued his explanation.

"A trickle of mana will let you control it intuitively, like most magic items. Once I send a signal through it that we're ready to communicate, that will allow Jes Fin Kaal to open a communication channel. I would ask that you refrain from speaking out while the channel is open. The exception being Mr Asano, whose participation was a requirement of ongoing negotiations. She will only speak to him going forward."

"Because they're probably working together," one of the gold-rankers said. He was unknown to Jason, acting as security for the government officials. "This man Asano is as suspicious as the messengers. He's been hiding from us and keeping secrets. It's fairly obvious he's working with them and I don't know why we haven't already peeled the secrets out of him, now that he's left his hiding hole. He was just using his aura to make a drink, for gods' sakes. None of us can move things with our auras. Only messengers can do that."

Jason let out a weary sigh.

"What's your name?"

"Ikola Goeth."

"Are you suggesting that I'm a messenger, Ikola?" Jason asked lightly.

"Why not?" Ikola asked. "You're an outworlder to my senses, but there was another outworlder in this city too. He turned out to be some magic snake egg planted by the messengers decades ago. There are still naga hiding in the ruins of the city that came out of that thing."

"See, now that's just frustrating," Jason said. "The last guy who spoke up—I'm assuming he's a mate of yours—got dragged out of the room."

Jason turned to Allayeth.

"Where did you have that thing take him?"

"Jason," Allayeth said. "I think you may be getting distracted."

"From what?"

"The man accusing you of having been planted by the messengers."

"What? Oh, right. Maybe you should probably give him his friend back?"

"Fine," Allayeth said. She turned to look at the door and everyone else did the same. No one had the nerve to speak up, Jason loudly slurping his beverage the only sound. After almost a minute, they heard dragging sounds as Allayeth's plant monster brought back in its bedraggled victim. The plant then turned into a cloud of dust and flaky ash, coating the nearest people. The man on the floor was covered in welts, visible through the shredded remains of his black clothing. As the man groaned feebly, Jason turned back to Ikola.

"Now," Jason said, "I was just saying that you accusing me like this is frustrating because if I make a move to intimidate you into silence, it just makes your words seem true. Would I like to take a power sander to your face for accusing me of being on the side of the people who levelled the city and killed I don't know how many people? Of course I would, that's only natural. But that wouldn't be productive. We're all on the same side, and we need to reach an accommodation based on cooperation rather than—"

He paused as the injured gold-ranker on the floor let out a loud groan of pain.

"—a pecking order based on the ability to perpetrate violence."

Jason scowled at the fallen man.

"Bloke, you're kind of undercutting me here. Get it together."

Ikola got out of his chair and Jason did the same, the fallen man between them. The elven gold-ranker was half a head taller and dressed entirely in black. Jason was wearing a cream suit with a pink shirt from the collection tailored for him in Rimaros.

"Is nothing serious to you?" Ikola asked.

"You accused me of being a traitor," Jason told him. "This meeting would get even more awkward if I took that seriously instead of in good humour."

"You think you're so special, don't you?" the gold-ranker accused.

"Yep. And so do you, which I suspect is the real reason you're so cranky. I'm going to sit back down and pretend you didn't level the kind of accusation that gets people murdering one another. I'm hoping that you'll also sit down, engage in some self-reflection or at least just sit quietly. I understand that, as a gold-ranker, you aren't used to being the guy standing at the back, but you're here as a guard. In case you hadn't noticed, there's a who's who of gold- and diamond-rankers watching us squabble like children and it's not doing any favours for either of our reputations."

Ikola glanced left and right, frowning in the unhappy realisation that Jason was right. He looked to be on the verge of stepping back but couldn't quite bring himself to let it go.

"You are a walking traitor flag and you get to attack someone, but I'm expected to sit down and keep my mouth shut?"

Jason opened his mouth to retort but stopped himself, letting out a sigh as his shoulders slumped.

"You're right," he said. "It's not fair, and I've indulged in the kind of arrogant behaviour that not only have I done time and again, but I've criticised in others. So, how about I apologise to the guy on the ground for overreacting when he had a go at my friend, and you and I both step back and we let this meeting go forward?"

"Which neatly avoids the question of whether you're a traitor when every indication is that you are."

Jason looked at Ikola for a moment and then turned to the Adventure Society director.

"I tried," Jason said. "De-escalation doesn't come naturally to me, which I think everyone saw pretty clearly. But I tried, I really did. I don't think we can move on to the next stage of this meeting with both him and me in the room, and I'm pretty sure you need me."

The director did not look happy with Jason or Ikola, but it was Ikola he turned to.

"Mr Goeth, I must ask you to sit down and refrain from making further interruptions. If you feel that you are unable to do this, I must ask you to remove yourself instead."

Ikola looked like he was going to argue but held his tongue. He helped the battered gold-ranker from the floor to his chair, frowning at the welts that should have already healed but remained bright red. He took his own seat with a dark glower and Musin turned his attention to Jason.

"And you, Mr Asano, I would advise you to be less provocative in how you act, as well as in how you react to others. I recognise that you have an outsized level of influence relative to your rank and you may feel the need to assert that influence when those of higher rank seek to suppress it. That being said, I think you will find that decorum will serve you better than acting out like a smug teenage aristocrat."

The people in the room who knew Jason all winced, except for Arabelle. Jason didn't respond to the director and, instead, quietly retook his seat.

"Thank you, Mr Asano," Musin said. "I will have you stand up again shortly once we activate the orb. As I was saying, prior to the interruption, once I signal that we are ready, the messengers will be able to open a channel for us to negotiate through. Jes Fin Kaal has made it clear that she will only negotiate with Mr Asano, whom I hope will take heed of my advice."

Most of the room's occupants glanced in Jason's direction, but he showed no reaction to them or Musin's words.

"If there are no more interruptions," Musin said, his tone indicating that it was not a question, "then we will begin."

He reached out and touched a finger to the orb.

"It's done."

The orb sat still on the table.

It continued sitting still on the table.

Emir surreptitiously checked his pocket watch and had his wrist slapped by his wife.

Jillet moved over to Musin and activated a small privacy screen behind which they talked unheard by the room's other occupants, but watched by all. There was a minor visible component that blurred the area enough to prevent lip reading, but body language was still visible. Musin variously nodded, shrugged, shook his head and held out empty hands as he and Jillet spoke. Finally, Jillet deactivated the privacy screen.

"...yes, I'm sure it's on," Musin finished, now audible to the room. His eyes darted back and forth and he slowly reached out to the orb as if that would somehow prevent everyone from noticing. His fingers brushed against it.

"It's definitely on," he said to no one in particular. "I was sure it was, and it was."

He was saved from the awkward moment by the orb emitting a soft glow.

"Right," Musin said. "If you would stand in front of the orb, please, Mr Asano?"

Jason got up and positioned himself in front of the table with a frown.

"This feels more like standing in front of a firing squad than I'm comfortable with," he grumbled.

Musin reached out and touched the orb again. A hologram-like image of someone's head projected from the front of the sphere, slightly off-centre and tilted down. This gave Jason a view of the top of the head and one ear.

"What am I looking at?" the projection of Jes Fin Kaal asked. Musin quickly turned the orb so the projection rose from the top and the messenger's face became visible.

"It wasn't clear which way was up," Musin said. "You should consider marking them so people can tell."

"It doesn't matter," Jes Fin Kaal said, her gaze now locked on Jason. "So, you are their king."

"I'm no one's king, lady, and I refuse to believe you said that for any reason other than riling up the other people in this room against me."

She smiled.

"Not a complete idiot, then, which I appreciate. It was an open question, given the research we've done on you. I admit that I've been anticipating our meeting for some time."

"Personally, I wished you'd invaded with the next monster surge. Once I'm gold rank, I could put you down myself instead of watching someone else do it."

"False machismo to make me think you're simple-minded enough to be led around by your own aggressive mindset? You can do better than that, Asano."

"I really can't. I actually am that simple-minded, so I talk about the films of Michael Dudikoff until people get distracted. People are starting to get wise to me, though: no one even asked me what a power sander was."

Jason had never wondered what a snake would sound like if it laughed until he heard Jes Fin Kaal do it.

"I was told you would likely use irreverence and references to your home world in an attempt to disrupt my train of thought. You'll have to do better than that, Jason Asano."

"Alright. Two strongholds. That's the price."

"You want me to relinquish two more strongholds in return for your working with us?"

"No," Jason said. "You attacked us. You infested people with those parasites, which is a kind of horror even I have trouble imagining, and I've been through some stuff. You killed people, took their homes and everything that matters to them and now you're here to make a deal?"

"I don't think that you will let anger guide you. I'm sure you've been informed by now that the threat below your feet is greater than any presented by me. You need us."

"No, we don't. With what you've done to this city, it's better to pack everyone up, relocate and write the whole region off. It's cheaper to contain the damage and rebuild elsewhere than clean up the mess you left behind."

"I very much doubt the people in the room with you agree, Asano."

"But you're not talking to them. You made it very clear that you would only talk to me, so here are your options: One, you abandon—"

"This is a negotiation, Asano. I'm not here to listen to your ultimatums."

"We aren't negotiating yet, lady. I told you that two strongholds is the price, but I didn't mean to get us working with you. That's the price for me to even listen to what you want."

"You think this tough-man act will work on me?"

"Nope. I doubt an axe to the head would work on you either, but if I get the chance, you'd better believe I'll check. If you want me to listen to anything you say, empty two more of your strongholds and destroy them behind you."

"It seems that I should have negotiated with the city officials after all."

"Probably," Jason agreed. "Feel free to do that. But if you're sticking with me, you know the price. Don't call back until it's done."

Jason slapped his hand on the orb and the projection disappeared. He turned to look at a room full of horrified faces.

"I thought that went pretty well," he said.

12

A MAN OF PRINCIPLE

In a room full of shocked faces, Arabelle stood up and moved over to Jason, the bouncy floor making it slightly awkward.

"You're playing things dangerously, Jason," she told him. "But you did well."

The Adventure Society director's expression showed that he was not in agreement, but he was not one to explode into bluster.

"Mrs Remore, not to disagree with an expert in the study of the mind, but I would appreciate your thoughts on what makes Mr Asano's... bold negotiating strategy the correct path."

"I don't know how much you are aware of messenger upbringing, Director," she said, "but messengers are born fully grown and immediately put through comprehensive indoctrination. Even those who have escaped the behavioural programming of that indoctrination still exhibit certain behavioural traits that may be, in part, driven by inherent physiological factors. Natural instincts, if you will."

"And how is it that you are so familiar with the messengers?" asked the leader of the local government delegation.

He was a bureaucrat who had reached gold rank through cores. This was his first time speaking up in the meeting, although declining to rein in his guard, Ikola, made a statement on its own. Arabelle turned to look at him, her expression ostensibly blank, yet somehow conveying the idea that she had found the man stuck to the bottom of her shoe.

"I didn't catch your name," she told him.

"Calcifer Bynes," the bureaucrat said. "Director of the Office of External Affairs. You seem to be more familiar with the messengers than the rest of us, Mrs Remore. I must confess a curiosity as to how that came about, given the violent reactions that messengers tend to have towards anyone who isn't one of their servants."

Arabelle smiled.

"Well, Mr Bynes—"

"Lord Bynes," he corrected. "Director Bynes is acceptable in certain contexts, where I am acting in my role as a representative of the city, although I would not recommend it. Addressing me as Lord Bynes at all times will save embarrassment for those who have trouble grasping the intricacies of proper etiquette."

"*Lord* Bynes," she corrected. "I'm afraid that some questions can only be answered through demonstration. I would be delighted to show you exactly how and where I've had the opportunity to observe messengers, including examples of both having rejected indoctrination and remaining in its throes."

Jason noticed the Knowledge priest, Jillet, listening with particular interest. Jason opened the portal to his soul realm next to Arabelle.

"How do people keep opening portals in here?" Emir complained. "That guy who installed the dimensional suppression was worthless."

"*You* installed the dimensional suppression," Constance pointed out.

"I distinctly remember getting in a guy."

"Yes. Then you kicked him out."

"Why would I do that?"

"He invited me to dinner."

"Oh. That makes sense."

Arabelle spared her old teammate a wry glance before turning back to Bynes and gesturing to the portal invitingly.

"You can find the answers on the other side of that portal, Lord Bynes. I can only assume you are willing, if not eager, to step through. Surely a man so unsubtle in how he throws around implications is only doing so that he might have the opportunity to investigate their accuracy. You wouldn't go implying that I am an unintelligent traitor only to not just imply but outright prove yourself both a hypocrite and a coward, would you? Please step through the portal."

"Mrs Remore," Allayeth said. "I am afraid that Lord… Bynes, was it? Lord Bynes does not have the level of refinement in his perceptual abilities that one might expect from someone of his rank. It is only natural that in his role as an administrator, he does not have the time for the kind of training that even most core users would manage. This is only to be expected, as why would he waste time with such exercises when he never encounters any monsters? Even during the monster surge, his aptitude as an organiser makes him far too useful to be on the front lines. After all, what is the value of just another gold-ranker, with a startling level of under-preparedness to face any monster, compared to a logistician of what I assume must be great capability."

Arabelle smiled as Bynes schooled his emotions enough that his lips pressing together hard was the only indication of his rage. Whatever the truth of Allayeth's claims about the man's perception abilities, Jason recognised that the man was skilled at keeping his emotions out of his aura.

"I believe I understand, Lady Allayeth," Arabelle said. "You're saying that Lord Bynes is ill-equipped to understand what he would be walking into through that portal until he sees it for himself."

"I am," Allayeth said. "While I am confident that Lord Bynes has a dazzling expertise in his chosen field of administration, that expertise understandably falls short on issues relating to adventurers and their activities. I'm certain that any implications he may have inadvertently made against a celebrated adventurer who has braved danger time and time again were entirely by accident. As such, I have no doubt that he would be more than happy to *quite explicitly* retract them. Of course, I may be incorrect and Lord Bynes was entirely deliberate in how he chose his words."

Allayeth's friendly smile plunged into Bynes' mind, found the most primal fear response he had and triggered it.

"If Lord Bynes was deliberate in his implications," Allayeth continued, "he would surely be happy to put his principles to the test. He would most certainly step through that portal, even not knowing what lies beyond. To do anything less would be to show himself a craven and insincere politician who mouths principles and exploits baseless accusations with neither the intention nor ability to interrogate their veracity."

The administrator sat silently in his seat, jaw locked. If it was only Arabelle, a fellow gold-ranker and outsider to Yaresh, he would have been able to shoot back. The woman was a century too early if she thought she was his equal in slinging mud.

A diamond-ranker who was also a native was another prospect entirely.

In politics, if a diamond-ranker said the sky was green, then all you could do was nod and agree. For all you knew, they could turn it green to prove you wrong if you had the lack of sense to gainsay them. Allayeth talking to him this way sent the same blunt message as having his guard dragged away by a plant monster—the only options were obedience or humiliation. From pretending she didn't remember his name to delivering an unpalatable ultimatum, she had used the power of a diamond-ranker to force him into a corner.

In his mind, Bynes scrambled for a fresh option, but only saw the two Allayeth had offered him. One was to apologise to the Remore woman, undercutting his prestige. There were enough people in the room that word would spread and his political influence would take a hit, requiring time to claw back. That would be an unpleasant but acceptable option if not for his father. The venerable Gormanston Bynes had been making noises about dignity of the aristocracy of late, and Calcifer could not afford to lose his father's support.

That left going through the portal. For some reason, neither of them seemed to believe he would be willing to go through the portal, which left him wondering why. There was only so far they would be willing to go, and he was almost certain it was all show. Allayeth's pet silver-ranker and Arabelle were not Lady Allayeth, and could not afford to match her brazenness. They believed that he would fear the mystery of the portal and fail to call their bluff.

The portal had appeared next to the Remore woman. He hadn't seen anyone call it up, but it was obvious enough, radiating Asano's aura. Allayeth's jibes about Calcifer's perception were not entirely without basis, so there was little else he could determine from examining it. The only other thing his senses picked up was some power on the portal's other side. It was much stronger than Asano, but Asano's aura infused the portal, masking the nature and owner of whatever lay beyond.

There was no doubt Asano was an anomaly, given his aura at silver rank. The general consensus was that he had one or more powerful backers using him as a proxy. There were the stories about him out of Rimaros, but Bynes was not stupid enough to accept them. Clearly outlandish exaggerations, he could no longer trust Havi Estos, his information broker in the Storm Kingdom.

Bynes stood up. He might not be willing to face off against monsters, but why should he? He didn't have the training or the experience. His battlefields were offices, salons and ballrooms; his weapons were information and innuendo. Just because he wouldn't take up a sword did not mean he was a coward. He was clearly expected to back off, so the way to fight back was to take the option they didn't think that he would.

Bynes was clued into political events enough to know that the diamond-rankers had been seeking out whatever was on the other side of that portal. Allayeth's colleague, Charist, detested politics and administration. Bynes had always been happy to help him out, taking on any and all tedious tasks and requests that Charist wished to avoid. It was more than worth the effort as the loose-lipped diamond-ranker was an information gold mine.

Bynes had no idea why Charist and Allayeth not entering Asano's portal was a topic of discussion. No silver-ranker, even a portal specialist, was able to call up a portal that diamond-rankers could use. What he did know was that the two diamond-rankers wanted information that was inside that portal. That secret was probably how Asano had become Lady Allayeth's pet.

If Bynes could deliver what Allayeth wanted to know, he could undercut Asano's influence. Or perhaps it would be better to give the information to Charist. Bynes had an existing relationship and, if played right, Charist could become a shield against Allayeth in the long term.

The two diamond-rankers had a long record of working together, their different styles making for complementary approaches. Below the surface, however, Bynes knew that relationships between powerful but very different people were delicate. If he was clever and careful, he might be able to pit them against one another, allowing him to profit. And with the entire city to be rebuilt, there was plenty of profit to be had.

"I am a man of principle," Bynes lied. "I want to see for myself where you have been consorting with messengers, Mrs Remore."

Arabelle's eyebrows went up in surprise and Allayeth had a delighted grin that Bynes tried not to let worry him.

"You're going through," Allayeth said. "I'm surprised, Lord Bynes; you have my admiration. I'm extremely fascinated about what happens to... about what you see in there."

As for Jason Asano, he was rubbing his temples like he had a headache.

"Do we have to do this now?" he asked. "I thought I was bad for derailing meetings, but you've all crashed this one into a school. For puppies."

"Regrets, Asano?" Bynes asked in a mocking tone.

"Look," Jason said. "I'm just saying that maybe we get this meeting back on track and we play who's brave enough to go through the mysterious portal later."

"No," Bynes insisted. "My character has been impugned. We must settle this now."

Jason frowned in confusion.

"So, what you're saying is, your reputation is more important than the cataclysmic event that threatens to destroy the entire city?"

"Of course not."

"Then, let's get back to the meeting."

"And leave my good name flapping in the breeze like a soiled flag?"

"Okay," Jason told him. "It doesn't sound like what I'm saying is getting through."

He held up his hands as if comparing the weight of two invisible objects.

"On one hand, we've got the city blowing up and the whole region being drowned in fire and ash. On the other, we have people thinking that you're bit of a prick. Which of those do you think is in more urgent need of address?"

"The disaster is months away, and we can resolve the issue of my reputation right now. Would you string my reputation out to be dragged through the mud until the city is saved?"

"Wow," Jason said. "Was not expecting you to choose your reputation over stopping a volcano from wiping out hundreds of thousands of people."

"You seem adamant about not allowing me through that portal, Asano. Do you have something to hide?"

"Uh, no. I'd just like to, you know, clean up a bit. I wasn't expecting guests. And also," he said, wheeling on Arabelle and Allayeth, "I never actually volunteered to participate in this. You two said he should go through the portal and you never even asked. Which is rude."

"You opened up the portal on cue," Arabelle pointed out. "Don't go complaining that you weren't completely complicit in what happens to Lord Bynes."

Jason let out a groan.

"Fine," he said resignedly, gesturing at the portal. "Go for it. If you have to. Which you don't."

"Lord Bynes," Ikola said. "I strongly advise against going through a portal to an uncertain destination. It was opened by a silver-ranker and can still accommodate you. That suggests a power behind it that is far greater than Asano, and one we know nothing about."

"Then it is time we dragged Asano's backer out of the shadows," Bynes said.

He threw Jason a disdainful glare, marched over to the portal and went through.

Jason turned to Arabelle and Allayeth.

"I don't know why you wanted him in there, but you were too enthusiastic about it. He probably would have backed out if he didn't think I was trying to avoid his digging up my secrets."

"Is he going to dig up your secrets?" Allayeth asked.

"Probably. Anyway, now he's gone, we should get back to the meeting, yeah?"

They looked around the room whose occupants were divided into two groups. The ones who knew Jason all wore long-suffering expressions. The rest looked like they had no idea what was happening, but there was a diamond-ranker acting strangely, which was a very good reason to be almost anywhere else.

"Regardless of what Lord Bynes is doing," the Adventure Society director said, "Mr Asano is correct in that the matter at hand is the impending disaster. For that reason, I would like to return to the topic of why Mr Asano's approach to negotiation with the messengers was the correct one. It was highly aggressive."

"That was necessary," Arabelle said. "Before Lord Bynes interrupted, I was trying to explain that messengers, like all living creatures, have natural instincts. For the messengers, their natural instinct is to respect strength and disregard weakness. It's a predatory instinct that divides everything into threat or prey. Obviously, messengers have higher mental functions that let them move beyond base instinct, but we are all driven by our instincts far more than we realise."

"You are saying that a more conciliatory approach would have hurt us," the director said.

"Yes," Arabelle said with a firm nod. "If Jason was anything but unyielding, Jes Fin Kaal would have lost any respect for him. She may have become much harder to negotiate with or potentially dropped out entirely."

"But that does not change the fact that we are negotiating from a position of weakness," the director said. "We have already stated that we will not give up this land. I understand the value of bluffing, Mr Asano, but if they call that bluff, we will fold."

"It's not a bluff," Jason said. "The messenger wants something. From me. And I'm not letting her dictate terms because you refuse to relocate. I'm prepared to walk away, at which point you can negotiate with her yourself."

Jason and the director stared at each other for a long time.

"This is not your home," the director said. "I can't ask you to throw yourself into the monster's lair for us. But relocating and allowing the disaster to take place is a far from desirable outcome."

"You don't need to worry about Jason," Arabelle assured the director. "I've been working with him for years, now, and what never changes is that he'll always throw himself into the monster's lair. However much he might whine and complain about it."

"Also, he wasn't just aggressive in that negotiation," Emir chimed in. "I'm not the only one who felt that was a little flirty, right?"

"Oh, he's always like that," Neil called out from the back. "You should see him with Clive's wife."

"Oh, gods damn it, Neil…"

Bynes burst from the portal at a full sprint, barrelling across the room in a mad panic. He stumbled on the bouncy cloud floor but didn't stop, scrambling through the door and down the hall in a gold-rank blur of speed.

1 3

EXPERIMENT

JASON WENT TO THE DOOR OF THE MEETING ROOM AND LOOKED OUT, BUT Lord Bynes was already gone. Being a monster core user didn't hurt his gold-rank speed and he had shot out like a rocket.

"Does he even know the way out?" Jason wondered aloud. "There was an elevating platform. It would feel weird to pause in the middle of a panicked flight to stop, calmly ride an elevator down and then bolt off in a mad dash again."

"He skipped the elevating platform," Emir said. Like Jason, he could sense the people in his cloud house. "He went out through a window."

Jason turned around to face Allayeth and Arabelle.

"Look," he said. "I played along, but can someone explain to me why we just ran that guy over the coals?"

"What did you do to him exactly?" Arabelle asked. "I've seen many kinds of fear, but what was coming off that man's aura was new to me."

"I've seen it," Allayeth said. "I've even felt it, but not like Lord Bynes. I'm finding my curiosity as to what lies beyond that portal of yours freshly aroused."

"Do try to control yourself," Jason told her. "You shouldn't let your curiosity be aroused in front of all these people."

"You say that," Allayeth told him, "yet you keep arousing it over and over."

"I'm not going out of my way to be arousing."

"I'm not sure I entirely believe that," Allayeth said. "There's only so arousing a person can be by accident, and given the frequency with which you are being arousing, I can only assume it is on purpose."

"I need you both to stop saying 'arouse,' and remember the importance of this meeting," Arabelle told them.

"We all might need that," Clive added, glaring at Neil.

"Especially while you're standing next to my mother, Jason," Rufus said.

"Ask Humphrey about Jason and mothers," Neil muttered. "I told you he was like that."

"I wish I was like that," Travis mumbled, glancing at Gabrielle. She, in turn, was glaring at Jason.

"See," she said to her fellow priests and priestesses. "What did I tell you? Moral turpitude."

"I thought turpitude was a thing you used to clean boats," Taika said.

"It depends on the boat," Jason told him. "I will admit, though, it does mostly make them dirtier."

The Adventure Society director looked on in a combination of confusion and horror. The fate of his city rested on a meeting where the silver-rankers brazenly ignored rank decorum, the gold-rankers were pulling pranks on city officials and even the diamond-ranker was spouting off innuendos.

"I think," he declared loudly, "that it is time to call this meeting to an end. I will discuss aspects of what is happening with the various interested parties in smaller group sessions. I will reconvene this meeting when it is appropriate or when we see any kind of response from Jes Fin Kaal."

He put on his best stern expression, panning it across the room.

"I *hope*," he added, "that we can all show some more decorum when next we meet."

The meeting broke up in short order. Rick Geller frowned as he watched Jason leaving with Arabelle and Allayeth, and got a slap on the back of his head from his girlfriend, Hannah.

"What was that for?" Rick asked, turning on her.

"I don't know," Hannah said. "But I'm pretty sure you deserved it."

Rick glanced back at Jason, the gold-ranker and the diamond-ranker as they disappeared through the door.

"Yeah, probably," he admitted in a resigned voice.

"Jason," Arabelle said as they walked through the halls of Emir's cloud palace. "What exactly did you show that man?"

"I'm curious as well," Allayeth agreed.

"You said you'd felt that kind of fear yourself," Jason said. "Where did you encounter something like that?"

"Every diamond-ranker has," Allayeth said. "You're silver rank now, and soon you'll begin to realise that once you approach the limits of silver rank, you can't just advance the way you have, training and pushing yourself. Monster core users can push through to gold, but that rather dead-ends them."

"He's not ready for that yet," Arabelle pointed out. "Not quite."

"That's fine," Allayeth said. "What we're talking about is the transition from gold to diamond-rank anyway. As you grow closer to the pinnacle of gold, you start to get an instinctive sense of something that lies beyond. Not diamond rank itself, but what lies beyond that."

"Transcendence," Jason said.

"Yes. Do you know much about transcendence?"

"I've picked up things here and there. Literally. The first magic item I ever got was transcendent rank."

Allayeth turned to him, wide-eyed.

"You've seen a transcendent rank item?"

"I've used a few," he said casually as they stepped onto an elevating platform. "I kind of go through them, now that I think about it. It might be one of my things."

"More than one transcendent item?" Allayeth said faintly. "What did they do?"

"The first one brought me back from the dead. For, I want to say the second time? Yeah, the second time. Took me back to my world while it was at it."

"To the other universe."

"Yep. That one was a consumable, so it was only ever meant to be a one-and-done. I had this magic door for rewriting reality and—"

"Rewriting reality?"

"I know, right? Thankfully, I'd just hit silver rank; I'd have Buckley's chance of remaking chunks of the planet at bronze rank. Anyway, the Builder left this door so some muppet would come along—in this case, me—and fix reality after it had been left a bit janky by the last bloke with his job. The magic door would let the Builder worm his way into the person that used it, but the Builder tried that with me once already and I wasn't having it. I wiped off the Builder's control, gave myself the old five-finger discount and ninja'd the door for myself. Later on, the World-Phoenix gave me this dimensional bridge thing, but I accidentally smashed that one and the Builder's door at the same time. I was storing them in my soul, but I gave the old soul a bit of what-for. They both ended up getting smashed and broken down for parts."

Allayeth looked at Arabelle who gave her a sympathetic shake of the head.

"Jason occasionally likes to push the limits of his translation power," Arabelle told her. "I'll explain later. For now, you were talking about transcendence."

"Uh, yes," Allayeth said, regaining her composure. "As I was saying, those of us who approach the peak of gold rank start to get a sense of what lies at the end of the path. A state of being that no amount of advancement can achieve. A state you can only begin to seek once every drop of mortal potential has been wrung out of you. The pinnacle does not lead to the next journey, but gives you a hint of where it begins."

"Moving beyond diamond rank," Arabelle said. "That is possible, then?"

"No," Allayeth said. "And that is rather the point. To transcend, you have to go beyond not just the limits of mortality, but possibility. The glimpses of the wider cosmos you gain as you approach diamond rank are soul-crushing. The truth of how insignificant you are seeps into the depths of your soul. You comprehend it in its complete and utterly stark fullness, right down into the depths of your soul."

"And that breaks people," Jason said.

"It can," Allayeth agreed. "For those who believe themselves important—and what gold-ranker doesn't—it can, indeed, break them. We are specks of sand on a beach that goes on forever, lasting only an instant before blowing away on the wind. The very world we stand on exists only for a fleeting moment in an insignificant corner of infinity."

The platform reached the bottom floor and they continued through Emir's massive cloud palace. There was a bustle of activity as people came through to be tested for world-taker worms and processed for housing and food allocation. The mass of people instinctively moved around them without even realising they were doing it. Jason observed Allayeth's aura manipulation producing the effect and took mental notes.

"The revelation of the cosmos and our place in it is too much for some," Allayeth said. "As you said, it breaks them. For others, it is a comfort to be a part of such grandness. It places the petty squabbles we all fight into perspective, revealing that they are, on a cosmic scale, meaningless."

"I always kind of liked it," Jason said. "Is that weird?"

"It's unusual, but not unheard of," Allayeth said. "Some face the revelation of cosmic magnitude with more acceptance. There are those for whom it does nothing; no effect at all. They are at one with themselves, who they are, and who they are not. Seeing their place in all things fails to change that. For those who are already in this state, moving from gold to diamond proves a relatively easy transition. For the rest of us, we have to try and reach that state. It doesn't have to be forever, but we need to find that equanimity for at least a time in order to move beyond gold rank."

"And you did that," Arabelle said. "As a scholar of the mind, I respect your ability to achieve such a condition."

"I spent years in isolation. Sometimes wandering the world, other times in uninhabited places, meditating for weeks or even months. Eventually, I found a peace through which I was able to surpass my previous limits. I'm not sure I could find that again if I tried. I know that fear we saw in Calcifer Bynes; a dread that reaches into the core of you. It takes who you think you are and makes you realise that you're infinitesimally smaller."

She looked at Jason.

"What I want to know," she asked, "is why I felt that same fear from Lord Bynes. He may be a gold-ranker, but he's not even close to the peak. Even if he were, he wouldn't sense what I described. A core user that does is the extreme exception, usually master craftspeople. Bynes is very far from that, so how did you show him the entirety of the cosmos?"

Jason didn't answer immediately, as they had reached the entrance to the cloud palace, moving through the waves of people. When they went outside, Jason's aura shucked off the heavy rain as they walked on a path of stone slabs set into the mud.

"You know your friend Charist is listening to us," Jason told Allayeth. "I'm not going to go giving up my secrets for free. I want information in return."

"What do you want?" she asked, her voice sober.

"You have to tell me everything about the sauce that was in that sandwich."

Arabelle slapped a hand over her face and Allayeth's eyebrows moved upwards.

"And I mean everything," Jason said. "Where you got it, what it's made of, what is the process. Are there variants? How are the ingredients cultivated? In what conditions? Who made it? Did they grow the ingredients themselves? How is it stored? Is there a difference when—"

"I'm serious," Allayeth said. "This isn't just about finding out something for a political purpose, here. We're talking about the fundamental mechanics of essence user advancement…"

Allayeth trailed off as Jason did something with his aura. The air around them shivered and the two women felt something lock into place.

"What is this?" Allayeth asked. "This isn't something you can do with a normal aura. This feels like a messenger technique."

"It has elements of the way messengers use their auras," Jason said. "It's something I've been working on. Essentially, it's an aura-based privacy screen. I based it on a lot of elements. Messenger techniques, certainly, but also examining how mine and Emir's cloud palaces obscure external senses. Plus, how gods secure their holy spaces. The inviolable places at the core of their temples."

"How would you even understand how the gods do that?" Allayeth asked.

"I know you've felt it," Jason told her. "You and your friend violated my home, forcing your way into the places your senses wouldn't penetrate. As much as I appreciate a good spicy sauce—and it's a lot—I haven't forgotten what you did. Now, can your senses penetrate this privacy screen without me noticing? I know you could smash them through it, but could you weasel them in?"

Jason felt a tingle on his aura senses.

"Maybe," she said. "Not quickly, at least until I examine the technique you're using some more."

"Then I want your word that anything you manipulate me into giving up stays with you."

"If I'm manipulating it out of you, why would you trust my word?"

"Call it an experiment. I like making friends and I don't care for having allies. I like you, Allayeth, but my judgement isn't always the best."

Arabelle made a coughing sound. Jason gave her a flat look but she maintained an innocent expression, saying nothing.

"Friendship requires the extension of trust," Jason continued. "I'm going to extend a little trust to you, Allayeth, and see where it takes us."

"You're an odd man, Jason," Allayeth told him. "You either dance around a point until the other person passes out from exhaustion, or dive on it like a shark on an unfortunate sailor."

Jason gave her a thin-lipped smile.

"There's a gate," he told her. "Through the portal. It connects what's on the other side of the portal to the wider cosmos. I used that to show Bynes what you described peak gold-rankers seeing."

"You showed him."

"Yes."

"You never left that room while he was inside that portal. And he was not in there for long."

"Both of those things are true."

She narrowed her eyes, peering at him.

"You have at least some measure of control on the far side of that portal."

He didn't respond, or even look at her as they walked along the path of muddy stone slabs.

"Who possesses the power I'm feeling through that portal?" Allayeth asked, more aloud to herself than in any expectation of an answer. "It's not just some natural force you're tapping into. There's a will behind it. I can almost feel it, but your aura on the portal is masking anything I can identify. Why has the entity behind that power given you so much control over it? Why do they trust you?"

"The owner of that power doesn't trust me," Jason said, drawing a sharp look from Arabelle that Allayeth didn't miss. Then he grinned.

"And that's as much as you're getting. It's time you tell me why you have it out for Bynes."

14

SPANKED

"GORMANSTON BYNES," ALLAYETH EXPLAINED, "IS ONE OF THE MOST prominent members of a powerful political faction here in Yaresh. It was his son, Calcifer, that you sent running off in a panic, but the father is the true threat."

She was still walking from Emir's cloud palace towards Jason's with him and Arabelle Remore. They were keeping a leisurely pace while others hustled around them under magic umbrellas, regular umbrellas or a pointed longing for umbrellas. Jason's aura was pushing aside any rain before it reached him or his companions.

"I first came across Bynes when I was working with the original refugee camp," Arabelle said. "This was before the attack when we were scrambling to get any survivors out of the towns and into the city while also keeping out any world-taker worms. You remember the scramble to get supplies coming in and the logistics in place to do that efficiently."

"I do," Jason said. His cloud building had been the original screening centre before it was eventually moved to Emir's.

"Bynes was pushing to get the budget assigned for that project cut. He was riling people up about the messenger threat, saying that funding should go to battle preparation. Gearing up for a counterattack."

"Bynes and his faction are extremely focused on consolidating and expanding aristocratic power," Allayeth explained. "They are also aggressively lacking in scruples regarding how their agenda is met."

"Which usually means they'd be happy to feed puppies into a wood-chipper," Jason said.

"Can I assume that a woodchipper is a device for turning large pieces of wood into very small pieces of wood?" Allayeth asked.

"You can."

"And I assume that placing small, adorable animals into such a device would remove a considerable amount of their innocent charm."

"I would characterise that as accurate, yes," Jason said.

"The main point," Arabelle said, "is that they are willing to stoop to significant lows."

"Like taking money from the refugee efforts," Jason said. "Why would he make a move like that? It can't make him popular."

"Oh, you'd be surprised," Allayeth said. "There are two things you need to know to understand Gormanston Bynes. One is his political faction, and the other is that political faction's agenda. The short version is that they are a cabal of merchant barons and old-money aristocrats. What they want is the ever-original money and power."

"What makes them interesting," Arabelle said, "is that while they do have combat-oriented people, they largely eschew the traditional power structure of personal power. Look at Ikola, a trained ex-adventurer, taking orders from Calcifer Bynes, a core user who's never faced a monster in his life. The one he's really serving is the father, not the son."

"For the long version, let me start with context," Allayeth said. "In any major population centre, political power is balanced between three forces. One power is the civilian government. In a kingdom, that's a royal court. In most city-states, it's a ducal administration. It also frequently includes guilds and associations outside of the Adventure and Magic Societies, along with the noble houses and any other families of influence. Arabelle's Remore family is a good example."

"Strictly speaking, I married into it," Arabelle said. "It's how I manage to go five minutes without telling people my family runs a school."

Jason snorted a laugh.

"The two societies, adventure and magic, make up another of the three major pillars of any city or country," Allayeth continued. "The third force is the collective churches."

"Judging by the much lengthier explanation of the first force," Jason said, "my guess is that local government is the problem here."

"Yes," Allayeth said. "The problem is one of balance. When the three forces are in balance, things work more or less as they should. Corruption disturbs that balance, having various knock-on effects."

"I've seen that before," Jason said. "Greenstone, where I trained as an adventurer, had a lot of rot. It got good people killed, including my friend Farrah."

"Didn't your friend Farrah just come to Yaresh?"

"The next time I came back from the dead, I brought her with me."

Allayeth, one of the few who could read Jason's aura, stopped and stared at him.

"You're not lying."

"Nope. You were talking about the civic administration in Yaresh?"

She shook her head and resumed walking as she continued her explanation.

"In Yaresh, the civic administration is considerably weaker than the churches and the major societies. This is because the civic pillar has one group that undermines the Duke for their own ends."

"Let me guess," Jason said. "A bunch of rich pricks."

"Yes. A collection of wealthy aristocrats, along with a few very wealthy merchant barons. They are known as the Aristocratic Faction. They own most of the land in the region and provide most of the jobs. They use that power and influence to co-opt their tenants and workers into certain ideologies. Playing on simplistic ideals and commonly held prejudices, they've built a power base of loud and angry people who rabidly support their policies. The very policies that keep them poor and ignorant."

"I've seen that before," Jason said. "A lot of countries in my world have suffered through that, my own included."

"What I just described is unpleasant," Allayeth said, "but not, in and of itself, crippling. The problem is that the Aristocratic Faction has done something extremely unusual in that they have focused on power structures completely divorced from personal power. No adventurers, no magical researchers. Just money and political influence."

"But political influence in Pallimustus is always tied to personal power," Jason pointed out. "Royal families get stuffed full of monster cores so they can stand at the top of the pile."

"But that is not a fixed rule," Arabelle said. "Look at the Sapphire Crown Guild in Rimaros. They have more personal power than the royal family, but they've been instilled with ideals of duty. To serve."

"Yeah," Jason said, "but Rimaros is an exception. They put their people through the hard yards. You think Zara is some monster-core-eating waif?"

"Not the best example," Arabelle acknowledged. "I already mentioned Ikola and how he was subordinate to Calcifer Bynes, despite being more personally powerful."

"It's part of an attitude the Aristocratic Faction promotes," Allayeth said. "They are trying to normalise their strengths of money and influence as being more important than personal power. The problem is, they're willing to undermine the structure they belong to. They don't see themselves as a third pillar alongside the city authorities. They'll happily undercut those authorities if it advantages them, then blame everyone else for the repercussions. And then they'll position themselves as the only solution to the problems they themselves caused."

"Why?" Jason asked. "What's their end game?"

"Bureaucracy," Allayeth said. "Each of the three groups brings their own strengths to the table, be it magic and monster hunting or communion with the gods. For civic administrations, it's the ability to run cities and countries. The day-to-day logistics of managing tens or hundreds of thousands is breathtakingly complex."

"I see," Jason said. "They're riling up the population, using that to enact policies and force through appointments to put their own people in the nodes of bureaucratic power."

"Yes," Allayeth confirmed. "Everything from department heads like Bynes through to magistrates and guard captains. Now, with the city fallen, you would expect them to back off. To let things rebuild before they resume their ambitions for control. Instead, they're using it as leverage. Rebuilding the infrastructure from the ground up, with their power baked right into the foundations. They want to rebuild a Yaresh where their control is in the very fabric of the city."

They paused to let a wagon train of building supplies go along a road they needed to cross. They all had the power to jump the road but chose to be patient.

"That's why Bynes worked his way into that meeting?" Jason asked. "Because influencing whether Yaresh is rebuilt here or elsewhere is critical to their plans?"

"More than that," Arabelle said. "If Yaresh gets saved from a fresh new disaster, the people behind that rescue will have influence."

"You already do, Jason," Allayeth explained. "Your actions during the Battle of Yaresh, along with your conflicts with myself and Charist, have put your name on people's lips. The mysteries surrounding you only make you more interesting. I'm now convinced that Charist was manipulated into pushing you so that you would be undermined. The Aristocratic Faction is a strong supporter of Charist, despite his ideologies being entirely centred around personal power hierarchies."

"How does that work?" Arabelle asked.

"Charist dislikes many of the responsibilities that come with his level of power," Allayeth explained. "Most diamond-rankers are wandering hermits. Those like Charist and myself, the Mirror King or your father-in-law, Arabelle, are exceptions. When we settle permanently in a city, we take on responsibilities by simple virtue of our power. The simple presence of that power has a ripple effect that goes unnoticed by the general population, but those in authority are very aware of it. I suspect that you have some experience with this yourself, Jason."

"Unfortunately," Jason said.

"The Aristocratic Faction do a good job of relieving Charist of annoying tasks that he would otherwise have to deal with. People seeking him out for favours or knowledge. He lets the Aristocratic Faction insulate him from that."

"Will Charist act on their behalf?" Jason asked.

"Not directly," Allayeth said. "Charist is extremely enamoured of personal power hierarchies. He sees what they do for him as natural deference to his rank and would never grant them a favour for it, if only to avoid setting a precedent. But through their service to him, they're able to filter the information he gets. I've been trying to get Charist more personally engaged in events, but with little success."

"So that the way this faction painted me, Charist saw me as a threat to the city."

"Yes," Allayeth said. "Only when Charist's approach was rebuffed effectively did he leave handling you to me. The Aristocratic Faction, however, did not give up so easily."

"Bynes tried to paint me as a traitor and it backfired," Arabelle said. "Bynes' lackey, Ikola, tried the same thing on you, Jason. They were there specifically to sow doubt and diminish our influence."

"What we did to Bynes will make him a laughing stock," Allayeth said, "but it's only one hit in a long and complex fight against the Aristocratic Faction. A good hit, but far from a finishing blow. We need to curtail their power and then do something about the Magic Society's corruption. If we can manage both of those, Yaresh has a good chance of coming through this with a functioning political system that will actually help rebuild it. But, as the Magic Society and Bynes are demonstrating, times of crisis are strong opportunities for those willing to exploit them at the cost of everyone else."

"You keep saying 'we,'" Jason said. "I hope you don't mean we three."

"No, I mean those of us that fight for the soul of Yaresh," Allayeth said, then sighed. "It is a challenge that seems increasingly insurmountable."

Jason let out a sigh of his own.

"I'm not great at intervening in political situations, as it turns out," he said. "I'm pretty good at reading them, though. And what I'm getting from this is that it's an internecine rat's nest that I can only make worse by sticking my big dumb head into the middle of. But you two just went and stuck it in for me."

"You didn't have to let him into that portal," Allayeth said.

"Don't give me that," Jason said. "Arabelle knew I'd do that the moment she suggested it. And you knew it too."

Allayeth glanced at Arabelle.

"What makes you think she was so confident?"

"Because she knows me," he said, then also turned his gaze on Arabelle. "Don't you, Mrs Remore? Why don't you tell her why I did it?"

"Because I wanted you to," Arabelle said. "I shouldn't have. You're right that involving you in the ground-level politics was a mistake. Given who and what you are, the circles you travel in, we should be treating you more like a diamond-ranker. Unless you know the local situation as well as Allayeth, here, you shouldn't be involved."

"Honestly," Jason said, "it's actually kind of great to see you make a mistake. You've always been this sage-like figure, talking me through every dumb thing I've ever done. It's nice to see that you can stuff up too."

"I guess I shouldn't apologise, then," Arabelle said.

"No, you should definitely apologise. I'm caught up in this Bynes nonsense now. His people will probably come after me."

"They may not," Allayeth said. "The Bynes family is not a loyal breed. Depending on how much his humiliation hits the father's reputation, he may cut the son out and move on. Not from the family, but you can expect Calcifer to become society wallpaper; seen and not heard. I think it's more likely that the Aristocratic Faction leave you be. They know you're not a soft target now, and you have too many mysteries. One of them just bit back, and smart political players don't pit themselves against the unknown if it poses any real threat. Not unless they have to. They probed and got bitten for their trouble. They're more likely to leave you be than risk making you an enemy."

"Well, that sounds nice," Jason said. "I just don't know if I have the kind of luck where the bad guys have a go, get spanked and then cut their losses."

15

BETTER AMBITIONS

IN THE EMPTY VOID OF A DYING UNIVERSE, ONE LUSH GREEN AND BLUE planet remained. Shielded from entropy by magic older than the ancient universe itself, some of the Builder's most powerful agents prepared to move it to a fresh, young reality. In a dimension ship, floating far enough from the planet to not fall into its orbit, a collection of prime avatars looked on. Each avatar belonged to a different member of the Council of Kings, the closest thing the messengers had to central leadership.

What the avatars were watching was an army of the Builder's most powerful tools, the massive golems called world engineers, orbiting the planet. The avatars observed as the world engineers wrapped the planet in threads of intrinsic-mandate magic, like a spider wrapping up captured prey.

Along with the avatars, the observation room of the dimensional ship contained Erigo Fin Desca, the Builder's new prime vessel. After Shako was taken by the Sundered Throne, the Builder had finally chosen his replacement. Erigo had originally been a messenger and still looked like one, but with heavy modification by the Builder. His wings were gleaming silver metal and his skin looked and felt like cold alabaster. His eyes were orbs of amber glass and his hair was entirely absent. His toga-like clothes had no fabric, and were instead made of tiny, interlocking shards of metal. With hues ranging from coppery reds to ocean-blue sapphire, they sparkled in glimmering waves of colour.

One of the astral king avatars was not watching the planet through the transparent wall of the observation deck of the spaceship-like dimensional vessel. Instead, he was looking over Erigo's clothes. This was the avatar of the astral king Jamis Fran Muskar, and he stood out from the other avatars, even compared to Erigo. Jamis was the only avatar whose wings had been completely absorbed into his body, making him look like a seven-foot-tall celestine with dark copper hair and eyes. Messengers, astral kings included, rarely hid their wings. He was also the only person in the room standing on the floor instead of floating over it. He wore shoes where the others had sandals or bare feet. Instead of diaphanous robes or draping togas, he wore fitted clothes in sober colours.

"How do you prevent pinching and chafing?" Jamis asked Erigo, still peering at his metal clothes. "Do you use magic, or perhaps some manner of conventional lubricant? So many of my fellows overlook the sensory pleasures once they become astral kings, but oiling oneself up is a delightful indulgence. All the better if someone does it for you."

"There are more important matters at hand than self-indulgence and the clothing choices of the Builder's new vessel," a woman told him. She was the prime avatar of Vesta Carmis Zell, the astral king controlling the messengers around Yaresh. Jamis turned to look at her, saying nothing. She held his gaze for only a moment before lowering her eyes. Jamis smiled slightly, then turned his attention to the planet outside.

"When this task is complete," Jamis said, "the price is paid. Zithis Carrow Vayel will have fulfilled his debt to us."

"His name is the Builder," Erigo corrected. "He is not one of our kind anymore."

"Our kind?" Jamis asked. "Do you consider yourself a messenger still, Erigo Fin Desca?"

"I am more a messenger than you, Jamis Fran Muskar. The astral kings are no longer messengers."

Jamis tilted his head, examining Erigo as if he was a painting.

"You are part of the Unorthodoxy," Jamis surmised. "Or perhaps, you were, prior to assuming your current position."

"I was," Erigo admitted. "I have moved on. There is little point fighting an oppressor that can turn you into a mindless drone and send you to fight your own allies."

"We should destroy you, traitor," one of the other astral kings said.

"Oh, don't bother with our little friend, here," Jamis told him.

"He thinks because he serves the Builder now that he—"

"I said don't bother with our little friend, here," Jamis repeated, cutting the astral king off. He then turned to look at him and raised an eyebrow to question if the astral king was done talking. The man stayed silent and bowed his head slightly, earning a friendly smile from Jamis.

"See?" Jamis asked the others. "We're all friends, here. Erigo Fin Desca has told us himself that he has left the Unorthodoxy behind. Perhaps we can even bargain some of the Unorthodoxy's secrets out of him, now that his loyalty lies elsewhere. If nothing else, it would not do to antagonise the Builder while he is still in the process of moving our planet for us."

"Wise," Erigo said. "You have received a fine reward when all you did was provide some low-level ritual magic."

"You truly have forgotten yourself as a messenger," Vesta Carmis Zell told him. "Adapting our magic so that the lesser species can use it was a task completely below us. Having our ritualists lower themselves to do so cost them dignity, which is more precious than Zithis Carrow Vayel can understand."

"I have told you his name," Erigo said. "I will not remind you again."

"We apologise," Jamis said. "Please excuse us, Erigo Fin Desca. We have internal issues to discuss, and I promise more civility when we speak again."

"I will go and supervise the proceedings directly," Erigo said. "See that civility is maintained the next time we speak or this planet goes nowhere."

Jamis gestured and the transparent wall rippled like the surface of a pond. Erigo floated through, accelerating swiftly in the direction of the planet. When he was gone, Jamis turned on Vesta.

"I recognise that you don't have any interest in our actual goals on Pallimustus," he told her, "but you would do well not to antagonise the Builder's servant. It is not yet time to make the Builder our enemy, and while you may not care about that…"

Jamis walked over to Vesta.

"…I do," Jamis finished. He stared up at Vesta, who would have stood taller than him even if she wasn't floating.

"Every astral king in this room," Jamis continued, "other than you, Vesta Carmis Zell, is focused on our larger goal and not some personal project."

"You have no say over my agenda or my actions," Vesta shot back.

"That is true, so long as you do not take something harmless and turn it into a problem for the rest of us."

"What are you talking about?"

"Your nascent astral king?"

"You mean the Asano boy? How do you know about him?"

Jamis responded with a laugh and no answers.

"I need him for the moment," Vesta said. "I will kill him when that need is done."

"I would recommend against it," Jamis said.

"He has to die. He's turning into an astral king. He has already started replacing my mark on the souls of my messengers."

"So? While this council ostensibly represents the strongest of the astral kings, there are many others. Even a few powerful eccentrics who have declined to be part of our little group. They are no problem to us, so what do we care if their number grows by one?"

"But he is not a messenger."

Jamis laughed again.

"I forget how young you are, Vesta Carmis Zell. I do not fear the rise of another original."

"Original? What does that mean?"

"It does not fall to me to teach you history."

"Asano threatens to become more than just an astral king. He claims domains like a god and employs intrinsic-mandate magic."

"An astral king with their own unique abilities?" Jamis asked in a mocking tone, clutching his hands in front of him. "That's never happened before. Whatever shall we do?"

"You're dismissive, but if left to his own devices, he can become a powerful enemy."

Jamis laughed once more.

"Every person here is an enemy to everyone else in this room, yet we work together regardless."

"You think Asano will work with us?"

"Perhaps. Forever is a very long time to say something will never happen. But, for now, his concerns are too small for the likes of us to care about or obstruct. With the exception of yourself, of course."

"And if his concerns grow larger?"

"Then it will be in concert with his power. He might have the strength to be a challenge to your agenda, Vesta Carmis Zell, but you are the one who chose to pursue a separate goal from the rest of us. You might find yourself in a position where he can cause you trouble, but that is not the case for the rest of this council. By the time he is powerful enough to fight for the purification artefact, it will already have been found and claimed. Preferably by us. He also has little interest in it. Like you, his goals and ours move in different directions."

Vesta narrowed her eyes.

"How do you know so much about him?"

"You said it yourself: he is a potential threat. Only a fool would ignore that, so I took an interest. And, as it turns out, I agree with you. He is a threat, but only a potential one. Should his interests and ours clash once he has enough power to be worth dealing with, then we will. But if we went around annihilating every potential threat, our species would spend their entire lives roaming the cosmos, smiting silver- and bronze-rankers. We'd have to start wiping out planets just to save time. That, I'm sure you'd agree, would be more trouble than it's worth."

"Asano is different. He isn't an ordinary threat."

"He is different, yes. The confluence of events, circumstances and powers that came together to shape him is extraordinary. But the cosmos is far more vast than you can imagine, Vesta Carmis Zell. At this very moment, there are more people with equally extraordinary stories than your mind is capable of comprehending. Let me assure you that the way to deal with these people is to leave them alone."

"If you know so much, do you know what happened to the diamond-ranker you all saddled me with?"

"Yes," Jamis said. "And since his killer's agenda does not interfere with ours, I will leave the matter be. If you want to pursue it, that is for you to do on your own. But, as with Asano, I recommend you follow my lead and let the issue lie."

"Even if I was willing to swallow my pride over a jumped-up silver-ranker, I still have need of him."

"Jumped-up silver-ranker? A moment ago, he was a terrible new astral king, ready to bring us all down with his unheard-of powers. You need to settle in your own mind if you're dealing with a genuine threat or an insignificant pawn. He can't be both."

"For now, he is the latter," Vesta said. "Left to his own devices, he will become the former."

"Then I advise you to leave him to his own devices. People like Asano, who find themselves at the crux of great events, have a habit of enduring everything thrown at them and coming back stronger. And those who placed them in the crucible are left forgotten in the ashes of history. Asano is not a threat to the agenda of anyone in this room except for you, and only because you are more interested in your personal hobbies than our collective interest. That is your prerogative, but Asano is only a problem if you make him one. If you do, you had best understand that problem will be yours. If you are foolish or incompetent enough to make him my problem, my first course of action will be to feed you to him. That may solve it right there."

"You would choose him over me?"

"You are the one who called him a future threat, and you were right. Today, you are a member of this council and he is some essence user that I can ignore. A hundred years from now, you will be in the exact same place you are now, but where will he be?"

"A century from now, I will not be in the same place," Vesta insisted.

"Right, your little project. Do you really think another soul forge will make that much difference?"

Vesta's eyes widened for the slightest moment before she regained her composure.

"Oh yes," Jamis said. "I'm fully aware of what you're after, Vesta Carmis Zell; I just don't care. I will give you my advice anyway, knowing full well that you will ignore it: Find better ambitions. Stop scavenging for power outside the group and turn your efforts to seeking out the purification artefact. Becoming a critical player in our greater plans will serve you better than carving your own path."

"Of course you would say that."

Jamis laughed.

"I am biased, it's true, but my advice stands. Asano has made an unreasonable demand of your Voice of the Will. Use it as a chance to withdraw and restrategise without losing face."

Vesta narrowed her eyes again.

"You've been paying very close attention."

"No, Vesta Carmis Zell, I have not. My information comes from paying a regular amount of attention without you ever noticing. Perhaps you should dwell on the ramifications of that when considering my advice."

16

THE INSTINCT TO KNEEL

INSIDE JASON'S SOUL REALM, HE AND HIS TEAM WERE SORTING THROUGH all the loot they had picked up during the Battle of Yaresh. With multiple loot powers and storage spaces between them, the sum total formed a small hillock of magical treasures piled up in a courtyard.

This was not the first session of sorting through the pile, or even the first pile. Items were sorted into things the team wanted now, things they would keep until they were gold rank and could use them, and a donation pile. This was the largest collection by far, with items donated for use in the restoration efforts where possible, or sold to fund it where not.

"I like having a flight item, don't get me wrong," Neil said as he patted his new belt. "Being wind-based worries me a little."

"What's wrong with that?" asked Sophie, the team's practitioner of wind powers.

"Other elemental magic might interfere with it. It doesn't matter if your fire wand stops working when you're standing on solid ground, but you want a flight device to be reliable."

"That's fair," Sophie acknowledged.

"It still doesn't seem fair that Humphrey got all the cool items," Belinda said. "He even got another die for the dice set that modifies his summons. He didn't even use them in the fight."

"Yes, because what that battle needed was even more summons,"

Humphrey said. "We could have distributed pamphlets to all the adventurers to explain which summons to attack and which ones to not attack."

"Lots of people used summons," Neil pointed out.

"Not a whole contingent of them," Jason said. "How many do you call up these days, Humphrey?"

"Twenty," Humphrey said. "Some of the rolls on the new die can change that, though."

"I would have loved to get my hands on that amulet that strengthens conjurations," Jason said. "I'll admit that Hump's armour and swords are more important than my cloak and shadow arms, though."

"You can have my gauntlets," Humphrey said. "This amulet is much stronger, but they do the same thing."

"As if you didn't have a stupidly strong amulet already," Belinda pointed out to Jason. "Not all of us have amazing items that grow stronger as we do."

Jason, Clive and Neil had the decency to look sheepish. Jason had the cloud house and his amulet, while Neil and Clive both had items claimed during the Reaper trials before Belinda joined the team.

"I want to know what Jason took from the diamond-rank messenger," Sophie said.

"Diamond-rankers drop diamond-rank items," Jason pointed out. "I can hold them for only a few seconds before my body has a negative magic reaction. I had to keep them all in my soul realm."

"We're in your soul realm," Clive pointed out.

"Fine," Jason said. "There is some stuff I'm looking into maybe using, to be honest, but it's all on the backburner while we deal with everything else. But if you really must—"

"Mr Asano," Shade interrupted, emerging from the shadow at the base of the wall. The whole team started jeering.

"You set that up so you wouldn't have to tell us," Neil accused.

"No, but I'll keep that in mind for the future," Jason said. "What is it, Shade?"

"The messenger strongholds, Mr Asano. The messengers look to be abandoning two of them."

Jes Fin Kaal watched from atop a domed tower as the messenger forces poured into the stronghold, consolidating their forces from the two abandoned locations. Another messenger flew up to join her in floating just over the dome. Hess Jor Nasala was only silver rank, but she had come to rely on him as her chief assistant and mouthpiece.

"The commanders continue to voice their objection to abandoning two more fortresses," Hess informed her.

"I am aware of their concerns."

"They have asked me to warn you that it will leave us in a strategically unsound position should events underground not go as we intend."

"Strategic position is irrelevant. If we do not get what we want from the natural array, there is nothing else here for us. Once affairs below ground are settled, whatever the outcome, we leave."

"They have further asked me to point out that if the servant races accept your terms only as a ruse to launch an attack, our position is compromised with only two remaining defensive positions."

"They won't," she assured him. "I've made sure their mediocre ritualists have enough information to confirm the threat to their city. The only reason they would compromise their chances of saving it by attacking us is if they intend to evacuate and give up on the region entirely. We still have informants enough in the city that I will learn their intentions with more than enough time to respond. But I believe that the concerns of the commanders go beyond the strategic, do they not?"

"Your insight is accurate, Voice. I believe the questions of strategy are to avoid reprimand for questioning your ideological soundness."

Kaal's slight smile didn't reach her eyes.

"They are unhappy over striking a bargain with the servant races."

"Yes, Voice. I must confess that I am also uneasy at the proposition."

"And why is that, Hess Jor Nasala?"

"Because it begs the question of what can they do that we cannot do ourselves? If they are lesser, why must we rely on them?"

"This is not a new question. You know the answer. If our people descend, they become tainted. It is not that the servant races can endure it because they are superior, but because they are already tainted themselves. The magic down there is able to stain the pure souls of messengers, but servant races are tainted already. That is how they endure. There is nothing new about sending servant races on tasks that are below us in places we do not wish to go."

"But this is different," Hess told her. "We are not just instructing our slaves to do our work for us."

"No," Kaal agreed. "We sent in our slaves and they lacked the will."

"Which means that we are not telling them to do as we bid. We are asking, and that is what has left so many of us, including myself, unsure about this course of action."

"You worry that we are putting the servant races on a level with ourselves by negotiating."

"Yes, Voice. That is our concern."

"Tell me your thoughts on Jason Asano."

"He is… troubling. He is not one of us, yet he also is, in the ways that matter. So much of what makes us superior is shared by him. And he is an astral king, or close to it. I felt his aura myself and…"

"…and?" Kaal prompted.

"I felt the instinct to kneel," Hess confessed.

Kaal nodded.

"He is not below us, yet he is not *of* us," she said. "It means that we are left with three reactions to choose from. One, we can deny and destroy him as an aberration. Two, we can accept that he actually is one of us. Or three, we can acknowledge that we are not the only superior beings."

"The overwhelming consensus is that the first option is the correct one, Voice."

"I happen to agree. But how would you do it? Mah Go Schaat tried to kill him and fell dead at his feet. Do you know how? Can you be certain you would not share the same fate? Would you be willing to fight him, Hess Jor Nasala?"

"No," Hess admitted. "I would not."

"Jason Asano will die. We will have him walk into the fire of his own accord, serving our ends even as he meets his."

"But is not manipulating him instead of dominating him a form of acknowledgement?"

"Yes, but in truth, we have acknowledged him many times. You yourself just said you would decline to fight him, and that decision would be a wise one. You saw the frenzy he put our people in during the attack on the city. You saw the ragged gold-rankers after they desperately escaped his pyramid fortress. We acknowledge others all the time, Hess Jor Nasala. Great astral beings. Gods."

"He is neither a god nor a great astral being. He's a silver-ranker."

"Yet, in defiance of everything we understand about astral kings, he is one of them. He is an enemy there is no shame in acknowledging, and there is no greater glory than destroying a worthy enemy. Especially when doing so gives you exactly that which you seek. Return to the commanders and tell them that if any amongst them have no need for glory, they may come and discuss it with me. If any of them accept that offer, prepare a list of replacements for me to approve as they will not be coming back."

The next large meeting to take place in Emir's cloud palace had several differences from the last one. The floor didn't bounce, and the government delegation had undergone some personnel changes. Calcifer Bynes was absent, as were his guards, Ikola and the one whose name Jason hadn't picked up before Allayeth had thrown the man into a portal. In the place of Bynes was another elf who looked much the same, but older.

The vast majority of the Aristocratic Faction in Yaresh had gained their ranks through monster cores. As a group, they valued money and political influence over personal power, but there was no escaping the fact that most of Pallimustus disagreed. This meant that any aristocratic family without standard-bearers to wield traditional forms of power would fall into irrelevancy.

For the Bynes family, the chief standard bearer was Gormanston Bynes. The father of the man who had left the previous meeting in such an undignified scramble, he was the new lead representative of the Yaresh civic administration. Unlike his son, he had no title; all he required to maintain his place in society was his name.

Gormanston Bynes had not a trace of monster core within his aura. He was not as pretty as his son, despite having the same gold rank. Where ranking up had given Calcifer the elegance of a palace, his father had the blunt, stark beauty of an impregnable fortress. A weathered fortress, with the signs of aging that took an extremely long time to show on a gold-ranker.

Gormanston was taller than his son with a broad frame that exuded speed and power. Unlike Neil, whose clothes played down his physique, he was an elf that showed off a physicality that was rare for his people. From his dress to his gait to the way he sat in a chair, Gormanston Bynes looked like a coil waiting to spring.

"So, that's the dad," Jason said from within a privacy screen. Another difference in this meeting was that the various groups were each under privacy screens. Following the messenger acceptance of Jason's terms, the various stakeholders were all looking to serve their various agendas. Jason hoped that most of those agendas involved saving the city.

"That's him," Allayeth said. She and Jason were their own little group at the front of the room with the rest of Jason's team at the back.

"He looks more serious than his son," Jason said. "Are you sure he won't be cranky about what happened to Junior Bynes at the last meeting?"

"I am. From what I know of the man, he'll be thankful for weeding out weakness. He has other children, and I'm surprised he came in person instead of sending one of his daughters. I imagine whatever he managed to get out of Calcifer about what's on the other side of your portal intrigued him."

Jason gave her a side glance, but she maintained an innocent expression.

"Yes, I'm also intrigued," she admitted.

"We can talk about it after the meeting," Jason said. "If I'm too important to kill, I might be open to a little show and tell."

They took their seats as Emir filled the room with cloud furniture. The director of the Adventure Society, Musin Heath, was once more at the front. He took out the box containing the box containing the communication orb, releasing the seals that prevented any spying by the messengers via the orb. He set the orb on the table and glanced surreptitiously at Jason. Jason gestured subtly with head gestures and Musin turned the orb back and to the side, adjusting until Jason gave him a nod.

"You realise that it hasn't gone unnoticed that only you, out of everyone in the room, can tell which way is up for the messenger's magical device," Allayeth told him.

"Anyone who knows anything is already aware that, magically speaking, I have more in common with the messengers than with anyone on our side."

Every privacy screen in the room shattered simultaneously as an overwhelming aura settled over the room.

"It's not just magically speaking," a disembodied voice spoke.

"Dude, I'm in a meeting," Jason said. "Also, now I have to explain the context of what you just said to everyone here if they want to understand it, and we were all using privacy screens for a reason."

"I just thought I could contribute," the voice said.

"That's a bucket of horse manure and you know it," Jason said. "Don't come in here with your half-arsed power-plays."

"What's a horse?"

"The bottom half of a centaur. Now sod off. I'm expecting a call."

"Would it help if I was here?"

"No! I'm pretty sure they hate your lot more than they hate me."

"That's true," the voice said. "If you need anything, though, just ask. We're all quite keen to kick them off our world."

"Yeah, because that's totally why you're making a spectacle of yourself."

"That's rich, coming from you."

"Yeah, well… shut up. Look, the blue ball is flashing; I have to take that."

"Fine," Dominion said, and his presence faded away. This left a room full of people staring at Jason as the communications orb gently strobed.

"He totally knows what a horse is," Jason muttered.

17

ACCEPTABLE TERMS

JASON LOOKED AROUND THE ROOM, THEN FOCUSED ON THE GENTLY strobing blue orb.

"Is no one else going to…?" he asked. "I'm just going to go ahead, then. If the evil angel sorceress thinks we're screening her calls, she might get cranky with the negotiations."

Jason stood up and awkwardly slinked over to the communication orb on the table. When he reached out and touched it, a projection of Jes Fin Kaal appeared over it.

"G'day," Jason said. "How've you been? Oh, right, you've been moving. That always sucks. It's why I keep my house in a bottle and just take it with me. That being said, it's always being used these days to screen for apocalypse worms or feeding homeless people, and those are both your fault, so… I'd appreciate you being less evil, I guess?"

"Are you done talking nonsense?" she asked.

"No," Jason said through laughter. "I'm really, really not."

"I have met your demands, Asano. It is now time that you listened to my proposal."

"Yeah, that's fair," Jason said, calming down. "I said I'd listen if you did the thing and you did the thing. So, let's hear it."

"The natural array deep underground is unstable. You know this as well as we do."

"I also heard that was your fault. You were messing about with forces you don't understand."

"I understand them perfectly well, Jason Asano."

"Oh, you didn't mess up and turn the natural array into a very slow time bomb that sends all your messengers squiffy? It sounds like you don't need us at all. Should I just hang up?"

"There is always the potential for unforeseen complications with magic, Jason Asano."

"Yeah, that's true," Jason acknowledged. "Your track record doesn't exactly fill me with confidence that you have a solution, though."

"The only reason anything went wrong in the first place is that we were unable to complete our task before we were forced to flee the array's effects. All we need is for someone less susceptible to the array's effects to complete what has already been started."

"To summarise, then, you messed up your evil plan, the after-effects of which threaten to destroy this city and a good chunk of the landscape around it. You propose that we finish your plan for you, giving you everything you want?"

"And saving the city."

"What's left of it after another of your evil schemes, yes. You understand why we aren't excited about the choice between annihilation and giving you everything you came here to get."

"Yes," Kaal agreed. "But as you say, one of your options is annihilation. That means you have to act on the alternative, however unpalatable."

"Unless I take the unmentioned option three," Jason pointed out. "I walk away."

Jason looked around at the people who were silently listening in.

"I know that the people in this room will still want to work with you," Jason continued, "but can you work with them? Will all your indoctrinated little drones stand for that?"

"It would seem that the messengers in your possession have been talkative. Since it no longer matters, I will ask this: was Marek Nior Vargas a part of the Unorthodoxy?"

"The what? Unorthodoxy? I thought your kind didn't have religions. If you're willing to put some information about that on the table, I might be willing to make some extra concessions. Actually, I do have my own messengers, as you pointed out. I might just go ask them."

"Then do so, but we are here for a reason. You do not want the city destroyed and you do not want to deliver to me what I want. But the nature of compromise is that you make accommodations to get what you want, Asano. Stomping your feet and demanding to get everything while giving up nothing is a child's tantrum, not a negotiating position."

"Where I come from, they call it budget appropriations. That never really works out, though, so tell me what you want from us."

"I need a force of your essence users to descend to the natural array and use a device that will stabilise it. I need you to lead it, regardless of rank make-up because, as you said, my people will not tolerate trafficking with someone who is not one of us."

"One of you? Are you trying to isolate me from my own people? I'm not one of you, Kaal, and I don't think your minions would like you saying I am. There are ways in which I'm like you, certainly, but your kind has too many flaws. You're inferior."

"You think you can anger me?"

"I think that you were once a freshly budded messenger, just like the rest of them. I think you may have moved past the indoctrination, but there are still some hooks left in you. That kind of treatment never goes away, not completely. It becomes part of you."

"You have a few stolen scraps of knowledge and think you know us?"

"Oh, I've looked deep inside your kind, Jes Fin Kaal. Did your astral king not tell you? She has to know because she felt it. She felt me reach inside her messengers and remake what they are. If Vesta Carmis Zell didn't tell you that, she sent you into this negotiation blind. And if she's been keeping secrets from you, I think we both know that she's hung you out to dry."

"My astral king shares and hides what she wills; it is hers to do so. If there are secrets she keeps from me, it is not my place to know them. You shall not provoke me this way."

"Won't I? You're not eating up the simple lies anymore, Voice. You can't be if you want to carry out your function with even a modicum of competence. Which means that you know the questions and see the contradictions. There's something wrong and you can feel it, but you're too afraid to ask."

"I have no interest in this discussion," Kaal told him. "If you cannot keep to the negotiation at hand, there is no point continuing this conversation."

"Alright," Jason said. "You wouldn't believe the truth anyway. It's hard to throw off a shackle when you think it's a lifeline, and it will take more than me to convince you. Instead, let's talk details."

Jason and Kaal went over the proposed operation in detail. A mixed group of silver- and gold-rankers would descend into the access shaft that the messengers had been keeping the surface dwellers away from. They would then need to navigate whatever state the underground denizens were in from the effects of the unstable array, set up a device provided by the messengers and keep it secure for as long as it took to activate.

"And you're confident that whatever kinks made the device go wrong in the first place have been worked out?" Jason asked.

"There were no 'kinks' in the device. The only issue was our inability to stay and keep it secure long enough to take full effect."

"Even if that's true," Jason said, "how do you know the old device will work in the new conditions? The magic is getting pretty soupy down there, by all accounts."

"We have been monitoring the magical conditions far more accurately than your primitive ritualists. The astral king has built a new device that will adapt to any variances in the magical conditions."

"Oh, someone built a dangerous thing and took every variable into account. That's definitely not the start of a thousand disaster movies."

"You have nothing to contribute but worthless doubt," Kaal told him. "You have neither the knowledge nor the power to understand the device, let alone craft an alternative. Your questions are pointless because you must accept the device we provide or none of this matters."

Jason sighed.

"I'm getting very tired of making choices I don't like because the alternative is a city blowing up or the planet getting sucked out through the side of the universe. Alright, we'll use your device."

"Of course you will; stop wasting my time. My being immortal does not mean I am willing to endure your vain attempts to confuse or frustrate me by indulging in irrelevancies from your world."

Jason winced.

"Oof, you've got my number. Alright, I think we have the details of the job covered. That leaves the price."

"Your city will not die. That is the price."

"It's not my city, and we've already talked about what happens if I walk away. There will be a price because, a few weeks ago, your people came in here and trashed the place, and you don't get to pretend that's acceptable. I wouldn't be too worried; the locals won't trust much of anything you give them. I looked at their list of demands and it's pretty much just a huge pile of spirit coins and the magic you used to knock up those fortress strongholds so quickly. The rituals shouldn't be that complex. They're confident they can scrub through them for any nasty surprises you slip in there, and they've got a city to rebuild."

"Those sound like acceptable terms. But what do you want for your part, Jason Asano?"

"I want Mah Go Schaat's study. I've been watching and I know you haven't managed to break into it yet."

"You have the keystone," Kaal realised. "You managed to loot it from Mah Go Schaat's body."

Jason felt auras stir with greed from various points around the room. The people in the meeting well-informed enough to know the name of Mah Go Schaat also knew how valuable his possessions would be.

"I do have the key," Jason said.

"And will you share the spoils with the people in that room with you?"

"It depends on what's in it," Jason said. "And how nice they are about asking."

"Are you sure they'll stop at asking?"

"They'll stop or be stopped," Jason said. "I hope for the best in people, but I've learned to prepare for the worst. But I'm going to pass you off to the city's representatives now. Give them most of what they want or I'll back out of the whole thing."

Most of the room's occupants were over the shock of a god's presence and had been listening to Jason's negotiating style with a mix of trepidation, horror and disdain. Jason patted the Adventure Society director on the shoulder.

"Good luck, cobber. Tell me how it goes."

Jes Fin Kaal and the occupants of the room then watched Jason saunter off.

Jason walked into the workroom in his soul space where Clive had a workroom set up. White walls were covered in Clive's notes, the walls taking marks from Clive's finger like a whiteboard. The tables were covered in notes and measuring devices secured from the Magic Society, showing every measurement they had managed to get from the magical emanations rising from deep below ground.

"Hiding from the people wanting to talk about Dominion paying you a visit?"

"Yep. How's the research going?"

"I have very little idea how to even prepare to examine this device the messengers will give us. There just isn't enough information to work with."

Jason looked around at the walls covered floor to ceiling in Clive's scrawled notes, along with tables piled high with folders, notebooks and crystals with aura recordings.

"Okay," he said.

"Obviously, we can't trust the device the messengers give us," Clive said.

"Agreed."

"But I have no confidence at all in deciphering what it does in any remotely practical timeframe."

"That makes sense," Jason acknowledged. "The data you have on the natural array is second-hand at best, and the messenger device will use magic more advanced than what this world has."

"It may even be uniquely bound to messenger magic," Clive said. "Our best bet is to bring the device into your soul space. You can copy it perfectly here, allowing us to disassemble and examine it safely."

"Not a chance," Jason said.

"Why not?" Clive asked.

"Because I think you're wrong about being able to do so safely. If I were a devious astral king—"

"Which you are."

"Hurtful, but to continue: I would look at someone like me, and a device like the one we're dealing with, and see an opportunity. Traditional soul implants, like star seeds, aren't going to work on me. But I'm just a half-cooked astral king and Vesta Carmis Zell is the real thing. She's also known for soul engineering."

"Soul engineering," Clive said with a shudder. "Necromancy but worse. It's almost unheard of in Pallimustus. The only example I've seen was that sword with a disembodied soul as a container, and that was in an astral space. It wasn't in Pallimustus proper."

"Well, this astral king is something of an expert, according to the messenger commander I've got locked up in here. She may well be capable of building something that can harm me if, of my own volition, I bring it past the defences of my soul."

"Such as a mysterious device you want to examine, thinking nothing can hurt you," Clive realised.

"Exactly."

"Then we're stuck trusting this device?"

"No," Jason said. "We may be able to go halfway. You know what most astral kings can't do?"

"I'm going to go with 'be humble,'" Clive said, getting a laugh from Jason.

"That's definitely true, but I'm talking about my spirit domains. The realm inside my soul is something every astral king has a version of. My spirit domains are something else, though. I don't have the same power there, because they're a claimed patch of regular reality instead of a homebrew universe. It might be enough to dig out whatever nasty secrets this device holds without letting it inside my soul. I'll have to take my cloud house off cafeteria duty long enough to turn it into a proper spirit domain, but we need to get a good look at this device without exposing my soul to it."

"Will that be effective?" Clive asked. "I genuinely have no idea how any of your strange soul powers work. This might be a good chance to discuss that, actually."

He started looking around the messy room.

"Let me grab a notebook and I'll start going through some... Jason? Oh, you disappeared, that's very mature. Come back here. I'm inside your soul, Jason. I know you can hear me!"

18

ACTUAL ADVENTURERS

Jason and Allayeth watched the cloud palace break down into thick fog that obscured the area and replaced the smell of ash and wet mud with a fresh, clean scent. It was slowly drawn into the cloud flask like a massive genie returning to its bottle.

"I'm surprised at how quickly the city accepted using messenger magic," Jason said. "Even if it is for construction."

"I believe that using it to replace your cloud palace is a large part of that," Allayeth told him. "I believe that the Adventure Society is on your side."

"We'll see."

"They understand what you've done and how hard you fought for the city during the Battle of Yaresh."

"Plenty of people fought as hard or harder."

"But not quite so loudly," Allayeth pointed out. "You made something of a spectacle of yourself, and more than once. But the way you did it, along with various other concerns, have left the non-adventuring portion of the city elite voicing various concerns."

"Other concerns?"

"You keep doing things the way the messengers do them. Your aura is like theirs and you've hardly been discreet in demonstrating this. During the battle, they challenged you in rather unusual fashion—what people are calling aura speech. You responded not just in kind but in such a way as it resonated over the battleground. Not to mention that you occasionally float around the same way they do, you still refuse to hand over the messenger prisoners, you won't—"

"Point made," Jason acknowledged. "Although I did most of that in direct opposition to the messengers. You said that the city elite were *voicing* concerns, not that they genuinely held them."

"I did say that, yes."

"So they're using me as an easy punching bag to rail against."

"Your rather bold way of conducting yourself has certain unconventional advantages, Jason, but there are very good reasons that most take a more decorous approach. When you mark yourself as an outsider, you make an easy target for exclusionary political tactics."

"I'm familiar with the tactic. On my world, my political enemies painted me as a shady, untrustworthy figure as well."

"How did that work out for them?"

"I don't know. I stopped paying attention, saved the world and got out. I wasn't in the best place back then. I say back then, but it isn't that long since I left. I've been working a lot on letting go of my anger and vengefulness."

"And how is that going?"

"Calcifer Bynes came out of my portal on his feet. A year ago, he would have come out in a bucket."

"That would have had ramifications."

"And that's always been my problem; people keep warning me of ramifications, without considering the ramifications of crossing me. So, I started to show them, but I didn't like where that took me. There's a saying on my world about people who fight with monsters and the dangers of becoming monsters themselves. I went further down that path than I like and it's taken me the better part of a year to walk it back."

"And have you?"

"Not all the way. I doubt I ever will. If you're going to fight monsters, you have to be like them, at least a little. The temptation is to be like them a lot. People like us have power, but the trap is in using it. It's so easy to justify every step until you find yourself somewhere you can't defend being. At that point, you have to either go back or change who you are, and that's when you lose yourself."

"He still has some way to go," Arabelle said, emerging from the fog that had once been a hospital. It was breaking down and pouring into the flask, but the process was a long one.

"Jason still struggles with it," Arabelle continued. "Less with the violence than his dark urges."

"Dark urges?" Allayeth asked.

"Oh yes," Arabelle said. "He has trouble standing still for more than a minute without explaining how dark and edgy he is to the middle distance."

Jason gave her a thin smile.

"Because I keep finding myself in circumstances that make me confront these issues all over again."

"And you always will," Arabelle told him. "You can whine about it for the rest of your life or learn to accept it without a near-constant stream of brooding monologues."

"I'm working on it."

"I know."

"Was there something you wanted, Arabelle?"

"Emir asked me again if you would be willing to speak with his associate."

"I've sensed her probing the cloud house. She hasn't been very polite about it."

"She's a diamond-ranker, Jason. She doesn't have to be."

Jason's expression turned hard and he glanced briefly at Allayeth, then shook his head.

"I am so very tired of being weaker than everything I have to deal with," he muttered. "Shade, grab the flask when it's done."

"Jason…" Arabelle said. He ignored her and opened a portal arch to his soul realm. When he went through, Arabelle made to follow but was repelled by the curtain of energy. The energy vanished and the arch vanished into the ground. Arabelle sighed, left with Allayeth as the cloud flask sucked in the seemingly endless mist.

"He normally responds well to some light teasing," Arabelle said.

"That was my assessment as well," Allayeth said. "Has something changed?"

"There is little I can tell you. Jason is under my care and I won't break a confidence. And even if he weren't, my first loyalty is to him, not to you."

Allayeth ran an assessing gaze over Arabelle.

"I have found that the people around Jason lack much of the fearful reverence most have for diamond-rankers. Is that his influence?"

"That, and when you spend enough time around Jason, you meet more than just diamond-rankers."

"Like Dominion randomly appearing in a meeting?"

"Yes."

"Why did a god choose to make that display? I don't believe for a moment that it was a simple whim."

"I have my guesses, but I would not presume to understand the reasoning of a god. Like people, how they portray themselves is no sure indicator of their true nature or intentions. Look at the god Deception taking the role of Purity without anyone knowing. For centuries, he warped the church towards the more exclusionary and intolerant aspects of purity as a concept."

"It still unsettles me that the other gods never informed us."

"The gods have their rules, just as we do."

"That fact also unsettles me, along with leaving me conflicted. I'm not sure if I like the idea of the beings that guide the world having rules I don't understand. It makes me wonder about their motives, which is an uncomfortable position to be in. I also wonder why the rules are there, and how they are enforced. To what degree can they act beyond their remit?"

"You should talk to Jason about it."

"He has answers?"

"No, but he enjoys the questions. As you saw, he treats the gods the way he treats everyone else."

"Why do they tolerate it?"

"You wondered why Dominion would appear before us all and allow Jason to talk to him like that. Perhaps showing us that he would was the point."

"I thought you wouldn't presume to understand the reasoning of a god?"

"That's why I said 'perhaps.' It was a guess."

"What does showing that he would tolerate Jason like that accomplish?"

"Do you look down on Jason, Lady Allayeth?"

"No."

"No? There isn't some part of you that looks at him and files him away under 'just a silver-ranker' in your mind?"

"Not *just* a silver-ranker, no. But he is a silver-ranker."

Arabelle looked at the spot where Jason's portal vanished.

"I wouldn't presume to tell a diamond-ranker what to do," Arabelle lied, "but I would advise against letting Lord Charist make any more oppressive moves towards Jason."

"I am not his keeper."

"Aren't you? I will take my leave, Lady Allayeth."

The fog had much diminished over the course of their conversation, but a goodly amount was yet to return to the flask. Arabelle walked into it, vanishing from Allayeth's senses.

The Adventure Society director, Musin Heath, was seated behind the desk in his office, stating at Vidal Ladiv.

"I'm sorry, they did what?" Musin asked.

"They took a contract, Director," Vidal repeated.

Musin ran his hands through his hair and let out a groan.

"Why would they do that?"

"They are adventurers, Director, and there is no shortage of contracts, as you know. After the attack on the city, there are too few adventurers and too many tasks."

"I'm well aware of that, Ladiv. I was the one who implemented the campaign to get the inactive adventurers who stepped up to defend the city to stay active. My point is that Asano is the focus of some very important events right now."

"I would point out, Director, that what you described seems to be Jason Asano's normal circumstance. If he didn't take contracts while embroiled in major events, I'm not sure he ever would."

"I would be okay with that." Musin let out a weary sigh. "What contract did they take?"

"I'm sorry, Director, but I have misspoken. It's *contracts*, plural."

"Multiple contracts?"

"There's an open sweep-and-clear for the northern regions. They've registered for that."

Musin nodded. "The northern regions have been underserved since we started focusing on the infested towns to the south. What else?"

"They've claimed a lot of the high-difficulty, low-reward contracts that most adventurers avoid. I spoke to the jobs hall officials and they said they were about to increase the listed reward on most of them. They even offered and Asano's team declined."

"I see," Musin said, then leaned back in his chair. "They're looking to rank up."

"That will take years. They'll be lucky to reach gold by the next monster surge."

"And if they don't get started, it'll take until the monster surge after that. Can you imagine what it's like being silver-rankers under so much gold- and even diamond-rank scrutiny?"

"Yes, Director," Vidal said flatly and Musin snorted a laugh.

"We've made you the message boy in a hailstorm, haven't we, Ladiv?"

"Asano's team also collected other contracts, Director. Based on the locations, they were choices to fill in the gaps of their intended route. It seems they will be heading out of the city and moving north-east. They'll make a large, zig-zagging loop and then return to the city from the north-west."

"How many contracts did they take?"

"Seventy-four."

"Seventy-four? How long is that going to take them?"

"They've reported three as complete so far, Director."

"They're delivering reports to the jobs hall through Asano's shadow familiar?"

"Yes, Director. They have estimated between four and nine days, but any number of factors make it hard to predict."

"And they've done three already. When did they take the contracts?"

Vidal pulled out his pocket watch.

"Approximately six-and-a-half hours ago, Director."

"They're keen, I'll give them that. At least if they're going to go off and do something, it's being actual adventurers. If that was the worst behaviour I had to deal with, I'd be the happiest Adventure Society director in the world."

Musin leaned his elbow on his desk and his forehead in his hand.

"Asano has obligations," he said. "The expedition to head underground is being assembled, with his team as part of it. He also needs to be present for the handing over of the thing he asked for from the messengers."

"I asked him about that before he left, Director. On the latter, he said that he will teleport in as appropriate. As for the expedition, sir, he made it clear that while he does not need to lead it, he will not be subordinate to it."

"Did you tell him that's not how Adventure Society expeditions work?"

"I did, Director. He said that once the Adventure Society has publicly redressed Lord Charist for invading his home, he would be happy to discuss institutional integrity."

The director closed his eyes and rubbed his temples.

"I'm getting a headache. Should that even be possible?"

"It seems to be going around, Director."

"And by going around, do you mean around Asano?"

"I do, although diamond-rankers tend to elicit similar symptoms. With the extended monster surge, they have been acting far more publicly than normal."

"I knew it," Musin said. "I knew as soon as I got the reports from the Rimaros branch that Asano would be a diamond-rank problem. I have no idea what they were thinking with this false identity business; he was obviously going to become very overt, very quickly."

"This is why you voiced your public support for Asano?"

"You're new to Yaresh, Mr Ladiv. One of the features of our—usually —fine city is that it has two diamond-rankers that are here on a near-permanent basis. One of the results of this is that anyone in my position is required to do their best to manage said diamond-rankers, which is roughly as easy as wrestling a tornado that just passed through a cooking oil warehouse."

"I don't think that's possible, Director."

"No, it is not. And Asano has that feel. The more I read the reports about what he's done, how he's done it and who he's done it with, the more I got that feeling. With a diamond-ranker, Mr Ladiv, all you can do is get on board or get out of the way. Maybe, just maybe, you can nudge them slightly in a direction that won't leave you spending the next month cleaning up after them. Once it was clear that Lord Charist had failed to pressure Asano and Lady Allayeth would be taking charge, I decided to get on board with Asano."

"You may pay for that politically, Director."

"That may be so, Mr Ladiv, but it's still the right choice."

"May I ask why?"

"Because the point of my job isn't accruing political power. The Adventure Society exists to protect the populace. Sometimes that means putting up with people who are a pain to deal with. For all of Lord Charist's headstrong bluster, Lady Allayeth's schemes and Jason Asano's brazen absurdity, each one of them acts in the cause of what they think is right."

"And we just have to hope that what they believe to be right is the same as what we do?"

"We can nudge, where we're able. I've found Lady Allayeth quite reasonable in that regard. She mostly ignores me, yes, but at least she listens first. Lord Charist and Asano don't seem as amenable, but I believe they hew close enough to my own sensibilities."

"Then you will not attempt to curtail Asano and his team's contract activities?"

"Have you read Asano's file?"

"It's restricted, Director. I don't have the authority."

"Well, suffice it to say that time and again, Jason Asano and his team have demonstrated not only that they'll do the right thing but that they'll spot it before most everyone else. Did you know that while Asano was still believed dead, his team discovered that the messengers were preparing to invade? That man Standish is some kind of magical genius. The Magic Society screwed him over and now they're desperate to get him back in the fold."

"And you want to avoid that mistake with Asano?"

"You're damn right I do. He already threatened to give up his Adventure Society membership. I think that was more to make a point than his actual intention, but there's no way I'm going to test that man's resolve."

"Because of what you've read in his file?"

"For a start. The messengers, who won't deal with anyone, will deal with him and think he's some kind of king. The god of dominion—the god of deciding who gets to be king—showed up for a chat, and not for the first time. If anyone is fool enough to treat Asano like a silver-ranker, they'll pay for it."

"Like Calcifer Bynes."

"Exactly."

"Are you concerned about his father?"

"Not yet. Asano clearly has a role to play, and Gormanston Bynes is nothing if not efficient in squeezing the value out of his enemies before putting them down."

"And after?"

"Bynes is part of the Aristocratic Faction. More than anyone else, they respect powerful backing. I'm hoping he looks at the beings standing behind Asano and backs off."

"Is that likely?"

"I don't know. Asano rolled his son, but Gormanston hates weakness, especially from his own people. He's also smart, and going after Asano now would not be. If anything, I think he'll try to use or ally with him. Asano may have the etiquette of an explosive device, but he is not weak."

19

BAD INFLUENCE

Like Jason, Emir had reclaimed his cloud palace as new buildings were swiftly fabricated in their place. As the area once used to hold visiting adventurer vehicles was being reclaimed by the city while they expanded their refugee and rehousing infrastructure, Emir had joined other adventurers in settling his vehicle outside the city walls. He chose a spot to the south not far from where the river emerged from the city, far enough from anything else that he could let it sprawl. The cloud palace took on its full form and size, primarily consisting of five massive towers. They made no attempt to hide their cloud nature and were stained in sunset colours of orange, yellow and teal.

On one of the many terraces adorning the palace towers, Arabelle looked out over the river. Before the attack on the city, the Yaresh River had been lined with buildings that serviced the water trade and the people who plied it: warehouses, small docks, taverns and brothels. Left outside of the city defences, those buildings had been thoroughly annihilated. What little remained was nothing but flotsam, having become stuck to the riverbank instead of drifting downriver like so much other debris.

"You look troubled," Emir said, joining her in leaning against the rail. "I'm guessing that your talk with Jason did not precipitate him meeting with my increasingly impatient diamond-rank guest."

"I'm surprised she didn't just hunt him down herself. He hasn't been hiding away in his special domain for a while."

"She's well-connected amongst diamond-rankers. I suspect she has a better understanding of who and what are standing behind Jason than we do. She's being extremely careful about pushing him directly, although her patience is wearing thin without his cloud building to poke at."

"Diamond-rankers aren't used to waiting or being denied."

"No, but the irritability of my guest is my problem. What is it that's troubling you?"

Arabelle didn't answer immediately. She let herself indulge in the quiet moment with her old teammate as they looked out over the river, thick with debris still being flushed out of the city.

"I worry about Jason. About my ability to help him. I'm meant to be the one with all the answers, but his experiences are beyond anything I've even heard of."

"You seem to be doing well. Compared to what I heard of his early days in Rimaros, he seems not so removed from the boy I knew in Greenstone. More seasoned, more haunted. I have seen it, though. The sharp steel inside him that comes out easier than it should."

"I won't discuss the particulars, Emir, you know that."

Emir nodded. "I know. I'll leave you be."

"I appreciate it. And don't be alarmed if you lose the ability to sense this part of the cloud palace for a little while. I'm expecting someone I can talk about it with."

"A divine visitation?"

"I'm a priestess, Emir; it's hardly out of the ordinary. The only reason the gods appearing to Jason is remarkable is that their personal visitations are rarely in public or to non-clergy."

"That's a rather good reason, Belle."

Emir had not long gone when Healer manifested next to Arabelle. She pushed herself off the railing to stand up straight.

"Oh, don't do that on my account," Healer said, leaning himself. After a moment of hesitation, Arabelle returned to her original position next to him.

"I dislike this," he said, looking out at the debris-choked river. "The land needs healing."

"Houses count as part of the land?"

"Are the houses built by people so far removed from the dams built on the river by beavers? The only real difference is scale."

"What are beavers?"

"You've never seen them? They're an animal that builds dams out of logs. Jason Asano's world has them as well, so I'm told, but his only have one tail and don't shoot venomous spines."

"Who told you that about Jason's world?"

"Gabrielle Pellin asks questions like the Knowledge priestess she is, and she is extremely pretty. Travis Noble has a habit of talking non-stop when he's nervous, and pretty girls make him very nervous."

"That's not ideal when magic makes everyone beautiful."

"No," Healer said with a chuckle. "Guardian almost sent one of his priests to rescue the boy."

"Why didn't he?"

"I'm not entirely certain. Something the boy said about a little bit of peril."

"I have no idea what that means."

"I decided it was best to not enquire further for myself. Perhaps you could ask the young man with the garuda powers. He's from Asano's world as well."

"I should ask him and not Jason?"

"I'm worried that Jason Asano is a bad influence on you."

"A bad influence how?"

"You presumed that a god would show up to speak with you."

"You did show up."

"Being right only makes it worse."

"I need to talk to someone. Someone I can discuss Jason's secrets with without betraying them."

"You can turn to your fellow clergy people. They have all taken the same oath as you."

"I'm not convinced the healer's oath is enough that a stranger will remain silent. Jason's secrets can change worlds. They already have, and will again."

"You don't trust the oaths my priests take? That you took?"

"You always see enforcement as a last resort, Lord Healer. Your oath is soft because you want people to do the right thing out of choice, not obedience, but that's not always the choice they make. I was in Greenstone. Aside from Neil Davone and Jory Tillman, you cast out an entire city's worth of your priests for failing their oaths. If you punish people for spreading Jason's secrets that they heard from me, it does not retroactively stop those secrets from having been spilled. I am your priest, Lord Healer. I follow your belief in personal responsibility, but that means taking responsibility myself."

Healer had a wide grin on his face.

"Listen to yourself. Hear the conviction. Do not doubt yourself or the guidance you give to those who need it. Not even with someone as unusual as Jason Asano."

The god placed a fatherly hand on her head.

"I am proud of you, child."

Arabelle closed her eyes.

"I don't know that my guidance is enough," she said. "How do I lead him when I don't know the way?"

"Then don't lead him. Walk beside him, with a kind word."

"Metaphors are nice, Lord Healer, but I need more than that. I need specifics."

"Then be specific in your needs, child."

"He's been getting better."

"And who defines better? He is different, but what makes one state superior to another? Who chooses that?"

"He does. He's getting closer to the person he wants to be."

Healer smiled. "You fear he is backtracking."

"Regressive behaviour is a normal part of recovery," Arabelle said. "My concern is that one of his negative behavioural triggers is being forced to endure the same patterns over and over. Or, more precisely, choosing to endure them because he believes it necessary. One of those patterns is being seen only by his rank when he is operating at a very different level, and this may be the most dangerous to him."

"Oh?" Healer prompted neutrally.

"It's at the core of the behavioural loop that took him to the state he asked me to help him escape. Jason acts out his principles, often regardless of the cost. It was a defence mechanism he developed to cope with his arrival to our world, but he learned the cost wasn't always his to pay. He learned that to yield when standing on his principles would cause more damage than it prevented."

Arabelle glanced at her god, who for all the world looked like a friendly older man, patiently listening. No divine aura pounding at her senses, no smothering presence choking off her ability to think.

"Jason's time on Earth repeatedly brought this balance between principle and compromise into conflict," she continued. "Time and again, he faced betrayals from those he needed to work with. He smothered his instinctive responses because retribution would have put his world in danger. He tolerated actions that, in our world, any adventurer would have killed over. Eventually, he was pushed too far, too many times, and his principles bent. He became more violent and less compassionate."

She sighed.

"Which brings us to where we are now," she continued. "Again, he's faced with the same pattern of people trying to use him with the belief that they can ignore any consequences because of his rank. I know the circumstances aren't the same, but they are close enough that I have concerns. My encounter with him yesterday suggests that he's done swallowing his responses. I think Dominion knows this, and that's why he made an appearance."

"You would presume to know a god's motives?"

"I have no right to assert what they were, but I have every right to guess."

"Bad influence."

She couldn't help but smile at the faint whiff of paternal indulgence, knowing that the god hadn't let that scrap of his aura out by accident.

"I think Jason Asano is done being a silver-ranker," she said. "I'm worried, both that he will undo the progress he's made and of the damage he will do in the process."

"Is that all that worries you?"

"It's selfish, but that may have been the final weight that collapsed everything he and I have built together in terms of his mental health. I conveyed Emir's latest request from someone very powerful who wants something from him. He left and the next thing I hear he's gone off on a spree of monster-hunting contracts. That's an old pattern, throwing himself into justifiable violence when he needs to vent negative emotions."

Healer let out a chuckle.

"You think this is funny?"

"I think I don't care for one of my most capable servants miring herself in self-doubt."

Healer held out a hand, pointing to nothing out in front of them. Arabelle then spotted a patch of darkness emerge from the shadow of a tree that had been snapped in half, not far from the palace. The shadow moved through the air in a blur until it floated in front of Healer's hand. The shadowy mass resolved itself into the shape of a person, the dark parts highlighted with white to resemble some of the formalwear she had seen Jason wear.

"Might I have an explanation of this indecorous behaviour, Lord Healer?" Shade asked.

"I need to look in on your contractor."

"Might I suggest following that by looking in on an etiquette tutor."

"What is it that Jason Asano does to people that makes them so willing to disrespect power?" Healer asked.

"He looks at that power," Shade said, "and asks if its behaviour is deserving of respect. Or, if it instead grabs people and leaves them dangling in the air to use as a scrying tool."

"A not inconsequential point," Healer acknowledged. "Still, damage done, so I may as well go ahead."

Shade turned back into a mass of shadow that then took the form of a ring, like a portal. An image appeared in the ring of Jason standing at what looked like a village street stall, jiggling a pan over an open flame.

"Can he see and hear us?" Arabelle asked.

"No," Healer said as they listened to Jason speak.

"...haven't managed to find potatoes," he was explaining to a handful of elves gathered around him. "Potatoes are—okay, now that I think about it, it doesn't matter what potatoes are. The point is that ibrilim powder serves much the same purpose as potato starch and I just realised I should never have brought up potatoes at all. Anyway, the powder will thicken the sauce, but be patient and give it time to do its work. Don't just keep pouring it in or it'll keep thickening and your brown sauce will turn into brown mud. This is something you'll need to develop from experience, as how much powder to use is always a judgement call..."

Jason trailed off and peered up at the ring, narrowing his eyes.

"Shade?" he asked. "I don't know who is messing with my familiar, but you'd best knock it off or I'm coming for you."

"It is I, Jason Asano," Healer said. The people around Jason dropped to their knees as the aura of the god washed over them.

"My point stands," Jason said, "and if you keep distracting me, it'll ruin my sauce. Let go of my friend or I'll start visiting your priests for purposes they aren't going to approve of."

The people around Jason went from kneeling to sprinting away.

"You would interfere with the good work my people do?" Healer asked.

"You interfered with my sauce."

"And that is enough to go to war with a god?"

"Mate, I was killing priests of Purity before it was cool. I know you're a generally okay bloke, but being a god doesn't give you a pass to be a turd. You let my guy go and I'll let it slide. This time. I don't know what point you're trying to make with this little display of provocation, or who you're trying to make it to, but let Shade go and sod off, or you and me have a problem."

The ring vanished and turned back into a shadow mass. It then burst like a dark firework as Shade destroyed his body.

"Did you see his reaction?" Healer said.

"Where you provoked my friend and he threatened my god? Yes, I saw, Lord Healer."

"Calm yourself, child, and look deeper. What Jason Asano demonstrated was balance. An odd balance, yes, but he lives a life where it must be so. He is stronger than he was before. Less likely to lose himself. You helped him find the place he is now, but the journey never ends. You know that. Have faith in yourself and your abilities as a healer."

"He just threatened a god!"

"And a year ago, he'd have been tearing through one of my churches by now. Do you consider threatening a god to be out of character for him?"

"No," Arabelle grudgingly acknowledged. "I suspect that it's kind of his thing."

NOT LIKE THE ONES WE KNOW

In a section of rainforest characterised by tall but intermittent trees rising above the canopy, Jason's cloud palace had taken the form of treehouses connected by rope bridges. The balcony of the largest treehouse had a sequence of hammocks hanging out over the jungle canopy below and most of the team was lying back, lazing and napping in the mid-morning sun. The missing members were Clive, Rufus, Sophie and Humphrey.

"Are they ever going to come out?" Taika asked, lying back with a plate of sliced fruit on his chest.

"Yeah, because you look like you can't wait to get up and get to work," Neil said.

"Leave them be," Jason said. "They're probably tired."

"From what?" Neil asked. Belinda snickered a laugh.

"Let's just say I beefed up the soundproofing on their treehouse last night," Jason said.

Humphrey and Sophie emerged from their treehouse together and everyone turned to look at them with huge grins. Humphrey pressed his lips together as he glared at them, then grabbed Sophie's hand. She looked uncharacteristically startled, going stiff for a moment before squeezing his hand as they moved over the rope bridge together. When they arrived at the central treehouse, Sophie panned her gaze over the team, challenging anyone to make a joke. Everyone hurriedly lay back in their hammocks,

Taika complaining as Jason floated a slice of fruit from Taika's plate through the air.

"Sorry, we got up late," Humphrey said. "We should probably get to it."

"We already got to it," Jason said. "We knocked off that nest of frog-hippo things right after dawn. Clive is out scouting the location of the next contract now."

"You sent Clive?" Humphrey asked.

"He sent himself," Belinda said. "He wants to broaden his adventuring skill base."

"And if something jumps him and he dies because he's alone?" Sophie asked. "He won't sense a gold-rank monster coming."

"He's got Onslow," Taika pointed out. "I wish I'd gotten a familiar."

"Plus, Shade is with him," Jason said. "And I'm keeping an eye on his aura."

"How far away is he?" Humphrey asked.

"About twenty kilometres that way," Jason said, pointing. "It's nice being out of the city. I can spread out my senses without picking up on thousands of essence users. Very relaxing. Also, Travis, Farrah, Gary and Rufus aren't too far from Clive either."

"They're putting up some kind of tower to run tests," Neil said. "Something about not blasting magic through a city."

"They're attempting to use magical resonance to communicate across relay points," Belinda clarified. "What they have now triggers the magical senses of everyone in the area. Essence user senses are too sharp, especially at decent rank. They're trying to calibrate it so that it uses ambient magic without disrupting that magic. Then, it will be like the background magic of any city filled with essence users, something people can just ignore."

"I'm pretty sure they're going to attract monsters as soon as they turn it on," Jason said, then furrowed his brow. "That might be handy, now that I think about it. We could crank the thing right up, draw in all the monsters and clean up. It could make our sweep and clear mission a lot easier."

"And how many monsters do you want to face at once?" Humphrey asked.

"I'm plenty used to fighting lots of monsters at once."

"And how many of those were gold rank? We're in a high-magic area,

Jason; the odds of bringing multiple golds down on our heads would be higher than I'm willing to tolerate."

"Fair point," Jason acknowledged. "Still, how convenient is that tower to set up?"

"It's about ten metres tall, so not very," Belinda told him.

"Shame," Jason mused. "There's potential there. Maybe the Adventure Society could set some up permanently and just turn them on when they want to lure in the unintelligent and aggressive monsters. Once they…"

Jason trailed off, floated out of his hammock and looked off into the distance.

"I think Clive has run into something," he said.

"Danger?" Humphrey asked as the others exited their own hammocks.

"Not sure," Jason said. "He's found the elementals, but there's something odd about their auras."

A circle of glowing runes appeared in the air and a portal appeared in the middle of them a moment later. Clive, covered head to toe in mud, squelched through. His equally muddy familiar floated through after him, the tortoise's big eyes looking mournfully out from a face caked in filth. The team rushed to gather around him, making sympathetic noises.

"What did you do to the poor little guy?" Sophie said.

"We need to get him into the showers and washed off," Belinda said. "Clive, go scrub yourself down in that creek over there."

"Seriously?" Clive asked, holding his arms out to his sides.

"Please don't drip in the cloud house," Jason said. "I know it looks like wood flooring, but it's not."

To make his point, the mud dripping off Clive and Onslow was being wicked away and absorbed by the floor.

"I know I put a lot of crystal wash in the cloud house, but even though it's diluted in the showers and the cleaning water, the supply isn't infinite."

"Oh, isn't it?" Clive asked.

"No," Jason said evasively, his eyes darting in Belinda's direction briefly before his shoulders slumped. "She told you, didn't she?"

"That you've been talking with Jory over a water link about setting up a dedicated alchemy facility exclusively for crystal wash? Yes, she has."

"Lots of teams have auxiliary adventurers," Jason said. "It's not strange to have an alchemist on call."

"It is when their only job is to make cleaning products," Clive said. "There aren't any alchemists doing that."

Clive frowned, his expression suggesting he had a thought he wasn't happy with.

"Okay," he said. "Yes, there are some auxiliary adventurers who are alchemists that mostly make cleaning products."

"There are?"

"Clean-up teams," Humphrey said. "You don't see them so much in smaller cities and low-magic areas where the adventurers don't specialise as much. In the bigger cities, they have teams dedicated to cleaning up after monster manifestations in urban areas. They literally clean up messes, clear out lesser monster infestations and hunt down any loose monsters summoned during larger fights. There are several teams of this sort in Yaresh leading the hunt for any leftover naga from the egg thing the garuda ate."

"As much fun as it is talking about soap," Neil said, "what put you in such drastic need of it?"

"You know how the contract said moderate-sized water and earth elementals?"

"Oh, they merged," Humphrey said.

"Ah," Jason said. "That's what I sensed."

"Yes," Clive confirmed. "We now have a very large mud elemental to deal with."

***

"Never again!" Neil declared as the team arrived back at the treehouse through Jason and Clive's portals.

"What?" Jason asked. The others all turned to glare at him. He, Sophie and Belinda were all clean while the others were covered head-to-toe in foul-smelling mud and worse-smelling ichor.

"Jason," Neil said through gritted teeth. "Not all of us can deflect mud when it's being flung everywhere."

"Why am I the problem? Sophie deflected it with her wind powers and Belinda had that hardcore magic umbrella."

"The issue isn't so much the mud," Humphrey said. "That would be an unpleasant but acceptable part of the job."

"The problem," Neil said, "is that someone used magic so that the mud monster could bleed and rot. So, when it turned into a mud tornado, it was also a gooey, rotting flesh tornado."

"Oh, come on," Jason said. "I already cleansed all the diseases you picked up from it."

He looked at the rest of the team.

"Okay," he said. "From your expressions, what I'm taking away is that you feel that cleansing the diseases after the fact isn't a sufficient response. I'm noting that for future reference so I can take a different approach next time I paint you in rotting corpse meat."

"Oh no," Neil said. "There's no need for 'future reference' because you don't get to fight any more mud elementals. No water elementals and definitely no wind elementals."

"But fire elementals are alright?"

"Absolutely not," Sophie said. "The smell of burnt, rotting flesh? No thank you."

"You didn't even get muddy," Jason complained to her. "In fact, I saw you wind blast a bunch of gunk away from you and onto Neil."

"It was you?" Neil asked, wheeling on the very clean Sophie. "I thought that was Jason."

"Why would it be me?" Jason asked. "I don't have wind abilities."

"We don't know that," Neil said. "You're always pulling out some nonsensical new soul power. It could have been spirit wind or something."

"Ghost farts. You think I'm making ghost farts."

"Ghost farts," Clive said, "is where I leave in search of an adult conversation. Or a shower."

The non-clean members of the team, which was the majority, made agreeing sounds and marched inside.

"Hey, don't forget that very lovely stream out there," Jason called after them encouragingly. "The crystal wash really won't last if you keep—"

They all felt a massive magical explosion with their supernatural senses, the sound following like thunder after lightning. They rushed back onto the balcony and looked out as a cloud of dirt and dust rose far above the rainforest canopy. It was dozens of miles away, but the mushroom-shaped cloud would have been easy to spot even without silver-rank vision.

"What is that?" Neil asked.

"Can't tell from this distance," Clive said.

Jason took enough crystal wash vials from his inventory for everyone and floated them to the team using his aura.

"We've still got a few minutes on the portal cooldowns," he said.

"Clean up while Shade turns into something fast and we'll fly there. We'll pick up the others on the way."

The black private jet was still some way from the mushroom cloud of dust when the plane dissolved into a cloud of shadows. Jason and his companions, now including Farrah, Rufus and Gary, all fell from it and into the air. Only Travis had been left behind, ferried back to the tree house by one of Shade's bodies in the form of a winged heidel.

"I can feel what you turned into," Jason scolded his familiar. "What's wrong with a regular Pegasus?"

"I believe you have more important things to hold your attention, Mr Asano."

As the team fell, Sophie activated her flight power, taking control of the wind around them.

Ability: [Leaf on the Wind] (Wind)

- Special ability (movement, dimension).
- Cost: Moderate mana-per-second.
- Cooldown: None.

- Current rank: Silver 4 (47%).

- Effect (iron): Glide through the air; highly effective at riding the wind. Can reduce weight to slow fall at a reduced mana cost. Ignore or ride the effects of strong wind, even when this ability is not in active use.

- Effect (bronze): Moderate control of nearby airflow while in use. Cost of gliding reduced to low mana-per-second. Strong winds increase your rate of stamina and mana recovery, even when this ability is not in active use.

- Effect (silver): Fly for moderate mana-per-second; highly effective at riding the wind. Gliding no longer costs mana. You can control the airflow around you, including using winds to carry others with you when you fly. Carrying others increases the ongoing mana cost and incurs a speed penalty, both scaling with the number of people carried.

Sophie's wind-based flight power could scoop up others to let them fly as well and she used it on Belinda, Clive, Rufus and Gary. Jason used his cloak to float while Humphrey, Farrah and Taika conjured wings. Neil plummeted as he fumbled at his belt buckle while tumbling end over end. Finally, he managed to activate the flight power enchanted into the belt and arrested his fall, waiting for the others to catch up in their more sedate descent.

"That's hilarious," Neil said to Sophie.

His words were sarcastic, but the team was sincere in voicing their agreement.

"Do you want to get healed or not?" Neil asked them. They all looked away with unconvincing expressions of innocence.

"Is anyone sensing anything from that cloud?" Humphrey asked. "All I'm getting is some kind of elemental energy. Jason, you have the sharpest senses."

"There is something in there," Jason said. "Lot of… creatures? Could be elementals. They're infused with elemental power, just like the cloud. I can only pick them out because it's more concentrated."

"If there are elementals, Jason has to leave," Neil said. "We just talked about this."

"Anything else?" Humphrey asked, ignoring Neil.

"Adventurers," Jason said. "We aren't the only team responding."

"Hardly a surprise," Sophie said. "You can probably see that cloud from Yaresh."

"Anyone we know?" Humphrey asked.

"Korinne's team," Jason said. "Rick's too; they came through a portal with a gold-ranker. I think…"

Jason trailed off and turned, narrowing his gaze at the plume.

"I know what's in there," he said. "Messengers, but not like the ones we know. There's something wrong with them."

"If they're infused with elemental power," Clive said, "that suggests that these are the warped messengers from underground that we heard about. I think they might not be underground anymore."

"Okay," Neil said. "Jason doesn't have to leave."

21

A JUICE NEWTON SITUATION

For essence users, summoned familiars occupied parts of their summoner when not manifested. Colin occupied Jason's blood, Shade his shadow and Gordon his aura. Clive's familiar, Onslow, became a magical tattoo on Clive's abdomen that he could tap into for elemental power.

Clive, like Jason, favoured practical combat robes, with his lighter colour preferences that made him a Jedi to Jason's Sith. Onslow's tattoo lit up, visible through the robes, transforming into energy that passed harmlessly through the fabric. The energy gathered together, manifesting into Onslow's familiar rune tortoise shape, his legs dangling as he floated in the air.

Onslow's shell expanded, detaching from Onslow himself, who became an adorable, child-sized humanoid tortoise. The sides of the enlarging shell were largely open, the gaps filled with a wind magic barrier. The team members Sophie held aloft with her flight power were moved inside, the two wind powers gently stirring the air as they came together without impeding one another.

The members of the team with self-propelled flight made their way in as well. They joined the others as they observed the humungous dust cloud, still some distance away. Like Onslow, the cloud was charged with elemental energy, but where his powers were in balance, the cloud had specific affinities.

Sensations of fire, earth, ash and magma pushed against the team's perceptions as they moved closer to the giant mushroom cloud. It increasingly loomed over them, dust and ash choking the air. It stung their eyes and left the air tasting smoky, bitter and dead.

They could see tall, angelic silhouettes moving through the murk. Some were making their way out of the cloud, moving to intercept teams of adventurers approaching through the air and across the ground. The terrain below was rough; the rainforest had been flattened for kilometres by the explosion that created the cloud.

Onslow approached the cloud at a steady but cautious speed as Clive used his Enact Ritual power to draw ritual circles made of golden light on the floor and ceiling. Belinda observed him, her eyes darting over the glowing diagrams.

"These aren't the usual protections you employ to protect Onslow," she said.

"No," Clive said, not pausing his work. "These are rituals for channelling elemental energy. They should be able to absorb at least some of any elemental power that comes our way, feeding it to Onslow. That will help recharge his elemental powers and reduce my need to feed him extra mana, all while offering additional protection. It's not as effective against physical attacks, but I have a feeling that we're heading into a firestorm."

The figures started emerging through the dust and ash enough that the team could make them out. As expected, they were messengers, but unlike the ones they were familiar with. Clearly altered by elemental energies, the messengers unleashed elemental attacks at the approaching adventurers. This did not yet include Jason and his companions, but many teams had rushed ahead with more speed than caution. Cones of fire, stone spears, streams of magma and clouds of ash were sent at the adventurers.

The elemental influence on these altered messengers was extremely evident. The group observed four subtypes, each conforming to one of the four power types of elemental attack being tossed around. The messengers were all naked, sexless and androgynous, like the dolls of children, stripped of clothes.

Two of the messenger variants were more visually spectacular than the others. Those throwing out fire also had flames rising from their heads instead of hair. The feathers of their wings alternated between glistening red metal and ruby-like crystal, fire playing across them. Their skin was black and fire shrouded their hands and feet. The ones throwing out magma had skin that was not just black but featured the hard gloss of obsidian. Their wings were obsidian shards outlined by magma, matching the glow of their eyes.

Farrah looked at the magma variants as they clashed with adventurers.

"They're stealing my whole motif," she complained.

"Perhaps if you hadn't given up adventuring to start a business, they would have been more respectful," Rufus suggested.

"Coming from a guy who gave up adventuring to become a teacher," she shot back.

"I'm in Jason's team now, aren't I? Anyway, it's an allowable diversion for me. My family runs a school."

Jason took a tray of liquor shots from his inventory and floated them to the group members using his aura.

"Oh, come on," Rufus complained. "I don't think this is the situation for drinking games."

"Oh, it's not just time for drinking," Jason said after the team downed their shots and he collected the glasses. He put away the tray and took out a cube the size of a basketball with concentric rings engraved on each side. "It's time to rock."

"Rock?" Clive asked, peering at the cube. "Is that some kind of earth element device?"

"No, it's an arse-kicking device," Jason said. He took a recording crystal from his inventory and fitted it into a small slot of the cube. He threw it out of Onslow's shell and it started to rise slowly into the air, blasting out noise. The magic enchanted into it projected the sound all across the battlefield.

"What is that noise?" Humphrey yelled.

"Metallica," Farrah said through voice chat. "Heavier than I'd normally go for, but if you're fighting flame-spewing angels from the bowels of the earth, it's not really a Juice Newton situation."

"What kind of juice?" Rufus asked. "I don't think anyone should go to Jason's planet. It makes them turn strange."

Jason and Farrah flashed grins at each other and leapt from Onslow's protective shell, shadows taking the form of black flying motorcycles under them and hauling away through the air. Jason's shadow cloak trailed behind him and Farrah conjured her fire wings that did the same.

"Why are you riding off on vehicles?" Neil asked through voice chat. "You can both fly."

"Because it's more metal," Jason said.

"Shade made those vehicles out of shadow-stuff," Neil said. "There isn't any metal."

"I was thinking that perhaps we should devise a plan before rushing off," Humphrey suggested. Taika, one of the few people that towered over Humphrey, put a meat slab hand on his shoulder.

"The music's playing, bro. Time to rock and roll."

Taika also leapt from the safety of Onslow's shell. He transformed into a giant golden bird and rocketed after Jason and Farrah, swiftly gaining on them.

"This is music?" Humphrey asked. "The guy just asked if he was evil, then said that he was!"

"I like it," Sophie said, then kissed him gently on the cheek. "See you out there."

In a blur, she was also gone.

"Does no one see the value in making a plan?" Humphrey asked. Rufus put a hand on Humphrey's shoulder, just like Taika had.

"Plans are great," Rufus told him. "But sometimes there's a giant explosion and you just have to go out and fight. Take it from a guy who failed as a team leader: it's not always about having a clever plan. Sometimes it's about getting out of your own way and trusting your amazing teammates to be amazing."

Humphrey sighed.

"Alright," he said. "Onslow, speed us up if you please."

Onslow accelerated the pace of his shell, propelling it closer to the dust cloud.

"I still say this isn't music," Humphrey muttered.

"What is that noise?" Korinne asked. "Is it some kind of sound attack?"

"I think it's music," Zara said.

"If someone is using a song essence aura to produce that," Korinne said, "I'm worried about the state of their mind."

"I believe it is Jason Asano," Orin offered. "I have heard this sound when I met with my uncle in the training room in Asano's vehicle."

"Why is he projecting it now?" Korinne asked.

"I don't know," Zara said, "but I think I like it. It makes me want to hit things."

"Good," Korinne said. "We've got no shortage of things to hit."

The other two elemental messenger variants didn't have flames for hair or parts of their bodies glowing magma, but they were no less a departure from the messengers the group had seen in the past. Those with an affinity to ash retained the shape of normal messengers but were entirely white-grey as if coated in chalk. Ash swirled around them and they fired off rough white orbs that exploded into clouds of obscuring ash and burning cinders. The last variant had affinities for earth and metal, looking like mosaic statues made from shards of stone and different-coloured metals.

Jason and Farrah were the vanguard as they headed for the cloud, now close enough that it covered the sky. They did not remain in the lead, however, with Taika and Sophie blazing past them as more messengers emerged from the cloud to meet them. Taika, in the form of a giant golden eagle, was the first to strike, crashing into one of the metal and earth messengers.

Ability: [Momentous Charge] (Swift)

- Special attack (movement, combination).
- Cost: High mana and stamina.
- Cooldown: Four minutes.

- Current rank: Silver 0 (01%).

- Effect (iron): Charge attack. Rapidly gain [Momentum] during the charge. Can culminate in a non-combination special attack.

- Effect (bronze): Can cover extreme distances and move through the air. The speed of the charge escalates over the duration of the charge.

- Effect (silver): The damage from [Momentum] is enhanced by your speed at the moment the attack lands.

- [Momentum] (boon, magic, stacking): When making an attack, all instances are consumed to inflict resonating-force damage. Multiple instances can be accumulated and instances are lost quickly while not moving.

Taika's first battle as a silver-ranker had been an awkward fight in the corridors of Jason's cloud palace. It was a situation that did not allow Taika to fully express his power set that excelled with wide open spaces and the chance to make long, charging attacks. His Momentous Charge had been accumulating power from the moment he had left Onslow's shell, unleashing it as he struck. He didn't peck with his eagle's beak or claw with his talons, instead ramming his head into the messenger, maximising the raw physical impact. Chunks of stone and fragments of metal burst off it like a sculpture struck by a cannon.

Ability: [Unstoppable Strike] (Swift)

- Special attack (movement).
- Cost: Moderate mana and stamina.
- Cooldown: One minute.

- Current rank: Silver 0 (01%).

- Effect (iron): Melee attack. If any instances of [Momentum] are triggered by the attack, they deal an amount of disruptive-force equal to the resonating-force damage.

- Effect (bronze): When combined with a movement-combination special attack, the physical momentum of that attack is extremely hard to impede. Physical barriers and constraints are struck with resonating-force damage. Magical barriers and constraints are struck with disruptive-force damage. Resistances to any effect that impedes motion are significantly increased for the duration of the combination attack.

- Effect (silver): The cooldown of this ability is reset when using a movement-combination special attack, allowing this ability to be combined with that attack.

The combination of powers, used under optimal conditions, made a wreck of Taika's target. Even so, no silver-rank being was easy to kill and the elemental powers of earth and metal reinforced the messenger all the more.

Taika did not stick around to finish the job, despite the messenger's condition. While he shared Humphrey's qualities of power, mobility and strength, their roles were similar but not the same. Humphrey was a brawler, using speed, power and toughness to make life hard for his enemies. His ability to keep up with enemies and sustain brutal levels of attack power made him an unrelenting opponent that often secured kills for the team. Taika was an initiator, using overwhelming speed and incredible burst damage to put enemies on the back foot. He was heavy cavalry, except giant and a bird.

Taika didn't have Humphrey's sustained damage, so he roared off in another charge attack as Humphrey teleported in to finish the severely damaged messenger. This new charge attack did not accelerate over time until it rivalled Sophie's pace, but it still let him move faster than anyone but her.

Ability: [Speed and Power] (Swift)

- Special attack (movement, combination).
- Cost: Low mana and stamina.
- Cooldown: None.

- Current rank: Silver 0 (02%).

- Effect (iron): Melee attack. Gains an instance of the [Relentless Attack] boon.

- Effect (bronze): When instances of [Relentless Attack] are consumed, gain that many instances of [Momentum].

- Effect (silver): May be used as a charge attack by increasing the mana and stamina cost to moderate, granting additional speed for the duration of the attack. Speed increase enhances flight more than ground speed. When combined with a non-combination special attack, a number of instances of [Relentless Attack] are immediately generated based on the damage dealt. Using this ability multiple times in succession progressively increases the mana and stamina cost.

- [Relentless Attack] (boon, magic, stacking): Consume all instances of this boon to reduce the cooldown of a special attack. The cooldown reduction has an increased effect on movement special attacks.

- [Momentum] (boon, magic, stacking): When making an attack, all instances are consumed to inflict resonating-force damage. Multiple instances can be accumulated and instances are lost quickly while not moving.

Taika's first charge attack had landed him amongst the enemy, so there were plenty around when he made his second. This gave him the chance to use an aspect of his shape-changing power as he flew to the next target, gathering air around his wings and shooting it off in bolts of compressed air. The damage was far from exceptional, but the bolts exploded on impact, sending messengers scattering. As a result, they had trouble forming up to meet the team following in Taika's wake.

Ability: [Block Out the Sun] (Wing)

- Special ability (shape-change).
- Cost: High mana and stamina.
- Cooldown: Four minutes.

- Current rank: Silver 0 (00%).

. . .

- Effect (iron): Bird form with high speed.

- Effect (bronze): Giant bird form with high speed.

- Effect (silver): Gather wind energy while moving. That wind can be used to make compressed air attacks. These attacks do not interrupt any movement special attacks in progress.

Taika's Unstoppable Strike power had its cooldown reset by being combined with his first charge ability, making it available to combine with his second. Taika struck the next earth-type messenger like a missile, smashing off chunks. The second charge power also generated the Relentless Attack buff, which Taika immediately consumed to reset the first charge power. As combining Unstoppable Strike again had let it reset its own cooldown, Taika once more launched the combination of charge power and special attack at the next target.

By this time, the team had engaged with the messengers that Taika's opening moves had placed firmly on the defensive. Sophie was barely visible, flickering between the messengers at a pace that made even Taika look slow. Where Humphrey was following up on Taika's big hits, she was following up on his air bursts, keeping the messengers from achieving any group cohesion.

The team, by comparison, were falling into easy synergies. Humphrey finished off the earth-type defenders Taika had already hammered, exposing the less-sturdy fire, magma and ash types. The fire and magma types output the most destruction, largely countered by Neil's timely shields and Farrah intercepting attacks. Farrah didn't just block the flames and magma but absorbed them, refilling the mana spent on costly attacks.

Farrah's blasted her Lava Cannon and Obsidian Shard Storm abilities at the ash-type messengers who were trying to impede the team with clouds of ash and burning cinders. These were being quickly dispersed by

Sophie's wind, Farrah's flames and Belinda, copying and locking the messenger's powers from the safety of Onslow's shell.

Rufus, despite the inability to fly, was harassing the fire and magma messengers in the backline. Clive opened a portal for him, and from there, he used the messengers themselves as platforms, showing off the agility he had been trained in from birth. His short-distance teleport powers, Flash Step and Flash of Moonlight, allowed him to move from foe to foe, leaving behind savage sword wounds before moving on.

With his flashy sun powers, Rufus was the light to Jason's shadow, both men moving from enemy to enemy. Already, butterflies glowing orange and blue were emerging from several messengers, seeking out more victims upon which to spread afflictions.

"See?" Rufus asked Humphrey through voice chat as the group dominated the messengers. "Sometimes you just have to trust the ability of your team."

"I still say this 'music' isn't necessary," Humphrey grumbled as Gary dropped past him, legs wrapped around a messenger. The huge leonid, covered in heavy armour was plunging through the sky, hammering the messenger with a short-handled mallet.

"Did anyone tell Gary he can't fly?" Neil asked, watching from Onslow's shell. "I think he's hitting it in time with the beat."

22

A MORE PRACTICAL PURPOSE

THE MUSHROOM CLOUD OF DUST AND ASH COVERED A HUGE AREA, AND all around it, teams of adventurers were clashing with the messengers altered by elemental power. One of the first things Jason had done upon coming into contact with one was to touch his hand to it briefly.

Converted Messenger (ash, silver rank)

- Messenger abilities suppressed.
- Able to conjure ash bombs.

The elemental messengers were noticeably weaker than the regular variety, most evident in their lack of aura control. Instead of the usual precise and oppressive force, their auras lashed out in waves of suppressive power, strong but inconsistent. Any well-trained adventurer could handle the intermittent spiritual attacks, fending off what was normally a messenger's strongest weapon.

They were also lacking in intellect; reduced to animalistic instincts.

They understood enough to work in tandem, but failed to move beyond placing the strong ones at the front and the destructive ones at the rear. They failed to adapt to any strategy but the most obvious, allowing the adventurers to get the upper hand.

On the ground, Clive and Farrah stood at the edge of a circle of scorched earth. The blast that had created the mushroom cloud had levelled a huge area of rainforest and Farrah had burned away the felled trees and crushed undergrowth to create a space for Clive to work. He drew a cubic ritual diagram from sparkling golden light, a box comprised of framework lines and floating sigils.

As he worked, a stray gobbet of magma the size of a motorcycle plunged through the air towards the cube. A stream of blue and orange light shot in from the side and transformed into Jason's familiar, Gordon. One of the orbs floating around Gordon turned into a shield and intercepted the attack.

"Thank you, Gordon," Farrah called up at him. He responded with a complex strobing of his orbs before turning back into a light stream and flashing away.

"Do you have any idea what that flashy-light language means?" Farrah asked Clive. "I have a translation power now, and I'm getting nothing."

"I also have a translation power, and I have no idea. Do you think Jason is just pretending to understand it?"

"No," Farrah said. "He'd do that to us, but he wouldn't do it to Gordon."

After completing the diagram, Clive chanted a brief incantation. Flames ran across the lines of the box for a moment before sputtering out almost immediately. He and Farrah walked around the cube that was twice as tall as they were, looking it over.

"Seems sound, Farrah said.

"Give it a test?" Clive suggested.

Farrah cast her Fire Bolt spell and the box absorbed it, much like she had the powers of the fire messengers. The flames were dispersed across the lines and sigils before being drawn in and vanishing. Farrah pointed out a section where the golden lines had dimmed noticeably as they drew in the fire.

"You might want to touch that up," she said.

"I saw it," Clive agreed. He redrew the section and repeated the incantation. Another test showed that the weak area had been repaired.

"Do we do a proper field test of this one first?" Farrah asked, "or go straight to the other three."

"Let's field test," Clive said. "It should be able to hold one."

They looked up at the sky where messengers and adventurers still clashed in the air. They both had sufficiently acute vision to pick out the distant figures, at least those close enough to not be entirely obscured by dust. Farrah pointed, using her aura to guide Clive's eyes.

"That one."

"Okay," Clive said.

Farrah moved into the cube, the golden lines tingling her body as they passed through her and strobing for a moment once they had. She stood in the middle of the cube, looking up. Clive pointed one arm at her and another to the sky and then incanted a spell.

"Exchange your fates."

Farrah vanished and was replaced with a fire-type messenger, while she appeared in what had been his place up in the sky. Now at the back of a messenger formation, she opened up on them with her strongest attacks. Down below, the flame messenger was barely fazed by the abrupt translocation, firing a blast of flame from its hands almost immediately.

Clive raised an eyebrow as fire struck the edge of the box. Instead of passing through the open space between the lines of the magical cage, the flames were contained by an invisible barrier. The fire messenger charged forward, bouncing off the same barrier.

"Adequate," Clive assessed, then proceeded to draw a second cube next to the first.

"That's a lot of butterflies," Jason said as he floated in the air, looking at a wall of blue and orange. The butterflies were so thick that they obscured the messengers behind them. Many of the butterflies were destroyed by attacks from the messengers, exploding in colourful blasts of disruptive-force energy. The gaps were swiftly filled as more butterflies spawned from the already-afflicted messengers.

"Is there some kind of limit on how many butterflies you can have?" Taika asked. He was back in his human form but had a pair of golden wings holding him aloft.

"Not numerically," Jason explained. "They aren't actual living things; they're energy constructs that look and behave somewhat like butterflies.

They come from an affliction that Gordon's orbs can inflict. The affliction continually takes tiny bits of mana from the target and turns them
into the butterflies. The butterflies carry all the afflictions of the person
they were created from, including the one that creates more butterflies. If
the butterflies can find an enemy before the bit of mana they're made of
runs out, they dump all the afflictions on the fresh victim. If not, they
peter out."

"Bro, I don't want to sound like I'm on the other team, here, but I
think it sounds better when you call them enemies, not victims. Otherwise, it sounds like you're rounding them up to do experiments on."

Jason pointedly avoided looking down towards what Clive was doing.

"I'll keep that in mind," he said, slightly too casually.

"How do the butterflies know who's an enemy?" Taika asked.

"You know, I have a few powers that only affect enemies, or affect
them differently from allies. I've never figured out to my satisfaction how
they tell the difference. It almost has to be some kind of aura interaction,
but that raises a lot of questions. As a test, I've tried forcing myself to
think of something as an enemy when it, strictly speaking, was not."

"Some *thing*, not someone?"

"I thought it would be best to try it on the most disdainful, despicable
thing I could conceive of, to make it easier to think of as an enemy, even
though it technically wasn't."

"What did you go with?"

"Frozen meals for one."

"You might want to try it on a person, bro."

"That never seemed very ethical."

"That's a good point, the whole victims-versus-enemies thing. You
know, you could probably wipe out a whole city with those butterflies. If
the city was full of your enemies."

"Being in a city full of enemies is something I'll generally try to
avoid."

"You say that, bro, but we all know what you're like. It'll probably
happen and it'll probably be your fault."

"You think there's a city full of people that hate me that much?"

"Bro, you blasted Metallica over the battlefield. I bet you freaked a lot
of people out."

"That does not warrant a city full of mortal foes."

"Also, I don't think you picked the right song to start with. It was
okay, but I would have opened with 'Master of Puppets' or 'Trapped

Under Ice.' Or maybe mix it up with some AC/DC. 'Thunderstruck' would be awesome to have a fight to."

"I'm waiting to fight someone with lightning powers to use that one."

"Bro, if the bloke you're fighting is the one with the lightning powers, wouldn't 'Thunderstruck' be you putting on a soundtrack for the other guy to kick the crap out of you instead of the other way around?"

"Huh," Jason mused. "You might be right."

"You should put it on now and we'll go find some more bad guys."

"No, most of the remaining messengers are staying in the cloud. They're aggressive but not completely unintelligent, and they've seen how badly they're losing against the adventurers."

"You can sense around the whole cloud?"

"Yeah. Hasn't your perception started filtering the sensations to get a better handle on the situation?"

"Nah, bro. That sounds like some next-level stuff."

"Well, you're silver rank now; welcome to the next level. Do some meditation practise and see how it goes."

"Bro, I'm flying in the air and we're still in a battle."

"Think of it like spiritual resistance training. I'll be your spotter."

Taika's expression turned thoughtful.

"Like doing bench presses with your soul."

"Exactly," Jason said. "Which leads me to one question: do you even lift, bro?"

"Bro, that's ice cold. Okay, let's do this."

They flew over to Onslow's shell and Taika sat cross-legged atop it, eyes closed. Jason stood watching over him for a moment, then some cloud material spilled out from the shrunken cloud flask hanging around his neck. It formed a chair for Jason to settle into, eating a sandwich and leafing through a book as he watched over Taika.

Rufus teleported onto the shell in a flash of silvery moonlight.

"What are you doing?" he asked.

"It's meditation training," Jason said.

Rufus' eyes rested on the sandwich.

"Yes, it looks like you're engrossed in contemplating the mysteries of the cosmos."

Jason gently waved the book in his hand.

"This is astral magic theory, so technically, I am. And the bad guys are pretty much done for; we're just letting the familiars get some practise in before the butterflies finish all the stragglers."

As Jason suggested, Gordon was floating around with Belinda's lantern familiar, shooting beams and bolts of force at messengers rapidly rotting away under the weight of Jason's afflictions. Humphrey's biscuit-loving, shape-shifting familiar was also present, Stash having taken the form of a woodpecker the size of a bulldozer. He hovered in place, wings buzzing like a hummingbird as his beak pounded at an earth-type messenger like a jackhammer. He quickly gave up on that approach, however, spitting out gobbets of rot caused by the afflictions.

"You could just join Taika," Jason suggested to Rufus.

"It does seem like it would be good perception training, trying to push your senses through all this obstruction," Rufus acknowledged. He was moving to sit down when Jason stood up suddenly, the cloud chair returning to the flask as he put away the book.

"What is it?" Rufus asked.

"The fight just finished," Jason said.

"What do you mean?" Rufus asked, then turned his head as he sensed what Jason already had: two diamond-rank auras moving through the air at blinding speed.

Charist and Allayeth had arrived from Yaresh, Charist flying super-hero-style while Allayeth sat in what looked like a throne made from glittering lights. They slowed down and split up as they approached the massive cloud. Charist gained altitude and vanished into the murk as Allayeth descended, making her way to one of the gold-rank adventurers for a quick discussion.

"We should regroup," Humphrey announced through voice chat. "How are things on the ground, Clive?"

"We're more or less at capacity here," Clive said.

"Very well, we'll converge on you. Jason, it might be time for you to take in that…"

He paused before reluctantly finishing.

"…'music' device."

"Bro," Taika said as he got to his feet. "I think Humphrey might like old-man music. Do you have any Foster and Allen?"

"No," Jason said. "I do have some young-people music made so long ago that the people who made it are old now. Do you think he'd like the Hollies?"

"If he doesn't," Farrah said, "I'm not sure he's on the right team."

"You don't get to say that," Humphrey told her. "You're not even on this team."

"She's right about the Hollies, though," Sophie said.

"Do you even know who that is?" Humphrey asked.

"Humpy, Jason and Farrah brought back a whole different world's worth of music. Have you not listened to any of it?"

There was resounding silence in the voice chat until, finally, Gary spoke up, his voice trepidatious.

"Did you just call him Humpy?"

"No," Sophie said, uncharacteristically flustered.

"No!" Humphrey said, just as fast.

Everyone fell silent again, each person connected to the voice chat almost hearing Humphrey's sweat as they waited for Jason to voice an opinion of Humphrey's new nickname.

"Well, I think it's sweet they're becoming more comfortable as a couple," Jason said. "Gary, where are you?"

"I'm riding to the ground by holding on to a messenger. I've left his wings alone so he can fly, but I'm too heavy in my armour and we're descending steadily. I figured out that if you hold one leg and one arm, you can kind of steer them."

"Isn't the messenger attacking you?" Humphrey asked, eagerly jumping into Jason's merciful change of subject.

"Yeah, but it's one of the fire ones," Gary said. "It's not accomplishing much. The heat's making my undies a little swampy."

As they chatted, Jason, Taika and Rufus moved from atop Onslow's shell to the inside with Neil and Belinda as it descended towards the ground. The sound projector floated down and into the shell as well, as directed by a control device Jason took out. He waited for the last song to finish before removing the recording crystal and turning it off, however.

They reached the ground and disembarked from Onslow's shell, which shrank down to encase the familiar, who resumed his normal tortoise form. Clive and Farrah stood by what were now four cubic cages, set out in a square. Each one was crowded with around a dozen messengers, each cube holding a different type, trapped and alive.

"That seems to have gone well," Jason said.

"You weren't the one who had to keep going in to be switch-teleport-ed," Farrah complained. "It got very unpleasant as they filled up."

Jason turned his head as he felt Allayeth's attention fall on them. A few seconds later, she arrived in a blur of her sparkling throne. She stepped off it and took a small bottle from a dimensional pouch at her waist. She unstoppered it and the cloud of lights was drawn in, after which she sealed the bottle and put it away.

"What do you have here?" she asked, looking over the arrangement of prison cubes.

"It's a prison array," Farrah explained. "It cyclically employs the elemental energy of the prisoners to reinforce the array. The prisoners themselves fuel their imprisonment through an energy drain that keeps them from having the power to break out. It only works because there are distinct elemental forces with uniform subsets that we can use to cycle the energy. You can't suppress elemental power with the same element."

"And you just happened to have a ritual array for exactly that?"

"Farrah is the array specialist," Clive said. "I just helped tweak the specifics."

"Meaning that I had an idea and Clive figured out how to make it work in about four minutes by himself instead of four weeks with a research team," Farrah clarified.

"Interesting," Allayeth said. "We should leave that discussion for now, however. Jason, I understand you have some kind of sound projector?"

"Yep. You want to make a request?"

"Tina Turner," Farrah suggested. "You don't know musicians from Jason's world, so just trust me."

"Thank you," Allayeth said, "but I had a more practical purpose in mind."

Allayeth took a recording crystal from Jason, made an announcement into it and then placed it into the projector and tossed it into the air. Her voice spread out, warning the adventurers to move away from the cloud.

Shortly after the announcement began repeating on a loop, a vast force of elemental wind appeared to everyone's senses, high in the sky. A massive vortex had formed and was drawing in the cloud, sucking it high into the sky. The adventurers who had been moving away from the cloud started moving faster, but a few were still sucked up with the cloud. Allayeth tilted her head back, sighing as she looked at the vortex, barely visible beyond the chaotically swirling cloud.

"He could have waited a little bit," she said. "No patience, that man."

"Out of curiosity," Jason asked, "how would you have warned everyone if you didn't have my sound projector?"

"I wouldn't."

"Okay," Jason said. "And now I know you a little better."

"Are you suggesting that I'm callous?"

"Definitely not," Jason said firmly.

"Good."

"Because I don't want to get sucked into a wind vortex like the sound projector you borrowed," he mumbled.

"What was that?"

"Nothing."

"It didn't sound like nothing."

"Oh look: there's a gold-ranker flying over here. He probably needs to talk to you about something very important."

23

EXPLICITLY ANTAGONISTIC

JASON AND HIS TEAM WERE NOT THE ONLY ONES TO CAPTURE SOME OF THE elemental messengers, although they were the ones to catch the most. Clive and Farrah's ritual cages were able to contain almost fifty of them, although the constructs would not last forever. The Adventure Society was sending containment vehicles in their direction, but in the meantime, all of the prisoners were being watched.

The cloud that had been choking the sky was now gone. The diamond-ranker, Charist, had created an air vortex that sucked up not just the cloud and the messengers inside it but a goodly number of the adventurers fighting those messengers. All of them were tossed into the upper atmosphere by Charist's potent vortex power.

On the ground, there was no shortage of adventurers, including those that had been tumbled around like clothes in a washing machine. Most of those had an unpleasant time being knocked around by the vortex, but through slow-fall or flight powers were able to return to the ground safely. The messengers had a less pleasant time of it as Charist killed most of them.

The absence of the cloud revealed a massive shaft descending into the earth, wide enough that a house could be dropped down it. The opening of the shaft was at the bottom of a hole made not by impact from above but explosion from below, making it less a crater than a massive exit wound.

Charist and Allayeth were discussing how he had approached the situation inside a privacy screen that both sealed off any sound and blurred the visuals just enough that no one could read their lips. Their body language remained obvious, however. Charist looked like a child caught doing something stupid by his mother as Allayeth jabbed her finger in his direction with every point she made. After talking about all the adventurers he had knocked around, she moved on to the messengers from the cloud that he hadn't killed.

"What inspired you to think that throwing them into space was a good idea?" Allayeth asked. "They can handle the cold, they don't need to breathe and they can fly. They're just going to come back."

"Then we'll kill them when they do."

"No, *you'll* go and find them now before they start showing up in little towns and villages across half the planet and killing everyone there."

"Find them? Do you know how big space is?"

"Unless you threw them to the moon, I don't see... you threw them to the moon?"

"Just a couple," Charist mumbled. "You know I threw them because I was prioritising rescuing the adventurers."

"Rescuing them from what?"

"From my air vortex."

"You couldn't have waited a little longer before using it?"

"How was I meant to know you were going to warn them all? It was something of an urgent situation, Aly."

"Don't 'Aly' me, Charist."

"Fine. But you shouldn't talk to me like this in front of the other adventurers."

Charist held out his arms, gesturing at the landscape around them. The blast and subsequent battle had devastated the landscape, leaving only a few felled trees strewn amongst the earth and stone exposed by the scouring of the surface. There were people everywhere, from adventurers to Magic Society researchers to city officials. More were arriving from Yaresh with every moment, in vehicles or through portals. All the people were focusing on three things: the giant hole in the ground, the caged messenger prisoners, and the two diamond-rankers in a privacy bubble.

"They can't hear a thing through this privacy screen," Allayeth said. "They can't even read our lips because of the slight blur effect."

"They can see me getting told off."

"You won't get told off if you don't throw people to the moon!"

"We both know that isn't true. Also, it was more *at* the moon than *to* the moon. It looks large, but hard to pinpoint from this distance."

"At least tell me you didn't throw them at the Mystic Moon."

"No, it was the regular moon. Which is a point of reference, at least. Do you know how hard it will be to track people down if they're randomly orbiting the planet?"

"Yes, Charist, I do. It's the reason I don't throw people into space. Much."

"Why you are so up in arms about this?"

"Because it's always the same with you, Charist. You drop in like an alchemy bomb and then leave me to clean up the mess. You insisted on taking the lead in dealing with Jason and you messed that right up. I had to step in and now everything is more complicated."

"You cleaned up my mess, did you? You got no more answers out of Asano than I did. Do you even see what he's doing right now?"

"Yes, Charist, I see it."

"And you called him Jason."

"That's his name, Charist."

"Are you sure you aren't a little closer to Asano than you should be?"

"Charist, you are very powerful. When that's what we need, that's good, unless you start throwing messengers at the moon."

"We don't even know if any of them got there. It takes a lot of precision."

"And you are a blunt object. You agreed to let me deal with J… Asano."

"We shouldn't have to deal with him. He's a silver-ranker."

"He's more than just a silver-ranker, Charist, and I think you understand that."

Charist peered at Allayeth in suspicion.

"You've had some success after all, haven't you?" he accused. "When did you intend to share what you've learned with me?"

"Once I have something worth sharing. Asano has given me hints, implications and little else. He's wary, as you might expect after we essentially ransacked his home."

"The man has too many secrets."

"And you don't?"

"No, Allayeth, I don't. I'm not you. Are you sure you aren't keeping things from me? Because I'm a 'blunt instrument'?"

"Charist, you have no concept of how many things I'm keeping from you. Now, go chase down those messengers you threw. Why exactly did you not just kill them with the others? And don't give me that nonsense about saving adventurers because most saved themselves. And you're a diamond-ranker; you can kill a silver as easily as throw one."

"It's fun tossing things into space."

"That's true," Allayeth acknowledged. "But you need to make sure you're throwing the right people. The ones who'll die."

She pointed at the sky.

"Now go."

"I don't want to go to space," he mumbled, earning him a raised eyebrow glare from Allayeth.

"Fine," he grumbled, and then shot into the air with a rush of wind that sent up dust, dirt and debris for more than a hundred metres.

"You didn't have to do that," Allayeth said quietly after dropping the privacy screen. "I know you can still hear me, Charist."

She moved to the ritual cages, their glowing golden light standing out against the brown, blasted landscape. In a blur, she appeared next to Jason, who was standing in front of them with some other adventurers. There was a portal nearby, a sheet of rainbow light in an archway of milky crystal.

"Don't think I haven't been watching what you're up to," she told him.

"What?" he asked innocently. "There are lots of adventurers watching the cages, not just me or even my team. Tell her, Korinne."

Korinne bowed deeply.

"It is an honour to be in your presence, Lady Allayeth."

"Well, that's not helpful," Jason complained.

"Jason," Allayeth said, pointing at a portal arch. "What is that?"

"It's a portal," Jason said innocently.

"That would be one of your mysterious portals to places unknown."

"It's known to me. Kind of. I more or less understand the... anyway, what does that matter? It's a perfectly innocent portal."

"You weren't trying to get some of the elemental messengers to go through it, then?"

"Maybe," he said evasively. "What's wrong with that?"

"The Adventure Society will be taking them into custody."

"We caught them. We've already got them in custody."

"You aren't isolated underground this time, Jason. You're surrounded by adventurers. Powerful adventurers."

"If you're going to be making threats, Lady Allayeth, then I think you'd best start calling me Mr Asano."

"It wasn't a threat, Jason."

"It wasn't? Then what happens if we say no?"

Jason's team gathered around him while other adventurers backed well off.

"I'm sorry, Jason, but you don't get to say no."

"Leave it be, Jason," Clive said. "These aren't our prisoners anymore, so let the Adventure Society take them."

Clive snapped his fingers and the cages vanished, leaving four dozen messengers in the middle of the adventurers, all of whom were startled at the sudden release. Jason's group rushed through the portal arch, aside from Jason himself. He watched as Allayeth conjured a vine whip in each hand, each one having nine thick lashes that ended in a Venus flytrap head. They looked similar to a hydra whip that Jason had used at bronze rank.

Compared to Jason's old whip, Allayeth's conjured ones had the superior power expected of a diamond-ranker. The heads dove down again and again as if bobbing for apples. With each bite, a silver-rank messenger died. The other adventurers contributed little more than containing the messengers as the whips did their grisly work, although some of the gold-rank adventurers contributed damage effectively.

After watching for a moment, Jason followed his companions through the portal. A gold-ranker moved to stop him but was spooked by a startling powerful spike of aura from Jason. It only startled the gold-ranker for a moment, but Jason used that moment to dart past him.

Jason appeared in his soul realm in one of the courtyards surrounding the central pagoda. In the constantly changing world of Jason's astral kingdom, the courtyards currently had slate tile floors and were divided up by trellises covered in brightly flowering vines. The team sat at a large round table in plush cloud furniture.

Jason joined them, tapping into the raw magic that he could shape into spirit coins as he did. Instead of turning the magic into coins, he had it take the form of trays full of refreshments and the team immediately started digging in.

"Bro, that was a total boss move," Taika told Clive.

"It did feel satisfying," Neil agreed, "but I can't help but wonder about the repercussions."

"I can't say I approve of releasing all those messengers," Humphrey said. "I know Lady Allayeth will handle them, but it still doesn't feel right."

"It felt right to me," Clive said. "Jason isn't the only one who doesn't like getting pushed around. We devised those cages, we filled them with messengers and then they want to swoop in and take them? For what? To hand them all over to the Magic Society for study? No."

"Am I the only one here that respects authority?" Humphrey complained.

His chair was a loveseat he shared with Sophie. She sidled next to him, taking his hand and intertwining their fingers.

"Of course you are," she said sweetly. "I was a thief, Lindy was a thief. She still is, more often than she strictly should be. Taika is some kind of criminal; I'm not clear on the details. Clive is definitely done after the way he was treated by the Magic Society, and I certainly don't have to explain Jason."

"I don't think you could," Neil said.

"I don't have a problem with authority," Rufus said. "Hierarchy is important in the management of institutions."

"I'm ambivalent," Neil said. "I could go either way, based on the circumstances. Which we should all agree is the smart approach."

"Well, you've got Rufus," Sophie said, squeezing Humphrey's hand. "That's something, at least."

"We've provoked the local authorities again," Rufus said. "That leaves the question of what to do next. Are we going to investigate this giant hole with elemental messengers geysering out?"

"Absolutely not," Humphrey said. "Presumably, these messengers have dug their way out. We have no real idea what's down there; all our information comes from sources that are unreliable or explicitly antagonistic."

"Agreed," Clive said. "I don't trust some half-cooked Magic Society assumptions based on a handful of sketchy aura readings."

"Or the Voice of the Will," Jason added.

"Anything we do here, we do with our eyes open," Humphrey said. "Between Clive and Jason—"

"Mostly Jason," Neil interjected.

"Between Clive and Jason," Humphrey repeated, giving Neil a sharp look, "we've demonstrated that we aren't going to be pushed around. That means we can't go back to playing good, obedient adventurers—"

"Which we're terrible at anyway," Belinda said.

"Could people stop interrupting me? We can't—"

"Yeah, stop interrupting Humphrey," Jason said. "He's trying to monologue through what we're... oh, I did it too, didn't I? Sorry, Hump."

Humphrey didn't resume talking right away, panning a disgruntled gaze over the table. He saw the rest of the group trying not to laugh and turned around. Behind his chair, his moustachioed twin was also panning his gaze over the group, but with comically exaggerated sternness.

"Yeah," Stash said in a gravelly imitation of Humphrey's voice. "I'm a very serious man who relies on my friends to provide my own familiar with biscuits."

"Stash, we've talked about this," Humphrey said. "Biscuits are a sometimes food."

"I'm a dragon! I'm not going to get fat!"

"It's not about getting fat. It's about self-discipline."

"You never let me do anything I want!" Stash yelled and ran off. Humphrey watched him go with a sigh.

"I think he's heading into the dragon equivalent of being a teenager," Humphrey explained. "The accelerated maturing of a bonded familiar means we got to this point early, but at least it shouldn't last too long."

"Are you sure?" Rufus asked.

"Being a bonded familiar accelerates the maturation cycle of long-lived bonded familiar beasts," Humphrey said. "It's why creatures like dragons allow their young to bond."

"Yes, I know that part," Rufus said. "But Stash will slowly develop as you go through silver rank, right? Which should take you about as long as a human goes through the juvenile stage. What you've got there, Humphrey, is a normal teenage boy. Who can shape-shift."

Humphrey leaned back in his chair, looking shell-shocked at Rufus' revelation. Sophie comfortingly patted his hand.

24

LEAP OF FAITH

Jason and his companions were sitting at a large round table in a garden courtyard of Jason's soul realm, nibbling at refreshments.

"There's no escaping the fact that Clive's actions will cause us trouble," Humphrey said. "That being said, we are under no obligation to hand over the fruits of our labour to the Adventure Society just because they assume they can take them. But it does complicate our interactions with them when we're meant to be part of a major expedition soon. One with significant political ramifications."

"Will that even be going forward now?" Neil asked. "We were working with the messengers because they're sitting on the hole leading down to the natural array, but it looks like these messed-up new messengers just dug an extra hole for us."

"If the Adventure Society wants to try and go around the messengers," Clive said, "I strongly suggest we stay out of it. As much as I detest working with this Jes Fin Kaal woman, she's not wrong about our knowledge of natural arrays being lacking. I know that I'm somewhat biased when it comes to the Magic Society, but their best researchers know less about natural arrays than Farrah does."

"You think it's better to trust this device the messengers are providing?" Belinda asked.

"It's not a good choice," Clive said, "but yes. We can at least examine that device and learn what we can from it while it's still up here on the surface. That's preferable to heading underground and trying to invent the field of natural array theory while neck-deep in whatever bizarre magic has been cooked up between the array itself and whatever the messengers did to it. All while dodging whatever elementally tainted messengers are left, the local residents, whatever has happened to them, and an astral space full of leftover Builder cultists."

"I'm halfway tempted to give it a go," Farrah said. "I'm an array specialist, and I spent years studying the grid on Earth. I even led the project to repair it after some idiots sabotaged it. That grid is the endgame for natural array research. It uses the principles of natural arrays to create an artificial array according to an entirely different paradigm. It uses natural landscape to create an array so large, it can cover an entire planet, yet doesn't interfere with any other arrays set up within its area. It's at a level of sophistication that goes so far past sophistication, it winds up back at simplicity. The elegance of it is like no other magic I've encountered."

She sipped at a cup of tea before continuing.

"This natural array theory, based on Earth's grid, is the foundation of what Travis and I are doing in terms of developing a communication system. Right now, we're building towers and using crude magical resonance. Give us ten or twenty years of more research and we'll be using mountains and oceans, and no one will even notice. Thirty years, tops."

"So long as the Magic Society doesn't realise what you're working with and interrogate you for your knowledge," Clive pointed out.

"Which is why I've been quiet about this natural array business when I'm not exclusively around friends," Farrah said.

"Maybe you should return to adventuring," Jason said. "Come back to this research when you're diamond rank and don't have to worry about that."

"It's what a lot of diamond-rankers do," Rufus said. "Look at that lady who builds cloud houses and has been chasing Jason around."

"No," Clive said, shaking his head. "That's the smart thing, yes, but that's not how it works. When you find something you need—and I mean *need*—to research, you're not going to wait. Not to reach diamond, which is itself an extremely uncertain proposition, or even gold. When that knowledge is waiting, just out of reach, all you can do is take the step forward to grasp it. Nothing else matters."

Farrah and Clive nodded a shared understanding.

"The grid on Earth is like the astral magic the messengers developed for the Builder cult," Farrah explained. "It's way beyond any local equivalent and was imported in. I suspect that it was the messengers who developed the magic that the person who built the grid on Earth used. That's what makes me suspect that the messengers aren't lying when they say they know what they're doing with this natural array."

"Do you think you understand this magic enough to figure out what to do with this natural array?" Humphrey asked Farrah. "Enough that you'd be willing to go down there without examining the device the messengers have promised us?"

"No," Farrah said without any hint of uncertainty. "I said I was halfway tempted, but that is the half that encourages Jason to do things. The other half is the part of me that tells him to not do things."

"We should listen to that half," Jason said. "Trust me on that one."

"I'll probably learn more from the messenger device than a messed-up natural array anyway," Farrah said. "But why not check out the device first and *then* the array? A little bit of patience and we get the best of both worlds. Well, best for my research. I've been to both worlds, and fiddling with them magically has been fairly catastrophic, historically speaking."

"So, that's a no to going down this new hole, then," Neil said. "Good, because not only is dropping down the big spooky hole something I don't want to do, but it also sounds like a euphemism for something I don't want to do."

"Then we carry on as we were?" Rufus asked. "It seems a little anticlimactic to just go back to the contracts we were on."

"Sounds good to me," Jason said. "There will be no shortage of adventurers looking to be part of whatever the response to this giant hole ends up being. I say we leave them to it."

Around the massive hole in the ground, dozens of adventurers and hundreds of Adventure Society functionaries were building an encampment that would beggar most towns. Flattened trees and underbrush were cleared away and magically recycled into building materials. Stone shapers smoothed out the ground and laid foundations.

Charist stormed into a large tent where Allayeth sat in a folding camp chair, looking out.

"Have you seen what they're doing out there?" he asked angrily.

"I have," she said. Her gaze didn't waver from the portal arch Jason and his team had vanished into. It still sat next to where Clive and Farrah's ritual cages had been. She had been watching it through the open tent flap for the hours it took Charist to hunt down the orbital messengers.

"They're out here building an outpost to go delving into the ground. How many of these people did they pull away from rebuilding the city for this? Look at how fast they're going. Those could have been people's homes."

"They could," Allayeth agreed.

"Do you know what the Adventure Society executives said when I asked?"

"The same thing they told me, I imagine."

"That while diamond-rankers don't answer to the society, neither does the society answer to them."

"Yes. That's what they told me."

"What is happening lately? What happened to the respect people used to hold for us?"

"I'm not sure that was respect, Charist. It was power and mystery, and our prominence since the monster surge began has stripped much of that mystery away. We still have the power, yes, but it's quantifiable for them now. They've seen us hit our limits against Mah Go Schaat. And against Jason Asano, who turned out to be the limit for Mah Go Schaat."

"Asano didn't kill a diamond-rank messenger."

"No. But a diamond-rank messenger tried to kill him and what happened? The messenger dropped dead and Asano ate his life force. When it comes to reputation, the story matters more than the details. However accurate they may or may not be, the stories around Asano are the stuff of legends."

Charist let out his frustration in a grumbling growl.

"I'm going to escort the messengers that were captured back to the city for proper containment at the Adventure Society campus."

He strode back out, leaving Allayeth still contemplating the portal arch. The freed messengers had been dealt with, but setting them loose had caused a rift between the Adventure Society and Jason's team. Normally, annoying even a prominent team was of no matter to the society. Things became complicated when that team had leverage.

The expedition to the natural array was important to the Adventure Society. It meant saving Yaresh instead of having to move the entire population and start over. Claiming the natural array would be a massive boon to the Magic Society, so the Adventure Society securing it would gain them a lot of influence with their sister organisation. The success of that expedition was largely contingent on Jason Asano, however, who was much less invested in it. That gave him an advantage over the Adventure Society that most adventurers didn't have.

Their stunt of releasing dozens of enemies in the middle of a bunch of adventurers could only have been worse if it hadn't been amongst adventurers that could deal with it. Allayeth still wondered what Asano wanted them for, trying to take them through his mystery portal. If releasing the messengers had produced casualties, it would have been an untenable situation. Even with everything safely contained, the society wasn't happy.

The director might have been an advocate for Jason in the past, but the other upper executives were done indulging him. Allayeth knew that they had reached out to the continental council to step in, which she considered an inadvisable solution. The society executives wanted to ramp up the pressure on Jason's team until they fell in line, but she was quite certain they would not, whatever pressure was brought to bear. It would only drive them to act more independently, not bring them to heel.

Jason had threatened to surrender his Adventure Society membership and Allayeth wondered if that might not be best. If they would only ever use the society for their own needs and never serve its needs, then what was the point? That was the privilege of diamond-rankers, earned through service and power.

One of the issues that the Adventure Society had in reining in Jason was his activities for the society. The society's stated purpose was protecting the populace from monsters and other threats, and Jason's record of self-sacrifice for that very purpose was beyond reproach.

His team was respected. Celebrated, even. They had a record of taking the jobs others didn't want, be that in Greenstone, Rimaros or now in Yaresh. When they weren't doing the scutwork, they were doing the exact opposite: fighting with the fate of thousands hanging in the balance. Their record made it all but impossible to reproach them for not acting in service of the society's political needs.

They had saved Greenstone from being invaded by the Builder's world engineers. Not only would the diamond-ranked constructs have annihilated the city and everyone in it, but the Builder invasion would have come three years early. In Vitesse, they discovered that the Purity church was summoning the messengers, revealing the coming invasion. In Rimaros, they were at least partially responsible for eliminating two of the Builder's three fortress cities. They convinced the immensely powerful

Dawn to wipe out one, and another was felled by a weapon designed by their companion. His team were then critical to breaking the Order of Redeeming Light.

In Yaresh, they continued to hold a prominence that was outsized relative to their rank. They had been on the front lines of the world-taker worm discovery, and Jason's cloud palace had allowed them to set up a processing point for handling the refugees. It would have otherwise taken far longer to get the logistics into place.

Jason's ostentatious aura display in the Battle of Yaresh had sent the enemy into a frenzy, exposing them to a costly counterattack. He had captured a contingent of messengers, including an important commander, and the enemy diamond-ranker had fallen dead at his feet for reasons still unknown.

And now he was a critical element in the expedition underground because the messengers refused to deal with anyone else. Combined with Jason's increasingly obvious messenger-like tendencies, from floating around on his own aura to his general sense of smug superiority, it made people nervous. But those were people in power. By reputation, Jason Asano was unimpeachable, and that reputation was spreading now that he had abandoned his false persona. His name had literally resonated over the battlefield in the Battle of Yaresh. The messengers had targeted him personally and paid a heavy price for it.

The Adventure Society branch in Rimaros had understood the difficulty in handling them. Jason had participated in some theatrics to demonstrate he was subject to society control, but his tolerance for such games had clearly come to an end.

As events currently stood, the Adventure Society needed Jason more than he needed them. He wasn't invested in saving Yaresh when there were real, practical reasons to just relocate the city. As one of the few people that could read his emotions, Allayeth knew his position on that to be his true opinion. He would rather relocate the whole city than work with the messengers, but, at least in that, he had acceded to the Adventure Society.

Allayeth also knew that if the society kept pushing, he would reverse that decision, abandon his society membership and walk away, albeit with reluctance. Contracts and the information that came with them were convenient, but if he and his team wanted to go killing monsters freelance, they could. With two loot powers on the team, they could easily get by without contract rewards.

Still staring at the portal, Allayeth let out a sigh. She knew that repairing the fraying relationship between Jason and the Adventure Society was the best thing for both in the long run. The problem was that both sides still needed to compromise when they each felt they had compromised enough.

If Jason walked away, it was likely the messengers would refuse to work with the 'servant races' at all. The natural array would inexorably destroy what remained of Yaresh and leave the region devastated. Once Jason no longer had that leverage over the Adventure Society, it would seek to redress the grievances with him it had previously put aside. That might come from the pride of gold-rankers or society executives, or it might be to shield the society's reputation so it didn't look like a silver-ranker was pushing it around.

Allayeth knew she had to be the adult in the room, take the squabbling children aside and force them to reluctantly shake hands. She had to be the glue that held them together, but wasn't sure how to do that. The Adventure Society would back her because she wasn't some silver-ranker; when she or Charist treated them with the disregard that Jason did, that fell within their expectation. It was the privilege of power.

Was the solution to show them Jason's power? She was convinced that his rank was not a true reflection of his abilities, but the details remained a mystery. Who was the backer who gave him whatever vast power lay beyond that portal? Why was he convinced that the truth had at least a chance of making her want to kill him? He was beginning to trust her, but not yet enough to open up. This latest incident was another setback.

Her gaze had not left the portal in all the time she had been sitting in the tent. She stood up, eyes still locked on it.

"It's going to take a leap of faith," she murmured.

She steeled herself for a moment, then strode over to the portal and stepped through.

25

GARDEN-VARIETY ARROGANCE

Jason's team was preparing to leave his soul realm when Jason went dead still.

"Jason?" Gary asked, prompting everyone else to look at him.

"What's wrong?" Humphrey asked.

"Allayeth has been staring at the portal the whole time we've been in here. She just got up and walked through it."

The group all looked at the nearby portal arch.

"She won't come out here," Jason explained. "I opened another portal in the gardens. Stay here."

"Is it a good thing that the god-like power he has here doesn't make him more imperious?" Neil asked. "Or is it a bad thing that he isn't less imperious when he's anywhere else?"

Dedicated portal specialists had power sets that synergised to expand the rank and number of people they could move with translocation powers. They supplemented this with specialised rituals and custom-crafted tools to further push those limits. But there was no combination of essence abilities or bespoke magic items that would stretch a silver-rank portal to accommodate a diamond-ranker.

That the portal could accommodate her suggested it was not produced by an essence ability. That made sense, as it felt like something apart from an essence user's magic. How much of that power belonged to Jason, and how much came from his mysterious backers, was one of the key questions she wanted to answer.

She hesitated as she reached the portal, just the echo of the power on the other side striking her magical senses. Her pause lasted only the briefest moment before she stepped through the arch.

The portal felt slightly off compared to others she'd used. The transition took the tiniest moment longer than it should have, which did not concern her. The dimensional forces she felt press against her soul as she passed through them did.

The time she spent passing through the portal was a fragment of a second, but she arrived shaken from the experience. Those with less than diamond-rank senses wouldn't understand enough be unnerved by the portal transition, but she arrived trembling. What those senses picked up on arrival was worse.

The physical space barely mattered as the spiritual environment felt almost like an attack. An aura of raw power and terrible will was as ubiquitous as the air. She had visited the ocean depths once, and the pressure on her body then was like the pressure on her soul now. She screwed her eyes shut and concentrated on rallying her spiritual strength. She struggled against the domineering power that demanded control, but fighting it was like trying to drink the seas.

The sense of someone else controlling her fate was something Allayeth had spent her entire adventuring career trying to overcome. Adrift in a sea of raw spiritual oppression, she staggered as she flashed back to the childhood memory still seared into her mind.

She was slung over one of the house staff's shoulders, bouncing up and down as the woman ran. Her arms stretched out helplessly in the direction of her parents' bodies, lit up in the night by the fires of their burning home. That was the last time she had felt so completely helpless against the world around her. Nothing in her adventuring career, from iron to diamond, had ever left her feeling so at the mercy of fate.

Until now.

Allayeth wasn't sure what had happened. She'd passed out or otherwise been rendered insensible, only to wake up in a chair. It had the incomparable comfort of cloud furniture, and was in a grassy circle surrounded by rainforest; a small, secluded grove.

The spiritual pressure was no longer pressing in on her, but its presence remained an inescapable threat. It felt like being in a cave while a monster prowled outside, too large to come in but too dangerous to get past.

She closed her eyes and took a slow, calming breath. The sense of threat she felt was unusual for a diamond-ranker, but she hadn't always been one. She was an adventurer and danger was her life. She used meditation to calm herself, to settle the whirling eddies of her soul. She didn't rush, fully reclaiming her equanimity before opening her eyes.

The sky was clear and blue but for a few clouds as white and fluffy as her seat. The lush green foliage and gorgeously vibrant flowers of the rainforest grove were a little too perfectly arranged to be natural. There was a creek merrily babbling by, raw magic radiating off of it. She had no doubt that if she drank from it, it would be just as nourishing as a spirit coin. The trails leading away from the grove were flat and easy underfoot. One invited her along a wide, seemingly natural path, leading into a false twilight created by the canopy. Another meandered along the creek past tantalising fruit trees. That fruit, the tropical flowers and the rich greenery filled the air with an aroma that was almost musical.

But under the beauty was a sense of foreboding that was as much a warning as the domineering aura suffusing everything. She had a distinct feeling that danger lurked in the shadows for any who sought to explore beyond the well-defined paths. The garden was beautiful but also a threat —a benevolent cage that promised safety so long as she remained inside it.

The other notable aspect of her environment was an unsettled mutability. It wasn't anything she could see, but her spiritual senses told her that everything around her was on the verge of shifting, like a tide at its zenith.

She wondered where Asano was. Did he know she was here? The chair she was sitting in was certainly his style. Taking a risk, she closed her eyes and pushed out her aura senses. The instant they reached beyond her body, they ran headlong into a wall of molasses. The world felt heavy, like the air on a summer day so humid that it was hard to breathe.

She reflected on the oddness of the comparison her mind had thrown out. She hadn't needed to breathe in well over a century. She wondered why that had sprung to mind, then trembled as she realised where it had come from.

Allayeth didn't have any real memories of her childhood, bar the one that remained crystal clear. It was too far back, long before magic had sharpened her mind. Or perhaps she didn't want to remember. What was left was little more than a collection of feelings, but her flashback had managed to dredge something up.

She was holding her father's hand, licking flavoured ice on a scorching day. That was all she got, not when or where or why. Tears formed in her eyes, something she hadn't done since she was a girl.

She had to spiritually heave to spread her senses even a little way past her body. She closed her eyes again, concentrating entirely on pushing her perception through the interference. It gave her a much better sense of the oppressive aura and, when she examined the aura more closely, her reclaimed equanimity shattered.

There was no mysterious power behind Jason. He might have cosmic allies like Dawn, but the power they had been wondering about, the power behind his mysterious portal, wasn't someone backing him. It *was* him. Literally, this was him; this place was an extension of Jason somehow.

She opened her eyes to find Jason sitting across from her in an identical cloud chair. He was wearing a floral shirt, tan shorts and sandals, topped with a broad-brimmed straw hat. In one hand, he held a half-eaten sandwich, and in the other, a glass of juice with a wedge of fruit pushed onto the edge. His eyes were fixed on her, curious and penetrating.

"Hello, Allayeth."

"It's you," she said in a shaking voice. "It's not some backer who we can't sense because you're imprinted on the portal. It's just you. All the things we attributed to… it's always been just you."

"Not always," he answered, his voice soft and his expression gentle. "I do have some remarkable acquaintances. You've met Dawn."

"Dawn isn't behind this place."

"She had her role. Unintentional and peripheral, yes, but a soul doesn't just get like this."

"How does it happen?"

"In stages. I promised to show you my secrets if you came here, Allayeth, not to explain them. Although you might tease some things out of me. If you ask nicely."

He gave her a smile unlike anything she had seen from him before. There was no trace of an underlying smirk, no ironic amusement. It was just kind.

"Are you alright?" he asked. "That memory you had earlier, it seemed rather intense."

Her eyes turned sharp.

"You saw that?"

"Just the emotions that came with it. You blasted them out pretty hard, but I contained your aura so that no one else in this place sensed it."

"This place," she echoed. "This is you. Not just the power but the physical space itself. Some kind of dimensional space, and I don't think it's an entirely stable one. Everything around me feels like it's paused in the middle of some otherwise constant transformation. How is it so powerful? Why does your aura permeate it like water in a sponge?"

Her eyes went wide as she had a revelation.

"Are we inside your soul?"

"Yes."

"How is that possible? How does that even work? Your body *is* your soul, like the messengers. If your body and soul are one thing, and we're in your soul, where exactly are we in relation to that? Did we shrink and are in your body somehow? What part of your body? Do I even want to know?"

Jason let out an easy-going laugh.

"We're not tiny people running around inside my eyeball or something. As you say, my body and soul are one. Physical and spiritual, neither fully one nor the other. That means the spiritual elements intrude on the physical realm, granting me certain abilities. It's why my spiritual expression—my aura—can manifest as a physical force. The messengers are the same. Where we are now is the opposite end: a physical intrusion into the spiritual realm."

"The astral."

"Yes. This is something akin to an astral space, but instead of being anchored to the world, it's anchored to me."

"Do all the messengers have one of these spaces as well?"

"They have the potential for them. Their spaces do not manifest unless triggered somehow. Such as by becoming an astral king."

"And that's why they say you are a king. Because you can do what their kings do."

"That's part of it."

"This space is unstable."

"Embryonic would be a more accurate description. I'm still new to this and this space has grown faster than my ability to manage it. I don't have all the tools to settle it."

"The tools?"

"I need something called a soul forge. There may be a way to obtain one from the natural array, or perhaps turn it into one. I suspect that is the true objective of the messengers, and likely what the device they intend to give us will do. It's also the main reason I'm quite certain they intend for me to die down there. They need me to get it, but they can't allow me to keep it."

"I think they intend everyone to die down there."

"I imagine you're right."

"But what makes you think that this soul forge is what's down there?"

"Something that Healer gave me."

"Healer, as in the god?"

"It would be weird if it was Healer the pre-loved amphora salesman."

"A god gave you a gift?"

"Don't be envious. Gods and great astral beings don't give you gifts, not really. They give you manipulation coated in a sweet candy shell. You take it, because they don't muck about when handing out the goods, but get ready to drop neck-deep into the brown. Nothing is just a gift with them."

Jason took out a fist-sized orb that glowed with gold, silver and blue transcendent light. A window popped up in front of Allayeth, startling her.

Item: [Genesis Command: Life] (transcendent rank, legendary)

The authority to create a life. (consumable, magic core).

- Effect: Give true life to an astral construct created from a dimensional space. The construct becomes a true astral entity, bound to the dimensional space.

- Uses remaining: 1/1

- You do not meet the qualifications to activate this device in the current space. Missing element: soul forge.

"What is this?" Allayeth asked, the screen blurring as she passed a hand through it.

"This is how I see the world," Jason told her. "Mostly."

"Mostly?"

"There are other elements."

Synthesizer music started playing and a black and white helicopter flew overhead.

"Sorry," Jason apologised as the music abruptly stopped. "I'm still learning to control this place properly and I occasionally get some reflexive Airwolf."

"I don't know what that means."

"It means that if you see a young David Hasselhoff wandering around, just leave him be."

"I don't know who that is."

"You'll catch up. Have you ever heard of a DVD box set?"

Allayeth stopped asking questions that only led to nonsensical answers and turned back to the message window still floating in the air.

"This is a description of the item the Healer gave you?" she asked, her eyes moving to the orb still in Jason's hand.

"Yes. You'll see the last line mentions that I'm missing something in order to use it."

"A soul forge."

"A suspicious man might look at something that he got from a god with a critical missing component and imagine it to be a clue as to what he might encounter in the near future."

Allayeth frowned, still overwhelmed by everything. The power of the place. The man behind that power, who had received enough gifts from gods and great astral beings to share the benefits of his experience.

"How did you get this power?"

"Which power? You'll have to narrow it down."

"To create this space inside your soul."

"I said you'd have to ask nicely if you want me to spill the beans. That felt a little curt and demanding."

"Are you going to keep hiding things from me at this stage? I'm inside your soul."

"Yes, I am. And yes, you are. Walk with me."

He stood and started walking. She did the same, falling into step beside him as they wandered along a gravel path that followed the creek. He didn't speak, and just as she was about to press him with more questions, she spotted a messenger flying in the distance.

"You let the messengers here roam free."

"No one is free here."

"Except you."

"Perhaps. I may be the most trapped of all."

"This is your soul."

"Yes, but obligations are chains. Metaphorical ones, but that matters in this place. If my behaviour out there changes who I am, it changes things in here as well. If your soul crumbles, Allayeth, it's a metaphor. For me, that metaphor is the earth and sky. If my soul crumbles, what becomes of this place?"

"You were right to be wary of showing us this. Of fearing we would kill you. If this is what's inside you now, and we allow you to go grow stronger, you'll be—"

"Monstrous?"

"No, unstoppable. Which makes it a problem if you choose to become monstrous."

"And now you have to decide if you're willing to risk that."

"If Charist saw this place, he would kill you as soon as he got out. Never let him know about this until you have the strength to stop him. Or do you have it already? Did you use the power of this place to kill the diamond-rank messenger?"

"No. I genuinely have no idea what happened there. I can tap into the power of this place while I'm out there, but it's never easy and there's always a price. Even trying to kill someone on your level would kill me first, and would fail miserably."

"Then tell no one."

"You may have noticed, lady, but that's what I was doing. You're the one who barged in here."

"At your standing invitation."

"You weren't meant to accept it."

"And if Charist does as well?"

"Then he stays here until I'm strong enough that he can't kill me."

"Are you going to let me out?"

"Should I?"

"Disappearing a diamond-ranker would be a mess I don't think you're ready for."

"That's why I'd appreciate you keeping Charist from ducking in for a look."

"You trust me enough to let me go?"

"I'm working on it. I like trusting people. It used to be that I would always trust them until they gave me a reason not to. The cost of making a mistake is too high for that now. There is so much riding on me that I can't risk that kind of mistake just for the chance at making a new friend. I have to be careful these days."

Allayeth nodded, understanding the burden of power and responsibility. She looked away from him, her eyes once more taking in the beautiful gardens around them.

"This is why you act like you're already a diamond-ranker, isn't it? You're just waiting for your rank to catch up to the rest of you. The power you have here, your spiritual strength. The circles you move in and the challenges in front of you. The gods and the great astral beings understand, but we mortals don't see it. How many of your problems stem from that disconnect?"

"Most of the little ones. The big ones see me for exactly what I am."

"I see why you act the way you do now. I think I would too."

"No," Jason said, shaking his head. "I was like this before I acquired all the power. I act this way out of garden-variety arrogance."

HOW TO REACH GOLD RANK IN THREE EASY STEPS

JASON AND ALLAYETH CONTINUED TO MEANDER THROUGH THE GARDEN OF Jason's spiritual estate.

"This realm is in a constant state of change," Jason explained. "At first, it was a metaphor. A mindscape I could enter while meditating. I found it after my first direct encounter with the Builder—I'm assuming you've read my Adventure Society records."

"Yes, although they left me with more questions than answers."

"Perhaps you'll get some of them. Someday. As I said, it was a mindscape, shaped fairly directly by my essences. After I died the second time, I was able to enter the space, just myself and my familiars. Then… other things happened. From there, it became more or less the genuine space you see now. Not as large, back then. It also became less rigidly defined by my essences. Their influence didn't vanish, it just blended together with other factors. I suspect it's related to how I view them and how that relates to my sense of self."

"It is," Allayeth said.

"That was a confident response. You have a lot of experience with dimensional soul realms?"

"No, but I understand how we, meaning all essence users, relate to our essences. Are you familiar with the idea that essences shape who we are?"

"I am. When I first arrived in this world, I met two people with different views on this. One thought that the essences we choose shape us, so she wasn't delighted with my sin essence. Or my doom essence. She didn't care for any of them, really. The other person, that's my friend Rufus, held that our essences are what we make of them."

"Neither was entirely right or wrong. At low rank, our essences are just tools, as your friend said. Things become more complicated at higher ranks, and attempting to engage with those higher truths too early can be detrimental to growth. It's why the Adventure and Magic Societies forbid sharing that information until it becomes relevant at high silver."

"I've heard pieces of this, from Rufus' mother and elsewhere. From what I can tell, we're talking about exploring essences and how they relate to who we are on a conceptual level."

"Yes. It seems absurd to not tell you. Seeing this place, the Adventure Society information restrictions seem a bit laughable. Starting around the peak of silver, the traditional method to advance stops being as effective. That's the balanced approach of training the body, training the spirit, and then pushing them both to the limit by fighting monsters. Advancement slows as you reach that point."

"At that point? Advancement feels quite slow now."

"The wall is only the beginning. You still need to train the traditional way until you reach the upper levels of silver, which will take longer than everything that came before put together. You can't reach the peak that way, though. Advancement gets even slower unless you know what you're doing. This is where those without strong mentors tend to fall down through lack of guidance. That's not always true, though. Charist, for example, had no one to guide him, but he moved quite smoothly from silver into gold. Some people just know exactly who and what they are. It's the complications that catch us up, so the process favours those who are—"

"Simple?"

"I was searching for a better word. Uncomplicated, perhaps."

"That sounds worse. It makes it sound like you're calling them simple and think they're too simple to figure that out."

"You may be right. In any case, they have an advantage over those who overthink things in coming to terms with their essences. It's not that essences alter our identities, not directly. What they do is find parts of our identities and latch on to them. They feed those parts of ourselves, fertilising and growing them until they are more prominent aspects of our personalities. I'm sure you've noticed that essence users, especially high-rank ones, are often overt in their behaviours. Larger than life."

"I've been a little guilty of that since I was an iron-ranker."

"I'd wondered about that, reading your record. It's a sign that your transition into and passage through gold rank will be a straightforward one."

"Are you calling me simple?"

"I'm definitely not calling you uncomplicated."

He let out a chuckle. They had followed the creek out of the rainforest garden and into a network of trellises with flowering plants woven into large, arching tunnels.

"Are you about to tell me how to reach gold rank in three easy steps?" Jason asked.

"Easy is relative. For example, the transition to gold rank is the one time that being a core user beats out advancement through training."

"Oh?"

"When you advance with monster cores, you can just throw money at the problem, buying cores until you hit gold."

"I assume that is prohibitively expensive."

"Oh, yes. There's a reason only royal families and the most established noble houses do it on a regular basis. It's often the last gasp of a house before it falls, in fact."

"How so?"

"Most noble houses start with some exceptional adventurer. Someone with skills like yours but who doesn't run around causing trouble everywhere."

Jason stopped short and Allayeth turned to look at him, seeing his expression turn hard.

"I don't run around causing problems," he said, his words clipped. "I run around solving them, and I'm getting pretty tired of people seeing it the wrong way around."

Allayeth had been slowly acclimatising to Jason's strange world with its domineering, ubiquitous aura. Suddenly, she felt all over again just how small her power was in Jason's realm. She'd almost gotten used to it, putting him at ease with some playful teasing, but his unexpected response brought the power dynamic crashing back to the forefront of her mind.0

"I'm sorry," she said.

"I'm not telling you how to think, Lady Allayeth, or forcing you to pretend you see me in a way you do not. But I get enough of people telling me what I am out there; I have no obligation to allow it in here. It might be best if you keep what you think of me to yourself."

"I'm sorry," she said again. "You always seemed comfortable with your rather erratic image. You certainly play into it enough."

His stern expression morphed into a troubled frown.

"I'm sorry," he apologised. "I hate people using their power to oppress me, yet I keep doing it to others at the drop of a hat. And you are right. The way I've conducted myself as an adventurer has understandably engendered certain impressions of me. I just wish that people would look past the way I do things to see the things I do."

"With respect, Jason, that is a desire shared by almost everyone ever."

Jason blinked, then laughed, breaking the tension. The world around them felt a little less oppressive.

"Come on," he said, resuming their walk. "You were telling me about adventurers and noble houses."

Allayeth took her place, walking beside him as they moved into another garden. This was a more cultivated area filled with rose beds. The flowers ranged from vibrant red to dark blue, with various shades of purple in between. The flowers all featured sharp, prominent thorns and their aroma was sweet but with a faint coppery tang.

She judged that this part of Jason's realm was heavily influenced by his blood essence. She let her senses taste the affinities of the aura hanging heavy around her. It was sinister and hungry, but bursting with life and something else she had trouble placing. She examined it for a moment before realising that what she sensed was immortality.

Her research into Jason confirmed that he had returned from the dead multiple times. It had also uncovered that the Builder himself had claimed that whatever power Jason used to resurrect had been expended, at least until he reached gold rank. What she was feeling now made her think that either the Builder was lying or the Builder was wrong.

"I've upset you," he said, seeing her caught up in contemplation.

"No," she told him. "This place leaves a lot to consider. About power and how much of it is tied up in essences. About you."

Jason nodded.

"I am increasingly drawn to the conclusion that essences are just shapes," he said. "I don't think they have power of their own. The soul is the power. Essences are just tools to shape that power to let us express it. The fact that even gods and great astral beings are helpless to breach a resolute soul shows us that the power was there from the beginning. I'm not sure that a soul has any limitations."

"You should advance to late silver as quickly as you can, Jason. I suspect that your passage into gold will be swift and smooth."

"Maybe I can beat the record," Jason said. "Dawn said she trained a woman who reached diamond rank before she was forty. I don't think the Builder counts because he was a messenger."

Allayeth stopped dead.

"The Builder was a messenger?" she asked.

"You didn't know that? His name is Zithis Carrow Vayel. He was a sixteen-year-old diamond-ranker when the great astral beings recruited him to replace the old Builder."

"Where are you getting that information?"

"I move in rarefied circles. You know this."

"I know that gods come to speak with you, even though you aren't a priest. I know that you held a meeting with the Builder and the World-Phoenix and convinced the Builder to abandon his invasion early. I know that there were a lot of questions about the exact relationship between you and Hierophant Dawn."

"And yet, people can't stop messing with me," Jason said. "They see the people I deal with, and instead of backing away, they covet that which is mine. Because of my rank."

"Are you truly surprised? Power is everything in Pallimustus, but your power is hidden away. The hints of what this realm represents are enough to drive people into a frenzy. You know this or you wouldn't have played the game of inviting Charist and myself to see it."

"Yes, well, you called my bluff and won that game."

"Did I? You could destroy me in an instant."

"But will I?"

She glanced at Jason before looking away. Her aura senses told her more about him than her eyes did in this realm. She felt unconscionable power, a savage will perhaps too eager to face challenges to its authority. An iron fist, but one that was held open, shielding those underneath it. It was the aura of a benevolent tyrant, and she was unsure what to do with it. Was it something to accept, to run from or fight against? But that was a fight she did not ever want. There was an unflinching resolve that lay under everything in this realm, like the core of a planet. It was his core, that stood strong in the face of gods and fought off the power of a great astral being.

"No," she said. "I don't think you'll destroy me. But I'm afraid of what happens to everyone else if you change your mind."

"Me too," he admitted softly. "What happens when you leave this place? Are you going to sell me out to Charist?"

"If I said no, could you tell if I was lying?"

"Yes. But honestly? I could probably compel you to both speak and speak truthfully."

"You would torture me?"

"No. I would rebuild your physiological makeup so that you were incapable of doing otherwise. Binaries are quite vulnerable in that regard, which is something Carlos Quilido is researching."

"Binaries?"

"People whose souls and bodies are connected but still discrete entities."

"So, almost everyone in existence."

"Yes. Altering the physical half of a person isn't hard, if you're not too worried about the final outcome. I won't do that, by the way. I don't quite know what I'm doing yet, and after I put you back together you would die the moment you left this place."

"Why would you even tell me you can do that? Aren't you afraid it will lead me to kill you the moment I get out of here?"

"I hope you don't. It wouldn't be good for my diminishing ability to trust."

The scent of the flowers filled her nostrils, reminding her of the power of immortality they held within them. She didn't think that that was an accident.

"Now," he said, "we keep getting distracted. You were telling me about noble houses."

"Right," she said distractedly, reorienting her thoughts. "Noble houses. They are usually formed when an outstanding adventurer is given a title for some great service to the local authorities. In the lifetime of that adventurer, they tend to flourish, but there comes a time when the adventurer is no longer around. When the founder dies or reaches diamond rank and steps into the background, the family must make their own way like a baby bird leaving the nest. They have to fly on their own or hit the ground hard."

"They need more successful adventurers to stay relevant."

"That or several gold-rankers. Some families have amassed so much wealth that they can just pay their way to maintain a cadre of gold-rankers through cores. Adventurers are better, though. They produce wealth instead of consuming it, and are more respected. But when a family is flagging, their coffers near empty and their highest rankers are silver, they sometimes throw all their remaining wealth into having at least one gold-ranker."

"But one core-using gold-ranker won't reverse their fortunes."

"No," Allayeth agreed. "Yet I have seen so many try anyway, clinging to the remnants of long-dead glory."

"How far can a core user go? We started talking about this because you said absorbing monster cores was an advantage for reaching gold rank."

"Yes, because it doesn't require that shift in approach from blindly fighting monsters to coming to grips with the complexities of self-revelation. But, once they reach gold rank, they stop dead. Once you reach gold, cores will no longer let you circumvent the need for self-exploration. It's possible someone could keep progressing with cores and reach diamond, but I've never heard of it happening. I don't think there are enough cores on the planet to get you to diamond."

"So, core use is ultimately a dead end. That's why the artefact Purity left behind is so appealing. But would the people who rose up through cores have the mindset to rise up?"

"Craftspeople would. Unlike adventurers, they push their limits by pushing the boundaries of their professions instead of fighting monsters. Their sense of self-reflection often outstrips that of an adventurer because of their focus on their craft. That self-revelation allows them to extract viable amounts of advancement from cores, giving them a path to diamond. If anything, I would guess there are more craftsperson diamond-rankers than adventurers. If they were freed from the influence of cores, I suspect the number of diamond-rankers would explode, and that's world-changing."

"I know of a diamond-rank craftsman," Jason said. "A weaponsmith who mentors my friend Gary. He helped him reforge my sword."

"There is also the woman whose attention you have been fending off for the last few weeks. I believe she made your cloud flask."

"She did. I haven't actually met her, though. I keep putting it off."

"I can't imagine she's happy about that."

"I'm told not."

"She's interested in the unconventional modifications you've made to your flask?"

"She's been trying to break in, is what she's been doing."

"What are you going to do about that?"

"Not much I can do, or need to. She's not getting in because I've connected the cloud flask to this place."

"Perhaps I could join you when you finally meet with her."

"I would appreciate that. I've always found diamond-rank backup to be useful."

She frowned.

"Did I just become one of the powerful people that always seem to be hanging around you?"

"I don't think of them that way," Jason said, "which is one of the reasons they choose to hang around."

"Then what do you think of them as?"

"Friends."

NIGH-IMPOSSIBLE GOAL

As Jason and Allayeth continued to meander through his garden estate, Allayeth had the chance to see much more of it. In the manicured gardens that didn't tower over them, she could see the looming pagoda at the centre of the estate. A network of small creeks flowed through everything, notable for the fact that they weren't filled with water but with unadulterated mana drawn from the astral.

"Have you considered opening a spirit coin farm here?" she asked.

"I have it on good authority that several gods like the economy where it is. I'm not above snubbing the gods, but not just because I can. Usually. And messing with the economy always ends up hurting the people at the bottom of it, while rich pricks like me make more money than ever."

"It would take a significant injection of coins to affect an entire economy."

"I know, right?"

They paused halfway across a massive rope bridge that spanned over a sharp gorge. The walls of the gorge were covered in thick moss and creeper vines. The bottom was shrouded in spray from a river that emerged from a cave, barrelled along the bottom of the gorge and disappeared into another cave.

"The underground areas stem from my dark essence," Jason told her. "They have some spectacular glowing mushroom caverns."

They carried on, passing buildings that ranged from gleaming glass and metal to old mansions reclaimed by nature to the point that they were hard to spot amongst the overgrowth. Oddly, she saw Jason, time and again. Meditating, sparring with himself.

"Avatars?"

"Yeah. I can only make them look like me in here. The ones in my cloud palace are the creepy cyclops fellas you've already seen."

Along with duplicates of Jason, she saw messengers. Some flew in the sky while others were wandering around, floating over the ground or even standing on it. Solitary messengers looked introspective and conflicted, while those in groups conducted quiet conspiratorial chats.

"What are you doing with them?" Allayeth asked.

"Stopping you from doing things with them. They won't talk, whatever you put them through. But you know that because you've tried it with the ones captured during the Battle of Yaresh."

"And other conflicts, yes. But you could make them talk in this place, couldn't you?"

"Yes. Silver-rankers I could make talk anywhere, I suspect. But that is a process I refuse to undertake unless the alternative is worse. Thus far, it's only ever been the one time."

"I'm not sure I follow your meaning."

They were in a section of garden that looked like a large rural estate gone to seed, the once carefully manicured gardens having grown out unevenly. Buildings were half-crumbled and mostly overgrown. Jason nodded at a dilapidated farmhouse where a messenger was perched in a crouch on the rooftop, wings spread out to balance her. She had no eyes for Allayeth, staring death at Jason.

"That's Tera," Jason said. "She doesn't like me very much."

"She's your prisoner."

"Being a prisoner she can accept. It's being free that she struggles with."

"I don't understand."

"Tera is a true believer in the messenger ideals. But she was going to die and I had to do things to keep her alive. Namely, I had to break her spirit."

"She doesn't seem broken. Just angry."

"Yes," Jason said with a smile. "It worked out as well as I could hope."

"Most people with a messenger obsessed with their death wouldn't call it working out well."

"The first messenger who obsessed over my death was the Builder, so anyone else is a bit tame by comparison. But I will have someone else explain Tera's situation and that of the other messengers. Do you know who Marek Nior Vargas is?"

"A messenger commander. A capable one. Also, the one you captured."

Jason nodded.

"Marek," he said. "Attend us, please."

Jason sat in a picnic chair that Allayeth was sure hadn't been there a moment ago. Failing to notice something happening that close to her was unsettling, and she was certain it was no accident. Jason was showing off. She checked behind herself and there was a chair for her too, plus a third when she looked forward again as she sat.

A messenger descended out of the sky, throwing a glance at the one Jason had called Tera. She continued to watch as Marek arrived, his wings folding back as he alighted upon the ground. Allayeth recognised Marek from having seen him across the battlefield while besieging messenger strongholds. He was less ostentatious in his appearance than most messengers, both in his garb and the way he carried himself.

He could have easily been a celestine adventurer with the wing essence if he was a foot shorter. He didn't stop at tucking his wings away but absorbed them fully into his body, something messengers could all do but rarely chose to. There was also something odd about the way he moved, and it took Allayeth a moment to realise what it was.

Marek didn't make every move as if the world around him was his to command. Messengers believed themselves inherently superior and it was reflected in their body language. It was odd to see its absence, especially in front of Jason. It was one of many traits Jason shared with most messengers.

"You know each other," Jason said, certain but sounding surprised. She assumed he read that from their auras, something she was not used to. It had been years since someone else could read her emotions while theirs were closed off to her.

"We have met on the battlefield," Marek said.

"Marek, if you would be so kind, would you tell Lady Allayeth how and why you came to be here?"

Marek looked at Jason.

"What should I hold back?"

"Nothing."

"Are you sure?"

"Lady Allayeth made a gesture of trust to come into this place. Diamond-rankers don't put themselves at the mercy of others very often. It's now my turn to put some trust in her."

"If you are sure," Marek said, his tone making it clear that he was not.

"I am," Jason told him.

"Very well," Marek said, then turned to look squarely at Allayeth. "The path that led me here started long ago, when I first became aware of a faction within the messengers called the Unorthodoxy…"

"What you're telling me," Allayeth said, "is that the messengers are an entire people made up of slaves who have been brainwashed into thinking they're lords."

"Yes," Marek confirmed.

Allayeth slumped back in her chair as she rubbed her temples in one hand, her mind churning away.

"That makes so much sense," she said. "The contradictory behaviour. The dissonance between attitudes and actions."

She looked up at Marek.

"I respect what you want to do for your people," she said, "but they are still invading our world. Still killing my people. We are going to keep killing them right back."

"And I respect that you have not asked me for information on the strategic disposition of my people," Marek told her. "My gratitude for what Jason Asano has done is close to boundless, but not quite. He has given me the chance to free my people, but I will not let the price be making it easier for you to kill them. I will not sell out my own kind, even when they are victims without knowing it."

"I understand. And when I said there was little I could do, I did mean little, not nothing. Here is what I propose: I attempt to sell the Adventure Society on Jason being given all messenger prisoners to contain."

"I'm not going to go soul-torturing every messenger we encounter to try and turn them from the dark side," Jason said. "Tera was an exception by circumstance, and don't think I'm going to go challenging messengers to reproduce that circumstance."

"I understand that. But from what Marek Nior Vargas just told me, you didn't torture him. He wanted this, and convinced his people to go along with it. The ones who are still stuck in their indoctrination you can contain safely here, but there may be others you can help."

"Not all of my people could bring themselves to open their souls to Jason," Marek pointed out. "Even willingly, fighting past the self-preservation instinct to make yourself that vulnerable is not easy. You expose the most core parts of your being, and one of my people died trying and failing to do that. Because she couldn't get there, the astral king was able to kill her because she still had a hold over her soul. Even here, she was not safe."

"I understand that," Allayeth said, "but they wouldn't fare any better in Adventure Society custody. Any time one of our messenger prisoners shows any intention of talking to us, they die. And the ones who hold fast and give us nothing are ultimately executed once we're convinced they are of no use to us. Here, they can be contained and maybe even turned around by messengers like you. And I imagine there are more like you, biding their time and hoping for an opportunity that they believe will never come."

"There are," Marek said.

"If we do as Allayeth suggests," Jason said, "someone should stay here when I let the rest of you go. To convince any Unorthodoxy sympathisers to let me free them from astral king control."

"Assuming you let us go at all," Marek said. "You yourself have voiced continuing doubt on this point."

"I admit that you trouble me, Marek," Jason said. "I've heard everything you have said to your people while you're here. You're an extremist."

"I must be extreme if I am ever to make headway against the astral kings."

"I agree. But being necessary doesn't stop you from being dangerous. You remind me of myself in that way. The problem with letting you go is how to do that without people like Allayeth here taking umbrage. Her senses are good enough, and she pays enough attention, that I can't just let you loose from my soul realm. And if I go far enough away that she can't sense me, someone else will."

"He's right," Allayeth said. "Many diamond-rankers that didn't go back into seclusion after the monster surge because of your people, Marek. They're always on the lookout for your kind, and if they sense Jason open a portal and let a bevy of messengers out, they'll kill you and probably him. I can possibly talk the Adventure Society and the Yaresh government into allowing you to take in all the messengers, Jason, but that is no certainty. What is certain is I can't convince them to accept you letting any messengers go. We will need an ally who is more compelling."

"Who do you have in mind?" Jason asked.

"Liberty," Allayeth told him.

"The goddess?" Jason asked. "That's a great idea. I never even considered that."

"That does not surprise me," Allayeth said. "My research suggests that, despite trafficking with the gods more than anyone who does not serve, you have an inherent distrust of deities."

"That's fair to say," Jason said. "I don't trust religion, I don't trust authority and I don't trust anyone with more power than one person should have. Vast cosmic power falls quite thoroughly into that range."

"You have vast cosmic power," Allayeth pointed out.

"Yes," Jason agreed.

"You don't trust yourself?"

"No."

"Yet you seek out even more power."

"Yes."

"How do you reconcile that with a lack of trust in yourself to use it responsibly?"

"I try to be patient and thoughtful in my actions. To consider my motives in making them, to see if the reasoning behind my ideals has been warped by my pride and vanity. Mostly, though, it is the same answer I gave to your earlier question: friends. A friend will support you when you are doing well and things are easy. A *good* friend holds you to account, even when it's hard."

His smile mixed sadness and happiness, his eyes holding a look of reminiscence.

"I've faced that danger more than once in the last few years," he said. "I've looked into the abyss and crossed line after line until I no longer recognise the man who was pulled into a magical world he didn't understand. Every time, my friends were there to help me find myself. To stop me before I went so far, there was no coming back."

He looked at Marek.

"Your kind are easy to hate, Marek Nior Vargas. You make it so easy to justify performing the most heinous acts upon you. I should thank you for that, in a way. It helped me, through my friends, realise that I was on a trajectory that had to change. That I had to stop escalating the violence and the terror before I become the very thing I was fighting. I would have taken ownership of you instead of setting you free, convincing myself that it was justified. For a greater good. But, as my friend Humphrey once tried to tell me, we can't always let our morals be relative. We have to choose for ourselves what our absolutes will be. Only once we've set our own objective anchor can we securely let ourselves ride the currents of circumstance, knowing that we won't drift too far."

"Mercy," Marek said. "That is the anchor you have set for yourself. We have discussed this before."

"Yes. Mercy won't always be possible, but it's what I want to pull myself back to after rough waters drag me away. But don't forget about the power of friendship either. It helps you secure that anchor. And this is something you should pay attention to. I've seen you with your companions here, and I know you feel friendship. But I also think you underestimate the power of it. Don't. You want to fight astral kings and I used it to defeat the Builder. You've set yourself the nigh-impossible goal of liberating your people, and the power of friendship is how you do it. How you and the companions you love and trust become the seed that grows into a mighty tree."

"I'm not sure how that works," Marek said, his expression uncertain, and Jason broke out into laughter.

"I hate to break it to you, bloke, but that uncertainty is not going away. Take it from a guy who's done the impossible enough times to know how it plays out; you'll always be uncertain, every time."

Jason turned back to Allayeth.

"Your idea is good. I'll seek out the goddess Liberty."

"Perhaps you should let me handle that, at least initially," Allayeth said. "I know that she will love what you have done with Marek and his companions, but the first approach should not be from someone whose idea of praying is 'oi, god, get down here before I get cranky.' They don't respond well to that."

"I've never said that. I don't think. Out loud."

28

WE SHOULD PROBABLY GET YOU
OUT OF HERE

"WE NEED TO TALK WITH MY TEAM," JASON SAID TO ALLAYETH. THEY were walking through an underground cavern lit by glowing fungus too bright and too convenient to be natural phosphorescence.

"Do they comprehend the magnitude of what this place means? Of what you are?"

"Their frame of reference is perhaps limited, for some of them. My mate Clive, maybe, and my friends that are priests probably understand the scope. Not many people have pushed their souls up against the will of a god or great astral being. Not in an actual conflict, which is when they show you the whole thing. Normally, they just poke you as hard as you can take to make a point."

"Will," Allayeth said, focusing on the one word of Jason's. "The will as an element of the soul is not normally something essence users explore until gold rank."

"Yeah, I've been learning from Amos Pensinata about controlling aspects of the soul in isolation. It's been really handy in expanding my perception without blasting my aura out like a beacon. We never focused on will because I already had a good teacher back at iron rank."

"Farrah Hurin was your aura teacher at iron rank. She shouldn't have had any grasp of will back then."

"I'm talking about someone else. From after Farrah died."

"I didn't see anything in your records. Are you talking about Carlos Quilido?"

"No. I'm talking about the Builder."

Allayeth flinched.

"You call it a teacher?"

"Him. He was a man once. A boy, really. I think he still is, in a lot of ways. It's almost like he's…"

Jason frowned as he trailed off.

"Like he's what?"

"It doesn't matter," Jason said, his tone firmly shelving the topic. "He was in the fullness of his power when he pressed his will upon mine and tried to get me to open the gates of my soul. He'd already claimed my body and then came for the rest. I didn't remember it for a long time, because he'd already claimed my brain at that stage. My soul remembered, sort of. Not exactly emotions but kind of. Only the things that impacted my will. Left a mark on my soul. I remember his will pushing against me when I had nothing left but my own to push back with. He schooled me in the nature of will in the most thorough way possible."

"That is not teaching."

"Maybe not, but I still learned. How to turn my soul into a weapon. He carved that into the surface of my soul as he flayed it, trying to break my will. After that, soul attacks came so easily. Naturally. Like breathing, back when I had to do that."

"I can make soul attacks. It's something you can do after you learn to differentiate your will. It's meant to happen at gold or diamond, not iron rank. It doesn't come easily either. It's hard to pinpoint your will so sharply, and there's an instinctive revulsion against doing that to another soul. You have to push through that to make a soul attack. I'm told it's possible to inure yourself to that, but I have no interest in doing so."

"I never had that trouble," Jason said, his voice low. "Not the difficulty and not the revulsion."

"I'm sorry. I didn't mean to bring up such dark memories."

"It's fine. What Carlos Quilido and Arabelle Remore did do was put me back together again after. They built me back strong."

"You rely on the people around you a lot."

"You don't?"

"I don't have a lot of peers. Charist is an inconsistent comfort."

"Your team?"

"I was the only one to reach diamond. The others died or couldn't make it past gold. We weren't as remarkable as yours. I can see many of your team members reaching the peak."

"There is no peak."

"Essence users can't go beyond diamond rank."

"Not with that attitude."

She looked at his teasing expression and couldn't help letting out a laugh.

She shook her head, then turned her attention to their current location in Jason's soul realm. They were entering a cenote, a sinkhole with water at the bottom and a hole leading to open sky at the top. A railed wooden deck ran around the circumference with two large grills and picnic seating. The light fell through the hole at just the right angle to illuminate the area perfectly.

Allayeth was looking up through the hole when a glass sphere floated overhead. Inside it, a red wet mass pulsed with internal light, like a massive, glowing heart.

"What was that?" she asked.

"You know how Jes Fin Kaal is a Voice of the Will?"

"Yes."

"And you know that makes her an extension of her astral king's will?"

"Yes."

"Well, I'm an astral king in progress. That's my Voice of the Will in progress. His cocoon was white before, and not so blood-soaked. I think he's about ready to hatch."

"I think I'd rather fight the messengers' Voice of the Will than that thing."

"I suspect that, once he comes out to play, so would the messengers."

———

Jason and Allayeth rejoined Jason's team in a courtyard lounge where the walls were covered in greenery and lotuses floated on a water feature of raw mana.

"But, to be clear," Humphrey said, "Lady Allayeth is the one who will go and talk to the goddess Liberty, correct?"

"To her high priestess in Yaresh," Allayeth said. "One does not just go speak to a goddess."

Jason's companions all turned to look at him, eyebrows raised.

"What?" he asked. "And really, who doesn't just talk to them? Isn't that what prayer is? Have I been getting prayer wrong this whole time?"

"Yes," Neil said.

"How is prayer meant to work, then? Is it catered? Is that why people take all those casseroles to church functions?"

"Is he always like this?" Allayeth asked. He'd been less erratic when they were alone, more vulnerable. Around his friends, he was more strange, but also plainly having more fun.

"No, but you don't want him the other way," Neil said, and the rest of the group nodded their agreement.

"You know I'm right here?" Jason asked. "You should wait until I'm gone to talk about me behind my back."

"Jason," Clive said. "You literally are this courtyard we're sitting in. You're the furniture we're sitting on. There is no behind your back."

Neil turned awkwardly on his picnic chair, twisting to look down at it with a concerned expression.

"I'm not always paying attention," Jason said. "I respect people's privacy."

"The goddess of Liberty might not be extremely open to you, Jason," Rufus pointed out.

"Something to do with the way you go around declaring things and then making everyone accept them whether they like it or not," Neil added, still looking uncertain if he should just be standing up.

"Dominion does seem to have taken quite a liking to you," Gary said. "He and Liberty are antagonistic forces."

"He would definitely make the worst possible approach," Belinda said.

"Like trying to trap the goddess maybe?" Sophie postulated. "Liberty would hate that."

"I totally know how he'd do it," Taika said. "He'd get a box and he'd prop up one end of the box with a stick. There would be a string attached to the stick so he could pull it and drop the box, and the string would lead to where he was hiding inside a fake bush that he made. The bait he put under the box would be a sandwich and a little card with the word FREEDOM written on it."

"You think I would try to catch the goddess of Liberty in a box?" Jason asked.

"Yep."

"That tracks."

"Sounds like how it would go, yeah."

Jason ran a hand over his face.

"Why would I do that?" he asked.

"No idea."

"Doesn't seem to matter."

"We never know."

"At this point, we just watch and lay the occasional side bet," Neil said. "Speaking of which…"

The team started taking out spirit coins and handing them to Neil.

"Did you make some of kind of bet on me?" Jason asked.

"Nope," Neil transparently lied as he stashed away his winnings.

"There may have been a betting pool on how long it took you to find a new transcendent being to out-rank Lady Allayeth now that you were dealing with diamond-rankers again," Humphrey said. "Belinda started it as soon as Lady Allayeth entered your realm and Neil picked 'immediately' as his time. Which wasn't fair, since we all—"

"I yelled it out first," Neil said. "You know the rules."

"You make bets like this enough that there are rules?" Allayeth asked.

"Yes," Belinda said. "And Humphrey has no room to complain because he picked the big battle in Yaresh for the next time someone much stronger than Jason came to kill him, died, and then had something absurd looted from his body."

Allayeth blinked several times, her expression nonplussed.

"What kind of absurd thing?" she asked.

"He still hasn't told us, so he's not going to tell you," Sophie said. "He refuses to until he figures out how to use it."

"I think I need the soul forge," Jason said. "I'm pretty sure there's a… look, that doesn't matter. We need to concentrate on the next step. We're going to have some cranky officials waiting for us if we just wander back outside."

"Sorry about that," Clive said sheepishly.

"Hey," Jason said, putting a comforting hand on his shoulder. "Who amongst us hasn't defied authority or committed a bunch of crimes or rewritten city-sized chunks of reality in their own image?"

"What?" Allayeth asked.

"Humphrey, obviously," Jason continued. "But the rest of us have all done something shady. Maybe not Neil. You need to get out more, Neil. Get drunk and steal a land skimmer or something."

"You leave Neil alone," Humphrey said. "He's a respectable young man. Now, what solution do you have for the problem of what awaits us outside? I assume you have one."

"Maybe not a solution," Jason said. "But I can probably put off needing to deal with it immediately. Give Allayeth time to calm things down."

"Am I meant to excuse the behaviour of your team?"

"Yep," Jason said. "I'm pretty sure I can use the archway on the outside as an anchor point to open a portal inside the normal portal range. Meaning that I can probably portal myself back to the tree house and then open up the soul realm, and out you all waltz."

He turned to Allayeth.

"Best if you scarper first," he said. "I don't want my portal arch to vanish and have them think I've absconded with a diamond-ranker."

"That's something else we need to discuss," Sophie said. "*Should* we abscond with a diamond-ranker? Are you sure you want to let her out with what she's seen?"

"We have to trust someone," Jason said.

"Do we, though?" Belinda asked. "I mean, the Adventure Society seems to get in the way more than help us. You only have to ask Clive what the Magic Society is like, and as for local government, you remember that guy you sent packing, Jason."

"What did you show him that sent him running?" Allayeth asked. "This whole place is certainly intimidating, and only more so the stronger your perception powers, I suspect. But not enough shake Calcifer Bynes to the degree it did. You told me it was something about a gate."

"You remember that big door?" Jason asked. "The vault-looking one with the long sign?"

"That sign was rather hard to forget," Allayeth said. "The Astral Gate Containment Centre and Standish Family Adult Recreation Retrospective, was it? I'm assuming the astral gate part is what so disturbed Lord Bynes."

"I wouldn't rule out the other bit just yet," Belinda said. "What Clive's parents were doing with those jellied eels is plenty disturbing itself."

"Those are not real images," Clive insisted.

"You haven't even seen them," Belinda said.

"Have you?" Clive asked in horror.

"No one has," Humphrey said firmly. "Because they don't exist. Jason is not going to create fake images of one of his friend's parents doing obscene things. Are you, Jason?"

"No," Jason begrudgingly admitted. "I recreated Clive's mum's voice a bit, but it's mostly just squelching noises over some videos from my world that Farrah put on a recording crystal."

"I need to get that crystal back, now you mention it," Farrah said. "A girl has needs. Do you know what it's like trying to get some action in Rimaros? Some gold-ranker got the fever over me, but he's about eighty and refuses to make a proper move until I'm at least half his age. No one else will go near me because they don't want to offend him, though, but I'm not waiting quarter of a century for my next tumble. The equipment needs to be taken out and fired up from time to time or it'll go rusty in the shed."

"Putting that aside," Rufus said. "Very, very far aside, we should return to Sophie's question of whether we should retain Lady Allayeth here. Do we let her out with however many of Jason's secrets she has managed to uncover? For my part, I am firmly against taking her prisoner. Prisoners taken in battle is one thing, but taking allies who know too much? I won't be a party to that."

"Jason said all that needed to be said," Humphrey declared. "We need to trust someone. I do recognise your concerns, Belinda, regarding the various institutions that have sometimes—often, even—acted with less integrity than we would like. But I am willing to bet that the people who have gained power by turning from duty to politics in the name of power are in the minority. That minority tends to occupy the upper echelons of those institutions, it's true, but even there I would wager that corruption is not ubiquitous."

Humphrey stepped out and turned to face the group as a whole, Jason keeping his mouth closed and trying not to cheer at Humphrey falling into a monologue.

"We have to trust," Humphrey said. "We just have to. There are far too many problems in the world for the people in this room to solve them all. Yes, we've encountered our fair share of people who have surrendered their integrity. They see Clive's mind or Jason's... whatever it is with Jason, and they seek us out. They're opportunists, hungry and shameless. But I promise you that there are countless people out there doing the right thing simply because it's the right thing. You don't see them because they aren't looking for glory or power. They're just looking to fulfil their duty."

He nodded to himself.

"Yes, they make mistakes. Anger, pride, vanity, greed; they lead us to make bad choices. But I have no doubt that most of the people in the Magic Society are just like Clive: trying to take magic and make the world a little bit better tomorrow than it is today. Do you think the people working in the Yaresh government are all looking to fill their pockets and raise their status? Some, yes, but I promise you that most of them are trying their best to put the city back together again and help the people who live in it. And I hope I don't have to tell you about adventurers. They are unquestionably more susceptible to the pride and vanity I mentioned, but every person in this room has seen them step up and risk everything because it was their duty to do so. And a lot of them never made it back."

Humphrey moved to Belinda and put a hand on her shoulder.

"I know that you have less reason to trust than most," he told her. "But we have to, even when it doesn't work out the way we hoped. Because if we don't, then what's the point? I was reluctant when Jason brought along two thieves and said they were going to be adventurers. Now look at you: you're glorious. This is not the team I envisaged building when I was growing up, and you'd best believe that I envisaged that a lot. But now my team is better than I ever imagined because I was convinced to trust when the smart choice was not to. So, I'm going to keep making that choice. And if any of you want to make a different one out of fear or anger or bitterness, then I'm going to talk and talk and talk until you all change your minds. And, as I've just demonstrated, I certainly can do that—"

Sophie shoved Belinda out of the way, grabbed Humphrey by the lapels and dragged him into a passionate kiss as the others all looked on.

"Does anyone else feel like this undercuts the gravitas of Humphrey's big speech?" Neil asked.

"It was such a good monologue," Jason said proudly. "It could have used more jokes."

Rufus moved next to Allayeth and leaned close.

"We should probably get you out of here," he said quietly.

THE QUESTIONS YOU'RE ASKING
DON'T MATTER

ALLAYETH WENT THROUGH THE PORTAL ARCH, LEAVING JASON'S SOUL realm. Jason and his companions all looked at one another.

"Do you think she bought it?" Belinda asked.

"Bought what?" Humphrey asked.

Sophie patted him on the arm.

"Don't worry about it," she told him.

"Don't worry about what?"

"Our 'plucky group of adventurers caught up in something crazy' routine," Rufus said. "Essentially, whether she believed that we were a quirky group forced into challenges beyond us by circumstance."

"That was a routine?" Humphrey asked. "Why didn't anyone tell me?"

"Because your mind would be constantly churning over the idea that you're faking something," Jason said. "And we weren't faking. We were just playing up our natural proclivities a little."

"That doesn't explain why you wouldn't tell me."

"Humphrey," Jason said, "you're as much a liar as I am a modest and humble churchgoer. You're one of those people who, when told to act natural, turns into a robot."

"What's a robot?" Humphrey asked.

"An overcomplicated golem," Farrah said.

"Shouldn't she have been able to read our emotions anyway?" Humphrey asked.

"Not here," Jason said. "In this place, I can limit her senses. But she's got more life experience than all of us put together. I doubt she needs her perception powers to read our body language. We just played up our natural inclinations so they didn't come across as false. But, Hump, you trying to act natural would have been a massive red flag."

"How she chooses to react to what she encountered here will play a big part in how things go for us moving forward," Rufus said. "If she supports us, things get a lot easier. The other diamond-ranker will stop pressuring Jason and the Adventure Society will be more accommodating. If she decides that Jason needs to be stopped before he becomes too powerful, things get a lot harder."

"Do we think that's likely?" Gary asked.

"I wouldn't think so," Jason said. "While it is possible that she was fooling me, I picked up enough of her emotions to think that she's going to support us."

"She didn't seem hostile," Sophie said. "The opposite, if anything."

"I think that I've accomplished something with her that I've failed to do many times in the past, to my cost," Jason said.

"What's that?" Rufus asked.

"Impart the magnitude of the powers and events he's at the centre of," Farrah said. "On Earth, the various factions only ever saw enough to covet. They never understood what he was doing or the price everyone would pay if they stopped him."

"That was on me," Jason said. "I never explained things properly. I was always angry or bitter. I never took the time to truly show people what I was doing or why. Sometimes that was necessary to avoid them trying to exploit me, but a lot of times, I was just too burned out. Honestly, I'd reached a point where I didn't feel the world deserved an explanation. It was my chance to be the bigger man, but my small-mindedness only made things worse."

He looked over at the portal arch.

"I may be in danger of doing that again. I think I should sit down with the Adventure Society director, and some of the power players from Yaresh. Explain it all from my perspective. Maybe then we can work together the way we should have from the start."

Jason turned to look at Humphrey.

"It might be time to stop trying to do everything myself, and show a little trust."

Allayeth emerged from Jason's portal arch and it closed behind her, sinking into the ground without a trace. She surveyed the area and saw that the outpost the Adventure Society was building had developed at a startling pace in her absence. She was in an outskirt area used mostly for storage, now filled with massive wooden crates reinforced by metal.

She levitated into the air using her aura, a trick any silver-ranker could do. She contrasted her skill with what Jason and the messengers could do and it fell significantly short. Even at diamond rank, she could only affect herself and the levitation was still quite easy to disrupt. After seeing the inside of Jason's soul realm, it made an apt metaphor for her own position.

She was powerful. One of the most powerful beings on the planet, but so much of what she found herself involved with was not from her planet. The Builder invasion, the messenger invasion. She was ostensibly at the end of her path to power and found herself poorly equipped to face it. Jason was far weaker, yet he was a part of that wider reality. Part of a cosmic community that she was not.

Those who were like her didn't see it. She and Charist had long ago become content to be large fish in a small pond, leaving Soramir Rimaros and his ilk to explore the realms beyond their world. She had put a box around her mind and was unable to clearly see anything outside that box. The Adventure Society was like her in this regard, their considerations limited by the constraints they unconsciously placed on themselves.

Seeing Jason's soul from the inside had broken her box. Now she was able to see what Soramir Rimaros, Dawn and even the gods had seen from the beginning: Jason Asano belonged to a wider world. For the first time in a long time, Allayeth found herself running into her limits and becoming dissatisfied with them. Perhaps there was a wider world for her too.

Diamond rank was the end of the path. Not only was this an absolute that had been taught to her from the beginning, but the very idea of reaching it was a dream few adventurers could reach. When she did, she had been satisfied. She had no need to roam out into the cosmos, placing herself at the bottom of a new ladder she had no idea how to climb. She'd already achieved every goal she ever set for herself, and it had been enough.

But now, the cosmos she had declined to explore was intruding on her world, and in Jason Asano, she had caught a glimpse of how the climb might work. There was a man so far below her, yet with so much further to go. He was not going slow down when he reached her level, let alone stop.

Allayeth looked at the outpost being built. The ragged hole that had been blasted outward was already covered in foundations that moved inward and down like a sunken theatre. Mostly, it was prepared ground; sealed foundation waiting for buildings to be placed atop it. Some buildings were already in place, though, and Allayeth watched as more were formed in just minutes through magic.

She could see that this was not crude stone-shaping. The expert construction combined rituals, essence abilities and expert design knowledge. Charist was right to be angry that this level of industriousness had been pulled away from the reconstruction of the city.

The rapidly forming outpost was an edifice to the opportunism of those with ambitions of power. They lacked the expansiveness of Allayeth's new perspective, seeing only the old squabbles. They didn't realise that power and the balance thereof had fundamentally changed. The Builder invasion had not been an isolated incident; it was an event that brought their world into a larger reality.

Although many of the people bustling about had seen her in the sky, they respected that her aura presence was undetectable, taking the hint and staying away. Only Charist had the perception to notice her aura and had set off in her direction the moment he had. It took him only moments to arrive, and when he did, he moved to float in the air beside her.

"You went through Asano's portal," he said in lieu of a greeting.

"Yes."

"Did you figure out how he could even produce a portal that you could use?"

"Yes."

"Did you find out what power is backing him?"

"Yes."

Charist rolled his eyes.

"Do you have any interest in giving an answer longer than one word?"

"The problem, Charist, is that the questions you're asking don't matter."

"Then what does matter?"

"Whether Jason Asano and whatever he has going on is good for us or bad for us."

"And?"

"It's definitely bad for the messengers."

"Tell me everything."

"No."

"No?"

"His secrets don't hurt us."

"And you expect me to take your word for that?"

"I'll be a little hurt if you don't. But I understand how some unknown agent of unknown power could potentially compromise even a diamond-ranker, so we should make sure that hasn't happened."

"How? There's no Church of Purity to check if you've been affected by something."

"The Church of Liberty. They can tell you if my free will has been compromised."

Charist nodded.

"Agreed," he said. "Let's return to Yaresh and we'll head straight for the temple."

Vidal Ladiv was not good at driving the flying skimmer he used to approach Jason's cloud palace, currently a series of tree houses linked by rope bridges. Out on an open balcony, Travis Noble was working on a device the size of a transit van. It was a clear mix of magical and technological elements, most prominently a protruding shaft of metal. A cloud of gemstones floated around the shaft as if held in place by magnets.

Travis looked up at the approaching skimmer, watching curiously as it arrived unsteadily at the edge of the balcony. Vidal left it floating next to the rail and awkwardly hopped from the vehicle to the balcony.

"You don't seem great at that," Travis said. "No offence."

"Not at all," Vidal said. "I hate this thing. Back in Rimaros, my water powers were more than enough to get me around. But this far inland, there aren't enough waterways to get me where I need to go. Mr Asano moving to a treehouse in the middle of nowhere certainly doesn't help."

"Are you sure you should be driving that?" Travis asked. "It's a flying car and you get around in it like a nervous kid in driver's ed. It seems like there should be regulations or something against that. Aren't people worried you'll crash it into some lady's stroller and kill adorable twin girls?"

"That's oddly specific," Vidal said, looking at the massive device Travis was working on. "What's this?"

"Right now? Annoying. If I can solve the cyclical alignment issues, it'll be a rotary beam cannon."

"Some kind of weapon? I thought you were working on a communication device."

"It's more of a comprehensive communication grid. Also, that's work. This is more of a hobby."

Vidal looked over the monstrous and complex device.

"A hobby?"

"Yeah. Something to do for fun."

"You're building a weapon the size of a trade wagon for fun?"

"If you can't have some fun with a rotary beam cannon, I don't think you can have fun at all. What brings you here, Mr Ladiv? Is it something to do with that giant explosion this morning? I saw the cloud getting sucked up into the air."

"Indirectly. Has Mr Asano returned yet?"

"Nope. Last I saw, they were all headed for the cloud. I don't even know what happened."

"Altered messengers broke out from deep underground."

"That was the explosion?"

"Yes."

"That seems weird. They dug all the way up to the surface and then made a big explosion for the last bit? Setting off something like that while underground with it is a terrible idea."

"The messengers were far from in their right minds."

"I won't blame them for that. I'm building a giant Gatling laser in a tree house in alternate-universe Brazil. I'm not entirely convinced that *I'm* in my right mind. For all I know, I'm in an asylum somewhere staring into the distance and yelling 'pew pew pew' over and over."

"Uh, alright. I need to talk to Asano."

"They aren't back yet."

"You don't seem worried about that."

"Jason once got stuck with a bunch of his gold-rank enemies in a dimensional space that was on the verge of ripping a hole in the side of the universe and wiping out our planet. Jason and one gold-rank vampire managed to escape, and the vampire ran and hid until Jason left the universe entirely. As for the dimensional space, Jason turned it into a magic city that his clan lives in now. It kills anyone who tries to get near it with ill intentions, and it's kind of a temple to himself. And that was before he had his team with him, so, no, I'm not worried that a bunch of second-rate angels with mental health issues will do them in."

"I don't recall seeing any of that in Asano's Adventure Society record. It must have been in the restricted parts."

"No, that was back in my universe, so it won't be in his local record. Now that I think about it, I'm not sure I should be telling you this stuff."

Travis looked at Vidal thoughtfully, then at the device he was working on.

"Can you go stand in front of that long metal bit?" Travis asked.

"No," Vidal said.

POLITICAL PRICE

On the balcony of Jason's treehouse, Vidal Ladiv was looking warily at the spherical device at the end of the pole he was holding.

"What exactly is this thing?"

"Don't worry about it," Travis said distractedly as he rummaged through a large box, absently tossing out crystals. "Just don't let it get too close to you. I've almost certainly resolved the organic proximity combustion issue, but better safe than sorry."

"What?"

Before Vidal could ask more questions, a portal arch appeared on the balcony. Jason and his companions emerged, with Farrah immediately looking at the spherical device.

"How did you resolve the organic proximity combustion issue?" she asked Travis.

"I put it on the end of a pole," he said.

"Oh," she said, and then turned to look at Vidal with sympathy.

"Don't let it get too close to you," she suggested.

"Travis," Jason said, "take that thing off him. Vidal, I assume you're here because the Adventure Society has decided how to punish us because we wouldn't let them steal all our prisoners."

Travis waved a rod in the direction of an open door. A construct creature that looked like a naked store mannequin walked out and over to Vidal with a rocking shamble. The construct looked like it had been hastily assembled, possibly while drunk, from whatever parts came to hand. Vidal was fairly sure the left forearm was a short length of sloppily painted tree branch.

"What's this for?" Vidal asked, clutching the very end of the pole to keep the device as far from himself as possible.

"Just hand it the thing," Travis said.

"You said this device was dangerous, and that construct does not look stable."

"It's fine," Travis said unconvincingly. "Hardly any explosives are left on it. After the incident."

"What incident?"

"I don't think he's allowed to tell you," Farrah said. "I don't remember the exact terms of the legal agreement, but the gag order lasted at least until the healers figured out how to stop the… I shouldn't say any more."

"I don't think he's got any confidence in your construct, Travis," Neil said. "Can't you just take it yourself?"

"I'm not going near that thing," Travis said. "And you should be grateful I'm not. You're the one who would have to figure out how to get healing magic to work through the interference."

"What interference?" Neil asked.

"The magic on my nethers if there's another testicular resonance event."

"Another WHAT?" Vidal asked as he tossed the pole and the device it was attached to over the balcony.

"Hey!" Travis said. "I was joking; it's perfectly safe."

The device hit the ground and exploded. Everyone turned to look at Travis.

"Okay, 'perfectly' may have been a slight exaggeration," Travis conceded.

Humphrey went to the rail and looked over. "I don't think it's going to start a forest fire."

"Of course it won't," Travis said. "It's way too wet here for that. Probably. I might just pop down there and spray some stuff to make sure."

He ducked through the door the construct had emerged from and came out with a red canister.

"Blue," Farrah said.

Travis looked down at the canister made a wincing expression and went back inside, emerging with a blue canister instead.

"Dodged a bullet there," he said and made his way over to an elevating platform. Fitting in with the motif of the treehouse, the platform looked like it was being lowered on ropes.

"It's fine," Travis called up from below. "It's all fine. There are no problems down—"

One of the construct's arms popped off and went sailing over the rail with the thrum of a spring being violently unsprung.

"It's fine," Travis called up again. "On an unrelated note, Farrah, could you wash down the construct from the green canister? Nothing dangerous is happening down here, but doing so very very quickly would be appreciated."

Everyone moved away from the construct that was now swaying on its feet.

"Isn't this the person who built the bomb that felled the Builder's flying city?" Vidal asked.

"Oh, yes," Farrah said as she went into the room, then came out with a third canister, this one green. "He's very good at making things that explode. Or shoot dangerous energy more or less on command. Emit poisonous gas, often on purpose. Liquefy… oh, not allowed to talk about that one either. You know, Princess Liara knows a number of excellent legal advocates."

She used her Obsidian Wall power to put up a wall of dark stone between the group and the construct, now making a fizzing sound as it turned lopsidedly on the spot. With their vision of it blocked, they watched Farrah spray white liquid from the canister into the space they couldn't see behind the wall.

"I'm not doubting his ability to cause destruction," Vidal said. "My concerns are more about stability. The bomb that took down the fortress city, he presumably built that in the city where I was living at the time. Where my mum and hundreds of thousands of other people were living, right?"

"It was a fun project," Travis called out from below. "It was interesting to… why is this thing turning the plants that colour?"

"Is this something I should be allowing to happen in my building?" Jason asked.

"It's fine," Farrah said, moving to put the wall between herself and the construct as dark, thick smoke rose from it.

"Why is there a skull drawn on the side of that canister?" Belinda asked.

"No idea," Farrah said as a hole corroded through the wall. She raised another one in front of it.

"We might have used a few experimental materials on the construct," she confessed. "Just trying to find things that can hold more magic than usual without dangerous resonance."

"Some might say that trapping an escalating magical energy inside a fixed matrix with no release mechanism is dangerous…" Travis called out from below.

Everyone waited in silence for him to continue until, finally, Jason spoke up.

"…but…" he prompted.

"But what?" Travis called back. "Why did everyone go quiet?"

"We were kind of expecting you to follow up on that last thing you said," Jason told him.

"No, I was done."

"Should we move to a different tree house?" Sophie suggested.

They all swiftly moved across a rope bridge to a different house built around another tree. Like all the treehouses that made up Jason's disguised cloud palace, it had a broad balcony. Jason called up a set of cloud-substance furniture for everyone that masked itself as wood to match the house. Despite the appearance, it retained the luxurious softness of cloud material. They took their seats with Jason and his companions all facing the single chair left for Vidal.

"Should we wait for Travis?" Humphrey asked.

"No," Travis called out. "Also, Farrah, could you bring me the yellow and purple canisters."

"I thought you couldn't get the yellow anymore after what happened to the bottling plant," Farrah called back.

"He said I could take the surviving stock so long as I promised to never come back."

"Just go," Jason told her.

She wandered off and Jason turned to Vidal.

"So," he said. "What has the Adventure Society decided to do about us?"

"To wait," Vidal said. "There are opinions ranging from revoking your membership to demoting you all to one star. The director has spoken up for you, but he couldn't override the entire executive council. The most he could manage was to refer it to the Continental Council. They will send an assessment officer to make a final judgement."

"How long will that take?" Rufus asked.

"I have no idea," Vidal said. "My guess would be a while, as this smacks of politics and the Continental Council really doesn't like that. Honestly, I suspect that the executive council in Yaresh made sure it came across as political to slow down the process."

"Why would they stall like that?" Sophie asked. "I assume it's so they can bend us over somehow."

"The expedition," Jason said. "They need us for that. But they want us to toe the line, so they're letting us know that there's disciplinary action waiting for us afterwards. They hope that will put us on our best behaviour and make us more compliant."

"They clearly haven't been paying attention," Belinda said. "We're not exactly a compliant kind of team."

"No team is," Humphrey said. "Not any of the good ones anyway. Adventurers have to be independent thinkers, able to take responsibility for their own choices."

"Agreed," Rufus said. "Any good Adventure Society branch respects that. It's when politics get involved that it goes wrong. I might not think much of the way they train adventurers in Rimaros, but their Adventure Society strikes the right balance between directing adventurers and trusting them."

"You look nervous, Vidal," Jason said. "Unhappy."

"I'm an Adventure Society official," he said. "It doesn't sound like you intend to make my life any easier."

"Don't forget what being an adventurer is about," Rufus told him. "It's not about the society and it's not about us. It's about helping people. Protecting people."

"I don't think you all being at odds with the Adventure Society will help a lot of people," Vidal pointed out.

"And I think that excuses like that are how people who have corrupted the Adventure Society's purpose get good adventurers to go along with bad intentions," Rufus shot back. "All that accomplishes is getting people to stay quiet while the poison spreads."

"Let's not pile it all on Vidal, here," Jason said. "He's just the guy stuck in the middle, telling both sides things they don't want to hear. That must suck. He's not a local and is just as new to the political situation here as we are. Plus, he doesn't have the same leverage we do to tell people to sod off."

"Thank you," Vidal said. "I had concerns about what I would be caught up in when the society assigned me to you as a liaison, but it has been more trying than anything I imagined. But I have a duty, and part of that duty is to give the society my best assessment of what you will do next."

"For now," Jason said, "we're going to continue the contracts we signed up for."

"Because it's about the people who need help," Rufus reiterated. "They don't care about the politics. They only care about the monsters threatening their homes and families."

"And we're going to help them," Humphrey said.

"Out of curiosity," Rufus asked, "how resistant were the people calling for our heads to bringing in the Continental Council?"

"The Aristocratic Faction is a political bloc that crosses all major institutions in Yaresh," Vidal explained. "They have members in any area prestigious enough and influence any place that isn't. This is hardly unusual as aristocratic families hold a firm grip on most cities. There are other political factions, of course, but my experience has been that most places have only two main groups with any real influence. One is a conservative faction, usually led by aristocrats and others with wealth and power whose interests begin and end with maintaining the advantages they've built up over generations. The other group is also usually made up of aristocrats and people with power and money. This group believes in making changes and doing what's right. They also believe that they are the only ones who know what's right, so they make sure the changes are all either made by them or by those they control. Also, what's right never seems to involve them giving up any of their money and power, oddly enough."

"That sounds uncomfortably familiar," Jason muttered.

"And we come from another universe, bro."

"Those two power blocs, or some variation of them," Vidal said, "exist in every state and city-state that I have had dealings with as an Adventure Society official. Where those political blocs exert a significant influence on the Adventure Society, that is where they start to lose track of that mission Mr Remore was talking about."

Rufus nodded.

"I sorry, Mr Ladiv," he said to Vidal. "It would seem that you have more passion and integrity than I have credited you for, and I apologise for that."

"Thank you, Mr Remore," Vidal said. "I have been far more involved with the Adventure Society here than any of you. I can tell you that while there is more political influence than I would like, the Yaresh branch is not as far gone as you might fear. The director, from what I can tell, is a good man. He manoeuvred the Aristocratic Faction into calling on the Continental Council, not realising how inured they are to the influence of local political forces. Only the proper adventurers in their faction opposed it, knowing the reality, but the director's timing was deft. So, to answer your question, Mr Remore, the only people 'calling for your heads' who resisted calling in the Continental Council were the actual adventurers who understood what that entailed. Now that they have time to explain it to their fellows, they are trying to reverse that decision."

"Will they be able to do that?" Rufus asked.

"There are no guarantees," Vidal said, "but I suspect not. The Adventure Society director tricked the Aristocratic Faction into expending too much political capital. They pushed too hard for the executive council of the Adventure Society to go up against the director. They won't get them to go up against the director a second time to undo the thing they were influenced into doing in the first place."

"The Aristocratic Faction members are nobility," Humphrey said. "Their rights are theirs by blood and can only be taken from them for transgressions on the level of treason. Any political setback for them is temporary."

Humphrey glanced at Jason before turning back to the group.

"The bureaucrats at the Adventure Society don't have the same security in their positions," he continued. "They will do what their political masters want, but only while it still benefits them. A nobleman can be seen taking wildly different positions from one day to the next because his family name will always place him on the upper echelon. Calcifer Bynes ran out of our large meeting all but wetting himself. He'll pay a political price for that public humiliation but it doesn't change the fact that he is and always will be a man of wealth, influence and power."

"A good example," Vidal said. "Calcifer Bynes is part of the executive council, and while he'll fade into the background for a time, he's not going anywhere. But the bulk of the group are career bureaucrats. They have suckled at the teat of larger political forces, but when their careers are in danger, they will act in their own interests. This is why they will almost certainly not revoke the call for Continental Council intercession."

"That makes sense," Rufus said. "Calling in the council and then telling them to go home before they arrived would have severe political repercussions."

"What can we expect from this Continental Council?" Belinda asked.

"Last time I got involved with them," Jason said, "they demoted me. Along with almost every adventurer in the city."

"You hadn't just let loose a cohort of enemies to attack adventurers, though," Clive said regretfully. "I think I've earned us all worse than just demotion."

Neil leaned forward in his chair to put a comforting hand on Clive's shoulder.

"Don't worry about it," Neil said. "Everyone here agrees with you."

"Yes," Humphrey agreed. "We've just been talking about the things that negatively impact the Adventure Society. The way we fight back against that influence is by remaining independent. The way they're meant to allow adventurers to be. If we had just capitulated, we would have been contributing to the problem."

"Look at you, fighting authority," Belinda told Humphrey. "You're turning into Jason."

Humphrey looked at her for a long moment, then took a plate from his storage space and held it out for her.

"Sandwich?" he asked in a deadpan voice and everyone but Vidal started laughing.

"This is a very weird team," Vidal said.

ORDINARY EVERYDAY
ADVENTURING

JASON'S TEAM HAD BEEN EXPECTING THE EMERGENCE OF ELEMENTAL-infused messengers to accelerate the plans of Jes Fin Kaal. Instead, they heard nothing as they continued taking and fulfilling contracts, Shade picking up new ones as he delivered their reports. For the first time in a long time, the team was all together for some ordinary everyday adventuring.

Jason's time on Earth, fighting in monster-filled proto-spaces and later full-blown monster waves, had allowed him to reach the wall that was the fourth stage of silver-rank faster than his team members. Once he reached it, however, Earth's lack of powerful threats had stalled him out. Through proto-spaces, monster waves and transformation zones, Jason had killed more monsters and other threats than the rest of his team combined. Even so, his progress had been limited by the threat those monsters provided.

Jason had reached a point where few silver-rank monsters were a genuine danger, even in massive numbers. He'd been throwing himself at whole herds or not using various powers to try and push his limits, but once he hit the wall, there was little progress to be made on Earth. The gold-rank threats were too few and too dangerous, as Jason was only willing to take on specific monsters of that rank. If the match-up was bad for his powers, he was unwilling to take them on.

The monsters of Earth had not been the greatest challenges Jason had faced on his home world, but those other dangers were not ones that he could resolve with just his essence abilities. He was forced to wield powerful artefacts, wade into dimensional anomalies and develop spiritual powers he barely understood even now. His understanding of the soul, reality and the wider cosmos expanded, laying out a pathway that would carry him into the distant future. In the immediacy, however, his essence abilities were left fallow, without growth.

Jason's need to rely on spiritual strength continued with his return to Pallimustus. Although his essence abilities did resume a glacial upward trajectory, Jason was again forced to rely on his strange new abilities, and at no small cost. While he convalesced from over-taxing himself, his companions continued fighting their way through the monster surge, slowly but surely catching up to him at the advancement wall.

Clive, Humphrey and Belinda, had an inherent advantage in the form of intrinsic human gifts. Their essence abilities advanced at a slight but measurably faster rate than others, too slight to be of value at lower ranks. Now they had hit the wall and every measure of growth counted, it gave them a slight edge. For Clive and Belinda, this gave them time to pursue magical study without falling behind the others. For Humphrey, it meant that he could be slightly ahead of the pack, which gave him confidence as team leader.

As their non-stop adventuring entered its third week, Jason was the first to take an ability beyond the fourth level of silver rank, but only by a matter of days. As the team ploughed through roaming monsters and cleaned up contracts, Jason's perception ability finally crossed the line just two days before Humphrey's.

Gary, Farrah and Travis were not taking part in the flurry of contract work. They were in Jason's soul realm, using the advantages it offered to advance their various professions. This left the team eight strong with the semi-permanent addition of Rufus and Taika. Rufus would resume teaching but was in no rush, having rediscovered his love of adventure when not burdened with the leadership role. As for Taika, his goal was Earth and the people he had left behind there. His passage home, however, was entirely reliant on Jason's ability to forge it.

Having shifted their base of operations in anticipation of new contracts, the team watched Jason's cloud flask produce a new cloud palace. They did so from the edge of a mountainous plateau, the cloud-stuff sliding down the cliff to form buildings hanging off the face.

"You have a lot more control over the camouflage version of your cloud buildings compared to Emir," Rufus said.

"Emir never uses his camouflage versions," Jason said. "His are always big and flashy. But yeah, my deeper soul connection gives me a lot more say in the structural details. Hey, who won the betting pool?"

"What betting pool?" Belinda asked.

"I know you make bets on me," Jason said. "Who had me down for the first one to get an ability moving past the wall?"

"That's not really the kind of thing we bet on," Belinda told him. "It's more like what country will declare war on you personally."

"What god you're going to offer a sandwich," Clive said.

"Which diamond-ranker you're going to hit on," Taika added.

"When you'll love up Humphrey's mum," Neil said.

"Neil…" Humphrey growled.

"I can't have been the only one seeing that dynamic," Neil said.

"Jason's like that with every powerful woman he meets," Rufus said. "We really should do a better job of keeping him away from princesses."

Shade emerged from Jason's shadow.

"You have the next batch of contracts?" Jason asked him.

"Not as yet, Mr Asano. I decided to postpone their acquisition as events appear to finally be going into motion."

"The messengers?"

"There is more activity than we have seen in the last few weeks," Shade confirmed. "More pressing is that Lady Allayeth asked that I convey a message. She is ready to meet with you and a representative of the Church of Liberty."

"Does she have a time and date?"

"She has designated a location far from Yaresh or any other population centre."

"I don't suppose she is setting us up for an ambush," Belinda wondered.

"That's why I'll go alone," Jason said. "If we misread her and it's some kind of ambush, I have the best chance of getting away."

Jason was using Shade as a vehicle to fly only a few metres over the jungle canopy. Shade's form was that of an Earth vehicle, a personal flight device that amounted to a chair in a roll cage with a series of drone-style rotors for lift and propulsion. It was, of course, all black, looking more aggressive and sinister than the vehicles it was based on. It also had more speed and the flight time was essentially infinite.

"I know what you're doing, Shade."

"I am conveying you through the air as directed, Mr Asano."

"You've been increasingly using Earth-style transport as I've been coming to terms with my time there."

"Magical vehicles are, for the most part, less practical than technological ones," Shade pointed out. "Obviously, living mounts and vehicles stylised in the form of living creatures are not as practical as purpose-designed vehicles. Even the more practical vehicle designs, like skimmers, demonstrate a level of inefficiency only seen on Earth when hooligans modify their own cars. Utilising magic to overcome the technical drawbacks of ordinarily non-magical vehicles offers the best of both worlds."

"That's well thought-out," Jason said. "But we both know that's not the primary reason. You're acclimatising me back to Earth with demonstrations of what's good about it. As I become less emotionally distraught about my time there, you're introducing the Earth elements you knew better than to pull out when I first returned to Pallimustus."

Jason snorted a laugh.

"I sound accusatory," he said. "I'm sorry, Shade; what I'm trying to say is thank you. You're always looking out for me."

"I'm glad you can face this with equanimity, Mr Asano."

Jason sensed the presence of a priestess from a good way away, the distinctive whiff of divine power hanging in the air around her. It had surprised him to discover that other people found divine power almost undetectable unless they were looking for it with intrusive perceptual probes. To his senses, it lit up like a beacon.

The location was a town, destroyed and abandoned. The jungle had reclaimed it to the point that there was nowhere to land even the small vehicle. The flight device exploded into a cloud of shadows like a magician's trick, Jason's momentum carrying him out of it to plunge through the air, angling his body. The shadows trailed him as he conjured his Cloak of Night that spread out like wings, turning his controlled fall into a glide.

A massive grin split Jason's face. A few weeks of doing normal jobs with his team and helping out people in need had done more for his mood than all the brooding introspection in the world. Sailing through the air, he was able to appreciate just how amazing the life he was living could be.

"I've got to stop saving the world," he muttered. Although his words were snatched away on the wind, Shade heard them perfectly.

"We both know that you won't step away, Mr Asano. Perhaps you should simply enjoy the moment and leave tomorrow to tomorrow."

"You're a wise man, Shade."

Although Jason had sensed only the priestess, two people were sitting on the low remains of a brick wall as Jason descended towards it. Allayeth turned to look in Jason's direction, the woman with her following suit. Jason swooped in, reducing his weight at the last moment as he landed on a soft-looking patch of moss that could still have hidden some awkward footing.

The two women stood as Jason dismissed his cloak to reveal a simple, casual suit underneath. The fabric was light and breathable, the effect enhanced subtly by magic to be comfortable even in the muggy heat. Jason mentally thanked Alejandro Albericci and his expert tailoring.

The priestess with Allayeth was not a gold-ranker but a silver, meaning that she was not the high priestess. Allayeth nodded at a section of road not too badly overgrown and they converged on that point. Jason looked around, seeing an incongruity in the ruins.

"What happened to this town?" he asked. "The remains of this building have been weathered about right for the monster surge, but this looks like years of growth."

"Guess," Allayeth told him and he took another look around.

"Plant monsters?" he postulated.

"Something like that," Allayeth told him.

"You didn't pick this place because it was the closest point that was both convenient and discreet," he said.

"Later," she told him. "For the moment, allow me to introduce Priestess Raelia Cass. Priestess, Jason Asano."

"G'day," Jason said, shaking her hand.

The priestess was human, compared to the elves far more common in the region. Her dark hair was wavy and long, setting off her typically attractive silver-rank features well. She looked like she was barely twenty-one years old and Jason guessed her to be close to his own twenty-nine.

"I've been warned about you, Jason Asano," she said, her voice curious, not hostile.

Jason glanced at Allayeth, who shook her head.

"Not by me," she said.

"My Lady," the priestess said, referring to the goddess Liberty, "likes to keep a wary eye on Dominion's favourites."

"That makes sense," Jason said. "I don't suppose you know how to get off that list?"

"I do," Raelia said. "I fear it is beyond you, however."

"Oh?"

"What Dominion likes in you is not the autocratic tendencies you consistently demonstrate," she said. "It is the fact that you rarely regret them."

"Ah," Jason said. "It's hard to be penitent when you feel no need for penance. I fear I will never be in your lady's good graces."

"While you have definite tendencies that she does not care for, Mr Asano, she knows that freedom is an important principle for you, despite your inclinations. More importantly, she respects that you are willing to act on that principle."

"How much do you know about these 'autocratic tendencies' of mine?" Jason asked.

"Nothing at all," she said. "My goddess has only told me that you have them. That you have a habit of deciding the way things should be and then moving the land and the sky to make it so, whatever anyone else might think. Or how they might be affected."

"That's true enough," Jason acknowledged. "But you do know what I want, right?"

"Lady Allayeth has made things clear. My goddess has qualms about participating as she cannot see into the astral space you are holding them in. She is all for freeing these people as any form of incarceration is unacceptable to her, but she also does not want invaders let loose to rejoin their kind's oppressive invasion. She would like to see the leader of your prisoners for herself."

"That's one of the reasons we're out here, then," Jason deduced. "So I can pop out a messenger or two outside of Charist's primary perception area."

"Yes," Allayeth said.

Jason didn't fuss about and immediately brought out Marek Noir Vargas. The messenger answered a lengthy list of questions, ranging from his intentions to his current state to the history of how he landed in his current situation. There were more questions about Jason himself than he was entirely comfortable with. Finally, the priestess allowed Marek to return to Jason's soul realm.

"The goddess is satisfied," the priestess announced. "She will aid you, but the important work must be undertaken by you, Mr Asano."

"I'm not afraid of a little hard work."

"Good. These messengers will need to be released into the cosmos, not just this world, and accomplishing that falls to you. When you do achieve this, the goddess will hide your actions. No one will see or over-hear, even should they be in a position to directly observe. The goddess Knowledge will not learn of it, even from your mind after the task is done."

"You can hide things from Knowledge? And keep it hidden?"

"Gods have the ability to overrule other gods when it comes to their own area of influence. Freeing people from your custody, having already freed them from bondage of the soul places this issue very much under Liberty's authority."

"I see. But until I figure out how to set them loose, she won't do anything."

"The gods exist to help and guide our actions, Mr Asano, not to act in our stead."

"I'm very onboard with that stance," Jason told her. "Any tips on how to gate these people out into the cosmos? I have some other interests in dimensional transgression that might dovetail nicely."

"No," the priestess said sternly. "On a wholly unrelated note, she wishes me to convey that choosing to claim the messenger's study was a very wise choice."

Jason's personal condition for working with Jes Fin Kaal had been the sealed study of the dead diamond-rank messenger.

"Good to know," Jason said. "Is that everything from your goddess? Can I turn my attention to whatever reason Lady Allayeth wanted to meet over?"

"You may. And if I may say, Mr Asano, you were far less difficult to deal with than the rumours have suggested."

"I'm a perfectly reasonable man."

"We just had such a good meeting, Mr Asano. Let us not start lying now."

32

DRUNKEN LIES AND MYTHIC LEGENDS

IN A GHOST TOWN LARGELY RECLAIMED BY JUNGLE, JASON AND ALLAYETH watched Raelia open a portal and leave through it.

"She held up well," Jason observed.

"She did," Allayeth said. "It didn't show in her body language at all. Do you think she was more scared of me or you?"

"I'm hoping you."

Jason smiled, but his expression was resigned.

"It's funny," he said, his tone suggesting that it wasn't. "I used to work so hard to be scary. I don't do that anymore, yet now people are starting to be scared of me by accident."

"Are you genuinely surprised? People don't understand your power or your behaviour. Your reputation is based on little-understood events that land somewhere between drunken lies and mythic legends. You have a problem with authority yourself, but authority is just the power to impose your will on the world around you. Everyone who tries to impose their will on you falls short, myself included. When you decide to impose your will, what happens?"

"You make it sound like I'm breezing through life, doing what I will."

"Aren't you? You're not getting everything you want, Jason, but when you truly need something to happen, has anyone ever stopped you? Gods? Great astral beings? Death itself? Somewhere near the top of the list of questions I still have is that there's been talk of you remaking chunks of reality. Putting aside how, tell me why you did that?"

"I had to. The dimensional membrane around my home planet was brittle and cracking. Dimensional events were punching holes in it that would have destroyed my world if I hadn't patched those holes."

"And when you went to do that, you already had the power to do so?"

"I kind of figured it out as I went."

"So, the universe decided to break down and you decided to not let it."

"That is an extremely skewed way of looking at it."

"But is there anything you do that can't be looked at that way? You need something to happen, or not happen, and you get your way, regardless of the people, entities or laws of nature pitted against you."

"I can see how that might seem like it's the case, but every instance was a mad scramble of exploiting circumstance, other parties using me as a proxy and a big wet sack full of luck."

"And I can see how it might not seem special when you went through these events one at a time. But there are only so many dogs you can murder before people start calling you a dog murderer."

"A dog murderer?"

"As a random example."

"That doesn't feel random. Do you think I'm running around murdering dogs?"

"No, Jason, I think you're running around doing impossible things. You have your own private universe. You keep a temple to yourself in a bottle that you hang around your neck."

Jason touched a finger to the miniaturised cloud flask hanging on the necklace with his magic amulet.

"Jason, *I'm* scared of you. When your rank catches up to everything else, a planet won't hold you. You'll be like your friend Dawn, needing to restrict your behaviour on planets like this so you don't break too much of them. And I'm not telling you anything you don't know. You knew that even a fragment of what you've shown me would alarm me to the point that I considered killing you. It's why you warned Charist and me off."

"That backfired. It might have warded off your friend, at least for now, but it didn't stop you."

"No. Charist doesn't like how evasive I've been, by the way."

"He's not scared of me?"

"I think he is, and that's the problem. He went to kick a rock out of his path and stubbed his toe, and now he's wondering what's under that rock."

"Will he be a problem?"

"I don't think so, but this tension between your team and the Adventure Society has gotten him more aggressive about getting answers from me."

"What did you tell him?"

"That he needs to stop thinking of you as a silver-ranker and start seeing you as a peer."

"And how did he take that?"

"He asked me why I think that. I told him that, if nothing else, there wasn't much point killing you. That I believe the Builder's assertion that you couldn't resurrect again until gold rank was wrong, out of date or a lie."

"You picked up on that, then."

"I felt immortality in your astral realm. Even if your ability to resurrect is limited, you've stopped ageing, haven't you?"

"So have you," he said defensively, getting a laugh from the diamond-ranker.

"Look, what is it you've brought me out here for?" he asked. "Something about this town and a plant monster?"

She sighed and looked around the town. Not a single building was intact and the ruins were all but buried in growth.

"What does this town tell you?" she asked.

"That something came through, trashed the place and left behind something that massively accelerated plant growth. These ruins aren't old enough for how much jungle is crawling over them. And there are no animals. Not bugs, not birds."

He concentrated his aura senses on the ground.

"No worms. Something's dug into the soil. Plant roots?"

"Fungus."

"Some kind of roaming mushroom creature? It consumes anything or anyone made of meat and turns them into super-fertiliser?"

"Something like that. Not quite so straightforward, unfortunately," she said. "Have you ever heard of an amalgeth?"

"No," Jason said. "Shade?"

"An amalgeth is a fungal monster," Shade said as he emerged from Jason's shadow. "An extremely dangerous one, from recollection. I believe that they are intelligent and able to shape-shift."

"Yes," Allayeth confirmed, "but that is only the beginning. In addition to being able to consume living things and take on their forms, they can mask their auras almost perfectly."

"That's why me," Jason said. "You want someone with a better chance to spot them in hiding."

"Yes. I know that you are getting ready for the underground expedition, but since you sent your familiar for another batch of contracts, I was hoping to convince you to participate in this one specifically. Your team won't be the only one on it."

"An expedition?"

"Similar to the one where the world-taker worms were discovered. Different teams investigating various towns. The teams have all been chosen for having at least one member with powerful or unusual senses. I wanted to use your auxiliary, Estella Warnock, until I realised what you've got her doing."

"You didn't bring anything down on her, did you?"

"No. I was careful."

"Thank you. Why are you delivering what amounts to an ordinary contract in person? To give my team and the Adventure Society some space before the adjudicator from the Continental Council shows up?"

"Yes. At my suggestion."

"Of course it was your suggestion. What lunatic would go around telling diamond-rankers what to do?"

She looked at him from under raised eyebrows.

"Tell me about this contract," he said and she rolled her eyes at his changing of the subject.

"This town we're in now was wiped out early during the monster surge," she said. "It wasn't discovered to be like this for weeks, with everything that has transpired over the last half a year. People aren't travelling and communication isn't what it was. When the town was discovered to have been wiped out, a team of adventurers was deployed. They found nothing alive that wasn't a plant or a fungus. Even flying insects wouldn't come near. They swept the region in case the population had been dragged off or they could discover what did it, but found nothing. There was a monster surge taking place, so they made a report, flagged it for further investigation and moved on."

"Why was it discovered now?" Jason asked. "I can't imagine Yaresh has so little going on now that people are making their way through the report backlogs."

"It was happenstance," Allayeth said. "The Adventure Society jobs hall had some records being moved so they could make repairs and someone stumbled across it. They happened to recognise the signs of an amalgeth and passed it up the line with a priority tag."

"You're worried about more towns being wiped out?"

"Yes. Most monsters don't reproduce, but the amalgeth does and its life cycle is extremely predatory. It infiltrates a population centre, usually small and isolated. It claims to be some kind of traveller in distress. Lone survivor of a monster attack or the like, trying to allay suspicion. At first, the creature does nothing. It learns to fit in and becomes part of the community. Then it starts taking things. Slowly at first. Herd animals. Pets. A person, if it thinks it can get away with it, but that usually comes later. They're patient, often timing their predations with active monster activity, to pass off the blame."

"I think I see where this is going. They slowly escalate until the townsfolk finally catch on that the new person in town is the bad guy, at which point the amalgeth goes ham and kills every living thing."

"Eventually, yes. But the infiltration is a process that takes months or years, usually. They are quite good at hiding the truth, and the more they kill before being discovered, the stronger they grow. The people and animals they kill become a supply of mutable flesh they can use to heal themselves or take monstrous forms when they finally reveal themselves."

"My familiar does something similar," Jason said. "You saw him floating through the sky in a glass cocoon. I call his collection of organic material biomass, which isn't strictly accurate, but video games use the term a lot."

"What are video games?"

"Okay, that would take too long to explain. But he keeps leftover biomass inside my soul realm, in a big pit. I don't have any of the paths leading to it; it's pretty gross. The amalgeth save their biomass up as well?"

"Yes. Then, once they are finally exposed, they absorb it and take on a hybrid flesh-fungal form. They go on a rampage, absorbing and killing every single living creature, collecting all that… biomass. Then they use it to form another of their kind, fully grown and with all the memories of the original. This process triggers accelerated plant growth over a fairly wide area. Then they both go off in search of new towns to infiltrate."

"So we don't know how many of them there are."

"No. I have checked several towns myself, uncovering and killing one. But I have an obligation to defend Yaresh in its vulnerable state, along with other responsibilities. That is why the Adventure Society has established this expedition. I have a list of locations and a map, if you accept the contract."

"I'll need to talk to the others, but I imagine they will say yes."

Jason's cloud palace was a string of buildings set on the face of a cliff, linked by a series of open stairs and elevating platforms. The buildings themselves looked carved from stone with the outfacing walls of each building made of single sheets of glass. Inside the largest building, looking out over miles of rainforest and out to the sea, Jason explained the contract to his team.

"I've heard of amalgeths," Clive said. "They always start at silver rank, but if they reproduce enough times, they advance to gold."

"Can we face one of them at gold rank?" Humphrey asked.

"It depends on the point of their life cycle they're in," Clive said. "If they've just eaten a town full of people, no chance. They can forgo reproducing to use all that accumulated biomass for combat. Even a silver-rank one at that stage would be extremely challenging to face. If we get them at the stage where they've accumulated a large supply of organic mass but haven't consumed a whole town, gold rank would be extremely sketchy, but silver rank wouldn't be too challenging. Early stage, when they're just starting their cycle, we'd have to be careful, but I think we could handle a gold."

"We'll need to scope out the amalgeth if we find one, then," Humphrey said. "Then we can assess whether to take it on ourselves or call in backup."

"I have some backup to call in right now," Jason said. "I know someone I suspect will be very useful, and he's just about done with his nap."

33

STASH WAKES UP FROM A NAP

SOPHIE AND HUMPHREY MADE THEIR WAY THROUGH THE BUILDING AFFIXED to the side of a cliff, arriving at a window wall with a gorgeous view of the rainforest below, stretching out to the distant coast. In front of the window was a huge mound of blankets. Humphrey yanked off the blankets one by one and tossed them aside as he dug his way through the pile. Finally, he revealed a dragon with rainbow-coloured iridescent scales. It was the size of a large dog and was asleep, hugging a full-sized plush replica of itself.

Humphrey struggled to maintain his stern expression for a moment before failing miserably.

"Okay, that's adorable," he conceded.

"Where did he get that thing?"

"From Jason. Once he gave up on the secret identity thing—"

"He was so bad at that."

"Yes, he was. But he said that if we're going to be famous, we should capitalise on merchandising opportunities."

"Meaning that he wants to make toys?"

"I think so."

"What for?"

"Money, I guess."

"Can't he just make infinite money?"

"He also said something about branding."

"As in, burning an ownership mark into people's flesh? That doesn't sound like him."

"He said it's a different kind of branding."

"So, he wants to make toy versions of us?"

"Of the familiars, I think. The one of Onslow does look pretty good. He also said something about a body pillow with Gary's picture on it. Who would buy that?"

"I would buy that. I would buy that immediately."

"He said he didn't know if there was a market for it. I asked him about a body pillow with you on it, but he said that would be a very bad idea."

"It would."

"Why?"

She turned to look at him.

"Really?" she asked.

"What?"

She stepped in front of him and cupped his face in her hands.

"My sweet, innocent boy," she said and then pushed up on her toes to gently kiss him. A groaning sound came from the floor.

"Eww, gross," Stash complained sleepily, a very twelve-year-old human voice coming from the dragon.

"It's time to get up," Humphrey told him. "We have to hunt some monsters."

Stash gripped a blanket in his teeth and pulled it back over himself.

"Sleepy."

"It's some kind of shape-changing monster," Humphrey encouraged. "That could be fun."

Stash flapped awkwardly at the blanket from underneath so it also covered toy Stash, then went still. Humphrey gave Sophie an exasperated look and she grinned.

"Stash," she said in a voice so sweet that Humphrey gave a startled shake of the head. "It's time to go see Colin."

The blanket exploded up into the air as Stash grew to the size of a horse, tucked his toy under one arm and did a three-legged dragon gallop out of the room.

"ONSLOW!" his voice bellowed from the hall. "WE'RE GOING TO SEE COLIN!"

A certain section of Jason's soul realm felt like an old English estate that had been abandoned to neglect. Tall hedges looked like they may have once been scraps of a hedge maze with sections variously absent or overgrown. What might have once been topiaries were now massive thorny bushes holding the vague shape of monsters.

The grass underfoot was thick and deep green. The hedges and bushes were a deeper green, sometimes almost black around the tips of leaves or thorny protrusions. The only elements of bright colour were blood-red berries that had the enticing allure of a trap.

Gothic buildings were visible over the high foliage, the ornate dark stone crumbling around the edges. The pathways never led to them, jutting up over long tall hedges or through passages choked with inch-long thistles with wet, black tips. Like old, abandoned temples, they had a few high broken windows where the remnants of stained glass showed just enough of what had once been depicted to indicate that the original images had not carried positive imagery.

Jason and his companions walked along the wide and winding grassy pathways. The tall hedges and ominous buildings meant that little direct sunlight reached them and what did was oddly muted. Given the clear sky overhead, there was a little too much gloom.

With Jason were Humphrey, Sophie and Clive, along with Clive's rune tortoise, Onslow. The last member of the group was Stash, who had taken the form of a celestine child. His hair and eyes were silver with dark chocolate skin and an unusual absence of moustache. He sat cross-legged, riding atop Onslow's shell. As they moved along the wide, grassy paths, Humphrey craned his neck to take in the looming surrounds.

"Jason," he said. "I know that everything in this place is a part of you."

"It's kind of hard to miss with his aura drenched everywhere," Clive said.

"Yes," Humphrey agreed. "And I've noticed that your aura shows variations depending on which part of your soul realm we're in."

"Yes, I've been cataloguing the differences," Clive said. "The differentiation was quite marked at first, but the zones have become more varied and complex over time."

"Like this vampire manor estate," Humphrey said.

"Vampires have creepy gothic castles in this world too?"

"Only really in stories," Humphrey admitted. "If they all lived in decrepit manors and abandoned churches then adventurers would find them a lot easier."

"I guess people who sleep through the day and feed on blood tend to inspire certain narratives," Jason reasoned. "I think it's mostly an act, though. My friend Craig is a vampire and he just plays it up so that naïve, attractive women will let him suck their blood."

"And you accept that?" Sophie asked.

"I checked it out," Jason said. "He never feeds too much, and they are *extremely* into it. Most vampires from my world were like that before the old ones woke up and everything went nuts. They had more of a 'luring people into their creepy mansion' vibe."

"Jason, your aura is never what I would describe as friendly," Humphrey said. "Not unless you're masking it. But it also seems to have that vibe that you mentioned. Domineering, predatory. Ominously well-suited to this particular environment."

"It makes sense," Jason said. "Dark essence, blood essence. I can see why my soul knocked out a place like this. Plus, this is where I store Colin's excess flesh pile."

"Excess flesh pile," Humphrey repeated under his breath, shaking his head. Jason watched him with a grin.

"You could have just called it biomass like you usually do," Clive pointed out.

"Yeah, but where's the fun in that?" Jason asked. "Oh, and I'd avoid getting too close to the bushes from here on in. They can be a bit hungry."

"What do you mean by hungry?" Humphrey asked.

"Hungry. You know, wanting to eat things. Namely us. Well, you. Colin has a lot of influence on this area, and while he's a good boy, he does also yearn to devour every living thing on the planet."

The others all turned to look at him.

"A bit," Jason qualified. "He yearns a bit. It's like when you have a hobby you're really into. Knitting, for example. Sometimes life gets busy and you might go for a while without finding the time to sit down for a good knit. You yearn to do some knitting. It's like that with Colin."

"Except, instead of wanting to knit," Clive said, "he wants to wipe the world clean in a nightmare of hunger and flesh and blood."

"Exactly," Jason said. "You get it. And Farrah says I'm bad at explaining things."

"I really hope you are," Sophie said.

"Why would you hope that?" Jason asked her.

"Because, Jason," Clive said, "your tone suggests you think you're saying something sensible as you explain how you look at an apocalypse the way other people look at knitting."

"Which is not sensible," Sophie clarified.

"It's all perspective, I suppose," Jason said.

"Yes," Sophie agreed. "It is a matter of perspective, but let me try and explain it in a way that might sink in: One perspective is the sandwich and the other perspective is the mouth."

"You're suggesting I'm losing the ability to see the point of view of the one that's about to get eaten?"

"None of us are foolish enough to claim knowledge of what's going on in your head, Jason," Humphrey said. "But I remember those talks we used to have back in Greenstone. About right and wrong. About duty and responsibility. I remember that you have a habit of representing yourself or taking a position that doesn't reflect your actual beliefs, just to make a point."

"Is that what I'm doing?" Jason asked lightly.

"Unless, a couple of minutes ago, you genuinely stopped caring about the deaths of everyone on the planet. And we both know that isn't the case, which leads to the question of what point are you trying to make?"

"Well, you mentioned those talks we used to have. When you boil them down, what was each one of those talks about?"

"Power," Humphrey said. "Who has it, and who should. What's done with it and what should be done."

"Exactly," Jason said, throwing out his arms to indicate the soul realm. "Every day, the power I have outside this realm gets a little closer to being the power I have inside it. I'm twenty-nine years old. By the time I'm thirty-nine, we'll be gold-rankers. How old will I be when we reach diamond?"

"You just casually assume that we'll all reach diamond," Clive said.

"Yep," Jason confirmed. "And once I reach that point, there won't be any limits on Colin's natural power anymore. He'll have the full strength of an apocalypse beast. I'll probably be worse, but let's put that aside for the moment and focus on just my familiar. If I tell him to wipe out a planet, will he say no? Wiping out planets is kind of his thing."

Jason stopped walking and let out a sigh. The others stopped as well.

"No one should have that power," Jason said. "But I will. What happens if I decide that an apocalypse isn't any more drastic than knitting?"

"Then we'll slap you on the head until your head gets right," Sophie said, exasperation in her voice. "You told us about your world. Did a culture not based on lording it over people with personal magic make things better? Or did people just pick something other than magic to be the power and use that to exploit the people without it?"

"The second one," Jason admitted.

"Then knock off with the sad-boy brooding," Sophie said. "I know it's kind of your thing, but in case you hadn't noticed, you have a habit of making enemies. The sort of enemies where having an apocalypse in your back pocket might not be enough."

"That's a good point," Jason acknowledged. "Balance of power. Balance of terror? I shouldn't worry about me when so many things are more powerful than I am and suck a lot more than I do."

"Good," Sophie said. "Now, can we get on with waking up your familiar?"

"We have to get Clive first," Jason said.

"What are you talking about?" Clive asked. "I'm right here."

"What is that?" Humphrey asked as he turned to look at Clive. Humphrey had spotted a vine that had crept close to Clive's foot. The vine, as if having heard it was noticed, sprang to life, wrapping around Clive's shin. It toppled him over as it withdrew, Clive yelping as he was dragged into a hedge.

"I told him not to get too close," Jason said.

"You're a bit covered in thorn marks there, Clive," Jason pointed out. "It looks like an extremely aggressive form of chicken pox. The little dots are bleeding a bit."

Clive was sitting on the grass, using Onslow's shell as a backrest as he glared at Jason.

"Jason, this is your soul," Clive said.

"It is," Jason agreed.

"Then maybe you should avoid having your soul drag me into thorn bushes that try to eat me."

"That's all automatic," Jason said. "If you could just change things because you want to, I'd have eye beams right now."

Finally, they reached a path to a cluster of buildings that wasn't blocked by a hedge or Clive-eating bushes. There was a large open square made of the same dark brick as the buildings. Clock towers sat at each corner, but the clock faces were warped. Instead of numbers, there were symbols in the old tongue, the language older than the planet they were standing on. The hands of the clock were actual hands, moving and grasping at the air.

"Those symbols instead of the numbers," Clive said. "I think they're some of the basic patterns that Gordon uses for that strange ritual magic of his."

"Yeah," Jason said. "Shade and I have been discussing how that magic is linked to me."

"We should talk about this," Clive said, opening his rune portal to pluck out a notebook and pencil.

"Not the time, Clive," Humphrey said. "That's not what we're here for."

"Exactly," Jason said, plucking a cup of tea from the air. "We need to focus. Hmm, this is a bit tepid."

Jason shot red eyebeams into the cup and steam rose from it. He took a sip and nodded.

"Much better," he said with a happy nod, then looked at the glare he was getting from Clive.

"What?" Jason asked innocently as Clive grumbled and put his notebook away. He continued muttering under his breath as the group moved into the square.

In the middle of the square was a massive, round metal door set horizontally into the ground. As they approached, the metal door slid out of sight, revealing a deep shaft some thirty metres across and twice that deep.

They moved to the edge and looked down. Instead of continuing the brickwork of the square above, the shaft's walls were rough-hewn stone, obsidian black. Set into the wall like pegs were stone stairs winding their way down. At the bottom was what looked like a roiling pool of blood, glowing with an internal light that painted the bottom of the shaft red. A strong stench of coppery blood rose up to greet them.

"Jason," Clive said. "This looks a lot like that chamber you took us to that one time."

"The place where they tried to sacrifice you," Humphrey said.

"Yep," Jason confirmed. "It's where they summoned a sanguine horror that we killed and I looted the awakening stone that let me summon Colin. Now it's his flesh pit."

"I really prefer the term 'biomass storage,'" Clive said.

"Clive, look at it," Sophie said. "That's a flesh pit. Or a blood-flesh soup. I'm not sure if that sounds better or worse."

Jason looked up just as a massive glass sphere floated into view over the buildings and hedges. Inside was a red mass that glowed from the inside, pulsing like a heartbeat.

"It's time," Jason said.

Cracks appeared on the glass like an egg starting to hatch. Each glass fragment dissolved into nothing as it fell away, larger and larger shards breaking off until the fleshy mass inside started poking out. The flesh looked like a giant heart—not the love kind but the meat kind. Finally, the weight of it broke through the remaining glass and it fell into the hole like an offcut tossed away by a butcher.

The mass dropped through the shaft, splashing into the pool below.

WELCOME BACK, COLIN

THE GIANT, FLESHY MASS SPLASHED INTO THE ROILING RED POOL AT THE bottom of the shaft. Jason winced at the sound, which, even through the echo effect of the shaft, reminded him of messing up a dive and doing a painful belly flop.

"That was a weird sound," Sophie said.

"Yep," Jason agreed.

"It sounded exactly like when you hit a very fat man with a very large fish."

Jason, Humphrey and Clive all turned to look at her.

"What?" she asked defensively. "I had a life before I met you people."

Humphrey opened his mouth to ask many, many questions, but was interrupted by a horrifying alien shriek. It reverberated up through the shaft with a nails-on-chalkboard shrillness that seemed to dig into the group's nerves. Jason moved to the edge to look down, the others quickly joining him.

The inside of the shaft was dark, the previous red glow no longer lighting up the bottom. The coppery tang of blood had gotten much stronger.

"Do we go down there?" Clive asked. "There are stairs, but I do not want to go down there."

"Are you scared of a hole just because there's a weird noise coming out of it?" Jason asked, then frowned as something occurred to him. "You know, I once asked your wife the exact same question *in a very* different context."

"Oh, go jump in a hole," Clive said bitterly. "Look, there's one right there."

"Fair enough," Jason said and leapt into the void. His cloak manifested around him and slowed his descent into the dark. Shortly after he jumped, a thrumming sound pulsed up from the shaft, each beat accompanied by a momentary glow of red light. Like the heartbeat of some long-buried monster starting to wake, it was filled with terrible promise.

Slowly floating down the shaft, Jason couldn't help but think back to his first day on Pallimustus. Captured by cultists looking to sacrifice him, trapped alongside people who were yet to become his precious friends. The cloak he now used and the perception ability allowing him to see in the dark were the only powers he'd possessed at the time. Faced with a neophyte sanguine horror, he and his new friends desperately managed to kill it before it had the chance to consume its way into becoming a world-devouring beast.

Jason's soul had reproduced that sacrificial chamber as he called up a sanguine horror inside it. Colin, as a familiar, was limited by Jason's potential compared to the sanguine horror the cult had summoned. Both Jason and Colin gained benefits from their connection, however, especially now the bond was closer than that of a mere summoned familiar. As for limitations, the day would come when that was no longer an issue for either of them.

As he drew closer to the bottom of the shaft, a jolt of excitement passed through Jason in anticipation. Like the original sacrifice chamber, the bottom of the shaft had a ring of open floor around the pit of blood. The floor was wet and red from when Colin's flesh mass crashed down from above, but the pit was still full to the brim, churning like a witch's cauldron.

The mass itself was submerged, only seen as a dark shape with each heartbeat strobe of light. The thudding sound that came with it was deafening at the bottom of the shaft, a thunderous echo that hammered at the ears. Combined with the bitter taste of blood choking the air, the bottom of the shaft was an assault on the senses. Sophie and Clive complained about it loudly as they descended on the back of Onslow's shell with Humphrey and Stash.

Jason ignored them, eyes locked on the blood pool filling the pit, fresh undulations roiling the surface with each pulse of light and sound. More and more, Colin's transitory state felt like the heart of some vast beast, torn from its body and yet refusing to stop beating.

The others fell quiet as they joined Jason in his vigil. Even Humphrey's rebellious dragon familiar watched in sober silence. The pulses of light slowed and stopped over time, the thudding heartbeat doing the same. The smell of blood did not fade, even growing stronger as the blood pool stopped churning and started draining like a bath. As it emptied, they saw that the mass inside it was gone.

The liquid continued to drain until it was revealed that there was no hole at the bottom, draining it away. Jason moved to the edge of the now-empty pool, looking down several metres. There was a humanoid figure lying prone and naked. It looked identical to Jason in shape but was entirely blood red. It was the blood clone form that Colin often assumed.

As they watched, the figure started to change. Portions of the body took on other shades, shifting from the monochrome scarlet. The skin texture shifted from the gloss of wet blood, although the hair retained that shine as it turned into Jason's usual shampoo-commercial black.

When the blood clone completed the transformation into an identical copy of Jason, Colin opened his eyes to reveal one difference remained. Instead of the blue and orange eye-shaped nebulas Jason had instead of eyes, Colin had red embers burning in a void. He pushed himself to his feet as a rust-red robe was conjured to cover his nakedness.

- Your familiar and bonded avatar [Colin] has become your [Voice of the Will].

- As a [Voice of the Will], the summoned vessel of [Colin] has been modified. The vessel can advance in rank without a new vessel being summoned. The cost to summon a new vessel if destroyed is significantly increased.

Colin lightly leapt the several metres out of the pool as Jason stepped back, his doppelganger standing in front of him as they looked at each other.

"You know what?" Jason asked.

"I'm a very handsome man?" Colin said in Jason's voice.

"Yes," Jason said with a grin. "Yes, you are."

"Neil isn't here," Sophie said. "If he was, I think he would say this is true love at last."

Jason and Colin let out identical chuckles.

"Okay, that's creepy," Clive said.

"Compared to the subterranean flesh pit we're standing in?" Sophie asked him.

"I guess not," Clive acknowledged.

Jason and Colin smiled at the interplay but quickly went back to examining one another over with assessing looks.

- The vessel of your [Voice of the Will] now possesses four distinct forms: swarm, the worm that walks, apocalypse beast, and Voice of the Will.

- Current form: Voice of the Will.

Form Four: [Voice of the Will]

- As a vessel for your soul, the Voice of the Will form has enhanced intellect compared to other forms. In this form, [Colin] loses the majority of his own abilities but can fully utilise the majority of yours. Abilities related to your nature as a nascent astral hegemon cannot be replicated. Essence abilities of the familiar, perception and aura types are not replicated but are replaced with other abilities.

- In this form, [Colin] may exert influence over messengers you have branded using your authority.

- Current number of branded messengers: 0.

"Nascent astral hegemon," Jason said, the phrase standing out. "Do you know what that means?"

"No," Colin said. "I assume—as I suspect you do as well—that it's related to your progress as a variant astral king."

"It says that you have enhanced intellect while in this form."

"Not that enhanced," Colin said. "Only to the same level as you."

"Hey…"

"I take it back," Clive said. "This is creepier than being in a subterranean flesh pit."

"Does it worry you?" Jason asked Colin. "Your mind degenerating as you take other forms?"

"It's not degenerating," Colin explained, "but merely changing. My other forms are all swarm variants requiring different levels of hive mind to function. The 'enhanced' intellect of this form is merely a re-tasking of mental ability because there is only one of me."

"That was very clear," Jason said. "And people say I'm not good at explaining things."

"They're right," Colin told him. "That's why you need a Voice."

Jason and Colin shared a grin as Sophie groaned.

"This is becoming insufferably smug," she complained. "That's tolerable when there's only one of you, but this is too much."

Jason and Colin both turned to look at Sophie, then back to one another.

"Another form?" Colin asked.

"Please," Jason said.

Colin held out an arm that turned back to monochrome red and started spraying leeches into the pit. They kept gushing out like water from a fire hose, half-filling the pit.

"I normally can't maintain two separate forms," Colin explained, "but in your soul realm, I can use the excess biomass to demonstrate the other states I can assume. Explanations come easier when they aren't just screeching the word 'hungry' over and over in a language that can't be fully expressed in just sound."

"Sure," Jason said.

Form One: [Swarm]

- Increased biomass capacity and hive mind cohesion range.

- Absorb life force to temporarily increase maximum biomass. Biomass must be consumed, discarded or stored within a certain period or be lost.

"The original swarm state," humanoid Colin explained, "doesn't have any fancy bells and whistles, just a butt-load of leeches. The advantages are that I can use more biomass than the other forms, and my hive mind won't start losing track of individual leeches until they're much further away. That allows me to spread out and eat a lot more people."

"Jason..." Humphrey said.

"Oh, come on, Hump," Jason said. "Are you going to tell a bird not to fly?"

"If it's flying off to eat people, yes. You and I have killed bird monsters together so they wouldn't fly off and eat people."

"Colin's a good boy," Jason said. "He's only going to eat bad people. Isn't that right, Colin?"

"It is," Colin said. "People who oppress others and live a life of violence."

"Exactly," Jason said.

"But not Jason," Colin continued. "He gets a pass."

"Hey," Jason said, turning back to Colin. "Whose side are you on?"

"Justice?" Colin suggested.

"Okay, let's try another one of those forms. Maybe one with a bit less lip."

Colin chuckled and the pool of leeches half-filling the pit started to shrink down. As it reached the size of a small mound, bloody rags emerged from the pile to wrap around it, encapsulating the leeches and squeezing them into a humanoid shape until it looked like an old movie mummy. More rags roughly wove together and draped over the figure as a hood and cloak. There were two small gaps in the face where the eyes would be and a larger one in place of the mouth. They revealed the leeches pressed together inside the rags, writhing and flashing rings of teeth. Some fell out of the mouth and eye gaps, tumbling to the floor like fat, carnivorous tears.

Form Two: [The Worm That Walks]

- Use rags to encapsulate worms and entangle foes.

"This is another form I've been using for a long time," Colin said. "Nothing new here. Fewer leeches, but more utility. Because I don't need the range or the multi-tasking of the full swarm, I can think a little more tactically in this state."

"Didn't you switch from the rags to red leather straps?" Sophie asked.

"I can use either," Colin said as the coarse cloth turned into neat leather straps, giving a much less ragged appearance. "I kind of like the rags, to be honest."

"What about the last form?" Clive asked. "That's something new, right?"

"Yes," Colin said. "My first, second and fourth forms are adaptations of ones I could already take. The third form is something new; a result of consuming the world-taker worm queen."

The leather straps wrapped around the worms turned back to rags and bulged outwards as the worms inside melded into a growing, singular form. The rags burst, revealing red limbs of thick, ropy muscle as the humanoid form bulked out.

"This better not be a Red Hulk thing," Jason said. "Red Hulk sucks."

As more of the rags burst, the figure in the pit diverged from the humanoid. The arms grew longer and a second pair grew out. The rag-wrapped head sank into the torso. What looked like closed eyelids all over the exposed flesh opened and closed, revealing themselves as mouths covering the body. Leeches emerged from the tooth-filled maws to crawl all over it and long, prehensile tongues emerged, themselves ending in toothy mouths. When the transformation was complete, it was a headless, four-armed monstrosity covered in gaping mouths, standing twice as tall as Humphrey even hunched over.

"Well," Clive said. "I guess that's my next nightmare covered."

Form Three: [Apocalypse Beast]

- The [Apocalypse Beast] form has a large biomass with enhanced physical strength.

- When the [Apocalypse Beast] form feeds on enemies, powers belonging to them are randomly sealed and become available to [Colin]. Weaker abilities are absorbed at first with additional and more powerful abilities absorbed with extended feeding. Using the abilities restores their use to the enemy they were stolen from, with any cooldowns for those abilities triggered.

- The [Apocalypse Beast] form is strenuous. Feeding on life force or consuming biomass is required to maintain it or it will break down into a swarm state.

"This form is physically powerful," Colin explained, "but also more agile than it looks. It's a form that will allow me to take some fights head-on while also bringing some of Jason's signature unpleasantness to the opponent."

"What do you mean by signature unpleasantness?" Jason asked.

"Jason," Sophie said, "your powers make people's flesh rot and blood leak out like sweat."

"I guess that is relatively unpleasant," Jason conceded.

The blood giant then turned into blood that splashed over the floor of the pit.

"Completing my transfiguration into a Voice of the Will consumed most of the excess biomass I had stored up," Colin said. "The blood giant form will consume it quickly as well without something to feed on. If you need a combat form that doesn't continually eat into my reserves, this Voice of the Will form can use most of your abilities."

"That's all very impressive," Humphrey said. "Now it's time to get out of here so you can show us your new abilities in the field. We have to find some shape-shifting flesh monsters and kill them."

Humphrey's expression turned awkward as he looked at Colin.

"No offence," Humphrey said, drawing identical laughs from Jason and Colin.

"What do you think is creepier?" Clive asked. "A blood ogre covered in mouths with tongues that have their own mouths, or there being more than one Jason?"

"I've got avatars all through this space," Jason said.

"Yeah, but they're perfect copies," Sophie said. "It just feels like some magic power. The Colin version of you is more real. He's just different enough to feel off, somehow."

"Uncanny," Clive agreed.

Colin walked over to Onslow where Stash had been sitting cross-legged, peering at Colin the whole time with an uncertain expression.

"What do you think, Stash? You've turned into Jason enough times."

"Don't know," Stash said. "You're weird."

Colin plucked a large biscuit out of the air, taking it from Jason's inventory. Stash grabbed it and bit half of it off in a single chomp.

"Welcome back, Colin," he mumbled happily, spraying crumbs.

In the Pallimustus equivalent of what Jason knew as the Pacific Ocean was an island named Jorganis. A small island almost entirely covered by a grimy city, it was a haven for those operating outside of the auspices of the Adventure Society, the Magic Society or any form of legitimate government. The city was ruled by whatever groups could take and hold territory, with districts changing hands regularly. The only permanent institutions were temples to gods that weren't allowed to set up in civilised society, at least not openly.

One of the local factions currently holding power was a coterie of vampires, mostly the ordinary variety but led by a group of energy vampires. Another group, currently pressuring the vampires hard, was a handful of messengers that had moved in and rapidly claimed a section of city, despite their small number.

One of the messengers, a gold-ranker, had decided to put an end to the vampire clan and invaded their core stronghold, which was an old stone manor. He broke through the roof, into the lounge used by the energy vampires. He laughed derisively as they grabbed him and tried to drain his energy. He tossed them away to all corners of the room.

"Pathetic," he mocked. "Your feeble powers cannot consume me. I am a gestalt being, inherently superior. You should kneel and be honoured, but killing you all is acceptable as well."

His disdainful expression turned to confusion as an ornate black and red blade jabbed out through his chest, impaling him from behind. A hand gripped his shoulder and drained his mana.

"Let's try this again, shall we?" a voice whispered in the messenger's ear as he fell to the floor. The other vampires scrambled over and fed.

"I wasn't sure what to do with this sword," the leader of the energy vampires said. "It came into my possession under some rather unusual circumstances, at a time when I was going through some drastic changes. One might even say I was born the moment I devoured the soul containing it and claimed it for myself. I went searching for its origin, hoping to find some kind of identity for myself."

The messenger lay helpless and twitching as the vampires fed.

"As it turns out," the vampires continued, "it's designed for killing your kind. The Builder, apparently holding some sentimentality for your kind, sealed it away. Until he inadvertently handed it to me."

The colour had faded from the messenger, his skin and wings turned an ashen grey. The vampire leader pulled out the sword and stood up while the others stayed crouched over their prey.

"Don't kill him," the vampire once known as Thadwick said. "We need to find out what he knows about the Purity relic."

35

OPTIMISM

Every building in the village was damaged, but at least the damage was minor. They had suffered an unusual sequence of attacks, starting with hundreds of lesser monsters that the locals had fought off themselves with shovels, pitchforks and even the occasional weapon. Days later, bronze-rank adventurers fought off a second wave of creatures, this time, hopping creatures akin to a lizard version of a wallaby.

Jason and his expansive aura senses had detected the third wave coming from kilometres away, giving the team time to rush in and intercept. The monsters were silver rank yet startlingly weak for that level. Monsters spawned on a scale ranging from few-but-strong to many-but-weak, and this was further down the numerous scale than the team had ever seen.

The silver-rank monsters were fist-sized balls of fur that bounced along the ground, quite adorable up until their teeth clamped onto flesh. Individually, the monsters had strength more in line with iron-rank monsters, which had cost the bronze-rank adventurers. Still in the village after the second wave, they had thought to mow down the tiny creatures and rack up the easiest silver-rank kills they would ever get.

It was a hard and swift lesson in the tyranny of rank. Although weak, the creatures still had the inherent damage reduction that high-rankers enjoyed against those below them. The bronze-rankers discovered why bronze to silver was considered the first true leap in power; their whole team had to stack onto each of the little creatures to take them down. Given that left the remainder of the swarm to overrun them, Jason's team needed to extract them in short order.

The newly awakened Colin proved to be the champion of the day. Of his four forms, the original leech swarm state allowed him to expand his collection of leeches more than ever, albeit temporarily, by feeding on life force. The creatures had no rank-based protection from him, allowing his numbers to rapidly swell as he consumed. That left their meagre vitality swiftly drained away by hungry leeches that used it to produce yet more leeches.

The fight was still annoying as the monsters could rapidly replicate themselves, turning it into a race between the monsters and Colin. The team helped as best they could, but their area-attack potential was limited. Jason tried his affliction butterflies that could also reproduce from monsters, but the afflictions killed the weak monsters before the butterflies could reproduce themselves. The most work, other than by Colin, came from Humphrey and his fire breath.

When the job was done, most of Colin's leeches were shunted into Jason's soul realm. The biomass Colin had stored there over time had all been consuming in his awakening, but this made a solid start to refilling the flesh pit.

Looting the monsters afterwards was also a pain, Shade doing most of the work of moving from body to body, lightly touching each one. Once he was done, Jason triggered his looting ability and each member of the group saw a lengthy window of collected treasures listed. Those without personal storage spaces had items appear around them, some on the ground but others above, loot raining down on their heads. Mostly, it was coins, but Sophie deftly avoided a falling dagger while Clive had a slab of meat wrapped in oiled paper slap him in the face.

"Sorry," Jason said. "I forgot to set the loot mode to master looter."

While they all set to picking up the loose treasure, Jason glanced over his list and frowned as he looked at one of the items.

- [Greatsword of the Makar Veen] has been added to your inventory.

"Who or what is the Makar Veen?" Jason asked.

"It's an order of warriors," Humphrey said. "It's just a legend, I think. I don't know that they were ever real, and if they were, I doubt the stories are accurate."

Jason opened his inventory and took out the sword, a two-handed monstrosity so ornately crafted as to become impractical as a weapon.

"Yeah, this is a real JRPG-looking sword," he observed. "It certainly looks more like a weapon from a story than something someone would actually use."

He held it vertically, the tip resting on the ground. Even sinking into the dirt a little, it was taller than Jason himself. Neil wandered over and held his hands a few inches apart, at roughly the size of the monsters from which the weapon had been looted.

"Looting powers are weird," Jason said, and Neil nodded.

"Especially yours," Neil said. "I know that most looting powers produce containers for things like potions and slabs of meat. But aren't yours a little elaborate?"

Neil held up a potion produced by his loot power: a semi-transparent red liquid in a small, clear vial. In his other hand was a potion he picked up from Jason's loot power. The vial was similar, but the liquid inside roiled as if boiling and had flecks of what looked like gold glitter. There was also a colourful label on the vial.

Neil held up the plain potion for the group to see.

"Frenzy potion," he said. "Not something I'd use, but a perfectly ordinary potion."

Then he held up Jason's with the fluid that churned in the vial.

"According to Jason's party interface, the exact same potion," Neil said. "Yet the label reads…"

He turned the vial to read the label out loud.

"…ACME Calm-B-Gone," Neil read. "Why doesn't it just say frenzy potion? These do the same thing except one looks weird and is labelled wrong."

Looting powers varied in both the type of goods primarily produced and the condition in which they were produced. Most loot from monsters was some variety of refined body part, imbued with magic. These were useful for rituals and especially crafting, from meat used in cooking to gallbladders containing bile used to treat metal in smithing.

Both Jason and Neil's loot powers produced spirit coins and could churn out almost any kind of item. Each tended to produce more of certain item types, however. Neil's power, Spoils of Victory, more frequently produced hard materials like chitin and bone, along with other simple-but-valuable commodities and crafting materials. It made Neil's power the consistent source of wealth that loot powers were famous for.

Jason's power was a lot more up-and-down in terms of the value of items produced. The monster parts he looted tended to be meat, which was less valuable than other crafting materials. On the other hand, Jason produced more fully crafted items than Neil, with ready-made weapons, armour and other tools fetching high prices.

Both men produced more potions and unguents than other crafted items, usually of the healing variety. Neil produced mostly potions compared to Jason, who usually got tins of topical ointment. Even when they produced the same item, though, the results were not the same.

"I'm pretty sure my version of the potion tastes better," Jason said.

"That sounds right," Sophie agreed. "Jason usually loots those annoying tins with the oily healing cream, but his potions always taste great. Most looted potions work fine but taste like an alchemist filled the vials with residue scraped from the bottom of a vat to get more money out of the batch."

"That's because it's exactly what they do," Belinda said. "Jory complains about it all the time. It's not all residue, but they definitely throw it in to bulk out the last few vials. It's why cheap potions often have that gluggy texture."

"How is Jory doing?" Jason asked.

"Last I heard, the Church of the Healer was sending him to Estercost to lecture on his potion-development methods," Belinda said. "The Magic Society hasn't opened the water link chambers to the public since the attack on the Yaresh, so I haven't talked to him since then."

"Neil," Jason asked. "How is Jory doing?"

"I don't know," Neil said. "Why ask me?"

"You both work for the Healer."

"Jason, prayer is a sacred and important practice. It's not there for me to casually ask how my friends are…"

Neil trailed off as he tilted his head as if listening for a distant sound, then glowered at Jason.

"Jory's fine," Neil grumbled. "He's in Cyrion, lecturing a bunch of Knowledge priests so they can start spreading Jory's ingredient research techniques."

Cyrion was the capital of Estercost, the same country that contained the city of Vitesse. It was also the main seat of House Geller, despite the family's aristocratic title coming from Greenstone.

"Humphrey, bro," Taika said. "Aren't all those people from Earth still waiting at your family's place in Cyrion for Jason to go claim them?"

"Yes," Humphrey said. "I've been getting increasingly less polite messages from my mother about it."

"Shouldn't we go sort that out, then?" Clive asked.

"No," Humphrey told him. "Mother's too controlled to be genuinely angry. Not when she can just rewrite a message before sending it. She's just faking it to make me feel pressured. By now, I'm sure she's found a way to leverage them to some political end. If we pulled up stakes and got Jason anywhere near there, she'd probably find a way to send us in the other direction."

"No offence, bro, but your mum sounds kind of twisty."

"Yes," Humphrey said with a weary sigh.

"Yeah," Jason said with a wistful sigh, getting a snort of laughter from Neil and a glare from Humphrey.

The latest iteration of Jason's cloud palace was a series of wooden buildings on stilts, rising from a swamp. Wooden walkways connected the buildings, almost enough to make for a small hamlet. Rather than being dismal, the bright summer sun reflected off the water and brought out the colours of the verdant plant life, making for a picturesque, if humid, locale.

The team's intended short sojourn on an open contract had extended to over a month as delays came in on all fronts. Farrah and Travis had finished up their experiments in Jason's soul realm and Jason portalled them back to Yaresh. He checked in with the Adventure Society before returning, discovering numerous delays, starting with the official from the Adventure Society's continental council. The messengers were also dragging their heels in providing access to the study of Mah Go Schaat, the dead diamond-rank messenger. It had been promised to Jason and he had no doubt the messengers were trying to break in before handing it over.

The team was lounging on an open deck, enjoying the fact that the flying insects avoided the building and its aura.

"Is the trade hall in Yaresh even operating right now?" Neil asked in Jason's absence. "I know the Adventure Society campus came through the attack better than most places but is the infrastructure for trade even in place? We've got a whole stack of loot to sell off."

"I asked Jason to check in with the Adventure Society while he's there," Humphrey said from the cloud hammock he shared with Sophie. "Last I heard, trade was open but under very strict controls. The Adventure Society is claiming anything useful for the reconstruction and paying in credit."

"You mean those bonds you only get the money for in a year?" Belinda asked. "Stuff that. We can just hoard everything and sell it at the next city."

"We're heading underground soon, with no idea how long that will take. We may not see a new city for a while," Humphrey said. "And while it may not benefit us as much, it wouldn't hurt us to contribute. We aren't exactly hurting for money and there's a city full of people who lost everything."

"Fine," Belinda grumbled. "We can let the stupid people have stupid houses."

"You know that it's alright to want to help people, right?" Clive asked her. "It's not going to hurt your hard-as-a-rock street-thief reputation to admit you want to help people. We won't think less of you for being nice or showing some basic compassion."

"We will probably make fun of you, though," Neil admitted. "Just for a bit."

Humphrey leaned out of the hammock, grabbed the leftover crust from a sandwich and threw it at Neil.

"Hey," Neil complained. "Don't waste food. It's disrespectful."

"Speaking of food, when is Jason coming back?" Rufus asked.

"He's already back, bro," Taika said. "I saw him wandering off with that weird sword he looted. He looked all broody; you know how he gets. I figure we give him an hour to get it out of his system and then kick him in the pants."

Jason was in one of the wooden buildings, sitting in a swinging hammock chair. The room was full of loose objects floating around as he practised his aura control. Only one object was unmoving, the Greatsword of the Makar Veen, hovering in front of him.

"The Makar Veen," he said. "From what the others described, they sound like the local equivalent of the Knights of the Round Table or the Paladins of Charlemagne."

"That seems accurate, given my knowledge of the respective legends," Shade agreed. "Why does that trouble you, Mr Asano?"

"Because it was my loot power, but not my legend."

"Ah," Shade said. "The idea of fate senses is still weighing on your mind."

"I've never heard of this legend. The fact that my loot power produced something related to it means that these fate senses are still intertwined with my interface power, right?"

"That is a logical conclusion."

"I don't like it. I don't want my subconscious to have its own special sense that I can't consciously access. I don't trust it."

"Nor should you, Mr Asano. Instincts are important, and your fate senses have allowed you to get this far. But without a critical mind to assess them, instincts can also lead you astray. As you know."

Jason nodded.

"What do I do when I don't know if and when these fate senses are guiding me?"

"Mr Asano, you went to rather extreme efforts to surround yourself with people you value and trust. When you feel lost on your own, let them be your guide. Listen when they tell you that you are wrong. And just perhaps, don't sit in your room brooding when everyone else is having a relaxing afternoon together."

"I'm not brooding."

"Of course not, Mr Asano."

"Bro," Taika said as Jason joined the others. "I'm not saying the dark and brooding thing won't help you pick up ladies. You just might want to consider the type of ladies it works on."

"Jason doesn't care about that," Neil said. "He has Humphrey's mum."

Another crust bounced off Neil's head.

"Do you not finish your food?" Neil complained.

"If you will pardon the intrusion," Shade said, emerging from a shadow. "It would seem that, after much delay, the messengers are preparing to move the study belonging to Mah Go Schaat."

"The what belonging to who?" Taika asked.

"The study belonging to the diamond-rank messenger," Jason said. "It was my personal demand for participating in this expedition the messengers will definitely backstab us during. They say they'll send word when it's ready, but I've had Shade watching it directly. It's in a big metal ball on top of a tower in one of the messenger strongholds, so easy to watch from a distance."

"It seems they have finally given up on attempting to break in and are preparing to move it," Shade said.

"That was a brilliant concession to ask for," Clive said eagerly. "It contains all the personal research of the diamond-rank messenger in his attempts to become an astral king. There's no telling what kind of trove it is."

"Won't the messengers just empty out all the good stuff?" Neil asked.

"As far as we can tell, they can't get in," Jason said. "The diamond-rank messenger wasn't on the same team as the rest of them. The Adventure Society even thinks that the attack on Yaresh was some kind of elaborate plan to get him killed since it didn't accomplish much else."

"And what makes you think you can break into this thing when the messengers couldn't?" Belinda asked.

"Optimism?" Jason told her.

36

MOTHERS

BOTH VEHICLES FROM EARTH AND THOSE FROM PALLIMUSTUS HAD THEIR advantages. Magical vehicles could accomplish things that nothing from Earth could match, especially at the high end. No rock star's private jet or presidential aeroplane could compare to what the cloud flasks like Emir's and Jason's could do. There was also the issue of fuel; spirit coins were far superior to anything Earth had regular access to, be it fossil fuels or renewable energy.

Earth vehicles, by contrast, were often superior in design, performance and utility, especially in the low- and mid-range price bracket. A station wagon or utility vehicle was more practical than a land skimmer. Even an expensive electric scooter was faster, cheaper and easier to ride than a personal floatation disk. A giant, hollow bird construct was far more impressive than a private jet, but also slower and far less space efficient. In addition, it had magic requirements, either high levels of ambient magic or someone with a specific kind of power to operate.

Earth was increasingly incorporating magic into technology. It would, in theory, eventually give them the best of both worlds. That was still some ways off when Jason left the planet, although he had seen some magical vehicles. The magically enhanced plane that had blown up with him inside it didn't fill him with confidence, even if the bomb responsible hadn't been magical.

In the wake of the transformation zone events that Jason had put an end to, Earth's ambient magic had risen. This led to aggressive moves to expand magical activity by the time Jason left Earth. Spirit coin farms were being established around the world, largely based on designs provided by Farrah. It was the drought of spirit coins that had restricted magitech research to critical projects, and an increase in their availability meant more everyday magic.

Jason was in the enviable position of already seeing what the best of both worlds looked like. The Reaper had given Jason a blessing that allowed Shade, a Shadow of the Reaper, to take the form of a mount. Mount, as it turned out, extended from magical shadow horse to void-black private jet. He frequently took forms that were similar to Earth vehicles but with superior designs. Some of that was magical influence, but mostly the designs came from worlds Shade had seen in his extremely long life. If he had seen higher levels of technology in action, he was happy to put it to Jason's use.

After making extensive use of this on Earth, Shade had carefully avoided Earth-like vehicles since their return to Pallimustus. Taking the form of elaborate constructs or bizarre monsters was much less efficient than technology-based vehicles, but Jason's feelings about Earth had been bitter. Shade had taken it upon himself to not offer reminders of that time; Jason had accepted the gesture with silent gratitude.

Time away from Earth, reuniting with his friends, and no small amount of therapy from Arabelle had helped Jason immensely. Once he started asking Shade to again use more practical vehicles, the difference in utility was not lost on the team. This was exemplified by the luxury cabin inside Shade's jet form as they flew towards a messenger stronghold with blinding speed.

Jason's cloud flask could produce what amounted to a flying pleasure yacht. It wasn't a match for Emir's ocean-liner-sized cloud ship as that required a gold-rank flask, but neither was ideal for short trips anyway. The cloud vessels offered peerless luxury and amenities, and they were far from slow. A high-tech private jet was faster, however, and Shade could assume that form in moments.

While certainly speaking to Earth design sensibilities, the jet-black aircraft was not an Earth design unless Shade was cribbing his blueprints from Batman. It was a VTOL craft, capable of vertical take-off and landing, and looked as if Lamborghini had built a spaceship.

Jason and his friends lounged in the passenger cabin eating snacks and looking out the windows at the clouds below. In the back of the cabin was

Melody, Sophie's mother. Normally imprisoned in the cloud palace, she remained under Sophie's supervision while the palace was tucked away in its flask.

It had been months since Melody's capture by Jason's team. She had spent that time interacting regularly with Sophie and Arabelle but remained mostly locked away. She had changed after time with her daughter and semi-voluntary therapy, becoming less hostile and manipulative. This had some unanticipated negative consequences, however.

Melody had been magically brainwashed by the Order of Redeeming Light, which itself was a creation of the god Disguise, masquerading as Purity. The so-called Flames of Redemption used to 'purify' people were developed from an extreme modification of lesser vampirism. The more she was able to fight the brainwashing it produced, the more the magical taint inside her fought back. The result was increasing mental instability as the separate aspects of her mind went to war, threatening to fracture altogether.

From the back of the cabin, Melody started furiously ranting, speckles of froth spitting from her mouth as she proclaimed the revenge that Purity would take on them all. Her aura was a wild mess and Jason reached out with his own, suppressing hers and forcibly stabilising it. It was a technique that stilled her mind and caused her to pass out harmlessly. Sophie caught her mother as she fell and placed her gently in a seat before Humphrey got up, walked over and pulled her into a hug.

Jason, Carlos and Amos Pensinata had pooled their knowledge of aura manipulation and Melody's condition to develop the calming technique. It only worked when Melody was suffering extremes of mental conflict. Carlos and Arabelle had diligently monitored her to check for potential long-term damage but found just the opposite. So long as Jason didn't use it too often, there would be no lingering after-effects, even saving her from doing herself more harm as her own aura tried to shred itself.

An aura was a projection of the soul, using the body as a medium. Melody's soul remained untainted, but the Flames of Redemption permeated her flesh like a cancer. With her body and soul at odds, the resulting aura projection was an ugly mess, which was what Jason had learned to shut down.

Jason's ability to assert himself against other souls had become a lot more refined. All he had known at first was how to make merciless soul attacks, which he had learned the hard way from the Builder. After months of studying under Amos and stealing messenger techniques, Jason had a lot more he could pull out of his toolkit. The technique he used to suppress Melody without harming her was the most specialised and sophisticated expression of that he had thus far developed. It didn't free her mind, but it did disrupt the brainwashing. It always knocked her out, but even if unconscious, she had a brief reprieve from undue influence.

Sophie and Humphrey moved up the cabin, his arm bundled around her protectively. They stopped in front of Jason, who stood. Sophie's face had a naked vulnerability she never would have let herself show when they first met.

"I'm willing to let you try," she said, her voice barely a whisper. Jason nodded, catching her in a quick hug.

Some time ago, Carlos had proposed the idea of taking Melody into Jason's soul realm where his power could potentially help remove the conditioning she had been put through. He would not be able to cleanse her and let her out without killing her yet, but Carlos believed that, with enough research, they could someday reach that point. Jason's soul realm had already hosted research for Farrah and Travis' communication network and Gary's experiments in smithing and metallurgy. Carlos was certain it could shortcut his own research by years, possibly decades.

"We'll sit down with Carlos and Arabelle and discuss it when we get back to Yaresh," Jason said.

Sophie had been going back and forth on trying to get Melody into Jason's soul realm. There was also the issue of getting her to go through of her own volition as no one could be forced through a portal. Another question was whether to let her meet with Callum Morse, who was in love with her and had been hunting for her for years. Given that Cal was almost as unstable as Melody had become, Sophie had flatly refused.

"Shade," Jason said. "Turn us back toward Yaresh. We can deal with the messengers some other time."

"We don't have to do that," Sophie said and Jason grinned.

"Everyone who thinks we should help Sophie's mum instead of going to get me a big magic ball, raise your hand," he said, not taking his eyes from Sophie. Everyone raised their hands except for Sophie herself and puppy Stash, sitting in Humphrey's seat. He raised a paw instead, waving it at Sophie.

High in the sky above Yaresh, Shade's jet form dispersed into a cloud of darkness, dropping his passengers into open air. Those unable to fly themselves were encased in black jet suits, the kind Jason's sister disapproved of his young niece using. Magic resolved some of the practical issues of the purely technological versions, notably heat and fuel, making them more sleek and practical than the Earth original.

From above, the city looked like the subject of a sustained bombing campaign. The shining towers and ziggurats of metal and glass at the heart of the city had been hit hard, many toppled or caved in. Even the most intact were scarred and blemished with the marks of high-level magical combat.

The rest of the city was made up of traditional elven design, with plant-shaped living trees combined with more traditional building materials. Many of the trees were dead, even uprooted entirely. Others were already in the process of repair, which meant specialised healing as much as masonry magic.

The small handful of almost undamaged areas stood in stark contrast to the rest of the city. The ducal palace and the campuses for the Adventure and Magic Societies had stronger magical protection than even the bunkers in which the populace had hidden throughout the attack.

As the team descended from the sky, flying adventurers rose from the city to challenge their approach. The team didn't begrudge the city being wary of invaders from the sky and happily identified themselves with their Adventure Society badges. The new spot for the adventurer vehicles was outside the city. Emir's cloud palace made an unmistakable landmark, but the team went into the city instead. They aimed for what once had been the area of Yaresh where visiting adventurers would park their large vehicles. It had weathered the attack on the city better than most, and the damaged vehicles had all moved on.

The adventurer vehicles were gone, a massive logistics centre in their place. It scrambled to provide the food, water, shelter, medical and hygiene facilities the almost entirely displaced population required. In the team's absence, the logistics hub had grown into a small town in its own right. The blank, seamless buildings told a story of stone-shaping for rapid construction while showing more care than the quickly tossed-up buildings from right after the attack. A few of those still stood, their rough walls standing out from the rest.

They landed in a large square, the open space used as a handy thoroughfare by hundreds at a time. They got some looks as they reached the ground, but a few odd adventurers weren't much of a spectacle. They found benches around the edge of the square and sat down to discuss the next move.

As was usually the case with major city squares, temples made up many of the buildings with prime frontal real estate. These newly built worship houses lacked the usual ostentation, however, being little different from the buildings around them. That was only true to the eye, however, as the divine auras coming from the sanctified grounds were unmistakable.

"Funny how these temples feel a lot like the cloud box you've had me cooped up in for months," Melody pointed out. "I'm surprised the gods put up with you, Asano."

She was once more awake and calm, although Sophie stood over her like a prison guard. Jason flashed her a grin.

"So is everyone else," he told her and she laughed.

"Are you sure you want to stick with the boring one?" Melody asked her daughter.

"Humphrey isn't boring," Sophie said, her voice heavy with the frustration of weary repetition.

"What is it with you and people's mothers?" Neil asked Jason.

"I don't have a thing with people's mothers," Jason said.

"Oh, come on," Neil said. "We've all seen you and Humphrey's mother together."

"Neil…" Humphrey growled.

Neil remained unintimidated, partly because he knew Humphrey and partly because Humphrey's stern visage was undercut by the tiny colourful bird perched on his head.

"When was the last time you saw your dad?" Neil asked Humphrey. "Are you *completely* sure Jason and your mum didn't quietly bump him off? Also, it undercuts how intimidating you are with an adorable bird on your head."

Stash's attempt at an intimidating chirp garnered immediate praise for cuteness that he lapped up. Immediately forgetting his support of Humphrey, he flittered to Neil's shoulder to enjoy gentle finger strokes.

"Traitor," Humphrey grumbled.

37

THE WHIMS OF PEOPLE LIKE ME

THEY WERE SEATED ON BENCHES IN A CORNER OF A CROWDED CITY square, a sea of people flowing from building to building and street to street. The temples were abustle, Jason recognising the closest as churches for Trader and Healer. The buildings had the symbols of their gods emblazoned on the walls in place of signs.

"Jason," Humphrey directed in his team leader voice. "You've worked with the recovery effort admin more than the rest of us because they used your cloud palace so much. Go get the current state of affairs from someone who isn't the Adventure Society."

"No worries," Jason said, dark mist shrouding him. It vanished a moment later to reveal him in a casual suit that would play better with harried administrators than his normal tan shorts and floral-shirt combo.

"Lindy," Humphrey continued. "Make contact with Estella and find out how her project is going. If she needs anything, get it. If you can't—"

"I can," she interrupted.

"Without stealing," Humphrey qualified. "And don't bribe anyone to do anything *too* egregious."

"Fine," she said grudgingly.

"Neil," Humphrey said. "When we left, Hana Shavar was in charge of this place. She's the high priestess of your church, so see if you can find and talk to her. I want you to do the same thing as Jason and get the current state of affairs, but from her perspective."

"I'll start with the temple," Neil said.

"No, she's in that building," Jason said, pointing to a building next to the temple, the largest one situated around the square. "I think it's a hospital, from the auras inside. Hers is on the third floor, opposite side to the temple."

Jason's companions all turned to look at him.

"What?" he asked.

"How are you sensing the auras in that building?" Humphrey asked. "Especially a gold-ranker."

"Uh, aura perception," Jason said. "My aura senses are pretty strong. Did you forget?"

"Jason," Humphrey said, "your aura is retracted. You shouldn't be able to blanket the area with your senses."

Humphrey's words were common sense in a city where powerful essence users kept their auras withdrawn. In addition to preventing them from bombarding every other essence user in range, any non-essence users could potentially be harmed by particularly strong auras, especially if the effects were stacked onto one another.

"Yeah, my aura is retracted," Jason said. "That's just polite. That's why I'm just extending my senses."

For almost every essence user, expanding their perceptual range meant pushing out their aura as well. Amos Pensinata had taught Jason how to project only his perception, such that only extremely sensitive people or those of much higher rank would notice. Jason had been working on it for months and was now capable of doing it effectively when not otherwise distracted. His attempts to pass the skill onto his companions had proven less than effective, only Farrah making any real inroads.

"You've come this far along," Clive said. "Your aura does seem fundamentally different to that of a normal essence user. I'm going to borrow some testing equipment from Carlos so we can—"

"Nope." Jason walked off, pointing at a building. "I'm pretty sure this one is main admin," he called back, not stopping.

"Come on, Jason," Clive called after him. "It's for advancing magical knowledge. That helps everyone."

- [Jason Asano] has removed [Clive Standish] from group chat.

"That's not very mature!" Clive yelled after the rapidly retreating Jason.

The team did some basic reconnoitring of the city's current state. Nothing was urgent; it was as much to practise information gathering as anything else. The team intended to be travelling for years, so the practise would do them good. It also helped them keep track of events in a city with no status quo as recovery and rebuilding continued. The population were refugees in their own land, unaware of the magic doom building up deep beneath the ground.

Nothing they found was too surprising. The official from the Continental Council was expected to arrive within the next day or two and the messengers had reached out to say they would be delivering the device to prevent the underground disaster within the week. Estella was almost done with her mission, having taken it as far as she could without an unacceptable risk of exposure.

There was a growing shantytown outside the walls that was increasingly a concern for city officials. These were people that rejected the official recovery program for whatever reason, from criminal history to distrust of city officials. The shanty town was outside the city defences, but they'd placed themselves between the walls and the adventurer camp.

With no urgent calls on their time, the group decided to travel on foot. They hadn't seen the destruction from any angle other than looking down on it from above. Humphrey pointed out that while literally true, it was also a metaphor worth acknowledging.

"Jason and I talked a lot about power dynamics back in Greenstone," Humphrey said as they walked debris-scattered roads, between buildings ranging from damaged to burned-out ruins.

"In fairness," Jason said, "I mostly ranted at him about ideas that I'd only read about and never had practical experience with. I've learned a lot about the difference between ideas in concept and execution since then."

"It's true that you were quite naïve," Humphrey told him. "But that was true for both of us. And you weren't always wrong."

"I never said I was wrong," Jason pointed out.

"Jason's ideas—" Humphrey continued, only to be cut off by Jason.

"They weren't my ideas," Jason's said. "I'm pretty great, but I'm not claiming credit for socialism. If nothing else, I like money *way* too much."

"What I'm *trying* to say," Humphrey said, giving Jason a stern look, "is that while I always felt a responsibility for people that came with being a Geller, I had never thought to question whether it was right that my name had the power it does. There's a world of people who never had the chance to escape the whims of someone like me."

"But you're one of the good ones," Sophie said.

"And that's the problem," Humphrey said. "That's what Jason got me thinking about. There are good ones, but there's no shortage of bad ones. The way we decide who gets that power isn't good. What if, instead of Thadwick, we had you, Lindy?"

"Then I'd probably have been an entitled turd sandwich as well."

"I don't believe that," Humphrey said. "I think, under all those layers, you like what we do. You like helping people, and all it took was giving you the chance."

Humphrey gestured at the destruction around them. Labourers cleared streets and loaded wrecked sections of building onto carts, hauling it away to be magically recycled into fresh building material. Guards were protecting them after a few instances where recovery resources were the target of violent looting.

"We get to walk through this city with impunity," Humphrey said. "Through this whole world, really."

He looked around at the devastated city.

"An attack like this..." he said. "Yes, we could have died in the fighting, but at least we would have died fighting. We need to remember that even when we put our lives on the line, we are privileged in a way that those we protect are not. We can't always choose our own fate, but at least we get to fight for it. How many of the people who never got that chance would have taken it if they had? How many, if they had the choice, would face the dark to protect the ones that can't?"

"Three," Belinda said.

Humphrey laughed, giving his head an amused shake.

"I'm a little more hopeful," he said. "After all, you and Sophie were given the chance, and here you are. Adventurers. Heroes, even. Helping people. And you can play bitter ex-criminal all you want, Lindy, but I know you like what we do."

"You're talking out the back of your pants, rich boy," Belinda told him.

"Yes, I am rich," Humphrey said. "The Gellers have more money than any other family in Greenstone. All you have is more money than most of them."

Belinda opened her mouth to retort before what Humphrey had said

286 | SHIRTALOON & TRAVIS DEVERELL

sunk in and she froze, mouth still open. The others stopped walking and looked at her with amusement.

"Really?" she asked.

"Belinda," Humphrey said, his tone full schoolteacher. "You're an active silver-rank adventurer. All those monster cores we sell, who do you think buys them? It's people like the Greenstone aristocracy. Their family coffers go into raising silver-rankers who never protect anyone. They're paper monsters. Think of all the opportunities you have at your rank. Why would you lord it over a bunch of bronze- and iron-rankers in a low-magic zone in an isolated corner of the world? Because it's the only place you can. Greenstone's silver-rankers are small people who spend all their money to make themselves feel big."

"He's not wrong," Neil said, himself a Greenstone aristocrat. "Anyone who wants to make something of themselves leaves. My family isn't a big deal in Greenstone because all of our talented people go off to make something of themselves. We don't have lingerers monster-coring their way to silver. The family doesn't support that. There are great reasons to live in Greenstone, but when you're an adventurer, it's a place to be from, not a place to be. The big families and their silver-rankers are literally making money at their spirit-coin farms and they sink it all into keeping up appearances. Monsters cores, imported goods. Do you have any idea how expensive shipping things to Greenstone is?"

"You're rich, Lindy," Humphrey said. "Extremely rich. I know Jason flat-out refused to churn out spirit coins for you, but don't think I'm not aware of all the extra moneymaking you get up to. I don't care if you're clever enough to make more coin than the rest of us from our adventuring. I know you put time and effort into making that happen. So long as you actually do the adventuring, I'm happy for you. Just don't rip off or hurt anyone that doesn't have it coming."

Belinda stood silent, looking at Humphrey, blinking in mild confusion.

"Come on," Sophie told her, grabbing her hand and pulling her back into stride. "Humphrey, be a dear and bring my mother along."

"I can walk by myself," Melody said.

"You can run off and be a menace by yourself as well," Humphrey said. "Be thankful we don't put a suppression collar on you. If I didn't love your daughter so much, I would have."

They walked in silence for a time, taking slow stock of just how devastating even the repelled attack of the messengers had been. Weeks of recovery efforts had removed vast amounts of rubble and debris, but there was more work ahead than behind. Many buildings were too far gone for anything but demolition.

Witnessing the reconstruction was an unusual experience for Jason. The elf city made extensive use of living trees, shaped by magic and integrated with more traditional construction materials. Many dead trees were uprooted and removed while damaged ones were salvaged in a process magically closer to healing than repair. New trees were put in place, their growth magically accelerated by essence abilities, rituals and significant amounts of compost and fertiliser.

They arrived at what had once been the entertainment district, where they had been part of the defensive force. It was no less devastated than anywhere else, making their efforts feel hollow, even knowing the people that had stayed safe in the bunker below ground. That had been a near thing. Monsters had burrowed through the defences and if Jason's duel hadn't spilled inside, the monsters would have. Fortunately, the people inside this bunker had lived.

"As bad as this is," Humphrey said, "it's inspiring to see people coming together for the common good."

"If only it didn't take so much damage to make it happen," Belinda said bitterly. "The time will come when all this is forgotten and people start crawling over one another to reach the top of the pile again. And the people already there will start kicking them back down because you're right, Humphrey: they aren't all good ones."

"On that cheerful note," Jason said. "I'm going to go. I sense some auras I recognise, so I'm going to go off and check on some people. I'll catch you all up."

WHAT'S WRONG WITH SIMPLE

BELLORY WATCHED AS THE PLANT ESSENCE USER RESTORED THE OLD TREE that had once formed the bones of her tavern. She could rebuild it, but it wouldn't be the same, especially not with the directions from the city officials. It would be bigger than ever, much bigger, spreading across multiple trees. A large establishment for lots of people, part of the morale-building exercises for which the entertainment district had been tapped. A large-scale cafeteria through the day and a place they could forget their troubles at night, if only for a little while.

She looked at a man hauling building materials that looked like they should crush him under their weight, his feet sinking into the dirt with each step. Valk Vohl seemed like a decent enough man, despite the noxious weeds that were his brother and father. Perhaps he had been one as well, before. She'd seen more than a few people whose decency had been dug out by what had happened.

For so long, her debt to the Vohl family had been a looming axe, waiting to drop. Then her debt had been shifted to more favourable terms, refinanced as part of some noble's conflict with Valk's father, Urman. Bellory hadn't cared so long as it let her squeeze free of the space Urman and Emresh Vohl had crammed her into. She didn't like being a game piece, small and powerless, but life didn't always offer the best choices.

None of that mattered anymore. Old problems like sketchy debts seemed so small now. Or maybe it did matter. People with money and power didn't keep it by letting folks off out of decency. What would happen when her new creditor came calling? Would the government even consider her the owner of this new tavern? She only owned a fragment of the land it would stand on.

As she watched Valk, lost in thought, he almost stumbled, looking with shock at something behind her. She turned, following his gaze to see a familiar face. She couldn't sense his aura, though, as if he weren't there. She swallowed a lump in her throat, not sure how to feel.

"John... no, Jason," she said. "Your real name is Jason Asano."

"Hello, Bell," he said. His voice was almost a whisper yet it carried over clearly. His smile was sad, his eyes hinting at loss. "I did tell you that I was a liar."

He wore a simple suit, unmarred despite the ash and dust thick in the air. She saw a flake of ash fall onto his suit and slide off, expensive magic keeping it clean. It was a far cry from the floral shirt and short pants he'd been wearing when they met and he went to work in her kitchen. The kitchen whose remains had been cleared away before reconstruction began.

"I saw you," she said. "In the bunker."

"I know. I sensed your aura. Less fear in it than most."

"I was plenty scared. I don't understand what happened between you and the messenger down there. But I know she was about to come at us. Until you stopped her."

Jason nodded.

"I was scared too. We had barriers around us. Anyone we touched would get hurt. Killed, for most people. All she had to do was charge into the crowd and it would have been a massacre. I probably shouldn't be telling you that, after the fact. I don't imagine it'll help you sleep at night. I was lucky I could get her to stop at all."

"Were you?" Bellory asked. "I didn't just hear you tell her to stop. I felt it. We all did. It wasn't just words, it was... a decree. Like the words of a god. Are you a priest?"

He chuckled, shaking his head.

"No," he told her. "I'm not a priest."

"Then what are you? I know it's not a cook for an adventuring team."

"Actually, I am, from a certain point of view. It's just not all that I am. It's complicated."

"And you live a complicated life, I bet."

"I do."

"And what was I to you? What were you doing playing kitchen hand? A simple little diversion? Tumbling some girl who owns a tavern?"

His expression looked hurt.

"What's wrong with simple?" he asked, then gestured at the city around them. "This is what complicated gets you. And I like being a kitchen hand. My sister is a chef; she's the one who taught me to cook."

"I'm sorry," she said. "That wasn't fair. I don't know where to put all this anger. People like me don't get to learn the truth people like you deal with."

Jason bowed his head, eyes locked on his feet.

"I want to argue with you," he said. "To tell you that really, I'm a normal guy. That's part of what brought me to your door, I think. The chance to pretend I'm something I'm not anymore."

He looked up, meeting her gaze.

"But I'm not better than you," he said. "That's not what I'm saying. And you deserve answers. Everyone does, but I can't offer that to everyone, so I'll offer it to you. I'll answer your questions, and I may have to be a little vague when it comes to dangerous secrets, but I'll do my best."

Bellory nodded.

"Alright. What happened with that messenger girl you were fighting?"

"I told you about the barrier we had around us. One of us had to kill the other or the barrier would kill us both. I found a way to save us both, but I had to do something very bad to her for that to happen."

"Why not just kill her?"

"Lots of reasons. Because a fight could so easily have caught all those people up in it, yourself included. Because the messengers are slaves and they don't even know it. Because my father told me that if I get the choice between ruthlessness and mercy, my choice shouldn't be about the person under my sword but about me."

"What about all the other messengers? You sent them through some portal. Why? Did you help them escape? There are so many rumours."

Jason nodded.

"That's where things get complicated. You might say I helped them. They needed to escape their own people more than mine, so I took them prisoner. They're still there, waiting for me to decide what to do with them. I'll show you, if you want, but you should be careful about getting too deeply involved with me."

"Then why are you here?"

"Selfishness, if I'm being honest. You and I had a good time, I think. A beautiful, simple night, and I don't get so many of those."

"Am I in danger?"

"No more than anyone else in this city."

"What does that mean? Is the city in danger?"

"There's always danger, Bell. And there are people to get in between it and the people just trying to live their lives."

He looked sadly around the construction site and the ruined city beyond.

"Sometimes we fail, and I'm sorry about that. There is something. I can't tell you about it, but there will be time to get to safety if we fail."

"If it comes to that, will it mean you're dead?"

"Probably not. I have ways around death."

She let out a disbelieving laugh.

"You have ways around death," she echoed.

He nodded.

"Sure, why not," she said. "I have another question."

"Go ahead."

"When you came in to fight that messenger, why were you only wearing your underpants?"

Jason burst out into laughter.

"I use conjured clothes when I'm fighting. Saves on expensive replacements. If you ever become an adventurer, always spend the most money on underwear. It's modesty's last line of defence. That barrier I mention prevented me from using my conjured gear. You saw me put it back on when I overcame the barrier."

"You have a lot of scars."

"Yes."

"Where did they really come from?"

"Fighting the Builder, mostly."

"Lots of people fought the Builder cult. They didn't end up covered in scars."

"I didn't say the Builder cult. I said the Builder."

"As in, personally?"

"Again, complicated. But yes."

"I thought the Builder was some kind of weird god."

"More or less."

"How do you fight something like that and live?"

"You don't."

"Right, I forgot. You have ways around death."

"Yes."

"Do you die a lot?"

"Not that often. More than most."

He plucked a piece of card the size of a large envelope out of the air, stepped closer and held it out for her to take. She looked it over. It was a certification from the Church of Death confirming four deaths for Jason Asano, current status: alive.

"You have a certificate?" she asked, looking up from it to his amused face.

He was closer now and she could smell him. That enticing fresh spring aroma, strange set against the earthy, acrid stench of the city. She held out the certificate for him to take back and he did, their hands lingering briefly when they touched. Their eyes met and then broke apart as they both averted their gaze. He pushed it into the air, where it vanished.

"The Adventure Society can be pedantic about that kind of thing," he told her. "Due diligence, you know? They don't like it when their members turn out to be undead abominations, so they check."

"Sure."

Unable to look directly at him for a moment, she spotted Valk Vohl, nervously edging closer after putting down his load. Jason followed her gaze to look at the man, who took the chance to speak.

"Mr Asano," he said, his voice hesitant. "I wanted to thank you for saving my life during the battle. And for not killing my family before the battle."

Jason looked Valk up and down.

"I remember you," Jason said. "You were here during the battle. Fighting to protect the bunker. Who are your family that I would kill them?"

"My name is Valk Vohl. My father—"

"Is Urman Vohl," Jason finished, glancing at Bellory. "I remember. And I remember your brother, coming for Bellory's tavern, looking for trouble. And later cowering in the bunker when he had the rank to defend it."

Jason paused, looking Valk up and down.

"The way you did."

Valk had the stain of hard work on his clothes and smeared into his skin. His face spoke to exhaustion, bags under the eyes. That was not a state easy for a silver-ranker to end up in. There was no question he'd been working relentlessly for weeks. Bellory watched as Jason took Valk's appearance in for a long, silent moment.

"You stood up when it mattered most," Jason said finally. "We all have a chance to be better than where we come from. To be better than the mistakes of our past. I need to believe that for myself, so it's not out of my way to believe it for you."

Jason sighed, glancing at Bellory again.

"Your father is going to forgive all the debts he is owed," he told Valk.

"He won't like that," Valk said.

"He'll like it less if I have to tell him in person. Ask your brother what happens when someone crosses me and I'm not a kitchen hand."

"I haven't seen my brother since the bunker was evacuated," Valk said. "We think he fled the city."

Jason closed his eyes. After a moment, he raised a hand and pointed.

"He's still in the city," Jason said and opened his eyes. "There's a displacement camp two kilometres that way. He's probably hiding his identity, which is easy enough amongst all those people."

"What would he be hiding from?" Valk asked. "The messengers are gone."

"From him," Bellory said, nodding at Jason. "Emresh and his goons gave Joh... Jason a beating. Then he saw what he can do when he's not pretending to be ordinary."

Valk nodded, remembering the sight of Jason draining the life force from a messenger. The dead messenger's scream that Valk only heard through his aura senses, not sure if he imagined it.

"I'll tell my father."

Jason turned to Bellory.

"Your debts will be cleared as well."

"I don't like being a helpless piece moved around in a game between powerful people who don't care if I'm knocked off the board," she said.

Jason nodded.

"The inability to fight for your own fate is a harsh reality," he said. "And sympathy from me on that is quite hypocritical. Fighting over my fate is all I seem to do, and it's been pointed out that I don't always allow others the same luxury. But helping is better than not, even if I am high-handed about it. And while you could rightly accuse me of many things, not caring isn't one of them. There will always be someone to tell you that you don't matter, but you do. To me, yes, but also, you just do. You matter."

"It probably won't help anyway," Bellory said. "Someone will come along and exploit all this once there's money to be made again. Take our land somehow and charge us to live on it. If it's not Urman Vohl, it will be someone like him."

"I'm no economist, and definitely not a politician," Jason said. "But I know someone. She has the skill set to help you."

"You mean the princess," Valk said. "The one from the Storm Kingdom."

"She's not a princess," Jason corrected. "Not right now. Technically. But yes. Shade, please ask Zara to keep an eye on land exploitation during the recovery."

"Of course, Mr Asano."

Bellory and Valk looked around for the source of the voice, having sensed no other presence. Jason offered no explanation.

"It was you," Bellory accused. "You had my loan refinanced."

"I didn't want to give you a handout," he said. "Just a chance to control your own fate a little."

"It wasn't just you," Valk told her. "Everyone in the entertainment district with debts to my father got the same deal."

"I told you not to go after Urman Vohl," she told Jason.

"I didn't," Jason said. "I sent a princess to do it."

"You sent a princess."

"She has bit of a crush on me."

Bellory let out an exhausted, disbelieving laugh.

"You weren't kidding about complicated, were you?"

"I was not," he said with a warm smile. "I'm going to go now. I have to catch up with my friends. I am glad to see that you came through that attack alive, Bellory."

"Thank you for making sure I did," Bellory said. "If monsters had come into that bunker instead of you, or if that messenger..."

Bellory shook her head, not completing the thought.

"I'm an adventurer," Jason said. "Protecting people from bad things is what we do."

He turned to look at Valk.

"Try to stop your father from being one of those bad things, Mr Vohl."

Valk nodded, wisely remaining silent.

"Will I see you again?" Bellory asked.

Jason turned his gaze back to her. "Do you want to?"

She didn't answer immediately, giving it some thought.

"No," she said finally. "I know that sounds ungrateful, but your complications could destroy someone like me without anyone even noticing."

Jason gave a slight, sad nod.

"It's not ungrateful," he told her. "It's smart. Which makes me all the sadder that we won't meet again."

He turned back to Valk.

"And you, Mr Vohl, should work very hard to make sure that we don't meet again either."

Jason's shadow rose from the ground behind him, taking on depth and substance as it assumed the shape of a person made from darkness. Jason held Bellory's gaze, his smile sad as he stepped back into the shadow, and vanished. The shadow then slid into the shadow of the wall and also disappeared. Bellory and Valk looked at one another before Bellory shrugged.

"I guess we get back to work," she said.

39

FAITH IS THE BANE OF INTELLECT

JASON JOINED HIS TEAM AS THEY PASSED BY A WORSHIP SQUARE. THE temples surrounding it were in better condition than most of the city's buildings, but not through any respect for the gods. The messengers had no compunction about defiling temples, but their objective had been mass casualties by breaching the bunkers shielding the city populace. The bunkers were not situated near the worship squares, leaving the latter relatively intact, although no part of the city had gone entirely unscathed.

All of the temples displayed signs of damage, but it did not stop the gods from showing themselves in force to offer solace and inspiration. This was backed up by their various clergy, found pitching in with recovery efforts throughout the city. The square was thronged with people and a half-dozen gods were present, their aura glorious but diminished so as to not be harmful.

Of Jason's many instances of soul damage, the first significant one came from a group of gods imposing their presence on him without such care. After he recovered, the result had been a toughening of his soul and an echo of divinity that had helped make his aura more intimidating. Realising that was their intention had not made the experience any more pleasant, and he had been a magical being. To normal-rankers, the uncontrolled aura of a gold-ranker could kill them, let alone that of a god.

As they moved past the worship square without going in, Melody, still under Sophie's careful watch, started muttering incoherently to herself. It was something happening more and more often as the dissonance between her magically brainwashed beliefs and the obviousness of their falsehood impacted her mental stability.

Jason and his companions continued through the city, taking in the misery of destruction and the optimism of unity. Old rivalries and grudges were put aside, at least for the moment, in a near-universal display of solidarity. Reaching the city walls, the group passed through a diligent security check at the gate. Their prisoner, Melody, caused questions, but their status as adventurers and the fact that they were leaving, not entering, smoothed things out swiftly enough. The checks upon their airborne entry had been far more rigorous.

Outside of the city, they quickly found the other adventurers' campsite. Along with the adventurers foreign to Yaresh, many of the local ones had set up camp. There was a temporary Adventure Society outpost as it was much easier to deploy from outside the city under current conditions.

A huge area of rainforest had been cleared out and tiled over using magic, essentially recreating the parking lot for giant vehicular homes that was now the city's logistics hub. This version was a lot nicer, being fully tiled rather than stone slabs set into mud. There were also patches of rainforest left intact and even cultivated, making it more like a pleasant park with tiled pathways winding between massive parking spots and tropical garden beds. It made Jason think of a trailer park for the super-rich, with people with multi-million-dollar recreation vehicles.

It was impossible to miss Emir's place, his cloud palace at full sprawl. Its five domed towers rose above all the other vehicles in glorious sunset colours. The group made their way through the park, nodding greetings to the many adventurers they passed.

Sophie, Jason, Arabelle and Carlos sat in armchairs made of clouds on a terrace, high on one of Emir's palace towers. Despite the excellent view over the rainforest, their expressions were grim as they discussed Melody.

"My concern is that my attempts to bring out Melody's original personality have done more harm than good," Arabelle said. "My success has only served to pit Melody's mind against itself."

"No amount of therapy can break down magically enforced indoctrination," Jason said. "We need to deal with that before we can move forward."

"For ongoing treatment, yes," Arabelle said. "But in the immediacy, we need to resolve the dissonance before it causes permanent harm."

"What we're dealing with is difficult," Carlos said, "but this disassociation between the baseline mentality and the influenced one may well be an important step. I suspect that it will be a standard stage in the finalised treatment methodology."

"You think that isolating the influenced mentality will assist in eliminating that influence?" Arabelle asked.

"I do," Carlos said with a firm nod. "Especially given that our initial treatment regime will almost certainly rely on Jason as a shortcut. From what Jason has described, his power is near-infinite inside his soul domain. But to make changes that will hold up outside of his domain, he requires a certain amount of knowledge for delicate processes."

"Inorganics are easy," Jason said. "I've been cranking out metals for Gary to play with for a while now. Living things are harder. I've been running some experiments with pot plants and things… haven't gone well. I've been studying a lot since then, but you're both healers. You know how much work it will take to get even the fundamentals down properly."

"I gave him material to go through," Carlos said. "In the meantime, I've been working on isolating the physical aspects of the mind manipulation, the way you've been isolating the mental, Arabelle. I believe that all of our efforts will be required to get this done."

"But for now," Jason said, "we want to take Melody into my soul space. I believe that I can suppress the effects of the brainwashing without harm, at least while she's in there."

"That's all well and good," Sophie said, "but how do we get her into your soul space? The old restrictions on entering the portal might be gone, but it's still a portal. You can't force anyone through one."

"A not inconsiderable concern," Arabelle agreed. "I can tell you now that Melody is likely to resist any active attempt to overcome her…"

She glanced at Jason.

"…I still don't like the term brainwashing."

"It's inaccurate since she no longer has one," Carlos pointed out. "Like any well-trained silver-ranker, her body has removed it and taken over its functions more holistically to remove a critical weakness."

"If you've got a better term, go for it," Jason said. "I just think that 'influence' is too vague and 'the physiological and mental effects of the Flames of Redemption' is too wordy."

"Thus, my use of your inaccurate but illustrative term," Arabelle said. "As I was saying, any attempt by Melody to actively overcome her *brain-washing* triggers what amounts to a defensive response from Flames of Redemption's influence. This triggers the episodes that we've all witnessed."

Sophie moved to the terrace balustrade and leaned on it with both hands as she looked out.

"The episodes are becoming more and more frequent," she said.

"Yes," Arabelle agreed. "I believe that any attempt to get Melody into Jason's soul space for treatment will trigger an episode and her refusal to use the portal. This leaves us with two potential approaches that I can see. One is to simply lie. We've moved Melody through portals before and she's gone willingly. The problem is that she's smart and Jason's soul realm portal is visually distinct from his shadow portals. At the very least, she'll ask questions. If we don't have very convincing answers, I think she'll go on the defensive."

"If that goes wrong, the odds of ever getting her through shrink considerably," Jason said.

"That's unacceptable," Carlos said, sitting forward in his chair, clenching and unclenching his hands. "Your soul realm offers us the chance to circumvent problems that have stopped research like mine dead for centuries. The number of people who could be helped by—"

"I know, Carlos," Arabelle said, cutting him off. "I wanted to put that option forward, but it's not the approach I'm advocating."

"Then what is?" Sophie asked.

"Playing to the weakness of the brainwashing," Arabelle said.

"Which is what?" Carlos asked. "I've been studying this for months and—"

"Carlos," Jason said. "Maybe give her a chance to answer before interrupting to ask why she hasn't?"

Carlos turned a glare on Jason before visibly relaxing, sitting back in his chair with a nod.

"Sorry," he said.

"No worries," Jason said. "Passion is good. Just make sure you use it rather than it using you, yeah?"

Neither mentioned the incident where Carlos harangued Jason to be an experimental subject when Jason had barely woken from a coma. Compared to Jason throwing Carlos across the room with his aura, Carlos backing down was considerable progress.

"What is the weakness in the brainwashing you're talking about?" Sophie asked Arabelle.

"The Flames of Redemption, the magical substance used to alter people by the Order of Redeeming Light, works differently than other, comparable processes," Arabelle explained. "Carlos, this is your area."

Carlos nodded.

"While the Order of Redeeming Light holds that the flames are divinely sourced, that is only partially true. The flames are an extreme modification of lesser vampirism, and I believe that part of that modification comes from Disguise, the god who was pretending to be Purity."

"The best information we have is that the order was founded within the Church of Purity only after Disguise took on Purity's mantle," Arabelle said. "Whitewashing vampirism and masking it as the power of redemption falls right into the methodology of Disguise."

"The Flames of Redemption are distinct from vampirism and other similar transformation curses and effects," Carlos said. "Most of those cause such fundamental transformations that any essence abilities are no longer useable. The conversion process the Builder cult uses is much the same. They tend to trade off the loss of essence abilities with a rank increase, but it is still usually an overall loss in power. Essence abilities are just too strong and too versatile."

"My mother still has her essence abilities," Sophie pointed out.

"Exactly," Carlos said. "That's what makes the Flames of Redemption different. The process to instil them is a lengthy and complex ritual, and the final result is a simultaneously lighter touch while also comprehensively altering the body. There are significant physiological changes— your mother is a human now, instead of her original celestine ancestry— but the primary change is in mentality. In many ways, it's a subtle change. It essentially plants one idea and everything else stems from that. It's almost elegant."

Sophie's face darkened and Arabelle winced.

"Bloke, maybe don't praise the craftsmanship of the evil god who brainwashed Sophie's mum."

Carlos also winced, realising what he'd said.

"My apologies, Miss Wexler. I'll just carry on with my explanation. I mentioned that mid-to-high rankers don't have brains and that their whole bodies take over the brain's function. The flames can't invade the soul to cause an inside-out, fundamental change in belief, so the mind must be changed by changing the body. And with no neatly contained brain to work on, a complex full-body alteration is required. Thus, the sophisti-cated nature of the change and the elaborate process to carry it out."

"I still don't see the weakness we're going to exploit," Sophie said.

"I think I do," Jason said. "Fundamentally, the Flames of Redemption alter the mind in one way: They instil an absolute and unshakeable faith in Purity. We've seen that. Purity not being Purity is common knowledge now and we've exposed Melody to that. But she always denies the truth, however apparent it becomes. We've even had to stop doing it because it keeps triggering her episodes."

"Yes," Arabelle said. "That absolutism is a safety mechanism against the kind of treatment I have been carrying out. It means that when a victim's reasoning comes into conflict with the brainwashing, the brain-washing goes from subtle to overt. A wall no amount of critical thought can overcome. The resulting dissonance causes the outbursts that we've all seen. Her faith is forced to override her normal sensibilities, almost to the point of having two minds."

"The brainwashing mostly employs Melody's normal mind," Jason said. "It just adds that one inviolable absolute: faith in a false god. But as any devout religious follower can tell you, their faith informs every part of their lives, from values to behaviour. Arabelle's therapy has effectively isolated the two aspects of her mind: the part that can examine things criti-cally, and the one with blind faith. The dissonance between them as the faith shuts down Melody's rational mind is the cause of Melody's episodes. Is that right?"

"Yes," Arabelle said. "Keep going."

Jason tried to avoid thinking of Rufus' mother—his own magical ther-apist—as a stern-but-sexy professor, and continued.

"That means that, hopefully, the brainwashed portions of Melody's mind are less able to rely on the rest of her when they're forced to freeze them out. We just need to get her faith response all riled up. If the only thing going through her head is 'Purity is real, Purity is real' on a loop it will override the critical thought she would otherwise apply to any manip-ulation on our part. We don't try to sneak Melody through the portal by tricking the brainwashing to not pay attention. We get the brainwashing to send her through by challenging her faith."

"And how do we do that?" Carlos asked.

"That's all me," Jason said. "Annoying the deeply faithful is kind of my thing."

"I was hoping for something a little more specific," Carlos said.

"It's easy," Jason assured him. "We just have to tell her that I'm more powerful than her god."

"And you think that's plausible enough that she'll go for it?" Carlos asked.

"Why wouldn't it?" Jason asked. "It's true. Kind of. In the right circumstances. From a certain perspective. Okay, it's not true, but I can probably fake it enough that it will trigger her need to demonstrate her faith. And that need…"

He nodded at Sophie.

"…is the weakness of her brainwashing. Its very nature is that one fundamental value, faith, overrides her intelligence. Faith is the bane of intellect. We use that."

"Jason, the gods can hear you," Carlos said. "You may want to clarify that you're speaking within this specific context."

Jason thought it over for a moment.

"No, I'll stand by it."

"How is it that the gods haven't struck you down yet?" Carlos asked.

"My working theory is that I'm too sexy."

Sophie went off to return to Melody while Carlos left to gather his research notes, leaving Jason and Arabelle alone. Jason got up from his chair and moved to the balustrade, occupying the space Sophie had left. Arabelle moved to stand next to him.

"You looked troubled," she said. "That's not just concern over Sophie's mother."

"No," he said. "I saw something, back in Rimaros. Someone tried to tell me something but they were stopped. The way it happened confused me at the time, but this conversation made me realise at least part of what they wanted to tell me. It's not the same, but I have an inkling of something."

"You're talking around it, Jason. I can't help you if you don't let me in."

He shook his head.

"Not this. I don't know enough, just guesses, really. Sufficient to do damage but not to do any good. Dawn might be the only person I could talk about this with, but she may know already. I'm pretty certain her boss won't let her tell me."

"That suggests you're talking about something on a dangerous scale, Jason."

"Oh, yes. I can't even imagine the ramifications if what I'm thinking is true, but I strongly suspect at least some version of it is. It explains so many things that didn't make sense to me before."

"What will you do about it?"

"Nothing. Not yet. I'm not even sure it matters anymore, and I don't have close to the power to keep looking into it. I might not until I've left diamond rank behind."

Arabelle let out a chortle.

"You know, when I'm treating people, talking about achieving diamond rank as if it's a given is usually a bad sign."

"We call it delusions of grandeur, back on Earth." He frowned, looking down. "Are delusions of normalcy a thing?"

Arabelle narrowed her eyes. "Where is that coming from?"

"You know I was roaming around under my false identity when we first came to Yaresh."

"I do."

"I saw someone today that I first met as John Miller. She got to see Jason Asano, dimension-hopping superhero warlock ninja. It's something I've done a bunch of times, but this felt different. Like I'd lost something. It used to be fun, you know? 'Hey, I've died a bunch of times.' 'Yeah, there's princesses everywhere and I got in a knife fight with a super god.' Why isn't it fun anymore?"

"Because it was only fun when you were an ordinary person surrounded by ridiculousness. Now you *are* the ridiculousness. Ordinary people now have crazy stories about the time they met Jason Asano."

Jason turned and looked at her, not speaking for a long time. Eventually, he turned his gaze back out off the balcony.

"Oh," he said quietly.

40
LISTING OFF ANIMALS

Sophie, Jason and Melody were in a blank room in Emir's cloud palace. Carlos, Arabelle and Emir were watching through a wall only transparent from the outside. Even knowing that her mother was more unstable than ever, Sophie was astounded at how quickly Jason sent Melody into a frenzy. She had already attacked them once, Sophie deflecting her strikes harmlessly. Melody eventually calmed a little and went back to verbal assaults.

"It's not going to work," Jason told Sophie as he gestured at his portal. It was the only object in the room that was otherwise blank and empty. "She's seen the truth, even if she can't admit it to herself. There's nothing we can do about that."

"What truth?" Sophie asked.

"That her false god isn't as powerful as I am."

Even knowing that Jason was putting up an act, Sophie was astounded at the man's gall. Not only did he look every inch as if he believed it, but his body language seemed astounded that it wasn't obvious.

"Even for you, that's arrogant."

"Not if I'm right."

Melody came to the boil as the other two ignored her, storming up to Jason.

"Your blasphemy—"

"Is easy enough to prove baseless," Jason said, cutting her off.

Melody staggered back as Jason unleashed the full power of his aura. He hid nothing, from the touch of the gods to the echoes of his battles with the Builder to the power of his soul realm, hidden behind a threshold. Sophie wasn't subjected to the brunt of it but still backed up to the wall herself.

Jason stepped forward as Melody stepped back, mentally reeling from Jason's aura barrage. She soon had her back to the wall with Jason standing in front of her. He was too short to loom, but he didn't need to. His presence was visceral, his aura almost a physical thing as it pressed against Melody. While she had backed off, however, Melody looked anything but intimidated, snarling like an animal, even snapping her teeth at him.

Sophie didn't recognise her mother. This wasn't the sharp woman she had come to know over the last couple of months. It wasn't the bold woman who went toe to toe with Jason in physical and verbal combat. This was the thing inside her, the taint that had desecrated her mind. Now it had suppressed that mind almost entirely, leaving little more than cruel, savage instinct. This was the so-called Flames of Purification, their true nature laid bare.

"Here's the truth, Melody," Jason said, his voice as calm as her face was wild. "I'm here for one reason: to rip the faith right out of you. I'm going to do that, and I don't think your god has the strength to stop me. Not in my domain. If you go through that portal, I can shut your god's power down like it was nothing. Your god is a fraud and you know it, even if you won't admit it to even yourself. But you know, deep down, that he's an illusion. A disguise. And through that portal, he's not even that. He's vapour, washed away by even the gentlest breeze."

"If you believe that, then you're a fool," Melody snarled.

Jason laughed in her face.

"Yes, I'm a fool," he said. "I never denied it. Which means that your god can't even stand up to a fool. You think your faith is so grand, but I can crush it as easily as I can break an egg in my fist. Your god is a lie. An obvious façade, depthless and impotent."

"YOU KNOW NOTHING!"

"You can say what you like," Jason said softly. "If you lack the faith to put that faith to the test, then all you're doing is screaming into the dark, shrinking from the fear that you're wrong. That your god really is an empty shell."

Melody raised her arms to hammer on Jason, but he gave his aura a physical force and pinned her to the wall. He frowned as he looked her over, watching her struggle.

"You're too weak," he observed. "I bet it's because your faith isn't the real deal. Someone slapped it together from recycled vampirism and shoved it inside you. Normally, something like that takes away your powers, but there's no denying you're a monster someone made when your essence powers go away. I guess even brainwashing can only go so far. I think when that poison inside you is taking greater control, the limitations of the source material start coming through. You can't use your strength the way you normally could. Can you even use an essence ability right now? I'll wait."

Melody said nothing, glaring venom at Jason.

"Wow, you really can't," he said. "I guess that's what happens when your faith is as fake as your god."

"My god has power beyond your imagining."

"Is that so?" Jason asked lightly.

His presence in the room surged. Sophie let out a ragged breath and the cloud-substance of the walls rippled like the surface of a pond. He brought his head close, whispering in Melody's ear.

"I don't fear your empty god because I don't have to," he gloated. "You know I'm right. You can feel my power, rattling your bones. Shaking your soul. And where is he? Your god is weak, and this is only a taste. A paltry echo of what I can do, almost as empty as your sad little deity."

"You are nothing before my god."

He stepped back and laughed.

"But I'm not before your god," he said. "You're before me, and your god is conspicuously absent. You see, everyone knows the truth now. Purity is dead and has been for a while. Someone else has been pulling a *Weekend at Bernie's,* but now the game is up."

"Spitting nonsense won't help you, Asano."

"My track record says otherwise, but you're right. Out here, our words mean nothing. The only way we can prove if your faith is real is if you come into my house, my domain. There, either your god has the power to sustain your faith, or your god is nothing. But you won't, will you? Because you know I'm right and that your god is just the echo of a power long dead."

He turned to look at the portal.

"That is your leap of faith. The only place you can prove me wrong."

He gave another mocking laugh.

"I'll be waiting, but I'm taking a book because we both know the truth. If you follow, you won't be able to deny it anymore, even to yourself."

Jason moved through the portal, Sophie watching her mother's expression. For a moment, something recognisable appeared, a spark of doubt. It immediately triggered a furious snarl of zeal and Melody stormed through the portal after Jason. A short time later, a wall vanished to admit Emir, Arabelle and Carlos to the room.

"I was worried he was going too hard," Emir said. "Being too obvious."

"No," Arabelle said. "Zealots, like any extremists, have various weaknesses. Denying the validity of their faith is one of the biggest. They'd rather be martyrs than let their beliefs be stepped on. That's a generalisation, of course, but it applies here. Jason pulled out the power influencing her and drilled on that faith so it kept shutting out Melody's rational mind. He made the thing that stops us from saving Melody the tool that gives us a chance to."

"And only the beginning of who we save, I hope," Carlos said. "Jason's realisation that Melody loses her original strength if the influence grows too controlling is interesting. It may be a means to validate my ideas about isolating the influence in order to identify and extract it. We should go in."

Arabelle looked to Sophie, still shaken. Sophie nodded, her usual stern expression snapping into place. She marched to the portal and stepped through.

The portal opened to a large grassy area in Jason's soul realm, the size of a sports field. Jason watched Melody as she came through the portal; he saw her face as she sensed the nature of his soul realm. She turned to him with ferocity in her eyes, but when she opened her mouth, no words came out.

"I made sound stop existing around you," he told her. "My voice probably sounds strange. That's because you aren't hearing it. I'm triggering your body's ability to process sensory information to make it perceive my words directly."

Melody moved to lunge at him but instead floated into the air, arms and legs flailing helplessly.

"I'm going to keep you there for the moment," he told her. "If you want to get down, I'd try prayer. That's why you're here, right? To prove your god is more powerful than me?"

Melody continued to rant silently, thrashing her limbs ineffectually.

"You'll have to forgive my taking the chance to villain monologue," he told her amiably. "I haven't gone full chuuni like this in a while and it's the little things that make life worth living, you know? So, please bear with me while I explain my evil plan. Oh, hold on. I need to set the scene."

Metal industrial-style walls rose from the ground, which itself turned from grass to concrete. Metal catwalks and large vats of chemicals appeared. A high ceiling formed overhead, strung with patchy fluorescent lighting that left the dingy warehouse full of shadowy nooks. A winch lowered a chain that wrapped around Melody, no longer suspended by levitation. Jason stepped back as a pit opened up underneath her, filled with molten metal. The radiant heat alone would have killed an iron-ranker and done a bronze-ranker significant harm, even with their resistance to non-magical damage. The pit was massive and the back of a lava crocodile surfaced briefly before slipping back into the liquid.

A watch appeared on Melody's wrist.

"It's got a laser in it," Jason explained. "Oh, a laser is… well, you'll figure it out or you won't. Anyway, evil plan. You probably didn't understand what I was saying about the body processing sensory information, but I've been studying medical texts. In preparation for today, in fact. Pallimustus has a surprisingly solid foundation of knowledge when it comes to human physiology, although it's still cavemen with sticks compared to what Earth has. Earth is the planet I come from, by the way. But, what I just said is only true when it comes to baseline humans. It'll hold pretty well for iron-rankers, but once you get into late bronze and silver, the rules get very different. Magic, you know?"

He rubbed his chin thoughtfully.

"Now, once magic gets involved, the knowledge base on physiology on Pallimustus gets a lot better. Healing magic, as it turns out, has a lot more to it than casting *Cure Light Wounds* and walking away. That works for your garden variety injuries, sure. Stabbing and whatnot. But magic can do some seriously nasty stuff to people, and I'd know. I damn near killed your daughter once and I barely touched her. That was at iron rank.

Trying to heal through what I do to people now? I have afflictions that make the healing kill you."

Jason sighed and shook his head.

"No wonder these speeches always get interrupted. Establishing context alone takes forever. Anyway, I've been studying healing magic theory to get a better sense of how magical bodies work. You see, I can do just about anything here, but if I don't know what I'm doing, it goes tits-up once you take it outside of my private little realm. I can rip that Flames of Redemption crap out of you right now, but you'd drop dead the second you left this place. Until I know how to do it right, the cancer stays in."

He shrugged.

"That's why I've been doing some book-learning. Once we figure out the details, we're going to help you and people like you. You might even be the key to curing things like vampirism, how good would that be? I don't need to be a total expert in healing magic, thankfully. I have people for that. But I need a solid grounding if we're going to make things work. Inorganic stuff is much easier than people. I've been making my friend Gary all kinds of metals to…"

He trailed off and shook his head again.

"I'm losing the thread here. I should have written this down, but I think there needs to be a certain level of improvisation in a proper villain speech, you know. A certain rough authenticity that plays off the unhinged charisma. Is that immodest to say? I'm sure it's fine. Anyway, the point is that I've been working with this bloke Carlos to try and get that stuff out of you for good. Sadly, that's not what's happening today. Carlos hasn't done enough research and I haven't done enough study to reach that point."

He looked to the portal, now set into one of the walls.

"Today, we're just going to try turning the external influence inside you off without removing it. We'll see where that gets us. Talk to the real Melody, whatever's left after years of having that artificial faith twisting her head around. I think we've gotten close already, which is why things have gone a bit wrong. You keep pushing her down, you being that Flames of Redemption crap. Are you sentient on your own? Can you think for yourself or are you just a mindless parasite? Maybe we'll get some answers today."

Jason looked at the portal again.

"Still not here," he mused. "Okay, I'm going to set this chain to slowly lower you down and then walk away assuming everything went to plan... oh, here they are."

Sophie, Arabelle, Carlos and Emir arrived through the portal and looked around at the creepy villain warehouse.

"Jason..." Arabelle said in a tone of long-suffering admonition.

"What?" Jason asked, the image of boyish innocence.

"What is this?"

"What is what?"

"This place?"

"I have no idea. It was like this when I got here."

"Really?"

"Yep. I think Gary might have set it up. Look at all that molten metal. He's probably taking a stab at industrial smithing."

"You're claiming Gary did this."

"Yeah, that kooky leonid. What will he get up to next?"

"So, there aren't iron sharks swimming around in that molten metal."

"Absolutely not."

"Or fire piranhas."

"I can, in all honesty, assure you that there are no piranhas of any kind."

"Lava crocodiles."

"Look, we can stand here listing off animals all day, but we're here for a reason."

41

I'M GOING TO CHANGE THE LAWS
OF REALITY

As soon as she entered Jason's soul realm, Sophie was blasted with heat. They were in some kind of industrial facility with a massive foundry pit of molten iron and her mother dangling over it from a chain. Sophie's ire rose as she watched Arabelle and Jason banter. She finally exploded as she flashed to Jason in a blur, grabbing his shirt and hoisting him into the air.

"Does everything have to be a joke to you?" she growled.

The amusement left his expression as he looked down at her from where she held him in the air.

"I've tried being serious all the time," he told her. "It didn't work out. The more I—"

"THIS ISN'T ABOUT YOU!" she bellowed and tossed him hard onto the ground.

Jason looked up at her, eyes wide with shock before his expression crumpled with remorse. The room around them dissolved into nothing, replaced with a grassy field the size of a football field, ringed with trees. The chains holding Melody dissolved and she floated into a chair that appeared under her, falling into it, unconscious. A glass box appeared around the chair, preventing her from rushing off. The radiant heat of the vanished foundry pit dissipated.

"I'm sorry, Sophie," he said softly.

"As am I," Arabelle added. "I have worked with Jason a long time and

I sometimes indulge him more than I should. He has a habit of affecting the behaviour of those around him; those of us that should know better have no excuse. I apologise, Miss Wexler."

Sophie glanced at Arabelle, giving her a curt nod, then realised Jason was no longer at her feet. He was standing a few feet away from her without having tripped her senses.

"I can sense the thing inside Melody," Jason said, neither his habitual half-smirk nor his usual tone of amusement in evidence. "The fact that the influence on her hasn't penetrated her soul makes it fairly easy to detect. It feels like a waterproof ball, caked in mud. I could strip it out of her right now, but it would shred her body. I don't know enough to rebuild it."

"Healing magic uses the soul as a model, right?" Sophie asked. "Can't you just use that to make her a body without that stuff inside it?"

"No," Jason said. "I can't access her soul to do that. Healing magic is intrinsically benevolent. A soul recognises that and works with it. I am a lot of things, but innately harmless and helpful is not one of them."

"Can't she let you use her soul for that?"

"No. The conscious mind requires considerable effort to overcome the inherent protectiveness of the soul. I saved all the messengers here by accessing their souls. There was one who, knowing that it was life and death, failed to overcome their inherent instinct and grant me access. At the cost of dying."

"Melody has had her soul under siege for years," Arabelle said. "There is no way it will let Jason in, even if her conscious mind recognises that she should."

"So, right now, the only option is torturing her soul until she capitulates," Jason said. "Which I flatly refuse to do. The Builder did it to me and I did it to one messenger. I don't know that I'll ever wash off the stains from either event."

"I know that Jason giving us a shortcut is the only reason any of this is possible," Carlos said. "But now we have a path forward, we should avoid any other shortcuts we don't have to take. Going slowly and being as sure as we can of every move before we make it is what we need to do. Miss Wexler, it's how we give your mother the best long-term prospects."

"There's no getting around that the trauma she has been in and is going through right now will be with Melody forever," Arabelle said. "Even if—when—we extract this thing inside her, the physical recovery is only the start. Sophie, you need to be aware that the effects of what she's been through will affect her mind the rest of her life. There will be years of recovery and permanent after-effects."

Sophie nodded.

"I've seen you working with Jason for years," Sophie said to Arabelle. "I know what my mother is going through is worse, but you've helped Jason, and he turned out alright."

"Thank you," Jason said brightly.

"Even if he is insensitive, self-impressed, self-important and too busy being what he thinks is clever to consider how his actions hurt the people around him."

Jason opened his mouth to retort and then stopped himself. After a moment, he let her words stand and returned to the previous topic.

"I need to learn healing magic theory," he said. "I don't have any, but in this place, I can have all the healing magic I like. The problem is, I don't get the instinctive grasp of how a type of magic works that comes from getting it as an essence ability. That's not a huge problem if I want to throw around lightning magic, but we're talking about putting people back together. I don't want to see what happens when they leave this place and I've got the healing wrong."

"Fortunately, all Jason needs is a solid foundation of knowledge," Carlos said. "The intricate details fall to me."

"And when will this study be happening?" Sophie asked. "Jason, we've been out adventuring for weeks. Months, almost. I've seen you cooking, fighting monsters, taking naps. I haven't seen you studying."

"You've all seen the replicas of me in here," Jason said. "Meditation, training swordsmanship, etc. You've sparred with copies of me. One of the buildings here is a fairly impressive library where I have a small army of avatars studying all day, every day. Mostly astral magic, that being my specialty, in a futile attempt to catch up to Clive's expertise. Since Carlos first proposed what we're doing now I added healing magic as well."

"Are you saying that you can just learn as much as you like by having copies of yourself all learning things at the same time?" Emir asked.

"I'd been hoping that was exactly what I could do," Jason said. "Alas, even magic has its limits. A silver-rank spirit attribute makes for a mind with powerful information retention and memory capacity, but there is only so much I can take in at a time. I tried absorbing too much at once and it left me unconscious for three days, and loopy in the head for weeks. Plus, the information didn't stick."

"You never told me that," Carlos said.

"That was when things were strained between us after you wanted to run experiments on the best ways to kill me," Jason said. "I was convalescing after I overtaxed myself portalling out of the underwater complex. I had a lot of time to do things like study."

"You should have told me. The potential for self-damage—"

"My team has a healer, Carlos," Jason cut him off. "He and Arabelle monitored me carefully throughout that time. They knew what I was doing before I did it and were waiting to look after me if anything went wrong. Which it did, and they were ready."

"Oh," Carlos said, deflated.

"The way it works is that I keep the copies of myself isolated from my mind until I absorb their knowledge. I stagger it, absorbing the knowledge of one avatar at a time until I hit the limit. It still allows me to absorb massive amounts of new information and the fruits of various training, none of which takes me any time. Hundreds of avatars means that for every hour that passes, hundreds of training and study hours take place. And all the while, I'm cooking or adventuring or, yes, napping. The only limit is how much my mind can take in before it starts burning out."

"Like the limitations on skill-book learning," Emir said. "You can only use so many skill books at once before they stop working and you do yourself harm."

"Exactly," Jason said. "It's pretty much an overcomplicated skill-book system. But we're getting side-tracked. What we're doing today is—hopefully—taking the first step in learning to extract this taint from Sophie's mother and others like her."

"Yes," Carlos said, perking back up. "Jason, now that you've examined her with all the power you have here, do you think you can suppress the Flames of Redemption without causing any harm?"

"Yes," Jason said. "In this place, I'm not bound to the usual rules of… anything. Not so long as I don't need to remain true outside of this realm. I can resurrect the dead. Absorb all that knowledge we were talking about in an instant. I suspect I could even…"

He stopped himself.

"Nope, not going to talk about that. But I can do things here that violate the laws of not just physical reality but even the laws of magic. I can sense the influence the stuff inside Melody is having. I don't understand what it's doing, or how, but I can make it stop doing it."

"And what if she needs that?" Sophie asked. "What if the stuff they put in her, the fires of whateverwhocares, is something she needs to survive now?"

"That shouldn't be an issue," Jason said. "I'm not going to take it away or change it. Or change her."

"Then how will you suppress the influence?" Emir asked.

"I'm going to change the laws of reality so that the Flames of Redemption influencing people isn't a thing. Think of it like throwing someone into the air by changing the universe to swap what up and down are."

The others all looked at him incredulously.

"What?" he asked. "Look, even if that approach creates unanticipated problems, I can undo everything. I can't fix any problems she came in here with if I don't know how, but I can revert her to the exact state she was in when she arrived. She'll forget anything that happened, although her soul would retain some emotional echoes. I can't touch that."

"Can you do that to all of us?" Emir asked. "Could you just reset us to the moment we entered and wipe our memories of whatever happened here?"

"Uh… no," Jason said unconvincingly, then quickly moved on. "What I can do is stop her from dying, even when something should definitely kill her. I can just turn off death long enough for someone who knows what they're doing to heal her body."

"What do you mean, turn off death?" Arabelle asked.

"I mean turn it off. As a concept. It's probably a bad idea unless I really need to. Easier just to bring someone back by reverting their state to when they first arrived here, still alive. As long as the soul hasn't floated off into the astral by then, of course. Once the Reaper gets it, it's out of my hands."

"Is it possible to trap a soul here?" Carlos asked. "Prevent it from leaving?"

Jason's face darkened.

"Yes, Carlos," he said, "but I can't just grab it and hold it. Souls are the ultimate rule-breakers, and I can't directly control one, even here. Gods and great astral beings are just as powerless, but there are indirect methods we can all use quite easily. The vorger, for example, turn people's own bodies into immortal prisons of twisted flesh. I could do that. Wouldn't even matter if the body was dead since I can just bring it back. Or even make a whole new body; it doesn't matter. As long as I only need to keep them in my realm, I can do whatever I like. But I don't like what I just described, Carlos. I don't like it at all. What the vorger do to people is unconscionable. My team and I spent half a year hunting down and freeing their victims. But I am curious as to your interest in trapping souls, Carlos."

"I was just asking," Carlos said. "Academic curiosity."

"There are some things you don't do, Carlos, whatever the payoff. I could lure a few hundred people in here, break them down to their component parts and rummage through what's left. I'd learn all I need to know about how bodies work in an afternoon, save myself all that trouble with avatars and the library. But I don't do that. You have a bad habit of throwing ethics out the window the moment you think it can further your research, Carlos. That's not a good look for a priest of the Healer."

"I know," Carlos said softly. "It's something my god and I talk about a lot."

"We keep getting off track," Arabelle scolded. "We need to stop following tangents."

"I disagree," Emir said. "Slow and deliberate was what we're going for, right? Jason's capabilities here are critical to what we're doing. I think that interrogating what Jason is capable of in this place is critical. We shouldn't wait for something to go wrong before finding out what he can, cannot or will not do."

Arabelle nodded, acknowledging the point.

Jason turned from Carlos, floating away like a messenger.

"I agree with Emir," he said. "I think we might be ready to begin, though."

"How do we start?" Sophie asked. "What do we do?"

"I'll suppress the effects and see if there are any adverse reactions," Jason told her. "If that works out, I'll wake her up. I think it's best if only you and Arabelle are here when Melody comes to. Emir, Carlos and I will absent ourselves, although I'll project a duplicate of Melody for Carlos to examine magically. It will accurately reflect any changes happening to the real Melody."

"You can duplicate my mother?" Sophie asked. "Like those avatars of you?"

"Only her body," Jason explained. "I can't recreate her soul, so the body will have no animus. It won't do anything. It will be closer to a reflection in a mirror than a person. Something for Carlos to examine so he can leave your mother alone for the moment. That way, Carlos can get his data and you can have as much privacy as I can offer."

"I'll need some time and a space to set up the tools and rituals for the examination," Carlos said.

A building rose from the ground at the edge of the massive clearing and Carlos vanished.

"Emir and I will walk over there while Carlos sets up," Jason said. "Is there anything you would like before I go?"

"Some furniture," Arabelle said. "And some food."

Jason nodded and furniture made of cloud stuff appeared. He conjured a few armchairs, a corner couch and a dining table with three seats. Then he made a large wooden gazebo with a round table in the middle with three dining chairs. A long side table appeared in the gazebo and was populated with a massive buffet.

"It's not just empty mirage food," Jason said. "I've infused it with raw mana, so it's really a pile of spirit coin variants that don't taste like licking a car battery."

"Thank you," Arabelle said.

Jason nodded and walked off, Emir beside him.

"I don't suppose you could get me something to eat?" Emir asked.

"I already have," Jason told him.

Emir lifted his hand to find it holding a sandwich.

"I didn't feel you put that there," he said. "That's a little disturbing."

"You don't have to eat it."

"I didn't say I wasn't going to eat it."

EXACTLY WHERE I WANT TO BE

ALTHOUGH HIS BODY WAS SITTING WITH EMIR AND CARLOS, JASON'S attention was on other places within his soul realm. There was only so much privacy Jason could offer Sophie and her mother, but he forcibly moved his attention away from where she and Arabelle were looking after Melody. Because of how his mind and perception worked in this place, he was able to compartmentalise the memories, the same way his avatars learned. He could access them later if necessary, a quirk of how his mind and perception worked in this place.

Jason distracted himself by focusing on Marek Nior Vargas, leader of Jason's messenger prisoners. The man was yet again working on plans for his uprising against the astral kings, his timeline measured not in months and years but decades and centuries. Tera Jun Casta, the messenger whose soul had been forcibly altered by Jason, was pretending not to listen as she stood at a remove.

Tera was still railing against her fate, regularly screaming bile at Marek and Jason. Marek, she yelled at in person, while her wild tirades against Jason were usually screamed into the sky. It was increasingly performative, Jason was sure, although the heavy self-deception made it hard to read the truth from her aura.

He hoped that her listening in on Marek and the other messengers was a sign that she was finding some kind of equanimity. Indoctrinated from birth, she felt that Jason had stolen her from grace and placed her amongst heretics. He hoped that she would come around on the nature of the astral kings and recognize the bondage in which she had been held, accepting that she would need to move on. His fear was that, once she stopped clinging to the shards of her old life, she would be an empty vessel, too broken to be refilled.

Tera Jun Casta was easy to think of as an enemy, yet she had been through more than any of them. Her soul branded, raised on lies and exploited her entire life. She was having so much trouble because her very sense of self had been constructed from the mechanisms of her oppression. Then, her liberation had come in the form of the worst violation, Jason himself torturing her soul until she opened it up to him that he might meddle with it. The fact that he had used that chance to set her free was immaterial to the trauma he had inflicted in the process.

Jason frowned at the thought of all the trauma around him, from Tera to Melody to himself. Those with the most power were the ones who did the most damage; astral kings, gods and great astral beings all were the agents of their misery. Their machinations hurt so many, and Jason knew that he was not absolved from being grouped among them. How many had been hurt by his decisions back on Earth? Excuses were easy to come by with a world to save, but how much collateral damage could he ignore? For all the people he saved, how many died because he chose one path over another? Thoughtlessly accepted a battle without regard for civilian casualties?

Jason had made a lot of hard, necessary choices, and he would make more in the days and years to come. He was no longer so naïve as to believe that he could do so without innocent people getting hurt along the way. He would make mistakes. He would fail. He would choose one life over another.

He had to resolve to not let himself become callous. To stop rushing ahead and letting others suffer the consequences. He needed to think before he acted, and heed the wisdom of the people around him. But he couldn't allow being diligent and thoughtful to paralyse him either. He wouldn't let his efforts to minimise damage prevent him from doing what good he was able.

He decided to ask Marek Nior Vargas to speak with Carlos and Arabelle about the kind of soul-based control the astral kings used on messengers. He didn't think there would be a lot of crossover between what was happening with Melody, but he guessed that the healers would be enthusiastic regardless.

Jason's attention was snapped back to Sophie, Melody and Arabelle when Arabelle spoke his name. A replica of Jason, one of his avatars, was brought into existence next to the three women. He saw Melody slumped in a chair, staring off into space, looking less catatonic than drugged. His all-pervasive senses examined her body for anything wrong, sensing that she was mostly healthy but extremely exhausted.

He was about to ask what happened but instead tapped into the memory of the events he'd been ignoring. Earlier, when he'd suppressed the influence on Melody, she had collapsed, caught by Sophie's lightning speed before she fell to the ground. Melody recovered her faculties after a moment, seemingly fine, and that was when Jason had stopped paying attention.

The memory began from there. His mind processed it in an instant, although it felt longer as it played out in his mind. He watched Sophie carefully help her mother into a chair as Arabelle fetched a glass of water. They started talking, Melody disoriented and confused. She complained of being tired after years of fruitlessly fighting the influence inside her. Arabelle, being a healer, monitored her condition, finding her tired but healthy, just as Jason had. Melody flagged quickly as the conversation jumped around, disjointed by her erratic sensibilities. Once she became non-responsive, Arabelle called for Jason, catching him up to the current moment.

"She's just tired," Jason assured Sophie. "Arabelle's assessment was spot-on, so far as I can tell. Physically, she's in excellent condition."

"What about her mind?" Sophie asked, none of her usual stoicism in evidence. "She was scattered, confused."

"This may seem counterintuitive," Arabelle said, "but her state of mind being where it was is exactly what we wanted to see. If she came out of that fully lucid, I wouldn't trust it. I would assume that the thing inside of her still had control. Given what she's been through, and for how long, what we saw was extremely encouraging."

"Physically, she's doing as well as we could have hoped," Jason said. "There don't appear to be any negative side-effects from suppressing the control on her."

"Which means we can leave her here long enough to get the rest she needs," Arabelle said. "For all the power Jason can wield here, that's the best thing he can offer her: a place to rest without that thing crawling inside her mind. And she'll need a lot of rest. Don't expect her to reawaken today."

"I doubt many could imagine what she's been through," Jason said. "Even me. My soul torture was over in a matter of hours, but Amos Pensinata went through extended spiritual tribulation, just as Melody has. Sophie, while your mother is sleeping, I would recommend you seek Lord Pensinata out. He can tell you at least some of what to expect. Maybe even what your mother is going to want and need as she goes through this, now that she's free of the influence. Even if that freedom is only temporary."

"That is an excellent idea," Arabelle said. "But you are right that her reprieve is only temporary; she isn't actually in recovery. Once she leaves here, the shackles on her mind go back on."

"Does she have to leave?" Sophie asked. "We've just been keeping her in locked rooms, and what is more secure than this place? It's still a cage, but it's bigger and nicer."

"I have no problem with that," Jason said, "but I think we should defer to Arabelle as her primary care physician."

"Her what?" Sophie asked.

"Sorry," Jason said. "Primary care physician. It's a term from my world that just means the person in charge of seeing to someone's medical care. They are the first port of call, tapping into specialists like Carlos as needed."

"Oh," Sophie said. "Why not just say healer?"

"Jason has introduced a number of terms from physical and especially mental care in his world that I have found useful to adopt. Specificity matters when it comes to healing. But as for your idea, Sophie, I think it has merit. Unless we see any detrimental effects over time, keeping her in Jason's soul realm until we have an actual treatment may well be the best thing for her."

"I also think we need to avoid jumping the gun on any kind of testing for removing what's inside her permanently," Jason said. "Carlos won't like to hear it, but I think she could use a nice, long time to get herself together before we let him anywhere near her."

"I couldn't agree more," Arabelle said. "I'll break it to him."

The team was assembling in the atrium of Emir's palace when Jason and Sophie emerged from his portal. Jason tooled up in full adventuring gear to match his team, shrouding himself in dark mist. It dissolved away a moment later, revealing him in his dark blood robes.

The team's Adventure Society liaison, Vidal Ladiv, had been sent to fetch them.

"So," Jason asked him. "The messengers finally turned up?"

"More the messengers of the messengers," Vidal said. "Rather than turn up in person, they've sent some of the people they've enslaved."

"Enslaved nothing," Allayeth said, the diamond-rank elf striding in through the mist door. "I've been fighting the messengers here for months, and they don't take slaves. Everyone that serves them joins up voluntarily."

Jason looked at her angry expression.

"I'm not sure that join or die is much of a choice," Jason said. "There's nothing wrong with biding your time and looking for the chance to escape."

"Except that's not how it works," Allayeth said. "It's join or die, yes, they don't get to choose. The messengers are just as good as you at reading emotions, Jason. They look for people who are demoralised by their power and accept that the messengers are superior beings. Anyone else, they kill outright. It's how they trust the people they take to infiltrate the city; their wills are broken. And speaking of the messenger servants, how is your auxiliary's project going?"

"Lindy?" Jason asked.

"Estella says she's gone almost as far as she can mapping out the network of messenger agents still in the city," Belinda reported. "She doesn't think there are any gold-rankers and it's mostly bronze-rankers in positions adjacent to power. Anyone with direct power is being watched too closely, especially now, and the messenger agents are laying low."

"And she's identifying them through the aura masks the messengers provide?" Allayeth asked.

"Yes," Jason confirmed. "They're hard to spot, but I saw one on a messenger agent in the weeks before the attack. Estella's fourfold senses make her even better than I am at picking them out. She's also an experienced spy, so I'm confident she's done a thorough job of mapping out their network. It's unlikely that we'll pinpoint them all, but she'll put you in a good position to sweep them all up at once."

"The Adventure Society has been carefully vetting teams to strike when ready," Vidal said. "We don't think any of the adventuring teams have been compromised, but we're checking anyway and focusing on using outside adventurers like your friend Rick Geller's team. The less time they've been in Yaresh, the less likely they are to have been suborned somehow. Of course, none of the teams knows what's going on yet. Most of the people who know about the plan are in this room."

"Estella wanted to know when we're moving forward," Belinda asked. "She's ready to present everything for the strike teams to act."

"Mr Ladiv," Allayeth said. "How is the readiness of the Adventure Society to move on this?"

"We're already finalising preparations. We're almost ready to bring teams in for briefing, immediately prior to deployment. If Miss Warnock is willing to come in today and present her findings in full, we can be ready to move as early as the day after tomorrow."

"Excellent," Allayeth said. "That is the day the Continental Council officials are set to arrive. We might get lucky and find some of the messenger spies sticking their necks out for slicing."

"Should I skip this and go find Estella now?" Belinda asked.

"No," Humphrey said. "I know we'll have gold- and diamond-rank backup, but I want the whole team on deck for this."

"You're a silver-rank team going somewhere with gold-rankers and a diamond," Vidal said to Humphrey. "And you think that *they* are your backup?"

"Yes," Humphrey told him.

"No offence, Master Geller, but I think Mr Asano is affecting the way you think."

"Mr Ladiv," Humphrey said, "Jason told the Builder to pack up and leave this planet—*and he did*. If that's where his kind of thinking gets us, that's exactly where I want to be."

43

AN IMPOSSIBLE ACT OF FORGIVENESS

THE MESSENGER ENVOY GROUP WAS SET UP NOT TOO FAR FROM WHERE THE adventurers were camped outside the city. There were no messengers amongst them, being comprised entirely of what they called the servant races. They had travelled along the network of roads winding through the rainforest, stopping at a clearing not far from the city. A heavy freight land skimmer had been used to move the large metal orb containing the study of the diamond-rank messenger, Mah Go Schaat. It was close enough to be visible from the towers of Emir's palace.

While the study was being delivered to Jason, his team was only part of a full convoy of vehicles being sent to collect it. The Duke of Yaresh, the Adventure Society and the Magic Society were all represented, a string of land skimmers flowing out of the city. Jason and his team joined them outside the city gate in two black skimmers, courtesy of Shade. Allayeth had joined Jason in his skimmer, along with Clive, Humphrey and Neil.

"Why so many people?" Neil asked. "This is something Jason is just picking up and taking away, right?"

"There are concerns that messengers are using this handoff as some kind of ploy," Allayeth said. "That is the stated reason."

"Stated?" Neil asked.

"Politics," Humphrey said. "The interactions with the messengers are important to the city. This means that the city's power factions need to involve themselves or they look irrelevant."

"In this case, they are irrelevant," Neil said.

"I'll bet that's not what the Magic Society wants," Clive muttered darkly. "They're going to try and snake the orb from Jason. Claim it's for the greater good of the city or some other transparent lie. Seriously, I'll bet money. Any takers?"

"No thanks," Jason said.

Amongst the convoy coming from Yaresh, there was no shortage of gold-rankers, all from the city factions. Jason's team included the only outsider adventurers involved. Allayeth was the representative diamond-ranker while Charist remained in the city in case the messengers were attempting something shady.

The highway was a little worse for wear after more than six months of neglect, starting back with the monster surge. In a rainforest, the plant life encroached fast, even on a magically sealed road. Weeds grew up through cracks and crawled across the surface from the edge. Trees started to over-hang the sides, although the road was still wide enough to allow the passage of the skimmers. The surface was even less of a problem, the skimmers floating around a metre over it as they hovered along the ground.

Jason looked around at the intimidating force riding in the vehicles around them. He picked up dissatisfaction aimed in his direction, mostly from the auras of the silver-rankers, but he didn't begrudge them for it. It was their city, their home, and it had been levelled to the ground. Now, they were heading to meet with agents of the force behind that destruction and they were self-invited hangers-on. It was Jason, an outsider, who was central to the interaction.

The convoy approached the spot where the messenger servants waited, a grassy clearing beside the road. There was a long, straight section of road leading up to them, allowing the convoy to see them from a good way off. They could sense them from even further, letting them determine the strength of the group.

The convoy slowed to a crawl, making a slow and careful approach. This was in spite of their senses revealing that the group from Yaresh was massively overpowered compared to the messenger envoys. Most of the messenger servants were bronze rank, with only a few silvers. They were also outnumbered.

The heavy freight skimmer amounted to a barge that floated just off the ground. On the back was a metal orb the size of a small cottage, braced in a wooden scaffold. There were also a couple of skimmers that had brought most of the dozen or so messenger servants, mostly elves. Clearly, this was not a force able to face what Yaresh had sent, but it was enough to handle most monsters that attacked the group in transit.

The elves were standing around, their auras pulsing nervous energy. They had known they would be outmatched in terms of power and there was every chance this mission would be their last. Traitors to Yaresh, which had suffered terribly under the messengers, they had to know they were likely to be killed outright. If any of the gold-rankers decided they wanted these people dead, they were more likely to be cheered on than admonished.

The one person with the absolute power to stop that was Allayeth. Having heard her opinion on the issue, however, Jason half-expected her to do the killing herself. As one of the few people present Jason couldn't read even a little, he was unable to predict what she would do.

"They're scared of us," Jason said, feeling Allayeth out.

"They should be," she muttered darkly. "They're traitors."

"Please don't execute them."

"Why shouldn't we?"

"Because we don't need to. It doesn't hurt us if they live. We're well past the point they could sneak into the city as spies."

"And what does mercy get us?"

"Mercy isn't a means, Allayeth. It's an end. Do you think killing these people would be some kind of justice?"

"They betrayed the city. Betrayed the world."

"And they will forever be outcasts for that. Once we kick the messengers off this planet, these people will be pariahs wherever they go. Can you honestly tell me that killing them is about justice? Or even punishment? That it wouldn't be about satisfying your own anger?"

"And what's wrong with that?"

"When I went back to my world, I was an unsheathed sword. My father told me something that I took far too long to internalise: That when I have all the power, and I'm choosing between life and death, it's not the person that I'm killing or sparing that matters. I'm what matters. Do I be ruthless or merciful?"

"It's not your city, Jason. It's easy for you to be self-righteous."

"Yes," he agreed. "It is. It doesn't make me wrong, though. These people were weak, Allayeth, not evil. They faced a power beyond their ability to confront and it broke them. They couldn't see a world where the messengers didn't conquer it, and they did the only thing that made sense to them in that moment: they gave in. If everyone had the strength to stand up against impossible odds, then everyone would be an adventurer. But they're not. Some people need protection, and those traitors? They are people that you and I failed to protect. Now, we are the great power before them, just as the messengers once were. And like the messengers, we have to choose their fate. Will we be ruthless, like the messengers, or merciful? Maybe even show a little glimpse of hope to people who served the messengers because their hope was dead."

"That all sounds very nice, Jason," Allayeth told him. "But the practical reality isn't like that."

"And it never will be if we aren't willing to try and make it that way."

"What would you do?" Allayeth asked him. "What would you try? You're famous for ridiculous choices. What would yours be here?"

"You're not going to like it."

"Tell me anyway."

"I'd forgive them."

"And what would that look like, from a practical perspective?" she asked. "Tell them that we're sorry that they got turned into traitors and open up the gates of the city to welcome them home?"

"Of course not. Trust but verify. Watch them, carefully. Those people would need massive amounts of counselling, so give it to them. Some you'd be able to help and some would be beyond help. You'd probably have to put those ones down, but not before getting some information out of them. You might even put them to use, let them think they've deceived their way into the city. It would make what Estella Warnock is doing a lot easier. Maybe, some of them come out the other side as people who can still live a life, even after all they've done. I hope that we all deserve redemption, so long as we're willing to work for it."

"What you just described is never going to happen."

"I know," Jason said.

"There are so many ways that would go wrong."

"Yes," Jason agreed.

"Then why?"

"Because why not try to make things better, even if it seems impossible? Killing is necessary sometimes, but it doesn't make anything better. At best, it stops something from getting worse. And if we're being honest with ourselves, sometimes justice is a word we use to mask indulging in our anger. That doesn't make anything better; it just makes us worse for having done it."

Allayeth shook her head.

"I did ask for ridiculous," she said. "I didn't know what to expect, but you want to help the people who turned to the enemies threatening the entire world. That's who they betrayed, Jason: the entire world. Wanting to help them is madness."

"So is getting in a knife fight with the Builder, or patching a hole in the side of reality by building a temple to yourself. Is forgiving all those people and having it work out well in any way possible? Probably not. But you'll never accomplish the impossible if you aren't willing to try, Allayeth, and I like the idea of an impossible act of forgiveness. I know that it's hypocritical of me to be saying all this, after the things I've done. And I know that you have much more life experience than me."

Allayeth's stern gaze cracked a little, showing a brief glimpse of amusement.

"Are you calling me old?"

"No!" he exclaimed quickly. "Well, yes, but in a good way. But the thing about youth is that it can be passionate. Idealistic. It can chase impossible dreams, and in doing so, be the change that pushes civilisation forward. I don't know about this world, but in mine, every generation makes society a little bit better. Showing compassion where their parents showed blame. Accepting outsiders where they were once excluded. And every generation before it looks back, calling them frivolous or selfish or caught up in foolish ideas that will never work. They claim that what they want is impossible. The reality is that positive change is closer to inexorable. And yes, there are some rough steps backward as well. But compared to even a century ago, society is transformed."

"I think that may be the first time I heard you say something good about your world," Neil said. "Normally, you just say it's terrible and there are flying wolves everywhere."

Jason groaned.

"No, that's not... look, *Airwolf* is—"

"Nobody cares," Neil cut him off.

Jason lacked the time to get the conversation back on track as the convoy's sluggish pace finally drew it close to the messengers' servants. The Magic Society contingent was the first to move, leaping from their skimmers before they fully came to a stop. There was one gold-ranker amongst them, a monster-core-using administrator; the rest were silver.

They were a mix of core users in society-branded robes and non-core users dressed more practically. They were most likely members of both the Magic and Adventure Societies, as Clive had once been. Jason could sense their emotions, the eager avarice towards the orb and the knowledge it contained.

"I told you they'd try and take it from you," Clive muttered bitterly. "Just like they took the elemental messengers we captured."

"I wonder what happened with that hole the elemental messengers dug up to the surface?" Neil mused. "The Adventure Society was building some kind of defence outpost on top of it, right?"

"Alongside the Magic Society," Clive said. "They're keeping very quiet about what's happening with it. It's harder to exploit something when people watch you do it."

"The outpost is being guarded and any messengers that come out of it are being captured," Allayeth said. "They're little more than mindless beasts. More monsters and elementals are coming out than messengers, though. In all of our discussions, the messengers refused to reveal how many of their kind were down there in the first place. And yes, all the messengers are being handed off to the Magic Society."

"They should be giving them to Carlos Quilido," Clive said. "He's the world's foremost expert on involuntary transformation and he's right here in Yaresh. But the Magic Society won't use him because then it wouldn't be the society taking the most credit for whatever they get out of the messengers."

"I recommend you bring that up with the Continental Council representatives," Allayeth told Clive. "I suspect they will be receptive to that line of argumentation."

"I don't suppose you can get them to back off here?" Jason asked Allayeth.

"I can, but I won't. I will go as far as I need to deal with the messengers, but that orb is a spoil that you asked for, Jason. If you want to keep it, you'll have to prove that you can, and that's politics. As a diamond-ranker, I stay out of such things."

"Your friend Charist doesn't," Jason pointed out.

"I am not responsible for Charist's integrity," she told him. "Only my own."

"Yeah," Jason said, resigned but accepting. "That's fair enough."

Humphrey let out an unhappy sigh.

"You know," he said, "for all that I said the gold-rankers were here to support us, I didn't want to go pushing people around. But you negotiated that orb for yourself, and I know why. Having them try to take it from you will not stand."

He hopped out of the skimmer.

"Let's go annoy the Magic Society."

Clive practically bounced out of the skimmer with a maniacal laugh that had everyone giving him wary side glances. He ignored them and marched off after the Magic Society contingent.

44

THE MANNER OF PERSON ONE
WILL BE DEALING WITH

THE TEAM MOVED TOWARDS THE MESSENGER SERVANTS WHERE THE GOLD-rank Magic Society official was already barking orders, both to his own people and the messenger servants.

"Get out of the way, you traitorous weeds! Get the control key for the freight skimmer off them and get it moving! I want this back at the campus."

"I'm afraid that's not where it's going," Humphrey told him as the team approached from behind. The gold-ranker was close to Jason's height, so when he turned, he had to look up at the much taller Humphrey. He glanced at Jason before turning back to Humphrey.

"Damn right, that's not where it's—" Clive started. Humphrey cut him off with a gesture, not taking his eyes from the gold-ranker. The gold-ranker glanced at Clive briefly, his expression dismissive as he locked eyes with Humphrey again.

"You must be the leader of Asano's little team. What were you called again? Team Snack? Team Brunch?"

Humphrey raised an eyebrow.

"Really?" he asked. "You think making fun of our team name will provoke me into doing something that will let you dismiss us out of hand? You think we didn't know exactly what we were doing when we chose that name?"

Humphrey ignored Neil's awkward cough.

"Look," the gold-ranker said. "It's all very nice that you get along so well with the messengers that wiped out our city. They'll only work with you probably because Asano there is still protected by the messengers that he saved from being captured during the invasion of Yaresh. But you're silver-rankers and you aren't to be trusted. For all we know, you're trying to bring something extremely dangerous inside the city defences to finish what the messengers started. Only the expertise of the Magic Society can handle something like this."

Behind Humphrey, the team members were different levels of riled-up, Sophie letting out an actual growl. Only Jason, Humphrey and Rufus demonstrated complete equanimity, while Clive burst out into uproarious laughter.

"...expertise..." he managed to choke out. "You..."

He couldn't get out any more words as he doubled over laughing.

Humphrey gave Clive an amused look before turning back to the gold-ranker.

"It seems that our own magical expert doesn't think highly of you, but I would not make the same mistake. I'm certain you know all about the dangers the messengers present. I'm guessing you took down many messengers during the Battle of Yaresh. Being gold rank, you certainly wouldn't have been cowering inside the Magic Society campus because it was one of the few truly secure zones within the city. But I don't have to guess, do I? The Adventure Society kept excellent battle records for all the gold-rankers in the battle. I can just look you up when we get back to the city and learn exactly what a brave son of Yaresh you are."

The gold-ranker's face turned ugly.

"What is your name, sir?" Humphrey asked him.

"I am Lord Warth—"

"Actually, I don't care," he cut him off, the smile dropping from Humphrey's face as his fake-friendly tone turned cold. "Your name and the pointless noise coming out of your mouth stopped mattering the moment you accused me and my friends of being traitors."

"You should show some respect, boy. In Yaresh, silver-rankers know better than to talk back to golds."

"And in Vitesse, the gold-rankers know that the respect rank commands is earned by living up to that power. That to be gold rank and act like a petty, greedy coward is to undermine the respect every gold-ranker worth the rank deserves."

"Those are bold words, silver-ranker. Although it is uncouth to stab downwards, most people know better than to issue such provocation. I would be well within my rights to demand a duel over your words."

Humphrey laughed out loud.

"Please do, Lord Warthington-Hampstead," Humphrey said, the gold-ranker's eyes growing wary at realising that Humphrey already knew who he was. "In the first place, I would be more than happy to place my good name against yours. I wear my accomplishments with pride and take responsibility for my failures. I don't have any cowardly shames or wretched, self-serving schemes to hide."

"It takes more than reputation to win a duel, boy. It takes blood."

"Yes," Humphrey agreed. "Funny you should say that, as I believe your natural predilection for cowardice has had you using duels as an empty threat. I imagine that is why you seem to have forgotten what the laws of duelling entail when it comes to crossing rank, so allow me to remind you. When a gold-ranker declares a duel against a silver-ranker, the silver can bring his entire team. I would be more than happy to pit my friends against whatever skills you have developed, sitting at home, slurping up monster cores."

"I'll take on your team, you little weasel."

"Really? Because, as the challenged, we can set the terms. What was it you said about duelling in mirage chambers, back in Rimaros, Jason?"

"That if you want to duel, you put blood on the line," Jason answered. "Anything else and you're a coward pretending to be a hero."

"I am not going to draw blood like a savage. I am a magical researcher. I have better things to do than run around, fighting like a thug."

"Oh please," Clive said. "You wouldn't know magical research if it referenced you in an appendix. I've looked into the fungus growing out of the Magic Society that they've appointed as their officials. I know exactly who and what you are. You're one of those political slimes oozing through the halls of Magic Society, using influence to get your name attached to other people's research. I've seen plenty of your kind."

"Now, be nice, Clive," Humphrey faux-admonished. "Just because you are both a prestigious adventurer and a famed magical researcher doesn't mean you should belittle other people for being neither. Take a little walk and calm down. Belinda, see he doesn't get into any trouble."

Belinda raised her eyebrows at being chosen as the one to keep someone out of trouble. She met Humphrey's eyes, seeing the ever-so-slight smile teasing his mouth.

"Alright, come on, Clive," she said.

"But I want to—"

"Nope," she said firmly, dragging him off by the arm.

"Sorry about that," Humphrey told Warthington-Hampstead. "We need to keep things civil."

"Civil? You have called me a coward to my face!"

"And you called me a traitor. More importantly, you called my team traitors, so the fact that your insides are still inside you is the height of restraint, I can assure you. You are a coward and a parasite, but you were wise not to actually challenge us to that duel. We would have seen you dead, and it wouldn't have been clean."

By this point, the Magic Society contingent had stopped trying to claim the orb and grouped up behind their leader. The two groups were arrayed before one another, behind Humphrey and the gold-ranker.

"Do you think I will stand for this kind of insult?" Warthington-Hampstead asked.

"Yes," Humphrey said lightly. "Because you're used to people seeing your rank, your political faction and your position in the Magic Society and backing down. But we're not backing down. Clive would take down the whole Magic Society, given half a chance. Once he reaches diamond rank, I think he might even take a shot at it."

"You think he'll reach diamond rank?" Warthington-Hampstead asked with a mocking laugh.

"I do," Humphrey said. "You should follow my and Clive's example, and find out who you're dealing with. Ask around about Clive Standish when you get back to the Magic Society. You'll find out soon enough. In the meantime, you need to decide if you're going to challenge us to that duel. You can send the little minions standing behind you if you like. Team versus team. We'll take them on, and hiding behind a bunch of silver-rankers will definitely prove that you're not a coward. If you can't muster up the courage for even that, then get your people away from that orb."

"You think you can throw me off with a false dichotomy, boy? I am taking that orb, and I won't be fighting you like a bloody-minded barbarian. What will you do about it? Attack us?"

"Oh, that won't be necessary," Humphrey said.

"What will you do, then?" Warthington-Hampstead asked. "You talk big, but what can you do without hiding behind someone else's skirts? Are you going to have Lady Allayeth force me to give it to you? I know your boy Asano is her little pet."

Humphrey smiled, his fury gone as if it had never existed.

"We both know she won't," Humphrey said. "And we don't need her to. You see, we're going to do things the way you do. You talk about power, leaning on the rank you bought with money. But you understand that when it comes to politics, the key is to find the leverage point and push."

"Oh, you fancy yourself a cunning politician now, do you?"

"No," Humphrey said. "I just happen to have a very solid fulcrum. You said that Jason here is Allayeth's pet. Do you remember why? It's because if he doesn't participate in this operation to go underground, the messengers won't participate. And if the messengers don't participate, it doesn't happen. Which means that instead of rebuilding Yaresh, it will have to be evacuated. The entire population will become refugees and you'll have to build a new city somewhere else. All while messengers and remnant monsters from the surge are roaming about. While the whole region is devastated by a magical disaster on a scale that none of us have ever seen."

"You're bluffing. You wouldn't let the city be destroyed."

"The city has already been destroyed, remember? You said that yourself. If the people in it would be killed, then you would be right that we wouldn't walk away. But, if anything, it would be easier to establish a new Yaresh somewhere else rather than deal with what's left of the old one, even with all the troubles. Jason advocated for that in the first place. He had to be talked into taking part at all. So, take your people and go home or you won't have time to try and fail to open that orb. You'll be too busy explaining how the population now needs to evacuate because you convinced us to leave this city in our dust."

The gold-ranker's face took on an increasingly savage sneer as Humphrey spoke, but he held his tongue.

"You'll pay for this, silver-ranker."

"Every action has a consequence," Humphrey told him. "If you need to find me for that, my name is Humphrey Geller."

The gold-ranker paled slightly.

"Geller?"

"Yes."

"As in…?"

"Yes. As I suggested before, if one anticipates a confrontation, it is best to learn in advance the manner of person one will be dealing with."

The gold-ranker's expression turned even uglier. His body language screamed reluctance, but the gold-ranker capitulated, ordering his people back to their skimmers with a tirade of angry shouts.

Left to their own devices, Sophie sidled up to Humphrey.

"That was incredibly sexy," she whispered.

"Agreed," Clive said enthusiastically as he strolled back to the group with Belinda.

"What?" Humphrey asked, wide-eyed.

The Magic Society contingent were returning to their skimmers and taking off, and Neil looked around at the rest of the Yaresh convoy. Quite a few had stopped to watch the spectacle of the team confronting the Magic Society, but most had gone to work. They had rounded up the messenger servants and were questioning them in a none-too-friendly manner.

"Why wasn't the rest of the group backing us up against that idiot?" Neil complained. "All these people here, and they leave us to stand up to a gold-ranker? That fool might not know the details of our involvement, but some of these others must. They were in the meeting where Jason said he thought they should evacuate the city in the first place. They knew we wouldn't stand for this."

"The man being a fool was the point," Rufus said. "I suspect he was carefully chosen. A fool, but one with enough influence and power to be an annoyance. He was used to test us. We're playing at a high level, now, in power and politics both."

"Wasn't the same true in Rimaros?" Neil asked.

"Not really," Rufus said. "We were involved with powerful political figures, but not the actual machinations of politics there. Princess Liara and Soramir Rimaros shielded us from that. Except for that final party, we were always on the periphery. Jason was meant to become more involved, but events overtook those intentions. That plan effectively died with Vesper Rimaros."

"This time, the local diamond-ranker isn't shielding us," Humphrey said. "She's leaving us to sink or swim."

"Humphrey, Neil and I understand the rules," Rufus said. "We've been raised on them from birth. It's a complex balance of etiquette and power. When to use decorum and when to put it aside. Who can be pushed and who cannot. The rest of you don't have that background, and Jason somehow has the exact opposite of it. He has a knack for figuring out when he's too important to dismiss and then swinging like a hammer in a glassworks."

"I only talked when Humphrey asked me to," Jason complained.

"Yes," Rufus told him. "It must have been hard for you. Well done on persevering."

"I don't just say whatever lunatic thing that pops into my… this is not convincing anyone, is it?"

The rest of the team all shook their heads.

"This is all well and good," Neil said, "but you think that idiot was sent here just to see how we'd deal with it?"

"Yes," Rufus said. "It's an event that all the political factions are sensitive to, but the stakes are ultimately low. This is just something Jason wanted, not the device that is critical to saving the city. That made it the perfect opportunity to see if we were able to hold our own in a political confrontation, or if we were worthless outside of combat."

"Why would the Magic Society go along with this?" Neil asked. "Doesn't this make them look bad?"

"If you think about them as a monolithic group, yes," Clive said. "But any group is a collection of individuals. Remember what Rufus said about the fool being a mix of power and annoyance? I promise you that someone a lot better at politics than him arranged it all. They picked up political points with the other factions by agreeing to have the Magic Society do it. Then he chose Warthington-Hampstead, whose power all comes from family ties to the Magic Society and the Aristocratic Faction of Yaresh politics."

"Exactly," Rufus said. "Either Warthington-Hampstead gets spanked and sent home, diminishing his influence, or the Magic Society gets their hands on the orb. The person behind it all reaps the political points from the other factions and either has an obstacle in Warthington-Hampstead removed or gets more influence in the Magic Society for having master-minded the acquisition of the orb."

"So, there's someone we can't see behind all this," Jason said. "Someone smart who put an idiot on the end of a stick and poked us with him."

"That seems likely," Rufus said. "The truly skilled politicians go unseen, leaving amateurs like us to be pieces on their board. We were played, but to an end that works out for us, so there's little point making an issue of it. That, too, is a demonstration of deft politics. Make the pieces on the board accept their position, even if they understand what they are."

"I don't like the taste of that," Jason said.

"Yes, and we know what happens when you decide to flip the board," Rufus said. "but don't do it just because you can."

"I know," Jason said. "I've seen Zara Rimaros do that on the big stage, and I've seen how it goes."

"I don't suppose that means you've reformed?" Humphrey asked him.

"No," Jason said. "It means I'll be more careful about picking my moments."

"Good," Sophie said. "I hate all of this. Leave me out of it until it's time to punch things."

"What happens now?" Neil asked. "They've tested us. What next?"

"Now, they know we won't be pushed around and can play by rules they understand," Rufus said. "We can expect an appropriate level of support, but also without being treated like children. And they know that we know they were testing us because you can bet they're all listening right now. That is political leverage all on its own. They know they owe us, now. Not a lot, but enough that we can use it, should we have the need."

45

BECAUSE IT'S HARD

JASON WAS USING HIS CLOUD-FLASK TO PRODUCE WHAT WAS ESSENTIALLY a combat recreational vehicle. The size of a large tour bus, it was comprised of cloud-substance encased in panels of various magical materials. The blue and green metal panels were not square but formed swooping shapes, reminiscent of the wind. The result looked like a hybrid between a bus and a swift pleasure yacht.

"This is the way to travel, bro," Taika said happily.

Belinda and Clive were floating around the metal orb on the heavy freight skimmer. They couldn't fly around with the ease of Jason or Sophie, but any silver-ranker could levitate slowly with concentration. The pair were attaching devices around the surface of the orb, designed to reduce the weight of the massive thing. When they were done, they dropped down to join the rest of the team.

"These were Belinda's idea," Clive said. "They're usually used in shipping."

"Also, occasionally for stealing things," Belinda added, getting an eye-roll from Clive.

"They only get used for loading and unloading," Clive continued. "They burn through spirit coins too fast to use them for an entire trip. Humphrey, Neil and Taika, you're the strongest of us by far, so we'll need you to move the orb once we activate the devices."

"Didn't you say those things will make the orb weightless?" Rufus asked. "Shouldn't that make it easy to move?"

"No," Clive said. "It won't fall to the ground anymore, but it still has what's called the echo of weight, meaning that it's still hard to shift."

"Are you talking about the difference between weight and mass?" Jason asked.

Clive turned to him with a curious expression, but before Jason could say anything, an overwhelming aura manifested.

"No," a female voice rumbled like thunder.

"Oh, come on," Jason complained to the sky. "I know this one. Kind of. More or less. Okay, fine. You're not even saying anything and I can practically hear your raised eyebrow."

The aura vanished.

"Ask Travis about it later," Jason told Clive. "Did he ever tell you about gravity?"

"Jason…" the voice rumbled, the aura returning.

"Seriously?" he asked the sky, throwing his arms out. "I was just asking a question. Bloody hell, lady, don't you have a precocious child to go inspire with a verve for learning? You've got to have better things to do than this."

Jason shook his head as the divine aura receded again.

"Gods, am I right?"

He looked around, seeing that everyone from both groups, the Yaresh convoy and the messenger servants, were all staring at him.

"Oh, like you've never seen gods before," Jason said loudly. "I know a bunch of you are priests; I can feel the divinity in your auras, so don't give me those looks."

Jason wandered over to his cloud vehicle, muttering discontentedly as he did.

"Bloody transcendent beings think they run the whole bloody cosmos…"

When Jason disappeared into the vehicle, the people all turned their attention to his team. Rufus pinched the bridge of his nose while Humphrey ran an exasperated hand over his face.

"We cannot take that guy anywhere," Neil muttered.

"I don't think my mum would like this," Taika said as he gave all the people looking at them an awkward wave. "She's pretty Christian."

"That's one of the religions from your world?" Clive asked.

"Yep. The god is kind of like the Builder, in that he's more on a creating-the-universe level than the gods here. Also, he doesn't like shellfish or mixed fabrics. I was never clear on why."

"Your mother didn't tell you?" Sophie asked.

"Well, there's this book with all the rules in it, but it seemed a bit sketchy to me. Mum used to make me read it, but then I'd ask questions until she hit me with a spoon."

The massive metal orb was heavy, even for a metal sphere the size of a cottage. Even so, it was slowly moving as Humphrey, Neil and Taika pushed on it, bracing themselves on the carry bed of the freight skimmer. Each of them had strength enhanced beyond the silver-rank norm, leaving them somewhere between the strength of a peak silver-ranker and a baseline gold.

The freight skimmer was floating at maximum height, some four metres off the ground, at considerable cost in spirit coins as fuel. It was enough that the orb, when pushed sideways, would float over Jason's cloud RV instead of into the side of it. The rest of the team were looking on, as were most of the Yaresh city representatives and Adventure Society officials. Those that weren't watching were busy interrogating the messenger servants. The Magic Society people had already left.

"It's a shame you couldn't make the cloud vehicle more like that freight skimmer, with a big flatbed," Rufus said.

"No, I could," Jason said.

"Then why didn't you?"

"So many reasons. One, see how it looks? It was completely worth House de Varco messing with us to get those upgrades to the cloud vehicles."

"You don't think having a giant metal sphere on top will ruin the lines?"

"Well, you can't have everything. And that wasn't even the main reason anyway."

"Which is?"

"Flatbed haulers don't have a lounge area."

"That's a good reason," Sophie said.

"Agreed," Belinda chipped in.

"Just to be clear," Rufus said, "you use a bunch of spirit coins to lift that skimmer under extreme load so you could sit more comfortably for the minutes it will take to get back to the city?"

"More or less," Jason said.

"Wealth is ruining you."

"Yeah," he agreed happily. "Anyway, I'm not taking it back to the city. Too many greedy little hands. I'm going to set up somewhere more remote, like when we were on the road contract last month."

"You know we won't exactly be hidden, right?" Belinda asked. "Hauling around a giant magic ball isn't what you'd call a subtle activity."

"I know," Jason said. "The Magic Society has drones above us as we speak."

"Drones?" Clive asked.

Jason pointed at the sky. "Little flying magical sensors."

The others craned their heads back, except for Clive, who looked at Jason.

"I don't see anything," Sophie said.

"You wouldn't," Clive said. "They shift colour, so they're hard to spot. They also fly around three kilometres in the air and are shielded against magical senses."

The others joined Clive in staring at Jason.

"What?" he asked, having continued to watch the orb the whole time.

Many of the people outside of the team, even the messenger servants, had been throwing regular glances at Jason since his interactions with the goddess Knowledge. Almost all of them had spoken with one god or another in their lives, some having done so many times. None of them had interactions like *that*, however. Gods were for worshipping, not for banter and certainly not for yelling complaints at. One might take issue with a god's priests, but not the deity itself. Belinda looked around at all the people watching, then turned to Jason.

"You know there are a bunch of gold-rankers here, right?" she asked. "Why not get them to move this thing?"

"To prove we don't need them to," Jason answered, not taking his gaze from the orb.

Belinda thought about his response for a moment.

"I can respect that," she said.

Some of the Yaresh group were still interrogating the messenger servants, but they had little of value to reveal. It was less that the servants were resisting than the messengers had made sure to not send anyone who knew any critical information. The interrogators had largely moved on to demands for the promised device from the messengers. The servant in charge, one of their silver-rankers, claimed to have no knowledge of the messengers' plans in that regard. Given how the messengers treated them, Jason was unsurprised to sense truth from the man's aura.

"You know," Jason said, looking over at the cloud vehicle. "I'm very happy with what House de Varco managed to do in terms of designing upgrades for the cloud flask. Maybe I should finally talk to that diamond-rank friend of Emir's."

Rufus let out an exasperated groan so uncharacteristic that the rest of the team all turned to stare.

"Please do that," Rufus told Jason. "Emir has been complaining to me constantly about asking you to do that because she's constantly complaining to him. Emir called my father to have *him* complain at me over water link."

"Not your mother?" Sophie asked. "She's right here where he can find her."

"Emir isn't stupid enough to do that," Rufus said. "He's right here where she can find him."

The others laughed at Rufus' thousand-yard stare.

"Why have you been putting the diamond-ranker off?" Clive asked. "She created your cloud flask, right? Surely there is a lot to gain from meeting with her."

"Yeah, but she tried to take it over," Jason said. "If she wasn't a diamond-ranker and a friend of Emir's, I'd have already done something about that."

"What do you mean, take it over?" Clive asked.

"She has some device or method to control the flask, even without the owner's permission. I sensed her trying to use it numerous times but she could never get it to work. It's not just connected to me by a normal soul-binding that restricts access anymore. It's an actual expression of my soul now, so even a diamond-ranker is locked out from messing with it."

"You didn't tell me that," Rufus said.

"I know you and Emir are close," Jason said. "And I know he's been bothering you about this. I didn't want to cause friction between you."

"I don't think Emir would still be bothering me if he knew what she was doing," Rufus said.

"He knows," Jason told him. "Emir's mindset is still caught up in ranks. It doesn't occur to him that a diamond-ranker shouldn't get what-ever they want, whenever they want. It's the wise approach. I just don't get the luxury of respecting power the way that self-preservation suggests. Too many people with too much power are always looking to take something from me. Still, it might be time to meet with this woman. Maybe she can offer some upgrades that will help us when we head underground. We don't know what we're going to face down there."

Humphrey, Taika and Neil finished moving the orb over the cloud vehicle and came down as Belinda and Clive floated up. They carefully disabled the weight-reducing devices in sequence to slowly lower the orb. It sank heavily into the cloud roof as wispy tendrils moved up to encase it, although they seemed unnecessary. It looked like a bomb would have trouble dislodging it.

"I think we're good," Jason said. "Let's get out of here."

Humphrey, Neil and Taika looked exhausted, trudging in the direction of the cloud vehicle's door.

"Good job, blokes," Jason said, slapping Neil on the shoulder. "I've got a very nice juice blend waiting for you inside."

Neil nodded his acknowledgement and they climbed the short set of stairs to the door. The rest of the team followed. Jason was about to be the last one in when he felt a surge of magic. He turned to see large thorns erupting from the ground, instantly and precisely impaling each and every messenger servant. The bronze-rankers had died immediately, as had one of the silver-rankers whose head had burst like a rotten fruit as the thick, sharp thorn passed right through it. The others died when the thorns sprouted smaller thorns, puncturing them all a dozen times from the inside out.

Jason looked over to Allayeth, whose gaze was fixated on the now-dead envoys. Sensing his eyes on her, she turned to look at him, expression unrepentant. With a blur of movement, she was standing in front of Jason.

"Something to say?" she challenged.

"No," he said sadly.

"You think I shouldn't have done that."

"Yes."

"I don't answer to you."

"No, you don't," Jason agreed. "You don't have to answer anyone but yourself."

She seemed thrown by Jason's lack of combativeness.

"Some things can't be forgiven," she said and then vanished in another blur, not waiting for his response.

Allayeth didn't join Jason and his team for the return to the city. Jason's cloud RV trundled along the highway with Shade driving, the rest of the team relaxing in the comfortable living area. Jason sat on a bench by the window, looking out, and Rufus moved to join him.

"You're disappointed in Allayeth," Rufus said.

"No," Jason said. "I never expected my little morality rant to change her mind. I'm disappointed that I didn't do a better job of trying, and it's not like I'm some paragon of virtue."

"I found it interesting that she came up to you like that. The way she said that she didn't have to answer to you made it feel a lot like she did."

"No," Jason said. "She knows that the one she has to answer to is herself. But I've been there, and I think she realised that after she killed them all. And why I asked her to forgive them instead."

"You've killed a bunch of helpless prisoners?"

"Not exactly. Once, back on Earth, some people came for me while my family was around. I don't know if I could have handled it better, but they had a weakness and I used it. Killed them all on the spot without moving a muscle. It was kind of the last straw for my family. It'd been coming for a while, but they didn't look at me the same after that. It seemed like the right choice at the time, but I know what it did to me."

"It was hard to live with?"

"No, and that's the problem. It made it easier to do the next horrible thing, and that's why I need to be better. Every time I justify some brutal action, it makes it easier to dismiss finding a better way as too hard. That's why I'm trying to force myself to find alternatives to killing a bunch of people, even when it isn't easy. Which it never seems to be with the things we do."

"I respect that," Rufus told him. "I don't know that it's a practical approach to adventuring, though."

Jason laughed.

"No, it's not," he agreed. "I'm well aware that there are hard, grim choices waiting for all of us. But I'll never do it if I never try."

Rufus nodded. "You don't give up on doing something that's right, just because it's hard."

"No," Jason agreed. "You don't. I've been thinking about these people the messengers have cowed into serving them. There has to be a better way to get through to them than impaling them on spikes."

"If mercy is the goal, it can't be hard to improve on that. You have something in mind?"

"Not yet. I'm still putting pieces together. The key has to be breaking the ideas the messengers have imprinted on them. Did you sense their auras? Those people are broken. Devoid of hope. The messengers have convinced them that the conquest of this world is inevitable, which crushed their will to struggle."

"Well, if anyone is going to disprove the myth of messenger superiority, it's you."

"Immodest as it is, I was thinking the same thing. I still need to work on how, but at the very least, I'll need some live messenger servants to try with at some stage. Can't have Allayeth massacring them all on sight. You're diplomatic in a way that I'm not; can you go to the Adventure Society? Get them to hand over the next bundle of messenger slaves we get our hands on to me?"

"I can try."

"Thank you."

Jason and Rufus leaned towards the window, peering out at a group of people around a pair of halted skimmers beside the road.

"Are they the Magic Society people?" Rufus asked. The team clustered around Jason and Rufus to look outside.

The skimmers containing the Magic Society contingent had stopped and were belching sickly green smoke. The people in them had gotten out and were variously dry-heaving or yanking off their clothes and tossing them away.

"What is going on?" Humphrey asked.

"No idea," Clive said, a little too quickly. "We should keep going, though. Those stink cloud potions are extremely clingy."

46

EVERYTHING ADVENTURERS
SHOULD BE

JASON TOOK HIS CLOUD VEHICLE A SIGNIFICANT DISTANCE FROM YARESH, away from the messenger strongholds and towards the eastern coastline. He set up a cloud palace atop a massive plateau cliff that offered spectacular views that stretched out to the ocean. They could see a handful of large towns dotting the coast, the buildings washed white and decorated with bold colours.

"Why are we so far from the city?" Sophie asked Humphrey. They were on a balcony, looking out at the ocean, her leaning into his large frame.

"We're still within portal range," Humphrey told her. "It's not an impractical location, given how many portal users we have. To be accurate, I'm a teleporter, not a portal user but—"

Sophie reached up to press a finger to his lips.

"You know how I'm always telling you that pedantically defining terms is sexy?" she asked him.

"Uh, no."

"Exactly. The only person who has ever said that is Clive's wife, and Jason made her up. And I didn't ask if we could portal back to the city conveniently. I asked why we came out here in the first place. Don't get me wrong, I'm happy to be away from all the cloying politicians, the sad tent camps and the smell of ash churned into mud. It's good to get out and just be somewhere quiet and beautiful together. But why set up so far from Yaresh?"

"To make a point," Humphrey told her. "That orb was something Jason negotiated for himself. It took no one but us to go collect it, yet every major faction in the city felt entitled to invite themselves along. Wanting some observers for any interaction with the messengers is understandable, but they swept in and took over. All those people? Testing us with that Magic Society fool? Having that many gold-rankers around was a message to us more than the messengers. This is our message back, reminding them that we aren't an asset for them to be used as they like."

"By moving to the middle of nowhere?"

"Yaresh is their sphere of influence. We have placed ourselves outside it."

"I think it's going to take more than that to convince them to not try and use us."

"Yes, but if we do things the diplomatic way before the Jason way, they can't say they weren't warned."

In his soul realm, Jason was sitting on a bench in a garden. Around him were leafy green plants with flowers whose scents were as sweet as their colours bright. Jason was examining a smooth, flat stone, turning it over and over in his hands. It was carved with an intricate web of lines and sigils, complex and precision-cut. As he continued to peer at it, Marek Nior Vargas descended from the sky on dark wings to land lightly on the grass.

"That is it?" Marek asked.

"It is," Jason said, tossing the stone to him. Marek did as Jason had, turning it over in his hands as he examined it.

"Definitely an aura keystone," Marek said. "A common device in securing our strongholds, but this is more complex than others I've seen."

He stepped closer to hand it back to Jason.

"Without Mah Go Schaat's aura, I don't think you can…"

He fell silent as the carvings on the stone lit up in Jason's hand. Jason grinned, waving the stone jauntily.

"How are you doing that?" Marek asked.

"I'm told that diamond-rank messengers are obsessed with becoming astral kings."

"Yes. The closer they get to the peak of power, the more they chafe at being beholden to those that stand above them."

"It seems that your boy Mah fell into that camp. This keystone is barely aligned to his aura. It seems like he took everything he had learned about the power of an astral king and imbued it into this key. It's not a terrible idea, since it's easier to replicate an aura, even a diamond-rank one, than the power of an astral king. Mostly, though, I suspect he wanted to feel like a big boy astral king by mustering up even an echo of their power."

"You're saying that any astral king could open it easily?"

"I imagine most astral kings are sufficiently powerful that they wouldn't need to. I'm the poor cousin of the astral king community, though. But yes, it was pretty easy to trigger. I did have to replicate elements of Mango Shot's aura, but I spent an absurdly long time devouring his life force. That left me with a pretty solid grasp on it. That bloke was a meal and a half, let me tell you."

"If you have an active keystone, Mah Go Schaat's study should just open for you, then. And, if you drained his life force as thoroughly as you suggest, then you should have some time before he comes looking for it."

"Comes looking for it? That guy's dead. I checked. I used a power on his body that only works on dead people. Are you saying that he might come back?"

"No, I am saying that he *will* come back. He's a diamond-ranker. They're extremely difficult to keep dead."

"Wait, are you saying that all diamond-rankers self-resurrect?"

"You didn't know that?"

"That would explain why the restrictions on my resurrection power lift after gold rank."

"I think you'll find that most of the diamond-rank monsters that appear during a monster surge aren't newly manifested but rising from dormancy as the ambient magic grows strong enough to wake them."

Jason groaned.

"The Adventure Society and their bloody secrets," he complained. "And now I have to worry about this guy coming back?"

"Yes. Even if their body is annihilated, diamond-rankers come back unless you take measures to prevent it. Once you become diamond rank yourself, your corpse-draining power *might* be enough, I don't know what the specific power is. The best you can hope for at your current rank is that you've extended the time before his return."

"Great, there was a secret clock on this the whole time. Here I was worried that the messengers were stalling because they were either trying to break into the study or booby trap it on me. Maybe they were just holding out for this guy to come back."

"Unlikely. Jes Fin Kaal detests Mah Go Schaat, and killing you does not serve her agenda. Your postulation of her trying to access the study for herself is almost certainly accurate and does not harm her astral king's interests. Jes Fin Kaal is detestable, but not a fool. For the moment, she has need of you. That said, do not think for a moment that she won't take the chance to establish dominance, should the opportunity arise."

"But no booby trap on the orb?"

"I cannot speak definitively on that which I have no direct knowledge of. I would be very surprised if there were. If nothing else, It would be hard for any kind of trap to go unnoticed unless she had successfully accessed the study. Even so, you should be diligent in examining the exterior before you open it."

"I've got my best guy on it. I don't suppose you or any of your people could help with that?"

"No, we are soldiers. The astral kings are careful in whom they allow to wield any power outside of our innate abilities."

Jason sighed.

"Alright," he said. "If Margo Shat is waiting out there like a time bomb, I need to stop faffing about and get to it. Anything else you can suggest, as my expert on messengers?"

"I do have a suggestion. You should foment insurrection amongst the messengers to undermine the astral kings."

"By letting you and your people go?"

"We are very motivated."

"I'm sure you are. But you also killed a lot of innocent people, and you don't care about that. Your only concern is your conflict with the astral kings, and if you can advance that by killing more innocent people, I have no doubt that you will. Which makes it hard to let you go."

"The greater good of pitting us against the astral kings—"

Jason stood as the air trembled and the sky darkened, blue shifting to bloody red as the soul realm reacted to his anger. Marek felt the world press in on him like a squeezing fist.

"I'm familiar with the 'killing ten to save a hundred' argument," Jason said in a voice of thunder echoing through a glacial canyon. "You would be well-served in not making it, Marek Nior Vargas."

The messenger set his jaw, matching Jason's gaze. He could not still the tremulation in his hands, however, held down at his sides.

"I can see this is a discussion for another day," he said, his voice carefully controlled.

"On that day, you'd best come up with a better argument," Jason warned, his tone cold but returning to normal as the sky shifted back to blue. "Otherwise, you might find me convinced that there is no salvation for you. Forgiveness is one thing, but mercy has its limits. Sometimes a beast has to be put down because it can't be trusted not to hurt people."

"Perhaps you can guide me towards an argument that you would find compelling?"

"Start by convincing me that your kind are even capable of compassion. If you can't manage that much, then I don't see any hope for you as a species. It would make your kind less a people than a thorny, poisonous weed. Avoided where possible and burned out to the roots when necessary."

The metal orb got its own building, resting in a cradle of cloud substance. Clive had set up a small forest of magical devices and was running every test he could think of. He could think of a lot of tests.

"It changed colour again," Clive said as he moved around the orb, peering at it so closely his nose was almost touching it.

"It did?" Belinda asked in a bored voice, looking up from the notebook she was using to record Clive's observations. "Are you sure?"

"I'm certain," Clive said confidently. "It went from a dark brassy colour to a slightly darker brassy colour."

"Fascinating," Belinda said in an aggressively unconvincing tone as she marked down a note. "Have you considered hiring a research assistant now that you don't have the Magic Society to provide them?"

"I hired you as a research assistant."

"Five years ago. We've kind of moved on since then. Pay an auxiliary adventurer to do it."

"Yes, I bet the Magic Society would love to position a spy next to me," Clive said.

"Who cares if they're a spy, as long as they're willing to organise your notes? I'm not transcribing these into your reference system, just so you know."

Clive moved to one of the many testing devices he had set up around the orb and was adjusting it when Jason walked in.

"What is that thing?" he asked, peering at the device Clive was fiddling with. "It looks like a backwards steampunk telescope with kaleidoscopic lenses."

"Is that a research device from your world?" Clive asked.

"No, it's what happens when a cosplayer eats too much sugar. Have you found anything?"

"No," Clive said. "Nothing that suggests the messengers have set any traps for us, anyway. That's not to say they aren't there, just that I can't find them. The messengers have a magical tradition older than this planet, so it's hardly a surprise their magic is more advanced than ours. If you give me a couple of weeks to—"

"No," Jason said, his tone firmly cutting off that proposal. "It turns out that the original owner is likely to come looking for it at an indeterminate time in the future."

"I thought he died."

"I've died plenty of times; I don't put much stock in it. As it turns out, those rumours about diamond-rankers being immortal have quite a lot of truth to them."

"Wait, what? Where are you getting that from? Those messengers you have locked up?"

"Yeah. I think it's on the Adventure Society's restricted information list. Right alongside secondary racial gift evolutions and pretty much anything that's ever happened to me."

"I think you're both missing the point here," Belinda said. "Which is not a shock since neither of you can make it through a conversation without going off on three tangents. You need to open this thing now before the big, bad diamond-ranker turns up looking for it. Let me remind you that we are a long way from support if he comes knocking on our door."

"You're right," Jason said. "Thank you, Lindy. Shade is already letting the others know, and we'll crack this egg as soon as we're all assembled. Clive, you might want to pack up your magic tools."

The team, minus Rufus, who was in Yaresh, were gathered in the one-room building with the orb. They had a blast wall between them and the orb, cloud material encased in the strongest materials Jason had fed into his cloud flask. They were ready to fight if something in the orb was waiting to ambush them. They were ready to contain it if it blew up or spewed poison gas. They were ready to run if none of that worked, three portals already in place for them to flee into. Jason's shadow portal, his soul realm portal and Clive's rune circle portal were arrayed behind the team in a line.

"You know that if there's a diamond-level threat in there, we're done, right?" Neil asked. "Nothing in this cloud building can stop it and we can't move fast enough to avoid it."

"Speak for yourself," Sophie told him.

"Well, if you live and I die," Neil told her, "you're going to have to do something for me."

"What?" she asked, her voice thick with suspicion.

"Just give someone a letter for me. You know, final goodbye stuff."

"You want me to go to Greenstone and find your mother?"

"What?" Neil asked. "No, the letter is for Clive's wife."

"Oh, come on!" Clive exclaimed.

"You don't have to go to Greenstone," Neil continued. "Just give it to anyone at the Magic Society. They'll know how to find her."

"Bro, that is ice cold," Taika said.

"Yeah, that might be crossing a line," Jason said.

"Does anyone have a writing implement?" Neil asked. "I haven't actually written it yet. Lindy, you were writing something earlier, right? I can just scribble it on the back of that."

"You are not going to write a letter to my imaginary wife on the back of my research notes!" Clive told him.

"Should I include a poem?" Neil asked. "What rhymes with glistening thighs?"

"Seriously, I think Clive is going to choke you out," Jason warned Neil.

"Lindy, get out one of my recording crystals," Sophie said.

"Good idea," Belinda said.

Humphrey let out a sigh.

"You know, I always knew I'd be an adventurer," he said wearily. "I used to lie awake at night, wondering what kind of team I'd have. Paragons, champions. Everything adventurers should be. Heroic. Dignified. People who gave respect as easily as they earned it. What happened to my life?"

"Uh oh," Jason said. "I think we finally broke Humphrey. Look, I'm just going to open this thing. Everyone, try not to die."

He pulled out the engraved keystone.

"Wait!" Clive exclaimed. "You can't just—"

The carvings on the keystone lit up. A panel on the side of the orb popped out and slid to the side. The team waited, frozen, for something to happen. For anything to happen. It didn't.

"Well," Neil said. "Is anyone else feeling let down?"

47

WHAT IS THE ADVENTURE
SOCIETY

RUFUS EMERGED FROM A SHADOW PORTAL IN JASON'S CLOUD PALACE, IN
front of the open metal sphere. A moment later, Jason emerged from the
opening and walked down the ramp.

"The Continental Council rep finally turned up?" Jason asked.

"Yes," Rufus said, then nodded at the orb. "Didn't that thing used to
be a different colour?"

The previously brassy colour had shifted over the last couple of days
to a glossy dark grey.

"Yeah," Jason said. "Clive is obsessed with figuring out why, but he's
also obsessed with everything else in there."

"Find anything amazing?"

"It depends on who you ask," Jason told him. "If the diamond-rank
messenger had any amazing magical relics, tools, weapons or anything, he
had them stashed somewhere else. Everything in there is about research."

"Clive is extra excited, then."

"Clive is fizzing like an alchemy experiment on the verge of going
very, very wrong."

"But you didn't want this thing for Clive, did you?"

"No. I've been letting events push back the larger mission for too
long. My hope was that this study would hold the astral magic secrets I
need to finish building the bridge between worlds. Since I accidentally

destroyed the artefact that Dawn gave me to do that, I have to do it the hard way now. The longer I leave it, the more Earth's dimensional membrane will break down."

"You've thrown yourself into some pretty dire situations, Jason. Have you ever considered what happens to your planet if you die?"

"The World-Phoenix won't put all her eggs in my basket. There's a plan B. And C and D. Dawn wouldn't tell me what these plans are, but she strongly implied it's best if I do it. The World-Phoenix will see the world saved, one way or another, but all it cares about is the dimensional integrity of that portion of the universe. The living things on the planet that happens to be there don't factor into its thinking."

"Did you ever consider playing it safe? Hiding away until the job was done?"

"No. If I had the choice again today? I probably would. But after I got back from Earth, I was so angry. I felt like a ball of magma with my personality plastered over it in a shell, slowly burning out from the inside. I'm still realising just how compromised my judgement became while I was on Earth."

"I remember," Rufus said. "After you came back, you seemed much the same at first. Then the cracks started appearing until Farrah and I were worried you were going to break altogether. She ran off to yell at a diamond-ranker she was so worried about you. A diamond-ranker. She's always charted her own path, but she never would have done that before we met you. You're a bad influence, you know that?"

"You're welcome."

Rufus chuckled, shaking his head. Then he looked over at the orb again.

"Does it have the astral magic you need?" he asked. "Or is it too early to tell?"

"Too early, but I'm extremely optimistic. Learning the material that's in there is going to be an absolute prick, though, even with my advantages. I've had the good fortune that most of my astral magic studies have been with materials and teachers from outside of this world. The astral magic here is a little backwards, as if someone's been deliberately slowing its development for centuries."

"You think there's some grand conspiracy?"

"I do. We know that the Cult of the Builder has been here a lot longer than the last few decades. That's just when they started their recruiting drive and allying with the Purity church to prime for the Builder's invasion. I think their original purpose was to make sure this planet doesn't become too dimensionally active. Our universes are fragile, especially mine. The Builder inherited the responsibility of ensuring that they don't collapse from the previous Builder, who caused the problem in the first place. From what I can tell, the World-Phoenix has been riding him about it for at least a few billion years."

"But the Builder didn't fix it. He used that fragility to set Pallimustus up for invasion, right?"

"Yep. The Builder has been band-aiding the dimensional integrity of our worlds just enough to exploit them for his own ends. That's why he left that magic door on Earth and I think his cult has been here on Pallimustus, maybe forever. Making sure astral magic doesn't advance to the point of causing trouble. The occasional diamond-ranker shooting off into the cosmos is one thing, but I think the real problem is Clive."

"Clive?"

"Clive, and all the people like him that came before. Geniuses that advanced astral magic beyond the invisible limitations put on it. If the Builder cult hadn't been busy with their invasion, I think it would have only been a matter of time before they found Clive and assassinated him."

"That suggests Clive might be more right about Magic Society corruption than even he thinks."

"Yeah. And now Clive has his hands on what I suspect is the most advanced trove of magical knowledge on the planet. Seriously, even a glance at this stuff showed off how dense the material is. Our diamond-rank benefactor didn't stock a lot of foundational material; he was all about the advanced stuff. I am maybe—maybe—ready to *start* studying what's in there, and that's with Dawn tutoring me for years and an innate sense for dimensional forces."

"A sense for dimensional forces?"

"Yeah. I spent months in the liminal space the Builder's door gave me access to, tweaking the fundamental building blocks of reality as I fumblingly repaired the link between our worlds. Then I was inside a space where I ended up reworking a pocket of reality. I did that twice. By the end of all that, I could feel the astral. You've seen my cloak, the way it blows around as if there's a different wind to the normal one?"

"Sure."

"I feel those winds. The flow of the astral. Impossibly far away, yet close enough to touch."

Jason stretched his hand out in front of him.

"I really can, you know. Reach out and touch it."

His hand dropped to his side and his voice returned to normal as he snorted a laugh.

"It's a very bad idea," he added.

"I remember that too," Rufus said. "You almost killed yourself boosting your portal so everyone could escape the underwater complex."

Jason nodded.

"Anyway," he said. "The point is that I have a lot going for me when it comes to studying astral magic. If nothing else, I've got Clive to research with, and for all my advantages, I'll never grok the theory like he does. But the materials in that orb are dense. Books and recording crystals where the knowledge starts somewhere around the point my current understanding ends. I am extremely confident that what I need is in there, but it's going to take years of study before I'm ready to use any of it."

"What about all those avatars helping you study?"

"That's already taking them into account. There are centuries of accumulated research in that orb. From a being with access to some of the most advanced magical knowledge in the cosmos. Then assuming I can get my head around all of that, I need to figure out how to design the rest of a half-complete dimensional bridge created by an artefact designed by the World-Phoenix, who had to crib notes from the Builder to do it in the first place."

"So, not quick, then."

"Dawn estimated ten years. Any guess I made at this point would be so ill-informed as to be pointless, but I can't see ten years as anything but an optimistic minimum."

"I thought it was ten years until something vague and menacing happened."

"Yeah, but it got pretty obvious that completing this bridge is going to trigger something I don't like. I think she's been so vague because she knows I'd do something drastic if I found out. Doesn't want me screwing up her boss' plan."

"That sounds like exactly what you would do. I'm just wondering why you didn't push."

"Dawn has done a lot for me. I know that she's always working toward the World-Phoenix's agenda, but Dawn has gone well above and beyond any duty she had. I know that she wouldn't put this on me if she didn't think it was for the best."

"That shows a lot of trust."

"She's earned it. And even her boss has done me right a few times. Even if its motivations weren't to benefit my wellbeing, they did, and that's worth something."

"I respect that. Clive's in there now, getting a start on research?"

"We aren't at that stage yet; it's going to be a while. He's taking stock of what's in there, seeing if there are any unpleasant surprises. I don't want to take any of this into my soul realm until we're as sure as we can be that it isn't all a complex play from the messengers to spike my soul. We're pretty sure it's fine, but I'm not going to bet my soul on pretty sure."

"You should pull Clive off of that for the moment. The Continental Council rep is in Yaresh and he wants to see the whole team."

"What's he like?"

"Angry."

"At us?"

"In general, from what I can tell. He already put an axe in someone's head. The woman was a gold-ranker, so she's fine, but it certainly set a tone."

"And here we were trying to be all diplomatic."

Gormanston Bynes looked around the Yaresh elite gathered in the largest of the Adventure Society campus halls. Most were silver, but every faction represented had at least one gold, including Gormanston himself. Although he was no stranger to the game of politics, he had only disdain for all but a handful of the room's occupants. His own people were not spared from this, but if he didn't wade into the mud, he would never pull his family free of it.

For far too long, House Bynes had allowed themselves to slide. Too much indulgence in the power left to them by the generations before. Too little maintenance of the foundations on which that power rested. Gormanston had tried to lead by example, but no one was looking for an example. They just saw him as another source of shade to laze in.

That was why he had started involving himself in the family's affairs. The aristocratic faction was just like his family: weak, foolish and oblivious to their own path to self-destruction. Claiming power within their impatient, short-sighted and self-serving ranks had only required turning up and not running his mouth. Decades later, he had accomplished little more than bailing water from a ship whose sinking was inevitable. He had reached the conclusion that the ship needed to be drydocked and burned down to ashes. Only then could a new one be built in its place.

The invasion of Yaresh and the events around it was not the fire that Gormanston wanted, but it was the one he had. Despite everything that had gone on, people were still bickering over reputation and advantage while the populace lived in tents, in the ruins of what had once been their homes. That was the last straw. To lead was a duty, and the elite of Yaresh had forgotten that entirely.

Today was the day the pieces started falling into place. The day that people started falling out of place. He would have liked to involve the boy, Asano, and his knack for being at the centre of events. He was a fine adventurer but too unpredictable. It was better to work around him than with him, letting the waves he kicked up become ripples before trying to navigate them.

This meeting was a perfect example. Most of the people in it believed that the Adventure Society's Continental Council representative had come to bring Asano in line. The ones who had no trace of core in their aura knew better. Every person in the room was a member of the Adventure Society, yet only a handful were truly adventurers. Outside of a monster surge, when they had to keep their benefits, none of them would set foot in a jobs hall.

The large double doors to the room slammed open to admit a massive man. Gormanston was large, one of the elves who had an unusually powerful physique. This man was his leonid counterpart, an angry, ambulatory hillock covered in snow-white fur. He wore hard leathers that looked adequately tough to protect him on an adventuring contract. If Jason had been present, he would have thought the leonid looked more like a bikie.

Behind him, almost invisible behind the gold-ranker whose aura was as imposing as his visage, followed Vidal Ladiv. If he was unhappy at being recruited into yet another high-rank mess, he did a superb job of hiding it from his expression and his aura.

"Is this everyone?" the man bellowed with the spine-tingling rumble that only leonids could manage. "Alright, gather up; this isn't a bloody ball, you pointless gronks."

Gormanston sent out a silent wish that was granted immediately as a silver-ranker stepped forward.

"You can't talk to us like that! Do you know who—"

He was cut off by the leonid grabbing his face, having closed the distance so fast that it would look like teleportation to anyone below gold rank. The leonid held his arm out straight and was so tall that it left the silver-ranker dangling by his head, arms scrabbling ineffectually at the leonid's arm in a panic. The leonid looked at the man as if he were holding up an article of soiled clothing and recited a quick spell incantation.

"*Unquenchable flame.*"

The man's head burst into flames that licked harmlessly at the leonid's hand, rising between his fingers. The screams of the silver-ranker were muffled by his covered mouth. The leonid marched back to the still-open doors, the burning man dangling from his grip, legs flailing. The leonid casually tossed him out and then closed the doors, cutting off the now-unmuffled shrieking. The moment the doors sealed, the room was plunged into heavy silence. The leonid turned, his grin that of a lion on spotting a limping antelope.

"I put an axe through someone's head and you idiots still haven't learned to read a room. Any silver-rankers who are looking to talk back to a gold had best make sure you kill some of us first, or you may find us disinclined to listen."

He strode back towards the group, many of whom involuntarily flinched. He stopped halfway across the room, occupying half of it with no one but himself and Vidal, quietly standing by the wall. Everyone else occupied the other half.

"My name is Marcus Hargrave Xenoria," he announced. "I am an adventurer and the man the Adventure Society saw fit to deploy to your city after hearing about the events that have taken place here. I have read the complaints lodged by the adventurers, both against the local Adventure Society administrative staff and against…"

He reached into his leather vest to pull out a folded, slightly crumpled sheet of paper.

"…sweet gods, are they really called Team Biscuit? Did they let one of their familiars pick the name?"

"Actually, yes, they did," Vidal said from over by the back wall. It was the first time many in the room realised he was there.

Marcus shook his head.

"Bloody young people."

He stuffed the paper roughly into his pants pocket and turned his attention back to the group.

"The point is, the people leading this city seem to have forgotten what the Adventure Society is. I'm told that everyone in this room is a member, which makes you both the city elite and part of the Adventure Society. That makes it a failure on your part."

He marched up to the group, looking down at one of the silver-rankers at the front.

"You. You're in the Adventure Society?"

The man nodded.

"I'll ignore the very obvious question of how for the moment and ask you this instead: what is the Adventure Society?"

The silver-ranker hesitated only a moment before answering.

"A collection of people who—"

The force of Marcus' hand hitting the side of the silver-ranker's head tousled the hair of some of the people nearby. Others were bowled out of the way as the man went flying. Marcus turned to the next one.

"You. What is the Adventure Society?"

The man didn't answer immediately, his eyes darting as he looked for a response that wouldn't lead to violence.

"A shield," he said finally. He looked up at the looming leonid, who narrowed his eyes.

"Go on," Marcus prompted.

"They protect—"

"They?" Marcus interrupted. "I thought you were one of us."

"I'm sorry, I—"

"Shut up!" Marcus roared, the silver-ranker stumbling back into the person behind him. The leonid turned and paced back, shaking his head.

"Exactly what I expected," he said. "Ladiv, bring over the list."

Vidal walked to Marcus while opening the flap on a satchel hanging from his shoulder. He took out a folder and handed it to Marcus, who removed the single piece of paper before tossing the folder away. Vidal's shoulders slumped only briefly before he moved to pick it up.

"What I have in my hand," Marcus announced, "is a very short list of names. I was firmly instructed to give you all a chance to prove yourselves before I finalised it, which is what I have just done. I would say I was disappointed, but that would have required me to have so much as a single expectation of you. I am now going to read this list, and if your name is on it, you still get to be a member of the Adventure Society when you leave this room. If anyone has a complaint about their absence from this list…"

Marcus' grin showed off how many very large teeth a leonid had.

"...I will be downright ecstatic to address your concerns personally. Any questions?"

The silence that followed was broken only by the quiet rustle of Vidal returning the folder to his satchel.

48
TRADITION AND DECENCY

THE GATHERED ELITES LOOKED AT MARCUS LIKE HE WAS A MADMAN WHO had somehow invaded the Adventure Society campus. Gormanston Bynes masked his contempt for their muttered outrage, carefully moderated not to draw the leonid's ire.

Gormanston's niece, Juniper, was next to him. At twenty-two, she had reached silver rank during the monster surge. Gormanston was not the only one in the room who frequently brought around young members of their families to gain experience, political and otherwise. He still had hopes for Juniper, if he could purge the influence of his idiot brother. The days to come would determine if she could be salvaged.

For her part, Juniper stayed quiet, listening and learning. It was the habit Gormanston liked most about her. Expression concerned, her gaze vacillated between her uncle and the leonid. Marcus was still grinning, waiting for the hubbub to die down or grow loud enough to have another excuse to intervene, not that he needed one. Finally, her anxiety won out.

"Uncle Gorman," Juniper whispered. "Are you going to—"

"Gormanston Bynes," Marcus bellowed happily, attention drawn by Juniper's quiet words.

He marched in their direction as if assuming the people in his way would rush to get out of it. He was immediately proven right and arrived in the rapidly emptied space in front of Gormanston. Juniper slid back and behind him slightly, Marcus's eyes following. Gormanston stepped to block his eyeline and Marcus shifted his gaze to Gormanston's face.

Gormanston was big for an elf, but Marcus was big for a leonid. Gormanston had the unusual experience of tilting his head back to meet someone's eyes, unintimidated by the looming figure.

"Gormanston Bynes," Marcus boomed. "I was warned that you might give me trouble."

"Look at my niece like she'd be fun to slap around again and you'll see what trouble looks like," Gormanston told him.

Marcus burst out in laughter.

"Your niece doesn't have to worry, Gormanston. She's even on my list of people not losing their society membership. Most of the list is occupied by the younger people in this room. They still have a chance to avoid the pitfalls of their elders, and the society recognises that. Of course, some are too far gone already."

"And who decides that?" another gold-ranker asked. "By what metric have we been judged?"

The man's name was Finneus Gallow, a monster-core user from Gormanston's own aristocratic faction. Not a true adventurer, but not an idiot either. He was a capable force in city politics. Marcus turned on him.

"A good question, Lord Gallow," Marcus said. "And one whose answer is found in another question. I would call it a simple question, but in a room full of adventurers that could not tell me what the Adventure Society was, my optimism is dampened. What, Lord Gallow, do Adventurers do? Actually, don't answer that."

Marcus wheeled back to look at Juniper.

"Lord Bynes. Surely your young niece is up to the task of answering such a simple question. I even promise to refrain from any penalty should I be unhappy with the answer."

Juniper looked up at Gormanston, who nodded, despite not shifting his glare from Marcus. Juniper came out from behind her uncle, looking uncertain as she mustered the courage to answer.

"Adventurers... fulfil contracts?"

"YES!" Marcus boomed, pointing a finger at her. "That is exactly what adventurers do. And tell me, girl—"

Gormanston shoved Marcus back.

"Her name isn't 'girl,' and you'd best remember that," Gormanston growled.

The room went dead still as everyone in it waited for the leonid's response.

"So it's not," Marcus said. "Young Mistress Bynes, you have my apology. But to finish my question, when was the last time you took a completed contract to the jobs hall?"

Juniper seeing her uncle stand up to Marcus had finally made her more confident about the power dynamic. She answered boldly.

"This morning," she told the leonid. "My team just got back from a sweep for any escaped world-taker worms in the southern districts."

Marcus gave a grin that made it very clear that Juniper's head would fit in his mouth.

"Very good, Young Mistress Bynes. It seems you have a winner here, Lord Bynes, although quietly killing her father off might be a good idea."

The freshly emboldened Juniper stepped around her uncle to retort but was stopped by Gormanston's gentle hand on her shoulder. Marcus grinned again and turned back to Finneus Gallow.

"And there we have it, Lord Gallow: Our metric for deciding who goes on the list. Those of you who have been living up to the promise of Miss Juniper Bynes will find their Adventure Society membership unthreatened. But if the only contracts you've taken were to prevent your membership being cancelled during a monster surge, then I'm afraid you shall find yourselves stricken off."

"That is unfair," Gallow said. "Long-standing policy has been that those who stand during the monster surge will maintain their membership once the dangerous times are over."

"YES!" Marcus growled, but this wasn't the gleeful roars he had let out before. This sound was savage and angry, sending silver-rankers scrambling away as he marched to Gallow. Gallow moved to back off, but Marcus grabbed him by the throat. Gallow didn't panic or fight, instead glaring back at the leonid, even as he dangled from his hand.

"Tell me, Lord Gallow, how are things now that the dangerous times are over? Had a fun few weeks, have you?"

"I am well aware that there are new threats," Gallow told him. As he didn't physically have a trachea, Gallow's voice was unimpeded by Marcus' grip. "My family home was levelled during the messenger invasion, just like everyone else's."

"Oh," Marcus said, putting Gallow down apologetically. "I didn't realise, I'm sorry. How is your family finding it in the tent camps where the displaced are housed?"

Gallow's lips pressed thinly together for a moment before he answered.

"My family is staying at the Ducal Palace."

"Oh," Marcus said. "Then I imagine you're all working hard to earn that privilege."

"Privilege is a birthright, not a prize for service."

"And Adventure Society membership is *not* a birthright, *Lord* Gallow, however much some people seem to think it is!"

Marcus' angry roars shook the chandeliers.

"Position in the Adventure Society is earned. Through service. The dangerous times, Lord Gallow, are extremely far from over. The monster surge was unlike any that has come before, and the after-effects are being felt to this day. Which include, let me remind you, not one, but two extradimensional invasions. The Builder may be gone, but he left a lot of danger behind, and I hope I don't need to explain the threat of the messengers. It is now Adventure Society policy that, in these extreme times, monster surge policy will be extended indefinitely. You work, and you work hard, or your membership is gone."

"That policy change was never announced," Gallow said. "You can't punish us under a policy before there was an announcement for us to react to."

The leonid once more made one of his sudden changes between roaring madman and calm predator, his voice growing placid. He turned and wandered away from Gallow as he spoke.

"Allow me to explain. Firstly, I will remind you all that the Adventure Society is an organisation built around volunteerism. Unless you are a functionary, official or executive directly employed by the society, then any member is free to accept or refuse any request the society makes of them. Of course, those who refuse too many or key requests may find that their star rating lowered and their benefits from the society withheld, up to and including their membership itself."

Marcus turned and looked back at Gallow again. The room was otherwise deathly silent, the people in it frozen as they listened to the leonid's monologue.

"Revoking membership," Marcus continued, "is the limit of what the Adventure Society will do. Any member unhappy with their treatment at the hands of the society may give up their membership, obviating any and all penalties. From that point forward, the society can and will do nothing to them, unless they start raising a zombie army or something equivalently unsavoury."

Marcus levelled his gaze at Gallow.

"My point, Lord Gallow, is that both the society and its members can walk away from one another at any point. If the Adventure Society decides it wants no more of you, then no more they shall have. But, I will acknowledge the issues of tradition and decency. It is, indeed, tradition to allow those who only act during the monster surge to maintain their memberships. Not a tradition I personally care for, but a tradition nonetheless. As such, I was instructed to make an announcement regarding this shift in policy."

"No announcement was made, by you or anyone else," Gallow said.

"What is it you think I'm doing?" Marcus asked, his tone suspiciously reasonable. "I was told to announce this change by finding the most worthless collection of self-aggrandizing, freeloading scum I could find bolstering their noxious reputations using our organisation and demonstrate in no uncertain terms that their kind are no longer welcome. You will soon hear, no doubt, that this meeting is being replicated all across the planet. In short, if you're not ready to stand up and fight the messengers or whatever other threat rears its ugly head, the Adventure Society has no place for you on its roster. As of this moment, any attempt to manipulate or leverage the Adventure Society, its members and its resources will be considered an attack upon it and responded to accordingly."

"And what about decency?" Gormanston asked.

Marcus turned slowly to look at him.

"You said tradition and decency," Gormanston said. "You've explained the tradition part. What about decency?"

Marcus took on one of his predatory grins, then slowly walked in Gormanston's direction.

"Decency, Lord Bynes, is that they wouldn't allow me to lock every worthless, fake member of the Adventure Society in a building and burn it down. Decency is that the contemporaries of your delightful niece Juniper will be watched and judged instead of purged with the fetid pond water from which they were spawned. Decency is that all the people not on my list will get a chance to go home and warn their worthless friends to surrender their Adventure Society memberships before I come and take them."

He arrived back in front of Gormanston.

"That, Lord Bynes, is the most decency I have to muster. Do you have a problem with that?"

Gormanston smiled, graciously inclining his head.

"I serve at the pleasure of the Adventure Society," he said.

The wary uncertainty on the leonid's face was the first time since kicking in the doors that Marcus didn't look completely in control.

"Now," Gormanston said. "I believe you had a list to read out."

Jason and his team were in a waiting room quite different to how they had found it. There was now a selection of furniture conjured by Belinda, plus one cloud chair. A buffet table had been set up along one wall where each person was filling a plate. Gary was working a grill, the smoke being absorbed into a dimensional range hood floating over it.

"Why are you here?" Neil asked Gary. "I thought you gave up adventuring."

"I did give up adventuring. I didn't give up barbecues."

Clive and Rufus left the buffet table with full plates. Clive's plate wobbled precariously in one hand as he gestured enthusiastically with the other, explaining a concept to Rufus. They sat down near Belinda, who was already merrily chomping away.

"The aura keys we use are, of course, nowhere near as sophisticated as the standard ones the messengers employ," Clive said.

"That's not even thinking about a specialised tool like the keystone for the orb," Belinda mumbled around a mouthful of food.

"Just so," Clive agreed. "But the basic principle is the same: take a specialised aura imprint and use it as a resonance key to open a lock."

"Bad security," Belinda said, then bit into a tyrannical pheasant leg.

"Indeed," Clive said. "There are numerous ways to replicate an aura key. Belinda, here, is an expert at doing so with simple devices. An aura manipulation expert like Jason or Amos Pensinata can simply use their own auras to do so."

Belinda said something unintelligible with her mouth full and Clive shook his head.

"What she was probably trying to say was that the problem with spoofing an aura key is that it takes time to get the aura signature correct, and any good security system will detect attempts to do so and have secondary security in place, usually alarms."

Belinda nodded as she swallowed her food.

"You can get around it," she said. "Just a matter of time. But what you really want to do is get hold of the key you need. With the right tool, you record the aura signature from it in a few moments and put the key back, leaving no one the wiser. Then you can go off and replicate the key at your leisure. I built little spider constructs to sneak into places and copy aura keys for me. They're hard to detect, and can enter or hide in places that I can't."

"The flaws of this security method are well known," Clive said. "The Magic Society knows all about it, but bureaucratic inertia means they're resistant to changes that would require sweeping infrastructure shifts across all the branches. So, instead of fixing the problem, they use makeshift solutions that introduce almost as many vulnerabilities as they patch. Take your average Magic Society official, for example. They carry with them a whole plethora of aura keys to various vaults, storage rooms and research stations, depending on their level of authority."

"That idiot we met the other day," Belinda said. "He'd have all kinds of access to all kinds of great stuff."

"But the Magic Society won't just let a buffoon like that wander around with those keys," Clive said. "They have countermeasures on everything from clothes to vehicles to dimensional bags to intercept tricks like Belinda's spider constructs. It stops people from exploiting members who might not have reached their high office through competence."

"It's a pain," Belinda said. "If you wanted to get in and replicate those keys, you'd need to get all the Magic Society people in the group to throw out all of their clothes, tools, bags, the lot, and then maybe cover it all in some very specifically tailored custom magic."

"What kind of magic?" Rufus asked.

"Well," Belinda said, "something that's beyond me. I had this idea for tiny rune stones, so small and light that they'd essentially be a powder, but that would take some highly precise ritual carving using processes I don't know. You'd need an innovative magic genius obsessed with esoteric forms of magic for that. If you did manage to make it, though, you could do some interesting things. For example, you could put it in some kind of delivery system that would spread and adhere to everything, but in a way that doesn't get people wondering what the powder is. You'd need the delivery system itself to be a distraction."

"Like a sticky stink potion," Rufus suggested.

"Who's to say," Clive told him. "Hypothetically, I suppose it's feasible."

The door to the room opened and a massive, white-furred leonid strode in.

"What is going on in here?" he asked.

49

DESTINY

Marcus made his way through the Adventure Society campus after meeting with the carefully selected nobility. It was fun going full bombast and pushing around some aristocratic slackers, but it was also exhausting to ham it up like that. Fortunately, the opposite approach was the correct one for his next meeting. He had been warned, in no uncertain terms, to never get in an outrageousness contest with Jason Asano. And when Danielle Geller gave out political advice, you listened.

It would have been nice to have someone of her ability advising him on the rest of the Yaresh political scene. He'd been prepared well enough for the most part, but they'd been way off on Gormanston Bynes. He'd been warned that Bynes would be the one most likely to derail his appearance, but Marcus was almost certain the man had actually been helping him.

"Ladiv," Marcus said to the celestine trailing behind him. "What did you make of Gormanston Bynes in that meeting?"

"He should have been fighting you," Vidal said. "Undermining, pushing for concessions that would minimise the damage to his faction while he got a handle on the new political state of play. Instead, his resistance was token, and transparently so. I think he knew what was coming, and instead of warning his people, is using it to burn off the useless underbrush. It felt like we did exactly what he wanted us to."

"That was my feeling as well. Can I expect the same kind of surprise from Asano? You were assigned to him for a time, correct?"

"Firstly, always expect a surprise from Asano. On any given day. you might get a foolish buffoon, a hardened adventurer or an enigmatic figure dealing with cosmic forces. If you're really unlucky, you'll get an unstable head-case that can and will annihilate anyone or anything that wanders into view. Mostly, he takes that out on Builder cultists or monsters, but there have been other incidents. I know of one where, at iron rank, he killed multiple adventurers in a shopping arcade."

"What did the Adventure Society do to him for that?"

"Promoted him to three stars."

"You're kidding."

"It was an isolated branch, the usual corruption. The Continental Council over there ended up taking over the branch for several months to clean house."

"He's three stars again now, right?"

"There was considerable debate at the Rimaros branch as to what his rating should be set at. A three-star rating is for contracts that involve large political messes. The director decided that if he had the kings and multiple diamond-rankers making personal inquiries as to what his ranking would be, claiming Asano wasn't dealing with high-level politics already would make him look like a fool."

"They showed you his unredacted file, right? What is your take on Asano?"

"Alone, he's more liability than asset. Emotionally unstable, unpredictable. Extremely erratic. Does not work well with others, outside of his own team. Unreliable by most metrics."

"Most?"

"Jason Asano's saving graces are twofold. One is that if he decides that something is worth doing, he'll kill himself to get it done if that's what it takes. He's literally done that. The other is that when he sets out to do something, it gets done. It doesn't seem to matter who or what gets in his way, or even if it's possible in the first place."

"Trouble, but worth putting up with?"

"A year ago, I would have said no. But just as the world started going mad, a madman from another world arrived and found himself at the centre of it all, over and over. He sacrificed himself to prevent the Builder invasion from starting early and miraculously returns just as it starts in earnest. I don't think that's a coincidence. The gods don't keep visiting him in public because they're bored. They're warning us that Asano has something to do here, and we'd best get out of his way and let him."

Marcus glanced at Ladiv as they continued navigating the halls of the Adventure Society's massive admin complex.

"I was told by someone that knows Asano," he said, "that he's easy to deal with if you look at him with the right perspective."

"That is information I could have used quite a while ago," Ladiv said. "Please share."

"I was told that if you think of Asano as a diamond-ranker, it all becomes easier."

"A diamond-ranker."

"Yes. This advice came from the mother of Asano's team leader who is a highly respected gold-ranker. She has known Asano since his first days on our world. She told me that Asano himself doesn't realise it, but his mentality is that of a diamond-ranker, and always has been. The indifference to authority, operating by his own rules and values, disregarding consequences. Involving himself in things that anyone with a functional mind would run screaming from. In a diamond-ranker, that's what we expect to see, but Asano has been doing it from the beginning."

Ladiv frowned, falling into silent thought as they continued through the halls.

"There are lots of people like that," Ladiv said finally. "Arrogant. Foolish. The universe slaps them down for it. But Asano keeps getting back up, doesn't he? Even when it kills him. I said that I didn't think that Asano's arrival was a coincidence, and now you say to look at him as a diamond-ranker. Suddenly, I start to see the pattern. The more time that passes, the more it becomes clear that the world around us is treating Asano like a diamond-ranker. He was iron rank when he gained a personal grudge from the Builder. The way Soramir Rimaros treated him baffled everyone, but if he was looking at Asano as a peer, then it all makes sense."

"The Council agrees with you that Asano is not finding himself in the middle of events by coincidence. Do you think Asano has some kind of destiny, set in motion by forces beyond our reality?"

"Asano was plucked from another world. I don't know if that's because he was chosen or if he was chosen because of it, but it seems clear that he has something to do that very powerful entities want done. I even think he's working on it right now. While I was travelling with his team, I heard the occasional offhand remark about some task he was putting off because of the monster surge. The implication was that it was an undertaking of some magnitude."

"What manner of undertaking?"

"I'm not sure, but I believe it involves taking something from the messengers. It's why we came to this city."

"Taking something from the messengers," Marcus repeated. "Something contained in a giant metal orb, perhaps?"

"I think that highly likely."

"Have you shared all of this with anyone?"

"The director of the Adventure Society here in Yaresh. It's all postulation and overheard asides, so I haven't made any kind of formal report."

"Do you think Asano knows more about the messengers than he's telling us?"

"I absolutely think that."

"Which makes me wonder why he doesn't share that information."

"That much is easy," Vidal said. "Imagine if every time you brought forth major information you were disbelieved, distrusted and dismissed."

"But surely that has changed now. Everyone is aware that Asano has access to sources of information the Adventure Society and Magic Society only dream of."

"Yes. But if you go from being ignored to people trying to take what you have, take over what you're doing or just take you out entirely, I can see why you might not be open to collaboration. And it's not just Asano. You know what caused Clive Standish to fall out with the Magic Society."

"I do."

"I know that Asano has considered giving up his Adventure Society membership altogether. He threatened as much to Lady Allayeth when their relationship was still more conflicted."

"It's not now?"

"No. I think she figured out the same thing you were told and started treating him like a peer. Now people are concerned that they're a little too close."

"She convinced him not to leave?"

"I think his team are the reason he won't. Not unless the society pushes them harder."

"Hopefully, this meeting will turn that around," Marcus said.

Marcus had been warned to anticipate the unexpected from Asano and his team, and that was what he got: a conference room in the heart of the Adventure Society being used for an outdoor barbecue luncheon, indoors. The conference table and formal chairs had been piled up on one side of the room where they were being casually snacked on by two giant tortoises, one of whom had a moustache.

A collection of lounge furniture had been put in the centre of the room, mostly conjured, Marcus guessed, from the uniform green colouration and the faint tingle on his magic senses. That would be the work of Belinda Callahan, one of two former thieves on the team. The one piece of furniture that stood out was made of cloud-material shaped into what Marcus could only describe as a throne.

The man sitting in it was unquestionably Jason Asano. As promised, his aura was something to behold, and Marcus immediately saw what people had told him about it feeling akin to a messenger's. There was more to it than that, though—marks from old battles, echoes of the divine and stranger things he couldn't identify. Most of all, there was a depth to it, as if Asano contained some unfathomable void.

Asano and his team were spread out around the room. There was a leonid working the grill wearing an apron with 'adventuring is more fun when you eat the bad guy' emblazoned upon it.

"What is going on here?" Marcus asked.

"You've never heard of lunch?" the leonid asked.

"I don't buy it, bro," said a man so large, he could have been a leonid shaved down as a disguise. "No way a bloke that huge doesn't know what lunch is."

"Hey, Vidal is here," an elf said. "Standing next to this guy is practically an invisibility power."

The elf had a large physique, which always stood out on their normally svelte species. He didn't assertively project power the way Gormanston Bynes did, his looser outfit de-emphasising his physicality. He looked more stocky than muscular, even a little chunky. Marcus knew this to be the team's healer who, alongside the team leader, was reportedly one of its more conventional members. He had clearly picked up Asano's casualness around high-rankers, however.

"Why don't you blokes grab a plate and sit down," Asano said.

"Always nice to break bread while having a chat. Unless you think that what you're here to tell us will spoil lunch."

Marcus grinned. He'd been warned that Asano liked to provoke people in non-aggressive ways to feel them out, and that had certainly proven true. He glanced at Vidal.

"The food's going to be good," Vidal told him. "As for whether or not they'll like what you have to say, that is for you to convince them."

"We'll eat," Marcus decided and wandered in the direction of the buffet table. He took a plate and piled it high with grilled meat, barely making a dent in the small hillock steaming away on the table.

"Tyrannical pheasant?" he asked.

"The team came across a huge wave of lesser monsters," the other leonid said from behind the grill. "We have a stockpile like you wouldn't believe."

Marcus looked over at him.

"You're not a part of the team, correct? You're Gareth Xandier."

"I'm retired. I'm not above swinging my hammer at a monster from time to time, but I'm focusing on my craft now."

"Are you from the Xandier clan of the Redwild Mesa?"

"No, I'm from the Xandier family of some little town you've never heard of."

"Oh, he's heard of it," Asano said, watching the exchange from his cloud throne. "He knows all there is to know about everyone in this room. He's just pretending he doesn't so he doesn't seem too creepy about it. Isn't that right, Mr Xenoria?"

"It seems you've done your research as well, Mr Asano," Marcus said. "And you saw me coming."

"I don't have time for that kind of thing," Asano said. "Humphrey's mum told us about you. Did you think you could ask her about me without her letting us know someone's looking? She's loyal to the Adventure Society, but she'll burn it to the ground if that's what her son needs."

"Let's hope it doesn't come to that," Marcus said.

He moved to sit opposite Asano, claiming a couch that fit him more like a chair. Asano looked at the pile of saucy meat on his plate and looked over to the buffet. Marcus sensed a subtle aura expression and a plate lifted off the table and portions of food started floating in the air to land on it. The plate then moved through the air to hover next to Marcus.

"Protein is important, Mr Xenoria, but you really shouldn't miss the full culinary experience."

"He's not wrong," Vidal said from the buffet table where he was piling a plate high with side dishes.

"What is protein?" Marcus asked.

"Something in meat that's important for normal-rankers," Asano explained. "I won't go into it further or Knowledge will get cranky at me again. My brother-in-law could explain it; he's a doctor. That's what we call expert healers where I'm from. I'd intended to bring him over with me, maybe advance healing on two worlds. Shame that didn't work out."

"Why didn't it?"

"My family grew reticent after I started publicly executing people."

"You're a ruler on your world?"

"No, it was extrajudicial. The opportunity came up and I took it."

"You don't have any more time for the authorities on your world than mine, then."

"I tried, Mr Xenoria, I genuinely did. I overlooked one betrayal after another, countless attempts to exploit me while I was trying to work with the people who should have been saving the world. But they were too invested in short-term power grabs to do their duty. In the end, I had to do it for them. Myself and a small team I put together. But the people who should have been working with me wanted what I had, and they came for us. My lover, my brother and my friend were killed. Most of the others I made go home to their families. After that, it was me, my friend Farrah and a silver-rank avatar of Dawn. I'm assuming you know of whom I speak."

"I do."

"The Adventure Society isn't as bad as the organisations in my world, I'll grant you. But there's no escaping politics and ambitions that blind people to the larger problems. Rimaros felt very familiar in that way. Wherever I go, people in authority can't seem to stop causing me the same problems. Are you going to be my next problem, Mr Xenoria?"

Marcus burst out laughing.

"You do quiet menace very well, Mr Asano. But no, I don't want to be your next problem. Just the opposite, in fact."

"I've heard that before."

"I imagine you have. The reason I am here is that the Adventure Society is undergoing a major shift in general policy. The sinecure memberships are being stripped out. Focus and resources are being redirected to the ongoing threats. Remnants of the Builder cult, leftover monsters from an unprecedented surge. Most of all, the messenger threat."

"We don't want any extra focus from the Adventure Society," Jason told him.

"So we have surmised. We know that you have some task before you. We know that powers larger than this world are invested in its completion."

"You want to know what I'm doing."

"Yes, but I'm instructed that if you are unwilling to share that information, I am to leave it at that."

Jason sighed.

"Meaning that you'll be doing something behind my back to find out, inevitably causing us trouble at the worst possible moment."

"You have a lot of trouble accepting good news, don't you, Mr Asano?"

"I don't know, Mr Xenoria. People like you never give me any."

"Then let me be plain about our intentions. We're going to get out of your way. Clearly, you've been doing very fine without an Adventure Society hand on the yoke. You'll need to be part of a much larger group when you go underground, as there are gold-rank threats down there. I'm glad that you aren't so stubborn as to try and cut the Adventure Society out of that expedition, as you have leverage enough that you could. But in the rest of your activities, we shall leave you be unless you come to us."

"You needed a meeting to tell us you would be leaving us alone?"

"We want to be clear that what happened with attempting to seize those elementally infused messengers from you won't happen again."

"That would be a lot more convincing if the Magic Society hadn't tried to grip my huge magic ball two days ago."

"That was politics."

"Isn't it always?"

"I've just come from a meeting where I stripped a plethora of adventurers of their society membership as they used it for nothing but politics."

"Not on my behalf, I hope."

"No. The same is happening around the world. As I said, there has been a shift in general policy. We will also be reallocating resources. For example, Carlos Quilido has been conducting research using a combination of funding from the Church of the Healer and the Amouz family of Rimaros. We intend to inject significant additional funding into that research."

"You'll have to take that up with Carlos," Asano said.

"He is travelling in your convoy. And views you as a critical element in making that research viable, from what I understand."

"Lindy?" Asano said, not removing his gaze from Marcus.

"What?" she mumbled from around a mouthful of food. "Sorry, I wasn't listening. Something about being sad because everyone's out to get you? We've heard it before, so I stopped paying attention pretty early."

Asano chuckled, unoffended.

"Have Estella take a closer look into Carlos' research assistants," he told her. "Their lips may have come a little loose."

She gave him a thumbs-up as Marcus gave him a rueful smile.

"I've gone and annoyed you when that was the opposite of my intention," he told Asano.

"Why would I trust this sudden change in attitude from the Adventure Society?" Asano asked him.

"You shouldn't, I suppose. Trust is built over time, and we've not done a great job engendering it from you, have we?"

"It's not like I don't understand," Asano said. "Why would you put stock in some erratic low-ranker who's constantly getting into trouble and disrespecting everyone? I like the Adventure Society, Mr Xenoria, I really do. But I've been operating outside of the frameworks they understand for a long time now."

"You're right. The purpose of the Adventure Society is to confront the unusual challenges that this world and its people face. But these last few years have seen those challenges become more unusual than ever. We're a large organisation and our movements are commensurately ponderous. While we've been catching up, you've been facing challenges we didn't properly see or understand. You're not alone in this. All around the world, people like me are having conversations like this with people like you. People who saw all of this coming and acted on their own when we were too blind and too slow to respond."

Marcus nodded at the lanky human eating a sandwich.

"People like Mr Standish, there."

"Me?" Clive mumbled.

"Yes, Mr Standish. You. Mr Asano, while you were back on your home world, Mr Standish warned us. He uncovered a critical transport and communication network used by the loyalists of the disgraced Purity church. He led some of the people in this room on an investigation that revealed the messenger invasion. He had to fight for all of that through a less-than-enthusiastic response from us and a worse one from the Magic Society. I imagine he's explained all of that."

"Great," Asano said. "All the people who did the hard work alone while your lot sat on their butts. Now that they've been proven right, suddenly, you're looking to swoop in and take over. Or maybe just take credit."

Marcus let out a wince.

"Honestly? Yes, that's pretty close to what we're doing. Not taking over, though. Just participating. Supporting the people who jumped ahead, like you. You said that you were operating outside of our framework. You're right, and you and your companions aren't the only ones. The Adventure Society wants to expand our framework. To give you what you need, even when that is getting out of your way and letting you do what you do. I know I'm not going to convince you of anything today. All I'm asking is that you keep an open mind. Don't shut us out and we won't try to box you in."

"So, we're back to you arranging this meeting—interrupting what we were busy doing—so you could not ask to do anything."

"We can help you if you need it. I know that tensions are strained with the Magic Society—"

"We can deal with the Magic Society," Standish interrupted.

Asano got to his feet.

"We should get back to the cloud palace," he said. "This is starting to feel just pointless enough that they may have been trying to lure us away from it."

Marcus also stood.

"Mr Asano, Danielle Geller was right about most things when it came to you, but not everything. She thought you would invite me to call you Jason."

"I haven't seen Danielle in several years. Last time we met, I was nicer."

Asano went off to vanish buffet dishes into his personal space. Belinda Callahan dismissed the conjured furniture and Asano floated the other furniture back into place, albeit now with a few gnaw marks. The group vanished through a pair of portals, leaving Marcus and Vidal behind. Marcus stood, shoulders slumped, with a plate full of food in each hand. Vidal only had one, leaving a hand free to fork lunch into his mouth.

"That did not go as well as I had hoped," Marcus said.

"At least they left us our meals," Vidal said after swallowing. "He didn't completely shut us out."

"How so? I feel shut out."

"He left us a pretext to talk with him again."

"And what's that?" Marcus asked.

"At some point, we have to return the plates."

THE NIGHTMARES NEVER
REALLY GO

In the cloud palace, Jason had an almost empty room where the walls were magic whiteboards made of cloud stuff. He and Clive had spent the better part of a week using the space to try and decipher the basics of the messenger astral magic, building a foundation for further study. As a result, the walls were covered in sigils, diagrams and notes. The one piece of furniture was a large table piled high with books, notes and scrolls taken from the messenger's study. It also held a selection of thin rods that produced various colours like whiteboard markers.

The pair stood in front of a particular section of wall as an exhausted Clive passed his finger over a sequence of sigils comprising a long, linear diagram.

"I don't understand how you made this leap," he said.

"It works, trust me," Jason said.

"I do trust you. I just don't see how you got to this from where we were."

"Okay," Jason said, pointing at a diagram right before the section Clive was indicating. "Here we have our transitional forces complete and give the process impetus."

"Yes, that makes sense," Clive agreed, then pointed to the section after the diagram he had a problem with. "But how does that process end up here?"

"It's about the inherent nature of the astral energy," Jason said. "Raw magic, uninfluenced by physical reality. It doesn't just move directly like water following the easiest course. It kind of undulates."

"Undulates?"

"Yeah. It's kind of…"

Jason held out his arms and waved them about slowly while waggling his fingers.

"…like that."

"Very helpful," Clive lied. "Look, Jason, it's great that you have this instinctive sense of dimensional forces, but we have to use it as a guide, not a shortcut."

"Isn't using it as a shortcut kind of what it's for?"

"No," Clive said. "If we keep taking shortcuts, we'll eventually reach a point where we can't move forward anymore."

He pointed at the section in question again.

"Take this," Clive said. "I trust that you're right in that this is how it works. We should test it, but whatever your astral sense is, it's always been accurate when it comes to the behaviour of dimensional forces. But it doesn't show us how or why. If we just accept that something works a certain way then, yes, we'll be able to move forward. But what happens when we need to draw on the same principles and they operate differently? In some way that your astral intuition can't guide us through? We dead-end because we don't understand the underlying theory."

"So, it's like maths. If we look up the answer in the back of the book, we won't know how to solve it if it comes up again."

"Yes, if I'm following you correctly," Clive said. "I suspect our educations were quite different. Now that I think about it, a comparison of different approaches could be very enlightening. Let me grab a notebook real quick and—"

"Clive…"

"Sorry," Clive said. "I know, on task. Look, your intuition with astral magic is going to save us immense amounts of time. It means that, in cases like this, we'll know the answer and can work backwards to figure out how it works. But we need to do that, or we'll reach the point where it becomes impossible to understand the next step because we've undermined our foundational knowledge."

"I know," Jason groaned. "This is why I didn't want to learn astral magic from you in the first place. What I want from a magical alternate reality is adventure and exciting new culinary experiences, not diligent study."

"You need to do this, Jason. I can help you, now and hopefully then, but you're the one that has to complete the bridge between worlds. It does have to be you, right?"

"Yeah," Jason confirmed. "I already used the device the World-Phoenix made to establish it on the other side. Now the device is gone, and we have to do it the hard way. Either that or half-done work has to be torn down so someone else can build a new one from scratch. Dawn implied that doing it that way would not be great for the people living on the worlds in question."

"Why does it have to be you? Now that we're getting into the mechanics of it, can you explain why someone else can't finish the job?"

"The device I used to build half the bridge already was designed in such a way that I'm intrinsically linked to the construction. I'm linked to the bridge, even half finished, much as I am to my cloud flask or my dimensional realms back on Earth. Anyone else trying to mess with it would get nowhere, at best. At worst? Massive backlash."

"Why was the device designed that way? I mean, we've both been studying otherworldly advanced astral magic for years now and I at least have a basic idea of how this bridge is meant to operate."

"You do?"

"Yes. It's the difference between drawing a picture of a bridge and drawing an architectural plan you could build one from, but I have a sense of the basic concepts. Enough that I don't see any need or reason to bind the creation to the creator. Maybe I'm missing something in the complexities we've yet to decipher. Gods know there are enough of those."

"I don't know either," Jason said. "I did ask Dawn why the device worked that way. She said that she asked the World-Phoenix to build it that way but refused to explain why."

Clive let out a frustrated sigh and ran his hands over his face, feeling the stubble.

"Let's take a break," he said. "Shower and shave, maybe a nice cup of tea. Nothing is better for study than a fresh mind, after all."

"You won't get any argument from me."

Not long thereafter, they were having tea on the cloud palace balcony. Still situated on a plateau clifftop, they enjoyed the vista spanning out to the ocean.

"I wasn't so sure about situating us this far from Yaresh," Clive said. "But a week of uninterrupted investigation of the messenger's study and its contents have been extremely welcome."

"Don't get used to it," Jason warned him. "I suspect we're about to get news."

Moments later, Allayeth swooped in on a flying device that looked like a cloud.

"I love those," Jason said, nodding at the cloud construct.

"Yours is rather more impressive," Allayeth said, her gaze panning over the clifftop palace.

"It's not bad," Jason acknowledged. "To what do we owe the pleasure?"

"The messengers have sent word that the device will be delivered to the city tomorrow afternoon. Final preparations for the expedition are being readied, but the Adventure Society wants the device thoroughly examined before the operation begins. And they want the region's top expert in otherworldly magic to do it."

"Clive is the region's top expert in magic from outside Pallimustus," Jason said.

"Yes," Allayeth agreed. "We would appreciate you travelling to the city by early tomorrow afternoon at the latest. Earlier, if you wish to be present for the handing-over of the device."

"I don't imagine the Magic Society were happy about the decision to give Clive first look."

"They were not," Allayeth told him. "The director of the Yaresh branch came to protest in person, and was quite aggressive about it."

"What happened?" Jason asked.

"It turns out that aggression is not the correct approach to take with this particular Continental Council representative. I wasn't privy to the meeting, but the director left in different clothes than he came in with and the lamp from that office was missing. The Magic Society then withdrew their protest over handing the device directly to you, although they've also filed a grievance with their own Continental Council."

"A lamp went missing?" Clive asked.

"Representative Xenoria requested a replacement after the meeting. It was his office. He did not disclose where it went."

"There are only so many places it could have gone," Clive mused. "The Magic Society director is gold rank, so he could survive having it—"

"Best not to speculate," Jason cut him off.

"Mr Standish," Allayeth said. "If you'll forgive me for being impolite, would you allow me to have a private conversation with Mr Asano?"

"Of course," Clive said. "Jason, I'll go give the orb's outer shell another check before we hand it over to Emir's friend. Make sure we didn't miss anything."

"Clive," Jason said, "You've scooped out everything there is to be found in there."

"We can never be sure, Jason. Hidden dimensional pockets, secret document compartments built into the shell itself. We're talking about a diamond-rank messenger's knowledge stash. We can never be confident we got it all."

"I'm convinced," Jason said. "Go have fun."

"It's not about fun, Jason."

"Uh-huh."

Clive didn't bother trying to get the last word on Jason and left him on the balcony and Allayeth floating outside.

"You'd best come in," Jason said.

She floated down to the balcony. Her cloud dissipated and was drawn into her belt buckle. She claimed Clive's vacated seat and Jason pulled an extra cup from his inventory, filling it from the teapot.

"If the device is delivered by another group of messenger servants, the Adventure Society has agreed to hand them over to you," she said without preamble.

"Alright," he said with a nod.

"That's your only reaction?"

"I guess the new Continental Council rep is proving as good as his word so far. If he keeps this up, I might even remember how optimism works."

She frowned and he gave her a gentle smile, not one of his habitual half-smirks.

"What were you expecting?" he asked.

"I think you know the answer to that."

"If you want judgement for killing those people, you've come to the wrong place."

"Why would I want that?"

"I don't know. Why would you?"

She scowled and sipped at her tea. Her eyebrows rose.

"This is excellent."

"It's one of the Mistrun teas from Clive's hometown. There's a river, the Mistrun, which is sourced from an astral space. The water is infused with life and water magic. It produces a mist that fills the valley it runs through. The valley is gorgeous, and the tea they grow there… well, you're tasting it for yourself."

She took another sip, closing her eyes and savouring it.

"I've killed a lot of people," she said, leaving her eyes closed. "Not so many by diamond-rank standards, as I've always focused on monsters. But by any other standard, I'm drenched in blood."

"I've also killed more than I'd like," Jason said. "Not to your degree, I imagine, but enough that adding to the number doesn't make a difference anymore. Not to what it does to me."

"Exactly," Allayeth said, opening her eyes and looking at Jason. "It shouldn't matter that I killed those people. I've killed more and for worse reasons. But it keeps playing on my mind, and the only difference is you. What you said. You've done me a disservice."

"I disagree, but I understand how you would feel that way."

"You think you know better than me?"

"No."

"Killing those people was right."

"I can see why you would feel that way too. Plenty would agree with you. Maybe even most. My thoughts on that issue are settled and I think you know that, which leaves the question of who you came out here to convince. I think you know that too."

"I don't like being ill at ease over this."

"Of course you don't. But perhaps you should be thankful for it?"

"Thankful?"

Her aura radiated anger and Jason reinforced the aura of his cloud palace to contain it. He didn't want it to impact the other people in the palace, or to advertise Allayeth's momentary loss of control.

"I'm sorry," she said.

"I understand. I once had a nightmare that unleashed the darker corners of my aura with my family nearby. One of the ugly steps that led them away from me."

Allayeth nodded.

"The nightmares never really go, do they?"

"I hope not. For the same reason I want to be ill at ease when it comes to killing. When I first came to this world, I arrogantly proclaimed that I would be the morally superior adventurer. No killing."

"And how long did that last?"

"Not long at all. Of course, I was a fool. Killing monsters quickly became killing people. And once I started, it became dismissively easy. To this day I'm still trying to find balance. I still feel that urge. I see people being foolish or selfish or just plain greedy and hurting others in the process. Sometimes a lot. It would be so easy to remove them from the equation."

"Sometimes it's necessary."

"Sure. But when we make that decision, we make ourselves judge and executioner. And that makes me wonder, is my judgement better than the people I'm judging? I used to think so, and I have been wrong about that so many times. The truth is, sometimes I'm the greedy, selfish fool getting people hurt. I'm too self-centred, I know that. I get people hurt when I don't think about consequences or refuse to listen to other perspectives. But change is hard. Sometimes it feels like any progress I make goes out the window the moment things get crazy, and things get crazy a lot for me."

"There is a responsibility that comes with the power at my level. You feel that more than most of your rank, I think, and it will only get worse as your power grows. Most diamond-rankers isolate themselves from that responsibility. Hiding away from the world or leaving it behind entirely. I think, for many of them, it's just cowardice."

"It's not an easy choice," Jason said. "Abdicate the responsibility or accept that sometimes, you're going to be wrong about decisions that affect so many people. Whole worlds, even."

Allayeth gave Jason a searching look and he felt her searching his aura more than was strictly polite.

"You're not being hypothetical, are you?" she asked. "You really are one of us."

"You said you felt ill at ease," Jason said, not answering her question. "I try to cultivate that in myself now. I want to be uncomfortable when I kill or make equally sweeping decisions for others. If I can find another way, I will."

"It wasn't for you to impose your values onto me."

"No, it wasn't. When I gave you my high-handed monologue, I was sharing my perspective. You don't have to agree, or even listen, but there aren't a lot of people that understand the positions we find ourselves in. The choices we have to make. I think that we should learn from one another as best we can. It's been my experience that other people help light the way. I can't speak for you, but when left alone, I start getting things wrong. Long enough, they start getting very wrong. I imagine you're a lot better than me, in this regard. You're not as young as I am. You have more experience. And Charist, I guess."

Allayeth let out a wincing chortle.

"I would never have a conversation like this with Charist. That is a man entirely comfortable with his own judgement. The best I can do is try and ameliorate the damage."

Jason refilled their cups and they both sipped at them.

"Well," Allayeth said, "the next bundle of traitors will be subject to your judgement. You've got your wish and they'll be handed over to you. These are the ones delivering the device, if that's how the messengers do it this time. The ones being rounded up in the city will be subjected to extensive interrogation while you are away on the expedition. They may let you have them once you return."

"That's reasonable."

"Have you figured out what you're going to do with them if you aren't going to execute them outright?"

"It may come to that; I've never denied it. I have put some thought into how to rehabilitate them, though. I have some broad ideas, but can only try and see how it goes. When the time comes, would you like to be there? To see if I succeed or fail?"

"To gloat or be proven wrong? Neither appeals."

"Sometimes what's best for us is neither pleasant nor easy. That's true for both of us, whichever way it goes."

"I still don't want to forgive the people who betrayed us to the messengers."

"I know. And I understand."

"Well, stop it."

"I'm sorry? You want me to stop being understanding?"

"Yes. I didn't come here to have you sympathise with me. You disagreed with me and it's gotten into my head. I came here to clarify my feelings so I can stop dwelling on it. I can't argue it out if you keep empathising with my position."

"I can see how that would be frustrating."

She gave him a pointed glare.

"Sorry," he said, fighting down an impish grin. "Look, Allayeth, I said I wouldn't judge you and I won't."

She sipped at her tea.

"I'm not like you, Jason," Allayeth said. "My adventuring career wasn't special. I wasn't special. I wasn't exceptional or famous. I was in a top guild, but you wouldn't pick me out of that guild over anyone else. I didn't have outrageous encounters or make enemies of cosmic entities. I've always been comfortable with who and what I was. And what I wasn't, which seems to be the hard part for people. It's why I think diamond rank came so easily for me. So many of my peers were striving to be great while I never expected to be. I accepted myself as I am, and that was the key, I think. Reaching diamond, and doing so relatively young, was the only thing about me that was impressive."

"You may not know yourself as well as you think," Jason told her. "You are special, and not because you're diamond rank; you're diamond rank because you're special. I wish I could be that at peace. I'm always concerned with the person I'm turning into, one way or another. It's why I think about this so much. I envy your settled sense of self."

They sat in silence for a while until Jason had to refill their cups again.

"This is truly excellent," she said. "Would you do something for me?"

"What's that?"

"Tell me about your time in the other world. That's where you made the really big choices, didn't you? Without people like me to stifle you. I'd like to hear about that."

He sipped at his tea while he gathered his thoughts.

"Alright," he said. "But I'd like you to tell me something in return."

"And what's that?"

"You mentioned the difficulty of reaching diamond rank. No one has told me how that works yet. Or even getting to gold rank, for that matter. For all those extraordinary encounters and cosmic enemies you mentioned, I'm still a silver-ranker. I know there are changes for how to advance into and through gold rank, but people haven't even told me that much yet."

Allayeth blinked in surprise, then burst out laughing.

"Are you laughing at me?" Jason asked with an affronted look.

"I'm sorry," she said, not looking at all sorry. "I shouldn't be laughing, but seeing you act like your actual rank is hilarious to me."

"Is the diamond-ranker having fun at the expense of the lowly silver-ranker, Lady Allayeth?"

"Don't begrudge me a little fun, Jason; it's the privilege of rank. And call me Ally."

51

UNMISTAKEABLE

MARCUS WAS IN A COMMAND TENT SET UP IN MARSHALLING YARD ONE, the largest on the Adventure Society campus. From there, he was organising the round-up of messenger-servant infiltrators, as well as the impending expedition underground. He stood behind a large table covered in neatly organised maps and reports. On the other side of the table was Rick Geller, along with his fiancée and team member, Hannah Adeah.

"Your team performed excellently during the sweep," Marcus said. "I've always found working with Geller-led teams to be a pleasure."

"Thank you, sir," Rick answered.

"You can call me Marcus," he told them. "I was hoping you could help me with a minor thing. I'm aware that you were brought all the way to Yaresh because of Jason Asano. After Lord Charist put him at odds with the Adventure Society, you were asked to come here and help smooth out relations."

"That's broadly accurate," Rick said. "The word 'asked' is the only part I would categorise as entirely wrong. And, frankly, the entire thing was unnecessary. Lady Arabelle managed to mend that fence herself and we were scheduled to go home, but the society was looking for outside adventurers. They wanted people they were confident hadn't been compromised by the messengers. Since then, we've been pulling ordinary adventurer duty."

"I know that you've been dragged around because of Mr Asano, so I apologise in advance for asking, but I was hoping you would be able to help me find him. I received word that he arrived in the city this morning, but he hasn't reported in. Last word was that he came in through the gate closest to the adventurer camp outside the walls, so he's in the city unless he portalled out. I was hoping you had an idea of where he might be."

"Well…" Rick began, only for Hannah to kick his shin.

"We don't know," Hannah said. "Genuinely, Rick is being an idiot, sir, not hiding anything."

"Well, now I have to hear it," Marcus said. "Otherwise, curiosity will be burning me up the whole day."

Hannah let out a weary sigh.

"If you want to find Jason," Rick said, "find a large group of highly attractive women. Adventurers and professionals, not socialites, preferably with at least one princess."

Hannah rolled her eyes.

"I didn't get the impression of Asano as a womaniser," Marcus said.

"Oh, he's not," Rick said. "That's just how it works."

"That is not how it works," Hannah said.

"Okay," Rick said, plainly disagreeing but not pushing the issue.

Marcus watched the exchange with raised eyebrows.

"Well," he said. "That's too fun not to test."

"Aren't you quite busy, sir?" Hannah asked him.

"I could swear I told you to call me Marcus. And what's the point of being in charge if you don't get to do what you want?" Marcus asked.

"Uh," Hannah said, "carrying out your duties and responsibilities to the Adventure Society and its Continental Council?"

Marcus frowned, then shook his head, his massive white mane whipping around it.

"Nope," he said. "That's far too good an answer for me to counterpoint, so I'm going to ignore it. Come along, let's go."

Marcus marched around the table and outside, leaving the other two to trail behind.

"Look what you did," Hannah scolded Rick as they followed Marcus out of the tent. They found him with an Adventure Society official attempting to explain his schedule. The woman's dismay at Marcus' response was quite plain.

"No, push all that back," Marcus told her. "Right now, I need to find a large group of women attractive to human sensibilities, so elves, celestines. Humans, obviously."

"I wouldn't rule out leonids," Rick told him, which got Marcus to turn around.

"Really?" Marcus asked, his tone intrigued, before turning back to the official. "Also, any royalty involved would be ideal."

The official looked at him as if he'd gone mad.

"I have no idea what is going on," she said, "but I am certain that anything on my list is more important than it."

"It's not as bad as it sounds," Marcus assured her, leaving her looking very unassured. "Can you please just tell me of any group that matches those parameters?"

The official gave him an unhappy glare but scratched her head in thought.

"Beautiful women and a princess," she mused.

"Adventurers would be ideal," Marcus said. "And a princess."

The look on the official's face did not imply that made it better, but she begrudgingly answered.

"Lady Allayeth has been taking Team Moon's Edge around, introducing them to the team leaders that will be going on the expedition with them," she said. "I believe she's scheduled to meet representatives of Team Storm Shredder right about now. The team leader and one Zara Nareen."

"I assume this Nareen is a beautiful woman since you're pointing her out specifically?" Marcus asked.

"Yes," Rick said. "She's also the former Hurricane Princess of the Storm Kingdom."

He failed to notice the look that the speed and certainty of his answer got him from Hannah.

"It's very complicated, as you'd expect," Zara told Jason. "Refinancing all those people in the entertainment district was complicated enough before the city was destroyed. When it was destroyed, that got worse, obviously, but the real problems came when the city administration fast-tracked the reconstruction here and started micromanaging while ignoring property rights. They only care about creating a morale booster for the populace, which is a fine goal, but untangling the legal mess is going to take years."

Jason and Zara, along with Zara's team leader, Korinne, were watching a building being constructed in the entertainment district. With them were Allayeth and Team Moon's Edge, a team of six women personally supervised and guided from their early careers by Allayeth. They were now all gold rank, Jason estimating that to be a recent development based on their auras. His senses also picked up Bellory, but she was inside her half-built tavern, several blocks and a dozen construction projects away.

"I'll take the issue up with the city myself," Allayeth said. "I can't make any promises, but I'll try and ameliorate the damage. I maintain a small staff here at the Adventure Society, so if you could provide all the relevant details, I'll look into it. Are you going to be joining Team Storm Shredder for the underground expedition, Princess?"

"I am," Zara said, glancing at Jason. "I didn't come to the team with the most sensible of intentions, but I have found my time with them highly rewarding. I am part of it for the foreseeable future, so long as they are willing to have me. Also, referring to me as 'princess' or 'your highness' in the wrong setting could be a minor diplomatic incident. Lady is fine, although Zara would be even better."

"Well, Zara, let me introduce you to some of the gold-rankers that will be joining you when you head underground. I wanted an all-women team as role models for young girls, and not just pretty faces with no skills either. Team Moon's Edge are all exceptional adventurers by any standard. Essences are the great equaliser, but there is still too much oppression of women amongst the normal-ranked section of the populace. Given that the normal-rankers are almost all of the populace, that is a problem. I don't expect…"

Jason and Allayeth both turned to look at the sky, the gold-rankers doing the same shortly after. A tent on the back of a flying carpet arrived at breakneck speed, stopping almost instantaneously. It descended to the ground and a tent flap opened to let out Marcus, Rick and a disgruntled Hannah.

"Lady Allayeth," Marcus greeted. "Mr Asano, I've been waiting for you. The messenger envoys will reach the city soon."

"I'm aware," Jason told him. "My familiar is tracking them. He tells me that so many others are doing the same that more people are watching than being watched. Also, there's an actual messenger this time. What brings you by, Rick?"

"Winning a bet," Rick said, accepting a gold spirit coin from Hannah and dropping it smugly into his pocket.

"No," Jason said with a slow, sad shake of the head. "You just lost, mate, and you lost hard."

Rick looked at him with confusion, then at Hannah. The expression on her face suddenly registered and his eyes went wide. Jason wandered over to pat him consolingly on the shoulder.

Jali Corrik Fen was unhappy. She didn't care if a few dozen of the servants were killed by their own, but now she had been placed on the chopping block. Jes Fin Kaal had assured her that the lesser races would not risk murdering her without gain, but she had always overestimated her foresight. There was no predicting what the foolish savages would do, and the logical choice was always a poor bet.

The device was much smaller than the study of Mah Go Schaat that Kaal had also foolishly handed over. There was no telling what secrets the diamond-ranker had left behind but, more importantly, what about when he came back for them? For once, Jali was glad to be a silver-ranker too unimportant to be caught between them—assuming she lived that long.

Jali scowled at the old wound that was her rank. All messengers came into being with inherent limitations on their power. They never knew until they reached that limit, but Jali had been born at hers. Forever destined to be at the bottom of messenger society, the moment of her creation was also the peak of her existence, cursed to never become more than she was.

The teachings said that she should not worry, that the least of the messengers stood above the greatest of everyone else. The other perpetual silvers seemed to revel in that. She couldn't bring herself to do so, and her treatment at the hands of messengers not so unlucky certainly didn't reflect any superiority. There had been times when she was treated little better than favoured pets from the servant races. It was certainly why she had been chosen to deliver the device. Jes Fin Kaal's confidence that the lesser races would not kill Jali was less about Kaal's certainty than Jali's expendability.

She schooled her dissatisfaction, a long-practised behaviour. There was an astral king's mark on her soul and she had no interest in being killed for suspected sympathies with the Unorthodoxy. No astral king was watching those bound to her that closely, but a spike in disaffection could escalate that attention very quickly. Jali had known others that disappeared and she was careful about keeping her emotions in check. If the other messengers learned that she'd started meditating to calm herself, something she picked up from the lesser races, she could face anything from derision to violent excision.

Jali moved smoothly along the road, bare feet hanging just above the flagstones of the highway. Months of poor maintenance had left them uneven and with growth forcing its way up between them. Behind her was a pair of the floating vehicles the lesser races made with their primitive magic. One had a pair of servants and the device which was the size of an average human male when crushed into a ball shape. The other vehicle was more servants in case of trouble.

Monsters were always a problem, but unlikely to have an interest in the device. It was the fractious people of the city that presented the real danger. One of the few things they could truly be relied on for was to turn on one another, and if they sent one of the gold-rankers, it would be a problem. Jali was unwilling to rely on the inherent superiority of the messenger species she had so often been assured of.

Even that was of limited concern. She could sense the plethora of spies tracking the group in what they probably thought was secret. The inability of almost any of the lesser species to properly contain their auras was laughable. She wondered if most of them had been sent to distract from any who were able to evade her senses as they surely had some stealth specialists worth the name. Jali had fought during the attack on Yaresh and knew that the lesser races had members that weren't so lesser at all.

If nothing else, the astral king's shadow familiar should be around, and she certainly hadn't sensed it. Many scoffed at the idea of a silver-rank non-messenger astral king, but Jali knew it was denial. Her fellow messengers had proven startlingly good at that, but the ones who had been there knew better. They had felt the aura. The urge to kneel. If anything, Jason Asano's incomplete state made it worse because he was less unknowable. Less was hidden, his aura whispering secrets of the infinite.

So many of her kind had been driven to fury by his very existence. He was antithetical to so much of what they had been told about not just who, but what they were. Oddly, those with potential beyond their current rank were affected most strongly. Most of Jali's kind, forever bound to silver, were shocked but not overwhelmed. The central tenets of messenger identity had not been kind to them.

The idea of meeting the astral king had left her intrigued more than afraid, and she was uncertain as to why. Mah Go Schaat, in all his power, had dropped dead at Jason Asano's feet. Marek Nior Vargas followed him into a hole in the ground with an entire company of messengers and never came back. There were dangerous whispers, especially amongst those bound forever at silver rank. Jali had kept well away from such talk, her caution proving wise when a cluster of Unorthodoxy sympathisers was purged.

There were other rumours too, ones that were allowed to flourish instead of being quashed. The concept of a non-messenger as an equal nudged closer to revolutionary thought than Jali thought would ever be allowed. Conveniently, these rumours played into Jes Fin Kaal's plan to use Jason Asano not by subjugating him, but as an ally.

Kaal was playing fast and loose with the teachings that formed the core of messenger society. Jali was certain that tied into their entire purpose in the region, which was not the same as that of other messenger groups. She was not privy to what their astral king wanted, but it felt more and more like they were courting disaster, discord and internal strife. If not for the brand on her soul, Jali would have run far and fast long ago.

They reached the location where she had been told to wait, a short distance from the city. There were large holes in the road rimmed with blood stains from the last envoy to meet with the lesser races here. Just as she was wondering how long she would have to wait, a single aura entered her senses from the impenetrable barrier of the city. She tensed upon sensing it, as it would be forever unmistakable to her.

Jason Asano was coming, and he was coming alone.

52

MONEY OR THE BOX

JASON SWEPT A COUPLE OF METRES OVER THE HIGHWAY IN A FLYING device that was little more than a seat in a roll cage with drone rotors. It was something he'd seen on the internet on Earth, with some sleek Shade modifications and, of course, finished entirely in black. Convincing the Adventure Society to let him go alone had been startlingly easy thanks to the Continental Council rep, who was bending over backwards to get on his good side. It was the opposite of what Jason had been dealing with from almost every authority group he encountered. He wasn't entirely comfortable with it either.

"You seem troubled, Mr Asano," Shade said, reading him perfectly as always. "You have a problem with Representative Xenoria being so accommodating?"

"I just don't want to be one of those people who use privilege and power to get special treatment. And yes, I know that makes me a huge hypocrite because that's kind of exactly what I want."

"I think I know you well enough to state that you only want special treatment to the degree that special circumstances warrant it, Mr Asano. Representative Xenoria seems intent on overcompensating, which I believe to be the source of your concern. As he has done swift work to demonstrate his sincerity with actions and not just words, perhaps it is time to reciprocate with a little gratitude and courtesy. Speak to the man and tell him that you want your circumstances to get special treatment as necessary, rather than you getting it as default."

"Have I ever mentioned how much I appreciate your wisdom, Shade?"

"Perhaps in passing, Mr Asano, but it is always welcome."

Shade's vehicle form made short work of the journey and they arrived at the waiting messenger envoy. The vehicle exploded into a shadow cloud from which Jason shot out, carried by momentum. He landed with practised grace in front of the messenger, the dark cloud drawn into his shadow and vanishing.

Jason could feel the nervousness of the non-messenger servants, standing amidst the blood stains of their predecessors. More interestingly, the messenger herself was also nervous. Her appearance was traditional messenger imperiousness. Her outfit was an odd mix of Roman senator and Roman centurion, and Jason would only have been elbow-high on her if she wasn't floating over the ground. She was literally looking down her nose at him from on high.

Her aura was a stark contrast to her appearance. It had the usual refinement of a messenger, not letting any loose emotion slip, but Jason had no hesitation in rudely and forcefully probing it to get a better read on her.

Jali felt his approach and watched him arrive in a device combining magic with technology not native to this planet. She was reminded that he was a cosmic traveller, like her. The vehicle disappeared and he landed on the ground, dressed in casual clothing, not combat gear. His outfit, solitary arrival and relaxed manner all indicated her being entirely dismissed as a threat. It was not something she was used to outside of her own kind.

He forced an aura probe on her, leaving her feeling vulnerable and exposed, although she schooled her expression and body language to show none of it. Her attempts to read his, in turn, were like trying to push a fish through a brick wall.

"Interesting," he mused, looking her over. "Why would Jes Fin Kaal send you, of all people? Is she testing you or me? Both, probably. More efficient that way."

"The Voice's intentions are none of your concern," Jali told him.

"They are very much my concern," he disagreed. "Jes Fin Kaal and I are working very hard to use one another while being used as little as possible. She didn't send a messenger on a whim or you specifically at random."

"You killed the last envoy. I am expendable."

Jason frowned.

"Low self-esteem? I didn't think your kind were capable of it."

"We have your device. Take it and kill us."

Jason narrowed his eyes.

"You're really miserable, aren't you?" he asked. His voice had actual sympathy in it, which stabbed her deeper than she liked. It also had pity, which made her angry.

"What I am doesn't matter, Jason Asano. I am here to hand something over and that is all."

He ignored her response and started pacing, distractedly rubbing his chin in thought. He stopped suddenly and turned his head to look at her.

"She wants to know if I'll try and turn you to the Unorthodoxy," he said. "That's interesting. She wants to know if I would, and if I could. And she wants to know if you'd turn. Does she know that you've shucked off the indoctrination already? She must, if she's taken a good look at you, but has she? Would she? Is a messenger supposedly trapped at silver rank even worth looking at?"

He returned to thoughtful pacing as Jali's mind raced. What did he mean by *supposedly*?

"Why didn't she have you killed already?" he wondered aloud. "Did she not know that your faith is gone? Did you? I can feel the self-control. It's all over your aura like it's your whole life. I suppose it is when there's an astral king who'll notice the moment you let your mind rebel, even if you do nothing about it."

"How do you know so much about us?" Jali couldn't help asking. "How are you an astral king?"

She could feel his astral king nature, but barely. The opposite of when he'd blasted his aura across the battlefield, he now kept it contained.

"So much of what you've been taught is wrong, but I think you know that. Your uncertainty and inner conflict are stamped on you, almost as deeply as the astral king's brand. You've had doubts for a long time. I have to imagine that the only reason you haven't been purged is so that you might lead them to others like you. But you're disciplined, aren't you? You never stopped toeing the line. Never turned to the Unorthodoxy. Funnily enough, that means you don't have any value to them because you're not leading them to anyone."

He nodded to himself.

"That's why they gave you to me. They want to know how much I got from Marek Nior Vargas and Tera Jun Casta."

He turned, locking his gaze on her as he felt her reaction.

"You know Tera Jun Casta," he said. "It makes sense. Both stuck at silver, bottom of the messenger pecking order."

"How have you even heard of her?" Jali asked. "She is hardly Mah Go Schaat or Jes Fin Kaal."

"She used a duel power on me."

"Then if you are here and alive, she is dead."

"No. I broke the power."

"That isn't possible."

He grinned.

"Make a list of everything you know about me. How many of them are possible?"

"Words are easy, Jason Asano. If she is alive, where is she?"

"I'm an astral king," he said. "Isn't it kind of obvious?"

"Your astral kingdom."

"Yes. Want to see it?"

"What are you doing?" she asked. "What do you want?"

"I want to know that there's hope for the messengers. That you're worth saving."

"You think you can save us? You think we need saving?"

"I can't save the messengers. I know a bloke who wants to try. But maybe I can save you, if you want that. I get the feeling that maybe you do."

"I have no interest in your judgement or your ploys."

He looked her up and down.

"I can feel it, you know that," he said. "The fear of going too far. Of having your astral king tear you apart from the inside out."

A white stone arch rose from the ground and filled with transcendent light. She could feel his power clearly through the portal, knowing his astral kingdom had to be on the outside.

"You've got a choice," he told her. "You can leave the device you brought and go back to your people. You can keep living in quiet desperation until Jes Fin Kaal decides you're more liability than asset. Or you slip and your astral king reaches out from across the cosmos and ends you."

"You have nothing to offer as an alternative."

"No?"

Tera Jun Casta stepped out of the portal.

"Asano, I don't know what game you're… Jali?"

"Tera," Jali said. Her equanimity was gone, her stoic expression giving way to the mix of fear and confusion she'd been hiding behind it.

"Why are you here?" Tera asked.

"Asano made a deal with Jes Fin Kaal. I'm delivering something."

Tera looked between her and the man standing quietly by the portal, letting them talk.

"I know that your faith in our people isn't as strong as it should be, Jali," Tera said. "I know that we grew apart because of that, but don't let this man take you all the way. Don't let him erase the astral king's mark. Unsealing your advancement potential isn't worth losing who and what you are. He took my very identity from me."

Jali blinked, stunned at what Tera had just said. *Remove* the brand? Unlocking rank advancement? The very concept flew in the face of everything she had been taught. That all of them had been taught. Just the idea of it was electrifying.

"He can do that?" Jali whispered as if saying it too loudly would shatter the hope like glass. Her emotions erupted, years of careful self-control bursting like a flooded dam.

"Through the portal!" Asano yelled as she felt his aura snap around her like a cage. "I can shield you in there!"

Something inside her twisted savagely. The astral king had felt the emotions she'd held back for so long and was killing her for having them. Her body and soul formed a unified gestalt and it was trying to tear itself to shreds. Asano's aura shoved her own down to nothing, his influence impacting her with the inexorable vastness of gravity. Her body's attempt to wrench itself apart slowed to a crawl, but the power driving it pushed back hard. Asano's influence was losing ground fast and would last only moments. She looked at Tera and saw her own horror reflected in the eyes of her fellow messenger. Tera could sense what was happening and her face twisted in reluctance as she warred with herself over some decision. With a grimace, Tera jerked her head at the portal.

"Go," she said to Jali, who stood shell-shocked. "GO!"

Tera grabbed her and marched her towards it, all but shoving her through. Jali let out a shuddering breath and stepped through the portal.

Jason let out a sigh as he watched Tera follow the other messenger, whose name was apparently Jali, through the portal. He had no compunction about letting a messenger die, but he was the one who had unsettled the woman enough that she drew her astral king's attention. Inside his spirit realm, Jason could stave off the astral king's influence for a time, but there was no getting around the access the astral king had to her soul. Not unless Jason went into her soul and removed the king's brand himself.

In the meantime, there was a cluster of very confused messenger servants standing around, unsure of what just happened. There were eight of them. It was fewer than Allayeth had killed, but he decided that might well be best. Better to try with a handful than wrangle a crowd, and he wasn't going to go easy. If it came to it, he'd put them down with no more hesitation than Allayeth had.

"I can see your emotions. I know your fear. It seems that you were told what happened to those that came here before you. Yes, these blood-stains are theirs. The ones that didn't turn entirely into rainbow smoke. You have a choice to—"

Jason was cut off as a gold-ranker blurred in front of him, faster than he could react. The gold-ranker placed a hand on Jason's face and another on his torso, then unleashed power into both. Jason's head and chest exploded, liquefied flesh raining down onto the highway. The top half of his body was gone, falling to the ground and breaking apart like a dry cake as it turned into a pile of leeches.

Inside his astral realm, Jason opened his eyes when his connection with Colin broke as the familiar's Voice of the Will form collapsed. He vanished, emerging through the portal in front of the leech pile and a star-tled gold-ranker. The man hesitated only a moment before moving faster than Jason could react to again. It wasn't faster than Allayeth, who was suddenly there, gripping the man by the throat. Savagely barbed vines were growing out of her skin and wrapping around the gold-ranker like a cocoon, suppressing his essence abilities and gouging his skin.

"Told you," Jason said. "You owe me dinner."

"I'll take this one to Xenoria," Allayeth said. "The three of us are going to have a nice, long chat."

She vanished with the gold-ranker, leaving Jason with the pile of leeches and a group of messenger servants more confused than ever. More leeches poured out of the portal like a stream, enough to reform Colin into his Voice of the Will form, identical to Jason.

"Good job," Jason told him. "If this lot choose poorly, you can use them to replenish your flesh stores."

They both turned to the messenger servants.

"As I—kind of—was saying," Jason told them, "you all have a choice. You can be the next set of bloodstains on this ground, or you can go through that portal."

One of the messenger servants mustered the courage to ask a question.

"What's on the other side?"

"Really?" Jason asked. "I thought between the naked bloodstains and the idea of being fed to Colin, here, you'd all be jumping to go through the portal. I'm not wrong in thinking that's a pretty obvious choice, right?"

"Not at all," Colin said. "Option one is to go somewhere unknown, and option two is being slowly devoured in the middle of the road by a pile of leeches with teeth."

"It's not exactly money or the box," Jason agreed.

"I don't think they understand how enthusiastic I am about the chance to eat them. I'm going to go for it with gusto because you rarely let me eat normal people. Monsters are fine, don't get me wrong, but what I'd really like to do is devour every living thing on a planet. They're not that, but they're a start."

Jason let out a groan.

"Colin, how many times do I have to say it? No blood apocalypses."

53

THE TASK YOU CAN'T SEEM TO MANAGE

IT WASN'T HARD TO GET THE MESSENGER SERVANTS IN LINE AND JASON was soon frog-marching them into his soul realm. These were people already broken by the messengers, so obedience in the face of power came easy. That Jason had clearly been in the position of power over the messenger had helped.

They had already surrendered to the idea that the messengers were all-powerful, becoming traitors in the face of the seemingly inevitable. If they were wrong about that, then where did it leave them? It was a question Jason was hoping they would all ponder, but not right that moment. Fortunately, a little bit of imposing aura projection got them following orders, something they were used to from the messengers.

Jason followed them through, arriving in his soul realm. He'd sent them to a different area than the two messengers, Tera and Jali. The servants arrived in a building that was somewhere between hotel, prison and mental ward. Arabelle was waiting as the unnerved people were guided away by avatars of Jason. The servants were all the more shaken seeing the multiple copies of him.

"Is this the same wallpaper as when I made this building?" Jason asked, looking around.

"No," Arabelle told him. "Also, the stairwells switched from switchback to curved."

Jason shook his head.

"I have got to get a handle on stabilising my soul realm. Everything keeps shifting around on me, and that's when it's meant to be there."

He fell into a chair that came into being as he sat.

"Are you alright, Jason? You look pale."

He nodded, but also flashed her a slightly pained smile.

"Shutting out an astral king from someone's soul isn't easy. I had to tap into my astral gate and extend my spiritual authority over her. I also had to guess that it was possible and figure out how to do it in about five seconds, so I'm pretty happy with how that went."

"Jason, I don't know what you're talking about. I didn't see what happened out there."

"The messenger they sent was borderline on throwing off her indoctrination. I think Jes Fin Kaal sent her to see what would happen. She has to be concerned about how I'll influence her messengers, and rightly so if there's more like this one. The astral king sensed she wasn't on board with team Cosmic Angel Nazi anymore and decided to scrag her. I managed to hold the astral king off long enough to get her into my soul realm, but she won't last long, even here. Not unless I excise that connection permanently."

"By digging into her soul? Like the others?"

"I like to think I do so with a little more finesse than 'digging' implies. I'll admit that it was a little rough at first, but it didn't take long to get a handle on it. It was easy. Instinctual, like understanding a newly awakened essence ability. It's an astral king thing, I'm pretty sure. I can only do the basics of soul manipulation, and only on messengers because their souls seem built for certain kinds of artificial alteration. It's almost like they're artificial themselves. I imagine anything more than that is what the soul forge I don't have yet is for."

"Yet? You're certain you'll get one?"

"Forever is a long time," he said, then nodded his head at the last of the messenger servants as they were led away. "I'm glad you agreed to help with them."

"I'm glad you asked. Not to offer offence, but amateurs bumbling their way through treating people who have experienced mental trauma is a very bad idea."

"No offence taken. At all. I am startlingly aware that I am not a mental health professional."

"I'm also glad that you're attempting this at all. Most people would dismiss these people as traitors."

"They are traitors," Jason said. "But that doesn't have to be the end. If we can redeem this lot, there's hope for all of us."

"I would like to start by working with them myself," Arabelle said. "There will be a time for you to come along and disprove messenger superiority, but immediately isn't it. I'd like to de-escalate their circumstances rather than take them from one extreme to another. That will just close them off."

"I'll leave that to your judgement," Jason told her. A shadow extended out to engulf him, and when it shrank back, he and his chair were gone.

"Yes," Arabelle said to the empty room. "Because why bother with the basic courtesy of a goodbye when there's a dramatic exit to make."

Jali and Tera were in a garden courtyard of sandstone tiles and flowering wall vines. There was a sun high in a clear blue sky. It was the location into which the portal had deposited the two messengers after they rushed through it.

"You're telling me to die?" Jali snarled. "I can feel her twisting me from the inside out."

"At least you'll die a messenger," Tera told her. "Not whatever I've been turned into."

"How are you anything but a messenger?" Jali asked. "One that's free? One whose power isn't chained to the ground while the people around her rise to new heights?"

"Asano stealing my purpose is not freedom, and infusing me with his power is no gift. I have been tainted for whatever dark purpose he intends for me."

"Dark purpose?" a male voice came from above. They looked up to see Marek Nior Vargas descending through the sky.

"Messengers go where they like," he continued as he alighted on the tiled ground. "Enslaving or wiping out entire planetary populations. Countless worlds across countless universes, an unstoppable swarm, consuming and moving on like locusts. What is that if not dark purpose?"

"It is glory," Tera told him. "It is the right of those that stand at the pinnacle to look down on those below them."

"So we're told," Marek said. "The lowest messenger is above the highest of any other race. Then there is us, a second hierarchy. Remind me, Tera Jun Casta, who stands at the pinnacle amongst the messengers?"

"Your sophistry will get you nowhere, Marek Nior Vargas," Tera told him. "Asano is no messenger, nor is he a true astral king. He's flawed."

"He is incomplete," Marek corrected. "Not flawed."

"Oh, don't sell me short, Marek," Jason said, stepping out of a shadow. "I can be both. I have depths we have not yet begun to plumb. Also, I didn't leave anything inside you, young lady. If I did, your dark agenda would be obsessively watching recording crystals of *The Greatest American Hero.*"

Tera wheeled on Jason, opening her mouth to speak.

Tera Jun Casta.

Jason's words weren't spoken. They came into being like the creation of light at the dawn of time, an act of will that defined the universe. The three messengers were suddenly and extremely aware of where they were. They were not just surrounded by Jason's power; his power was everything. The ground beneath them and the sky above. The air brushing against their skin and the sweet scent of wildflowers. They were in a reality where they alone were alien and their continued existence was at Jason Asano's whim.

He gave them a friendly smile.

"Tera," he said softly. "We both know that you waved Jali here into my astral realm so that she wouldn't die. Maybe now, instead of telling her to die for your beliefs, you might want to give that action you took some thought. Examine why you did that. See how those beliefs hold up when you have the courage to be unflinchingly honest with yourself."

Jason made a flicking gesture and Tera was gone as if she'd never been there.

"Marek," he said, "leave me to speak with my guest."

"Asano, I think it would be best if—"

Jason looked at him and Marek felt it. His sense of balance lurched as if Jason's head had stayed where it was and the rest of the universe turned to position Marek in his eyeline.

"I wasn't asking, Marek Nior Vargas."

Marek didn't respond, taking to the air with a beat of his wings.

"I…" Jali said hesitantly, stopping as Jason turned to her, even though his expression softened.

"What were you going to say?" Jason asked gently.

"Marek Nior Vargas is a respected war leader, even amongst my kind. I've never seen someone like him scared before."

Jason nodded and sat, a chair appearing under him. A stool appeared behind Jali, backless to accommodate her folded wings. She turned and looked at it for a moment before sitting. She turned her gaze nervously back to Jason.

"You know Marek, then?" he asked casually.

She shook her head.

"I know of him. I'm too insignificant for him to know me. He's one of the commanders, amongst the strongest. I always paid attention to him."

"Why?"

"There were rumours. That perhaps he was like me."

"A doubter in the messenger orthodoxy?"

"I have nothing to do with the Unorthodoxy."

"I don't care if you do or don't. That is Marek's battle, not mine."

"Then he is? Part of the Unorthodoxy?"

"He is now. As for before this, I don't think he dared. I'm not sure that it's an actual organisation as much as an idea. How can you have a resistance movement when your soul is enslaved and your master will sense the rebellion inside you? Marek is free to be a rebel now, but you should be wary of him. I believe that he has a trap for you, although I doubt he sees it that way."

"A trap?"

"He's going to offer you a false dichotomy, but that is a concern for later. There are more pressing issues at hand."

She nodded, her whole body looking shrunken.

"How long do I have?" she whispered.

"A few days, without intervention."

She gestured around them.

"Isn't this place intervention?"

"This is hiding. Intervention is less gentle but more permanent. May I ask for your full name?"

"Jali Corrik Fen."

"I'd say I wish we met under better circumstances, but these are the best we could ask for, even if it doesn't feel like that right now."

"I'm dying."

"Yes, dying. Not dead. Because I was there the moment your astral king decided that you were no longer worth the power she's leaching from you. I don't know how many people in the cosmos are both willing and able to help someone in your situation, but I suspect calling them excruciatingly hard to find is a profound understatement. Yet, here I am, sitting right across from you. If I were you, I would consider that about as good a circumstance to meet under as I could ask for."

"Is what Tera said… can you truly—"

"Yes. True freedom from the astral king, but not without its own unpleasantness."

"I've heard of messengers changing allegiances between astral kings. Being traded like they were from the enslaved races…"

She paused, looking scared.

"What's wrong?" he asked.

"You looked angry. In this place, I could feel it. Like the air getting hotter."

"I don't like the way the messengers treat people. I think you know that the astral kings treat the rest of the messengers like you all treat everyone else. I hope you reflect on that, in the days to come, and consider what it means for how you conduct yourself around others."

"Do I have a choice? What Tera said. It means that you can overwrite my astral king's brand on my soul with your own, doesn't it?"

"I can. I've never done it, and I hope I never reach the point where I make that choice."

"Then what about Tera? Marek Nior Vargas? No astral king would let you hold their messengers here, especially Vesta Carmis Zell. How have they not been killed?"

"Because I didn't replace their brand with mine. I replaced it with their own. They are free."

"Then why would they obey you?"

"Because I can annihilate their physical forms, leaving the ragged remains of their souls purely spiritual, and then kick them out into the astral for the Reaper to take. Good old-fashioned tyranny."

"Why? Why are they here? Why am I here? What are you doing with us?"

Jason leaned forward, looked down at his feet and sighed.

"I hate this," he said.

"You hate using us?"

"I hate that your species has so much power and the concept of compassion never occurs to you as a motivation."

He looked up at her before continuing.

"I hope that's cultural, Jali Corrik Fen. I genuinely do. I'm rather hoping that you'll be the one to prove it. You're quite different from the other messengers I've met and that's a very good thing. But those are my ambitions, and we should put those aside for now. The issue at hand is keeping you alive and setting you free. From Vesta Carmis Zell, to be clear; you're still going to be my prisoner until I decide otherwise."

"How?"

"Well, step one is a doozy: you have to let me into your soul. That's sometimes the hard part. I've had a messenger desperately wanting to let me in, but they couldn't bring themselves to do it. Couldn't fight past their instincts, even to avoid death at the hands of your astral king."

"I can't believe that Tera Jun Casta let you do that."

Jason bowed his head again.

"She didn't," he whispered.

Jason felt the surprise in her aura.

"You're ashamed," she said. "You did something to her, and you're ashamed."

Jason forced himself to meet Jali's gaze and gave a confessional nod.

"She used a duel power on me. If neither of us killed the other, it would have killed us both. The only way to save us was to force her to let me into her soul and turn the ability off."

"Why not just kill her? She was trying to kill you."

"Peace has to start with someone. Sometimes it seems impossible, but that can be when the effort is most important. There was another way, and I took it. Compassion, like I just said. But I may have gotten it wrong. As you said, she would never have let me in. Not until I tortured her soul until she broke. Compared to that, just killing her might have been mercy. She hasn't taken any of it well. Not what I did, or what that means for her. To her. I hadn't done that before and I don't know how much damage I inflicted in my ignorance. I don't know if any of who she was is even left after what I did."

"She's not very different from when I knew her," Jali said. "I would say angrier, but no. We were friends, once. Neither of us took being limited to silver rank well, but we learned to deal with it in very different ways. I questioned. Reasoned. I had to be careful not to go too far, but the others knew about my doubts. It left me isolated. Untrusted. Tera went the other way. Absolute zeal. Unflinching dedication to duty, to the messenger race. Do you know what happened to us when you unveiled your aura during the attack on the elf city?"

"Rage. Frenzy. A general agreement that killing me should be at the top of the to-do list."

"You are an affront to everything we've been taught about ourselves. Especially our aspirations. It's why those like me, locked at silver rank, didn't react. Except for those like Tera."

"The ones who kept the faith, even when the faith didn't keep them."

"Yes. What you've done is take everything she built her life around and shatter it to pieces."

"That is the impression I've gotten. I'm hoping that time changes things for her. I'm hoping that you change things for her as well."

Jali looked at him like he was some oddity that washed up on a beach.

"You mean that, don't you? You truly have compassion for her. Someone that used a power on you that guaranteed one of you would die. And you feel ashamed for what you had to do to accomplish the impossible task of keeping her alive instead of killing her."

"Is that so strange?"

"Strange?" she asked with a laugh, surprising Jason. "It is, without question, the most bizarre thing I've ever seen. I have never heard of someone feeling compassion or shame over a messenger. Not from my own kind and certainly not from any other. Not anywhere, not ever."

"Don't you think that's sad?"

"Everyone sees us as enemies. We even see ourselves that way. When the astral kings come into conflict, we make war on one another."

"I admit that I have some trouble mustering up any good feelings for the astral kings," Jason said. "But the rest of you are slaves, and I suspect most of you don't even know it."

"I knew," Jali said in a whisper.

"I can do something about that. If you let me—"

"Yes."

Her answer was firm and confident.

"As I said, it's not so easy. Even when you want it."

He stood up and his chair vanished.

"I'll give you some time to process your thoughts."

"I'd rather we do this immediately."

"It was only minutes ago that you were a loyal messenger. Minutes."

"If I was loyal, I wouldn't be here. You'd probably have killed me."

"Perhaps, but even so."

He gestured at an archway in the wall that hadn't been there the last time she glanced in that direction. It led to a garden path running between beds of white and red flowers.

"Wander as you will," he told her. "Anywhere that lets you in, you are free to go. I'm not always paying attention, but if you speak to me, I'll hear it. If you want or need anything, just ask. Food, drink. To talk with other messengers here. A zeppelin in the shape of your own head. Just be aware that things might go a bit wobbly on you. I'm still getting a handle on remaking reality with the astral throne and stuff tends to shift about a bit."

He frowned.

"Which suddenly makes me worried about the people back on Earth that live in places where I remade reality. Oh well, I'm sure it's fine. Anyway, take some time and let your mind settle as best it can. I know what it's like to have everything you think is true turn out to be breathtakingly wrong. I'll find you soon enough and we'll talk again. I'll explain everything in detail about what my entering your soul and changing things entails."

"And then you'll do it?"

"Yes."

She turned to look out through the archway.

"I don't…"

When she turned back, he was gone. Her senses didn't register his absence because they told her that he was everywhere.

Jason emerged from the shadow of a tree atop a cliff. Marek Nior Vargas was standing on the ground instead of floating over it, looking out at a lake below, the shore occasionally dotted with sprawling lake houses. There was also a house in the middle of the lake, carved from a massive iceberg. Jason went and joined him in taking in the view.

"You'll talk to her if and when she wants you to," Jason told him.

"She should have the guidance of her own kind."

"The guidance of her own kind gave her a lifetime of misery. It indoctrinated her so thoroughly that she believed the most heinous acts were righteous. What she needs is time and space to think, finally free of the guidance of her own kind."

"And your guidance is better?"

"The comments on a trailer for an all-female movie reboot are better than anything your people can offer. But on the bright side, she may accomplish the task you can't seem to manage."

Marek turned to look at Jason.

"What task?"

"Convincing me that your entire species is worth anything more than killing on sight."

54
WORTH SAVING

MESSENGERS RARELY TOUCHED THE GROUND. IT WAS THE REASON MAREK Nior Vargas had stood out to Jali; he often stood on the ground, walking instead of floating. This act had drawn a lot of negative attention, leaving many wondering, as she had, if he was as loyal a messenger as he proclaimed.

Jali had decided to follow his example, her feet grounding her both literally and figuratively. It was unusual feeling the weight of her body holding itself up instead of floating with her aura. She suddenly realised why so many messengers lost their composure when grounded in a fight; the sensation was slightly unsettling. In the middle of a combat that was already more difficult than anticipated, it would be enough to throw them off further.

Rather than shrink away from that uneasiness, Jali embraced it as she moved through the gardens. As the gardens changed, so did the textures under her feet, from neat tiles to dirt tracks. Sometimes the change in the gardens came as she walked from one to the next. Other times, the gardens changed themselves, the world shifting with a lurching sensation. Open lawns and topiaries became small huts and bridges winding through bright flowers. A shift later, she was on a narrow dirt path twisting through dense green foliage. The thick canopy left her in false twilight, surrounded by shadows. She quickly discovered that the shadowy foliage was full of sharp, hidden thorns that, at a taste of her blood, started rapidly growing. Forced to hasten her step to leave them behind, she was happy when the world lurched again, leaving her somewhere else.

One garden was a complex network of water channels with drifting waterlilies carrying brightly flowering orchids and lotuses. She thought she glimpsed one in which a rabbit in a top hat was painting a watercolour, but the gardens changed just as she spotted it. It was gone so fast, she couldn't be sure that it wasn't just her imagination.

She passed red flowers that smelled of blood yet were somehow sweet and enticing, despite the coppery tang. The dissonance seemed to bypass her nose and take place in her mind, as disorienting as everything else. Another garden was set out in strict right angles, the flower beds holding black and white flowers in regimented rows and columns. The flowers had no smell, but Jali had a very strong sense that straying from the path would be extremely bad.

Jali was staring at her reflection in a still pond when the world lurched again. She found herself underground, a river streaming past reflecting the room's rainbow light. That light came from phosphorescent fungus crowded across the walls and ceiling, glowing with brilliant light that shifted through kaleidoscopic hues.

The ground was too flat for a natural cave, despite it otherwise seeming that way, and a blanket of soft cool moss cushioned her feet. It meant that she didn't need to watch her step and could instead look around at the cavern's beauty, lit by the fungal luminescence. She spotted a tunnel leading downstream, and another leading up. An angry voice growled out from the downstream tunnel.

"Bloody gods, Jason, will you ever stop changing things about?"

Jali's first instinct was to go in the other direction, but on a whim, she moved towards the voice. She entered the tunnel as clanking sounds of metal being tossed around echoed out. Heat radiated from whatever destination awaited her, soon becoming strong enough that even a silver-rank messenger felt uncomfortable. The fungal lights gave way to stones embedded in the walls, also shedding light. She recognised them as nodes of lava-watch granite, a stone that absorbed heat and converted it into light. She had seen them used for illumination in volcano foundries.

As she continued down the tunnel, the clanking grew louder, accompanied by a growled muttering only intelligible in short snatches.

"Where did you put my damn anvil, you skinny, ridiculous... oh, you have got to be kidding."

The tunnel changed from a mostly natural cave to a roughly hewn passage, the floor going from flat and padded with moss to polished smooth. It was hot on Jali's bare feet, but she didn't float up to relieve the pain. She saw an opening ahead, lit by the orange forge light of a smithy. She reached the chamber that, like the tunnel, had rough-cut walls but a polished-smooth floor.

The large room was a smithy, centred around a massive forge fire in the middle that radiated the room's light and searing heat. There was enough infrastructure for a half-dozen smiths to work at once, from more forges, currently cold, to bellows, tool racks and benches. They were all scattered, and tipped over, with loose tools, ingots and chunks of scrap metal scattered at random. The major absence was an anvil, but the room's solitary occupant revealed where it had gone.

A leonid in a heavy leather apron was leaned back, hands on hips as he glared at the roof. He seemed unaffected by the heat, despite his thick fur. Jali followed his gaze to spot an anvil affixed to the ceiling. The leonid moved his gaze from the ceiling to her, saying nothing. He just stared, his expression unreadable.

Jali got no read from the leonid's aura beyond his silver rank. Asano's kingdom seemed to restrict aura senses to whatever Asano wanted them to see, one of the many things that made the place feel alien. Even to a cosmic traveller like Jali, it was strange, and she wondered if all astral kingdoms were like this. This was the only one she'd been in.

The leonid kept staring, saying nothing. Jali looked back, uncertain of what to do. Everything she'd been told her entire life said that when faced with a non-messenger, the only options were to kill or dominate. She didn't know what she wanted, only that it wasn't to do either of those.

"You're the new one," the leonid said, his voice an unfriendly rumble.

"The new one?" Jali asked.

The leonid turned away and went back to cleaning up the room, picking up scraps of metal and tossing them in a corner.

"Jason's started collecting messengers," the leonid said, not bothering to look at her as he worked.

"Collecting?"

"He thinks that maybe you're worth saving."

"You disagree," she said, an observation and not a question.

"Plenty of folks need saving," he told her. "None of them deserved it less than you and your kind."

"You know me well enough to be certain that no one in the world is less deserving?"

The leonid stopped what he was doing and turned to look at her.

"Were you part of the attack on the city?" he asked.

"Yes," she admitted.

"Then that's all I need to know. I fought in that battle too, and faced more than a few of your people. Every single one of them started out the same. So proud, so confident. No more purpose than to kill us to prove they could, sowing fear and spreading terror. And they liked it. Thought it was sport. Innocent people, slaughtered in the street. Homes brought down on the heads of the families living in them. It takes a special kind of evil to look at a street littered with dead children and laugh."

He growled, the echo of it filling the chamber with his presence. She was suddenly very aware that while her height was larger than his, her teeth were not.

"Your kind," he continued, almost spitting the words. "They float above it all, beautiful and untouchable. But then you show them that they can be touched. You can see it in their eyes, the moment they realise what's about to happen, that they aren't as invincible as they thought. When they realise that they're about to die, filthy and broken, after thinking they'd live forever. That the superiority they believed in was nothing. It's not so hard to drag your kind down to the ground."

He glanced down, seeing her feet on the floor instead of floating over it. His eyes panned back up to her face, staring again. She wasn't sure how to respond, so she said nothing.

"Are you just going to stand there?" he asked finally, "or are you going to help clean this mess up?"

"I... you'll have to tell me what to do."

His eyes narrowed in an assessing gaze.

"Jason's soul realm decided to move my smithy," he said. "Tossed everything around, dumped my material stores on the floor while warping half of them into useless scrap. Just grab any twisted chunks of metal and chuck them in that corner for now."

He pointed to a corner where he'd been doing just that, a small pile of scrap metal heaped in there already. She looked around and saw there was no shortage of metal to add to it. She was about to reach out with her aura to move the closest chunk but stopped herself. Instead, she walked over, picked it up and threw it. The leonid glanced at her briefly before resuming the clean-up.

"I'm Gary," he told her, his tone still hostile, although not quite as angry.

"Jali Corrik Fen."

"Well, I'm going to call you Jali," he grumbled. "That thing where you use people's full name all the time is bloody annoying."

Jason watched, unnoticed, as Gary stalked off to find his way back to the surface. Jali moved to follow until she felt a prick of aura directed her way and turned to spot Jason. She glanced at Gary, but Jason shook his head and she remained silent, letting him walk away. Moments later, his voice came rumbling down the tunnel.

"A bloody beverage station? I want a forge that works and a way out, not a drink. I mean, yeah, I'll take a drink, but I don't want to be wandering around these tunnels all day."

Jason chuckled and wandered in the opposite direction, towards a wall that became an upward-sloping tunnel as he reached it.

"Isn't he your friend?" Jali asked, hustling in an un-messenger-like fashion to catch up. The tunnel was dark, although that impeded neither of them.

"He is my friend," Jason said. "He's also gotten about a mountain's worth of rare and expensive materials conjured up for his metallurgy experiments. The price of that is getting messed with from time to time."

"So, you wrecked his forge?"

"No, that was my soul realm going wobbly, the way I warned you it would. I just didn't want to waste the opportunity for a little fun."

"I think he might have killed me, if not for you."

"Probably. I'm having trouble getting people to leave the people you've enslaved alive, let alone you lot. If I don't keep the actual messengers in here, you'll be tortured for information, then tortured for visceral satisfaction, and then eventually killed. I'm glad he didn't kill you, though. He's a joyful man by nature, and a symptomatic carrier; his joy is infectious. I don't want him to lose that again."

"Again?"

"The people of this world have seen a lot in the last few years. You and yours are just the latest thing. One more group that doesn't care about who or what you destroy in your greed for whatever it is you came for."

He sighed.

"I don't want to talk about all that. I know you didn't make those choices and I think you're a long way from ready to engage with that discussion. In some ways, you messengers are like children raised in a cult; all you know is the indoctrination. It's hard to have a conversation about a world you only see through a single, myopic lens. I'm guessing that you're feeling very lost right now, away from everything you know."

She nodded. Further up the tunnel, she spotted daylight promising release from the darkness.

"I said you should take some time to let your thoughts settle," Jason told her. "The reality is, you're dealing with so much that doing so isn't really possible. In which case we might as well begin. Do you still want me to go into your soul and cut off the leash?"

"How... what does that entail?"

"Basically, I knock on the door of your soul and you open it, or not. If you let me in, I erase the brand the astral king has on your soul."

"You said something about replacing it with my own brand, and not yours. I don't have one. I'm not an astral king."

"Not with that attitude. The brand isn't a big deal, more of a finger-print of the soul. We just have to figure out what yours is and use it. Then we take off the limiter that's holding your rank down. You were never inherently limited to silver. Your astral king has been feeding on your potential. All the power that should have gone to you ranking up has been going to Vesta Carmis Zell instead."

"So, all the messengers who can't go past silver..."

"Absolutely can. No messengers are locked to silver or gold. That's all just astral kings feeding on them. It lets them set up useful hierarchies and drain large amounts of power. The messengers aren't just slaves without knowing it. They're also food."

Jali bowed her head, her walk becoming a trudge as she considered Jason's words. She seemed oddly small, even as she towered over him.

"The good news is," Jason told her, "I can take you out of that cycle. I'm even getting pretty good at it. It's a whole different thing now compared to when I bumbled through cutting Tera Jun Casta off from your astral king. I worry that my fumbling might be responsible for her instability, at least in part. But she's got more than enough things causing that, so I don't think I'll ever know."

Jali looked down at Jason.

"Why go to such effort to be compassionate to her? She tried to kill you. The messengers have done so much. Your friend Gary pointed out that there are so many that need help, and we are the least deserving."

"Mercy and compassion aren't about deserving. Or they shouldn't be, not if you genuinely want to make things better. Compassion can be hard to give, and so easy to give up on. I did that for longer than I'd like to admit. Mercy and compassion are so often regarded as pointless, weakness or all cost and no payoff. I once showed mercy to a man who tried to murder me, and that choice saved my soul. When I was alone and in the hands of my enemies, that man whose life I spared turned out to be working for those enemies. He betrayed them to run for help, for me. They realised he was gone and what he was doing and turned on each other. Their inattention gave me the chance to fight off the star seed they implanted in me before the Builder could force me to open up my soul. And my friends came and got me after he led them to me."

"You fought off a star seed?"

Jason nodded.

"That was the beginning of my soul becoming what it is now."

They emerged from the tunnel into a garden that was wild and untamed, like a jungle with an incongruously neat garden path running through it.

"Even now," Jason said, "with all my soul has become, I'm not sure it was worth what I went through. What the Builder did to my soul. And I did the same thing to Tera Jun Casta, only worse because she didn't escape me. I kept going until she broke. Knowing what that is like, I'm not sure I can ever make up for that."

He smiled sadly.

"Compassion isn't always easy and you don't always get it right. But imagine if we could break the hold the astral kings have over the rest of the messengers. If, instead of an army of indoctrinated slaves, you were just ordinary citizens of the cosmos, like the rest of us."

"I don't know what that would be like," Jali said. "I've never known anything but my people as they are. My tasks. A life of obedience. Just a few hours ago, the very idea of wondering about any of this was dangerous."

"As demonstrated by the nasty lady trying to tear you apart from the inside out," Jason said and stopped walking. "Are you ready to do something about that?"

They were in a grove with a stream trickling by, the path forming a little bridge passing over it. He turned to face her and she nodded firmly.

"I think I've been ready for a long, long time. How do we—"

Jason vanished and she fell unconscious on her feet, toppling into a bush.

55

NOT YET

JASON STOOD ALONE ON ONE OF SEVERAL TOWERS OF A CASTLE. UNDER A bright blue sky, rolling hills, woodlands and vast plains of grass stretched out to the horizon, all in the colours of early autumn. The air was clean, a breeze taking just the right edge from the heat of the sun.

"Wow," Jason said to himself, as much about his presence as the vista. All the messengers whose inner realms he had entered previously had resisted to some degree, even the most willing. Jali was so open that not even her basic instincts mounted a defence against his intrusion. He'd practically tripped and fallen into her.

He couldn't imagine what her life had been like, living under a tyrant where not even her own mind was a haven. An existence where letting herself dwell on her doubts, on the iniquities of her life would lead to that life being snatched away. He couldn't help but think of Tera Jun Casta's ilk, the zealous, and imagine that they were better off. At least they were ignorant of their mind prisons, not forced to walk a tightrope of their own thoughts. At least those like Jali, the messengers with doubts, would be easier to save if the chance arose.

Jason floated into the air and away from the castle to get a better look at it. A complex of buildings rather than a single edifice, it wasn't like a real castle. It was more akin to something from a fairy tale or even a video game, with grand arches and towers jutting high into the air. There was a grand gate with a moat and a drawbridge, the moat fed by a nearby lake that sparkled in the sunlight.

Entering Jali's inner world was a very different experience from when he had plunged into Tera Jun Casta's soul. That had been rushed and incautious, lack of experience and the time constraints led him to jump in and start messing with things, not even forming an inner world to inhabit.

Jali's inner world was only possible because, like Jason himself, she was a being whose soul and body were one. Only a soul with a physical aspect could form a physical space that others could physically visit. Jason had a soul realm before becoming a gestalt entity, but the only ones that could join him inside it were his familiars, who were already anchored in his soul.

Forming a physical space inside messengers as a tool to liberate them was something he developed working with Marek and his subordinates. The idea was to minimise harm, but refining the process had been not without missteps. His early attempts involved forcing the formation of the inner worlds and the messengers had instinctually fought back, like a spiritual immune system. This forced him to suppress that resistance, doing the opposite of his intention to have minimal collateral effect.

He learned that the key was to trigger the messengers to subconsciously form their inner worlds themselves. Not only was it faster and easier, but came so naturally and without resistance that it felt like jumpstarting an inherent ability.

Jason suspected he was tapping into an aspect of the messengers that was part of their ability to progress to astral kings. Maybe even an aspect of what diamond-rank messengers like Mah Go Schaat were looking for. Jason worried he was creating a gaggle of future astral kings, but that was a problem for another day.

The soul spaces of Marek's people had not been exciting. It was all concrete blocks and empty landscapes, like a Soviet bloc country colonising a desert planet. They were blank, utilitarian and passionless. Jali's inner realm was a breath of fresh air—beautiful, vibrant and rich. It spoke to a longing for something more than the life she was trapped in.

This brought him to the next step of the process, which was finding Jali. Jason had full command of his soul realm and full control of himself when projected into someone else's. The messengers he helped were never in the same situation. In each case, they were locked away somewhere, bound by the strictures put in place by their astral king.

Floating in the air, Jason closed his eyes and extended his senses, swiftly finding Jali's location. She was somewhere under the castle, deep in a basement or dungeon. He could force his way directly to her, but this castle was the central construct of her soul. He wasn't going to smash a path right through the middle of it.

The large castle gates were shut, the gates themselves blocked by a portcullis. As he didn't want to trigger any defence mechanisms, he decided to take a longer route with less resistance. There was a stairwell leading down on the flat roof of the tower he had been on, so he returned to it and used that.

He made his way through the castle, finding no signs of occupation. Unlike the outside with its fresh air and pleasant breeze, the interior was stagnant and musty. Rooms and halls, corridors and massive chambers, all dust-filled and empty, with even the doorways having empty hinges. That also meant no lighting, but Jason's ability to see through the dark worked even here.

Only one chamber contained anything in it at all: a throne room complete with throne. Sitting on the throne was a blurry, ghost-like figure, too indistinct to make out any details but rough size and shape. It was a messenger, complete with wings, and larger than normal. It would easily stand head and shoulders above Jali, who already left Jason looking like a child.

As he watched the figure, he occasionally spotted sharper details flickering into place for a fleeting moment. Dark hair, olive skin. He suspected the person he was glimpsing to be Vesta Carmis Zell, Jali's astral king. This was the manifestation of the brand he would need to erase. He wouldn't do so before finding Jali, however, and resumed his search.

Jason found his way to the underground levels without too many pointless digressions into dead ends. Finally, he came to a doorway that actually had a door in it. Made with heavy wood and reinforced with metal bands, he could sense immediately that this was not a part of Jali's realm but a representation of the astral king's control.

Upon trying the door, Jason was unsurprised to find it locked. He placed a hand on it and started imposing his will. It resisted for a moment before dissolving into mist and vanishing, but with an incongruent sound of shattering glass.

The now empty doorway opened into a massive cylindrical chamber. The doorway was situated high up on a wall, opening onto empty air. There was a narrow column in the centre of the room, barely wide enough to stand on. It reached the same height as the door and Jali was balanced precariously atop it, waving her arms unsteadily as she fought for balance. At her back, her wings were bound in thin wire, so tight that they cut into her, drawing lines of blood. She had spotted him and looked his way with panicked, pleading eyes.

There was a loud splashing from below and Jason glanced down. The bottom of the chamber was flooded and filled with spinning blades like massive fans. Anything that fell into them would swiftly become nothing more than a red stain in the churning water.

He realised that, like the door, this whole room was not part of Jali's inner realm. This was more control put in place by the astral king. Jason felt no compunction about forcibly making changes.

He concentrated at his feet and a bridge extended out from the base of the door, swiftly reaching the column. Jali was moving even before it was complete, leaping onto it and barrelling towards Jason in the doorway. He stepped out of her way, letting her through into the hallway.

"Let's get rid of those, to start with," he said and the wires digging into her wings snapped and fell away, dissolving before they hit the floor.

"Thank you," Jali said, looking past him and into the strange chamber he'd just rescued her from. "What is this place? One moment we were talking and then I was in that room. I feel powerless. I can't fly. I couldn't even speak until you took those things off of my wings."

"Part of that is in your mind," Jason told her. "Another part is very much not, and that's what we're here to eliminate. You're extremely powerful here if you can get your head around it. We just need to excise the things holding you back. Like the door that was here—and the wires on your wings. They're all metaphors."

"Are we inside my soul?"

"Yep. Slid right in, not even a token resistance. That's great for this specific situation, but probably not good in a broader sense. I don't know if you were just extremely ready for this or if there's a problem with your soul defences, but you should look into that later."

"How do I look into something like that?"

"No idea. Given that I might be the person with the most soul expertise I know, that's probably not great news for you."

He looked up at her towering over him.

"Sorry," he said. "I imagine you'd rather hear something more encouraging right now."

"I still don't understand what's happening. This is my soul? This is a soul space, like your astral kingdom?"

"Yes. Well, like mine before I got an astral throne. It's like the more I become one with the astral throne, the more it messes with my soul realm. Like it's sifting through my soul to figure out how to absorb itself into me more fully. My rank is too low, so it causes side effects. Your soul realm should be nice and stable."

Jali looked down the dingy, unlit hallway, then back at the chamber she'd been trapped in.

"I don't think nice is the word."

"Oh, you might be surprised. Especially once we clean out the space a bit. We need to find the things that don't belong in your soul—myself excluded—and get rid of them. The first time I did this, with Tera Jun Casta, I didn't do any of this visualisation and I didn't work with her at all. I just did what I had to, crudely making blunt, inexpert changes. I was under time constraints and it was my first time doing anything like that."

"This is more than just visualisation," Jali said. "This is realisation. An actual space that you've forged from my soul."

"No," Jason corrected. "All I did was give you a subconscious prompt, and you made all this yourself."

Jali looked around again.

"My soul is a dark, damp hole with a massive torture room," she said morosely.

"Again, no," Jason said. "The torture chamber here isn't you. It's Vesta Carmis Zell, and it needs to go."

"How?"

"I'll do it, but I want your guidance to cut out something this large. Take my hand."

He held out his hand and she took it. They stood side by side in front of the door, Jason trying not to feel like a child being helped across the road.

"Feel what I do," he told her. "Focus on what feels wrong, but don't try to change it. Just let it happen and trust your instincts."

Jason pushed his will into the large chamber, pressing up against the lingering influence of the astral king. In person, the astral king would have scattered Jason's will to the wind, but this was an old, unattended remnant. Even projecting into Jali's soul wouldn't help her as the astral king would be using distant influence through a vessel that Jason was already breaking down. Through his direct connection to Jali, he was much more powerful than the astral king would be here.

The room was crumbling, brickwork tumbling into the water below.

The water itself steamed until the water and blades were obscured and fell silent. The column collapsed and disappeared. Behind the original brickwork was natural stone, the round room becoming an uneven cenote, the steam vanishing to reveal clear water below. It was gently flowing, part of some underground river that Jason guessed was connected to the lake.

The walls were covered in moss and vines. Balconies emerged from the walls, also strewn with vines blooming with colourful flowers. Doorways appeared in the walls, making the balconies accessible to some network of rooms and passages beyond. One of the balconies appeared right in front of them.

The ceiling crumbled away to reveal open skies above. A domed framework then crawled over the hole until it was completed and glass filled the gaps in the frame. The final part of the transformation was a waterfall that spilled over the edge, splashing into the river below.

"Better?" Jason asked as he released Jali's hand.

She stepped through the doorway onto the new balcony in front of them, leaning on the balustrade as she leaned over to look up and down.

"Better," she said with a smile that split her face. It was an expression of earnest joy and wonder, unlike anything Jason had seen on a messenger before.

"Think you're ready to fly yet?"

Her wings unfurled, the previous signs of injury gone—not just healed but absent, even the blood that had spilled from the wounds removed. She rose into the air, a massive panel in the dome sliding open to let her out. As soon as she passed through it, she shot into the sky.

"You think taking one insignificant pawn from me will accomplish anything?" a female voice asked from behind Jason. Instead of turning around, he walked through the door and placed his hands on the balustrade. It was a little high to be strictly comfortable, being scaled to messenger proportions.

"It's not about you," he said, looking up at the sky. "Not yet, anyway."

56

SOMETIMES, VIOLENCE IS THE ANSWER

JASON TURNED TO LOOK AT VESTA CARMIS ZELL. SHE WAS EXTREMELY tall, even for a messenger, filling the doorway that had easily accommodated Jali. The astral king didn't look different from other messengers, height aside. She had the usual exquisite beauty, with olive skin and dark hair cascading over her shoulders. The wings spread out behind her were like that of a hawk with a gorgeous and complex brown and white pattern. Her physique was athletic rather than delicate, muscular but lean and powerful.

"How many of my messengers do you intend to steal away, Jason Asano?"

"I think we both know that the only one that was really yours was Tera Jun Casta. The others were wavering enough that you'd have killed them off sooner or later."

"They are mine to kill. What is your plan? Undermine me by stealing away every messenger that wavers in their faith?"

"I don't have close to enough time for that, and I already said that this isn't about you. It makes sense that's a concept you have trouble getting through your head, though. Maybe it's an astral king failing? A friend recently had to remind me that everything isn't about me either."

"Perhaps your plan is to goad me into me annihilating all of my forces with anything but the utmost zeal, thereby diminishing their numbers."

"You're not a great listener, are you?"

"You are an arrogant fool."

"Yep," he agreed cheerfully.

"What are you even doing here, Asano? Playing around in the soul of some nothing woman that you or any of your friends could kill out of hand? You have a task before you."

"It was your Voice of the Will that sent her my way, and I don't think she was picked at random. She wanted to see what would happen when I got my hands on one of your straying sheep. If you have a problem with that, take it up with Jes Fin Kaal. As for the job I have to do, take that up with your Voice as well. She was meant to have that device to me weeks ago."

"You have it now."

"And I'll get the job done. I'll take your mysterious device into whatever is going on underground. There we'll find whatever trap you've set to go off and dump us in the brown stuff while giving you exactly what you want."

"Yet you will go anyway, confident that you can outmatch me and get what you want instead."

"We did agree I'm an arrogant fool. I think that's an astral king trait as well."

"The mark of an astral king is pride. Dignity. Power. You are a silver-rank buffoon. To call you an astral king is technically correct, but you represent none of what makes us what we are."

"Well, technically is the best kind of correct, so I'll take it."

Anger and disappointment crossed her face.

"I wanted to see what manner of man you are for myself, so I projected myself here to see this mortal who had reforged himself into an astral king. But you're an idiot."

Jason erupted into laughter.

"Yes," he choked out, still laughing. "Yes, I am. And you're stuck dealing with me."

They both looked up to see Jali descending through the air, the open panel in the glass dome closing behind her. She slowed as she recognised Vesta, landing behind Jason, her body language hesitant.

"Pathetic," Vesta said. "Hiding behind a lesser being? You are—"

Vesta vanished at a casually dismissive wave from Jason.

"That lady sucks," he said as he turned to look at Jali.

"That was Vesta Caris Zell," a shell-shocked Jali told him.

"Yep. Have a nice flight?"

"She was here."

"Yeah. Kind of, but not really. I mean, yeah, but nah. But yeah. But nah."

"What?"

"All she can send here is an echo, through the remnants of what influence we haven't cleared out yet. That's how come I can give her projection the punt; she doesn't have the juice to do anything in here."

"The brand is what's left. It's the crux of her power over me. It's what she's killing me with, so I would say she has considerable power here."

"Yeah, she can't do that while I'm in here. Didn't I mention that?"

"No!"

"Are you sure?"

"Yes!"

"Oh. Uh, sorry?"

He absently scratched the back of his neck and then plucked a pair of fruit drinks in coconut shells out of thin air.

"Take one of these as an apology," he told her.

"This is serious."

"No," Jason said, shaking his head. "This is over and Lady Macbeth in your chair up there can't do a damn thing about it. You see, I have this ability to stabilise any physical reality I'm inside. The World-Phoenix designed the power so I could repair holes in the universe, but it turns out that it works on messenger souls because they have a physical aspect. You have to take their souls and make a physical reality out of them…"

He waved his hands at the space around them, careful not to spill the drinks.

"…but then you're good to go. So long as I'm inside your soul, Vesta Carmis Zell can't make any inroads. It's too stable for her to mess with. You're safe."

"The World-Phoenix designed an ability for you?"

"Yeah. You know how great astral being blessings work, right? She knocked me up a custom job. You know how it goes. A few great astral beings want to manipulate you to serve their agendas while you need to come back from the dead occasionally and save the world a few times. It's win-win. You've been out in the cosmos; I imagine this is all old hat to you. Anyway, let's go finish the job we came in here for."

Jason meandered down the hall, sipping on one of the drinks. The other he left floating in the air in front of Jali. She watched him, wide-eyed, as he casually wandered off.

"Who are you?" she called after him incredulously.

His void cloak manifested and wrapped around him like a hole in the universe. Silver lights that seemed like distant stars emerged from it, shooting ahead to illuminate the dark hallway.

"I'm just like every other guy who periodically saves the world," he called back. "I just look better doing it."

She shook her head and followed after him, then stopped, turned around and grabbed the drink before continuing.

Motes of light floated up from Jason's cloak to light up the throne room. The blurred figure was still sitting on the throne, aspects of Vesta Carmis Zell's appearance flickering in place for the briefest moments.

"That's it," Jason said.

"That is the astral king's brand?"

"It's taken a different form in every messenger's soul space that I've seen," Jason told her. "Engraved plates, crude carvings on a wall, elaborate tapestries. The other messengers had pretty boring souls, with the brand being the only interesting thing in them. Almost a shame to get rid of them, really."

Jali turned to glare at Jason.

"Yeah," he acknowledged. "I knew that was too far as soon as I said it. I'm just saying that I appreciate your dramatic flair."

"What do I do?"

"You be thankful," Vesta said, "that another astral king, even one unworthy of the name, has claimed you as a pet."

Jason and Jali looked up at the throne where Vesta was now fully manifested. Jali shrank back before steeling herself, spreading her wings out wide and glaring back at the astral king. Fear marked her expression, but so did determination. Jason stepped back with a grin.

"Better a pet than food," Jali said, spitting the words at Vesta.

Vesta stood up from the throne that was on a platform atop a short set of stairs. She floated down them slowly, coming to a stop in front of Jali. Jali was tall, even by messenger standards, but Vesta was an edifice. That she was floating while Jali stood only heightened the difference.

Both women had powerful, athletic physiques. Vesta was dark, with the wings of a hawk and the sharp beauty of a knife. Jali's features were rounder, her skin fairer. Her hair and wings were the light brown of a fawn's fur. She was soft to Vesta's hardness, prey to her predator. Even so, she stood her ground, nervous but determined as Vesta looked down on her with superior disdain.

"You are no messenger," Vesta told her. "No more than your new owner is a real astral king."

"Astral kings are the ultimate power," Jali said. "So, astral king, where is your power? Why am I alive if you want me dead?"

"You believe that you are safe from me?"

"Not at all. I know the power at your command. The forces you can send after me. I was the least of your might, an afterthought you could throw away. I know what you can do and it terrifies me. But now I've seen what you can't do. I've seen your limits, and that is what scares you. That the illusion of the astral kings as limitless and inviolable will break and the messengers will realise what you are and what you've made us. You fear that we'll fight to be free."

"You will never be free."

"I am free. Prove me wrong."

"Replacing one master with another isn't freedom, you foolish child."

"You think—"

"That's enough," Jason said, cutting Jali off. "She's chucked the bucket of water on you, wicked witch. Time to pack up your flying monkeys and melt away."

Vesta turned her glare on him.

"Do you think that building an army of my discards will allow you to challenge me? Do you honestly believe that will work?"

"I guess we'll see," he told her. "The day will come when you and I will have a reckoning, but for now, you need me, remember?"

"You will never come into power enough to pose even the meagerest threat to me."

"You don't need to worry, then," he told her with a grin, then sipped from his drink.

"I will leave this worthless messenger for you," Vesta told him. "You can have her; use her however you like. An army of her kind is nothing to me."

"You say that like you have a choice," Jali said. "Get out of my soul."

Jali marched through Vesta's projection, which flickered as she did, then floated up the stairs to the throne as Jason and Vesta watched.

"You won't—"

Vesta was cut off when her projection blinked out of existence, the moment Jali took her seat. Jason rested his drink in the air as if putting it on an invisible shelf, and clapped.

"Well done," he told her.

"Please erase the brand now."

"You just did."

"That shouldn't be possible."

"Why not? It's your soul. Admittedly, I helped. I stopped Vesta from interfering, but you are the one who placed yourself in the spot that she has occupied your entire life. None of the other messengers did that. I had to remove it for them."

"Even Marek Nior Vargas?"

"Yes. I know you think you're ordinary, Jali. You're not."

"Did Vesta show up when you were freeing the others?"

"No. I think she wanted to know why I was bothering with you when the device to be taken underground is finally at hand. I'm sorry for talking over you while you were speaking with her, by the way. You were about to tell her something I realised she didn't know, and I don't want her to."

Jali's brow crinkled in thought.

"I was about to tell her that you weren't enslaving us but freeing us."

"Yes," Jason said. "I realised that it would never occur to her that I would release you instead of claiming you for myself. The idea of giving up power in the name of compassion is something she can't conceive of."

"Why does that matter?"

"Because you were right about what the astral kings fear. It isn't me, a rogue member of their club. Even if I reach transcendent-rank, I'll just be another one of their number. Plus, we'd all be immortal, so it's not like we could kill each other. What they fear is losing their hold on the rest of the messengers. They built a control system on faith, and nothing is more poisonous to faith than knowledge. The Unorthodoxy is what threatens them, not me."

"But if you're setting messengers free," Jali realised, "then you're giving the Unorthodoxy the one thing it needs most: the ability to grow their numbers outside of astral king control. And suddenly, you become much more important to eliminate."

"Exactly. Right now, the only astral king that cares about me is Vesta Carmis Zell, and she has a vested interest in keeping me alive. At least for the moment. If the other astral kings become motivated to see me dead, my life will get very hard, very quickly."

Jali stood up from the throne and descended the stairs, walking instead of floating. She kept her eyes on Jason the whole time as she walked up to him.

"Why are you doing this?" she asked. "All of it."

He smiled, looking up at her.

"You keep asking that question," he said. "The answer is still the same: because I want to be kind. I want to make things better. Sometimes, violence is the answer, but the best it can do is remove something that would otherwise make things worse. Violence can't make things better. That takes kindness. Forgiveness. Redemption. Making the stupid choice and hoping that others will make it with you."

He let out a self-deprecating laugh.

"At least, that's how I hope it works or I've bet heavy on the wrong horse."

"I think that I would like to bet on that horse as well."

"Great," Jason said and her drink floated over from where she had left it by the door upon entering the throne room. "Now, finish your drink and let's get out of here. I've got quite a lot going on today."

57

WELCOME ABOARD

THE MESSENGER DEVICE WAS AN OVOID CRYSTAL HELD SUSPENDED IN A rectangular frame of metal. The frame was some kind of magical brass variant, based on the colour and the magic Jason sensed from it. The crystal was very dark blue and perfectly smooth. The entire device was about the size of a bathtub.

"We have managed to confirm that the central part of the device is some manner of crystal," a Magic Society official said. Jason hadn't bothered remembering his name.

"You can confirm that it's a crystal," Marcus echoed.

"With a high degree of confidence," the official said, his two flunkies nodding confirmation.

"Can you confirm that it's blue?" Marcus asked.

"Not at this time. Initial assessment seems to indicate that, but until we apply spectral—"

"That's it?" Marcus asked at almost a roar.

"We are also relatively certain that the framework is one of magical brass variants."

"You've had hours to go over this, and that's all you have?"

"If you would let us take it back to our campus—"

"No," Marcus cut him off. "Out."

They were inside a large tent in Marshalling Yard One on the Adventure Society campus. The tent was empty aside from Jason, Marcus, the

Magic Society officials and the device. Marcus waved the officials out, their reluctance turning to haste as they saw his expression.

"Well," Marcus admitted, "your friend Standish wasn't wrong about them finding nothing. I didn't think they'd be stupid enough to send their most politically powerful researchers instead of their most competent ones. Where I come from, Magic Society officials know how to let their skilled researchers do the work and then exploit them after. What kind of idiots try to do it themselves?"

"You felt their auras," Jason said. "There's no way you missed that level of self-delusion."

"Yeah," Marcus grumbled. "I just needed to complain out loud. I detest incompetent people."

"Then you really shouldn't have talked Clive into leaving."

Clive had an hour with the device before agreeing to let the Magic Society have a look. Marcus had convinced him to do so to ease political tensions, in return for placing Clive explicitly in charge of all magical investigation during the expedition. This had already been the case, but Marcus had now made sure that every member of the expedition understood the consequences of ignoring that directive.

"Standish only had an hour with the thing. Did he get any further than 'it's probably a crystal'?"

"I did," Clive said as he entered the tent. "The device is very focused on astral magic, which is good for us. The only advanced magic from outside our world that I've had the chance to extensively study is astral magic, which also happens to be my specialty."

"What do we have?" Jason asked.

"It's complicated. Most of the device serves as what's called a dimensional differentiator. You see, there are a lot more layers to reality than most people realise. Jason understands this better than almost anyone, having spent a lot of time in the most fundamental reality layer of his home planet. That was the bottom layer, the most foundational, where the Builder—or you, in this case, Jason—can mess with the underpinnings of existence. The top layer is the world we know and live in, while everything in between is where the material of reality comes from. If you think of the bottom layer of reality as a kitchen, the middle layers are ingredients and the top layer is the cooked meal."

"Is that analogy even close to accurate?" Marcus asked.

"No," Clive said. "But unless you've got five spare years to study astral magic, it's what you're getting. The cooked meal comparison works well enough, though. You see, the natural array taps into those middle layers of reality. Trying to access them from the completed layer of reality, though—the completed meal—is like trying to extract an egg from a cake that's already been baked."

"Is that something you do?" Jason asked. "Is that why you suck so much when you cook anything but eels?"

"Let's keep on topic, shall we?" Marcus said.

"Thank you," Clive said gratefully, giving Jason a flat look. "You have to remember what it is we're heading into underground. Whatever the messengers have turned it into, it started as a natural array; a sequence of manifested essences and alchemy stones that, through wild coincidence, formed a naturally occurring magical pattern. A pattern tapping into those middle layers of reality."

"Are you saying this device is designed to isolate the dimensional layers associated with the aspects of the natural array?" Jason asked.

"Exactly," Clive said. "We know that the essences and stones that comprise the array are exactly what you'd expect from deep underground. Earth, fire, metal, etc. It's as much as we've managed to sense from the surface, but the elementally infused messengers that came from underground would seem to confirm that. The natural array is tapping into the layers of reality related to that. Primal elemental dimensions. The device is designed to isolate those dimensions, thereby removing the elemental aspect of the natural array, leaving only the underlying magical matrix."

"Wouldn't that cause the matrix to collapse?" Jason asked.

"Yes," Clive said, "but—"

"Can we get an explanation for someone who isn't an astral magic specialist?" Marcus asked.

"This device is designed to extract the egg from the cake," Jason said.

"That doesn't help," Marcus said. "I'm not really tracking the analogy anymore."

"Then stand there, be quiet and look like a total bad-arse," Jason told him. "You're super-good at it."

"Thank you?"

"You're welcome," Jason said. "Now, Clive. This thing isolates the elemental aspects of the natural array from its core magical framework, leaving behind a neutral matrix. I assume the second function of the device is to use that matrix for something."

"Yes," Clive said. "I just have no idea what. It's past my level of understanding, and I mean way past. Give me a decade with the material from the messengers' study and maybe."

"That's alright," Jason said. "I think I might know what it's making. What the messengers were trying to make in the first place, and why Vesta Carmis Zell has been willing to put up with all the losses and resource cost operating here has been."

"You know what it's making?" Marcus asked.

"It's a guess, but a guess that fits," Jason said. "There's a thing called a soul forge. I don't know what it is exactly. If it's an actual, physical thing or a loose magic matrix or something else. But every astral king has a soul forge. Every astral king but one."

"This Vesta Carmis Zell doesn't?" Marcus asked.

"No, she does," Jason said. "I'm the one who doesn't. Which is why she is definitely going to try and have me killed before I can claim it for myself. Letting me get involved at all is a gamble, but she's been hamstrung by her own propaganda. If the messengers handed this device off to anyone but one of their own, she'd have a religious uprising on her hands and need to kill off her own army. I'm barely close enough to count as one of their own, being an astral king."

"What are you basing this conclusion on?" Marcus asked.

"For one, the messenger commander I've captured. He suggested it as a possibility, as Vesta Carmis Zell is a practitioner of soul engineering. It's a crafting profession that is as ethically fraught as you'd imagine from the name. Having an extra soul forge would apparently be massively beneficial, although he wasn't certain as to how."

"Can you trust a messenger as a source?" Marcus asked.

"To a degree," Jason said. "He was far from certain, in any case. The other thing tipping me off was a gift I received from the Healer. It's an item that I'll only be able to use once I have a soul forge."

"That is a more reliable indicator," Marcus agreed. "Gods love to give hints instead of just telling you things outright. Except Knowledge. I'd take her as my patron deity if my entire life wasn't built around violently destroying people and things."

"Regretting your life choices?" Jason asked him.

"Absolutely not," Marcus said. "Violence is the best."

Jason and Clive shared a glance.

"Next question," Jason said, "is what happens when the device goes off. In theory, it isolated the elemental aspects of the array and creates a soul forge. Will that stabilise the magic down there, prevent it from reaching critical mass and blowing up Yaresh?"

"That, I can't tell you," Clive said. "I'm not an array specialist, let alone a natural array specialist. And once ours arrives, she won't be able to figure anything out until we get down there for her to look at it."

"You do have one, then," Marcus said. "I looked for one and the Magic Society said there's no such thing. That natural arrays are too rare to be a specialty field of study. Then I went to the Church of Knowledge. They told me to leave that to you, Asano, and I trusted in that. I'm glad to have it confirmed."

"We know someone," Jason said. "When I mentioned this whole thing, though, she told me to let the city blow up and she had her own stuff to deal with. She's done a lot for me over the last few years, so I didn't push. Clive is the one that got her on board."

"How do you even have a natural array specialist?" Marcus asked. "Without the Magic Society knowing, no less."

"She spent several years studying a planet-wide array that operated on the principles behind natural arrays," Jason explained.

"The adventurer you resurrected on your home planet," Marcus realised.

"The Reaper resurrected her, not me. The World-Phoenix convinced him because she was worried I'd go nuts and let the whole planet die instead of saving it. Which was a good call, as it turned out. How did you get her to sign on, Clive?"

"Wait," Marcus said. "Can we go back to the part about the great astral beings—"

"Nope," Jason said. "Clive, what convinced her to sign up?"

"I asked her to."

"That would do it, yeah," Jason said.

"That's it?" Marcus asked. "You just asked?"

"Do they not have friends where you come from, Mr Xenoria?" Clive asked.

"You think it's strange that I don't have a friend who is a specialist in something no one is a specialist of, and is willing to drop everything and follow me into the bowels of the planet to an unknown and extremely dangerous situation? Just because I asked?"

"Yes," Jason and Clive said as if it was the most obvious thing in the world.

"Wow," Marcus said. "I may need to get better friends."

"I'm sure yours are fine."

"I have a friend who won't let me forget about the time I took his slice of pie. That was three years ago."

"At least your friends didn't all sleep with your imaginary wife," Clive grumbled.

"What?" Marcus asked.

"It doesn't matter," Clive said, looking defeated.

"Uh, alright," Marcus said. "Make any final preparations tonight. At first light, we'll do the final briefing and go. Make sure that friend of yours is here."

Farrah was portalled in by a Rimaros gold-ranker arranged by the Adventure Society. The society was under instruction from Marcus to accept any reasonable request from Jason and most of the unreasonable ones no questions asked. She arrived at the Adventure Society campus portal square, with the portal closing immediately behind her. One of Jason's portals opened next to her immediately after and she stepped through, arriving outside the city in front of Emir's cloud palace.

Most of the adventurers not native to Yaresh were set up outside the city, with many of the native ones as well. They had their own portal square in front of the cloud palace that was the centrepiece of the adventurer camp, and Jason, Rufus and Gary were all waiting. Night had fallen hours ago and lanterns staved off the dark.

"I thought you already agreed to go on this expedition," Gary told her. Her response was inaudibly muffled through his fur as he pulled her into a devouring hug.

"It was up in the air," Farrah repeated after being released. "Are you going?"

"Gods, no," Gary said. "You may have only semi-retired, but I've committed. I'll get back to fighting monsters in the next monster surge."

"You're not going?" Jason asked him.

"No, thank you," Gary said firmly. "I'm going to stick to my smithing."

"And where is your forge?" Jason asked.

"Uh, you know that, obviously," Gary said. "It's in…"

Jason grinned as realisation struck.

"…your soul space," Gary finished limply.

"Welcome aboard," Farrah said, reaching up to slap him on the shoulder.

Gary hung his head back and sighed. Then he perked up and started laughing as he pointed at the sky. Everyone's gaze followed his finger and spotted a bright red light in the sky. An airship that looked like a water vessel except flying and on fire was moving through the sky, leaving a sparkling trail behind like a comet. Rufus groaned and slapped an exasperated hand to his forehead.

"You're burning through spirit coins, you idiot," he muttered.

"You know who that is?" Jason asked.

"Yes," Rufus grumbled. "Please let my mother know that my father is about to arrive."

Gabriel Remore plunged out of the sky, trailing fire the same way his airship had. Jason stood off to the side as he reunited with his wife and son, laughing quietly as Rufus acted like a surly teenager. Gabriel exchanged greetings with Gary and Farrah, his son's old team, before wandering over to speak with Jason.

Gabriel looked a lot like Rufus—tall, dark and muscular, but with hair. He wore it in colourful beads, but instead of tight to the head like Emir wore them, his trailed down to his shoulders in chains.

"I like your hair," Jason said as they shook hands.

"I like your ludicrous power and ability to come back from the dead. Do you have any idea how crazy the stories about you are?"

"Honestly? The reality is probably more absurd than what you've heard."

"I can't wait to hear all about it on this expedition."

"You're coming along?"

"I asked Marcus to keep it a secret so I could surprise Roo."

"Dad," Rufus called over. "I told you if you call me that, I'm going to tell Mother about the cooler box under the deck at—"

"That's fine!" Gabriel hurriedly choked out. "Understood, son. Not a problem."

He leaned closer to Jason to whisper conspiratorially.

"He can be so ruthless. Doesn't care about his old dad at all—"

"Silver rank now," Rufus called over. "My hearing is very, very good."

Gabriel grumbled under his breath as he placed a hand on Jason's shoulder.

"Never have kids," he told Jason.

"What was that?" Arabelle asked in the tone of a gun being cocked.

"Nothing, dear. Love you."

58

QUICK AND CLEAN

YARESH WAS NO LONGER LIT UP AT NIGHT. THE TREE BUILDINGS WERE toppled, lanterns no longer draped from the branches. The metal and glass ziggurats no longer shined in the city centre, having been annihilated in the fight between the garuda and the naga genesis egg.

Only a handful of patches in the city still shone in the dark. The most prominent was the Adventure Society campus, left largely intact despite being the starting point of the garuda fight. Some less important outbuildings where the fight had broken out were nothing but rubble, but the defences on the core areas had kept them intact as the fight spilled through the shining buildings at the city's heart.

The Magic Society campus and Ducal Palace boasted similarly effective protection and were all but untouched. The only other places that came close were the underground bunkers. Many of them were still being used to house the displaced populace, along with the tent cities dotted through the city ruins. The lamps lighting up these sad encampments were nothing compared to the shining city of the past and made up most of the city's night-time illumination.

With the vast reduction in light pollution, the stars were more visible in the night sky. It was poor consolation, but Jason still took advantage. He was reclined in a cloud chair, floating high above the city after leaving the Remore family to their reunion. Gabriel's arrival also reunited his old team with Arabelle, Emir and Callum Morse.

Jason had been studiously avoiding Callum and his continual petitions to see Melody. Arabelle claimed that Callum was improving now that everything was in the open and she could work with him, but the man's aura still felt dangerously unstable to Jason. Perhaps his old team would help balance him out; it certainly worked for Jason.

"Mr Asano," Shade said.

Jason sighed.

"You know, Shade, we're going underground in the morning. I can't help but wonder how long it will be until I see the sky again. There's a lot going on down there, and what little information we have is months out of date."

"It could only be a few days," Shade pointed out. "Get down there, trigger the device and leave."

"Do you really think it's going to be that simple?"

"Of course not, Mr Asano. But a positive outlook is more likely to achieve positive results. The anticipation of negative results can be a self-fulfilling prophecy, something I believe you understand."

"I suppose I do."

"Even if the messengers get what they want, that is hardly the end of the world. A phrase that is not hyperbole when addressing your activities, so be thankful for that. If the astral king gets her soul forge and this region avoids explosive destruction, that is at least an acceptable outcome. The astral king will take her prize and leave, allowing the city reconstruction to begin in earnest."

"I don't think the messengers see it the same way. I'm guessing the idea of me taking the soul forge for myself is a risk they are cognisant of, assuming that we're right and that's what they're trying to make. They'll be after my head, whatever the outcome. And what if I do get the soul forge? What happens when I become an astral king proper? Do I suddenly jump to transcendent-rank? Am I stuck out in the astral with a letterbox on my head?"

"Since when are you afraid of vast cosmic power, Mr Asano?"

"Power reveals who you are. On Earth, my relative power was enormous and I don't like what that did to me. Am I better now? I feel like I am, but what if I'm wrong and I become too powerful for my friends to correct me?"

"Do you believe that you will be so out of touch that they need to?"

"There's a chance. Even if it's an outside one, doesn't the damage if it happens make the risk worth considering?"

"I am not sure you should take your moral imperatives from terrible films about superheroes fighting each other, Mr Asano."

"You've seen that movie?"

"You assigned one of my bodies to Mr Williams' shadow."

"Right, Taika actually likes that movie. At least I know one person with worse judgement than me."

"Mr Asano, if you're waiting until you become a perfect man, you'll be waiting forever. Literally. You're ageless and it will never happen."

Jason laughed.

"Thank you, Shade. Once again, your perspective offers sage guidance."

"You are welcome, Mr Asano."

"So, what's up?"

"Lady Allayeth would like to see you."

"No worries. Say, did you notice that Jali and Allayeth have the exact same hair colour?"

"I don't pay attention to most colours. They seem pointless."

"That explains a lot. Does she want to see me about that guy who tried to kill me?"

"Yes. She is awaiting you outside the interrogation room."

"I can sense it. Any idea why Humphrey is there?"

"Lady Allayeth requested his presence to identify the man."

"Interesting. Thank you, Shade."

The chair under Jason dispersed, the cloud material being drawn into the tiny flask hanging from his necklace. He let himself fall, still lying back with legs crossed at the ankles and hands behind his head. Eventually, he shifted his weight to let his legs drift up, pointing him at the rapidly approaching ground. His cloak manifested around him and then flumed out, spreading like wings to turn his plummet into a breakneck swoop over the city.

Racing into the Adventure Society campus, he careened between some of the few buildings left standing in the city. Finally, he plunged into one of the many night-time shadows, vanishing as if it were a hole in the wall. Inside a nearby building, Shade emerged from Humphrey's shadow and Jason emerged from Shade.

"What's going on?" Jason asked.

"They've gotten the man who attacked you to talk," Humphrey said. "They brought me in to confirm his identity."

"You know the guy? I didn't recognise him."

"You wouldn't, although you have met," Humphrey said. "You only saw him very briefly back when you were still iron rank. Your aura perception was weak enough that you wouldn't have sensed his aura to recognise. Not from a silver-rank stealth specialist."

"The man who attacked me was gold."

"You're not the only one who gets to rank up, Jason."

"Now you've got me curious. Who is he?"

"A former member of the Greenstone nobility, which is how I recognised him. Lawrence Sparnow, also known as Mr Sparrow in certain unsavoury circles. He vanished from the city after kidnapping you for Cole Silva and hasn't been heard from since."

"He's the one that grabbed me and handed me over for star seed implantation."

"And was paid quite well for his services, it would seem. Using that money as a seed, he built a lucrative criminal enterprise. With the supply of monster cores being so high during the extended surge, he managed to accrue enough cores to hit gold rank."

"What is he doing here?"

"Some of that we can only guess," Allayeth said, coming through a door to join them in the hall. "The people that hired him were extremely careful about not exposing themselves. As best we can ascertain, the aristocratic faction who aren't happy about how things are going politically were looking to tip over the fruit cart. They wanted to kill you, Jason, to change things up by getting the expedition cancelled. Force the city population to be evacuated and founded again elsewhere."

"So, pretty much what I predicted would happen."

She rolled her eyes.

"Yes, Jason. I remember our bet."

"Would killing Jason even stop the expedition at this stage?" Humphrey asked. "We have the device, and the hole the elemental messengers dug to the surface. We don't need the underground tunnel the regular messengers have been sitting on."

"Perhaps, perhaps not," Allayeth said. "The messengers were about to hand off the device when Jason was attacked, but they hadn't done it yet. They might have snatched it back if Jason died. Also, I don't imagine you and your team would still be willing to participate in the expedition if he did. At this point, Clive Standish and Farrah Hurin are more important to the expedition's success than you are, Jason."

"They're willing to let the city be destroyed?" Humphrey asked.

"The aristocrats are on the back foot right now," Allayeth said. "The arrival of Marcus Xenoria and the unexpected support he has gotten from key figures in the aristocrats like Gormanston Bynes have left their power scattered. But the aristocrats still represent a majority of resources and power in Yaresh. Needing to rebuild would recentre their importance and let them re-establish their influence, building it into the very foundations of the new city."

"Can you use this against the Aristocratic Faction?" Humphrey asked. "We don't want any more interference in an expedition that already has too many uncertainties."

"I doubt it," Jason said. "I'm guessing they used this guy precisely because he was outside of their power structure. They'll have used enough cut-outs and blind meetings that there'll be no linking them to it."

"That's exactly what happened," Allayeth confirmed. "We'll try and make the connection, but for all they're mediocre at adventuring, the Aristocratic Faction excels at scheming. That's why it takes unpredictable outliers like Jason and Marcus Xenoria to force them out of their old patterns and slip up."

"My question," Jason said, "is what was the guy doing here in Yaresh that they could find him to hire? And why would he take the job? Surely he wouldn't have missed how much attention is on me right now. I'd have thought he'd be anywhere but here."

"He was already here to kill you before the aristocrats found him," Allayeth said. "He heard that while you were in the Storm Kingdom, you caught up with the man who hired him to kidnap you."

"We did," Jason said.

"He worried about you coming for him next."

"I had no idea where he was."

"He imagined the man you caught believed the same thing. I'm not sure you understand the magnitude of the stories around you, Jason, and the impact they have on people that hear enough of them."

"I understand fine. Every prick that hears them either dismisses them as lies or tries to crack me open and shake the secrets out. Kidnapping me, breaking into my cloud house, seducing me."

"Seducing you?" Humphrey asked. "Who did that?"

"No one yet, but a bloke can dream. Wait, did anyone try it? Am I just forgetting? Surely someone's tried it by now. Did I not notice? Should I be paying more attention to this stuff?"

Allayeth looked nonplussed as Humphrey shook his head.

"Shade," Jason said. "Has anyone ever tried to seduce me for my secrets?"

"Numerous times, Mr Asano," Shade said. "They normally leave confused before you realise."

"Wait, are you saying that I'm so repellent to women that they run off before I even notice?"

"I wouldn't concern yourself, Mr Asano. They weren't your type."

"Really? I love confident, assertive women. You'd think that's exactly what you'd want in a seductress. I know I do."

"Jason," Humphrey said. "I think you'll find that perhaps your type had shifted somewhat."

"Shifted where?" Jason asked.

"Upward," Humphrey told him.

"Flying women? I hope you're not talking about messengers because while they do have more startlingly attractive people who look twenty-five than a teen drama, they are off the table on principle."

"No, Jason," Humphrey said. "I'm saying that it's all princesses and diamond-rankers for you these days."

"It's not my fault they're the only ones around. I have to flirt with someone. I'm a magical being, Humphrey; I live on raw magic and repartee, and the astral only supplies me with one of those."

"Jason, you do not live on banter."

"I might. You don't know how astral kings work."

"Can I please say something?" Allayeth interjected.

"Of course," Jason said.

"Always, Lady Allayeth," Humphrey said. "We always have time for diamond-rankers, don't we, Jason?"

Jason gave him a flat look.

"For your information, Humpy, the last two women I was intimate with were a bartender and a tavern owner."

"And did either of them know your real name?" Humphrey asked.

"I wasn't looking to get married. My type is quite inclusive when you—"

"Gentlemen," Allayeth interrupted again. She was not used to being overlooked by silver-rankers and was finding the entire experience bizarre.

"Sorry," Jason said.

"Apologies, Lady Allayeth," Humphrey said.

"Jason," she said. "Explain to me how you can be out here having such a frivolous conversation when the man who handed you over for star-seed implantation is in the next room? He's responsible for what must vie for the worst experience of your life."

"He's not responsible for anything," Jason said. "The hammer pushes in the nail, but it's the man holding it who builds the house. That guy means nothing to me."

"Are you sure?" Allayeth asked. "I'm not certain I could be so detached about someone who delivered me to such a fate."

"People try to kidnap or assassinate me a lot. If I took it all personally, I'd spend my life hunting down people for bloody reprisals, and that's no way to live. I'm more interested in how he ended up here, coming after me."

"I told you that stories around you can be rather extreme," Allayeth said. "According to him, the fact that you escaped the Builder's star seed that he delivered you to had always worried him. He feared what someone capable of that would do if you ever caught up with him. Then he heard you died and that anxiety went away. He concentrated on building a criminal empire, to some success, and achieved gold rank during the monster surge when the surplus of cores drove prices down."

"They still can't have been cheap," Humphrey said. "Not for enough monster cores to hit gold."

"But there was unprecedented availability, even if the price was still out of reach for most," Allayeth said. "Sparnow has been very successful running a criminal enterprise so disgusting, I don't want to say what he was doing out loud."

"That's not new," Humphrey said. "His predilections came to light during the trial of the men who had Jason kidnapped. Part of his payment was facilitating his appetites."

"After the Builder decamped, the story about Jason's involvement spread. It gets less well-known the further you get from Rimaros, but certain people always hear things. Sparnow had become powerful enough that he was such a person, and he realised that Jason had returned from the dead."

"He must have loved hearing that," Jason said.

"Sparnow immediately decided to make Jason dead again," Allayeth continued. "He knew that if he didn't kill you before you ranked up again, Jason, it wasn't going to happen. He headed for Rimaros, where he heard about the other man. The one who hired him to kidnap you in the first place."

"Killian Laurent," Jason said. "He didn't do so bad out of getting caught. I imagine he's in a Magic Society basement somewhere, parcelling out enough nuggets to keep himself alive until he can execute an escape."

"Sparnow doesn't have the value this man Laurent had, and he knows it," Allayeth said. "He has nothing to offer in return for staying alive other than the names of others who share his debased leanings. For him, capture meant death and he knew it."

"So, he came looking for the one person he thought would be motivated to hunt him down," Humphrey said. "Only to effectively hunt himself down."

"Travel was hard during the surge," Allayeth said. "By the time travel routes opened up and he arrived in Rimaros, your team had moved on. The secret identity thing threw him off for a while, but when messenger servants started asking questions in Rimaros, he traced you here. He arrived in Yaresh shortly before the attack on the city and he's been looking for a chance to kill you ever since."

"But Jason has been roaming around the wilderness or spending time with gold- and diamond-rankers," Humphrey said.

"Exactly," Allayeth said. "Meeting the messenger envoy alone presented a small but predictable time window. It was a risk, but Sparnow is a stealth specialist. His power set is assassination-based, so he planned to get in, take Jason down and then escape before anyone responded."

"I told you that the Aristocratic Faction caved on letting me go alone too quickly," Jason told her.

"I already told you that I remember the bet, Jason."

"What next?" Humphrey asked. "Can we use Sparnow to bait the Aristocratic Faction into making a mistake and exposing themselves? Trying to get what's left of the city destroyed is outright treason."

"We don't have time for the kind of investigation it would take to catch the aristocrats' tail," Allayeth said. "It is happening, but it's unlikely to dig out proof and doesn't help us now anyway. As soon as the expedition is away, we're going to hold a trial for Sparnow to see if we can spook the Aristocratic Faction into making a mistake. It's unlikely, but worth trying. Then Sparnow will be executed, unless the mercy you've been pursuing extends to this man, Jason? As the victim, your voice will make an impact on the sentencing. And if you're willing to forgive messengers and the people who betrayed us to them…"

"He's not part of an indoctrinated slave race or a prisoner broken by fear," Jason said. "He's a depraved predator."

"Do you want to be the one to do it?" Allayeth asked. "We don't anticipate getting much out of a trial, so if I let you in there right now, no one will say a word."

"No," Jason said. "I have no interest in vengeance and I'm not going to take joy in someone's suffering, even someone like him. Using my powers on a gold-ranker is a slow and ugly way to kill."

"He deserves slow and ugly, from what I've heard," Allayeth said.

"It's not about what he deserves, or what I want. The only reason to kill him is that the only thing he has to offer the world is poison. Keeping him alive would be doing harm. Once you have everything he knows about every other predator he knows, put him down. Quick and clean."

Allayeth nodded.

"I'll get it done," she said and went back through the door.

Jason sighed and leaned against the wall.

"I hate making a choice like that," he said. "I know I'm a hypocrite, with all the people I've killed, but when killing is the best option, it feels like I've failed to find a better way."

Humphrey leaned against the wall next to Jason and nudged his shoulder.

"Don't apologise for moral growth, Jason."

"Are you sure it's growth? It feels so murky. Am I doing the right thing with the messengers?"

"I don't know," Humphrey admitted. "I never used to get confused about right and wrong before I met you. Now I just do my best. Sometimes I'll get it right and sometimes I won't, and then I'll do my best to fix that."

"When did you get so smart?"

"Meaning that you thought I wasn't?"

"Uh…"

Humphrey chuckled and looked over at the closed door.

"What was that bet Lady Allayeth kept mentioning?"

"After the aristocrats didn't fight me on picking up the device alone, I bet her that they would try to have me killed."

"What did you get for winning?"

"Nothing important. It doesn't matter."

Humphrey looked at Jason from under raised eyebrows.

"Fine," Jason grumbled. "She has to buy me dinner."

Humphrey shook his head.

"And if she won?" he asked.

"I had to buy her dinner."

"That sounds like you set up a bet where you win either way."

Jason grinned, pushed himself off the wall and slapped Humphrey on the shoulder.

"And your mum thought you'd never get your head around politics. See you at breakfast."

Humphrey watched Jason drop into his shadow like it was a hole in the floor and vanish. He then looked again at the door through which Allayeth had left.

"Maybe Rick has a point."

WHAT WE'RE WALKING INTO

THE EXPEDITION MEMBERS, ALONG WITH ALLAYETH AND MARCUS, WERE in a briefing room aboard an airship owned by the Adventure Society. This included Jason's team, Rick's team and Korinne Pescos' team as the silver-rank combat contingent, along with a team from the Magic Society. The team of researchers had been, to everyone's surprise, swiftly approved by Clive. It turned out the society officials didn't want to go on the incredibly dangerous mission, so they sent the competent researchers they kept in the basement doing work the officials could claim credit for.

The gold-rankers included Team Moon's Edge, the all-female team trained by Allayeth. Rufus' parents, Gabriel and Arabelle, had reformed their old team with Emir, minus former teammate Callum Morse. As they didn't trust Callum's current mentality for this mission, he had been swapped out for Emir's wife Constance. She had known them all for years and had trained with Callum leading up to gold rank, so she at least had some familiarity with the group.

The remaining gold-rank participants were Amos Pensinata, Carlos Quilido and Hana Shavar. Amos joined because his nephew was on one of the silver-rank teams while Carlos was the closest they had to an expert on the elemental messengers. Hana was a powerful healer, important to Yaresh but wouldn't allow any of her subordinates to join such a critical mission.

There was no bronze- or diamond-rank element to the expedition.

Bronze-rankers were too weak and diamond rank too strong for the massive fluctuations in the ambient magic. Sometimes it grew so saturated that it created anomalies that could kill a bronze-ranker outright. Other times, it dropped to almost nothing, like on Earth when Jason first returned home. Gold-rankers without a ready supply of gold spirit coins would be swiftly debilitated, rendered comatose, or even die.

A diamond-ranker would have it worse. Even if a sufficient supply of diamond spirit coins could be mustered up, which they couldn't, it was uncertain if they would even be enough. Allayeth argued that she could duck into Jason's soul space if necessary, but had eventually been convinced otherwise. If dimensional forces somehow blocked Jason's soul portal at a point of absolute low magic, she could be crippled and killed as the magic-parched world sucked the life right out of her.

The briefing began with making sure that none of the expedition members were missing any critical details. The basics had already been disseminated, but it was easy to miss something or other.

"To summarise," Marcus said, standing at the front, "you'll be entering through the hole we have secured, determining if the device does what the messengers claim, and then activating it if it does. The key threat is the unstable elemental magic pervading the underground area. This is the same magic slowly building up that will eventually destroy this region if we don't stop it. Mr Standish, if you would?"

Clive got up and moved to the front, Marcus shifting aside.

"Let me reiterate," Marcus said, "that Mr Standish is in command of all magical investigation in this expedition. I don't care if you're gold rank, I don't care if you're Magic Society; when it comes to investigating the magic, his word is first and last."

"Thank you, Representative Xenoria," Clive said. "The nature of the magic we will encounter remains unknown in the specific, but we do know some of its general trends. It is elemental in nature and appears to have a transformative effect on the body and mind. Our best information is that being an essence user offers considerable but not total protection. Strength of will also seems to play a considerable part. The messengers attempted to send some of their servants, but the messengers kill anyone whose will they don't break and those people did not do well."

"How reliable is this information?" Constance asked.

"Not as much as we'd like," Clive said. "A lot more comes from the messengers than what we could detect from the surface. Fortunately, within the last day, we've had access to a somewhat more reliable source. Jason?"

Jason got up and joined Clive.

"I know there have been a lot of questions about the messengers I've taken prisoner personally. What I've been doing with them and why. What information have I gotten from them? Some of that I've passed on already, mostly big-picture stuff with nothing specifically actionable. The initial group of messengers I captured weren't part of the messengers' original underground foray where they caused this problem in the first place. I couldn't use them to confirm or deny the information Jes Fin Kaal has been giving the Adventure Society. The messenger I captured most recently is another story. She's lower rank, but she was there in person."

"How can we trust any of the information they gave you?" asked the leader of Team Moon's Edge, Miriam Vance.

"That's a fair question," Jason said. "I've taken the messengers away and you have no idea where I put them or what I'm doing with them. But there are people in this room that have. Lady Allayeth has seen them. I had her speak with them just today so that someone you trust could allay your fears as much as possible."

"Anyone is free to speak with Lady Allayeth after the briefing," Marcus said. "In the meantime, Mr Asano, please continue."

"The latest messenger I captured was sent to us, in part, because she had little value to them. There are a lot of reasons for that I don't need to go into, but suffice it to say she was as close as the messengers get to a low-level drudge. She was part of an expendable group the messengers use for tasks like watching over the world-taker worm nests where there's a good chance of being killed by adventurers."

"I thought they were all meant to be superior beings," Gabriel said.

"They're indoctrinated to believe that they're superior to us, but ultimately, that's just a method of control. They're slaves and are used as such by the astral kings. They have an internal hierarchy, where the lowest messengers are told they're still above everyone else."

"You make them sound like victims," Miriam said.

"They are," Jason said. "Incredibly dangerous victims. Put them down if you get the chance; do not attempt to take them alive on the basis of compassion. Now, to get us back on track, these expendable messengers made up most of the group sent underground in the messengers' initial attempt to suborn the natural array. Only a fraction of them escaped when things went wrong."

"And this messenger was one of them?" Miriam asked.

"Yes. She has first-hand accounts of what's down there."

"We have detailed information that will be handed out with your packets at the end of this meeting," Marcus said. "For now, a quick summary, please, Mr Asano."

"There is an underground city," Jason said. "A magical variant of smoulders have been living peacefully with the natural array for an unknown period. During the monster surge, one of the earliest-arriving group of messengers somehow found this city and burrowed down to it, looking to claim the array. To complicate things, a group of Builder cultists followed them, looking to claim an astral space also located down there."

"Is the astral space related to the natural array?" Emir asked.

"We don't know," Clive told him. "This whole operation is built on incomplete and unreliable information, and I think we all know how that usually plays out."

"Mr Standish," Allayeth said. "Are you attempting to convince the members of this expedition to pull out?"

"No," Clive said. "But if just explaining the situation makes it sound like I am, that should tell us all something."

"The decision has been made, Mr Standish," Marcus said. "I won't force anyone down that hole, but you have had ample chance to back out."

Clive looked at Jason, who shrugged. Clive sighed before continuing.

"Each of you will be provided with elemental resistance items, which we believe will help stave off the corrupting effects of the magic down there. You'll also receive potions designed to purge your bodies of the elemental affinities magic they'll absorb in the process of natural mana recovery."

"How confident are we that will work?" Arabelle asked.

"Jason?" Clive said.

"Obviously," Jason said, "we can't trust Jes Fin Kaal and her messengers. While she has, so far as we can tell, mostly played things straight, she has also kept things from us. According to the messenger I just captured, certain messengers were significantly more resistant to the influence of the natural array's elemental energy. Those messengers were the ones who themselves possess elemental powers of the affiliated types, mostly fire, earth and metal."

"If the messengers have people that can go down there," Gabriel asked, "what do they need us for? As it was explained to me, they want us to go down there because they can't."

"They don't have the numbers," Jason said. "Elemental powers are fairly rare amongst messengers. Their local forces have between ten and twenty messengers that fit the bill, none of which are gold rank. They don't have the power to go down there and face what's waiting for them."

"Which is what?" Miriam asked. "Since it's waiting for us as well, what are we dealing with?"

Clive stepped back as Jason took centre stage at the front of the briefing room.

"The best information we have," Jason said, "is that we're walking into a three-sided war already in motion. There's an underground city down there and the native smoulders were, as of several months ago, largely unaffected by the unstable natural array. They've been modified by the array's power for centuries. They may be immune to the power building up or just resistant, changing slower than the messengers. For all we know, it could be making them stronger and they'll resist us trying to shut the array down. Hopefully not, as they're our best bet for any kind of alliance down there."

"Assuming that the escalating elemental energy hasn't turned them into mindless monsters, the way it did the messengers," Clive added.

"Yes," Jason agreed. "Which brings us to the second faction, the element-infused messengers. We don't know how many of them are still down there, but their numbers should be limited. A lot of them dug their way up and were killed on the surface. Fortunately, almost all should be silver rank."

He took a slow, weary breath.

"The third faction is the Builder cult. A lot of cultists couldn't get back to the fortress cities before they dimension-shifted out, and we can safely assume that this lot were left behind. They were trapped with a lot of resources and significantly greater numbers than the messengers, and they holed up in the astral space, sealing it off. Hopefully, they'll stay there and we won't see them, but I don't think we'll be that lucky."

"We also don't know if the astral space has shielded them from the natural array's magic," Clive said.

"That's right," Jason agreed. "They may be bunkered down and unaffected, or they might be an army of elemental monsters by now."

"So, to sum up," Farrah said. "We're going underground into a situation we don't understand, filled with unstable magic we don't understand, so we can fight enemies we don't understand in order to do something we don't understand but will probably give our worst enemies exactly what they want. We possibly understand what that is, but it's a guess. Also, to pre-empt questions, I am trying to get everyone to not do this. I've got my own stuff going on, and if my friends weren't going on this extremely ill-advised mission, I could get back to that."

Marcus hung his head, letting out a groan that sounded like a passenger jet spinning up its engines.

"I'm going to stop things here before someone actually convinces you all to pull out," he said. "We expect to arrive at the tunnel in around an hour, so I want you all to take that time and review the supplemental material you'll be given as you leave this room. Please direct any questions to me or Lady Allayeth."

Marcus looked over the side of the airship at the fortress town below. Built over the top of the hole blasted out by the elemental messengers, it was a spiderweb of reinforced bridges with buildings on them, with a ring of larger buildings around the perimeter.

"This was built in a few weeks?" he growled. "People in Yaresh are living in tents and bunkers while this many construction resources were diverted here?"

"Politics," Allayeth said. "The Aristocratic Faction is strongly allied with the upper echelons of the Magic Society in Yaresh. This was intended to be a way for both of them to take greater control in the messenger conflict. We pushed back as much as we could, but if the Duke went to war with the Aristocratic Faction, the city administration would have collapsed in the infighting and made things worse."

"I was given a surprising amount of leeway to cause trouble," Marcus said. "Normally, a local government wouldn't let this much power swing to the Adventure Society, but now I'm seeing why."

"The Aristocratic Faction isn't broken, but they're on the back foot now. You'll find a lot of these buildings are empty shells after resources were diverted back to the city. Now things are only getting started there and we have this half-finished mess."

"Have you been into the chasm?"

"Some way down, until the ambient magic became unstable."

"Does it stay anywhere near as wide as the aperture as it continues down?"

"Yes, although it's not uniform. Some sections are akin to an over-sized mineshaft while others are more twisty and cavernous. There are even sections that are honeycombed with smaller tunnels instead of one massive one."

"How did they do this? Displacing that much earth when digging up from below would be hard even with magic. By all accounts, the elemental messengers are fairly mindless, so I don't imagine they have any engineers."

"It looks like they used mixed methods, from what I saw. There was evidence of dimensional displacement, stone-shaping, magma tunnels. Clive Standish suspects that their elemental powers allow them to create or annihilate matter that is substantively elemental in nature by tapping into different dimensional layers."

"Don't you start. I tried listening to that man explain layers of reality, and I'm not doing it again. Although Asano did give me a slice of rainbow layer cake in an attempt to explain it with visual aids. Delicious, but ultimately futile."

"You never studied any magical theory?"

"I did meet a scholar who told me I was an expert in applied kinetics, whatever that is."

"You didn't ask?"

"I didn't get a chance before I beat him to death with a fruit cart."

"How exactly did you wind up as a Continental Council executive?"

"They like to have different people for different situations. I usually get sent places where they need someone to cut through the politics. Not literally, obviously. Unless we want to. We get quite broad discretionary power and I find an axe through someone's head on the first day helps set a tone."

60

WHAT KIND OF ADVENTURER

THE EXPEDITION TEAM WAS STANDING ON A PLATFORM THAT HUNG OVER one side of the hole. A strong wind blew through the town and over the aperture, creating a low, ominous roar. No one could resist going to the edge and looking down into the roughly circular chasm that was hundreds of metres across. It was a hungry void, devouring what sunlight made it past the bridges and buildings arching over it.

After peering over the edge, the group gathered to examine the vehicles lined up on the platform, waiting to carry them down. Their construction was rough and industrial, designed and assembled with only function in mind. Each looked like something between a crab and a centipede, with hollow backs that contained space for six plus a driver. The seats reminded Jason of amusement park rides, with bars and belts designed to hold people in place through some wild bucking. There were even roll cages over the top of each seating area.

Allayeth, standing in the middle of the platform with Marcus, grabbed everyone's attention with a burst of aura projection. Once everyone had gathered around, she started talking.

"The crawlers won't be as fast as descending through flight," she explained, "but magical conditions are uncertain. These vehicles are designed to operate with maximal reliability and will continue functioning at very low levels of ambient magic. Only those with essence abilities that allow them to employ specialised magical tools can operate them."

That was a standard concern for low-magic zones and had been the norm in Greenstone. Both Belinda and Clive had appropriate abilities.

"If the crawlers detect extreme magical abnormalities or massive fluctuations in ambient magic," Allayeth continued, "they will automatically secure themselves to the walls. This is to prevent them falling in case of malfunction, and this mode will need to be manually overridden to continue."

"A final reminder of command structure," Marcus said, taking over the briefing. He gestured to the elven leader of the team trained by Allayeth.

"Miriam is your tactical commander. When the fighting starts or something else goes wrong, she is in charge. For secondary commanders, those of you not in teams have already been assigned temporary groups. If you can't remember your assigned sub-commander, please jump into the hole now and save us all some time."

Allayeth gave him a sharp look; an unrepentant shrug was the closest he came to accepting her silent criticism.

"Clive Standish is in charge of magical operations and investigation," Marcus continued. "When the magic gets weird, and it will, you do what he says, when he says it. If you don't, I won't need to punish you because you'll have died like an idiot."

"Mr Xenoria..." Allayeth said through gritted teeth.

"Lastly," Marcus continued, "Jason Asano is operations commander. Outside of combat, he has the last word in what you will do and how you will do it. I know that it's unusual to have a silver-ranker in command of a team with a gold-rank contingent, but it's appropriate for this expedition, given his unique qualifications. He has had more experience with cosmic forces and exotic dimensional spaces in the last six years than the rest of us in our entire careers. Combined, probably. The man got in a knife fight with the Builder when he was iron rank, for gods' sakes."

"Strictly speaking, only I had a knife," Jason said. "Also, it didn't go well. I mean, we stopped him from activating his world engineers, but he did kill me."

"Jason," Arabelle spoke up. "Remember when we talked about focusing on professionalism?"

"Sorry," Jason said. "Look, everyone, we all know the chain of command; the org chart was in all our packets. Marcus just said he wanted to yell it at everyone so it sank in. As long as you actually read the thing, you know who command falls to if I die or turn into a universe or something, so let's—"

"I'm sorry," Miriam Vance cut in. "Did you just say you might turn into a universe? It sounded like you said you might turn into a universe, but that would be an insane thing for a person to say because people don't turn into universes. I can't help but feel like I'd be more comfortable with an operations commander who understands that."

"That is exactly why Mr Asano is in charge," Marcus said. "I did say he had unique qualifications. The fact is, he regularly operates outside of any scenario that makes sense to the rest of us. You may have heard about him convincing the Builder to leave the planet. That's a simplification, but not inaccurate. I'd also like to thank him for deciding to share some of his considerable secrets."

"Such as being able to turn into a universe?"

"A small universe," Jason said. "And to be honest, I'm two-thirds universe already. And I will be honest. Mostly. More or less. The fact is, everyone on this expedition is taking a huge risk, and you deserve something approximating the truth of what we might be walking into. I've already shared some of this with Lady Allayeth and Representative Xenoria in the planning stage. And, as I said, I'm on the way to being a living universe. Lady Allayeth has seen it for herself. She's also promised to help me murder any Magic Society pricks who try to kidnap and experiment on me. Just throwing that out there."

His gaze moved to the Magic Society contingent, his reptilian smile giving them chills.

The crawlers made their way down the walls of the shaft. Just as their appearance suggested, they had been built for practicality over looks or, as became swiftly apparent, comfort. At first, Jason had found it fun, the amusement park seats proving indicative of the ride. A couple of hours in, he reflected that there was a reason park rides only lasted a few minutes. Hanging from the straps and bars holding them in place as the crawlers clunked downwards became very old very fast.

Some of the passengers had means to make things more comfortable. Jason was one of those, calling some cloud stuff from the miniaturised flask on his necklace. It slipped between him and the bars and straps of his seat, smoothing and cushioning his ride. With so many elite gold- and silver-rankers, many others likewise had items and abilities that offered comfort. For those that didn't, some requested through Jason's party interface to make their own way down. This was immediately refused by Miriam Vance.

Miriam had joined half of Team Biscuit in one of the crawlers so she could continue talking with Jason. They could have used the interface, but she wanted to question him in person. Clive was driving, with Humphrey, Sophie, Rufus and Stash as the other passengers. Stash had enjoyed the experience at first, taking the form of a celestine version of an adolescent Humphrey with silver eyes and hair.

It did not take long before Stash started complaining to be let out, Humphrey and Sophie repeatedly calming him down. It was a sign of his growing maturity that he actually stayed put, despite his complaints, instead of turning into a bird and flying off. He did shift his form to be significantly rotund, however.

"It's for cushioning," he insisted.

The jerky ride where everyone was hanging face down was not conducive to conversation, even through voice chat. But once Jason had padded his ride and Miriam did something similar with an air-conjuration power, she continued probing him with questions.

"So, you're turning into one of the messengers' leaders, but that isn't the same as turning into a messenger?"

"No," Jason said. "Astral king seems to be an end-state for messenger advancement, but being a messenger isn't a requirement. Messengers are capable of developing the aspects required to become an astral king naturally, although we don't know how that is triggered. The diamond-rank messengers are all obsessed with that secret, by all accounts."

"But there are unnatural means of developing those aspects?" Miriam asked.

"I'd prefer to use the term artificial," Jason said. "But yes. The elements that make someone an astral king can be acquired through external means. It's the way I'm doing it, and it turns out I'm not the first. Clive dug out some records in the diamond-rank messenger's study that are old even by cosmic standards. These records seem to imply that the messenger race itself originated with astral kings who weren't messengers because the messengers didn't exist yet."

"It's not definitive," Clive called back with a grunt from where he was piloting the crawler. "Is the ride getting any better? I think I'm slowly coming to grips with this thing."

"Not getting better so much as less awful," Sophie told him. "But you're doing well, Clive; keep it up."

Jason smiled to himself as Sophie casually supported her teammate. It was worlds away from the porcupine she had been when they first met.

"The documents I found contradict messenger indoctrination, which is some piffle about having always existed as the living will of the universe," Clive continued, his tone distracted as he drove the crawler. "There was reference to messenger precursor astral kings it called 'originals,' although whether they were the actual source of the first messengers I don't know. There was nothing on where the birthing tree planets came fro— WHO PUT THAT BLOODY ROCK THERE?"

The crawler jolted hard, slamming Jason against the restraining bar even through his cloud cushioning.

The crawlers moved slower and far less comfortably than the adventurers would have descended under their own power. Upon reaching a sloped section of the shaft that became almost horizontal for a long stretch, they called a stop to rest. A small army of relieved adventurers got out to stretch their legs, a handful of familiars frolicking around them. Jason and the others from his crawler stood next to it, stretching out their limbs.

"Are you sensing that?" Jason asked Miriam who nodded.

"Elementals," she said. "We were expecting them sooner or later."

Elementals weren't monsters in the strictest sense. They were still the result of a magical manifestation, but rather than form a body entirely from magic, they were real elemental matter, infused with magic. The result was an animated and aggressive mass of elemental substance. Most elementals were comprised of earth, air, fire or water, but many variants existed based on the environments in which they appeared.

Jason's early career in Greenstone had included mud elementals in the delta and sand elementals in the desert. A silver-rank water elemental known as an elemental tyrant had left the first and still largest of his scars after almost killing him. An elemental had once emerged from the Greenstone sewerage system during Jason's time there, a battle he was grateful to have not participated in.

"I'm only sensing silver-rankers," Jason said. "Given that elementals are as subtle as a bridge collapse with their auras, I don't think I'm missing any gold-rankers amongst them."

"Then you should take them on alone," Humphrey said.

"You can't sense how many there are," Miriam told him. "There are at least a hundred of them."

"Good," Humphrey said. "A lot of the people in this expedition see Jason as a political appointment. Someone who is important to the mission but doesn't have their respect as an adventurer. The way Representative Xenoria introduced him didn't help with that."

"I don't think getting him killed will help with that either," Miriam said.

"It will when he comes back," Sophie muttered. "He always does, usually with some ridiculous new power."

"Commander Vance," Humphrey said. "Jason repeatedly finds himself at the nexus of grand events. This leads people to overlook the fact that he is, in fact, an excellent adventurer. This expedition is filled with guild elites, hand-picked for this mission. I would hold Jason up against any of them. There is a fight coming which makes how to face it your decision. If you want to see what kind of adventurer your operations commander is, now is the safest chance you'll get before the magic goes weird on us."

"Also, he's already gone," Sophie pointed out.

Miriam looked around and saw that Jason had, indeed, slipped away without her aura senses registering his sudden absence.

"How?"

She expanded her senses over the distant elementals, swarming up the tunnel. She noted shadow creatures spreading out amongst them and sensed Asano right in the middle.

***

Elementals surged upslope along the tunnel, covering the walls, floor and roof. They were all conglomerations of loose elemental material, from formless masses to highly specific shapes. A mound of earth slid along the tunnel as a deer made of tiny stone fragments pranced alongside it. There was what looked like a child's crude attempt at a clay tortoise, except the size of a small house. A winged gorilla made of magma loped along, taking to the air in long, gliding leaps.

The only light was shed by the more fire-related elementals, mostly magma creatures glowing in the dark. Shade's bodies went unnoticed, but when Jason strolled out of one, it was a different story. His cloak of stars shone brightly, draped around him to the point that he looked engulfed in a starry void.

Jason walked with hands clasped leisurely behind his back. A shadow arm drew his sword, Hegemon's Will, that Gary had forged for him. He used his Doom Blade ability, but instead of conjuring a dagger, the power was bestowed on the sword. The rune letters running down the black blade turned from white to red.

- You have invoked the effects of [Ruin, Blade of Tribulation]. All properties of that weapon have been imbued into [Hegemon's Will]. Necrotic damage will be inflicted in addition to physical damage.

In contrast to Jason's slow meander, the shadow arm flickered around Jason in a blur of motion, the speed, reach and flexibility beyond what his natural arms could achieve. The blade did little more than scratch the elementals with solid physical forms, while those comprised of fire or smoky ash seemed to flinch from the blade's touch. Each hit landed special attacks, delivering affliction after affliction, Jason chanting spells that did the same.

"Bleed for me."

"Carry the mark of your transgressions."

"Your fate is to suffer."

Elementals surged at Jason, only to pass harmlessly through one of Shade's intangible bodies, Jason having already moved on. He didn't rush, always stepping into a Shade body with perfect timing to casually avoid attacks.

The greatest weakness of elementals was their mindlessness, without even the mental capacity of the simplest insect. Combined with the relative slowness of the mostly earth-type elementals, their inability to learn allowed Jason to lead them around by the nose, delivering afflictions with impunity. His mobility moved him from one area of the fight to another, the imbecilic elementals always playing catch up.

- [Castigate] has inflicted [Mortality], [Sin], [Mark of Sin], and [Weight of Sin]. You have gained [Marshal of Judgement].
- [Haemorrhage] has inflicted [Blood From a Stone], [Bleeding], [Sacrificial Victim] and [Necrotoxin].
- [Punish] has inflicted [Sin], [Price of Absolution] and [Wages of Sin].
- [Hand of the Reaper] has inflicted [Weakness of the Flesh], [Creeping Death] and [Rigor Mortis].
- [Hegemon's Will] has drained mana and inflicted necrotic damage, [Corrosion], [Vulnerable] and [Hegemon's Tribute].
- [Leech Bite] has refreshed [Bleeding] and inflicted [Leech Toxin] and [Tainted Meridians].
- [Inexorable Doom] has inflicted [Inexorable Doom], [Inescapable] and [Persecution].

The oppressive weight of afflictions left stone bleeding and magma rotting like a week-old corpse. The elementals ignored their unnatural suffering, having no sense of fear, pain or even the self-preservation instinct of an animal. They kept pointlessly chasing Jason around as he strolled through them, moving in and out of Shade's bodies.

If Jason went through the elementals one by one, destroying them all would take far too long. He had the endurance for it, able to replenish himself by feeding on afflictions, but it was better to send his dark powers spreading through the enemy.

In a surge of aura, Gordon appeared above Jason's head, his massive, nebulous eye blazing in the dark. His floating orb eyes shot out, seeking out afflicted elementals to sink into. Those elementals immediately started spawning butterflies that carried their afflictions to fresh victims.

Jason had not done well fighting large groups of late. The affliction-spreading butterflies were extremely effective if allowed to do their work, but it was a more complex process than poison clouds or just affecting huge crowds. He lacked the variety of simple and effective methods that traditional affliction specialists had access to, although he found himself not regretting their absence. As an affliction skirmisher, he wasn't stuck behind a team, mindlessly throwing out spells and left helpless if something went wrong.

He considered his independence and versatility well worth the trade-off of not easily and efficiently blanketing an area with his powers. That trade-off was real, however, as the complexity of the afflictions-spreading butterflies as a medium offered a key failure point for intelligent enemies to target. The butterflies were all but unstoppable after reaching a critical mass, but could be shut down with sufficiently swift and diligent action. During the Battle of Yaresh, the messengers had been swift to eliminate any butterflies, and even their own monsters once they were affected. This had shut down Jason's ability to have a massive impact on the tactical situation.

The higher rank the enemies, the smarter they tended to be. The elementals were the opposite of intelligent, however, and the butterflies were soon swarming over them in such a thick cloud, it was hard to see. The darkness of the tunnel was gone, the glowing butterflies filling the space with blue and orange light. The display was as beautiful as the results were ugly as stone oozed rotting pus and fire shed black, poisoned blood that was immediately boiled to steam.

The stench of tainted, coppery blood and rancid death filled the air. It would have choked anyone that needed to breathe. The days of Jason failing to bleed enemies just because they had no blood, or to rot enemies because they had no flesh were behind him. His powers made the impossible possible, which was the purpose of magic, after all. The afflicted elementals were now vulnerable to that which they should have been impervious, marking the time to finish things. Jason held out his hands and his palms grew slick with blood that seeped through his skin. A moment later, leeches erupted from his hands, geysering over the elementals.

Normally, Colin would not be able to feast on creatures of stone and earth, but Jason's afflictions had left them susceptible to his predation. Only the fire and magma elementals could hold him off, their heat slaying any individual leeches that grew close. Jason ignored this, the elementals too stupid to capitalise on it. Colin devoured the others, growing his leech swarm faster than it burned away.

The elementals Colin couldn't devour, Jason took care of. He drained the foul afflictions from all the fire and magma elementals at once, leaving holy afflictions in their place. The clean light of transcendent damage destroyed them from within, eating away at them even faster than the bleeding and the rot. Jason used his execute ability, Verdict, to detonate that power, finishing off the individual elementals that seemed to be holding up the best, like the giant clay tortoise.

From that stage, the massacre ended in short order. Shade was already moving through the dead by the time it was over, touching them to make them lootable.

"This should be a good haul of quintessence," Jason mused.

"Indeed, Mr Asano," Shade agreed. "Miss Farrah and Mr Standish may put them to good use in rituals during our time underground."

Jason triggered the loot, rainbow smoke rising from the remains of the elementals. Unlike ordinary silver-rank monsters, this did not eliminate the bodies entirely. Aside from those annihilated by transcendent damage, the elemental substance remained, stained and deformed with blood and necrosis that shouldn't have been possible. Remnants painted the walls and dripped from the roof, Jason's cloak deflecting rancid gobbets as he stood amongst the remains, judiciously pouring crystal wash down the length of his fouled blade.

GARY'S OLD TEAM

"You were being optimistic," Jason told Humphrey. "If you kill a whole parcel of monsters in front of some elite adventurers, the result won't be an awed crowd. It'll be a cluster of wildly self-confident people explaining how they would have done it faster and looked better doing it."

"Actually," Clive said from the driver's seat, "they mostly complained about the smell. You left a lot of disgusting goo back there and we had to take the crawlers right through it."

Clive had been the man to drive their crawler through the foul remains of the elementals. As he said, the stench had been potent.

"Something dripped on my head while we were going through there," Rufus complained. "I washed it off, but I can still feel it, like a phantom limb. I need some crystal wash to get rid of it."

"There's nothing wrong with soap," Jason told him.

"Jason, I just want the others to stop overlooking you," Humphrey said. "If someone decides they know better than you and choose to ignore your orders, it could be disastrous."

"I appreciate the thought," Jason said, "but most of the people on this expedition are our friends, remember? The Adventure Society didn't trust enough of the locals to not be compromised by the messengers."

"This expedition being full of our people is the source of the problem," Humphrey said. "People think you've been put in charge because of the important events you keep getting caught up in. They don't think you earned your command of this expedition through adventuring."

"And they're right," Jason told him. "I'm a silver-ranker, Humphrey. The best silver-ranker in the world doesn't get put in charge of gold-rankers unless there's some extremely extenuating circumstances. And I went off to kill those elementals alone because you suggested it, but it all felt very performative. I'm not the same guy who faced off with Rick and his team in the mirage chamber way back when. I'm an adventurer to do the job, not to show off."

Jason's teammates shared a glance, even Clive dropping his attention from driving to crane his neck around.

"What?" Jason asked.

A coughing sound came from Jason's shadow.

"Is everything alright, Shade?" Jason asked.

"Of course, Mr Asano. I just had something caught in my throat."

"Shade, you don't have a throat."

The massive numbers in which the elementals appeared the first time proved to be the norm and not the exception. Even a monster surge rarely saw monsters appear in such concentrations, reminding Jason more of the proto-spaces and monster waves back on Earth. Elementals weren't the only monsters to appear, although they were the majority. Even when other monster types showed up, there were always at least a few elementals tagging along.

The expedition's first truly challenging battle came in a vertical section of the shaft. Gold-rank spider moles dug out through the sides of the shaft and started hitting the crawlers with webs, sending the expedition into chaos. Torrents of thick, viscous webbing hit the slow-moving crawlers in rapid succession, striking even before the dust cleared from when the spider moles burst through the rock and into the tunnel.

Along with the spider moles were diamond-tooth worms, whose rank was only silver. They had oily, sickly grey skin and maws full of crystalline teeth stained by ichor. Like the spiders, the worms erupted from the sides of the tunnel, smashing through the rock. They didn't fully emerge, however, jutting from the sides of the tunnels like cilia. They flailed their lengthy bodies, the teeth for which they were named able to shear through the metal of the crawlers.

Finishing up the onslaught was the usual smattering of elementals, although there was an unusual deficit of earth types. This time, it was gaseous elementals that exploded when exposed to fire before reforming, along with flying fire elementals to set them off.

Miriam Vance swiftly took charge, firing off commands through Jason's voice chat. The expedition was in a mess, scattered and pinned to the walls by viscous webbing. The gold-rankers fought their way free of the webbing with abilities or raw strength. They were swiftly deployed to intercept the gold-rank spider moles before they could wreak havoc amongst the weaker adventurers.

The spider moles were the clear threat, as they were gold rank, whereas the worms and elementals were silver. They were massive spiders with long bodies covered in long, stiff bristles. Their heads were squat-faced, more like a pug dog than a mole, despite the name. They also had an array of special abilities, which was common in gold-rank monsters. Along with the viscous webbing that had caught up the crawlers, they could project an alternate type of web that was razor sharp and laced with poison. At close range, they could fire bristles from all over their bodies that were forearm-length needles, also sharp and venomous.

The spider moles each had eight strong but wiry legs that let them scurry along the vertical surface of the tunnel, despite their massive size. Oversized claws dug into the rock walls and could burrow through armour as swiftly as they could earth and stone. The rapid ambush through the walls demonstrated just how fast that was.

The other ability facilitating the ambush was the power to mask the auras of not just themselves but the other monsters as well. Even Jason and the gold-rankers hadn't sensed them until the trap was sprung. Overall, the spider moles weren't especially powerful by gold-rank standards, but they were numerous. More importantly, the disarray in which the expedition of elite adventurers had been left was an important lesson: Even a less powerful monster could be extremely dangerous in the right environment.

With the crawlers stuck to the walls and the adventurers stuck inside them, the monsters had easily seized the initiative. The gold-rank adventurers had swiftly escaped the webbing and moved to engage the spider moles at Miriam's direction. Many of the silver-rankers also extracted themselves quickly and Miriam had them divide into two groups. One group was tasked with taking the fight to the monsters, fending off the explosive elementals and worms biting at the crawlers. The rest of the group were tasked with protecting the vehicles while extracting the adventurers unable to free themselves from the gold-rank webbing.

Jason's team was part of the protection and extraction group. Sophie, Humphrey, and Taika intercepted monsters. Jason's sword was able to corrode and rot the webbing quite well, while Rufus, Farrah and Gary all had powers to burn through them. Belinda and Clive worked on freeing the crawlers, not just the people inside them, while Neil watched over them all. He tossed barriers onto his team and threw Life Bolt spells at any injured adventurers the team released.

Their familiars also went to work. Gordon's disruptive-force beams were highly effective against the flaming and gaseous elementals. Belinda's astral lamp familiar, Shimmer, was equally effective with its rapid-fire force bolts. Stash turned into a flying fire octopus, burning tentacles effective at tearing webbing from the vehicles.

Leeches slithered up the wall, unimpeded by massive patches of webbing that painted the sides of the shaft. The adhesive in the webs slid right off Colin's slick leech bodies as they crawled over and through. Colin was on a mission to prove the tunnel was only big enough for one set of horrifying toothy worms.

Onslow was serving as a bunker for Neil, Clive and Belinda to work from. It was also a place to bring freed silver-rankers into, giving them a moment to gather themselves and prepare before joining the fight.

Dead monsters were soon falling down the shaft, be it severed worm halves or the crystalline powder left behind by the elementals on their deaths, smoky white for gas and orange for fire. Shade's bodies floated through the air, touching them for Jason to loot. He did so immediately, the monsters trailing rainbow smoke down the shaft as they fell while disintegrating. Not all the dead monsters fell, many landing in the web patches, including the ones holding the crawlers in place. More than a few adventurers had a heavy sprinkling of elemental power over their bodies.

"Such a waste," Clive muttered as another cloud of dust drifted past Onslow's shell. "So many good ritual materials, falling down a hole. I hope you're getting that elemental powder as loot, Jason."

"Haven't been taking the time to check," Jason said.

While continuing to cut away the webbing and free adventurers, Jason did take the time to occasionally cast his Blood Harvest spell. Catching every enemy corpse left by his own side in a considerable range, Jason drew in bright red streams of life force from across the battlefield.

- You have gained health, stamina, mana and [Blood Frenzy] from [Blood Harvest].
- Health, stamina and mana have exceeded normal values due to ability [Sin Eater].

- [Blood Frenzy] (boon, unholy, stacking): Bonus to [Speed] and [Recovery]. Additional instances have a cumulative effect, up to a maximum threshold].

With the preponderance of monsters, Jason had no shortage of bodies to drain the remnant life force from. That mostly meant worms as the elementals couldn't be drained unless his Blood From a Stone had made them vulnerable to blood magic. As he was busy freeing adventurers, he hadn't had time, although he got a few windfalls in the way of spider moles as the gold-rankers started to shave their numbers.

Even the lingering life force in just a few of the gold-rank corpses was a massive amount to Jason. By the time all the adventurers had been released, he had buffed himself powerfully.

- You have gained health, stamina, mana and [Blood Frenzy] from [Blood Harvest].

- Your [Speed] and [Recovery] have reached maximal levels for your current rank. Further instances of [Blood Frenzy] will be replaced with [Blood of the Immortal].

- [Blood of the Immortal] (boon, healing, unholy, stacking): On suffering damage, an instance is consumed to grant a powerful but short-lived heal-over-time effect. Additional instances can be accumulated but do not have a cumulative effect.

. . .

By the time Jason and his team launched themselves into the fight proper, Jason was flush with stolen life force and lightning fast. He even rivalled Sophie for speed, although she still managed to make him look sluggish. Her speed was always active and supported by years of experience and multiple supplemental powers. Compared to the grace, elegance and efficiency with which she soared around the space, Jason was a clumsy oaf. He was fast enough that he didn't feel in slow motion compared to the spider moles, though, which was good enough for him. He wasn't going to hunt them, but he wouldn't be blindsided by raw speed.

The team was variously flying or ensconced in Onslow's floating shell. The battlefield they joined was a disorienting mess of shrieks, roars and explosions, magic light strobing in the dark. The lights on the crawlers were mostly still obscured by webbing, leaving the flashes and blasts of magic to light up the chaos. Projectiles slammed into giant worms and elementals exploded into flames. Tentacles reached out of portals to grab monsters and tear them apart, magic lighting shining on their glistening skin. That was one of Amos Pensinata's abilities.

Jason had queried Miriam about adding his butterflies. The tactical commander said no, which Jason understood. In a messy flying battle where allies and enemies were all mixed up in the dark, the benefits they offered would not be worth the extra chaos.

The adventurers might have started on the back foot, but the battle was slowly but inexorably turning in their favour. The spider moles were certainly smarter than the elementals, but animal cunning wasn't a match for gold-rankers in coordinated teams. While the monsters had the numbers, the adventurers would inevitably claim victory. The question was how much victory would cost.

The crawlers had already been hammered, but assessing how badly would have to wait until the fight was done. The more important threat was to the silver-rankers, a destroyed crawler irrelevant next to a dead adventurer. The most vulnerable group were the magic researchers, the only part of the expedition not made up of guild-level elites. They had been freed from the crawler they were trapped in but didn't join the fight. They were hunkered down on top of their vehicle, hoping to avoid attention.

Jason's team was directed to retrieve them so they could be sheltered inside Onslow. They set out immediately, but they were on the far side of a battlefield full of chaos. Magic and monsters were flying around and a stray blast of gold-rank webbing could easily take a silver-ranker out of the fight, even if it was unlikely to kill them.

They started making their way across the shaft, fighting their way through. Gary was the only one left behind, to protect and tend to the largest group of now-empty crawlers. Several had taken some hefty damage and his forge powers went to work restoring them. He also fought off enemies threatening to damage them further, mostly the snapping worms writhing from their holes in the wall. Their filthy diamond teeth might have sliced through the metal of the crawler frames, but they broke on the humungous head of the enormous hammer in Gary's hand, so large it looked like it should tip him over from the weight. Gary grinned as he shoved it into the maw of another worm looking to take a bite out of him, watching its teeth shatter like glass. This popped up another message from Jason's party interface.

- [Gary's Medium Hammer] has resisted [Shear Metal].
- [Craftsman's Ire] has inflicted retaliatory resonating-force damage.

Gary yanked the hammer free and swung it in a wide arc. It crashed into the side of the worm, smashing it into the wall with a wet squelch.

As he dealt with worms, Gary's old team members were with Jason's team as they continued across the shaft. Jason's team took their standard approach to aerial combat, with Humphrey, Sophie, Jason and Taika in flight, alongside temporary member Farrah. She was encased in obsidian armour that glowed magma hot around the plates. Wings of fire carried her along, somewhat ponderously with the heavy stone armour. Not ponderous was her flailing chain sword, shards of obsidian threaded on a thick strand of lava.

Farrah's sword was especially effective against the worms, more and more of which kept bursting from the walls. Their length was such that they could reach more than halfway across the shaft without leaving their holes; no fliers were completely out of reach. Any that extended Farrah's way found her sword corkscrewed along its body, obsidian shards digging into it and lava rope searing its ugly flesh. That only lasted a moment, though, as Farrah retracted her weapon back into a normal greatsword shape. As it did so, it chewed up the worm like a red-hot meat grinder, leaving the dead remains to drop limply against the wall.

Rufus didn't fly, but it was hard to tell as he sailed through the air. He used the enemies themselves as platforms, leaping from the wall to a worm's head to even kicking off a hairy spider mole to vault through the air. When there wasn't a foe to stand on, one of his two short-range teleport abilities could reposition him perfectly. His sun sword carved chunks from the worms while his moon sword slashed through the fire and gas elementals, leaving them diminished in size.

Rufus demonstrated his increasing synergy with his new team as he moved through the air. Belinda, doing her usual job of versatile mixed support, conjured platforms in the air for Rufus to use as stepping-stones before they fell away.

Jason laughed riotously on seeing Rufus hopscotch a series of falling platforms, shadow-jumping nearby to give him two thumbs up.

"It's a-me, Rufus!"

Rufus was taken aback when Jason appeared right in front of him and slipped. His foot missed the platform and his head bounced off it instead, sending him spinning down into the darkness of the shaft. Jason winced.

"Oops."

"Jason!" Humphrey snarled.

"Sorry."

Rufus teleported atop an approaching worm and buried his sun sword in its body. Using it as a handle to hold himself in place, he glared at Jason but only for a moment. The sword flared bright enough that light shone from inside the worm and Rufus ran along the creature's body towards the wall in an implausible display of balance. He dragged the sword, still deep in the creature and moving as if through the air and not the dense flesh of a giant silver-rank worm. Rufus reached the wall and started running along it, leaving the worm's two halves dangling, dead.

Jason floated in the air, watching in awe.

"Holy crap, that looked awesome."

"Jason!" Humphrey scolded again.

"Sorry."

62
HIT POINTS

THE MASSIVE VERTICAL SHAFT WAS THICK WITH BATTLE. THE GOLD-RANK adventurers were doing their best to keep the fight with the spider moles away from the crawlers and the lower-rank adventurers. The silver-rank adventurers had even more to deal with, as at least the spider mole numbers weren't increasing. Gas and fire elementals kept pouring in through holes in the wall. Even more prolific were the toothy worms, continually burrowing their way out of the rock to extend from the walls like tentacles.

Worm after worm dug through and extended their sickly grey bodies in search of something to devour. The metal of armour or the crawlers would do, although the way the monsters grew agitated at the smell of blood revealed their true preference. As the battle continued, they just kept coming until the shaft was a vertical, fleshy forest. As the worms could reach more than halfway across the shaft, there was no escaping them. They could only be fought through, which was exactly what Jason and his team did. The team was in the process of making their way to the Magic Society research team, to secure them inside Onslow's shell.

Jason suggested he go ahead alone and portal the researchers to Onslow, but Humphrey nixed the idea. While Jason going off alone was barely acceptable, portals had become unreliable as the expedition drew closer to the natural array. Instantaneous teleportation, like Humphrey's and Jason's, still worked, but sustained dimensional apertures—portals—

quickly grew volatile and exploded. This included dimensional bags and certain storage spaces, like Clive's portal-based storage, which the expedition discovered at the cost of some supplies.

The expedition had back-tracked to a safer level and transferred the most important supplies to the crawlers in magically reinforced bags, which made any threat to the crawlers more dangerous. Along with the gold-rank coins to sustain the most powerful members of the expedition, substantial ritual materials would be required to activate the messenger device.

Jason had argued that he could probably stabilise his own portals by tapping into his astral throne, but Humphrey said no. Along with the uncertainty of that working, he didn't want Jason debilitated from drawing on his astral king powers too much. Jason had argued that he would probably be fine, losing the debate at the word 'probably.'

Thus, the team continued to slog their way across the shaft, fighting through elementals and worms while dodging stray blasts of webbing and poorly aimed projectiles from the gold-rank battle.

Farrah focused on the fire elementals, her Child of Fire ability making a mockery of them. Even completely immolated, their flames didn't so much as singe her hair. Even more ridiculously, her own powers were burning creatures that were themselves made of fire.

"How does that make any sense?" Jason asked.

"You made a rock bleed to death," Farrah shot back.

"I will not apologise for being awesome."

"What was that?" Farrah asked. "You were trying to explain how I'm the one doing ridiculous things, but I couldn't hear it over the sound of you coming back from the dead over and over."

"Oh, like you've never come back to life."

Neil opened a voice channel to Rick Geller.

"Rick, I know your team already has a healer, but would you be open to recruiting a second?"

"Are you seriously contacting me to CRACK A DAMN JOKE right now?" Rick roared back.

"Sorry," Neil said contritely and closed the channel.

"Can we please demonstrate at least a little discipline?" Humphrey growled.

"Sorry, Dad," Belinda said meekly.

"Belinda…" Humphrey admonished.

"Are we not meant to call you Daddy?" she asked. "Because Sophie said—"

"LINDY!" Humphrey bellowed, not through voice chat but out loud, audible even amongst the pounding of explosions and the sizzling zap of spells going off.

Humphrey continued to grumble but let it go. Partly it was because he knew they weren't going to stop, but mostly because the banter hadn't slowed them down. Neil was throwing out his short-lived barriers with pinpoint timing. Jason flickered through the shadowy battlefield, loading afflictions on worms not yet engaged by adventurers. Belinda was blasting attacks from the wands she had in each hand, duplicating spells used by Neil and Clive, and also conjuring platforms for Rufus to use.

While Humphrey told himself he preferred stoic professionalism, he let the banter slide so long as the team was getting the job done. Even if the other team leaders made fun of him sometimes.

"Look," he said in a voice of resigned annoyance. "At least avoid hitting team members in the head and dropping them down the shaft."

"Yeah, that was my bad," Jason said.

Humphrey himself was in charge of handling the gaseous elementals that were not only explosive but also inflicted unpleasant afflictions on anyone they overran. Humphrey detonated them from out of range of his companions, either with his fire breath or flaming dragon sword. They reconstituted shortly after, but couldn't detonate again for a while. That was when he moved in with his Spirit Reaper attack.

Ability: [Spirit Reaper] (Magic)

- Special Attack (melee, dimension, drain).
- Base cost: Low mana and stamina.
- Cooldown: None.

- Current rank: Silver 4 (71%).

- Effect (Iron): Inflicts additional disruptive-force damage and drains mana. Has additional effect against incorporeal or semi-corporeal creatures.

- Effect (bronze): Inflict [Stunned] on incorporeal or semi-incorporeal entities.

- Effect (silver): Inflict [Radiant Echo] on incorporeal entities.

- [Stunned] (affliction, magic): Briefly be unable to move, use abilities or control already active abilities. Fully reactive abilities and effects can still be triggered. The duration cannot be refreshed by applying [Stunned] again and being affected multiple times in succession has diminishing returns.

- [Radiant Echo] (affliction, damage over time, magic, stacking): Deal ongoing disruptive-force damage.

The special attack shredded the gaseous elementals, even stunning them briefly while he went to town. He wasn't the only one to do so, with the team's familiars backing up him and Farrah.

Stash turned into a floating orb monster, effectively an inflatable skin ball. Known as a gusher, it used compressed air attacks that made a comical noise that Stash was a little too enamoured with. Fortunately, the attacks were as effective at dispersing the elementals as they were at repli-cating flatulence sounds.

Gordon's disruptive-force beams were highly efficient at tearing apart the insubstantial elementals. The attacks of Belinda's familiar, Shimmer, were likewise effective. The sentient ornate lamp bobbed through the air, shedding silver light and firing rapid streams of force bolts. Belinda's other familiar was the echo spirit, Gemini. She turned into a blurry replica of Humphrey and tore through the elementals with a force sword.

Jason was the member of the group that roamed the furthest from Onslow. Shadow-jumping came as naturally to Jason as walking by this point and trumped even Sophie's mobility in the current conditions. With darkness and shadows everywhere, it wasn't so much a shadow jump as an unrestricted teleport with no cooldown.

For the most part, Jason worked on loading the worms that kept popping out with afflictions. He focused on the ones not fighting adventurers, which weren't hard to find as their numbers grew.

"Are you sure I shouldn't be dropping butterflies?" he asked Miriam.

"Not yet," the tactical commander responded. "We need to finish the gold-rank monsters, extract the crawlers and make a tactical withdrawal. Then will be the time to unleash indiscriminate chaos."

"Yes, Ma'am."

Jason was able to move around the shaft almost with impunity, but he didn't make a great combat reinforcement. He was able to arrive swiftly, but anyone needing urgent help was looking for immediate impact. Someone to start their enemies on the path to a slow, miserable demise wouldn't pull their bacon out of the fire. What Jason could do was act like a cleansing wand.

One of the stronger weapons available to the spider moles was a venom that impeded healing. While they didn't bite, it laced their bristly hair and the razor-sharp net variants of their webs. They also spat it out at close range.

The venom was something the gold-rank healers could handle, but when a stray net blindsided a silver-ranker, that was another issue. Rank disparity had a lot of effects, one being that afflictions were more resistant to under-ranked cleansing.

When Rick's fiancée Hannah was shredded by razor webbing, her twin, Claire, had trouble cleansing it. Jason appeared out of nowhere, drew the poison out with his Feast of Absolution power and vanished again within a few moments. Rick sent a quick thanks through voice chat before going back to fighting worms.

Jason's team was slowly but surely carving a path towards the researchers still hunkered down atop their vehicle. What should have been open space in the middle of the shaft felt like hacking through a jungle made of carnivorous worms. The silver-rank teams tried to avoid inter-fering with one another, but the larger hazard was the gold-rank battle.

The gold-rank adventurers worked hard to keep their conflict away from the silver-rankers and the crawlers. Their collateral damage could all too easily eliminate expedition members or critical supplies. They did fairly well at this; while the spider moles had the numbers, they were weaker than the adventurers. The occasional monster still managed to escape the battle while the adventurers were too occupied to pursue, however, and went after one of the silver-rank teams.

Most of the silver-rank teams could put up a unified front against one gold-rank monster. They didn't have to win, just hold it off until the gold-rankers corralled the monster back into their fight. Winning was certainly an option, though, with Rick's team getting revenge for Hannah's poison razor net experience.

The most vulnerable group were the Magic Society researchers, the only team not made up of guild-level elites. They were silver-rankers, but not a combat team, and had been hunkered down on their vehicle since Team Storm Shredder cut them loose. When Jason's team was only halfway across the shaft on their mission to retrieve them, Miriam sent a warning through the command channel of the voice chat.

"Team Biscuit! Loose spider mole on the researchers! Can you handle it?"

Humphrey couldn't see the researchers to teleport to them and he looked to Sophie, the team's expert defensive interceptor. She was tied up helping a team that had suddenly been swarmed with a half-dozen extra worms, just as their defensive specialist was struck by a stray blast of gold-rank webbing. She couldn't abandon them until they freed their team member.

"Jason," Humphrey said.

"On it."

The battlefield was a mess of auras and magic. The spider moles were also able to interfere with aura perception, which was what made their ambush possible. Even Jason had to focus to punch through the noise and pinpoint the researchers. He did and then immediately vanished.

A spider mole lunged through the air, having launched itself from the wall of the shaft. The Magic Society researchers in its path didn't just wait helplessly, blasting projectiles and raising barriers. The damage was negli-gible to the gold-rank monster with its inherent damage reduction against lower-ranked attacks. The barriers did a better job of slowing it down but were still smashed through in short order.

Just as the spider mole was about to crash into the researchers, a swarm of shadow arms yanked them out of the way. They were left dangling from the wall like cuts of meat, but the monster had missed them, so they weren't actual cuts of dangling meat. The monster's squat face roared, but Jason appeared on its back before it could move on the researchers now being passed hand-to-hand along the wall by the forest of shadow arms. He distracted the monster further by plunging his sword into its back.

Jason's speed was buffed to the point that his reflexes weren't entirely eclipsed by a gold-rank monster. Eight legs were a lot, however, and only three were occupied holding the monster to the wall. The rest snatched at Jason on its back, reaching for him with flexibility beyond any real spider. Needing the spider mole's attention squarely on himself, Jason tried to dodge rather than shadow-jump away, buying time for the researchers until a gold-ranker came to the rescue.

Jason's attempts at evasion lasted roughly zero seconds, his feet impeded by the monster's sharp, venomous hair that punched holes in his boots.

- You have resisted [Spider Mole Venom].
- You have gained [Resistance] and [Integrity] from ability [Sin Eater].

Each of the monster's legs ended in prehensile feet with three long talons. One foot wrapped around Jason's torso and another around his legs, the talons digging deep into his flesh. Jason tried to shadow-jump from the creature's grip but it didn't work. This was expected when deeply impaled with monster parts, but he tried anyway.

Jason's body resisted the monster's tugging for a brief moment before he was torn in half. Flooded with life force from all the enemies he had drained, fed even more by his potent regenerative powers, Jason had stacked up several times his normal maximum. As a result, he was near-unkillable until that life force had been chewed through. Some of that was consumed to immediately regrow his legs, the new ones flicking from the bottom of his torso like shaking a rug.

Life force was an odd thing, especially when it came to magical bodies and going beyond normal maximums. It sometimes made the body seemingly impervious, other times triggering near-instantaneous bodily restoration. Jason related having excess life force to having hit points that needed to be shaved off before he could take any meaningful damage. It would take more than being ripped in half to finish Jason off, but the monster seemed keen to oblige.

He also reconjured his armour, not liking his bare unmentionables so close to all those bristles. His boxer shorts were not conjured and were still on his old legs. The spider mole had tossed them away and they'd stuck to the webbing-encased crawler below.

The monster moved Jason to dangle helplessly in front of its ugly face. It was like a mole's face but pushed right in as if it'd been hit by a train but was too damn ornery to die.

"I don't suppose we could talk things through?"

It shrieked in Jason's face, coating him with phlegm.

- You have resisted [Spider Mole Venom].
- You have gained [Resistance] and [Integrity] from ability [Sin Eater].

The monster's talons squeezed, digging into Jason like fingers digging into a ripe peach. At the same time, bristles erupted from its body, shooting off in every direction. It left the spider mole's wrinkly skin exposed for a moment before the hair grew back, almost as fast as Jason's legs. The bristles pin-cushioned Jason and quite a few of them hit the researchers that were still not that far away. Jason immediately croaked out a spell.

"*Feed me your sins.*"

Feast of Absolution drained the venom not just from the spiked researchers but every adventurer affected by afflictions in a wide area. Trails of red stained with ugly purples, whites and yellows flowed into Jason from all directions.

- You have absorbed [Spider Mole Venom] from multiple allies.
- You have absorbed [Smoke Toxin] from multiple allies.
- You have absorbed [Gaseous Bloat] from multiple allies.
- You have gained stamina and mana.
- Stamina and mana have exceeded normal values due to ability [Sin Eater].
- You have gained multiple instances of [Resistance] and [Integrity] from ability [Sin Eater].

With Jason held right in front of the monster's face, the multicoloured light streaming into him obscured the monster's vision. This prevented it from noticing the mass of leeches seeping out of Jason's discarded legs below.

The spider mole continued to squeeze, blood oozing around its talons, soaking down its legs and onto its body. The monster had animalistic cunning, but not the intelligence to pay attention to that blood and how oddly lumpy it was. The spider mole likewise failed to notice that those lumps had teeth. Oblivious, the monster concentrated on crushing Jason in its grip, surprised at his resilience. Jason's excess life force was being rapidly consumed to keep him alive.

As Jason's spell ended and the monster no longer had the light of the spell in its face, it finally realised what was going on below. Jason's boxer-clad severed legs were now completely buried under a mound of purplish red flesh that had melded together from a massive pile of leeches and was now adhered to the wall. The mound undulated and shifted, Colin still in the process of taking a new form.

The spider mole looked down and shrieked at it, only half-coating Jason in venomous phlegm this time. Seeing the flesh mass as the greater threat, it flung Jason aside with gold-rank strength. It was so hard that he moved horizontally along the wall, barely starting to arc down by the time he struck a rocky protrusion like a bug on a windshield.

63

SURPLUS TO REQUIREMENTS

JASON LAY SPREAD ACROSS A ROCK LIKE DEEPLY UNPLEASANT JAM. COLIN, in an incomplete apocalypse beast form, continued battling the gold-rank spider mole. Leeches had crawled onto the monster's body, moving between the stiff, venomous bristles and biting into flesh, draining health and delivering afflictions.

The monster flailed with surprise and rage, distracted from Colin's flesh mass continuing to take shape below it. A slit formed in the mound and opened like an eyelid, but instead of an eye, it was filled with rows of jagged shark teeth.

Ropey tendrils shot out of the maw, each tendril with its own mouth on the end. They looked like smaller, dark red versions of the wall worms and their teeth buried themselves in the flesh of the spider mole. They ignored the bristles they impaled themselves on, draining blood to replenish what leaked from the wounds.

The spider mole immediately started fighting back. Still anchored to the wall by three of its legs, the remaining five slashed at the tendrils and the flesh mound from which they had emerged. Gold-rank claws carved troughs into the silver-rank flesh of Colin's still-coagulating form.

Colin healed swiftly by draining health from the spider mole, shooting more tendrils to replace those severed by the monster's claws. Even so, Colin was being torn up faster than he could heal. His apocalypse beast form hadn't finished taking shape, and with all the health it drained going to regeneration, the transformation halted, incomplete. Even with Colin inheriting Jason's ability to ignore the suppressive effects of rank disparity, the power difference between gold- and silver-rank was just too great.

Jason had been painted across a rock jutting out of the stone wall. He snapped back to consciousness as his body snapped back into shape, consuming most of his remaining life force surplus.

The rest had already been squeezed out of him by the spider mole before tossing him aside.

Groggy from the rapid succession of bodily destruction and reconstruction, he peeled himself out of the gore staining the rock and floated into the shaft using his aura. Still overloaded on mana the way he no longer was with life force, he reconjured his Cloak of Night. His robes technically weren't his to conjure, but a fresh set draped over his body and immediately absorbed the blood coating him. It was Colin who created the robes, the swarm entity still partly existing inside Jason.

Jason never let Colin fully emerge, always keeping a portion of his biomass in reserve. This way, Colin's vessel could never entirely be destroyed. That small amount of extra biomass was separate from the strategic reserve Jason maintained in his soul realm as well. That was excess that Colin couldn't keep or use after overfeeding.

Jason had started claiming that excess for himself, storing it up to return to Colin at need. They had even taken the time to build up a stock before the expedition, knowing they would probably have a use for it. Seeing how much damage Colin was going through, that would clearly be the case.

Jason shook his head to clear it and expanded his senses to take stock of the situation. Colin was fighting a losing battle against the spider mole, but it seemed like the monster had forgotten the researchers and Jason, focused fully on Colin. Then Jason noticed something that left his face twisted with anger.

"What are you doing?" he snarled at the gold-ranker floating in the air nearby. The thick cloud of silver lights shimmering around the bottom half of her body reminded Jason of a cartoon genie.

"So, you are still alive," the gold-ranker said, hands clasped casually behind her back as she floated in the air. "I thought as much, despite your condition, given that your familiar's vessel remained intact. Although not for long, it would seem."

Her name was Valetta, one of the members of Team Moon's Edge. Her aura was restrained to avoid the spider mole's attention.

"Why are you just floating there?" Jason asked.

"I wanted to see if you could win. All this talk about the mighty astral king; I wanted to see what the fuss was."

"At least save the research team!"

She glanced over at the researchers, dangling from shadow arms sticking out of the wall. They were out of range of the spider mole's fight with Colin, but not so far that the monster couldn't be on them in moments.

"It stopped bothering with them," she said. "Besides, saving them was what you were ordered to do, not me."

"I'm guessing you were ordered to help me, though?"

"Yes. And if I'm sure you'll need it, I will. Your familiar is holding on much better than I expected, even if it isn't going to win."

Jason held back a snarling retort, turning his attention back to the researchers. They didn't have any flying devices on them, but they weren't helpless either. Jason reconfigured the shadow arms to give them what amounted to a ladder to give themselves more distance. The next priority was to keep the spider from finishing Colin and going after them or him.

The spider mole was definitely worse for wear, looking emaciated from the life-draining that had kept Colin in the fight. Colin looked far worse; his incomplete apocalypse beast utterly savaged by the monster's claws. The original mass of flesh had been torn to ribbons and he was no longer capable of sending more tendrils to drain life. Without them, he was not going to last much longer.

For a long time, Jason had instinctively gesticulated when using various powers, but it wasn't truly necessary. He didn't need to point his hand at a thing to move it with his aura or target it with a spell. Jason didn't move as he drew on his power, floating motionless in the air. Only his eyes moved, blazing rage from within the darkness of his hooded cloak.

Jason's soul realm portal opened in the air above Colin and the monster, hovering in the air as a horizontal ring. The sheet of energy inside the ring flickered and stuttered, the elemental forces in the ambient magic attempting to make it explode. Jason grimaced as he tapped into his astral gate to reinforce the portal's dimensional integrity. The flickering stopped and the portal snapped solidly into place.

Jason called on the strategic reserve of biomass he kept in storage and dumped it out through the portal. It geysered down in a deluge of thick and viscous fluid; red, purple and sickly white, all mixed together. Somewhere between blood and molten flesh, it gushed over Colin and the spider mole, painting them in gore.

The meat soup looked like it should be splashing off them and continuing down the shaft like a waterfall, but not so much as a single drop was wasted. Instead, it curved through the air or crawled off the spider mole to inundate Colin, completely obscuring him in the liquefied flesh.

Despite Colin's obfuscation, the spider mole didn't let up its attacks, legs delving into the deluge to slash blindly with shovel-sized talons. It shrieked as it did—whether in fear, pain, rage or all three, Jason couldn't tell. As the gore rained down on them both, the monster kept flailing in a frenzy.

As the downpour finally slowed, a tree-trunk arm emerged from the meat waterfall. It had no skin, just ropey muscle shining wet from the thick fluids painting it. At the end of the arm was a hand with eight fingers, each terminating in a dark heavy claw. The hand reached out and grabbed the rock wall, fingers easily digging into the stone.

The spider mole immediately lashed out at the arm, only for another to emerge and intercept the attack. A third and fourth limb came into view as the downpour from above slowed and finally came to a stop. Colin's full form was revealed as he absorbed the last of the liquid.

Colin's body was an uneven sphere, ugly and lumpen like a tumour. No longer adhered to the wall of the shaft, he was held in place by three of his eight arms, the same as the spider. His arms jutted from his round body at seemingly random positions, with no sense of up and down or left and right. Between the limbs, eye-shaped mouths covered much of the remaining body, ringed with hooked, jagged teeth.

The mouths let out an alien shriek that scraped against the soul in a horrifying aura assault. The soul attack combined the immense power and domineering cosmic authority of Jason's aura with the sanguine horror's infinite alien hunger.

The screech gouged at the senses, leaving only Jason unaffected. The spider mole flailed and shrieked back at Colin in panic. The researchers screamed and tumbled from where they'd been climbing the walls, shadow limbs once again grabbing them before they fell. Even the gold-ranker, Valetta, was visibly shaken.

Despite being taken aback, the gold-rank monster didn't flee but lashed out with renewed freneticism, its legs a blur as they thrashed at Colin. Despite Colin's now-complete form, there was still no getting around the difference in rank and the spider mole took large chunks out of him. Even so, Colin was better able to fight back, reconstituted and reformed while the monster was still drained and afflicted from earlier.

Fresh tendrils shot of out Colin's mouths to clamp onto the monster's flesh and resume draining it, sustaining Colin for the fight. The spider mole slashed at them with its claws but had less success than previously. Not only were they thicker and tougher, but Colin's arms ran interference. It wasn't enough to keep them from being severed, but it slowed the process down.

Jason closed the portal to his soul realm, only a little worn down from tapping into the astral gate to maintain it. He floated past Valetta as he opened a voice channel to Miriam just long enough for a simple message.

"You can call your team member back," he said. "She's surplus to requirements."

Jason vanished and reappeared on the spider mole's back, shadow arms reaching down to anchor him to the bucking monster. He drew his sword, still buried in the monster's back from when the spider mole had grabbed him. The monster didn't seem to notice, caught up in the battle with Colin. To a massive gold-rank body, already brutalised, withered from life drain and covered in rotting, bleeding ulcers from Colin's afflictions, a sword wasn't especially impactful.

Jason immediately made use of those afflictions, casting a spell.

"Suffer the cost of your transgressions."

The Punition spell created an immediate surge of necrotic damage for each of the dark afflictions on the target. The monster's flesh rapidly rotted, turning a dark and hideous yellow. Its spiky hair, weapons in themselves, turned brittle and crumbled or fell out entirely. Even so, the fortitude of a gold-rank monster was so outrageous that the damage was still far from enough, not even slowing it down.

Jason's powers were extremely mana efficient and his mana pool, like his life force, could be extended well past his default maximum. This meant that he had a large supply to use on his one mana dump spell. Punition normally had a thirty-second cooldown, but ramping up the mana cost could reduce that or even remove it entirely. He left the first casting with a ten-second cooldown, giving him time to cast a few other quick spells and make some special attacks.

None of this fazed the monster, who continued to focus on Colin as the threat. The spider mole still had the power advantage, but the tide was slowly turning as the monster weakened under the blood draining and afflictions. The pace was glacial, however, another reminder of the absurd resilience of gold-rankers.

With additional afflictions in place, Jason's spell came off cooldown and he used it over and over, dumping massive amounts of mana into removing the cooldown entirely. Doing so also gave a much shorter incantation.

"*Suffer.*"

"*Suffer.*"

"*Suffer.*"

Miriam Vance was caught up in the latter stages of the larger spider mole fight, the monsters finally starting to drop in number. Gold-rank monsters, even the less threatening ones, just took so much killing before they'd go down. Even so, she couldn't help but notice the bizarre magic and auras she was sensing from the direction of the magic researchers. She'd gotten an odd message from Asano suggesting the gold-rank monster was handled, and now that she had a spare moment, she focused her senses in that direction.

Miriam's eyes went wide as she sensed what was possibly the most horrifying thing she'd encountered in her career. The aura alone coming out of it made her senses flinch, but there was something familiar within it as well. Her face paled as she realised that *thing* was Asano's familiar. As for Asano himself, he was riding the back of the monster, tied down to it with shadow arms as he chanted a spell over and over.

Finally, she sensed Valetta, safely backing away, restraining her aura to not get caught up in the fight. Miriam could also sense the researchers nearby, hanging from more shadow arms that had to be Asano's doing. Valetta only watched the fight instead of going to rescue them or help Asano.

Miriam's expression tightened with rage.

Many essence users had power sets that carried combat through stages if it went on long enough. Their battles could be almost narrative in structure and, for Jason, that narrative was oddly religious. At the beginning came sin. Pestilence, poison and unholy power. Then came absolution.

"Feed me your sins."

The spider mole's life force shone from within its body, the natural red almost entirely obscured in the ugly colours of affliction. All that taint flowed out of the monster, filling the air with sickly yellow, purple and blue light, so thick that Jason was completely obscured for a moment. As the poisons, curses, diseases and unholy afflictions departed the monster's life force, they left something behind in their place.

After absolution came penance. The monster's body lit up with bright light, the transcendent damage of the Penance affliction. Unstoppable, unavoidable. All but inescapable. It went to work on annihilating the monster from the inside out.

Even through all of that, the gold-rank monster endured. But Jason wasn't done. His Doom Blade power involved conjuring weapons, but his soul-bound blade, Hegemon's Will, could absorb the abilities of those conjured swords instead of having them manifest. Jason held out his sword, red runes pulsing down the length of the black blade. Jason used his power and the runes turned from red to a clean, radiant blue.

- You have invoked the effects of [Penitent, the Blade of Sacrifice]. All properties of that weapon have been imbued into [Hegemon's Will]. Disruptive-force damage will be inflicted in addition to physical damage.

The second form of Jason's Doom Blade was double-edged in more ways than one as the Price in Blood affliction increased the damage Jason and the monster dealt to each other. It was always a risk to employ, but the monster was occupied fending off Colin. For all that Jason was ravaging the spider mole with his powers, Colin was the one eating it.

Every blow from Jason's blade made the damage grow. Every strike not only escalated the Price in Blood but also delivered the special attack, Punish. In the beginning, Punish had been a tool of necrosis and sin, but the story of Jason's battle had changed.

Ability: [Punish] (Sin)

. . .

- Special attack (melee, curse, holy).
- Cost: Low mana.
- Cooldown: None.

- Current rank: Silver 5 (42%).

- Effect (iron): Inflicts necrotic damage and the [Sin] affliction.

- Effect (bronze): Inflicts or refreshes the duration of [Price of Absolution].

- Effect (silver): If the target has any instances of [Sin], they suffer an instance of the [Wages of Sin] affliction. If the enemy struck has no instances of [Sin] but does have instances of [Penance], they do not suffer [Sin] or [Wages of Sin]. They instead suffer transcendent damage from this ability in place of necrotic damage and suffer an additional instance of [Penance]. Instances of [Penance] do not drop off for a short period.

- [Sin] (affliction, curse, stacking): All necrotic damage taken is increased. Additional instances have a cumulative effect.

- [Price of Absolution] (affliction, holy): Suffer transcendent damage for each instance of [Sin] cleansed from you.

. . .

- [Wages of Sin] (affliction, unholy, stacking): Suffer necrotic damage over time. Additional instances have a cumulative effect.

- [Penance] (affliction, holy, damage-over-time, stacking): Deals ongoing transcendent damage. Additional instances have a cumulative effect, dropping off as damage is dealt.

Jason used a holy weapon to smite the monster with a holy attack. Over and over, blow after blow, the damage grew with every strike. Jason entered an almost zen-like state, a combat trance. He rode the wild thrashing of the monster, his body going with the flow. His senses expanded, taking in his surroundings. He absently noted that some wall worms had emerged nearby, prompting Valetta to finally rescue the researchers.

Time blended into itself. Jason didn't know how long it had been when the monster showed signs of finally flagging. The seemingly unkillable monster began to crumble, proving that even gold-rankers had their limits. The spider mole grew weaker, taking an extra limb from the fight with Colin to clamp itself to the wall.

The monster became sluggish and unstable, no longer trying to take down the ravaged Colin but fight him off, desperate to escape. Colin didn't allow it, tendrils still buried in its flesh. The familiar was still not as strong, but the gap had closed, and Colin's arms were dug into the wall. This kept the monster held fast for Jason to finish the job.

For many essence users, their powers were a reflection of who they were. Humphrey's were strong and straightforward while Sophie's were swift, elusive and unassailable. Belinda's required clever invention while Clive's had a complexity requiring someone steeped in the underlying rules of magic.

Jason's powers were the ideals of faith from the culture in which he had been raised, turned into horrifying weapons. His enemies were sinners because he declared them so, then forced them into atonement by the sword. They were delivered into misery and suffering on the path to a slow, terrible demise.

Then came the end.

"Mine is the judgement and the judgement is death."

Jason's execute power was called Verdict and looked like the wrath of a righteous, unforgiving god. A great column of transcendent light poured down, leaving Jason and Colin unharmed as it excised the monster from reality, vanishing in a plume of rainbow smoke.

The light faded, leaving Jason floating in the air. His sword was held at his side, runes blazing with light through dripping ichor. His eyes shone in the darkness of his hood, an implacable, imposing figure. Then he noticed the two elementals about to touch and explode.

"Oh shi—"

64

PRIDE

It was no longer possible to see the forest of worms down the shaft. The butterflies filling the space had turned it into a lake of glowing blue and orange. The expedition group were above it all in stone-shaped alcoves or on conjured platforms.

Jason floated over the centre of the shaft with frazzled hair and half his beard scorched off. Being crushed, impaled and smashed into walls had left his hair largely intact, but the explosion of fire in his face had not. Jason was perfectly capable of regenerating burnt flesh, but restoring his best physical feature required alchemical intervention.

As he watched the glowing lake below, Miriam Vance floated up to him, feet shrouded in a small gold cloud.

"It's going well," she said. After finishing the gold-rank monsters, the expedition extracted the crawlers and escaped up the shaft, leaving Jason to go to work.

"Why am I the only dedicated affliction user?" he asked. "A more traditional one would be more useful against these numbers."

"We weren't anticipating these numbers," Miriam said. "More importantly, the strengths and weakness of affliction specialists are well known. They're powerful, yes, but famously bad at self-reliance. They need teams around them. In fights like these where a messy ambush has us attacked from all sides, they'd be about as much use as the research team."

Jason didn't answer. Instead, he glanced over at Korinne Pescos and the rest of Team Storm Shredder, in an alcove being debriefed by Amos Pensinata. They were a typical Rimaros team built around high-damage range specialists, originally two but now three with the addition of Zara. The rest of the team served to maximise their effectiveness.

The chaos of the ambush had been a hard lesson in the value of individual capability, the team coming close to losing people in the early stages of the fight. The silver-rankers had been largely sheltered in their progress through iron and bronze, and this journey was meant to season them to the harsh realities of adventuring. That was exactly what they had gotten, and Jason was confident they would grow from the experience. Their team mentor, Amos Pensinata, was making sure they took the right lessons.

After a long pause, Miriam spoke again.

"We need to talk, Operations Commander."

"Yes, we do," Jason agreed. His voice was soft and sober with none of his usual joviality.

Miriam sighed and activated a privacy screen. It was an extremely high-end device that blocked sound and most forms of magical surveillance. It also blurred the interior to those looking on, preventing techniques like lip reading.

"Valetta," she said.

"Yes."

"I'm sorry. She's my team member and it was my mistake. She's the strongest person in the team, which is why I sent her. I knew she didn't like you, but I never thought she'd do that to you."

"It doesn't matter what she did to me. I've been betrayed by the people I'm working with enough that I just expect it now. But she didn't move to save the researchers until she absolutely had to. She's one of the most powerful assets in this expedition and she was wasting time on a personal grudge."

Miriam nodded.

"I overestimated her discipline and underestimated her dislike of you."

"Where did that come from?" Jason asked. "I picked up that she didn't think much of me when we did our expedition meet and greet, but that's normal. People tend to like me a lot or hate me immediately, with not a lot of ground in between. But what she did goes beyond dislike. If that's going to be a problem to this degree, she can't be a part of this expedition."

"It's the way you act around Lady Allayeth," Miriam said. "Or, more accurately, the way Lady Allayeth acts around you."

"Oh," Jason said. "You're saying Valetta is—"

"Not like that. Lady Allayeth means a lot to us all, but she took Valetta out of…"

Miriam sighed.

"The particulars don't matter," she continued. "Suffice it to say that Lady Allayeth is the sun in Valetta's sky. She isn't jealous of you. She just thinks you're unworthy of Lady Allayeth."

"Allayeth and I aren't—"

"You don't have to be. We know her better than anyone. How she is around different kinds of people. And we've seen how she is around you."

"Barely. You've seen us together, what? Twice?"

"It's enough."

Jason let out a long breath.

"If Valetta is a liability," he said, "she can't stay. Is she salvageable?"

"I think so. But she's a team member and a friend, so I'm biased. And I missed that she'd do what she did, so my judgement is clearly not what it should be on this. Whatever you decide to do, Operations Commander, I'll support it."

"Even if I decide to kill her?"

Miriam went very still.

"Is that something you're considering?" she asked.

"No."

"Then why would you even suggest that?"

"Because I wanted to see your reaction. You'd kill me before letting me have my gold-rank friends take her out, wouldn't you?"

"Yes. And you know if you try, this expedition is done, right?"

"I do. I just wanted to know that you'd go all the way for your team member. If she's worth that, then maybe she isn't a complete write-off."

"I'm not sure I like the way you do things, Operations Commander. Provoking people so you can gauge their reaction might get that reaction you're looking for, but they're still provoked."

"And I'm not sure I like where you put your trust, Tactical Commander. The wrong person in a critical role, you could kill us all."

They both nodded, each acknowledging the other's point.

"I'll talk with Valetta," Jason said. "I want a sense of where she's at."

"We can—"

"Just me," Jason said. "I need to know that she can respect my authority, not just yours."

"My understanding is that respecting authority isn't something you do well yourself."

"You're right. It's why I tend to avoid expeditions. But we're in the situation we're in."

"It's easier when you're in charge."

"Yes. That's not particularly fair, but if fair mattered, I wouldn't have a problem with authority."

Valetta was isolated from her team, standing alone in the plain alcove where Miriam had left her. Miriam's anger had been savage, with only the privacy screen holding in the loud berating she had given. Valetta knew she'd gone too far. She'd didn't understand why everyone made such a fuss about Asano. Why was he placed on the same level as Miriam? Why would Lady Allayeth treat him like that?

She hadn't realised how much resentment had festered away until she found herself watching him fight that monster. She'd seen him hammered into the rock wall with a force that would kill most silver-rankers and thought, for a moment, that he was dead. When he got back up, she'd felt relief. If her pride had killed someone, that was not something she was sure she could live with. And if that person was the expedition leader, it would have been the end of her career, and rightly so.

But most of those thoughts had come after. In the moment, even as she was glad he lived, her pride wasn't done. She should have acted then. Done what she was ordered to do. But admitting she was wrong was hard, especially to someone of lower rank, and pride was always easier than humility. Only after the fact did she realise how badly she'd handled everything. How close she'd come to letting innocent people die. Asano didn't deserve that, whatever she thought of him, and the research team certainly didn't. It would have ruined her life, making her the only person who would have gotten what they deserved.

After the extraction, Miriam had come to find her immediately. At least she took Valetta aside and put up a privacy screen before verbally tearing strips off of her. Miriam's anger had cut Valetta to the core, but it was Lady Allayeth's disappointment she was dreading. More than anything, she wanted to live up to the potential the lady had seen in her. To make the most of the opportunities she'd been given. If Lady Allayeth gave up on her, Valetta knew that would break her in a way she couldn't come back from.

She sensed Asano's approach. He floated in, still scorched and dirty from the elementals that had exploded in his face. His hair was mostly burnt off, only seared, comical tufts remaining, yet there was nothing humorous about the thunder in his eyes.

He activated a privacy field, not through a device but by somehow making his aura block out sound. She's seen messengers do something similar to block sound attacks, but hadn't realised it was possible for anyone else. He moved like a messenger too, using his aura to push himself around.

"I want to apologise," she said.

"I don't care. I want to know if I can trust you."

"I won't do anything like that again."

"You shouldn't have done it the first time. Words are easy, and your actions tell a different story."

She nodded.

"You know that if anyone in the research team had died, we wouldn't be having this conversation," he said.

She nodded again.

"I… I don't know what to say," she told him. "It would just be words."

Jason nodded.

"No one died," he said. "But those researchers are shaken. Badly. If you'd gotten them out, they wouldn't have been that close to the fight. To the soul attack my familiar made. You felt it too, right?"

"Yes."

"Would you have liked to take that at silver rank?"

"No."

"As of now, and until myself or the tactical commander says otherwise, you are responsible for the safety and wellbeing of the research team. Talk to Arabelle Remore and do everything she tells you. All you have to do is your job. Then, once we get back, maybe I'll suggest to Miriam that Allayeth doesn't need to hear about this."

Valetta's eyes went wide.

"Why?" she asked. "Why would you do that for me?"

"People were hurt. Traumatised. But no one died, which means you didn't screw up so badly that we have to get rid of you. That is only true, however, if you can demonstrate that you're an asset to this expedition, not a liability."

His expression softened, as did his tone when he continued.

"I know what it's like to make a mistake out of pride or self-confidence. To get others hurt. We don't deserve to be judged only by the worst things we've done. Not so long as we try to do better. But, just so we're clear, there won't be a third chance for you. This expedition is too important for that."

He dropped the privacy screen and floated out of the alcove, leaving Valetta alone.

Jason sat in his cloud chair over a platform conjured by Belinda. He let out an unhappy sigh as Shade rubbed hair-removal ointment into his scalp. He needed to excise the charred remains of his hair before using growth ointment to get it back.

Normally, silver-rankers had the physiological control to grow hair back normally, but the elemental energy in the area was interfering. As soon as Jason tried to grow it back, the new hair spontaneously combusted, leaving an unpleasant stink. That same smell permeated all through the expedition as others found themselves in the same situation as Jason.

Most of the team was sitting around, resting or checking equipment. Humphrey was off conferring with other team leaders and Jason knew he would be required soon. It was still the tactical commander's show right now, but he would be part of the discussion on moving forward.

"How do I have a headache?" he asked wearily. "My head doesn't have any of the things that can give you a headache in it."

"It's possibly psychosomatic," Shade suggested. "Would you like me to do your beard as well?"

"You should, bro," Taika said.

"It's bad?" Jason asked.

"It's basically a soul patch, plus a line running along your jaw. You look like an old child actor that hasn't gotten acting work since the nineties, was on drugs for a while but kicked it about ten years ago and is now super wholesome and in a Christian rock group."

"That sounds extremely specific," Jason said.

"Just a generalisation, bro. It would be weird if there wasn't someone like that."

"I'll take your word for it. How are the crawlers?"

"A lot of them took a beating, but Gary thinks if he cannibalises the worst one, we can get all the others up and running."

Jason sensed some nervousness in Taika's aura.

"You're uncertain about continuing on?"

Taika nodded.

"It's starting to feel like one of those movies where the expedition to do the important thing starts shedding people until the last, desperate survivors finally succeed at the cost of their own lives. Are we stealing the Death Star plans, bro?"

"I don't know, Taika. If you want to go back, I won't judge."

"Nah, bro. I'm in it as long as everyone else is. I'm just saying, if we were saving the city to stop everyone from dying, I would understand all this risk. But can't they move everyone and keep them safe?"

"Sure," Jason said. "The populace can be evacuated, but we're looking at a blast that makes most nukes look tame. Blackened skies and environmental devastation this world won't see again until it gets an industrial age. What really got me on board was the soul forge, though. I want it. I can't help but think there's a fight with the messengers coming. Something that goes beyond just this world and what they want here. I don't have any reason to think that, but I do. My instincts are screaming it, and Shade thinks my instincts are some kind of weird fate magic."

Jason let out a long sigh.

"If I'm right, and when that day comes, we need to be able to handle astral kings. Or at least have a chance."

"I'm going to be honest, bro: I don't know if I'm down for that."

"I know," Jason assured him. "Back to Earth, where you can take care of your mum. Don't worry, brother; I'll get you there or die trying. Or both. Probably both."

THE GREATEST ENEMY OF ALL

THE UNDERGROUND CITY OF CARDINAS WAS RULED FROM THE CITADEL OF Pillars, if ruled was even the right word. It had been a harmonious place for centuries before the cultists and then the messengers burrowed down from the surface world. They had paid the price for their intrusion, each in their own way, but that was little comfort to those left living with the ramifications. Or dying with them.

The central room of the citadel's top floor had been the council chamber, but was now the war room. There was no council anymore, just Lorenn; the others had fought valiantly and died horribly. Anything organic the elemental messengers got their hands on was fed as compost to their perverse tree.

Lorenn had seen the tree in that early battle where they had come so close to victory, only to fall disastrously short. That was when they had the numbers and the territory to mount an offensive. Now the elemental messengers had both and what remained of their populace had only a losing battle for survival.

The other cities were lost, as was most of Cardinas. Fewer than ten thousand of the brightheart smoulder had survived, yet that fraction felt so large crammed together in the citadel cavern, especially with the cultists taking up their own space.

Lorenn stood alone in the middle of the room, the heidelshoe-shaped desk arcing around her. In front of her was a model of the city, every cavern and tunnel. It tapped into the natural array to maintain a live depiction of the city's state, which grew increasingly dire with each cycle. Most of the map was covered in sickly green—the influence of the elemental messengers. It showed where the roots of their foul tree had burrowed through the rock and its vines crawled over every surface.

Lorenn looked up through the glass ceiling at the fire blazing across the ceiling of the cavern. It was said that the cycle of flaring and dimming reflected something called 'the sun' on the surface world, but that interested her not at all. The surface world had given them the cultists and messengers, so it could keep any other horrors it had to itself.

One side of the double doors swung open to admit Marla. Marla was a fire aspect, her skin markings, eyes and even hair the yellow-orange of steel in a forge. With the bold glow against her dark skin, she was extraordinarily beautiful. Lorenn had always been jealous, the smoky greys of her own ash aspect far less appealing. Marla was a physical embodiment of what it meant to be a brightheart.

"Councilwoman," Marla said without preamble. "I've completed the assessment of our food supplies. With only two growth chambers left, we can only last a few weeks. A month at the outside."

"Even with the new rationing levels?"

"Yes, Councilwoman. We need to—"

"We've talked about this, Marla. That discussion is over."

"And so are we, Lorenn! We can't feed our own people, let alone these cultists from the surface."

"If not for those cultists, Marla, there would be no one left to feed. You think I keep our agreement with them out of honour? If you can tell me how to hold this cavern against the elemental messengers, I'll cast them out myself."

Marla glowered, then looked down, unable to meet Lorenn's eyes as she voiced her suggestion.

"We're trying to defend too much ground," she said. "That's why we are forced to ally with the cultists. If we retreat to the remaining growth chambers, our own forces are enough to hold them."

"Those won't fit more than a third of our remaining population. Less if we don't want to overcrowd the chambers and their ability to produce food."

"Yes," Marla said, steeling her resolve to meet Lorenn's eyes. "But those are numbers we will be able to feed."

"At the cost of leaving most of our people to die."

"If we do nothing, *all* of our people will die."

Lorenn's stoic expression cracked, tears welling in her eyes.

"All of our people will die anyway," she sobbed. "I don't see... I don't know what to do!"

For a moment, Marla was startled at Lorenn's breakdown, then rushed forward to gather her in a comforting embrace. Lorenn stiffened for a moment, then leaned into Marla. Lorenn was uncertain how long they stayed like that, holding each other silently.

"Maybe..." Marla said before shaking her head and trailing off.

"What?" Lorenn asked.

"The hole the elemental messengers dug to the surface. Perhaps we could try and fight through and lead our people up."

"No," Lorenn said. "The tainted power of the natural array has the monsters and elementals in a frenzy. We couldn't get past that with all the population in tow, even if we somehow got them all past the elemental messengers. The only way to escape that way is if we took only our fighters and abandoned the populace entirely."

Marla nodded. Neither had to say that they would die with their people before fleeing alone. They looked at each other, their expressions soft, only to harden at the approach of a familiar but unwelcome aura.

Lorenn had gathered herself together by the time Beaufort arrived. The elf was the head of the Cult of the Builder's forces and their uneasy ally. The gold-ranker had given up his essence powers and was some manner of semi-artificial monstrosity, although he only revealed such on the battlefield. In his normal guise, that of a beautiful elven man with long blond hair, his aura revealed no such thing.

"Has Marla convinced you?" Beaufort asked.

"Of what?" Lorenn asked.

"Come now, Lorenn. The choice may be hard, but the calculation is easy. If you retreat to the growth chambers, you buy yourselves time and can abandon our uneasy alliance. All it will cost you is your honour and most of your people."

"No, Beaufort," Lorenn said. "Our alliance stands."

"That's good because I bring the single resource that we need the most yet possess the least."

"What's that?" Marla asked, her voice heavy with suspicion.

"Hope from above," Beaufort said smugly.

"Your allies from the surface?" Lorenn asked, unable to keep the hostility from her voice. Despite their grave need, she could not bring herself to be happy at the prospect of more surface invaders.

"Not allies," Beaufort said. "Not of mine. They're enemies, including a man who is, perhaps, the greatest enemy of my Lord Builder on this planet. We call him the Defier."

"Then why do you seem happy?"

"Because he will help us. It is his nature."

"He'll help you?"

"He'll help you. He may keep us alive, albeit as prisoners, if only because we helped you first. Even if he kills us, it is better to die fighting an enemy of the Lord Builder than as mulch for the elemental messengers and their filthy arboreal project."

"And how do you know this Defier is coming?"

"We call him the Defier because over and again he has kept our lord, the Builder himself, from obtaining that which he desires. He even stole some of the Lord Builder's power. We felt him coming, likely when he used his aura in battle."

"It sounds like he's not your enemy," Marla said. "Or that you aren't his. It sounds more like he's the enemy of your weird god and you're just the flunkies he carves through."

"The Builder is not some mere god," Beaufort said, his tone a warning. "I will admit that the second part of your statement is not entirely without accuracy. The Defier has demonstrated a consistent ability to overwhelm our lord's vassals."

"How powerful is he?" Lorenn asked.

"That is a question with a complicated answer. In some regards, he is but a silver-ranker. In others, he may be the most powerful being on this planet."

"How do we get him to be the second thing, then?" Marla asked. "One more silver-ranker won't help us."

"You might be surprised," Beaufort said. "Many have underestimated the Defier and paid the price, even the Lord Builder. We left the astral space because we knew we would die there if we did not find a way out. We had hoped an alliance with you would be enough, but it was not. I am going to have to restrain my people to prevent them from attacking him on sight, yet I will put my faith in the Defier. The Lord Builder hates him, yet also acknowledges him. What you choose to do is, as always, up to you."

Marla and Lorenn looked at each other.

"I will leave you to decide how to respond," Beaufort said and gracefully withdrew.

Marla closed the door before discussing it with Lorenn.

"What do you think?" she asked.

"We can't trust him," Lorenn said.

"No. But he seemed oddly confident in an enemy."

"It could be a ruse. Stopping us from abandoning the cult and holing up in the growth chambers."

"Perhaps. But as that would be just prolonging the inevitable, is there anything to lose by waiting for this Defier?"

In the wake of the gruelling battle, the expedition was resting. Once the crawlers were back in acceptable shape, they would set out, but until then they were taking a well-earned break. On a conjured platform sticking out of the wall, Miriam was once again probing Jason with questions about astral kings.

"So, your familiars are Voices of the Will, like Jes Fin Kaal?"

"No," Jason clarified. "Colin is a voice. Shade isn't, but Gordon and Farrah are somewhere in the middle. They have a bond with me, but it's not the full-blown connection of a voice. Farrah, can you let Miriam ID you?"

Farrah wandered over from her conversation with Clive to shake Miriam's hand.

Farrah Hurin

- Race: Outworlder (Human)

- Essences: Fire, Earth, Potent, Volcano

- Voice of the Will (Nascent).
- Transition to Voice of the Will unavailable.

. . .

"Colin was only able to make the transition because he got a significant boost from eating the world-taker worm queen. That allowed him to overcome my shortcomings as an astral king by going through a metamorphosis."

"I'm not going to become a messenger if I become your Voice of the Will, am I?" Farrah asked.

"Colin didn't," Jason pointed out. "Besides, the process is voluntary. I won't pressure you into going all the way. I'm all about consent."

Farrah shook her head and wandered off, muttering about childish boys. Jason was about to resume his explanation when Amos Pensinata appeared in a blur of speed.

"I need a gold-rank team, no time to explain."

Miriam raised an eyebrow at Jason, who nodded confirmation. Miriam immediately started barking orders.

"Arabelle Remore! Your group is on Amos Pensinata. Right now!"

Amos became a blur once more, shooting off down the shaft. Arabelle, Gabriel, Emir and Constance followed a moment later.

"We need to know what that's about," Miriam said.

"Lord Pensinata has the best senses in this expedition," Jason said. "I asked him to push out his range to see if he could pick up anything ahead of us. Looks like he saw something time-sensitive."

"I'll deploy a silver team to follow and relay information."

"Yeah," Jason said, suddenly morose. "That's a good idea."

"What's wrong? You disagree?"

"It's not that, it's just… you did the raising one eyebrow thing. I still have trouble getting it right. I'm meant to have all this perfect physiological control, yet I still can't do it more than half the time. At best."

She watched him wiggling his eyebrows with grim determination.

"You are a very odd man, Operations Commander."

―――――

The messengers had better magic than was available on Pallimustus. This included the communications orb that Jes Fin Kaal had used to communicate with the powers of Yaresh while negotiating the expedition details. Another such orb was being used by three gold-rank men, further down the shaft beyond the expedition's location. One of them held it in hand as an image of a messenger floated over it, berating them.

"...not slowing them down enough, priest."

"They're your beacons," the man holding the orb said. "If the monsters they attract aren't good enough, what do you expect us to do? Import bigger ones?"

"We don't have the numbers to make our way down in force," the messenger said. "We have to navigate downwards with extreme care and patience. Even with the delays Jes Fin Kaal engineered, we will be pressed to set up in time. You need to slow them down more."

"And what exactly do you suggest?" the priest asked. "An arrow sign pointing up that reads 'this way down?'"

"Don't be flippant with me, priest."

"And don't you tell me to do something you have no idea how to accomplish, just because your plan isn't working properly. Or do you have any better—"

The priest dropped the orb and launched himself down the shaft mid-sentence. His two companions sensed the rapidly approaching gold-rank auras almost as fast and likewise fled, one of them snatching the dropped orb as he went.

TAKING THE POSITION OF A GOD

THE EXPEDITION WAS WAITING ON THE RETURN OF AMOS PENSINATA AND the other gold-rankers that had taken off down the shaft. Jason and his companions sat around a pair of tables playing board games while they waited, discussing advancement to gold rank. Glow stones floated above each table to light them up while a large privacy screen kept their conversation private. It also saved the rest of the expedition from Neil's loud complaining when games went badly.

"You're saying that it's basically what we thought," Neil said. "It's about how we relate to our essences. Is it my go? I'm playing the barracks."

Belinda groaned as he put down his card.

"Why do you always go with a military strat?" she complained. "You're the healer."

"Not in this game," Neil told her. "I'm allowed to play how I like."

"Yeah, gold-rank is about the essences," Jason confirmed as he put down a card. "I'm playing the west trading post."

"I think what we're looking for are specifics," Clive said. "That's what Allayeth shared with you, right? I'm playing an apothecary."

"Yeah," Jason said. "What it comes down to is the way that essences affect us."

"That's not a thing," Rufus said from the other table. "Don't tell me you've come around to that nonsense Anisa was hawking about essences tainting our pure souls."

"She wasn't right," Jason said, "but she wasn't entirely wrong either, from what I'm told, and it gels with my own experiences. Essences don't impose themselves on our personalities when we absorb them. What they do is find aspects of our personalities that are already there, and that they resonate with. They then heighten those aspects over time, drawing out those parts of us and making them more central to our identities."

"I don't know if I buy that," Rufus said.

"I do," Humphrey said. "Essence users, especially adventurers, are all strong personalities. You could even say that the stronger the personality, the stronger the adventurer. I think what Jason is saying is that it's not so much changing who we are as concentrating the elements that make us who we are. Haven't you ever noticed how much people just seem to fit with their powers? Lindy's powers are twisty and versatile, Clive's are complicated and rely on magical knowledge. Neil's powers are understated, but with the chance to really make a show of things from time to time. His protection magic is oddly hostile but always there when we need it. Jason's powers are all at once elusive, flashy, domineering and terrible, yet also merciful and benevolent. But always on his terms, and when he decides to put an end to something, it ends."

"That doesn't sound flattering," Jason said. "But I think you're right. I've been considering this a lot since Allayeth told me about this stuff, so let's take me as an example of how an essence affects a person. When I first came to this world, I ended up in a knife fight with the first person I met. I accidentally killed him and I completely lost it. I wasn't a violent person. The only fights I'd been in were children's scuffles. So, when I killed the guy, I had a meltdown."

"You're talking about Landemere Vane," Clive said.

"Yep," Jason said. "If I was going kill anyone, he was a great pick, but that didn't matter. I just lost it afterwards. Anyway, I ended up killing more people that day. All cannibal cultists, but I didn't have a lot of time to think about it. It was all in a rush of action and I was concussed from multiple blows to the head. Plus, I was pretty sick from spirit coin over-use."

"You're lucky you were normal rank," Sophie said from Rufus' table. "I used a coin when we fought the Builder and his cult in the astral space. I was only bronze rank and I had to be carried up that tower. I'm going to move my guy here."

She moved her teal Sobek miniature.

"You can't end on a water space," Humphrey told her.

"Yes I can, because it's the big crocodile man. I can end on a water space and I count as being in all the zones he touches."

"That doesn't sound fair," Humphrey complained.

"No, she's right, Humphrey," Jason said. "Now, by the time everything calmed down that first day, I'd seen so much crazy stuff. Crossing realities, finding out magic was real, surviving an evil cult. Getting brain damage, getting healed from brain damage, seeing a kitchen full of chopped-up body parts. And I'd killed people. Again. A good handful of people. I was building up to another proper breakdown. But first thing the next morning, I absorbed the rest of my essence set."

"You're saying you became okay with killing because you got a bunch of evil powers?" Gary asked.

"Not exactly," Jason said, "but kind of, I suppose. Since Allayeth told me about this stuff, I've been trying to explore it as I meditate. She said I won't be able to sense those connections properly until I'm closer to the peak of silver rank, but I think I've caught the edge of them."

"Jason," Humphrey said. "How are things going with the gold-rankers?"

"Oh, come on," Sophie complained. "You just want them to come back because you're losing and you don't want to merge with Rufus."

"I hate the merge mechanic," Rufus complained. "We should have just played *Blood Rage*."

"I'm still halfway through repainting the minis," Jason said.

"I thought Shade already painted them," Rufus said.

"Yeah," Jason said. "He painted them black, and now I have to paint them with actual colours."

"I still assert they looked excellent," Shade's voice came from Jason's shadow.

Jason extended his senses, punching through the interference of the element-laden ambient magic to observe the gold-rankers.

"They caught up with those three guys and they're fighting now. Ooh, Rufus, your mum has some nasty abilities. And people say I'm the one with the evil powers."

"My mother does not have evil powers," Rufus insisted.

"Jason, we were talking about your evil powers," Clive pointed out.

"Right," Jason said. "So, I was shaken by killing people, and pretty moralistic about it too."

"He wanted us to not kill a bunch of Red Table cultists just because they were prisoners," Gary said, shaking his head. "What else were we going to do? Spend a week hauling them across the desert, giving them who knows how many chances to escape, just so they could be executed in a city?"

"The point is," Jason said, "my attitude changed. Swiftly and drastically, without me even noticing. It was only a few months later that the barge full of sand pirates came along, you remember? That was my first big expedition, and I killed a lot of people. I don't even know how many. It was only afterwards that it even occurred to me to question it. I just went there and killed people because I was told to."

"I remember that," Farrah said. "We talked about it because you were worried you were turning into a bloodthirsty monster without realising it."

"Bloodthirsty," Jason echoed. "That's the operative word. I'm convinced that it was my blood essence finding the parts of me that are capable of violence—we all have them, after all—and bringing them to the fore. Something else that Allayeth told me is that the essences don't just amplify aspects of our personalities at random. It brings out the things we need. And what I needed, for better or worse, was a propensity for violence that my life to that point had never required. Suppressed, even. I was lucky enough to grow up in a culture where violence was neither needed nor wanted."

"That's definitely not the case here," Neil said. "Still, you could have been a healer or something, right?"

"Sure," Jason said. "I could have held out for different essences. But I took the ones I had, and they responded to that choice. I think it's fairly obvious that my dark essence drew out my tendencies to deceive, obfuscate and confuse. My sin essence brought out the authoritarian tendencies that got Dominion's attention."

"How does that work?" Taika asked. "Shouldn't sin bring out all the nasty parts of you? Making you all lazy and horny and murdery?"

"I'd say tyranny is pretty nasty," Jason said. "Remember that the essence draws on my nature, meaning my understanding of sin. And sin isn't about some objective right and wrong; it's about transgression against a certain position on what's right and what's wrong. Good and evil. You can check any religious text for examples but, in this case, the position in question is mine."

"Religious texts," Neil said. "Because those positions you're talking about are normally held by gods. Jason's sin essence put his mind in a place where he's taking the position of a god, arbitrating what constitutes good and evil."

"Exactly," Jason agreed.

"Wait, what?" Neil asked. "You're agreeing with me?"

"You're not wrong," Jason told him. "The powers we awaken are a reflection of what our essences represent to us. Clive has been telling me as much since the beginning. People who attack me or my allies within my area of influence—within my aura—are literally burdened with sin."

"This does fill in a lot of gaps," Clive said, nodding thoughtfully. "Certain things make a lot more sense when looked at with this in mind. Especially around the way people try and cultivate specific power sets. Certain choices I've wondered about suddenly make sense if there was a gold-ranker who knows all this guiding the process."

"Why is any of this restricted information?" Belinda wondered. "Is it that bad for people to know all this?"

"If this is true, then I was taught something that was explicitly wrong, by people who unquestionably knew better," Rufus said. "I don't think my parents were trying to hamper me. Maybe the knowledge too early somehow impedes advancement in the early ranks."

"I think it's more likely that it affects personal development than power development," Jason said. "Although, all this suggests that it's the same thing in many ways. Think about your mother, Rufus. She understands how people work better than most. I think she made sure you thought your essences didn't affect your personality so you didn't get caught up thinking about it."

"You think that would be a problem?" Rufus asked.

"Absolutely," Jason said. "Look at me. One of the first things I asked the goddess of Knowledge was if magic changed the way I think. She said that my mind was my own, which I suppose is technically true if the essences use what's already there. She told me to remember that everyone changes, all the time, whether they're magical or not. I've been thinking about the changes I've gone through since becoming magical almost constantly."

"He has," Farrah agreed. "Really, really a lot."

"And there's the problem," Jason said. "I've been obsessing over my behaviour, my choices and the changes I'm going through. And now my mind is extremely messed up. I think they keep this stuff secret because it's healthier to go through this process without constantly second-guessing everything you do."

"But now we're silver rank," Clive said. "The changes our essences have wrought are largely settled. The high-rankers around us have been dropping hints about this stuff for a while because we're ready to start exploring it."

"That would explain some of the things my mother has been saying when I've spoken to her over water link," Humphrey said.

"Your mother has been hinting at weird stuff and you didn't wonder about it?" Neil asked him.

"She's always trying to nudge me in one direction or another," Humphrey said. "It's easier just to go with it."

"Not always," Sophie pointed out.

"Yes, not always," Humphrey said, his tone implying it was a much-repeated response. Jason narrowed his eyes, peering at them thoughtfully for a moment, then grinned.

"What?" Belinda asked him.

"I think Danielle is looking forward to grandkids," Jason said.

The gold-rankers returned to the expedition, landing on the largest stone platform. Expedition members swiftly gathered around them as Amos, Gabriel and Emir each dropped what was probably a person under all the blood. Arabelle conjured javelin-sized needles that pinned the prisoners to the floor, piercing all their limbs and their torsos several times each. She then conjured a transparent jar above each and red life force started trickling from the needles to fill the jars with red liquid.

"That will stop them from regenerating too fast," she said.

"Bro," Taika said to Rufus. "Your mum is kind of hardcore."

Jason nudged Gary on the arm.

"You knew she could do this stuff, right?" Jason asked.

"Yep," Gary said.

"Then how am I the guy with the evil powers?"

"She's prettier than you."

"Thank you, Gareth," Arabelle said. "That's very sweet of you."

"Gary," Rufus said through gritted teeth. "That's my mother."

"Yeah," Jason said, "but it doesn't matter whose mother she is, or how prettily her dark chocolate hair tumbles down over her shoulders; that is a classic evil power right there."

Rufus glared at Jason.

"Dark chocolate hair?" he growled. He was about to continue when Humphrey placed a commiserating hand on his shoulder.

"Don't," Humphrey said in a hollow, trembling voice. "Engaging only makes it worse. It doesn't stop them, it doesn't help. Nothing helps."

Miriam and the rest of the expedition looked on, their levels of befuddlement relating directly to how well they knew Jason and his team.

"Operations Commander," she said warily. "I recommend we move on to questioning the prisoners."

"Right, yes," Jason agreed, then panned a scolding look across his team. "You're all being very silly during a serious time and you should all be ashamed."

Neil opened his mouth to protest but was silenced by a gesture from Humphrey.

Jason glanced at Hana Shavar. The Healer high priestess had been oddly quiet, given that they were dealing with priests of an antagonistic faith. He had wondered if she would be opposed to rough questioning, but all he got from her aura was quiet determination.

From the gold-rankers that had captured the prisoner, Emir's wife and chief of staff, Constance, stepped forward. She held out a sphere that many recognised.

"That's a messenger communication orb," Miriam said. "Are these people working with the messengers or did they take it from one of the elemental messengers?"

"I'd ask," Gabriel said, "but even after getting juiced like this, it's not easy to get a gold-ranker to talk. We can all hold up to a lot of pain."

"Not all pain is the same," Amos Pensinata growled and everyone felt his aura surge.

Jason had learned a lot from Amos about how to effectively wield his aura, but not all the learning was one way. Jason had an aptitude for soul attacks from which Amos had learned a lot. With his even more powerful aura, the result was formidable. The reaction from the prisoners was not what anyone had expected, however.

The three bloody prisoners started screaming, but only for a moment. Amos' aura was thrown back dismissively, washing over the expedition in a twisted, chaotic form. Every silver-ranker other than Jason was staggered, some even falling over. The research team was the worst affected, but the wave swiftly passed. A new aura shrouded the prisoners, unmistakable in its divinity.

The auras of gods were both overwhelmingly powerful and extremely specific. Only the most neophyte iron-ranker, new to having aura senses, would fail to identify which god they were faced with. Even for a god they had never heard of, the nature of a deity was plain to see.

The god Destruction's voice rumbled like an avalanche.

"The souls of my priests are mine to toy with, not yours."

The force of the divine will pushed out like a wave. The silver-rankers scrambled away, abandoning the platform for others more distant. The gold-rankers backed off except for Amos, and even he looked strained. Only Jason was wholly unaffected, to his incredible surprise.

The gods impressing their will on Jason after he released many of their followers during the Reaper trials was one of his most formative experiences as a young adventurer. It had left him spiritually battered but ultimately became the first time that enduring spiritual tribulation led to his soul growing stronger. The gods had made him stronger the hard way, along with marking him with an echo of the divine.

Now that power washed around him like a river flowing around a rock. Jason probed with his aura, finding the divine will equally impervious to him as he was to it. Pushing back was less like a river moving around a rock than a droplet of water landing on a mountain, only to slide away unnoticed. But the feedback from his probe confirm one thing: he was not subject to the will of the gods any more than they were subject to his. His best guess was that his status as a nascent astral king had somehow excised him from their power, at least as they applied to mortals of the world they oversaw.

He had no doubt the gods could still affect him perfectly well within their sphere of influence. Knowledge would still know everything he knew, and if Destruction wished to destroy him, he could. But a general expression of divine power was not something by which Jason was influenced any longer.

Jason stepped up beside Amos but Destruction ignored him, as if he weren't there at all, facing off against Amos and his defiance of the god.

"What are your priests doing down here?" Amos growled.

"Whatever I will," Destruction rumbled. "You and those pathetic winged creatures are squabbling like children, not realising that it is my palm on which you perform your petty dance. Do as you will, mortals, it matters not. My desires are inescapable."

"For every one of your servants I find down here," Amos threatened, "I will find one of your hidden temples. I will raze them to the ground or bury them in whatever hole they're concealed in."

The god's laugh was like thunder.

"You threaten the god of destruction with destruction? There is nothing you can do to me, mortal. Destroying my temples only fulfils their ultimate purpose. Annihilating my worshippers only aids them in providing their greatest service. There are always those hungry for power to replace them, more than I could ever need. Those who hunger for power, not to dominate but to destroy. To fight me is to lose before you begin."

The god's presence vanished and the priests exploded in a visceral mess. Jason used his aura to shield himself and Amos, creating a wedge of clear space behind them while the rest of the platform was painted red.

"Well," Gabriel said, walking up as he pulled a vial of crystal wash from his potion belt to tip over his head. "That could have gone better."

CONFIDENT GUESSES

THE EXPEDITION'S GOLD-RANKERS, PLUS CLIVE AND JASON, WERE HAVING a strategy meeting before resuming their descent down the shaft.

"Unfortunately," Miriam said, "Destruction's involvement doesn't change anything."

"Unfortunately?" Gabriel asked.

"Our plan is so vague," Jason explained, "that there aren't enough specifics to change. We're still heading down and trying to use this device while stopping whatever counter-plans anyone down there has. 'Anyone' now including at least one god, the cult of a great astral being, two varieties of messenger, whatever the natives have going on, and whoever else has managed to sneak down there while the Magic Society was building a town on top of the hole. With blindfolds on, apparently, given that anyone can just stroll down here."

"At least we've confirmed that the regular messengers aren't playing us straight," Gabriel said.

"Yes," Emir agreed. "They've gone from 'almost to certainly going to betray us' to 'actively betraying us.' There's that."

"It does bring up an interesting question," Jason mused. "What kind of agreement did the messengers make with Destruction?"

"They wouldn't accept anything that robs them of their prize," Miriam said. "I don't see the messengers joining hands with the god of destruction unless they're very confident about getting what they want, although Destruction seemed to think he'd gotten one over on them."

"I think it's more likely that either the device doesn't do what it says on the tin," Jason said, "or that Destruction had some way to trigger the cataclysm anyway, once the device has been used."

"Assuming that the devastation level we already anticipate is enough for the god of destruction," Clive said. "Perhaps he has some way of amplifying the effect with divine power."

"Oh, thank you for that," Emir said. "I was just thinking that I wasn't anywhere close to worried enough, and here you come to clear that right up. That's tremendous, Clive, thank you."

"Perhaps a mix of all those scenarios?" Constance suggested, bringing things back on topic while giving her husband a stern look. "Destruction has some means to sabotage the device, but the messengers are convinced he'll only use it after it has given them what they want."

Emir was primarily an ideas man and the face of his treasure-hunting organisation. As Emir's wife and Chief of Staff, Constance was the detail-oriented half of the pairing, which sometimes made her closer to a babysitter than she would admit to liking.

"None of this matters," Amos said. "Asano said it: nothing's changed. We go down and we figure it out on the spot."

"He's right," Miriam said. "We don't have enough information for speculation to be useful. Let's get moving."

The teams clambered into the remaining crawlers, now in various states of disrepair. Three had lost their roll cages and two had been jury-rigged back into functionality by Gary. One crawler had been a complete write-off, cannibalised for parts. This left a few members of the expedition stuck clinging to the remaining roll cages.

Most of these people were gold-rankers, but Jason was also among them. With multiple means of flight and a demonstrable resistance to exotic magic, he was less likely to plunge down the shaft if thrown off. While he waited for his crawler to load, another divine aura manifested right beside him. This time, it was not just an aura but an image of a bookish woman in brown robes.

"Knowledge," Jason said. "It's been a while."

"Are you still piqued I didn't tell your friends you were alive?"

"Now that you ask, I am a little bit, yeah."

"I did not know for certain, so it was not right to tell them. I'm the goddess of knowledge, Jason, not of very confident guesses."

"Yeah, Gabrielle told me about the same. You keep her away from Travis, by the way; he's a sweet boy, but utterly hopeless with women."

"That is between him and Gabrielle. It is not for you and me to interfere."

"Yeah, I'm sure you're staying out of the relationship between your priestess and a guy who represents possibly the largest store of alien knowledge ever to arrive on this planet."

"This discussion is not why I'm here, Jason."

"Yeah, but it's fun, though, right?"

She snorted a small laugh, to the startlement of the expedition that had stopped loading up to gawk at the encounter.

"Are you teasing me, Mr Asano?"

"You're the one asking questions you already know the answer to. Which is all questions, I guess. You're here about Destruction?"

"Yes. I wanted to remind you of certain facts, starting with that I am the goddess of knowledge, not him. He does not see all and he does not know all. Especially not what has transpired on other planets."

"What does Earth have to do with any of this?"

"I cannot tell you what Destruction had planned, any more than I could reveal that Disguise was masquerading as Purity. Such things are the affairs of other gods, operating within their primary spheres of influence. What I can do is remind you of things you already know, such as the means by which you saved your world twice over. I suggest you keep the methodology in the forefront of your mind."

"Oh, oblique advice on solving a problem instead of just telling me. At least it's not an ambiguously worded prophecy, I guess."

"I have already—"

"Yeah, spheres of influence, I get it. I don't suppose there's anything you can just straight-up tell us?"

The goddess shook her head with the expression of a mother indulging her child more than she knew she should.

"Beaufort's intentions are what he claims," she said. "You do not need to second-guess his agenda."

"And who is Beaufort?"

"Someone whose agenda you would otherwise second-guess. He still has people in Yaresh, especially in the Magic Society. These were mercenary agents, not true believers that departed with the others, but they've continued to watch your activities with care. Even down here, the information they've gathered has been fed to Beaufort. He understands your power and your importance to what happens next. He will work with you honestly."

"I have an unpleasant suspicion of who you're talking about. Which means that I won't want to work with him, will I?"

"You will not. But he knows that this expedition is the only chance he has at survival, or even a clean death."

"I'm inclined towards clean death."

"That is for your group to decide, but be aware that you will need the strength of his forces."

Jason groaned. "That's just fantastic."

"Just remember my words, Jason. How you saved your world. You will need to push for it in this world, triggering it yourself. But you have the power, I promise you that, but I cannot promise you will wield it effectively. That falls to you."

"Do you think it will come to that?"

A smile teased the goddess' lips.

"I already told you, Jason: I'm not the goddess of very confident guesses."

Jason let out another groaning sigh.

"Of course you're not. Nothing but to get to it then, I suppose. Oh, and Knowledge?"

"Yes?"

He gave the goddess a genuine smile, free of his signature half-smirk.

"Thank you for helping us."

The goddess' smile was the first light on a warm spring morning.

"You are trouble to work with, Jason, but I'm determined to get some use out of you yet. Just try not to die *too* often."

"I'll do my best, but you know how it is."

"Yes," she said. "I do."

Miriam and Jason were once again sharing a crawler with half of Jason's team. Jason was hanging off the roll cage like it was a jungle gym as the crawler made its way down the rough wall of the shaft. Miriam activated a privacy screen, drawing immediate complaints from Clive in the driver's seat.

"How am I meant to steer this thing when everything is blurry? It's bad enough driving by the light of glow stones with shadows dancing off every lump in the rock."

"Apologies," Miriam said adjusting the brooch that generated the screen. The sound barrier stayed in place while the visual blurring disappeared.

"Thank you," Clive said, still grumpy.

"Operations Commander," Miriam said, "I was hoping to get more insight into what the goddess told you. Firstly, you saved your world twice?"

"Yeah," Jason said. "It's a very long story, but the short version starts with the understanding that the dimensional membrane around my world is extremely fragile. Brittle, almost. Smash a big enough hole and it might not close again. My entire planet is far too vulnerable to being annihilated by astral forces, leaving a giant hole in the universe where it used to be. I know a lot of people have wondered how I got caught up with great astral beings, and that's the answer. They needed someone who could move between worlds, powerful enough to change things but not so powerful I break them in the attempt."

"That all sounds bad," Miriam said.

"Relying on a guy whose greatest skill is eighties action-adventure television trivia to save the world is not great, no. But reality has mechanisms to help repair itself, especially our two worlds, for reasons I'm definitely not going into now."

"Yet you have time to mention your stupid sky dog stories," Neil pointed out.

"Don't give me that, Neil, you know damn well it's *Airwolf*."

"Operations Commander," Miriam said pointedly.

"Sorry," Jason said. "So, reality tries to repair itself. As the magic in the world I come from became unstable for reasons I also won't go into, dimensional spaces appeared to repair damage that started randomly appearing in the dimensional membrane."

"Randomly appearing?" Miriam said. "That also sounds very bad."

"Yep. These dimensional spaces were dubbed transformation zones. They appear and plug the hole as best they can before vanishing, but the area is left changed."

"Which is why they're called transformation zones?"

"Precisely. It affects the people too, shifting their very species. I'd be interested in what Carlos Quilido made of that, but that's for another day. These changes are left like scars on reality, but the world manages to limp on. But if you get a transformation zone appearing right on top of an astral space, it all goes very wrong. Seeping ulcer in the side of the universe wrong."

"He's massively simplifying the reality of the dimension forces involved to the point of not being accurate," Clive pointed out.

"She's just looking for the general idea, Clive," Jason said, "not a lecture on dimensional membrane theory."

"Are you sure?" Clive asked. "I can still elucidate the basics while driving. I think it would be useful in helping her grasp the context of—"

"Extremely sure, Clive, but thank you," Jason cut him off. "Anyway, the next thing you need to understand all this is that I have a specific power. The World-Phoenix gave me a blessing. Custom designed, just for me. You can sense how my body and soul are fused, like a messenger's?"

"Yes."

"That's only one aspect of it. Another is that I have a stabilising effect on the physical reality around me, and a third is that I have an easier time slipping through dimensional boundaries. I can walk right through a sealed astral space aperture, for example."

"Or into a transformation zone?" Miriam guessed.

"Exactly. A transformation zone is essentially a zone of reality that is in flux. I had to go in and fix it, and I did not know how. I pretty much ran on instinct. I did this twice before my world's magic stabilised and the transformation zones stopped appearing. The first time, the results were passable but not ideal. The second time, I did a lot better. In the course of affecting that first zone, I was transformed a little as well. In shaping the zone, I also shaped myself. I gained the power to imprint on reality, which is how I managed to stabilise the transformation zone completely."

"Imprint on reality," Miriam said.

"Yes."

"Like a god creating sacred ground?" she asked.

"I love working with people who are quick on the uptake," Jason said with a grin. "No offence, Neil."

"Just so you know," Neil said, "that whole sacred ground thing means that when he says he fixed the zones, he did it by turning them into temples to himself. To himself. I think that officially makes him the most self-aggrandising man in the cosmos."

"Sacred ground," Miriam repeated thoughtfully. "Like your cloud building?"

"Yes," Jason said. "Just larger and fixed in place when I reshape a transformation zone."

"Really?" Neil asked. "The guy is building temples to himself. Why aren't people more outraged by this?"

"Just ignore him, he's a priest," Jason told her. "They get so touchy when you assume the role of a god, even if it's just a little bit. It's not a big deal, Neil."

"He does have something of a point," Miriam said. "I can't help but feel that a silver-ranker creating temples to himself should be a matter of concern."

"Thank you. Finally, someone gets it," Neil said.

"I'm quite certain there are people that grasp the import," Humphrey said. He had thus far stayed out of the conversation, quietly sitting next to Sophie, their fingers interlocked as they held hands.

"You realise that your god didn't say anything about it when he came to visit me," Jason told Neil.

"What?" Neil asked. "When was this?"

"Just before the messengers invaded Yaresh. He even gave me a present."

"What kind of present?" Neil asked.

"Not sure. Can't use it until I get a soul forge. Something about creating an astral entity."

"I think we should stay on topic," Miriam said. "Was Knowledge saying that you'll need to forcibly trigger one of these transformation zones?"

"I think she was, yeah. Which is a whole thing, let me tell you."

———

It wasn't just at Allayeth's insistence that Team Moon's Edge had been assigned to the expedition. They were the local Yaresh team least likely to have been compromised by the messengers, due to Allayeth's close over-sight of them and their famous personal loyalty to her. The icing on the cake was that the team had multiple members with elemental powers. One of them had the iron essence, one the earth essence and one with both the fire and earth essences.

The two earth essence users were useful in mapping out the shaft well ahead of their location, only powerful sense-masking abilities like those of the spider moles preventing them from accurately determining the geography around them. This allowed them to notify Miriam as they finally approached their destination. She called the expedition to a halt to make an announcement through voice chat.

"Our earth users have picked up on a massive cavern system below. They've also noted that the rock within the areas they can sense appears to be riddled with what looks like tree roots to their senses. What that means, we can't be sure. We'll move ahead with caution but be ready for heavy combat. It may come from the walls again, as with the spider moles and the worms."

"I can use my senses to poke around and see if I can get an idea of what those roots are," Jason told Miriam. "My concern would be if the bad guys notice me looking and send an army of elemental messengers."

"Amos Pensinata might be a better choice," she said.

"Possibly," Jason said. "But when I heard roots, my hackles went up."

"Why?"

"Because with how deep we are underground, how likely are we to run into trees?"

"Not very."

"Exactly. But what we do have is messengers and something that the messengers tried to turn into a soul forge. I may be shooting in the dark here, but I can't help but think about the fact that the messengers are birthed from trees. My concern is that maybe there's some twisted version of a messenger birthing tree down here. It would explain how the number of elemental messengers is suspiciously high. The regular messengers never told us how many they lost, but the estimates I got from one of my messenger prisoners made the number that came out of this shaft they dug a bit suspect."

"You're suggesting that the elemental messengers have been reproducing?"

"It's just a guess based on too little information," Jason said. "It tickles my instincts, though. Messengers don't have a child state. They come out fully formed, naïve but complete with language skills. They get pushed through indoctrination and sent right off to join the evil army. If they're making more of these elemental messengers, who seem kind of mindless and angry, they'd be ready to go, fresh off the vine."

"Meaning that there could be countless numbers of them down there."

"I don't think that's entirely true," Clive said. "Even with magic, you don't get something from nothing. Even when material appears to be conjured from thin air, it's really drawing magic from the astral and shaping it. The same way magic manifestations turn into monsters or essences. But these elementals are real creatures, not summoned monsters. This suggests that they would need a source of material that originated in reality."

"They're elemental creatures," Neil said. "Could they just use rock as the material?"

"Maybe," Clive said. "I think it's more likely that they need living matter, at least in part. Most likely, the natives already down here. They may have all been turned into elemental messengers."

"That's a grim thought," Jason said. "But the question remains, should I try taking a peek at these roots? I may be able to confirm or disprove some of this speculation. Equally, I may bring a bunch of elemental messengers down on our heads. Or up under our feet, I guess."

Miriam brought some of the other gold-rankers into a voice channel to discuss it. They ultimately decided that more information was worth the risk of a fight that was inevitable anyway, and at least they could prepare. Platforms and alcoves were stone-shaped from the walls, setting up defensive positions for ranged and support members of the group. The crawlers were secured higher up the shaft.

While all this was happening, Clive used specialised equipment to run a series of tests on the ambient magic. The elemental energy was much more pervasive; even Jason was no longer willing to attempt opening a portal. Clive made a list of other potential effects on essence abilities, not all of which were negative.

For essence users with the right essences, their powers were likely to be more powerful, but harder to control. Gary, with his fire and iron essences, and Farrah with her fire, earth and volcano essences, fell firmly into this group. The gold-rank elemental essence users from Team Moon's Edge would be even more impactful.

Once everything was ready, Jason reached out with his senses, his team all around him.

"This preparation may have all been for nothing," Belinda pointed out.

"Uh, nope," Jason said, his voice an octave higher than normal.

"Those roots are some weird messenger stuff alright. And I'm pretty sure they noticed me checking."

"That was quick," Taika said.

"Yep," Jason agreed. He drew his sword, the white runes on the blade turning red as it slid from the sheath. "Just so you know, there seems to be quite a lot of them."

68

YOU DON'T DO IT BLINDLY

JASON AND MIRIAM STOOD SURROUNDED BY OTHERS AT THE EDGE OF A platform. Leaning out to look down they saw the seething mass of elemental messengers coming up the shaft.

"How are there this many?" Miriam asked, her voice hollow.

The shaft was thick with elemental messengers, rising like a cloud. In the dark, fiery powers flared and sparked, casting the ocean of winged figures in ominous light and dancing shadows.

"Does this count as a lot?" Jason asked.

She was about to shoot him a retort, then remembered what she'd seen while going over his record. Asano's Adventure Society badge kept a record of everything he had killed, from people to monsters to anything else. The vast majority stemmed from his time on his original world, and the numbers involved were outlandish to the point of implausibility. She'd had the Magic Society check the numbers several times and still suspected that shifting between worlds had altered the badge somehow. According to the record, he'd done more killing than she had, despite his much lower rank and vastly shorter career.

The number of monsters he'd killed at silver rank had gotten him to the wall in record time, but no further. Despite culling silver-rank monsters at a rate that made a monster surge seem tame, his advancement had almost stopped and the reason was obvious: What he was fighting didn't pose a significant threat. Armies of monsters, according to the numbers recorded by his badge, and other things besides. She had wondered about something called living anomalies, which she had just learned were monster-like entities that existed in the transformation zones he'd talked about.

She had never entirely believed the reality of his numbers, thinking that somehow the badge was tampered with or affected by travel between worlds. But standing beside him as he looked down at an army of elemental messengers rising through the dark she realized that he was completely calm.

Even Asano's powerful aura couldn't entirely mask his emotions from Miriam's gold-rank senses, and while nervousness rippled through the rest of expedition, he was completely relaxed. If anything, he was oddly centred, his normal self-amused attitude fading away. While everyone around them steeled themselves for battle, he gave off a sense of being exactly where he was meant to be. When he gave her a side glance, a slight smile playing on his lips, she realised she'd been probing his emotions with a little more force than was strictly polite.

"Don't worry," he assured her. "Fighting armies from another dimension is kind of my thing."

She was extremely interested in learning more about Asano's time in the other world, but this was not the moment. For the moment, she was just happy to have someone standing beside her who looked at the largest collection of enemies she'd ever seen like they were a long queue at the sandwich shop. He flashed her a reassuring grin that vanished as he conjured his cloak, his face vanishing into the hood.

Humphrey's strongest singular attack was called Unstoppable Force. It delivered massive amounts of the two most powerful forms of damage, short of transcendent.

Ability: [Unstoppable Force] (Might)

- Special Attack (melee).
- Base cost: High mana, extreme stamina.

- Cooldown: 1 Minute.

- Current rank: Silver 5 (16%).

- Effect (iron): Melee attack with massive momentum, dealing large amounts of additional resonating-force and disruptive-force damage. Requires a heavy weapon.

- Effect (bronze): For each enemy struck the cooldown of this ability and the cost of the next use of this ability are reduced.

- Effect (silver): Attack generates a blast wave of resonating-force and disruptive-force damage originating from each enemy struck.

Unstoppable Force was not a rare ability. One of the most common powers from one of the most common essences, it was the quintessential example of rare not automatically meaning best. It was also the opposite of complicated, famous as the most straightforward and iconic of all special attacks. It simply took a regular attack and added the magnitude of damage countries signed treaties to prevent. It was the ideal power to thoughtlessly swing at an enemy and still get tremendous results. But Humphrey could do better than that.

Racial Gift: [Hero's Sacrifice]

- Sacrifice your health to enhance the power of your special attacks.

Humphrey's twice-evolved human gift turned life force into power. That had been a risky move at bronze rank, but at silver, he had health to burn. Another of Humphrey's signatures was combination attacks, allowing multiple special attacks to be used in a single strike.

Ability: [Dive Bomb] (Wing)

- Special Attack (movement, combination).
- Base cost: High stamina.
- Cooldown: 20 seconds.

- Current rank: Silver 4 (89%).

- Effect (iron): Accelerate down to attack a target from above; can be combined with normal or special melee attacks. Physical damage from these attacks is increased. No falling damage is suffered when using this ability, even if the attack misses.

- Effect (bronze): A resonating-force shockwave is produced from the impact point.

- Effect (silver): All damage from melee weapons and melee special attacks combined with this ability is increased, regardless of damage type. Striking enemies and obstacles other than the designated target does not end this ability unless the attack's momentum is fully arrested.

Dive Bomb was a special attack purpose-built to strike from above. Normally, Humphrey set it up with his flight and teleport powers, but the horde of enemies pouring up the shaft presented a dream scenario. By targeting a foe deep behind the frontline, anyone and anything that got in his path suffered the full effect of his powers without consuming them, until the attack against his target was resolved.

Humphrey signalled his intentions to the team.

"I'm pulling a *Battlefield Earth*," he warned them.

"Which one is that again?" Taika asked through voice chat, still learning the team's strategies. "Also, why did you let Jason name the tactics?"

"It's the one where Humphrey pulls a move that was always going to end in a massive bomb," Jason told him.

"Bro, that's a stretch."

Humphrey ignored them and triggered his abilities. Combining Dive Bomb, Hero's Sacrifice and Unstoppable Force, he picked the furthest enemy he could sense as the target, deep in a mass of elemental messengers too thick to see through. Plunging out of the expedition forces, he crashed through the enemy like a meteor. Ramming into anything between himself and the target, he ploughed through without slowing. Every impact came with a pair of shockwaves from Dive Bomb and Unstoppable Force as he bowled through enemies, knocking them away like bowling pins.

Not every foe was sent flying away. By less than a fifth of the way to the target, Humphrey's dragon sword had impaled enemies down the full length of the blade. Further foes were struck by the tip and blasted away or even torn in half, Humphrey passing through mists of blood and viscera. The impaled enemies suffered shockwave after shockwave until they too were torn apart, making room for fresh meat.

Projectiles bounced off Humphrey's dragon wings and his dragon armour. Barriers of metal and stone were conjured in his path, but he tore through them like they were tissue paper. A gold-ranker moved to intercept him and bounced right off, doing no more than shuddering Humphrey as he continued down.

Resonating force was exceptionally effective on tough, rigid enemies like stone and metal affinity messengers. Disruptive force was effective against the semi-tangible states of the ash and fire messengers, their advantage turned to vulnerability as Humphrey scattered them like fog before a gust.

Finally, Humphrey struck his chosen target. The gold-rank messenger was fifteen feet tall, bigger than even the largest of normal messengers. His body was obsidian black, complete with glossy sheen, and Humphrey's sword plunged into it, the combined impact and shockwave tearing the leftover enemies from his blade.

For all the power of his attack, Humphrey knew it was far from enough to take down a gold-ranker. Even as the shock of hitting the enemy still reverberated through his sword, he was reaching for a consumable item on his belt.

Humphrey had a standard adventuring belt, enchanted to shield his potions and other sundry items from incidental damage. He touched a small ceramic disk held in a custom sheath. The ludicrously expensive, single-use consumable turned to powder.

- You have used [Greater Man-Catcher].
- Your next short-range teleport within 5 seconds can bring along a hostile enemy you are in physical contact with. Target can be up to gold-rank or one rank higher than the teleport power, whichever is lower.

Humphrey used his teleport to return him to the expedition force and bring the elemental messenger with him. Gold-rank allies pounced on the messenger as Neil's Life Force bolts landed on Humphrey, restoring his health.

Hitting so many enemies had reset the cooldown on Unstoppable Force immediately and Humphrey dived back into the fray, this time using it more conventionally. At the same time, he requested access to the expedition command channel. After being allowed to join he gave a brief report of what he'd sensed while deep behind enemy lines. Before leaving the channel again.

He joined Taika in his fast-moving, hard-hitting disruption of the enemy forces. The messengers were too mindlessly aggressive for tactics or strategy, failing to fully capitalise on their numbers or adapt well to the strategies of their enemies. Humphrey and Taika, the team's high-impact adventurers, were able to put them on the back foot and lead the way for the others.

"Good to have you back, bro. I saw your death-dive. You don't muck about."

"Thank you."

"Yeah," Taika continued. "You fight the same way Jason makes life choices."

"What?"

Miriam accepted a chat request from Humphrey Geller.

"Commander," his voice came through. "I just got a sense of the far side of the enemy. It was hard to be sure with so many auras, but I think they were being attacked from below."

"Any further details?"

"No, Commander, I'm sorry. It was brief and my senses aren't like Jason's or Lord Pensinata's."

"Thank you," Miriam said and cut off the channel. She had one perpetually open to Amos Pensinata, who had the strongest senses in the expedition by far.

"Pensinata," she ordered. "What can you give me on the far side of the enemy forces?"

"I will have to pull back from the fight and concentrate to reach through all these auras," he told her. That was not an inconsiderable draw-back, given that he was one of their strongest individual combatants, but it was worth the loss.

"Do it," she told him, then returned her attention to the battle.

Jason took his usual role in such large-scale conflicts of loading up as many enemies as he could with afflictions. He wouldn't be immediately impactful anywhere, but his total damage across the course of the fight would rival or eclipse most gold-rankers. The exceptions to this were the adventurers with elemental powers related to earth or fire. They, unsurprisingly, were the shining stars of the battle. The elemental messengers were all enhanced as well, however, so the adventurers needed to pick their targets well, not using fire to attack fire or earth to attack earth.

Gary and especially Farrah were likewise punching well above their normal weight. Gary was an impassable wall, moving around the makeshift battlements the expedition had set up. He shielded ranged attackers, held barricades under assault and blocked attempts to collapse the stone platforms by attacking the points at which they were attached to the shaft walls.

Farrah was an outright demoness, from her lava and obsidian whip sword to storms of obsidian shards and the heinous lava cannon. Oddly enough, one of her most useful powers was her perception ability. It allowed her to see through smoke, ash clouds and other obscuring factors in a battlefield already poorly lit. She also benefited from an expedition worth of auras including the shared, enhanced mana recovery that was a highlight of Jason's team.

Unfortunately for the expedition, a handful of bright stars did not make up for the enemy's advantage. While some adventurers were boosted by the enhanced elemental magic, *all* of the messengers were. If they weren't too stupid to do anything beyond rush up the shaft in a shapeless horde, the expedition would have been overrun. Teamwork, tactics and strategy were the counterbalancing factors, and they worked— at least while the adventurers were still fresh.

The horde's number suggested that Jason's theory of a birthing tree had merit. This was further supported by the mercifully small number of gold-rankers on the other side. If the horde had been spawned from a birthing tree, none would have had time to advance. This meant that the gold-rankers amongst them almost certainly came from the original messenger group. As a consequence, while the silver-rank horde could be churned out quickly, every gold-ranker they lost would be a massive blow.

Seeming to recognise this, the strongest messengers hung back from the fight. Although still animalistic, the gold-rank elemental messengers had a higher order of cunning, and the wits to understand the danger. As a result, the gold-rank adventurers were free to cut loose, forming the solid core of adventurer defence.

"Tactical Commander," Amos said through his direct channel to Miriam. "There is a force attacking the elemental messengers from below. They are Builder cultists and appear to be trying to force their way directly towards the shaft."

"Any indication if they're trying to reach us or simply trying to use the shaft to escape the underground?"

"Not that I saw."

"It seems unlikely that this is the moment they would pick to make a break for it," Jason said.

"This is meant to be a private channel," Miriam said.

"Yeah, but it's my communication power."

"So, you have heard everything anyone has said through those channels."

"You don't need to worry, Tactical Commander," Jason assured her. "I take privacy very seriously. Although I did hear you talking with your team member Alice, but you shouldn't worry about that either. Just go to an alchemist and they'll give you a topical cream."

"This is hardly the time, Operations Commander," Miriam said.

"I'm just kidding, I don't listen in. I just sensed you talking with Lord Pensinata after he extended his senses so far and I jumped into your channel to hear what he found."

"I have reported," Amos said. "Am I free to return to the battle?"

"You are," Miriam said, then she and Jason shifted to the command channel.

"Do you think this Beaufort that Knowledge mentioned is the leader of the Builder cult?" Miriam asked.

"I do," Jason told her.

"Do you think they're trying to reach us?"

"Yes."

"So, we have a choice to make. Our people are holding off the messengers for now, but we're going to run out of mana before they run out of bodies to throw at us. Long before, from what we're seeing. We can either back off and see if your butterflies can thin them out, or try and fight down to the Builders, form the alliance Knowledge seems to think we'll need and hope they have some kind of redoubt we can all escape to."

"That's my read as well."

"You're the operations commander," Miriam said. "Your job is to decide what we do. Mine is to figure out how, and to tell you if we can't. Or shouldn't."

"You favour pulling back?"

"It's what my instincts are telling me. But I'm not the operations commander for a reason. This whole situation is a series of choices I'd rather not make. You were put in charge because you're the one who has been through madness that most of us wouldn't think possible, let alone be willing to confront. You know how to crest that wave."

"I think you may be overselling me, but I also think you're right about my instincts being the ones to follow here. Now that Destruction is involved, I don't think walking away and assuming we can safely evacuate the city as a backup plan is still on the table. This is getting that full-blown, save-the-day, god-level-enemy feel. Like the One Day War in the Storm Kingdom or some of the stuff on Earth."

"So, what are you saying?"

"That sometimes you have to take the big risk. But you don't do it blindly. I'm going to sneak through the enemy, talk with this Beaufort bloke, and we'll see how it goes from there."

OF A MIND TO KILL YOU

BEAUFORT'S BODY CONTAINED FAR TOO MUCH METAL TO FIT WITHIN HIS elven frame. When not in his war form, most of it was contained in a dimensional space created by his star seed. In almost every instance, that was a convenience, the star seed even shielding the dimensional space from most interference. Most was not all, however, and every time Beaufort opened the portal within himself to extract the additional material, he felt the elemental energy attempt to seep in and corrupt it. It failed, of course, as it was nothing next to the power of the Builder, but the process of shifting into or out of his war form was excruciatingly painful.

If he was allowed his preference, Beaufort would have remained in his war form at all times. This was not possible—or, at least, very ill-advised —because of the need for diplomacy. They needed the brightheart smoulders to work with them, and they would not take well to a fifteen-foot metal skeleton with occasional patches of living flesh. For reasons that escaped Beaufort, people seemed to especially object to the metallic skeleton not being shaped like bones. Beaufort's true body was an industrial construction of dark iron girders held together with heavy bolts, all practicality and no pointless flourish. It was the beauty of simplicity and function.

To Beaufort, his form was so much more perfect than his old elf body, which now served as little more than a disguise. Diverging significantly from the humanoid norm, he had two extra arms, each longer than his legs. They were each capable of wielding a variety of magically enhanced weapons, and while it pained him to swap them out through his internal portal space, the results were worth the discomfort. It took more than a little suffering to deter a true servant of the Builder.

Carving a path through the horde of elemental messengers demonstrated the glory of what the Builder had turned him into. The messengers weren't intelligent, but possessed cunning enough to reserve their gold-rankers and spend their replaceable silvers. This meant that Beaufort and his fellow golds could burrow deep into the enemy, raw power overcoming the massive deficit in numbers.

This was a crucial moment for the Builder cult forces, one where everything could fall apart. It might have been wiser to make a break for the surface once the Adventure Society expedition and the messengers had exhausted themselves on one another. Beaufort had decided against that move; it was an all or nothing play against extremely long odds. They would need to make it up the shaft, past the retreated expedition and whatever else they ran into along the way. Then they would face the doubtlessly formidable defensive outpost on the surface.

The elemental messengers that excavated the shaft in the first place had dug their way up and never come back. That was the point at which their gold-rankers started acting with more caution, and Beaufort was going to do the same. Whatever his approach, their chances of survival were slim, but he would massage those odds as much as possible. Whatever indignities he had to swallow and whatever price he had to pay, so long as he was alive, there was a chance of someday rejoining the Builder's forces.

As making a break for it was a fool's errand, that was not the cult's purpose in striking out against the elemental messengers. They were there to get the attention of their greatest enemy, the one they could sense battling above.

They could feel Asano's presence as he went to war with the messengers. In some ways, it was more imposing to the cult than the entire messenger army, and more than a few of his people were unhappy about Beaufort's intentions. Even Beaufort himself felt an instinctive revulsion over joining hands with the Defier. When Asano's presence grew closer, a stir passed through the cultists.

"He's coming."

The dark battle, lit by flaring spells and flaming wings, felt purpose-built for Jason's combat style. Used to spending the battle amongst the enemy, he drifted in and out of shadows, his sword in constant motion as he chanted out spells. His shadowy form was all but invisible to the eye and aura senses both. Only Amos Pensinata had even a chance of pinpointing Jason as he moved through a battlefield blanketed with his aura. All that could be seen were the glowing runes of his black blade, one more blur of red in the chaos of fire magic.

Jason's aura power, Hegemony, caused everyone who attacked his allies to suffer the Sin affliction. Sin had little impact on its own as all it did was amplify the rare necrosis damage type. Jason and Colin were the only ones in the battle fielding that damage type, so anyone not engaged by them could ignore it. For that reason, the messengers had been accumulating it without bothering to cleanse it, leaving them drenched in Sin.

The special attack, Punish, was extremely weak as attack abilities went. It inflicted Sin and added a small amount of necrotic damage to a weapon strike. Normally, that was barely worth noticing, especially to a silver-ranker, requiring Jason to escalate with countless attacks before it became worthwhile. That strategy had been Jason's very first approach to combat when all he had was a small handful of powers. It was slow, inefficient and something he had long left behind. But now, with an army of foes loading themselves up with Sin, Jason's humble special attack was suddenly a formidable weapon.

Jason moved amongst the enemies with impunity, their elemental powers ill-suited to catching or even sensing his passage through the dark. He was not entirely alone, with a few other members of the expedition delving through the enemy. Assassin-types and other stealth specialists sprang attacks that provided Jason with useful distractions while he occasionally returned the favour.

Unlike assassins, Jason didn't go for the kill. Some foes he left to slowly die of afflictions, the elemental messengers lacking healing powers. Those truly laden with Sin, he maimed with a single strike. The small amount of necrosis delivered by his attack was amplified to such a level that the merest touch of his sword parted flesh like a chainsaw through long-rotted meat. He aimed for wings, shearing them off and sending the messengers tumbling down the shaft.

As he continued his descent through the enemy ranks, Jason reached the messengers unaffected by his Sin affliction. Too far from the frontline, or the topline as it was in the vertical shaft, they were waiting for enough room to fight. Combat on the wing took space and there were so many messengers that those in the rear needed their brethren to fall and make room. Having not made attacks, they were untouched by Sin, so Jason switched tactics.

Even Jason's senses had a hard time making anything out through the chaos of battle, but he sensed his proximity to the messenger gold-rankers. Refraining from the frontline of battle, they were hanging back in the area Jason had now reached. They did not seem to have sensed him, the elemental messengers having weaker perception than their original recipe counterparts.

Miriam didn't like Jason's butterflies adding chaos to where the expedition was fighting, but thinning out the backline and distracting the gold-rankers where the expedition wasn't fighting seemed like a good idea. If the butterflies were allowed to run rampant then that was all to the good, but he suspected the gold-rankers would step in. They might have been reduced to animalistic maniacs, but their caution suggested that the gold-rankers weren't completely foolish. If they were too busy shutting down butterflies to engage the expedition at a critical moment, that was good too.

As anticipated, the gold-rankers were smarter than the weaker and presumably freshly birthed silver-rankers. They recognised the threat of the butterflies and moved to intercept while Jason had already moved on. The gold-rankers had no attention to spare him; it was hard to contain the butterflies once started, especially with potential victims so plentiful and tightly packed. The gold-rankers were too busy culling their own people and destroying butterflies to pursue him as he went into total stealth mode out of caution. Poor perception or not, they were still gold rank.

A trident shot from Beaufort's arm, trailing a chain behind it as it flew towards a messenger at blinding speed. It punched into the messenger's body and each prong injected it with volatile liquid metal. With a yank from Beaufort, the messenger was flung into a group of other messengers before exploding as the volatile metal was agitated. It hardened with the blast, digging into the other messengers as shrapnel before melting again, turning lava hot as it seared them from the inside.

The gold-rank attack was devastating to the messengers, killing some and leaving the others too hurt to continue the fight. Unfortunately, some of the elemental messengers were highly resistant to metal, heat or both. These Beaufort lunged at, even as he retracted his harpoon chain. One of his other arms produced a ceramic axe shrouded in blue energy. The axe was less effective against earth types but carved up the metal, fire and ash varieties handily.

Beaufort looked around for fresh enemies; this was less a case of finding one than picking one. No matter how many the gold-rank Builder cult vanguard slaughtered, the silver-rank messengers kept coming, fearless and unabated. Beaufort was about to fire off another harpoon when the rotting carcass of a messenger landed on it from above, bouncing off with a wet squelch before continuing its path down.

Corpse rain was not an unfamiliar occurrence as casualties from the battle above dropped down the shaft. But more and more, they were showing signs of massive necrosis. Some fell while largely intact, a wing rotted away as if by some heinous disease. Others were masses of rotting flesh, occasionally leaving a trail of butterflies in their wake, glowing blue and orange.

Beaufort knew about those butterflies and knew to stay clear, directing the cult away from anywhere they spread. He extended his senses to look for dangerous conglomerations of the butterflies, discovering that the most powerful messengers had rallied in response to the threat. He left them to it, leading his cultists away from the butterflies and the gold-rank messengers to the side of the shaft.

"He's close," Beaufort muttered to himself.

Moments later, he felt Asano's aura vanish from above entirely. He stopped fighting, gesturing at his fellow gold-rankers to keep his location clear of enemies.

"You're already here, aren't you?" he asked, looking around at the dark.

A shadow on the wall opened blue and orange eyes.

"You have lost much in letting yourself become a monstrosity," Asano's icy voice said. "Your senses are too weak."

"Everything is a trade-off," Beaufort said. "The Builder does not look; he creates."

"He steals. He kills. How many have you killed in this world, Beaufort? What have you built?"

"I have helped build the future. A humble contribution to the Builder's grand design."

The cultists around Beaufort started to realise who was amongst them.

The gold-rankers held themselves together, although their auras were thick with barely restrained hatred. The silver-rankers did less well, few even launching themselves in Asano's direction. Beaufort's will spread through the cultists, freezing the attackers in their place. It didn't stop many from screaming hostility, roaring "DEFIER!" over and over.

"Defier?" Asano asked. "What happened to rejector?"

"You have done far more than reject the Builder's embrace, Asano. Many have fought against him, yet few have defied him so successfully as to deny that which he wills."

"I don't know about that name," Asano said, his voice softening from glacially hard. "I didn't love 'rejector,' but 'defier' feels like it would fit someone else out there better. Look for more of me kicking your boss back and forth across the cosmos, though; I'm not done with that prick."

Rage stirred through the cultists and Beaufort suppressed them again.

"We should kill him," one of the other gold-rankers said. "It would be worth our deaths."

"But would not achieve his," Beaufort warned. "The Lord Builder has warned me that Asano is well suited to fighting we who serve great astral beings. He does not want to use our own star seeds as weapons against us, but he can. There is a reason he sent others to kill him."

"They failed," the other gold-ranker growled.

"Of course," Beaufort said. "If even our Lord finds dealing with him an issue, what chance does some god playing pretend have? Asano, if you know my name, and have come this far without attacking, I can only assume you're aware that we need each other."

"I've been told."

"Then I would thank you to not provoke my people. It will only hurt you in the long run."

"Yeah. I did the same with Shako, and he killed me. On the other hand, here I am, and where is he? I'm told I should use you, Beaufort. That your intentions are honest. I'm of a mind to kill you anyway."

"Then do it or stop preening," Beaufort said. "In case you failed to notice, my people are holding off an army of these abominations so we can have this little chat."

"You can't see it," Jason said, "but my eyebrows shot right up at Erector Set Skeletor calling someone else an abomination. You're not wrong, though. If we're going to work together, we'll need somewhere to sit down and talk this through. Do you have some kind of redoubt my people can fight their way to?"

"That's why we're here: to lead your people back to the surviving locals. The messengers have overrun most of their territory and they're holding on to one last bastion."

"That all sounds like too much to explain here and now. I'll bring my people down, but they won't trust easily."

"More easily than mine trust you."

"But I can't make mine freeze if they get stroppy, so you don't get to provoke them the way I've been poking at you, understand?"

"Then I would ask that you reciprocate. From this point forward."

"Fair enough."

The blue and orange eyes closed and Beaufort sensed Asano's aura once again surge far above them.

70

HUMUNGOUS HAIRY HANDS

JASON STEPPED OUT OF A SHADE BODY THAT WAS STANDING ON THE expedition's main defensive platform. Ranged attackers were arrayed along the barricaded edge or firing through holes in the platform itself. Stone-shapers were repairing damage as the platform was attacked from below.

"Tactical Commander," Jason said through the voice chat's command channel.

"It's good that you're back," Miriam responded. "Your voice chat grew increasingly unreliable the further you went. How did it go?"

"I jabbed them to see if they'd yelp, but this Beaufort character seems to have them on a tight leash. I think we can operate alongside the cult so long as we keep a lid on our own people as well. I still don't like it, but if life were easy, we wouldn't need adventurers. If Knowledge thinks it's the way to go, I'm inclined to trust her on it."

"I heard you were disinclined to trust gods."

"Sure, but on one hand, we've got the most knowledgeable entity in the universe, who has every reason to want all these interdimensional invaders off her planet. On the other, we have what information we've gleaned from the regular messengers. The ones we've just confirmed are setting us up for a sudden but inevitable betrayal. In this instance, I'm going to pick the side that doesn't have an explicit reason to kill me personally. That I'm aware of."

"Then what's the move? Does the Builder cult have somewhere we can hole up?"

"They're claiming that they've shacked up with what's left of the locals, who I hope haven't all been converted to team Builder. They have some kind of secure holdout position where we can sit down and hash out what comes next."

"And you don't think it's a trap?"

"I think that's why Knowledge made an appearance. If she hadn't, I'd almost certainly think it's a trap. Too much of our information is based on what our enemies have told us."

"Then we'd best go get some information firsthand, don't you think?"

"I do," Jason said. "I'm just not sure how we get through this sea of elemental messengers without losing anyone."

"Leave that to me, Operations Commander. You've done your job and figured out what we need to do. Let me do mine and figure out how."

⸻

Jason was familiar with small group tactics from working with his team, but the coordination Miriam demonstrated over the entire expedition was well outside his expertise. With a fresh objective and a good sense of the obstacles ahead, Miriam developed a plan and set the expedition into motion.

It began by retrieving the supplies from the crawlers that she now chose to abandon. The supplies were distributed to various familiars and adventurers who could carry them with powers ranging from telekinetic shells to conjured cargo netting. Most important was the messenger device that was moved into Onslow's shell along with many of the adventurers.

Onslow's shell served as a miniature flying fortress, with a child-sized humanoid tortoise as its pilot, commander and adorable team mascot. The shell proved especially effective against the elemental messengers as the rune tortoise's powers were also elemental in nature. Clive had set up a potent magical array to absorb elemental energy, which proved to have numerous benefits.

The array fuelled Onslow's powers not just from absorbing messenger attacks but also by drawing elemental energy from the ambient magic. This allowed Onslow to fire off his abilities rapidly without drawing on Clive's mana, as well as creating a zone where elemental power was less prevalent in the ambient magic. This reduced the impact of the local magic on abilities and devices negatively affected by it.

Most importantly, absorbing elemental attacks made Onslow's shell a safe haven. Until and unless the gold-rank messengers arrived with the power to overload Clive's array, Onslow's shell was the most secure location within the expedition. Miriam didn't let that go to waste, having Onslow grow his shell to maximum size and loading it up with adventurers. This gave protection and mobility to ranged attackers and healers that would otherwise be fixed behind battlements, too vulnerable or immobile to reach key areas of the battle.

The next stage of Miriam's plan was to detach the defensive platforms from the walls and let them drop, adventurers still aboard. The platforms carved a rapid downward path, plunging the expedition into the heart of the enemy. The elemental messengers reacted swiftly and it was not long before the platforms were smashed out from under the adventurers.

This signalled the next phase of Miriam's plan, capitalising on their downward momentum with a wild blitz formation that gave up cohesion for a hard and fast assault, digging them further down through the enemy. This tactic only continued for a brief period, the messengers demonstrating the losses an incohesive assault accrued. Allowing it only long enough to make the most of their downward momentum, Miriam directed the expedition into a more regimented approach. Switching from an all-out pace to a controlled descent, the expedition assumed what Miriam called a drill formation.

The formation was cylindrical, like a drill bit, with the gold-rank adventurers forming the tip that bit into the messenger forces and allowed them to drill down. The frontline-suited silver-rankers formed the threads of the drill, spiralling around the more vulnerable adventurers in the middle. These were the researchers, backline healers and less mobile ranged attackers, along with the adventurers and familiars serving as porters.

Onslow was an exception, swiftly proving himself the most valuable member of the expedition. In addition to porting critical supplies, he was also a one-tortoise cavalry. Nigh impregnable and loaded up with adventurers otherwise unable to reach the frontline, Onslow's arrival at any point of the defensive line was a stabilising presence. He was also a way station for adventurers in need of healing, respite after draining their mana pool or rescue after their means of flight was compromised.

While Miriam's multi-stage strategy was proving effective, it was as true on Pallimustus as on Earth that no plan survived first contact with the enemy. Without the crawlers, every member of the expedition was required to fly or use an equivalent technique, and some fared better than others. Many with lesser mobility powers or reliant on external devices found their positions precarious. Shared flight like Sophie's Leaf on the Wind power were the least effective as they were often easily compromised, and if the one using the ability fell, anyone they were carrying fell too. Using familiars and summons as mounts was more effective as they could usually endure quite a beating.

While Onslow was the most obvious example of this, there were many others. Adventurers rode doubled up on griffins and other, less familiar flying creatures. One of the strangest was Stash in the form of a monster called a grippler. A grippler was a hulking creature whose bread-van-sized body was round and hairy with no discernible head or sensory organs. Six implausibly long arms, something like those of an orangutan but with too many elbows and oversized hands, were spaced evenly around the body in a ring. At the underside of the body, the hair concealed an orifice that blasted extremely unpleasant gas downwards to keep it aloft.

"Humphrey?" Jason asked through the team's voice channel.

"Yes, Jason?"

"Did your familiar turn into a headless hexapedal orangutan that flies using the power of farts?"

"What's an orangutan?"

Rick Geller's team had been adopted by Stash, more or less voluntarily, and he was flying them around the battlefield in mostly the directions they wanted. They weren't wildly comfortable with being held in Stash's humungous hairy hands like a toy, but it was proving effective. Only the team tank, Neil's friend Dustin Kettering, kept up his complaints beyond the early stages of the battle.

Stash's massive hand was gripped around the legs of Dustin's heavily armoured body. His torso, arms and head were covered in conjured diamond spikes variously stained bloody and scorched black from striking elemental messengers.

"I am not—"

Dustin was interrupted as Stash brought him down like a spiked mace on a messenger.

"—A BLOODY MELEE WEAPON!"

"Just bear with it," Rick's sister, Phoebe, told him. "You've taken out more of them than any of us."

"It's alright for you," Dustin shot back. "He isn't... oh no..."

Stash smashed Dustin and Rick together like a child playing with toys, several messengers caught between them. Dustin's weight and spike provided crushing force while, on the other end, Rick had set his spear against Stash's hand and impaled the messengers with the impact.

"Good job, Stash," Rick said happily.

"This is a pile of heidel shi—"

Dustin was cut off again as he was used to hammer a sturdy metal-type messenger like a recalcitrant nail. The rapid blows proved Dustin the sturdier, although he did have to conjure fresh spikes alongside swearing profusely at the gas Stash had waved him through.

Phoebe was a pugilist, like a more damage-oriented version of Sophie. She was using one of Stash's hands as a platform, the familiar holding his palm flat for her to launch from, strike multiple enemies and return. She couldn't fly, but pinballing between foes was very much in her wheelhouse.

"Stash, sweetie," she asked. "Could you pop me over to see Dusty for a little bit?"

Stash stopped waving Dustin around and brought the hands holding them together so they could be face to face. Phoebe was standing on an open palm while Dustin was still tightly gripped.

"Dusty, is it really that bad?" she asked.

"Yes!"

"Oh, come now," she said and tugged off his helmet. She planted a gentle kiss on his cheek before pushing his helmet back down as his face turned red.

"Thank you, Stash, dear," she said.

"Wait—" Dustin yelped before resuming semi-voluntary mace duty.

"What was that?" Phoebe's brother yelled in her direction, not bothering with voice chat.

"I thought he deserved a little reward," Phoebe told him. "He's doing very well."

"Do you know what that's going to do to team cohesion?" Rick asked.

"Oh, we don't fraternise between team members?" Rick's fiancée, Hannah, said. "I'll have to remember that."

"What? No, that's not... she's my sister... oh crap."

Along with familiars like Onslow and Stash, summons were proving their worth. Not just mounts and supply transit, their expendability made them valuable frontline fighters. The aerial nature of combat meant that not all summons were of use, however. Neither Farrah's magma elemental nor Gary's forge golem could fly, so the adventurers hadn't summoned them.

A summon that was proving effective was a giant insect that carried both people and supplies inside its hollow carapace, much like Onslow. It was faster than the rune tortoise but not as resilient, lacking Onslow's hard shell and the protection of Clive's magical array. For this reason, it served to secure the people in the middle of the formation instead of running around the frontline, and the supplies it carried were less critical.

Neil's chrysalis golem couldn't fly any more than Farrah or Gary, but he had summoned it early in the battle anyway, when the expedition was still on the platform. He'd gotten some odd looks from other adventurers when he directed it to walk off the platform where it immediately plunged into the enemy and out of sight.

Ability: [Chrysalis Golem] (Growth)

- Summoning.
- Cost: Very high mana.
- Cooldown: 6 hours.

- Current rank: Silver 4 (78%).

- Effect (iron): Summons a chrysalis golem.

- Effect (bronze): Shoots spikes while in the chrysalis state.

. . .

- Effect (silver): Chrysalis state resolves more quickly and the resulting form is better adapted to the environment.

The fundamental ability of a chrysalis golem was to enter a near-indestructible chrysalis state after suffering critical damage. This hadn't taken long as the messengers pounded on the massive weight barrelling through them.

In its chrysalis state, the golem was a large and mostly inert lump of crystal that shrugged off attacks as it continued bowling messengers out of its path. Its singular activity was to rapid-fire crystal spears in every direction like an explosive gemstone echidna. When the golem emerged from the chrysalis, it took a new form shaped in reaction to the attacks it had endured. As of silver rank, it was also much better at adapting to the environment it was in.

Silver rank also reduced the gestating time for the post-chrysalis state, and the result was far more well-defined than the crude giant it had been. It vaguely held the appearance of an elemental messenger, except made of diamonds and even larger, some twenty-five feet tall with a massive wingspan. It also didn't have humanoid arms and legs, instead boasting mantis-like bladed limbs. Those limbs, along with diamond-sharp wings, slashed savagely at the messengers, often sending them tumbling with their own wings sheared off.

The messengers responded to the golem now ascending towards the expedition with savage brutality that didn't actually accomplish very much. The problem with their narrow variety of attack forms was that they were easier to adapt to, and the golem had added their technological and biological distinctiveness to its own.

Stone spears and metal limbs shattered the golem's crystal surface, scattering shards that did not fall away but swarmed like angry hornets. Clouds of razor-sharp crystal swept over the messengers, metal and earth types largely unaffected, but others found their wings and flesh flayed away. The golem's missing crystal regrew swiftly, restoring it to wholeness.

The golem ignored fire and magma attacks entirely as they splashed harmlessly off it. The only effect was a red glow that built within the golem until it was shining bright red. Eventually, the golem sent that energy shooting off, striking a cluster of the sturdier messengers, earth bodies exploding and metal bodies melting.

As domineering as the golem was, the messengers proved resistance was not entirely futile. For all that the golem had adapted to their attacks, the sheer weight of numbers was overwhelming as it fought its way back to the expedition. The messengers weren't smart, but they could tell the difference between attacks that worked and ones that didn't. The fire and magma types backed off, leaving the more effective earth and metal types to hammer at it.

These messengers were largely impervious to the shard swarms and their attacks did do damage, even if it was rapidly repaired. Enough blows in rapid succession meant the damage accumulated faster than it could be recovered. One of the golem's limbs was lost, then a second. Damage building up on the wings slowed it down until it was struggling to stay aloft.

Seeing that the golem was on the verge of falling, the messengers lunged in for a final attack with renewed vigour. A bubble-shaped barrier snapped into place and exploded outward, flinging the attacking messengers into their fellows, all tumbling in clusters of tangled wings and limbs.

Ability: [Burst Shield] (Shield)

- Special ability (recovery, retribution).
- Cost: Moderate mana.
- Cooldown: 20 seconds.

- Current rank: Silver 5 (38%).

- Effect (iron): Create a short-lived shield that negates an incoming attack and explodes out, knocking back nearby enemies and inflicting concussive damage. High-damage attacks of silver rank or higher may not be entirely negated.

- Effect (bronze): Inflicts [Vibrant Echo] on anyone affected by the blast.

- Effect (silver): Inflicts [Slow Learner] on anyone affected by the blast.

- [Vibrant Echo] (affliction, damage-over-time, magic, stacking): Inflicts ongoing resonating-force damage.

- [Slow Learner] (affliction, magic, stacking): Retribution damage you suffer is increased. Attacking a barrier while subject to this affliction extends the duration of the barrier and allows it to block an additional attack. Additional instances have a cumulative effect.

Onslow drifted low in the formation as Neil shot out his barrier and armour abilities to shield the golem, barely visibly through the throng of messengers. Belinda aided him by duplicating and resetting his powers, as Neil did himself using his power-resetting magical tattoo.

Miriam directed other adventurers to help; she had sensed the effectiveness of the golem and soon the Slow Learner affliction of Neil's ability proved its value. Repeated attacks against his barriers extended their duration and let them block more attacks until the messengers themselves were keeping them perpetually up while the golem regrew the damage it had suffered. The messengers might have the intellect to realise what attacks did and didn't work, but analysing the effects of an essence ability was beyond the freshly birthed silver-rank variants.

"I love stupid people," Neil said happily as the golem fought clear of the throng to join the expedition.

"No you don't," Belinda pointed out.

"You're right," Neil said. "Let's kill them all."

71

ECHOES OF THE DEAD

WHILE MANY OF THE ADVENTURERS EXCELLED USING FAMILIARS, SUMMONS and flight powers as platforms from which to battle the messengers, not all fared as well. The most vulnerable were those relying on external flight devices. Some were fine, usually those with the most elaborate and expensive devices. Former Hurricane Princess Zara rode a two-headed Pegasus made of sapphires that not only provided transport but added to her combat power.

Zara specialised in wide-area ranged attacks, so having her construct mount cracking heads with its hooves and biting with its twin heads was useful. It even shot sapphire feathers from its wings that punched through flesh and bone like a railgun, or struck bodies of stone and sent spiderweb cracks spreading through them.

Zara's exceptional flying construct was the exception, a precious item she had inherited from her Aunt Vesper. Even a princess from one of the most powerful nations on the planet was lucky to have it; most of the flight devices were not as impressive.

One of the more popular flying tools in Yaresh was a cloud that one person could fly around on. Those used by the expedition were based on metal and air, rather than water and air, functioning something like magical nanoswarms. The versions that relied on water magic were not brought along, under the assumption that they would fail quite quickly.

The elemental energy of the local magic still seeped into them, but their metal makeup was compatible with that power.

At first, it went well; the local magic even supercharged the performance of the metal and air clouds. But as that power built up, it became more than the devices could handle. Overcharged with elemental energy, devices started failing in various ways. Most commonly, they just dispersed, dropping their passengers as the tiny fragments of metal scattered. Other clouds did the same, but the fragments combusted, burning up in a shower of sparks. A handful behaved extremely oddly and collected together in a swarm that dove down into the enemy, attacking any messenger they passed over. This wasn't effective, since they were tiny bits of rounded metal that couldn't do much more than get in the messenger's eyes. It was far from worth all those clouds dumping their riders.

The expedition reacted swiftly when an adventurer lost their ride. Miriam had anticipated this from the moment she ordered the crawlers left behind and had preparations in place. Falling adventurers were snagged up with a variety of powers, from swooping familiars to anyone who could bring others along on a teleport. Shade bodies appeared out of nowhere to turn into personal flight devices, although this was a last resort. Shade's vehicle forms were not built for the rigours of combat and a few rescues had false starts as a flying motorcycle or personal flight suit was destroyed by a messenger attack.

Miriam's drill formation proved effective but grew increasingly shaky as they descended through the messengers pressing endlessly on all sides. Each flight device that failed, each adventurer that had a flying summons destroyed out from under them was a fresh gap in the defences.

Casualties were healed up and sent back to the line, but there was inexorable attrition. They had yet to suffer any deaths, but some injuries were too severe to heal quickly without essence abilities that required ritual magic to use. Neil had an essence ability, but he had neither the time nor the space to use it. Onslow's shell was normally a good space for such magic, but it was crowded with adventurers and being rocked by continuous assaults. Onslow's defences were holding, but it was not an environment conducive to careful and precise ritual casting. There was a reason that Clive's use of combat rituals was so unusual.

Despite the attrition, the expedition was proving the power of guild-level elite adventurers. Strategy, intelligence and preparation paid off as they withstood an army that would have swarmed across the surface world like the wrath of a vengeful god. The messengers, while numerous and powerful, were also thoughtless, reckless and unskilled, most freshly spawned.

The elemental messengers simply weren't the threat that regular messengers were. Aside from the gold-rankers being smart enough to stay away, they lacked any sign of coordination, strategy, tactics, or even self-preservation. Trained and experienced adventurers could not only do better, they could also exploit those weaknesses to maximum effect. The enemy lacked the variety of powers that regular messengers possessed, let alone essence users.

Versatility was what made well-trained essence users the most powerful force at any given rank. As for the elemental messengers, a stream of fire versus a cone of fire, or a stone spear versus a metal one did not make for a complex mixture of attacks. It was so predictable that the expedition had brought a massive supply of potions and tools tailored to counter and resist exactly those attacks. It was this preparation, more than anything else, that had prevented any deaths in the face of so many enemies.

While the adventurers showed their worth, the weight of numbers remained an inescapable fact. And while the expedition held almost every advantage, that didn't make the messengers weak. Elemental energy had supercharged their powers and the tools and potions of the adventurers wouldn't hold out forever. Mana pools dwindled and exhaustion crept in, even silver-rank stamina lasting only so long.

"We're lucky they still haven't committed their gold-rankers," Miriam said over the command channel.

"I can sense them," Amos responded. Miriam had looped him in as his superior senses made him the best early warning system they had.

"Are they showing signs of moving to attack?" Miriam asked.

"They are still working to contain Asano's butterflies," Amos reported. "With enemies so tightly packed, they are extremely hard to suppress."

"They are suppressing them, though?"

"Yes."

"Perhaps we should have included a traditional affliction specialist after all," Miriam said. "But even our most pessimistic projections never predicted numbers like these."

"Their gold-rankers are thinning out their own numbers for us," Amos pointed out. "Not enough to practically diminish the whole, but there are areas where their numbers are less dense now. We should aim to pass through those areas they've already culled themselves."

"We don't want to go close enough to tempt the gold-rankers into an attack," Miriam said.

"They're following the spread of the butterflies," Amos said. "I can direct us towards an area they've moved on from."

"Then please do."

Both the Builder cult and the expedition were battered and spent by the time they came face to face. The tension between them almost led to disaster as they paused, each ready for confrontation. The ceaseless torrent of messengers did not care for the tension of the would-be allies and continued their attacks unabated. The defensive lines of both groups threatened to collapse, pushing the two groups almost back to back.

The adventurers and the cultists both had cards left up their sleeves, their last resorts held back for emergencies. Long cooldown powers, potent abilities that exhausted most of what mana they had left. For a blazing moment, the messengers were the ones overwhelmed. It was enough pushback for the expedition and the cultists to reform their lines and achieve a reluctant but functional joint formation.

The final stretch down the shaft had the cultists and especially the expedition all but spent. It was the time for high-endurance combatants to shine, such as Jason and Sophie. After fighting through countless enemies, they had grown stronger instead of weaker. With boons stacked high, they rivalled some of the gold-rankers for raw power and took on core defensive roles in the formation.

Sophie was all but invisible, a streak of motion that appeared only to intercept an attack and hit back far harder than she normally could. She fended off attacks with her hands, feet, shins and forearms.

"Did I just I just see you block a fireball with a headbutt?" Jason asked.

"Shut up and fight!"

"Ooh, strict nanny."

"Jason!"

"Sorry, Hump."

Jason's speed was also blinding, although his jerky pinball movement was crude next to Sophie's graceful flow. He also intercepted attacks, but instead of negating them, he just took the hits. A few were blocked by a pair of shields generated by orbs borrowed from Gordon, but many more impaled, lacerated, burned or even decapitated him. He burned through life force, only to draw even more from the enemies. Jason's Feast of Blood power drained all enemies in a wide area, and the messengers filled the space around the expedition like bricks in a wall.

More than a few of the cultists were keeping an eye on Jason as he fought. Beaufort ignored them so long as their combat performance didn't suffer, although even he was sometimes taken aback. When something bounced off him, he grabbed it, discovering it was Jason's severed head. He looked around to see Jason still fighting, his hood masking if he had a replacement head or was simply still fighting without it.

He watched Jason suck the life out of a whole raft of messengers. The vibrant red of their life force was draining into Jason in so many streams that it looked like a tide of blood. The messengers were left as withered husks and fell out of the air, more moving in to replace them immediately.

Beaufort tossed the head aside and went back to fighting.

Jason and Sophie weren't alone in growing stronger rather than weaker over the course of the battle. For all that they approached gold-rank performance in certain metrics, neither held a candle to Team Moon's Edge's berserker, Alice. She was just as buffed as Jason and Sophie, but at a gold-rank baseline, rather than silver. She was less a combatant at that point than a living zone of annihilation at the front of the formation.

Arabelle Remore was also quite powerful, floating by herself, surrounded by massive jars. Alternately filled with red life force and blue mana, she seemed isolated and vulnerable, which was part of the trap. Any messengers who came close found their life force and mana yanked out of them and added to the jars.

Throughout the battle, Arabelle had been accumulating vast amounts of life force and mana. She spent them in massive quantities, showering the expedition with mass healing and the enemies in crippling medical maledictions. Their silver-rank, largely elemental bodies should have been immune to them, but Arabelle didn't care about affliction immunity any more than Jason did.

Like many adventurers, especially from Vitesse, Arabelle dabbled in different roles while maintaining her position as a healer. She was not an affliction specialist and only had a couple of grim powers as trump cards. Doing anything more with her afflictions would take someone else, and

Jason was happy to oblige. He drained all the toxins and diseases Arabelle bestowed, leaving transcendent damage in their place.

Battling their way down the shaft, the uneasy allies formed a grudging acceptance of one another. That acceptance was heavily reliant on the leadership of both sides, each with their reasons to want the other dead. Every adventurer knew that the cultists were either invaders from another universe or, worse, traitors who had sided with them. They were all disciplined, but Miriam still gave a few stern reminders of the situation in which they found themselves. As for the cultists, Beaufort's iron control was the only reason many of them weren't shrieking their hatred and fear at Jason.

The shaft ended in an underground chamber that seemed impossibly vast. Only his ability to see through the dark allowed Jason to see across the kilometres of width and depth as the group descended through a vast hole in the roof. His amazement was undercut by a pervasive stench of death that seemed to infest even the magic around them.

The elemental aspects of the ambient magic around them had grown consistently stronger as the expedition made its way down from the surface. It had grown to surround them oppressively, like being seated between two sumo wrestlers on a domestic economy flight. But, on entering that vast chamber, all that was pushed aside. Like a river full of corpses flooding over an embankment, death washed over everything. Aura and magical senses alike were muted, quashed by a lifeless dread.

Most adventurers of silver and especially gold rank had seen horrors. The kind of threats that produced mass civilian casualties were the most important for adventurers to confront. Whole towns wiped out by plague zombies, vampires feeding on herds of livestock and sending them on a rampage as hideous ghouls. The lingering energy of death in this chamber dwarfed all of that.

Very few members of the group were unaffected; even the cultists that had seen it before. Jason and Farrah were able to endure it the best after their experiences on Earth. The city of Makassar had seen hundreds of thousands die, then raised up using foul necromancy. They had spent days wading through the dead, returning the unliving mockeries to rest. The result of infighting between the factions of Earth, this had been a critical point for Jason. His time on Earth had already made him harder, but that was the beginning of his descent into savagery and the edge of madness.

"Do not linger at the top of the shaft," Beaufort warned, driving the group down into the open space. "The messengers won't follow into the heart of the chamber."

True to his word, the messengers swept out of the shaft like a swarm of insects and turned off in the direction of the nearest wall. They streamed out of the shaft, like a waterfall that eventually ended. As if the expedition no longer existed, they hurried off. Jason watched them vanish into a massive hole torn into the wall of the chamber, which was otherwise covered in buildings carved into the rock. The massive hole was far from the only damage, but Jason didn't look further as Beaufort addressed the entire group.

"They will not tarry here," Beaufort said, "and they are right not to. We must also move with haste, but avoid getting close to anything. We will move through the air, staying clear of the roof and the walls until we reach the far side. Most of all, stay high above the ground."

Beaufort led them in the opposite direction from where the messengers went and towards the furthest end of the chamber. As they moved, Jason continued to examine their new surroundings. It was an abandoned city, with buildings rising from the floor, hanging from the ceiling and carved into the walls. Signs of destruction were everywhere, with wall buildings caved in, floor buildings collapsed and the roof buildings fallen to the ground below. Holes pockmarked every surface, each large enough to drive a small car through. The ground was covered in some kind of organic substance, lifeless and inert.

"This is the largest chamber of this underground realm," Beaufort explained as he led the group on. "It was the home to the vast majority of the brightheart smoulders. Now there is nothing but the echoes of the dead. The messengers avoid this place, even withdrawing the roots of their foul tree. Without their wariness of this chamber, we would not have lasted as long as we have."

"I'd like to hear more about that tree," Jason said. "I already suspected…"

He trailed off and turned to look behind them.

"Beware behind," Amos said, beating him to the punch.

Soon the others sensed the spectral entities that had followed them, having emerged from the roof buildings closest to the shaft. Many had dived in amongst the messengers who scattered like panicked birds, a stark contrast to their previous implacable behaviour. Others came for the expedition and their reluctant cultist allies. Miriam swiftly deployed those with effective powers to intercept, Jason included. The entities were weak, mostly iron and bronze rank, with a scant few silvers, and were dealt with swiftly enough. The expedition continued on.

"Most things in this chamber have little power," Beaufort explained, "and lack a physical form. That is not always the case, however, and the danger of death, twisted to wretched purpose, is underestimated at your peril. I can promise you that."

Beaufort continued to lead them on, staying well away from the buildings above and below. Jason occasionally spotted movement, seeing various shapes meandering about. Some looked like messengers, stumbling like zombies. Others were plodding, shapeless forms like sluggish earth elementals. All had auras stained by death.

Reaching the far side, Beaufort led them towards a circular gate set midway up the side of the chamber. It was built into the wall, unlike the ragged hole the messengers had used. It was massive, large enough to pass an airship through, and blocked by an enormous stone roller. More normal-sized double doors were set into the middle of the roller, each constructed of metal and etched with protective sigils. The buildings around the gate had all been caved in, the destruction too thorough to have been anything but methodical.

"We make sure nothing gets too close to the gate," Beaufort explained. "It's an ongoing effort."

"Why is the gate so high in the wall?" Miriam asked.

"This was for flying vehicles and festival parades, so I'm told," Beaufort said. "The doors are new. The ground-level entrance to the next chamber is too much of a risk."

A half dozen guards stood in alcoves to either side of the doors. The alcove on one side held cultists that looked normal but whose auras reeked of the Builder's magic. On the other side were smoulders, but not like those Jason had seen before. They appeared fairly normal for their kind, stocky with dark skin and brightly glowing eyes. Their exposed skin showed runic markings that glowed a little more than normal, closer to that of the runic people, although that wasn't unheard of. Smoulders and the runic were quite similar, with their dark skin and glowing features, much as humans and celestines were identical in most visible regards. Seeing three smoulders with those features all at once was a little odd.

More than their physical features, it was their auras that differentiated these smoulders from the norm. They each had strong magic, but not that of essence users. These people were imbued with elemental power, much like what the expedition had been sensing all the way down the shaft. In these people, though, it was less erratic, cleaner and more stable.

Beaufort moved out ahead, sharing a look with one of the smoulder guards.

"We wondered if you would return at all," the guard said. "The enemy you spoke of is amongst these people?"

"He is," Beaufort said.

"Then you had best deliver him."

The red runes on the guard's skin glowed brighter for a moment and the carved sigils on the doors glowed at the same time. Both runes and sigils faded and the doors swung open.

72

CITADEL

THE SENSE OF DEATH FROM THE PREVIOUS CHAMBER VANISHED THE moment the expedition passed through the double doors set into the giant gate. The pervasive elemental influence on the ambient magic snapped back into place so sharply that Jason doubted it was natural. His suspicions were only raised by the elemental power feeling a lot more stable than it had in the shaft. He reached out to Clive through voice chat with an idea.

"Can't say," Clive responded. "There are a lot of variables I'd have to check. Definitely not with a regular portal, but your soul portal... maybe."

The arrival of a combined force of adventurers and Builder cultists did not, unsurprisingly, go unremarked. A defensive squadron rose up to meet them, mostly travelling on flat floating rocks. As Beaufort worked to calm a visibly agitated defence commander, Jason and the other expedition members took in the last bastion of the brightheart smoulders.

While not as vast as the one they had just left, the chamber was still implausibly large and, to Jason's sensibilities, more impressive. Buildings were again carved into the walls but not from the ceiling and floor, with a significant exception. Massive pillars rose from the floor and descended from the ceiling to suspend a massive citadel in the very centre of the chamber.

The pillars themselves were some of the largest towers Jason had ever seen, but they weren't just solid supporting posts. The windows and balconies showed that the pillars were occupied spaces. As they were not solid, Jason doubted they could hold the weight of the massive citadel without some kind of magic. It could be enchantment, but he suspected the whole chamber had been carved out of some high-rank magical stone. Normally, that would ping his magical senses, but the ambient elemental magic blanketed everything.

The citadel itself was a confusing mess of different design elements. It looked like someone had taken sculptures, frescoes and buildings in a dozen clashing architectural styles and attempted to meld them together with magic. Badly. There was gothic statuary, time-worn crenellations and scattered murals with no cohesive theme. Some looked like defensive measures that were uselessly suspended in the air, while other parts were artistic and without practical purpose.

"Can you make any sense of this design?" Jason asked Miriam. They were standing at the front of the expedition atop Onslow's shell, flanked by their respective teams.

"I'm recognising elements of architectural designs I know," Humphrey said. "Old, though. Historical buildings more than anything modern."

"Valetta, you're an architect," Miriam said. "What do you make of it?"

"Master Geller is correct," Miriam's teammate said. "This is an amalgam of design elements from the surface, but all centuries out of favour. Look at the pillars. They reflect the buildings we saw in the previous chamber and are likely a reflection of the architectural style of the people that dwell here. The architectural abomination in the middle is almost certainly the result of a dimensional prefabrication disaster."

"Which is what, exactly?" Miriam asked.

"A dimensional accident," Clive said. "I've never seen a building like this in person, but I've seen recordings. Always in extreme environments."

"I think it's safe to call this massive underground chamber full of elemental power an extreme environment," Neil said.

"There is a construction technique," Valetta explained, "for establishing buildings in extreme environments. Underwater is the most common."

"Like that village under Sky Scar Lake, near Greenstone," Clive said. "That was modest compared to this massive building, but they still probably portalled in materials rather than carting them down through the water."

"For more involved builds and more extreme environments," Valetta continued, "building sections are pre-fabricated for rapid assembly. Then they're brought to the location in dimensional spaces or through portals."

"But some extreme environments," Belinda said, gesturing at the space around them, "aren't friendly to dimension magic."

"Precisely," Valetta said. "If the dimensional magic goes wrong in just the right way, you get something like this."

"Most likely what the first smoulders to arrive here brought with them," Miriam said.

The conversation ended as Beaufort returned.

"We're heading in," he said. "Most members of our groups will be placed in one of the ready areas used for quick mobilisation. I'll be taking your leadership to meet with that of the brightheart smoulders right away."

The group landed on a set of three clustered balconies, none individually large enough for the whole group. The expedition went to one and the cult to a second. Beaufort and the expedition leadership, Miriam, Jason and Clive, landed on the third. The larger groups were escorted into the citadel by wary guards while the leaders were guided by just one, a smoulder named Marla.

Jason got a close-up look at more brightheart smoulders as they moved towards the upper levels of the citadel. Normal smoulders were all fire-aspected, their eyes and often hair reflecting this. Their skin markings normally stayed subdued. All of that was prone to change with essences and racial gifts, and the brighthearts all demonstrated this to some degree.

The skin of the brighthearts remained the traditional obsidian black while their other features changed with elemental affinity. Iron and ash were usually shades of dull grey, while fire and magma glowed brightly. Fire aspects were the most common, although they were also the most likely to have their skin markings lit up.

Marla seemed to have a less common affinity, her aura radiating strong metal energy while her characteristic features glowed red-orange. That was striking enough on her eyes and skin markings, but the effect on her hair was flabbergasting. In a world where magic made everyone beautiful, she was one of those that truly stood apart, like Sophie, Rufus and Zara.

Marla led Jason and the others towards the upper reaches of the citadel. Their route was far from direct, but Jason didn't think they were getting the run-around. The issue was that the citadel's interior was just as bizarre as the outside, if not more so. Corridors zigzagged, the floors awkwardly undulating instead of staying flat. Stairwells led up and back down again without any access to other levels.

The doors were eclectic in design with some doorways simply empty, revealing what was on the other side. Most of the rooms were relatively ordinary, although many had slightly distorted measurements giving them an unnerving optical illusion quality. One room was just a slanted shaft with a rail for some kind of transport set into the wall.

"You must have all manner of stone-shapers down here," Clive said. "Why haven't you fixed this distorted building?"

"This underground realm is called Cardinas," Marla explained as they walked. "This citadel was formed by accident when our ancestors first descended to the natural array. It has been a monument to their early efforts, serving as a museum and school. We also hold government in the upper levels, which is where we are going. Until this crisis, it hadn't served as a residence in centuries."

"What kind of government do you have?" Jason asked.

"We had a ruling council of nine," Marla said. "Three were elected from the gold-rankers, three from the normal-rankers and three from the guilds. Now only Lorenn remains, the others having sacrificed everything to keep the rest of us alive. She is the last, and the burden lies heavy. I ask that you address her as Councilwoman Lorenn or just Councilwoman."

"I'm sorry to ask such a grim question," Miriam said, "but how many of your people are left?"

"Fewer than ten thousand now. Less than one in twenty of what we had before the messengers came, but even this few we struggle to feed. Aside from the citadel chamber, we have only two growth halls remaining. The growth halls are where we grow our food and purify the air. Most of our remaining citizens have advanced to iron rank and can sustain themselves on elements other than air. Most of the others died as our remaining growth halls were overtaxed and the air grew too thin. The children and the elderly were the first to…"

"Don't," Miriam said in half a sob. "I am sorry for asking such a thing."

Jason paled at the thought of watching thousands die as the air grew too thin, most of the population gasping desperately through their final moments. For all the horrors Jason had been through, he realised these people were going through worse. A society without children was a society without hope.

"Many of the children live still," Marla said. "We've moved them to the growth chambers where the air is strongest."

Unbreathable air was no impediment to the expedition members who were all silver-rank and above. The air underground would have killed them long before they reached the bottom of the shaft otherwise.

"If most of our people hadn't died," Marla continued, "we would have starved by now. We are rationing heavily, but we've already seen the first starvation deaths. We can't sustain ourselves on spirit coins like you surface people, and they can't be created from the magic here anyway. We grow moss, fungus and other plants that thrive on the heat of magma vents. They take on elemental properties that sustain us very well. Or did, when we had enough growth halls for all. But those were the places the messenger tree claimed first."

Jason had more questions about the tree but couldn't bring himself to ask. The three adventurers all had pained expressions, shoulders tensing and fists balling. Beaufort was fine. It reminded Jason that the cultist had the same name as Thadwick Mercer's father. Beaufort Mercer wasn't a villain like his namesake or his son, although the trio did share a significant deficit of empathy.

Marla led them to a large room where a horseshoe-shaped conference desk curved around a model that floated in the air. It looked to be made of coloured sand that Jason realised must depict the full underground realm. It was a surprisingly vast network of chambers and tunnels, although most of the map was obscured by a green glow. The largest chamber, which showed the shaft leading out through the top, was shrouded in darkness. One small chamber stood out, having a shifting glow of warm colours, reds, oranges and yellows. The only areas of the map not obscured were at one end. One chamber had a very clear depiction of the citadel, while two chambers branched off from it.

Waiting for the group was a weary-looking brightheart with the washed-out markings of an ash type. Having come close enough to sense a few of the smoulder now, Jason could tell them apart with his magical senses. The differences were much like those between the elemental messengers, although the comparison only went so far. The elemental messengers felt corrupted and twisted while, in the brightheart, that power felt natural and balanced. The woman got up from where she had been sitting at the desk, going over lists spread out in front of her.

"I am Lorenn," she said as she moved around the long desk to greet them. "You, as I understand it, are Beaufort's enemies."

She paused, sensing something, and narrowed hostile eyes on Jason. "You're like them," she accused.

"In some ways," Jason said, realising she meant that he shared the gestalt nature of the messengers. "But, in some ways, so are you."

Lorenn gave him a long look, their eyes locked as no one said anything. Finally, she nodded.

"They are a mockery of what we are," she said. "I suppose they are a mockery of what you are as well. I was not expecting the leadership of the group Beaufort was so insistent on retrieving to have more silver-rankers than gold. Although he assures us you are dangerous, I hope you understand I was hoping for more."

"I won't bother trying to convince you with words," Jason told her. "You'll see our actions soon enough. My name is Jason Asano, operations commander for this expedition. This is my tactical commander, Miriam Vance, and our magical expert, Clive Standish."

"Do not underestimate Asano or Standish," Beaufort told her. "They may be silver rank but they were giving the Builder black eyes at iron and bronze rank. The surface messengers have marked them both as personal threats as well."

"Wait, what?" Clive asked. "Since when do the messengers know me by name?"

"Clive, you're the bloke neck-deep in messenger magic with that study trove," Jason pointed out. "You know more about the messenger device than they'd like and we didn't clear out all the spies until right before we left."

"Oh, great," Clive said.

"So long as you can do something about the elemental messengers," Lorenn said, "I don't care what you are."

"Dealing with them is why we're here," Miriam said.

"No," Clive disagreed. "It's not. We came here because the natural array has become unstable. Councilwoman Lorenn, I presume you are aware that the core aspect of your people's predicament is the disruption of the natural array by the messengers."

"Yes," she said. "This citadel chamber is the site of the echo array, a powerful artefact that allows us to affect the array. We have been using the echo array to fight the corruption of the natural array by the messengers and their tree, but we have only been able to slow it, not stop it."

"We know little," Clive continued. "Most of our information on your people is just guesswork. One of those guesses is that the natural array is central to your civilisation, and the power that transformed your ancestors."

"That is an accurate assessment," Lorenn told him.

"At the risk of being insensitive," Clive told her, "are you aware that the natural array is likely beyond salvaging?"

"It would be strange to come back from what has happened," Lorenn said. "We have accepted that with our minds, but doing so with our hearts is more difficult. The array has been the centre of our society from the beginning. Cardinas, our civilisation, is only possible because of it. It is responsible for not just who we are but what we are. For many of our people, accepting its loss will be one source of despair too many. But the truth is, it is lost, whether we accept that or not."

"Most likely," Clive said.

"To be open and honest," Jason said, "we are here to neutralise the threat of the natural array. The odds of doing that by restoring it to its original condition are close enough to nil as to make no difference. We have forged something of an uneasy alliance with the messengers—the regular ones on the surface, not the ones you have here. Like the Builder cult, they are our enemies. We hope that the cultists are more honest with their dealings, though, as we know the messengers are working against us for their own ends."

"The messengers want to turn your array into something called a soul forge," Clive said. "They cannot do it alone as this place corrupts them."

"So they struck a false bargain with us," Jason said. "Send us here with a device they claim will stabilise the array. We believe it will finish the job the messengers started when they first came here and change the array into a soul forge."

"Or that's the intention," Clive said. "They may have gotten this attempt as wrong as the first."

"But if it does work, they intend to take it somehow," Jason said. "Then kill me and probably leave the rest of you to your fates."

"Why you?" Lorenn asked.

"Let's sit," Jason said. "We can introduce ourselves and explain everything from the beginning. And then we would like to hear about things from your end."

He glanced at Beaufort.

"Both of your ends."

73

THE IMPOSSIBLE

JASON, CLIVE AND MIRIAM SAT IN THE COUNCIL CHAMBER WITH Beaufort and the two brighthearts, Lorenn and Marla. The adventurers explained the Builder invasion, the messenger invasion and the expedition. Some of it Lorenn had already learned from Beaufort, although it was clear his explanation had been coloured differently in certain parts.

Beaufort then took his turn to recount the cult's story. It amounted to invading Cardinas but having no interest in the natural array. Instead, they fought their way into the local astral space, which was a rather unique one. Where other portal effects were disrupted by the array, the astral space aperture was extremely solid. Clive postulated that the astral space had formed alongside the array and could be the key to understanding how to stabilise it.

"I'm going to need to study that astral space," he said. "Trying anything without understanding how it relates to the array would be foolhardy. The failure to do so may be what went wrong with the messenger's attempts to hijack the array in the first place."

"That won't be easy," Lorenn said. "The astral space aperture is unclaimed by the messenger tree, which cannot tolerate its power, but we are cut off from it."

Marla stood up and moved around the horseshoe desk to the floating model of Cardinas in the middle. She pointed out the chamber that glowed with shifting red, yellow and orange light.

"This is the astral space chamber. You see how it's cut off from us by messenger-held territory but remains unclaimed. The energy there repels the messenger tree somehow. We don't know much else as we only have access to this projection, created by the echo array. If the chamber falls, it will be marked by the green, which represents the tree's domain."

Beaufort continued his story. The cult had been fighting for access to the astral space and the arrival of the messengers had been their opportunity. The brighthearts had been scrambling to react to a second incursion and the messengers quickly became the priority. The natural array was sacred to the brighthearts, and while the cult had ignored it, the messengers aimed straight for it. The brighthearts refocused their defenders on the messengers and the cultists were able to make their way into the astral space and seal it off from the inside.

"Our plan from this point was the usual," Beaufort explained. "Use our astral magic to sever the astral space from this universe so the Builder could claim it. It didn't work. The astral space proved a little too unique and our astral magic didn't work."

"Didn't you have people capable of adapting it?" Clive asked.

"Our people can use the magic," Beaufort said, "but our magic users have only so much expertise. Much of the magic required is built into the artificial components of their bodies. They don't fully understand the magic they're using."

Clive let out an exasperated groan.

"Mr Standish," Miriam said. "I would appreciate it if you didn't bemoan a lack of competence in our enemies."

"I'm just so sick of it," Clive complained as he ran his hands over his face. "Why is everyone so stupid?"

"That's a little hurtful," Jason said.

"I'm just saying that if you're going to use magic, the fundamental energy of the cosmos that is the most powerful and therefore dangerous thing there is, then maybe you should learn how it works before sticking your hand in it and wiggling about."

"We were trying," Beaufort said defensively. "We were still working on how to adapt the magic when you, Asano, convinced the Builder to leave this world and take no further astral spaces. We were trapped underground and couldn't get back to a fortress city on the surface, so we were left stranded."

Lorenn looked at Jason. "You forced a great astral being to back off?"

"More 'convinced' than 'forced,'" Jason said. "'Bargained,' might be more accurate. The Builder and I have a history."

"So Beaufort has told me. Yet all you tell me are stories of making alliances with your enemies."

"Yes," Jason said. "I've done it before, and every time, it feels like swallowing poison. But sometimes you have to do something ugly to prevent something worse."

Lorenn nodded.

"That, I understand," she told him. "As the messenger tree overtook more and more of our domain, the Builder cult came to us with an alliance."

"We were close to being cut off from everything by the elemental messengers," Beaufort said. "If we weren't going to claim the astral space, we needed to return to the surface and look for a way to rejoin the Builder. The elemental messengers had control of the tunnel the messengers had dug, and those regular messengers were waiting at the top. As for our digging machines, the brightheart had long destroyed them."

"Last I checked, you and the regular messengers were allies," Jason pointed out.

"An alliance based on usefulness and power. If we handed ourselves over to the messengers now that the Builder is gone, we would have no leverage. The messengers would only accept us as slaves, yet we would not be acceptable slaves to them. They only take slaves who are broken and have accepted messenger superiority."

"I'm familiar with their practices," Jason said. "They wouldn't take you because of your loyalty to the Builder."

"Yes. There are no forcibly converted amongst my people. We sacrificed those in the early fighting against the brighthearts. All who remain are true servants. None would be acceptable slaves, so the messengers would kill us. That left the other tunnel up, where the Adventure Society is waiting. I know they will likely kill us as well, but we at least have a chance at survival. I bet the lives of my people on mercy. Your mercy, Jason Asano."

Jason grimaced.

"Your boss told you to try that, didn't he?"

"The Lord Builder observes you still," Beaufort admitted. "He saw a weakness and told me to exploit it."

"You openly admit it?" Miriam asked.

"He knows it doesn't matter," Jason said, not taking his eyes off Beaufort. "If my mercy was so fragile that the Builder's opinion could break it, it's not worth relying on. He also knows that what waits for them on the surface isn't good. Letting them live isn't the same as setting them free."

"The cultists are detestable," Lorenn said. "It was not an easy choice to accept them, but we are not warriors. Our losses against the cult and then the messengers showed us this. Until the invaders came and the array was disrupted, no monsters attacked our chambers. The elementals were placid, even working with us in the forges and construction yards and growth chambers. We had known nothing but century after century of peace. We needed the Builder cult to teach us war."

She turned a cold gaze on Beaufort.

"They taught us. Fought for us. But we do not forget why they came here in the first place, or how many they killed before they started protecting us."

Lorenn and Marla told them the story of their people, starting with the Builder invasion. Much of that had been covered by Beaufort and she focused on the messengers. They had arrived in the midst of the bright-hearts already fighting a war they were not expecting or ready for. The messengers punched their way directly into the most sacred space in Cardinas, the natural array chamber, and worked their terrible magic.

The results went horribly awry. The messengers fled, many of them left behind as their own failed workings twisted and corrupted them. The damage had been done, however, and worse than the messengers them-selves was the tree they left behind in the natural array chamber.

"After the cult joined us, we made one attempt to purge the tree when the messenger numbers were still low. We reached the chamber, and that is the only time we saw the tree itself, a twisted, ugly thing. But we failed to take the chamber back. The gold-rank messengers were too strong. That was the beginning of the true days of horror."

She paused, a pained expression on her face.

"The tree roots burrowed through stone to invade the rest of our domain. The growth chambers were first. We didn't know why until we realised it was taking anything that was or had once been alive."

"Organic matter," Jason said. "Using it as base material to make more messengers?"

"Yes," Marla confirmed. "It seems to prefer plants, but meat will do. The tree's roots spread and the messengers grew in number. Our every loss was their gain. The main city chamber was where we made our stand.

Without it, and the growth chambers attached to it, most of our people would die."

"And die they did," Lorenn said. "We, so far as I know, are all the brighthearts that exist. Almost all of us died in three cycles."

"A cycle is their equivalent of days," Beaufort explained.

"We thought it was over," Lorenn said. "With that many bodies, the messengers would be countless. And their numbers did grow, as you saw. But something about all that death took a turn. The bodies were tainted and started to rise. Spiritual remnants appeared, echoes of departed souls mirrored by death magic. The roots withdrew and a gulf of death opened between us and the messengers. This chamber, and the two growth chambers attached to it, are on the far side of the main chamber from everything else."

"The roots couldn't grow around?" Miriam asked.

"It seems not," Lorenn said. "We suspect the expanded distance is too far from the natural array."

"Or maybe the tree didn't think of it," Jason said. "Trees aren't known for their developed problem-solving skills."

"The messengers made some attempts to cross the death chamber and attack us," Marla said. "They failed. We can hold them at the gates long enough that they draw too many of the dead and are forced to withdraw."

"Eventually, they seemed to give up," Beaufort said. "That was when they started digging the shaft up to the surface and you know what happened from there. Their initial scouting party to the surface didn't come back and they've been quiet since. Until you showed up. We believe they were consolidating in preparation to move up in force, processing the organic matter they'd already taken and spawning as many of their kind as they could. I knew you were coming because the Builder warned us. When the messengers started swarming up the shaft, we knew you were close."

"What I would have liked to do," Jason said, "is evacuate everyone. Write off the expedition, get all the brighthearts out and then say to hell with it and evacuate Yaresh. Let the natural array explode and take the messengers with it. But I don't think it's that simple anymore."

"We're fairly certain that the surface messengers have sent people other than us down here," Miriam said. "Some of their own kind that already had elemental powers and can resist being corrupted. More importantly, the god of destruction has taken an interest."

"I don't think Destruction's goal is to make sure the array blows up,"

Jason said. "I think his goal is the tree. I think he wants it to become some kind of apocalypse beast that devours every living thing on this planet. Even just doing a vast amount of damage before it gets stopped would satisfy him."

"What we're saying is that we can't leave the array alone," Miriam said. "We have to deal with it and then we can *all* go to the surface."

"Losing the array is a blow our people may not recover from," Lorenn said. "We have already lost so much. But I have accepted that if we are going to last as a people, we need to leave our home behind."

"And we'll take you," Jason said, then inclined his head at Beaufort. "We'll even take them. But the array must be dealt with. As for your people, I had an idea of how we could maybe do something for them. I can't promise anything, but we can at least look into it."

Clive had left Miriam and Jason to strategy while he worked on exploring whether Jason's idea was viable. Roped into helping were the Magic Society research team and some of the brightheart magic experts. Along with a staggering understanding of elemental magic, they understood how to manipulate the echo array that could, in turn, influence the natural array. He'd been given a large room along with all the magic supplies that the expedition, the brightheart and even the cult could muster.

"The idea," Clive explained, "is to create an area where the elemental energy that pervades the magic here is excluded. We'll be running some viability tests, but the basic premise is to use the messenger device to isolate the elemental aspects within a small area and absorb them with the excellent elemental mana lamps our new brightheart colleagues have provided."

"We're trying to create a space where we can open a portal?" asked a member of the Magic Society group.

"We are," Clive confirmed. "Opening a portal to the surface most likely won't be an option, though. Transportation portals are the most susceptible to elemental interference, and we won't be able to completely excise the elemental energy. We're hoping to make our dimensional storage useable and pull out all the supplies we were forced to stash."

He panned a stern gaze over the group, lingering on the brighthearts.

"What I'm going to tell you next stays in this room. I know that Marla has already explained the need for secrecy, so I won't harp any further. We are going to try and establish this portal viability zone to evacuate the civilian population."

"That's not possible," one of the brighthearts said. "Portals have limits and opening and closing enough of them to move ten thousand people would turn the most carefully refined ambient magic zone into pure turbulence."

"Correct," Clive said.

"Then what aren't you telling us?" the brightheart asked. "For one thing, where would the portal lead? You just said yourself that transportation portals won't work, and I haven't heard about any other underground cities nearby. Are you looking to send the whole population into the astral space? That's not an environment that most of the population will survive for long."

"All true," Clive agreed.

"And even if you got portals working, enough of them in quick succession would undo any preparation we made to balance out the ambient magic. It would only work if you had one portal that could stay open and accept any number of people through it."

"Yes," Clive said.

"If all you're going to do is stand there and agree that everything you want to do is impossible, then what are we doing here?"

"The impossible, obviously," Clive said.

EVERYTHING IN MY POWER

DESPITE BEING DEEP UNDERGROUND, THE GROWTH CHAMBER WAS FILLED with light. Level after level of stone lattices and catwalks were overgrown with luminescent flora creating a glorious light show. Jason's soul realm had underground areas with glowing fungus, but this place put them to shame. Moss, vines and fungal growth climbed over everything, shedding light in every shade of the rainbow to weave a kaleidoscopic tapestry.

Miniature aqueducts carried water down through the chamber in a complex series of troughs and channels. Water could be seen running off the edge of troughs to splash down in pools that emptied into more channels, spraying up mist in the process. That mist spread out, floating through the chamber to leave the abundant flora with a patina of dew.

"I never imagined something like this down here," Jason said, his voice filled with wonder. "How does it work when the magic here is filled with fire and magma affinity? Where does the water come from, all the way down here? That's magic making it mist that way, yes?"

He was walking through the growth chamber with Lorenn, the leader of the brightheart people. Three of her aides travelled a respectful distance behind.

"You are aware of what a natural array is?" Lorenn asked.

"A bunch of essences, awakening stones and quintessence that just happened to manifest over time in such a way that complex magical interactions are generated."

"Yes. While most of the components of the array are fire, earth, ash and similar types, at the heart of the array, there are three essences that create balance. One plant, one life and one water essence. You are no doubt wondering how such essences could manifest so far underground."

"That's exactly what I was wondering, yes."

"Our scholars theorise that these were the final elements of the array to manifest. The idea is that the rest of the array was in place and the components were already interacting, and that created a magic imbalance. As more magic manifested, that imbalance created an environment where those manifestations took forms that rectified that imbalance. There's a wellspring of water that is conjured into being underneath the array and passes through natural tunnels in the stone, ending up in the growth chambers."

"So, these growth chambers formed naturally, rather than being dug out?" Jason asked.

"Originally, yes, although we expanded them all. The citadel chamber and the growth chambers were the only natural ones. The pillars in the citadel chamber were already there, although they were solid when our ancestors found them. After the citadel was rather disastrously brought into being in the middle of them, they were hollowed out, reinforced and shaped. That was where most of our people lived until our population grew and we eventually created the Great Chamber."

"How did that work?" Jason asked. "Where was all that rock displaced to?"

"It was used to fill the tunnel our ancestors used to arrive here in the first place. They came in not straight down but at a long angle from the west to avoid the people in the surface region directly above us. Our people had discovered the natural array and wanted to build a home around it. They feared those without elements in their blood would see only something to be exploited, so we reached this place with the elves above never even realising."

"I'm pretty sure that was the right call," Jason said.

"The opening of the Great Chamber was the beginning of our peak as a civilisation," she said proudly, then bowed her head. Her voice became a mournful whisper.

"We call it the death chamber now."

Jason grimaced.

"I am left in awe at what you've accomplished here," he said. "Hanging gardens of light hidden impossibly deep underground. Even in a world of magic, this place is a wonder. But it feels wrong to take joy in what you've made here when your people are surviving on the ragged edge."

"Do you truly believe that you can help us?" Lorenn asked.

"That's the plan," Jason said, doing his best to offer a reassuring smile. "Once you've saved the world a few times, you start to wonder what's next. Saving whole species makes sense."

Lorenn raised her eyebrows sceptically.

"I know I can come off as flippant," Jason said apologetically. "But while my manner might sometimes make it seem otherwise, I promise my actions are undertaken with the utmost seriousness. I will do everything in my power to help your people. And between you and me, that is a lot of power."

"You'll have to forgive my doubts," Lorenn said. "It's hard to imagine a silver-ranker saving us all. What you describe doing seems... unlikely."

"I know. It took me a long time to get used to it as well. As for addressing your doubts, would you be willing to take a look at my aura if I completely opened it up to you? I don't know how sensitive the aura senses of your people are."

"Not as sharp as an essence user," Lorenn said, "but adequate. My understanding is that our ability to sense magic rather than auras is stronger, especially with elemental magic."

"That makes sense. I'm going to open up my soul, so please take a look. You'll have to push your senses in because I don't want to expose everyone else here in the chamber. It would probably kill some of the children."

Lorenn raised her eyebrows again and Jason gave her a wry smile.

"You'll see."

He felt her senses make an exploratory push into his aura and opened a gate in the restraints every essence user employed to hold back their auras. He watched Lorenn's eyes grow wider as she explored the strange and twisty depths of the power that reflected Jason's soul. He smiled until her expression turned from shock to horror.

"What are you?" she half-whispered as she withdrew her senses.

"Ouch. I'm in a transitional period. But you sensed the power, right? I can't whip it out and slap people in the face with it, but it's impressive to look at. Well, I suppose I can, kind of. My aura is only an echo of that power, but even that is enough to be used as a weapon."

"This place you said you can take my people. You called it a soul realm."

"I've called it a lot of things. But yeah."

"And this soul realm is yours."

"Yes."

"Meaning that it is shaped by what I just saw?"

"Strictly speaking, what you just saw is shaped by it. But more or less, yes. Councilwoman, I want to be clear about what I'm proposing before we move forward. The soul realm isn't just some dimensional space that's influenced by my soul. It is my soul. If your people enter it, they'll be inside my soul. Which means, amongst other things, that they will be completely in my power. It doesn't matter if they're gold rank, or what abilities they wield. The moment they arrive, my power over them becomes absolute, utter and inescapable. I could kill them in an instant or trap them there for eternity."

"Are you trying to convince me to not do this?"

"I just want you to understand exactly what you're leading your people into. I'm essentially asking you to put the fate of your entire people in the hands of someone you've known for all of a few hours. Someone who could easily annihilate them once you have. That's not a revelation I want you having when half of your people are already in my soul realm and some kind of riot starts."

"But do we genuinely have a choice?" Lorenn asked. "If we're choosing between no chance of survival and betting everything on a stranger, that's not a choice at all."

"You could wait it out. Hope we can beat the messengers and lead you all out of here."

"But you think we'll all get dragged into this transformation zone you talked about."

"Yes," Jason said. "I think this whole underground region will be dragged into the fragmented dimensional space that is going to form, and everyone here with it. But if your people are in my soul, they'll be protected. Not to mention having air to breathe and food to eat. Which brings us to the reason we're here."

Lorenn nodded, then waved to the aides trailing them. Two were bronze rank while the third was a silver who approached in response to Lorenn's gesture.

"You want samples of all the plants we have here," Lorenn said to Jason.

"Yes," he said, nodding his confirmation. "I can reproduce the plants in here. Organics are a lot trickier than inert material, though. I'll need as much information to understand what I'm dealing with as I can get. My understanding is that your people need food rich not just in magic but magic with a high elemental affinity."

"We don't strictly need it, but it's vastly more efficient. Our normal- and iron-rankers can get by on ordinary food. Our bronze-rankers as well, although they need a lot of it. We wouldn't have had nearly enough for everyone if that's what we were using. There may also be some sickness if it's not elementally rich, especially given how weak and starving our population is."

"I can work with that," Jason assured her. "To make sure I can produce what you need, what I need are samples of everything, and not just of the plants. The soil, the stone, the water. Any fertiliser and anything else you use. The more accurately I can replicate this growth chamber, the better I'll be able to produce food that will sustain your people. The further I am from understanding their needs, the longer it will take to figure out how to produce something they can consume without exacerbating any issues."

"This is Hilda," Lorenn said, introducing the aide. "She'll see to it that you get what you need."

Hilda was a magma type, her hair a mix of obsidian black and glowing orange. Her eyes and skin markings shifted between glossy black and glowing orange in a slow, heartbeat pulse. She looked young to Jason's eyes, around twenty or even younger, which was highly impressive for silver rank. He knew that rank and species difference could easily be fooling him, but her aura had a feel to it he associated with youth.

"I greet you, Lord Asano," she said.

"Oh, none of that," Jason said. "I'm not even Lord of the Dance, although I can twinkle my toes when the occasion calls for it. I'm Jason. Call me that and we'll get on just fine. Unless you're a terrible person or something, which would be unfortunate. I'm sure you're great."

"I'm going to go," Lorenn told Jason. "I've been away from my duties too long as it is. Hilda, I was told by Mr Asano's companions that if he starts getting… odd, I should just nod and wait for him to finish, then only address anything that actually made sense. I pass that advice on to you."

"Who told you that?" Jason asked. "It was Clive, wasn't it? He was the one that came with us to meet you."

"Before I go," Lorenn said, ignoring Jason's questions, "I do have a concern about something you've told me here. If this soul realm is actually within your soul, what happens to the people in it when you die?"

"Die permanently? I honestly have no idea."

Jason moved away from Hilda and tapped a pin in his robes, activating a privacy screen in which Lorenn moved to join him.

"I have a couple of deaths in me before we have to worry about what happens to the people in my soul."

"A couple of deaths?"

"You know how vampires work? Feeding on life force they can use to recover even from what should be thoroughly lethal injuries?"

"Yes."

"Well, I'm kind of like that, except I devour the life force of messengers and use it to resurrect myself. It takes a lot of them to get a whole resurrection's worth, but the one thing we're not short on down here is messengers. My concerns are failing, not dying."

"You are a strange creature, Jason Asano."

"So people tell me. I'd appreciate you keeping the resurrection thing to yourself, by the way. I normally only share those details with my closest companions, but with the trust you'll need to put in me, I think you deserve some trust in return. It's the only assurance I have to offer."

"Then I thank you for that."

Lorenn departed, leaving Jason with Hilda.

"What quantities are you going to need for each of your samples?" Hilda asked him.

"Well, for the plants, I'll need one full plant of each type, including root systems and whatever it's growing out of. I noticed that some of your plants look to be growing straight out of the rock..."

Clive and his ritualists were confident they could create a zone where Jason could open his portal but were unsure how long they could maintain it. With almost ten thousand people to move, from across three chambers, getting them to the portal would be a massive logistical challenge.

The bottom of the citadel chamber, amongst the pillars, was chosen as the portal site. It was the easiest place to funnel people from the growth chambers, and those in the citadel chamber would only need to descend, not climb their way up. Even so, the citadel chamber posed several challenges, the biggest being the citadel itself.

The citadel wasn't well designed for one person to navigate, let alone thousands at once. More historical artefact than functional building, the only practical way to move from the upper pillar to the lower was a series of elevating platforms that moved around the outside of the building. They were not even close to sufficient to move the numbers required in a short time frame.

The pillars faced similar, but less urgent issues. They all had elevating-platform shafts, along with stairwells, but they were not designed to move the entire populace all at once. One bad incident when every level of the stairs was packed with people could spell disaster.

The decision was made to take the time to get the populace down to ground level, lined up and ready to go before the portal was opened. The major risk was what happened if the portal couldn't take everyone at once and there was a lengthy break as the elemental energy was purged again. As more and more people arrived at ground level, it increasingly became a sports arena with no food stands and no public bathrooms.

Jason watched proceedings from the air, sitting in his cloud chair. He sighed.

"A lot of people are going to poop in my soul."

75

CONTROL THE POT

Jason watched the brightheart population migrate towards the ground level in preparation for moving through his portal. The base of the chamber was little more than rock carved flat for the most part, aside from the roads moving between the pillars and the growth chambers. They, at least, were flagstone paved and lined with garden beds, although the plants had long since died. Outside of the growth chambers, the lack of good air and people to care for them had left the moss, vines and fungus withered and brown.

Illumination for the tight-packed lines of brighthearts was provided by glow stones. The local variety had a yellow tinge, as they were crystals charged with fire energy. They were carried by brightheart officials, forming chains as they guided their people down. Jason couldn't see into the pillars, although he could sense the mass of people through their auras. He felt their fear and confusion, along with an undercurrent of despair born of too much misery and too many deaths. Hope was in disastrously short supply.

There hadn't been time to hold massive meetings and explain everything to the brightheart population. That left most with a tenuous grasp of why they were being moved, leading to uncertainty and unease that spread like a virus. There were systems in place to disseminate information, but anything beyond the practical basic was counterproductive. Too many details would just lead to confusion as large groups did not handle context and complex ideas very well. Any information given out would be distorted as it spread in a game of telephone thousands of links long.

What made the process of moving everyone work was the trust the brighthearts had in their leadership. This led to minimal pushback against the officials working to get and keep everyone moving.

The residents of the upper pillars that linked the citadel to the ceiling had to be ferried around the outside of the citadel as part of their descent. Elevating platforms were in constant motion, but they could only move a fraction of the required number. Spiralling ramps had been stone-shaped around the outside, hastily enough that the structural integrity of the slap-dash design was a concern. Not only would a collapse slow the process and get people killed, but it would make the population wary of the process entirely.

Gary had joined the brighthearts in establishing the ramps. During Jason's time back on Earth, Gary spent a couple of years helping small towns with their defensive infrastructure, in readiness for the monster surge. That time building walls and reinforcing structures to withstand monster attacks left him with experience that was paying off again. Expertise in shoring up swiftly built structures against significant strain was exactly what the brighthearts needed. They also had their own experts, as well as some deep earth metals that got the smith in him excited.

Miriam flew from the upper levels of the citadel on a flying motor-cycle that was mostly black with a few embellishments in dark grey. She pulled up next to Jason's floating cloud chair as he observed proceedings from on high.

"This vehicle type is very convenient," she commented.

"Yeah, vehicle design in Pallimustus is pretty bad," Jason said. "A private jet that's a giant construct eagle is awesome, don't get me wrong, but a plane is just more practical. That being said, most motorcycles don't fly. I think the police in Dubai might have them? Dubai is a city in the world I come from that's pretty much the capital of doing weird stuff because they have too much money."

"I don't know the vehicles you're describing. Except the bird one. How did it go with Councilwoman Lorenn?"

"There's a reason I'm not the leader of my team," Jason said. "I think I did acceptably, but my mediocrity when it comes to maintaining a diplo-matic demeanour is well documented. It's not a field in which my instincts lead me in the right direction. How goes the tactical planning?"

"I've been consulting with Marla and Beaufort. They're the local equivalents of my role as tactical commander. Their knowledge of the local terrain, conditions and enemy disposition has been valuable in plotting out the next stage of the mission. Standish has been working with us to set the objectives and we've been figuring out how to make that work."

"We have a plan of action?"

"We do. Objective one is the astral space chamber and we've plotted out an approach that we think will meet with the least amount of resistance. We're not sure if the messengers will attack us once we claim the chamber or if they're as wary of it as their tree is. Either way, we have plans in place to hold the chamber while the ritualists learn whatever it is they need to learn from it."

"And then it's on to the natural array chamber and the tree itself," Jason said. "I assume that will be the hard part."

"A safe assumption. Moving to objective two requires that Standish is confident in activating the device effectively after what he learns studying the astral space chamber, however. We have contingencies involving a retreat to the citadel chamber or into the astral space if Standish thinks we need to revise our approach. That will be for you and him to decide in the field."

"But the hope is that we move onto the natural array chamber," Jason said.

"Yes. We'll need to operate under the assumption that the messengers will spare nothing in defending the tree. We've established a series of different scenarios for going in, securing the area around the tree and performing the ritual."

"One of those scenarios being to kill all the messengers?"

"Yes. The last scenario because it's the least viable. Even with the addition of the brighthearts and the cult to our forces, we would most likely exhaust ourselves and fall before their numbers were expended. But assuming we can secure the site and activate the device, that's where things get uncertain. I do not like uncertain, Operations Commander."

"We work with what we have, not what we want."

"I know. But turning on the magic device given to us by our enemies and then waiting for those same enemies to sabotage us and hope we can work around them is as bad a plan as I've ever been involved in. That's assuming that only the regular messengers interfere and not the god of destruction."

"It is very bad," Jason agreed. "But it can be done, trust me. Saving civilisations from destructive cosmic forces is kind of my thing. I've had to deal with transcendent-level enemies and the fact is, they're incredibly restricted when working within physical reality. If Destruction had the power to wipe us all out, he would. If he was as confident as he put himself across, he wouldn't have been talking to us; he'd have just been doing what he wanted. Take it from someone who's been on both sides of the confident bluster when world-level stakes are in play: that guy is not as confident as he seems."

"Are you as confident as you seem?"

He chuckled.

"I've briefed you on transformation zone events, which Knowledge thinks is the key, and I can see why. Whatever the sabotage ends up being, it's going to involve dimensional magic. Probably trying to lift the soul forge out through the side of the universe, the same way the Builder steals astral spaces. Given that the device itself is already playing with the dimensional membrane, I may not need to push the transformation zone into forming. The messengers do not care about dimensional integrity."

"But you can push it over the edge if they don't?" Miriam asked. "You have the power to do that?"

"It's not about power as much as the right tool for the job. I have something called an astral gate that allows me to manipulate dimensional forces. Think of it like a normal-ranker who can't push a nail into a board, but give them a hammer and it's easy."

"So long as they don't hit their thumb."

"Very true," Jason said with a laugh. "I was warned not to use the astral gate until I'm diamond rank at least."

"At least?"

"Yeah. I disregarded that advice almost immediately, of course, and brought the hammer down on my thumb pretty damn hard. I imagine you heard about it."

"The incident in Rimaros where you spent months in recovery?"

"That's the one. Spiritual damage is a real prick, let me tell you."

"*At least* diamond rank?" Miriam repeated.

"Yep."

"Since I started working with you, Asano, it's felt like I'm swimming over very deep water. I'm not used to that as a gold-ranker."

Jason burst out laughing.

"Try dealing with great astral beings at iron or bronze."

"I would point out, Operations Commander, that my question is about confidence. You strike me as a man who starts giving context until he forgets what he was talking about in the first place."

Jason laughed again.

"You figured me out pretty quick. Okay, the point I'm slowly meandering towards is that a transformation zone is exactly what we need. The good thing about a transformation zone is that it's all-encompassing. It'll take everything that's going on and throw it into a big pot. All this uncertainty, all these factions and whatever weird magic is going around, all into the pot. That means we aren't dealing with all these unknowns anymore; we just have to control the pot. If we do that, we win."

"And you think we can do that?"

"I've done it before, and more than once. There are differences this time, I'll admit. You've set up a meeting for me to brief everyone on how transformation zones work?"

"Yes."

"Good. Long story short, a transformation zone is a bunch of territories. We claim enough territories and I can remake reality."

"It's that easy?" Miriam asked sceptically.

"No, it's that simple. And it does start easy. Taking territory means eliminating anomalies, which are rather weak in the beginning. The more territories get claimed, though, the more dangerous the unclaimed ones become. But our people are solid, so I'm more worried about challenges I didn't have to deal with on Earth. There, I was the only one with the power to properly claim territories."

"Because of your ability that will let you trigger the zone?"

"Uh, no. It's a different power, one of my outworlder racial gifts. It was a somewhat related power that was forcibly put through a secondary gift evolution the first time I was in a transformation zone."

"Operations Commander, talking to you makes me feel like I've led a boring life, and I once discovered an underwater dome city on the back of a giant turtle."

"Okay, that is awesome and you're totally telling me that story, but later, when there's booze. What was I talking about?"

"Challenges you didn't have on your home planet."

"Right. In the second transformation zone I was in, others were competing for territories. They weren't real competitors, though. They had no idea what they were doing and no way to reshape a giant mass of reality in a state of flux. I have to assume that the messenger saboteurs have at least one astral magic expert with them, meaning that they may be able to figure it out. And then there's the messenger tree. It may not have a mind, but I bet it has a will. I'm betting it will try and take over the transformation zone the way it's been taking over this underground domain. Whether it can do something with it or not doesn't matter. It'll be a disaster either way."

"What kind of disaster? What will happen if either of them wins over us?"

"Some variety of bad. Maybe they get what they want, be it a soul forge to take away or a base from which to spread arboreal doom. Or maybe they screw up and the whole place blows up the way we came here to stop in the first place. The transformation zone is the thing we need, but it won't let us just win and it won't solve all our problems. It solves one problem: the uncertainty you were talking about."

"By throwing everything into a pot."

"Exactly. It takes everything coming for us, whether we know it or not, and puts it in front of us where we can fight it. And a fight is something I know you can handle."

Miriam nodded.

"Alright," she said. "That makes things feel more manageable. I think you did instil me with some confidence. Thank you, Operations Commander."

"I'd say it's what I'm here for, but really I'm here to discuss different ways to trick Mr. T onto planes while you have no idea what I'm talking about."

"Then congratulations because I do have no idea what you're talking about."

"Mission accomplished."

Miriam sighed, rolling her shoulders as if she'd just shrugged off a weight.

"I finally feel like there's a path forward I can actually make out. Thank you, Jason. Everything should go fine and we just have to hope nothing unexpected prevents the transformation zone from forming."

Jason's jaw dropped.

"Why would you say that?"

———

Farrah met Jason outside the room that contained the echo array. They both had guides to help them navigate the citadel.

"How is it going?" Jason asked as Farrah came out into a hallway that didn't run quite straight.

"Is that a friend question or an Operations Commander question?"

"Operations Commander."

"Well. I'll be ready to brief you and Miriam before you're scheduled to open the portal."

"That's good. Should I have asked how you're doing as a friend question?"

"No, I'm fine," Farrah told him. "You look like something's weighing on you, though."

"Uh, yeah. We've got this thing where we're trying to stop two different sets of evil angels and a god from doing some super-evil stuff. And some lunatic put me in charge."

"No, that's not it. This stuff is old hat for you."

"Old hat? How much time did you spend with my grandmother?"

"Stop trying to derail the conversation, Jason. What's going on?"

"You're not going to like it."

"Just tell me."

"Okay, fine," Jason said. "It's about taking all these people into my portal."

"And?"

"And it's been a while since I had people in my soul realm for extended periods. Back when my family were in there, my spirit realm was more spirit and less realm. But now I've got the astral throne and it's much more of a physical reality."

"Isn't that a good thing?"

"Mostly, sure. But when Emi was living in there, she was kind of frozen. I mean, she could walk around in there or whatever, but she was in kind of a stasis, biologically. She didn't get hungry, I don't think she was aging. And she didn't... you know. What if that isn't the case anymore?"

Farrah let out an exasperated groan.

"The poop thing again?"

"Yes, the poop thing, again."

"We've got a lot more to worry about than that, Jason."

"Says the woman not about to have ten thousand people start taking dumps inside her soul."

"They're mostly iron rank, except for the children."

"They aren't essence users, Farrah. They don't eat spirit coins and they still have those biological functions."

"Are you sure?"

"Oh, I'm very sure. I spent hours learning all about their growth chambers so I could replicate them. Guess where they get their fertiliser?"

"Well, there you go, then," Farrah said.

"What do you mean, there I go?"

"Think about it," Farrah said. "You're trying to effectively replicate the growth chambers in your soul, right? Which means you'll need their fertiliser. You need them to poop in your soul. And if they can't, because your soul still stops people from needing to, then you'll have to use your power to replicate all that poo yourself."

Jason's eyes went wide in horror.

76

IT HAPPENS BECAUSE I WANT IT TO

THE MEETING ROOM IN THE CITADEL WAS MORE OR LESS RECTANGULAR. Jason and Miriam were already waiting when Farrah arrived. She found the two commanders in the middle of a contentious conversation, their voices escalating in volume as they argued.

"...can't believe you would say that," Jason said.

"Are you still complaining about this? It was a fair assessment of risk."

"It was tempting fate!"

"Fate isn't real."

"That was what I thought until I got destiny magic."

"What is destiny magic?"

"I'm not entirely sure!"

"Why are you angrily shouting a confused statement like it's an accusation?"

"I don't know! Maybe so I don't lose argumentative momentum!"

"Talking to you makes no sense."

"Isn't that the truth," Farrah said from the doorway. "Perhaps you should let an old hand take over, Tactical Commander."

Miriam looked embarrassed for a moment before she schooled her expression. Jason was shamelessly unembarrassed and gave Farrah a cheery wave.

"You're here to brief us on your study of the echo array?" Miriam asked.

"I am," Farrah said. "The brighthearts were kind enough to give me access to the array and their ritualists."

"What have you learned?"

"The surface messengers will need to access the natural array if they want to sabotage the device activation. We assumed that they would try and get as close to the array as possible, but I no longer think they'll be going for the natural array itself. I think they'll go for the echo array here at the citadel. I suspect it would be just as good for their needs, if not better."

"We do know their numbers are unlikely to be high," Miriam said. "It makes sense for them to avoid the natural array if they can. They can also safely assume that the bulk of our power will be sent to the natural array, to fight through the messengers. They will only have whoever they can muster with elemental powers, if your messenger prisoner is to be believed, Operations Commander."

"She also said that any gold-rankers the messengers bring will be ringers," Jason added.

"Ringers?"

"People brought in from the outside. The astral king we're dealing with, Vesta Carmis Zell, doesn't have any gold-rankers with elemental powers left. If any turn up down here, they'll be one she had to bargain away from other astral kings."

"How likely is that?" Farrah asked.

"The messengers are slaves, whether they know it or not," Jason said. "The question isn't whether Zell could trade for them, but if she had the time for them to arrive from whatever parts of the world they were in."

"And the messengers kept delaying handing over the device," Miriam said.

"Exactly," Jason agreed. "I think we can anticipate seeing some of them down here."

"But they still won't have the numbers to charge into a fight between us, the cult, the brighthearts and elemental messengers, will they?" Miriam asked.

"I'd consider it highly unlikely," Jason said.

"Then a small force attacking this place after we've emptied all the combatants to attack the tree makes more sense," Miriam said.

"It's also a strong move if you want to interfere with the natural array while we're trying to use the device on it," Farrah said. "If they have good array and astral magic specialists with them, they could wreak havoc."

"Could we destroy the echo array?" Miriam asked.

"No," Farrah said. "Not unless you want an extremely powerful and completely unpredictable backlash from the natural array we're trying to stabilise. In my assessment, that would be worse than bugging out and letting the messengers have it. At least their sabotage is within our plans, unlike an uncertain magical disaster."

"Then we'll have to leave a sufficient defensive force to protect it," Miriam said.

"Agreed," Jason said. "We couldn't destroy it anyway because we may need to let them have it, depending on how things go. If we end up needing a transformation zone, we'll probably need the sabotage to help weaken the dimensional boundary. I can't just muster up a transformation zone whenever I want. It's a defence mechanism of the world, not an ability of mine. The best I can do is act as a fulcrum to make sure it happens if the conditions are right. Even that much I'm only confident of because of the goddess of knowledge."

"We can work on contingencies before we brief the teams," Miriam said. "Moving on from the echo array as a potential vulnerability, have you learned anything from the echo array we can use, Miss Hurin?"

"That's the good news," Farrah said. "I suspect I got more from examining the echo array than I would from the natural array itself. It amounts to an artificial extension of the natural array, less elegant but more comprehensible. It uses a lot of the principles I managed to decipher by studying the grid network on Earth. I suspect that I'll be able to give Clive a much better understanding of the device, and probably help create a stable zone for a portal as well."

"This messenger device we brought with us," Miriam said. "It's designed to turn the unstable array into a soul forge, yes? Something the surface messengers will attempt to steal."

"That's our best guess," Jason said. "You already knew that."

"Yes," Miriam said, "but you never explained what a soul forge is. Not what it does—that's something to do with astral kings and I don't care right now. I'm talking about what it is, as an object. Is it the size of a loaf of bread? Of a wagon? How much does it weigh? Is it fragile? Will we be able to move it? How are the messengers expecting to take it? Especially if they approach the echo array instead of the natural array itself."

"I don't have any answers," Jason said. "At best, I have guesses. I'm not even certain the soul forge will have a physical form; it may be a purely spiritual construct that gets drawn straight into the astral. Or maybe it's a tree. The messenger tree may be a corrupted soul forge that the messengers want us to cleanse so they can swoop in and repot. I won't know until I encounter it for myself, but I'm guessing the messengers plan to yank whatever it is out of the universe without ever getting close enough to the natural array for us to fight them. Having the echo array as a proxy only makes that easier."

"That's at least actionable information," Miriam said. "I'm going to organise a defensive force to protect the echo array in our absence. If we can stop the intentions of the surface messengers, perhaps we can succeed without needing to rip a hole in the universe with your transformation zone, Operations Commander."

Miriam strode out, giving Farrah a nod as she passed.

"I'll go too," Farrah said. "I need to discuss the messenger device and the echo array with Clive."

***

The brightheart stone-shapers had put up small barriers to guide the thousands of people ready to enter the portal in switchback queues like an airport check-in desk. Jason and Lorenn were at the spot where the queues converged. Clive, Belinda and the ritualists had roped off a wide area and set out a large ritual diagram. It was sealed under glass produced by one of the brighthearts and magically reinforced. The thousands of people about to trample over it would otherwise have disrupted the magic.

Clive arrived riding Onslow. After dropping Clive off, the rune tortoise turned into a cloud of colourful lights that sank through Clive's shirt to become a tattoo on his torso.

"Clive," Jason said. "I always wondered, does the big chest tat help with the ladies?"

"No," Clive said. "Turning it into an adorable tortoise they can feed lettuce leaves to helps with the ladies."

"I can see how that would work," Jason said, holding out his fist. Clive rolled his eyes apologetically at Lorenn but still gave Jason the fist bump.

"You do realise," Belinda said to Jason, "that by 'helps with the ladies,' Clive means women kept hitting on him while he was feeding Onslow and he shoos them away like annoying flies."

"Still counts," Jason said. "If anything, knocking them back counts even more. High standards, showing some class. Nice one, Clive."

Clive eyed Jason suspiciously waiting for a reference to his nonexistent wife. It didn't come, to his surprise, yet that left him feeling more uneasy than relieved.

"Are we ready to begin?" Lorenn asked.

"We already have," Clive said. "The echo array is calibrated and the ritual is working. Once it reaches a critical threshold, we should…"

There was a pulse of magic that passed over the adventurers and the brighthearts like a wave.

"…get a sense of when it's ready," Clive finished.

Jason extended his magical senses. He could feel the elemental power being held back at the edge of the ritual circle. Some still permeated the area within, but it was greatly reduced. He concentrated on calling up his soul portal as cleanly as possible, making as small a ripple in the ambient magic as he could manage. He balanced stability against the need to make the portal arch larger than normal to let people through faster.

The arch rose from the floor, the width of a large set of double doors. Unlike the dark crystal of Jason's normal portals, the soul realm arch was a milky crystal with swirling motes of blue, gold and silver light floating inside it. A sheet of rainbow energy filled the archway as the portal activated.

Jason looked at Lorenn.

"You wanted to go first," he told her. "We're on the clock, so let's get it done."

He moved through the portal arch. Lorenn hesitated only a moment before following.

Lorenn had never used a portal before. She had heard of them in the old stories; some of the ancestors had such powers before their people became brighthearts. Stepping through one and suddenly being somewhere else was disorienting.

"Keep moving," Asano told her. "You've got a few thousand friends on your heels."

The reminder snapped her back to attention and she looked around as she followed him, already striding away. They were in a cavern, or perhaps a large tunnel, an underground river running along it. The walls were natural stone and covered in glowing fungus, not the same ones as in her home but not too alien either.

What was alien was the absence of the elemental power that had surrounded her since birth. It was as if sound had suddenly stopped existing, a fundamental part of reality suddenly absent. At least the surroundings had a subterranean familiarity. The old stories spoke of the open sky on the surface, something she had a hard time imagining. If her people had walked out under some vast emptiness, she could easily imagine a panicked stampede.

The tunnel was quiet but for the underground river flowing along its stone channel.

"This is your soul?" she asked. She needed no confirmation; the question was something to fill the quiet while she reined in her unease. In this place, the familiar pulse of elemental energy was absent, replaced with Asano's presence. It permeated everything, benevolent but with ominous undercurrents just beyond her senses. It was like feeling the breath of a sleeping monster she couldn't see in the dark.

As they walked, the world around them was changing. The cavern was expanding and forming a massive circular chamber. Natural walls became worked stone and a dozen massive archways were set all around. The river now flowed into the centre of the room with a series of small bridges crossing it. It reached the centre of the new chamber and poured into a hole right behind the portal, spilling down into the darkness.

The portal arch was in the middle of the chamber and people were already coming through. Lorenn found herself floating into the air alongside Asano as the chamber filled under them. The first through were Lorenn's officials, who were also floated into the air. Lorenn and the others went to work calming people as they arrived, although that didn't seem to be a large problem.

"I'm using my aura to create a naturally placid environment," Asano told her, floating close. "It's not mind control as such. You know how groups can start thinking as a whole instead of as individuals?"

"I'm the leader of an entire people. I am tragically and intimately familiar with the phenomenon."

"We call it pack mentality where I come from. This technique fosters that, but it doesn't impose anything. Strong individualists will be unaffected and other emotions that diverge from the group push it back easily enough. But for moving some people who just need a nudge in the right direction, it's useful."

Asano had assured them he could create space to contain all of their people and Lorenn was seeing him do so in real time. They had worked out a layout based on his assurances and it was happening right in front of her, although there were certain changes, like the river. Somehow she could feel the complex expand, tunnels and broad stairwells leading off from the arches of the central hub. Some led to peripheral hubs, others to dormitories and even growth chambers that were forming, flora and all. It was all lit up by luminescent plants or glow stones in familiar warm or soothingly cool shades.

There were signs over each archway, indicating where they led. Lorenn had a mysterious certainty that everyone shared her understanding of the layout, however, making the signs unnecessary. She felt it as a suite of chambers came into being and immediately understood they belonged to her. There was a meeting chamber, an office and a small residence.

She saw her people already moving off, each also apparently having a sense of the places that belonged to them. Children were breathing deeply, able to do so for the first time in a long time. Lorenn sensed cafeterias, but fresh fruit and mushrooms were materialising out of nothing into people's hands. Normally, they would be wary of such a thing, but food had been too scarce for too long and they immediately dug in.

"How?" she asked.

She looked at Asano floating beside her. He shook his head instead of responding, his eyes closed in concentration.

"Replicating the elemental power is harder than I thought," he said through gritted teeth. "I'll have to tap into some things I didn't want to, which may leave me weakened."

"You don't have to."

"The growth chambers need it if I'm going to maintain them, and I need them so I can replicate your food properly. Organics are still hard for me to get right."

A small cloud appeared under Lorenn's feet, solid but with a comfortable give, like plush carpet. She saw the same happening with her similarly floating officials and she instinctively understood how to move it around.

"So I don't accidentally drop you," Asano said, "I'm going to go and have a sit-down. Find your spot, guide your people. I'll add some meeting halls once everyone has a place to stay."

"I don't understand what's happening. How do I know that I have a place here? How do I know where it is?"

"Because I want you to," Asano told her. "That's how everything works here; it happens because I want it to."

He vanished and she turned her attention back to her people, still pouring through the portal. They were moving off in orderly lines, calm and merrily eating with barely any guidance from her officials. She watched, somewhat at a loss until she felt elemental power come flooding in, putting her at ease.

MORE URGENT WITH YOUR WARNING

JASON AND LORENN WERE THE LAST TO RETURN TO THE CITADEL CHAMBER through the soul realm portal. Everyone left inside was staying for the duration. The portal closed and Jason nodded at Clive.

"Sorry you didn't get to spend long in the rooms I set up for you," Jason told Lorenn.

"I'm more interested in putting the plan into action than resting, although you look like you could use it."

"I'm getting better at tapping into my astral gate, although it still takes it out of me, even when I'm working entirely in my soul realm. The astral gate is the thing I used to draw the elemental aspects out of the magic my realm draws in. I didn't manage to fully replicate the elemental magic out here, sorry."

"You did better than that," Lorenn assured him. "What you produced is closer to what the natural array was like before the messengers came. What you failed to replicate was the instability."

"Oh, uh... good, then?"

Clive was shutting down the active ritual that had kept the portal mostly free of elemental interference for the hours it had taken to evacuate the population. He and his ritualists, Magic Society and the local bright-hearts, had managed to keep it functioning the whole time. They chan-nelled magic through their bodies to maintain the portal for hour after hour as people shuffled into Jason's soul realm, but they were at their limits.

Clive stepped down the ritual in stages rather than let all that elemental energy crash back in. As the ritualists released the power flowing through them one by one, they dropped to the floor for some much-needed rest, not even looking for furniture.

"Brighthearts, thank you," Clive said to the contingent of local ritualists. "Your stamina carried us through. As for you Magic Society members, you are all embarrassments to your organisation."

"Hey," one of them complained. "We gave it our all."

"Yes, you did wonderfully," Clive agreed. "You were all excellent; I couldn't have asked for more. None of you belong in the Magic Society."

"Uh…"

With no way to open the portal without another draining and elaborate ritual, the civilians were now sealed in Jason's soul realm. Everyone still outside was a combatant, either staying to defend the citadel and the echo array or setting out with the main force. Lorenn mustered the brightheart forces, the largest group, while Beaufort gathered the cultists. Miriam organised the adventurers, which amounted to stopping anyone from wandering off. That was as much wrangling as adventurers were likely to tolerate, especially high-rank ones.

"I'm still unclear on our contingency plans," Gary said to Jason. "Do we want the messengers to sabotage the echo array or not?"

"If we can fight our way to the tree and keep the messengers off the echo array, that's the best-case scenario," Jason explained. "If we can stabilise the natural array without having to rewrite a chunk of reality, leaving it with a dimensional scar in the shape of my head, that's a good thing. More likely is something going wrong and we need the transformation zone just to make sure all the weird stuff that went wrong is caught up in it. That way, we can deal with it all together."

"Which is when we pull back and let the messengers think we left the place unguarded?"

"Pretty much."

"And if they notice us doing that and wonder why we're leaving all the doors open? Or don't notice us and wonder why we left all the doors open?"

"Then our defensive team mugs them and does the sabotage themselves. That's why Clive and Farrah have had Ramona from Miriam's team working with them and studying their notes. We can't spare Clive or Farrah, but, after Clive, she's the best magic expert we have here."

"You can spare me, though," Gary said. "I can be a lot more effective with the defences in place here than as part of the attack force. I asked the Tactical Commander to add me to the group staying."

"So that's why you're asking about the contingencies."

"Yeah. The briefing told me what they were, but not why. Now that I think about it, it also didn't mention what happens when we win."

"That's because we have no idea. At least we know what happens if we lose."

"We all die?"

"Yeah. And then I make a break for it, see if I can get back to the surface to warn them before I die two more times."

"Two more times?"

"It's all these messengers I've been draining. I've got two resurrections in the can, so it'll take three kills to drop me permanently."

"That must be nice."

"No, Gary. If it comes to that, the rest of you gone... I think dead might be better."

Jason sighed.

"Well, that got dark. Who else is hanging back to defend with you?"

"Rufus and his parents, plus some of the brighthearts and half the Magic Society researchers. Not a lot of golds, since we're probably letting the bad guys through anyway."

Jason nodded.

"I knew Clive was splitting up the researchers. They won't be great in a fight and Ramona may need help with the echo array. We have to take some of them to help Clive and Farrah, though."

Jason glanced at Miriam, who was looking in his direction.

"Time to go play boss man," he said. "At this point, I'm pretty much a mascot with Miriam in charge, but I have to at least wander around looking confident."

"Are you confident?" Gary asked.

"Relative to what's going on? Yeah. As these situations go, this one's pretty good. There's a lot of gold-rankers around, that's not new, but some of them being on team good guy is. There's a god looking to interfere, but at least it's not a great astral being. The evil army is a bunch of elemental messengers, not vampires and their ghoul minions, so I guess that part's a wash. It could be worse."

"So you think we'll win."

"I think we will, yeah. If I didn't, I'd be hatching some insane scheme to get us out of here. My real concern is how many people that victory is going to cost us. Fighting our way to the tree is going to bleed us."

"Good thing I'm staying behind, then. Nice and relaxing for me."

Jason chuckled.

"You might not want to get too comfy, mate. These things have a way of going pear-shaped."

The main force set out from the citadel chamber through the massive gate. The gate was a tunnel boring through the wall to the next chamber, a wall thick enough to have entire buildings dug into it. At the end of the tunnel was a massive stone slab that had been rolled aside to let the group pass through. Brighthearts made up around two-thirds of the force, all silver- and gold-rankers, but also the weakest. These people were new warriors, used to lives of peace, although the last few months had blooded them sharply. Even so, it was the cult and adventurer groups that were the stronger powers.

Flight was accomplished through a variety of devices. The cult had flight tools that seemed unaffected by the elemental magic, along with some vehicles that could accommodate a few others. Once again, familiars and summons did a lot of the work, although some would be precarious should combat impact them. Shade was counted amongst these, serving as vehicle transport for many of the brighthearts.

"I wish I could use my cloud flask for this," Jason told Emir. "I don't think a vehicle made of air and water is the best idea down here, though, heavily upgraded or not."

"Wise," Emir said.

Only a few of the brighthearts could fly under their own power. Those that could were usually ash types like Lorenn, along with some of the fire types. Those with metal, earth and magma affinities required outside assistance.

The passage across the death chamber took place almost entirely in silence. When they reached the other side unmolested, Lorenn gestured for Miriam, Jason and Beaufort to approach.

"What's the issue?" Miriam asked.

"Nothing came at us in the entire chamber," Lorenn said. "Not even a few loose spectres."

"I take it that's unusual?" Jason asked.

"It's unprecedented," Beaufort said. "I've had crossings where some genuine threats came after us, but mostly, it's something fairly weak. I've never before been left entirely alone."

"Especially with a group this size," Lorenn added. "There's a reason I warned everyone before we entered the chamber. That normally attracts trouble, which is why it's a problem for the messengers. They like to travel in hordes."

"You think something is going on in the dead zone?" Miriam asked.

"Yes," Lorenn said. "I'm inclined to take small mercies, but I don't want to dive into messenger territory, only to find an undead horde at our backs."

"I don't see an alternative to moving forward," Jason said. "Not unless you want us to dive into the bottom of the death chamber looking for trouble, which is self-defeating as methods to avoid trouble go."

They looked to their destination, another gate. This was open, the edges cracked and crumbling, roots poking out in various places. The roots were dark brown, almost black, looking more like stone than wood. Beyond the gate was darkness, although Jason could see what looked like an empty chamber beyond.

"We should hasten," Beaufort said. "The tree will have sensed us by now. Messengers will already be on the way."

Beaufort was proven right. The messengers arrived like a river soon after the group entered the chamber. As the united forces crossed the threshold of the gate, the permeating sense of death was replaced with elemental power, but unlike that of the citadel chamber. This energy was turbulent and volatile, pressing on the mind like half-heard music from a downstairs neighbour. It was enough to annoy but not distract as the force battled their way through.

Battling through the endless supply of elemental messengers was reminiscent of the descent through the shaft. Fortunately, each new batch had failed to learn the lessons of their predecessors and fell to the same tactics. The adventurers and their allies learned with each new battle while the messengers did not. Not only did they lack the intelligence to share experiences and strategies, but most of those attacking the adventurers died, without even a chance to share their knowledge.

With new messengers still being churned out by the tree, these messengers could have been as little as a few hours old. Messengers were produced to be battle-ready, only heightening Jason's suspicions that they were artificial in origin. As Clive was convinced that Jason was somehow linked to that origin, he expected to find the answers once he was an astral king. Assuming he got through the current situation alive.

The expedition moved with purpose. They fought through the first chamber, down a tunnel too narrow to allow the messengers to swarm them, then through a second where they were again attacked from all sides. One more tunnel led them to the astral space chamber and respite.

As the expedition had hoped, the messengers refused to enter the chamber. They were even wary of the tunnel leading into it, giving the expedition some breathing room. The root system that poked through every wall was still evident in the hall, but there was no sign of it in the chamber itself. The chamber was small, relative to others they'd seen, although still the size of a gymnasium. With so many people in the expedition, there wasn't a massive amount of spare room.

The walls and floor were carved in the same style Jason had seen in the citadel room's pillars, although more elaborately. The chamber had something of a cathedral feel to it, complete with an astral space aperture in place of an altar. Clive and Farrah immediately dragged the researchers in that direction while Miriam organised a defence of the entrance, an opening in one wall around twice the height and width of normal double doors.

Jason moved down the hall at a more sedate pace than Clive, who all but cracked a whip over the heads of his ritualists. The wall carvings were frescos depicting what he guessed was the arrival of the brightheart ancestors to the underground realm. Unlike the tunnels, the carvings hadn't been shattered by countless roots punching through, although there was some crumbling. It looked like there had been a mid-strength earthquake with no one to clean up afterwards.

Beaufort followed behind Jason and they arrived at the aperture, a circular sheet of red, orange and yellow energy that floated in the air. Clive and Farrah were already setting up testing devices as Jason extended his senses towards the portal, finding a seal in place that locked the aperture from the other side.

"You shut the gate behind you," Jason said.

"We did," Beaufort confirmed.

"Clive, the portal is sealed from the inside," Jason said. "Will that interfere with your tests?"

Clive let out a groan as he glared at Beaufort.

"Yes," he told Jason. "Can you go through and shut it down?"

"Sure," Jason said, weaving past the Magic Society researchers as they unpacked magical tools and supplies. As non-combatants, they had been put to work as pack mules.

"Asano," Beaufort called out. "You might want to wait until I... and he's gone."

Jason vanished through the portal, ignoring the seal that would have prevented anyone else from getting through. He appeared on the other side and was immediately blasted with fire and impaled multiple times by a series of elaborate mechanical traps.

"Rude," he croaked as Gordon appeared and used his beams to cut the offending blades from the mechanism, freeing Jason to yank them from his body.

Jason's regeneration quickly repaired his body as he kicked away the damaged trap device and broke the sealing ritual on the ground around the aperture. Having done so, he took a quick look around before leaving. There wasn't much to see, just a natural stone tunnel with a red glow coming from around a bend.

The elemental energy was more balanced here, free of the influence of the messenger tree. It was even more placid than in the citadel chamber, closer to what he'd created in his soul realm. It was probably a reflection of the natural array's original state. He went back through the aperture to inform Clive and Farrah.

"Oh, that's excellent," Farrah said. "That will give us the baseline readings we've been missing."

"Go," Clive said. "I'll finish setting up here and join you."

"Is there anything carnivorous in there?" Jason asked Beaufort.

"Probably," Beaufort said. "It spawned the occasional monster. Bronze and silver rank, mostly. We never saw a gold, but I wouldn't rule it out. How did you avoid the trap?"

"I didn't," Jason said, pulling back his hood to reveal his blackened and bloody face and charred hair before pulling it back up. "I'm just not worried about anything your kind can do. That said, you could have been a bit more urgent with your warning. Did Admiral Ackbar teach you nothing?"

"No, because I don't know who that is."

Jason went and found Valetta, the gold-rank architect studying the walls with a more educated eye than Jason had.

"Can you go into the aperture, please? Someone needs to be on watch in case a monster wanders in on the researchers."

Valetta nodded and walked towards the aperture.

"Oh, and Valetta?"

She stopped and turned with an enquiring look.

"If a monster does show up, don't just watch them fight it to see what happens, alright?"

She opened her mouth to fire off a retort but stopped herself, responding with a nod instead. Not long after she had followed Farrah through the portal, Jason and every gold-ranker present all snapped their heads to look in the same direction, as if they could see through the walls.

"What is that?" Miriam asked.

"Death," Amos Pensinata answered. "A lot of death."

A LITTLE BIT ODD

THE SILVER-RANKERS IN THE GROUP IMMEDIATELY SAW THE CONCERN ON the faces of Jason and the gold-rankers. Jason stepped right into Clive's personal space, arresting his attention.

"Clive, how long until you've learned enough here that we can try and activate the device without it being so much of a gamble that we may as well not bother?"

"Jason, what is—"

"How long?" Jason snapped as his aura rolled out like a military parade. Normally, he masked the authoritarian aspect of it, but now it choked the room such that even the gold-rankers were taken aback.

Clive frowned, but his mind went to work, eyes darting left to right, unfocused as he processed.

"Six minutes, but I don't like—"

"Then start," Jason said, already wheeling on the Magic Society researchers. "Figure out which supplies are essential for activating the device. Everything else gets left behind."

Jason turned to face Miriam, but she pre-empted him.

"We'll be ready to move in six minutes," she said.

Jason spared one second for an appreciative smile and sharp nod before heading for the aperture and passing through. Farrah had barely arrived and was still pulling tools out of one of the packs the Magic

Society members had been lugging. She took one look at Jason's face and stood up.

"What is it?" she asked.

"The death chamber just went active. Like Makassar, probably worse."

"Oh. How long?"

"Five and a half minutes. As much as you can get that Clive can use, then out. Ditch anything you won't absolutely need."

Jason didn't wait for a response before leaving and Farrah didn't give one. More than any other members of the expedition, they understood the sudden appearance of monster armies and fell into their old rhythm as they had on Earth. When he emerged from the portal, Miriam was wrangling the silver-rankers, cultists and brighthearts. Miriam sent one of her team members, Alice, to update him.

"The messengers that were amassing outside of this chamber pulled back," she told him. "Even the roots sticking through the walls in the tunnel outside pulled back. It's like the tree is scared."

Jason nodded and they headed for the gold-rank adventurers who were in huddled discussion. Along with Emir and Constance were most of Team Moon's Edge, Amos Pensinata and Hana Shavar, high priestess of the Healer.

"...must be what Destruction was actually after," Emir was saying as Jason and Alice joined the group.

"You think this is Destruction?" Jason asked.

"Destruction wasn't too fazed by us taking out his priests," Emir explained. "We all assumed that he was after the natural array, and that he believed we couldn't do anything about it. Either he gets his big blast as it reaches critical instability or the tree turns into some kind of apocalypse beast, turning every living thing into elemental messengers."

"Now," Hana said, "we think his goal was the death chamber all along."

"Undeath priests," Amos said. "You can feel the divine power in the death energy."

"Well, some of us can," Emir muttered.

Jason probed the energy with his senses and did find a touch of the divine. It was an utterly foul power, rancid like the fluids spilling from a plague-ridden corpse.

"The Church of Undeath is one of the few reliable allies the Church of Destruction has," Hana explained. "After Destruction didn't seem worried by the loss of his priests, I should have guessed what was happening the moment we came across that chamber full of the dead."

"What we missed doesn't matter," Constance said. "What we do now does."

"Asano," Amos said. "You once told me that you've encountered death on this scale before. That was a necromancer?"

"Yeah."

"This will be worse."

"Undeath priests are the most reviled people in our world," Constance explained to Jason. "More than Pain priests, even more than messengers."

She looked over at Beaufort getting his cultists into formation, ready to leave.

"The Builder cult might be the only ones who come close," she said, "given that they desecrate living bodies along with the dead."

"It's more than just how despicable they are too," Emir said. "The things they can do with the dead…"

He trailed off with a shudder.

"We came across one of their operations once when we were on a treasure-hunting contract," Constance explained. "I've never seen such horrors."

"The Church of Undeath does not act frequently," Hana said. "We don't give them the chance, and by we, I mean everyone. The Adventure Society and the Church of Death especially. So, they lay dormant for generations at a time, making plans in the dark. When they finally get that chance, it's like their god has been saving up his chances to intervene in the world. Expect to see some dark miracles."

"The plan doesn't change," Jason said. "It accelerates. From what I can sense, all that death energy has undergone a fundamental change. Presumably to undeath energy. It also seems to be spreading. Lord Pensinata?"

"Agreed," Amos said. "It seems to be devouring the elemental energy somehow."

"Undeath magic is hungry when the god of undeath gets involved," Hana said.

"Which is why we can't let it have the natural array. His priests could use that power to create powerful and unusual forms of undead. As it is, we can expect to see grave and pyre elementals."

"I don't know what they are and don't have the time to ask," said Jason.

"We don't know how much the messengers will back off before fighting back," Emir said. "There's no doubt they'll defend the tree, but we might have a short window to make a run at the tree without too many messengers in our way."

"Or we might try," Constance said, "and get pincered between the messengers and the undead."

"We're going," Jason said, his tone brooking no dissent. "Whatever we encounter, we encounter. My concern is the people we left in the citadel. The undeath taint on the local mana is interrupting the elemental energy that previously infused it. That's still affecting the range of my communication power, but can you communicate with your bodies in the citadel, Shade?"

"The connection is growing stronger," Shade said as he emerged from Jason's shadow. "This foul power is the opposite of everything my progenitor stands for, but undeath trembles before true demise. This power is antithetical to my nature but it does not impede me. Once the elemental power has diminished further, I should be able to communicate with the citadel. I would strongly recommend against attempting to shadow jump there through me, however."

"We've got more than enough to be going on with here," Jason said. "If other people could do that it would be more disappointing. Still, coordinating with them will be good, given what's happening. I hope they're alright, being right next to the death chamber."

"We can't do anything for them from here," Amos said. "I'm not sure we can do anything for ourselves. I'm sensing the undead rise as the priests create them."

"Rank-for-rank," Emir said, "even powerful undead can't match adventurers on our level."

"Not when the numbers are even," Amos said. "I'm already sensing bronze-rank undead in the tens of thousands. Silver in the thousands. Less than a hundred gold, but that number grows with each passing moment."

Arabelle and Gabriel Remore floated towards the massive gate halfway up the wall of the citadel chamber. They were carried on an ash cloud created by Gabriel, whose fire powers were enhanced by the elemental energy. But as the undeath energy seeped through the wall between the citadel chamber and the death field beyond, he could feel that advantage eroding away.

"Priests of Undeath?" he asked, knowing the answer but hoping he was wrong.

"Yes," his wife confirmed.

"Even if we joined up with the other group, do we have the numbers to handle this?"

"No."

"Course of action?"

"Around two hundred thousand brighthearts died in that chamber, along with who knows how many messengers. Nothing short of rewriting reality to change the situation entirely will get us out of it."

"Good thing that's Asano's plan, then."

They arrived at the short tunnel that led through the wall to the gate. The massive stone slab had been rolled back into place after the expedition departed, but the magically warded doors set into it were open. The brightheart guards stationed in the alcoves on the outside of the slab were retreating inside and their leader gestured urgently to the approaching adventurers.

"Mr and Mrs Remore. My name is Yokas. We need to seal the doors so their wards can help resist the death energy, but there's something you need to see."

Gabriel floated his cloud to the door and they looked out into what had been darkness the last time they passed through the chamber. That was no longer the case. The death chamber had once been the main home to the brightheart population, with buildings carved into the walls and hanging from the ceiling, along with sprawling across the ground. Many of them had crumbled under the assault of the messenger tree root system that itself had abandoned the place as it became a hall of death. The glow stones had long dimmed and the luminescent flora had died, leaving it dark, empty and ruined.

Most of the chamber was unchanged, dilapidated and half-collapsed, but now washed in an ominous purple light. The source of the illumination was a cluster of buildings on the ground, at the centre of the ruined brightheart city. There, the building had been wildly transformed. Towers were warped, sections of stone bulging like blisters and shining with the purple light. The light pulsed in a slow heartbeat rhythm, in sync as if the buildings were a single organism.

Other buildings, half-ruined already, had been crudely reassembled with sections of masonry held in place with massive bones, skewering the stonework like chunks of meat. The results looked oddly like the buildings themselves had somehow been turned into zombies.

The affected area continued to spread as they watched. Massive bones, like the legs of giant spiders, raised up chunks of masonry and returned them to broken buildings. Stonework pustules distended out like pregnant bellies and started to shine with purple light. The affected area of the city was growing at a rate that would reach them in a couple of hours, perhaps less.

"I'm going to go ahead and say that's bad," Gabriel said.

"The ground level of the citadel chamber is already under siege," Yokas said. "The gate down there has been sealed entirely for months; we filled it in with rocks and fused them together. The undead are coming through the wall instead. The buildings dug into the wall left it hollowed out, and while we filled and sealed the holes as best we could, there was only so much we could do."

"Zombie brighthearts?"

"Some, yes. The ones that are just animated people seem to retain at least some of their elemental power. There are other things too, though."

"That shouldn't happen with reanimation," Arabelle said. "The priests of Undeath must be using their god's power to feed on the elemental magic. Using it to create more powerful undead."

"They definitely are," Yokas said. "We've seen things out there that aren't right. Some of them are big; you'll see them wandering around the buildings if you give it a moment. It might be best not to, though."

"I'm worried about the messengers from the surface," Arabelle said. "We don't know how they intended to get into the citadel chamber, but now we need them for Jason's plan. If they've been caught up in the... are you sensing that?"

"It's a little hard to miss," Gabriel said as they looked at the city.

Tainted magic energy surged from somewhere within the expanding undead metropolis.

"It's been doing that," Yokas said. "We think it happens when they make the big ones."

"There's something else," Arabelle said. "Something alive. There."

She pointed at a section of the city, just outside the limits of the current expansion. Several figures rose into the sky, shooting towards the gate. These were messengers from the surface, not the elementally transformed ones, and they were fleeing for their lives. They shot into the air, making a beeline for the gate from which the adventurers watched them.

Messengers were not small, standing from seven to ten feet on average, but what came after them was much larger. It held the vague shape of a messenger, flapping enormous wings as it pursued the real thing. There was no mistaking it for the real thing, however; it was a heinous abomination.

Beyond the size, around twice that of a regular messenger, the body was much bulkier. It was not some giant messenger raised from the dead either, but an amalgam of other creatures, parts crudely sewn together with dead tree roots. The flesh had been taken from messengers, brighthearts and what looked to be some monsters, their corpses somehow preserved instead of turning to rainbow smoke.

Whoever or whatever had created the abomination had not found a way to build a large head from the parts it had available. Instead, the broad shoulders were topped with five messenger heads that appeared to do nothing, lolling like the corpses they were.

The messengers fled from it, a gold and several silvers. One of the silvers carried a bathtub-sized object that looked much like the device the messengers had provided the expedition. As they fled, the heads of the monstrosity woke up. Their mouths opened wide and their heads swivelled in unison like the clown ball game at a fairground, but not as creepy. Fleshy tongues shot out, the only part of the creature that looked like living flesh. They whipped forward, dancing with prehensile agility to wrap up the silvers. Only the gold-ranker was nimble enough to avoid them and kept bolting for the gate.

"Husband," Arabelle said. "Fetch."

Gabriel shot off, leaving a trail of flame in his wake. Arabelle levitated in the air, the one way that essence users could employ physical force with their auras, if far less effectively than a messenger.

"Would you like me to take the form of a mount, Mrs Remore?" Shade asked from her shadow.

"Thank you, Shade."

A cloud of darkness emerged from her shadow and took the shape of a giant crow with glowing white eyes. She sat cross-legged atop it, riding the gentle undulations as it held itself aloft with the slow flapping of wings.

"I went with a darkwind crow," Shade explained. "It is not native to this world but is highly popular in—"

"I am sure the history is fascinating, Shade, but perhaps when events are a little less urgent."

"I apologise, Mrs Remore. I get rather out of sorts when my bodies are isolated from one another. Mr Asano's niece repeatedly talked me into exercising bad judgement while most of my bodies were with him in isolated astral spaces."

A trail of fire led from the gate, past the gold-rank messenger to where the silver-rankers were entangled in tentacle tongues that were now growing barbs that sank into their flesh. Gabriel arrived in a literal blaze of glory, his sword the yellow-white of molten steel, flames dancing along the blade. He swiftly went to work, not on liberating the messengers but cutting loose the magical device. The tongues had wrapped around the messenger carrying it and the device both, so Gabriel cut them away with a sickly sizzle of flesh.

As soon as the device fell loose, Gabriel snatched it up and shot away. The messengers he left to their fate, the monstrosity content to feed on them as he made good his escape.

"Any word from Jason?" Arabelle asked as she watched the proceedings.

"Not yet, Mrs Remore, but I am starting to get a sense of my other bodies as the elemental energy diminishes. I imagine that communication will be possible soon."

The gold-rank messenger trailed a cloud of embers behind him as he flew. He arrived in front of Arabelle and stopped in place. After glancing at the guards who had weapons at the ready, he held up his hands.

"Take me to your leader?" he asked, then glanced back. "Quickly, please? This new job sucks donkey balls."

Arabelle and the guards looked at the messenger in startled silence as Gabriel arrived behind him.

"Is it just me," Gabriel asked, "or is this messenger a little bit odd?"

79

DUBIOUS ALLIANCE

ONSLOW'S SHELL WAS STUFFED FULL OF ADVENTURERS AND BRIGHTHEARTS as the expedition moved through an empty tunnel. The cultists could propel themselves, but, even if they couldn't, Clive wouldn't allow them on anyway. Clive was on top of the shell, along with Neil, Belinda, Rufus and other non-fliers that couldn't fit inside. Belinda had conjured a flat surface for them to sit on, atop a frame that held it fast to the sloping lid of the shell.

Neil brushed stone powder from his hair, not for the first time since re-entering the tunnels. The roof had been riddled with protruding roots the last time they passed through and now there was nothing but empty holes. Crumbling stone had been dropping onto their heads and clouds of stone dust drifted slowly down.

The expedition moved in wary silence, following the guidance of Lorenn. They had been expecting to fight tooth and nail, but the messengers had packed up and left. Tunnels they'd claimed from the brighthearts in long, bloody conflict were now abandoned and empty.

"This is eerie," Clive said. "The messengers fought us for every step we took on the way in."

"We're flying," Belinda pointed out. "We didn't take any steps."

He turned his head to give her a flat look.

"Hey," she said. "I'm not the one complaining that we *don't* have to fight our way through an army that flies and breathes fire."

"It does make you wonder what's waiting for us at the end, though," Rufus said.

"I see that everyone's optimistic today," Belinda said.

"I might be optimistic, you don't know," Neil said. "Maybe what's waiting for us at the end is snacks."

"There's an undead army coming," Belinda pointed out. "We are the snacks."

"Now who's short on optimism?" Neil asked.

"Nothing wrong with a little hope," Jason said as he approached through the air, his cloak spread out like wings. "It takes hope to find the light in the dark. Give up and you'll miss it."

He landed on the platform and his cloak gathered around him. The result looked like a human-shaped portal with a pair of glowing eyes.

"That would be very inspiring," Neil said, "if it didn't come from a void monster here to snatch away children in the night."

"That's a little hurtful," Jason said.

"No, that's what you look like," Belinda said, the others nodding their agreement. "Look, you're even spooking the brighthearts."

Jason turned his gaze on the other occupants on top of Onslow's shell. Some of them flinched back.

"Your aura doesn't help," Rufus pointed out. "You're pushing it out pretty hard and it's feeling a bit... strict."

"I need everyone following orders, be they mine or Miriam's."

"Yeah," Neil said, "but your particular brand of authority is less 'obey or die' and more 'to transgress against my will is a sin that shall render thee unto damnation.' I know we want everyone sharp, but there's such a thing as too on edge."

"Did you just use 'obey or die' as the example of something I'm worse than?" Jason asked. "It's not that bad, is it? Rufus?"

Rufus absently scratched his chin while awkwardly looking off to the side.

"Oh, come on."

"Mr Asano," Shade said, one of his bodies stepping out of Jason's cloak. "I have managed to re-establish a connection with my bodies in the citadel chamber."

"Thank you," Jason said, then turned to his team members.

"I'm going to project my senses through Shade. Do me a favour and make sure I don't fall off while I'm distracted."

"I'll do it!" Neil said.

"Anyone but Neil," Jason said.

Neil groaned. "I knew I was too enthusiastic as soon as the words came out of my mouth."

Arabelle, Gabriel and Yokas, the gold-rank brightheart guard, escorted their messenger prisoner to the citadel, flying formation around him. A silver-rank guard carried the device Gabriel had liberated from the messengers as they were being snatched by the undead monstrosity in the death chamber. The doors to the death chamber were now closed and sealed, their warding magic in full effect.

"You're suspicious, I get that," the messenger said. "I don't think there's much I can say that will turn you around on that. I need to speak to Jason Asano."

"He's not here," Gabriel growled. "Even if he were, we don't have time for that."

"Yeah, no kidding. No one likes a surprise zombie army, especially Asano. Last time he fought one, he went dead-voiced murder machine on them all, and he never really came back from it."

"He came back from it," Arabelle said.

"Not on Earth. He became a recluse after that, and when he did show up, it was to conquer parts of Europe or kill a bunch of people with his mind. I saw him do that on TV."

Arabelle observed their prisoner with a frown.

"How much time did you spend on Asano's world?"

"A lot more than he ever did."

"You have a lot of explaining to do," she told him.

"Yeah, but like your henchman said, we don't have time for that."

"Henchman?" Gabriel said. "I'm her husband!"

The messenger looked from Arabelle to Gabriel and back to Arabelle.

"You could do better," he told her. "I know we don't have a lot of time to spare, but you and I could—"

"You don't seem too worried about the death of your fellow messengers," she said, cutting him off. She'd learned how to keep Jason on track through years of counselling. Compared to that, this messenger was an amateur at conversation derailment.

"Those poor saps worked for Vesta Carmis Zell," the messenger said.

"We'd have just had to kill them anyway once they realised I've already rigged the device to help Asano."

"You're claiming that you don't work for Zell?" Gabriel asked.

"Yes and no. It's complicated. You're not going to trust me and Asano is the only one who can fact-check the details of my story."

"Before you speak with Jason," Arabelle said to the messenger. "Let's start with your name."

"Boris Ketland. You can call me Boris."

"That's not a messenger name," Arabelle pointed out.

"Right, sorry. My real name is Boris Ket Lundi. I haven't used that in a looong time."

They landed on a balcony platform where Marla was waiting for them with a pair of offsiders. As Lorenn's second-in-command, she was in charge of the citadel. As the group landed, Boris looked her up and down, taking in the glowing orange hair and delicate features.

"Hey, I'm Boris. How you living, girl?"

"Chain him," Marla said. One of her offsiders was a gold-rank metal-affinity brightheart who conjured chains that wrapped around the messenger.

"Oh, I like you," Boris said as his wings vanished and he shrank to human size, the chains falling to his feet. The guard moved to replace them, but Marla stopped him with a gesture. She looked at the device being carried by the guard.

"Do you know how to use that?" she asked Boris.

"Sure do. I also know why Asano needs me to, and it's already rigged. Take me to your echo array chamber, let me knock out a ritual circle and we're good to go. But as I told the unsatisfied wife, here, you won't trust me. I need to speak to Asano so I can convince him and he can convince you."

Shade rose out of Arabelle's shadow.

"Convince me of what?" Jason's voice came from the familiar.

Gary had joined a group of brighthearts reinforcing the wall between the citadel and the death chamber. The problem was that the wall had been hollowed out centuries earlier and turned into level after level of buildings. Gary's earth, iron and forge essences, along with his knowledge of defensive structures, complemented the abilities of the brighthearts. They were shaping stone and metal, shoring up the barricades that filled the building interiors. Gary then went to work, refining and strengthening the materials used, along with improving the barricade designs to be more effective.

"These were our government administration buildings," Kollas told Gary as they climbed the stairs to the next level. She was a metal-shaper and the leader of the detachment.

"I thought your government was run from the top of the citadel," Gary said.

"The council chamber is up there, and a few office and staff areas for the council and their staff. The actual business of government is all the people who keep it running, though, and all that was here."

Her expression darkened.

"My wife worked in one of these buildings. When the Builder cult invaded, she signed up for the new defensive force. We had no idea of how to fight at all, back then. The casualties were…"

She shook her head to clear it as increased her pace up the stairs.

"Now we're fighting alongside those same cultists," she continued, spitting out the words.

Gary couldn't think of anything that sounded supportive rather than trite, so he stayed silent as he followed her up the stairs.

"The lower levels are fairly secure as is," Kollas said, her brief spate of melancholy absent from her voice as she changed the subject. "We've all but filled them in, piling them with rock and fusing it into solid stone. Less attention was paid to the defences the higher we go, but none of it was ignored. Now we need to strengthen some of the mid and upper levels."

Their stairwell was just inside the buildings, on the citadel side. Being inside the wall, Gary could sense the undead on the other side. They were massed at the bottom, but some were climbing the wall as well.

"Do you think the wall will hold?" one of the other brighthearts asked nervously.

"I know it will not," Kollas said. "We have to do our best to make breaches as hard for them as possible. We work to stop any major breaches and make repairs after the minor ones that will be coming."

"What about setting weak points?" Gary asked. "Create funnels. Kill boxes."

"That would be nice if we had more people to put on the other side of those funnels. We're kind of doing that by focusing our resources on the lower levels. At least we can make them climb for the weaker points. In the end, we're not trying to win. We're trying to not die until your friend yanks us all into an astral space or whatever he's doing. It all sounds a bit crazy to me."

"Sometimes crazy is the only plan that will work," Gary said. "That's when you need Jason."

"You claim that you're from Earth," Jason said through Shade.

"Yes," Boris said. "And I know that leads to about a thousand questions that none of us have time for. What I have to say next will lead to a thousand more."

"And what's that?" Jason asked.

"I'm with the Unorthodoxy."

"That makes no sense."

"Tell me about it."

"Vesta Carmis Zell would never send anyone down here without a brand on their soul."

"Correct. I'm going to need you to help me get rid of that, by the way. I've got another twelve days or so before she breaks through the thing keeping her from exerting control over me."

"How is that even possible?"

"Zell likes to think that she's the best soul engineer in the cosmos. She's not. Messengers all tend to think they're the best whatever in the cosmos."

"But not you?" Jason asked.

"No, even me, although I happen to be right. I'm the best lover in the cosmos."

"Why should I believe any of this?"

"You could have Marla check real quick. Well, not *real* quick. I am the best lover in the cosmos."

"Anyone can tell you that I love some quality banter as much as the next guy," Jason said. "But there is a time for it to stop, so any more of this and I'll have them kill you because I don't have time to put up with you. Why should I give you even the slimmest modicum of trust?"

"Because you don't have time not to, which everyone keeps saying. I promise that I am downright eager to explain all this once we don't have an army of undead we need to deal with. We need to trigger the transformation zone."

"How do you know about that?"

"The Cabal has managed to gather a lot of information on you, and I've seen you use transformation zones on the news."

"You're with the Cabal? The Cabal on Earth?"

"We *founded* the Cabal, but that doesn't matter right now. When Vesta Carmis Zell started shopping around other astral kings for elemental messengers, my real astral king realised what was going to happen down here. Zell's plans aren't exactly a secret amongst her peers. Once we figured out how much the dimensional membrane here would get battered by what Zell was doing, we realised how you would respond. As I said, I've seen you using transformation zones before. I pitched a plan to my astral king and was fake sold to Zell to make sure you succeeded. It was going fine until the undead army no one expected raised their flag."

"Why do any of this? The Unorthodoxy doesn't care about this world."

"No, we care about you. I don't know how much you know about us, but the Unorthodoxy is scattered and lacking in allies. We hide because we lack the strength to fight, and nothing ever changes. You're shaping up to be the largest shift in the game state in millennia, but you aren't any use to us if you die while you're still mortal. And getting on your good side now seemed like a good idea."

"You know how to use the device you have?"

"Not a problem. I was never put through messenger indoctrination, so I was never told what I could and couldn't learn. I'm the best astral magic specialist on this planet."

"Second best," Jason said.

"Jason," Neil said, shaking Jason's shoulder.

His eyes snapped open.

"What is it?"

"You'd best go up the front."

Jason realised that the expedition had come to a halt. His cloak flared out like wings and he flew forward while reaching out to Miriam through voice chat.

"What's going on?"

"We caught up to the elemental messengers."

He reached the front of the group where the gold-rankers were set up in a defensive line. Clive was behind them, riding on a black flying bird with white eyes. They were near the end of a tunnel leading into an open chamber. At the entrance was a row of gold-rank elemental messengers, a mirror of the expedition's frontline. Jason moved next to Clive and Miriam turned to look at him.

"They haven't attacked, or even made aggressive moves," Miriam said. "They're trying to communicate with hand gestures."

"Anything you've managed to make out?"

"My translation power is picking out bits and pieces," Clive said. "These were originally messengers from the surface, so they have the capacity for language, but I doubt that language includes a hand-signing component. But it's obvious what they want."

"And what's that?" Jason asked.

"An alliance," Miriam said.

Jason's eyebrows shot up.

"That's... unexpected."

"We need you to make the call, Operations Commander," Miriam said. "Do we fight our way in, or try to deal with them?"

Her eyes glanced at Beaufort briefly, the cultist in line with the other gold-rankers.

"We don't understand how they think," she said. "It's a risky proposition, even compared to our other dubious alliance."

"According to Marla," Jason said, "the undead are expanding some kind of territory through the dead zone, infusing the buildings with their tainted mana. They expect it to reach the wall in less than two hours, and they don't expect to hold out much longer after that."

"You're saying that we don't have a lot of time to do this."

"I am. I'm going to go have a chat."

"You're going to go over there? Miriam asked.

"Yep."

"With all those gold-rank messengers whose minds have been warped by unstable magic."

"Yep."

"You have the power to come back from the dead, right?"

"Yep."

"Okay, good luck."

Jason floated through the line of gold-rankers and towards the messengers. One of their number floated out to meet him, a fire type whose body seemed to be made up almost entirely of diamonds and rubies that shone with internal light. The only part of her that looked organic was her long red hair, and even then it had the metallic sheen of celestine hair.

The messenger immediately started to communicate through large gestures, her meaning plain. She gestured at her own people and then at Jason's, followed by putting her hands together, fingers interlocked.

"Can you understand me?" Jason asked.

The messenger nodded.

"You want to ally with us against the undead."

Nod.

"What assurance do we have that you won't massacre us the moment we enter your territory?"

The messenger looked frustrated, her mouth opening and closing repeatedly. Finally, her face took on an expression of exertion and she spoke one word in something between a growl and hiss.

"Need."

"You need us?" Jason asked.

Nod.

"Here is the best offer I can make," Jason said. "The dead are too numerous. Even together, we can't kill them all. Especially not if you are especially vulnerable to them, and I think your actions have proven that to be the case. Do you understand what I am saying?"

Nod.

"And do you agree?"

The messenger's face showed reluctance, but after a moment, it nodded.

"Alright. The only way we have to overcome the undead is to trap them in a distorted reality, and us with them. This whole underground domain, in fact. Including your tree."

The messenger opened her mouth to release a feral, hissing roar, her face twisted with rage. Jason didn't react, waiting for her to stop before continuing as if nothing had happened.

"Once we are all inside the distorted reality space, we will all have to compete. Our people, your people and the undead. The winners take everything and the losers lose everything. That is the only offer I can make you. Every other path I see leads to your people and mine joining the ranks of the dead."

The messenger wasn't happy but turned and floated back to her people while Jason stayed in place. The gold-rank messengers gathered in a huddle. They did not speak, and while they made occasional grunts, snarls and hisses, Jason did not believe that was their means of communication. He sensed a complex interplay of elemental magic that he believed to be their language, his ability to sense it even teasing at his translation power like words half-heard through a wall. Finally, she returned.

"Will you let us in?" Jason asked. "We will need access to the natural array to perform our magic."

More reluctance on the messenger's face didn't stop her from making a jerking nod.

80

COME LIKE A TSUNAMI

THE EXPEDITION MOVED FORWARD WITH EXTREME WARINESS. THE elemental messengers ranged ahead of them while scouts were left behind to monitor the approach of the undead. Miriam and Jason were atop Onslow's shell in the middle of the formation.

"I'm surprised that the messengers went along with this," Miriam said. "This isn't just mutual defence against the undead but reshaping the reality their tree is in."

"I'm not sure how much of what I explained they really understood," Jason told her.

"You may be overlooking something," Clive said.

"Oh?" Jason asked.

"As best we can tell, the messengers aren't in charge. The tree that made them this way is. We think the tree has some kind of will, but does it have intelligence? Yes or no, I think the tree's objective is its own welfare, not that of the messengers it created. Whether it understands your proposal or not, we know it recognises the threat of the undead. Perhaps it has realised that your proposal is the only escape from them."

As the expedition moved through the tunnels and chambers, the brighthearts amongst them grew increasingly angry. These places had once been the homes where they lived. Where they grew their food, where they had played as children. Everything they had ever known had been stolen from them and left to ruin.

Once they reached the areas still claimed by the tree, it became so much worse. These places were unrecognisable, overgrown with vines and moss, but not the kind they were familiar with. Everything was washed in a blood-red light that came from the plants themselves, sickly red veins running through vines and leaves. Most disturbing were the pods, some empty and others containing half-grown messengers floating in murky fluid. They hung from the walls and ceilings in clutches.

All this had been made from the brightheart dead, tens of thousands of them. The material processed by the tree; the fertiliser used to grow it. This was a defilement of their entire species, their families and friends churned up and reused like sacks of manure.

Lorenn worked to keep her people calm, although Jason could feel the volatility in their auras. They were on the verge of boiling over, which would be a disaster in their current location. Attacking the messengers this deep into their territory would get them swarmed on every side. Jason considered trying to clamp down on them using his own aura but decided the risk was too high. He trusted Lorenn to keep her people in check, knowing their trust in her was strong.

Stone and steel erupted as the wall exploded, raining debris through the spreading cloud of dust. Yellow glow stones set into the wall around the breach dimmed as purple light shone through from the other side, the intrusion of undeath energy sapping their power.

Gary came tromping downstairs from above, followed by a massive iron golem that glowed with internal heat. He had summoned his forge golem after the first breach, the two of them being the main force of their response team. The others were stone and metal shapers who would repair the breach once Gary and his golem had beaten the undead back.

This breach was on the third level of twenty-six, the lower levels suffering the heaviest assaults. Other response teams were scattered across the walls, reinforcing where they could and reacting when they had to. Most of the assaults thus far had been streams of bronze-rank enemies, with a few silvers mixed in. The power level of the undead was climbing with every breach, however. Silvers and even the occasional gold were amongst the attackers in growing numbers.

The weaker undead were animated brighthearts and elemental messengers. Many retained elemental powers, breathing fire or lobbing small boulders. Gary deflected the projectiles with his shield and ignored the flames as he waded into the throng, pushing back the horde. He and his golem were like construction machinery, shoring up riverbanks against the flood.

When they had pushed back enough, Gary conjured a barrier that would only hold for moments, but that was enough. He and the golem pulled back and the element shapers filled the gap, restoring the barricades. The restored barriers weren't as strong as they were pre-breach, but they would do for the moment. The defenders knew they were plugging holes in a dam that would ultimately give way entirely. The best they could do was buy time.

Gary saw the stricken faces of his brightheart support team and placed a hand on the shoulder of Kollas, their leader.

"I know it's hard seeing your own people come at you like monsters, trying to take away what little you have left. Just remember that they aren't the ones we're fighting; they're the ones we're avenging. They are not our enemies but the victims of our enemies. Save your rage for the ones who turned them into weapons and sent them against you. Stay strong and remember that you're also fighting for the people you've lost, not just the living."

Jason and Miriam moved to the front of the group when Lorenn signalled them.

"We're approaching the natural array chamber," she said. "You're about to see the tree."

Jason had been expecting some level of reluctance on the part of the messengers to let the expedition into their most sacred space, but there was nothing. Clive's thoughts on the primacy of the tree's will seemed to be accurate, with the elemental messengers being little more than puppets. It was only the tree that mattered.

None of the chambers and tunnels they had encountered thus far had been sealed. Any construction they contained, from buildings to the doors and gates had been demolished, red-veined plants crawling over the few shattered remnants. The array chamber was different, with roots forming a solid mesh over the entrance to the chamber. As the expedition approached, those roots withdrew, the mesh unravelling to reveal the chamber beyond.

The room was awash with red light. At its centre, the leafless tree grew like an enormous pillar, its branches digging into the ceiling and its roots into the floor. The bark had a craggy, stone-like quality to it and lava trickled from numerous points like sap. The result was a tree that looked halfway to being a volcano.

Pillars of natural stone filled the rest of the chamber like a forest. The walls, floor and pillars were all covered in vines and moss from which flowers grew in abundance. Those flowers shone blindingly bright, giving the room its red-alert tint.

Jason could sense the array under it all, essences and awakening stones embedded in the walls, floor, ceiling and pillars. He could feel their interplay, creating a power far greater than the sum of its parts. He could also feel its instability. The tree sat at the centre of the elemental power like a black hole, warping and twisting everything around it.

Jason floated forward alone. The messengers didn't move to stop him and he gestured back Lorenn and Miriam when they moved to follow. He reached the tree, the trunk spread out in front of him like a wall. He extended his hand and touched it.

Birthing Tree (corrupted)

- This birthing tree is the result of a failed attempt to create a soul forge. Lacking the proper environment to grow, it has adapted a local energy source, corrupting it and being corrupted in turn.

Jason could feel a will pressing against his own. It was powerful but young, scared and erratic. It tried to claw its way into him, but he sensed no maliciousness. To expand was its nature and he felt how unsettled it was at having been forced to pull back from its claimed territory. This was not a malevolent force, Jason realised. It was an animal, wounded and confused, following its instincts.

The tree's will was strong, but it was a leaf in a hurricane next to what Jason had once experienced from the Builder. Jason fended it off easily, suddenly feeling pity for the tree, a warped living thing that did not even understand its own nature. He impressed his own will on it, his intentions not to destroy the tree but to heal it. There was a susurration in the chamber, a breeze that should not appear underground rustling the glowing flowers.

Jason nodded to himself, then turned and floated back to the group. On arrival, he was already snapping off orders.

"Clive and the ritualist team, get to work. Miriam, set up a defensive perimeter however you think best. We need to hold this chamber long enough for the ritualists to do their work. Councilwoman Lorenn, you and your people know these chambers, so please coordinate with the Tactical Commander. I seem to communicate with the messengers passably, so I'll do my best to play liaison."

If the undead attacking the citadel chamber wall were just an army of reanimated brighthearts and messengers, the wall blocking them from the citadel chamber would never fall. They had elemental powers but used them crudely, lacking the finesse to stone-shape their way through. Instead, they blasted ineffectual attacks at the walls, getting nowhere.

The messengers had lost the power of flight in their transformation to the walking dead, even if their wings remained intact. The magic that allowed their flight had been lost, although some of their elemental powers remained. They were larger and stronger than the brighthearts, but still far from enough to shatter the barriers blocking the internal sections of the citadel chamber wall. The adventurers and brighthearts had reinforced them well.

The encroaching power of undeath would eventually overtake the wall, at which point its fall was inevitable. The priests of Undeath were unwilling to wait that long, however, and had already started deploying more powerful undead.

The rank and file, the brighthearts and messengers, did not require direct intervention to create. The priests had been quietly developing a self-perpetuating system while everyone believed the death chamber was quiet and empty save for some spontaneously risen spectres and zombies. The priests had carefully measured out enough threat to make the brighthearts and messengers wary without triggering a retaliatory response. That left them free to make their preparations.

The first undead the priests had animated to serve as manual labour. From there, they established the spawning pits in which they seated the power bestowed by Undeath. These were the heart of this new domain; not only would they animate any corpse thrown into them, but they would spread the influence of undeath energy.

The greater that influence spread, the more powerful the undead created. This was why the first waves had been weak bronzes, but more and more silvers emerged with every passing moment. As for the source of the bodies, the undead were tossing in one corpse after another. The tainted death energy of the chamber was preserving them, even high-ranking bodies not dissolving into rainbow smoke.

The preservation of bodies was the very reason Undeath had sent the priests so deep underground. A massive supply of corpses, death magic gone wrong and a well-hidden location was a veritable wish list for the Church of Undeath.

Silver rank was as far as the pits would ever raise the undead, so the priests also had their part. It fell on them to create individual undead that could reach greater heights, custom-building gold-rank undead one by one.

Garth Larosse was a priest of Undeath, and was himself an unliving thing. He stood at the same height as a messenger, some nine feet tall, his skeletal body wrapped in a dark green cloak. The silhouette it formed showed that the body underneath, formed from the skeletons of a dozen monsters, did not conform to humanoid norms. Beneath his hood, a skull with glowing red eyes watched the undead crawl from the spawning pits.

He was the leader of dozens of Undeath's priests, all gold and silver rank. They had already claimed any prime corpse material for their more elaborate creations, while anything else went to the pits. Most of the corpses were brighthearts and messengers, but there were monsters as well. Anything relatively intact would eventually crawl back out while loose limbs and other chunks were consumed as fuel to spread the influence of undeath in the ambient magic.

The priests did get an occasional treat when the pits spat out some abominations of flesh made from fused random parts. They weren't especially powerful, but the priests did find them hilarious, with arms sticking out of faces and eyes in the back of knees. They tended to stumble around, accomplishing nothing, and sometimes just exploded without warning.

Garth knew that hordes did not matter for the moment. Barely controllable, he left them to their impotent scratching at the wall blocking them from the citadel chamber. The weak masses were for overrunning the enemy once their defences broke.

Garth and his priests had been focused on crafting their more powerful undead. Bespoke abominations, exalting the glory of Lord Undeath, he who would claim the world. None of them were strong enough to put down the strongest defenders, unfortunately.

If they had more powerful creatures as base materials, that would be a different story. As a boy, Garth had seen an undead dragon. In that moment, he had understood that he would forever serve the god of undeath. The concept of such power at his command was a dream that he had never lost.

This task, deep underground, was that chance. The gold-rank messengers and adventurers that currently opposed them would become the core of a new army. As for the tree, even Undeath himself was excited at the prospect. Garth had felt the god's eagerness each time they communed.

But first, this underground realm needed to be captured. Left to his own devices, Garth would have ignored the citadel chamber where the last of the brighthearts had hidden away. The expansion of the undeath influence would claim them soon enough. But the lord had manifested in person to instruct him to wipe them out. Although the god did not say as much, Garth knew there was a threat there that had to be eliminated sooner rather than later.

The gold-rank abominations they had would not break through the wall any faster than waiting for the undeath influence to reach it. For this reason, Garth and his priests had created a wasteful but effective-for-purpose form of undead. One of Garth's priests, Jeff, insisted on calling them boomers, an idiotic name that had sadly caught on amongst the rest of the clergy.

The boomers were simple creations. A mound of flesh on four legs, the flesh was overcharged with volatile elemental power. If detonated amongst their own forces, they were a liability, but they had forces to spare. So long as they were effective at breaching the wall, it didn't matter. When they could at least enter partway into the walls before exploding because of the old buildings, it was all the more effective.

With preparations to take the citadel chamber progressing, Garth called up his servant priests.

"The wall to the citadel chamber will soon collapse," he announced. "It is time to turn our attention to our next objective and make sure our preparations are in order. The messenger tree is the greater objective, and while there is no wall to stop us, the tunnels and chambers between here and there will be filled with defenders. Make sure the lesser undead do not depart yet. They will be wasted if we allow them to trickle in. Hold them back until they are ready to inundate the tunnels like a wave. When they come, they will come like a tsunami."

There was a smothered snort of laughter and the red light in Garth's skull sockets dimmed in frustration.

"I swear to Undeath, Jeff, if your uncle wasn't a rune lich…"

81
PUT UP OR SHUT UP

THE FIRST MAJOR BREACH OF THE WALL WAS ON THE FIFTH FLOOR. IT began as a minor breach, the wall blasting out in a cloud of stone dust and rubble. Gary's team was the first to respond, with the leonid once more moving in to block the gap. That was when he saw one of the creatures responsible for the explosions, little more than a glowing blob on four legs. He threw his hammer, trying to kill the thing before it marched into the hole, but something slammed into place to block his attack. A more powerful undead, something like a jet-black mantis with quick, jerking movements and arms ending in chitinous shields. If not for the aura it emitted, it would be hard to tell it was undead.

Gary's hammer flew back to his hand as the mantis creature moved forward, protecting the thing behind it. Gary hunkered behind his own shield as he backed off, knowing what was coming. He yelled at his support team to run.

The blast destroyed the shield mantis creature. Ironically, this also shielded Gary and his golem from the full blast, although they were still both thrown out from the wall to drop five storeys down. The wall itself was not so shielded and had already been weakened by the blast that caused the first breach. The floor above collapsed, taking that level's barricades with it and leaving a two-storey hole for the undead to pour through. They had to climb over the mound of rubble that had dropped from above, but that was barely an impediment.

Gary and his heavy armour left spiderweb cracks in the ground when he landed in a crouch. He slung his massive sledge-like weapon, Gary's Medium Hammer, over his back. The magical bandolier he wore over his conjured armour held it conveniently in place. He then plucked a tiny hammer that was dangling from his belt, the handle barely long enough for his hand to grip. Normally, he would keep it in his dimensional pouch, but they were still unreliable and he'd had a feeling he'd need it.

Gary's strength rivalled gold rank, so he didn't just stand up from a crouch but launched himself straight up into the air, armour and all. He reached the level of the hole he'd been tossed from, even a little higher, and threw the tiny hammer in his hand, Gary's Big Hammer. The hammer grew comically in size as it flew, landing in the hole and grinding the undead crawling through into paste. The hammer wasn't done growing as it landed, expanding to fill the entire gap, even cracking some of the stone wall around it.

Gary landed on a flying stone platform flown under him by one of the gold-rank brightheart guards.

"That's quite a weapon, Mr Xandier."

Gary took his medium hammer from his back.

"Bloody expensive, though, and it's a one-use item unless you find a giant looking for a new hammer. It cost more than this one," he said, gesturing with the hammer in his hand.

"Then we thank you for the expenditure. We can't afford a lot of breaches like that."

They both surveyed the wall from the air, minor breaches happening all over.

"I don't know how long we can hold this," Gary said. "I hope Clive is working fast."

Clive was working fast. There were nine platforms set up around the tree, all of which needed to have individual ritual circles. Each circle had to operate not only in response to the environment but to each other.

Clive, as it turned out, was one of the greatest minds on Pallimustus when it came to the understanding of magical theory. While astral magic was his speciality, there were a handful of other fields in which he was well-versed. That did not make him the same as a specialist in those fields, however. Without the people around him, their endeavour would have failed already.

Like almost everyone, Farrah was not the equal of Clive in magical theory. Even so, she was still a respected expert in her field of array magic. Array magic wasn't a flashy field, and every speciality had at least a fundamental grasp of it. It was only when delving into the more nuanced aspects that being an actual specialist mattered. Clive's fundamental understanding of array magic was exceptional, but what they needed now went far beyond the fundamentals.

It had swiftly become evident how the original attempt by the messengers to transmute the natural array failed. The complexity of the magic involved boggled even Clive's mind. Not only was the natural array a paradigm of magic with which he was too unfamiliar, but the interplay between the array and the environment was too much for him to actively track while conducting multiple interlocking rituals.

The interactivity of multiple arrays was an aspect of array magic well outside the fundamentals. Understanding the nuances took too much study for anyone but array specialists, many of whom focused on just that aspect of it. As for natural arrays, Farrah's study of the grid on Earth made her one of the few true experts on Pallimustus.

Carlos Quilido was proving a surprisingly useful asset in decoding how the natural array's magic had been twisted by the efforts of the messengers. With the tree as a reference, the expert in magical corruption helped Farrah work backwards from what the natural array was doing now versus what it should be doing, had the messengers not made their ill-fated attempt to turn it into a soul forge.

Clive was in charge of all the magical theorists currently scrambling to test and retest the ambient magic and set up the foundations of the ritual diagrams they were slowly assembling. He was the foreman on the worksite, overseeing the activity according to the design given to him. Farrah was the architect from which the design originated.

Belinda was of more direct assistance than Clive. Her unconventional training was a mixture of self-teaching, assisting Clive and practical application under often adverse and usually illegal conditions. When it came to speciality knowledge or executing known magic with precision and efficiency, she fell short of Farrah and Clive. When it came to quick and dirty solutions to problems cropping up with improvised magic, she left both of them in the dust.

"That is a wildly inefficient magic conduit," Clive pointed out as he observed Belinda adding to one of the ritual circles.

"The problem isn't efficiency," Belinda told him. "We've got magic shooting out of our arses in here. The problem is getting that magic to work for us without blowing up or turning us all into elemental mind slaves like these messengers."

Farrah wandered over to examine Belinda's work.

"She's right," Farrah told Clive. "What she's doing here exchanges the magic without causing interference with the source or destination points."

Clive frowned, not annoyed at being wrong but with curiosity.

"Can you make notes on what you're doing for me to look at later?"

"No, she can't!" Farrah told him. "We're trying to go fast, remember?"

Clive's face scrunched in a reluctant grimace.

"Fine," he acceded.

"Can you check in with Jason on how they're going with the other device?" Farrah asked him. Clive's expression was back to business at the reminder.

"Yeah," he said. "None of this means anything if they don't get it done at the other end."

"Destruction tricked the surface messengers as well," Boris explained as he crawled around on the floor, drawing out a ritual circle with the messenger device at its centre. It was situated in a room directly over that containing the echo array in the citadel. Assisting and checking on him was Ramona, the gold-rank ritualist from Team Moon's Edge.

As they worked, Boris was explaining more about his involvement in their current circumstances. His audience was Marla, the brightheart commander, and Jason via Shade.

"Jes Fin Kaal believed that Destruction wanted a massive explosion after the messengers successfully claimed the soul forge," Boris explained. "That was the deal. Of course, that's not how it was going to work, since all the destructive power would be absorbed into the forge itself. Kaal thought she was playing the god, but she was the one getting played. She never realised whose priests she granted access to the messenger-controlled tunnel. I was expecting to find Destruction priests waiting for us, not Undeath ones. We ran, and that's where Gabriel and his sexy wife came in."

"You're already on thin ice," Jason's voice came from Shade's body. "You will treat Arabelle Remore with respect, whether she is present or not."

"You're not exactly famous for treating people with respect yourself," Boris pointed out.

"You're right. Do you know what I am famous for?"

Boris froze for a moment before resuming his work.

"Nothing but respect for Mrs Remore," he said. "Almost done, by the way."

Boris and Ramona drew out the final chalk lines to complete the diagram, then placed materials in various locations within it. A clay bowl full of powder, small piles of quintessence gems and several stacks of spirit coins. After they were done, Boris turned to Shade.

"We can go on your word," he said. "The device on this end is ready for activation."

"Thank you," Jason said.

"Asano," Marla said. "The citadel chamber won't stand much longer. The wall is already breached in a dozen places and we can't plug holes as fast as they're appearing. More and more of our forces are being pulled from plugging holes to dealing with the undead that have already made it through."

"How long can you hold?" Jason asked.

"Could be an hour or two. Could be a minute or two. One or two major breaches will see us overrun. Two hours is our limit, though. After that, the encroaching undeath zone will expand to the wall and they'll have us."

"We'll be as fast as we can," Jason told her.

In the natural array chamber, Jason opened his eyes. He looked for Clive and spotted him already heading their way, sitting on Onslow who was currently the size of a dining table.

"How is the preparation on the other side?" Clive asked.

"They're ready. Now they need us to be before they get overrun. They're a lot closer to losing the echo array than I'd like. How long on our end?"

"Once we've calibrated for the incredibly complex and constantly shifting elemental energy that itself is being pressured by the encroaching undeath energy? Less than a minute."

"And that calibration?"

"I'm hoping another four hours. Definitely no less than three, maybe as many as six or seven."

"We don't have that time. I don't suppose you padded those estimates so that when I ask you to do it faster, you can say yes?"

Clive closed his eyes and let out the groan of someone trying to explain over the phone to their grandmother how to fix her email.

"Jason," Clive said, "the messengers screwed up. Again. The device, as calibrated by them, wouldn't have worked. They designed that thing without access to the astral space we examined and without access to the tree. Their arrogance made them think they could get it right without those and they were wrong. Very, very wrong. We've got Carlos deciphering the corruption in the ambient magic. Farrah figuring out how to set up an array in this bizarre magic environment. If we didn't have Belinda, we'd spend half our time finding workarounds for a hundred little problems and magic incompatibilities. My job is to adapt all that to the device so it can actually do the thing it was designed to. This is the most complex improvised multi-aspect array ritual I've ever heard of. If any one of us wasn't here, you'd be looking at days to pull all this together. If at all."

"Okay," Jason said. "I'm just saying that the citadel doesn't have the time you need. Not probably doesn't. *Does not.*"

"If the citadel needs more hours, you need to find them. If we're going to try activating the device right now, we might as well wander out and let the dead eat us. If the timing is impossible, then it's time for you to do something impossible. It's kind of your thing, right?"

Jason let out a groaning sigh.

"I'll see what I can do."

Clive headed back to the ritual being set up while Jason flew over to where Miriam was directing the defences. The undead were streaming into the tunnels like a river now and the defenders had been employing a measured withdrawal strategy. The adventurers, cultists and brighthearts were the frontline while the elemental messengers made ranged attacks from the rear.

This had frustrated some of the other defenders until one of the elementals got careless and was caught by an undead surge as the frontline pulled back. The defenders had watched the power drain out of him in an instant, like a plug had been pulled. Moments later, he was back on his feet and fighting for the enemy.

The divine power infusing the undead had proven a major problem. It was draining many of the attacks against them of their power before they had a chance to make an impact. This was especially true for attacks made with elemental power, leaving the messengers with limited combat value. It affected other powers as well, especially the more overtly magical ones. Conjured projectiles were effective, but blasts of energy were diminished or negated entirely. Gordon's butterflies gained no traction, growing dim and vanishing as soon as they neared the undead. They didn't even explode as normal when destroyed.

Jason didn't try deploying Colin. The leech monster fed on life force, and while he could chew up dead organic matter, the poisons that were his main strength would be ineffective. Without Jason to make the undead vulnerable first, their dead flesh would be largely impervious. Given that he didn't want to risk an army of undead worms coming at them, Jason kept Colin inside his body, boosting his regeneration. Once things got hairy, he was probably going to need it.

The defenders reaped countless undead for every inch of surrendered ground, but the dead kept coming and there was only so much ground to surrender. There was still some way to the array chamber where they would need to make a final stand, but that moment was coming.

"How long on the ritual?" Miriam asked Jason as he approached. "At the current rate, they'll reach the array chamber in a couple of hours, and I don't trust that estimate. Right now, we're only seeing the dregs of the undead, and we know they have stronger ones."

"They're currently dividing their efforts between us and the citadel chamber," Jason said. "If the citadel falls, it doesn't matter if things accelerate here because we'll already be done. Even so, we need more than a couple of hours."

"How much more?"

"Somewhere between three and seven hours from now. And by the two hours you estimate it'll take the undead to reach the array chamber, the citadel expects to be gone. Maybe long gone. Their wall is already looking shaky."

"Operations Commander, I'll do everything I can to buy us as much time as possible. Even putting aside our less-than-ideal allies, the adventurers here represent an incredible amount of power. I'll spend our lives if that's what it takes, but I can probably get you the hours you need here. But I can't do anything about the citadel."

"I know."

Miriam frowned, her commanding voice lowering to a near whisper.

"Operation Commander. Jason. I know you like to talk about doing the impossible. If that is anything more than just talk, now is the time."

"Why do people keep asking me to do the impossible?"

"I haven't known you that long, but you kind of talk about it a lot. Wasn't that the whole reason they put you in charge?"

"Just between you and me? It's a lot easier when it's just talk. I guess this is why they say put up or shut up."

"Does this mean you're shutting up?"

"You're right; you haven't known me that long."

82

MIRACLE

THE WALL BETWEEN THE CITADEL CHAMBER AND THE DEATH CHAMBER WAS leaking like a sieve. Gary moved from breach to breach in a rush now, as did the other teams, yet a half dozen gaps were spilling undead into the chamber. The undead that made it through went for the pillars holding up the citadel as defenders moved to intercept them.

Arabelle Remore was a particular star, draining the magic from the undead. Robbed of the force animating them, they fell inert. The hideous monstrosities were returned to a state of gruesome but otherwise ordinary carrion. The magic Arabelle took was collected in a floating ethereal jar. It followed her around as she moved, like a duckling filled with the heinous power of the unliving.

Inside the jar, the corrupted energy of undeath was purified, turning it back into the power of untainted natural death. That death energy was poison to the undead, clashing with the twisted energy inside them with explosive results.

Arabelle's power to drain the undead of their energy was more effective against the lower-ranked undead. She drained the hordes that poured through the breaches, purified their energy and then launched it at the more threatening foes that shambled through. This detonated them, turning them into weapons against their own side.

These stronger undead were either gold rank or powerful silvers. They were easy to pick out from the ordinary undead who were animated messengers and brighthearts, alongside the occasional subterranean monster. The most dangerous undead were bespoke creations, freakish and varied. Some were amalgams of monsters, messengers and brighthearts, hacked-up parts roughly sewn together with tree roots. Others looked like intact creatures that had been warped through flesh-shaping into nightmare fuel that existed nowhere in the natural world.

The crudely stitched horrors, like the five-headed giant messenger Gabriel had seen, were the most physically powerful. The flesh-shaped monstrosities tended to be more agile and had superior special abilities, like the armoured mantis that had stopped Gary from blocking a breach.

The siege of the citadel chamber turned slowly but inexorably in favour of the undead. Their forces continually grew stronger, from mostly bronze-rankers to almost all silvers, with gold-rank monstrosities scattered amongst them. The demand for gold-rank intervention on the defender side escalated as more of the hard-to-kill abominations forced their way through the breaches. Some of the larger ones didn't even need the explosive undead, forcing their way through with raw physical power.

Finally, a tipping point was reached. There were too many gold-rank undead for the defenders to respond to. Even with adventurers like Arabelle being the equal of two or more of their enemies, the gold-ranked undead were not quick to eliminate. New abominations arrived faster than the existing ones could be put down. More and more of the undead made it into the chamber, attacking the pillars unchallenged. Some were already showing dangerous cracks, and if enough fell, the citadel would fall with them.

Gary found himself fighting alongside Gabriel in a major breach, holding off a wave of lesser undead while Gabriel sliced apart a pair of golds. Gabriel had split his attacks so the monsters fell together, giving Gary the chance to blast their remains and the silver-rankers with a sonic roar. The roar thundered through the gap, hurling the enemy out through the breach and back into the death chamber.

Gary and Gabriel took a brief moment to rest while Gary's brightheart team stepped in to repair the breach. Gary could have helped, having his own powers to shape stone and metal, but he didn't have the mana to spare. Such large workings were mana intensive and it was more efficient to refine the work of his support team once they were done. He pressed his hands to the barricade wall, subtly altering the material with small but critical alterations to the structure.

"Did you see how close that purple light is getting to the other side?" Gabriel asked grimly.

"Yeah," Gary said.

"Once it reaches here, this wall goes from our territory to theirs. Once that happens, there won't be any more time to buy."

"Then let's make sure we at least hold that long," Gary said with a fierce grin that Gabriel returned.

"There's no quit in you, is there?"

"I tried quitting once. It didn't work out for me."

***

The bodies of the undead were already rotting by nature. The dark power that animated them also arrested further depreciation, staving off decrepitude and collapse. Jason's necrotic powers not only obviated the power staving off further decline but massively accelerated it. His blade smashed away chunks of flesh like hitting water balloons with a stick, liquefied corpse meat sloughing away in wet clumps. The afflictions he left behind finished off the undead while he was already moving on to the next.

It was a rare chance for Jason to act as a more traditional frontline fighter, although very much in his own mode. His swirling cloak rendered him all but invisible in the patchy light of glowing red flowers and dancing shadows. He shadow-jumped from area to area, one moment carving a path through the rank and file and in another loading a powerful undead with necrotic afflictions. The sword Gary made for him reaped the undead like a harvester's scythe.

Clive had been brought into the command channel of Jason's voice chat to keep Jason and Miriam updated. He had remained silent except for when Miriam asked for progress reports as she balanced the safety of the defenders with how much they had to slow the progress of the undead.

"Progress?" she asked again.

"We're getting a solid handle on how we need to calibrate the rituals," Clive reported. "I'm extremely confident in getting this to work, and at the lower end of my original time frame. Maybe three more hours. That's the good news."

"And the bad news?" Miriam asked.

"If the undead make it into the array chamber, everything changes. The undeath energy will affect the array and then we're done. The undead have to be kept out of this chamber at all costs. *All costs.*"

"Alright. Thank you, Clive."

Miriam opened a personal channel to Jason.

"We can't hold them outside of the array chamber for three more hours," she told him bluntly. "We just can't. I can start pushing back harder and slow the progress, but we'll see casualties. Once those start mounting, it'll leave us on much the same timeline, but with fewer people left."

"The citadel won't last three more hours anyway," Jason said.

"No," Miriam agreed. "If you've got any miracles you've been hoarding, I'd really like you to take them out now."

"Wouldn't that be nice," Jason said. "But I'm not a…"

Jason vanished, shadow jumping into the backline to emerge from Miriam's shadow.

"What is it?" she asked.

"I actually do have a couple of miracles in my pocket," he said. "They won't help us here, but maybe I can trade them."

"With who?"

"The other people that have miracles, obviously. I'm going to have to do something I don't like."

"I don't care what you like, Asano. If you have something you can do, then do it."

"Yeah," Jason agreed. "I just never thought I'd be relying on the power of prayer."

***

The undead assault on the citadel chamber grew worse, not just in the power of the undead but the coordination with which they were operating. It became clear that the Undeath priests were directing their forces once their more powerful creations entered the fray.

Gary's Big Hammer had plugged the first major breach, but more had come. The gold-rankers were increasingly occupied holding them, many too far gone to be sealed, tying up the gold-ranker defending them for the rest of the battle. Gary's forge golem was gone, sacrificed to take out a gold-rank abomination Gary and his team eliminated without needing a gold-rank adventurer.

The golem had self-detonated, coating the abomination in molten metal while inside the breach. Gary's support team had then shaped spears of metal and stone from the walls, impaling the undead dozens of times over while closing the breach at the same time.

Gary watched another large breach explode out, right below his current location. His footing shook as the bottom half of the stairwell he was on collapsed. He looked around and realised that, once again, there were no unoccupied gold-rankers left to respond. He gave his support team a grave look and nodded downwards.

"Let's go."

"Gary, that's a massive breach," said Kollas, the leader of Gary's brightheart support team. "We can't hold that alone."

"I can hold it," Gary told her. "At least long enough for you to seal the breach behind me."

"What? No! If we cut you off out there, it'll take a miracle for you to survive."

"Then do me a favour and start praying."

"Gary, I've been praying for the last two hours."

Gary's reassuring grin wasn't, his leonine face looking like he'd just spotted prey. He stepped off the shattered stairway to drop into the breach, landing in a cloud of stone dust, thick as fog. The undead were already pouring through, silhouettes in the cloud backlit by purple light. He let out a roar that cracked stonework, blasting them back with sound and force. The stone dust roiled wildly, lit up with purple light.

Only one undead had held firm through the blast, a gold-rank beetle-like creature made of stitched flesh with hundreds of eyes sewn into its body. It radiated out an aggressive aura, pressing down on Gary's with gold-rank might. This was not the aura of a living thing but an artificial aura, instilled into this monstrosity by its creators.

Gary's aura buckled under the onslaught but didn't break. The creature's aura probed for weaknesses to exploit and found nothing. Years of training with Farrah and then Jason had refined Gary's aura into a fortress. The raw power of gold rank threatened to crush it whole, but Gary held fast with raw determination. Aura combat was one of the few places where willpower could tip the scales of rank, if only a little.

Gary didn't let the spiritual battle pause the physical one. He was coated in armour of dark heavy steel that glowed red hot between the plates and his hammer lit up the same way. The monster was gold rank, but designed for spiritual assault. That didn't mean the fight would be easy, but it would be possible.

Behind him, Gary's support team frantically called for him to return. He called out to them without turning or slowing his stride.

"It has been an honour," he yelled back. "You know what to do."

He conjured up a stone wall, reinforced with a metal framework. He didn't have time to reinforce it properly and spent as little mana as he could. It was to make a point, not a barricade. The stone and metal-shapers on the other side would do that.

The abomination was bizarre, little more than a flesh mound with six legs and a patchwork body, covered in eyes. It neither retreated nor advanced at Gary's approach, continuing its spiritual barrage. Behind it, the undead horde was rushing in after being flung back by Gary's roar. He shifted his stance and raised his hammer.

The undead were a unifying force. The brighthearts, elemental messengers, cultists and adventurers each counted two members of their alliance as bane foes, yet the undead brought them all together. An all-consuming, existential threat, the undead turned even nemesis into ally.

Miriam was on overall command, directing a slow withdrawal through the chambers and tunnels. Each new wave of undead was forced to crawl over the remains of the last. The wide-open chambers were surrendered relatively quickly, being harder and more costly to defend. The tunnels were the true battleground, the tight confines turned into kill-boxes. The undead paid dearly for every inch, sometimes forced to dig through piles of their own fallen to advance.

Jason stood well behind the backline in one such tunnel, head bowed and eyes closed. His starlight cloak had been dismissed, showing a face stained with the grime of battle.

"I know you're watching this closely," he whispered. "I know you are more against the undead even than those of us likely to die to them. You know what I need."

"That," a warm female voice said quietly, "was a very mediocre prayer. And rather demanding at the end."

Jason smiled, raised his head and opened his eyes. The goddess of death stood before him in the guise of a stocky, middle-aged woman with a colourful dress. She gave off the warm feeling of a matronly tavern keeper.

"You may not have heard," Jason told her, "but prayer isn't really my thing."

"Oh, I've heard."

"And I heard you normally show up as a stern-faced man in this region."

"Do you want me to?"

"No, I like you this way," he said, glancing over at the ongoing battle. "There's enough cold and grim from the other side."

"I agree."

He looked around and saw that only he seemed to have noticed the goddess.

"What do you want from me, Jason Asano? You know people who keep resurrecting aren't exactly in my best graces."

"You like me more than the undead, though."

"Yes. But if you want a miracle, you need one of my servants or a grand sacrifice. And despite what people cannot seem to stop believing, I have no interest in the sacrifice of lives."

"I know," Jason said. "Death is just one part of the cycle."

"Do you know? You seem determined to escape that cycle."

"I don't think there is an escape. I think some cycles are just a lot larger than others."

"I would like to think so, but my remit does not reach beyond this planet, which itself will have its time."

"I have two resurrections," Jason said. "You can have them. I offer that as my sacrifice."

"I decline," Death told him. "It is not enough."

83

DEATH KNOWS HOW TO WAIT

"TWO RESURRECTIONS AREN'T ENOUGH?" JASON ASKED THE GODDESS Death. "Even as justification for doing something you must want to do anyway?"

"The purpose does not make the sacrifice cheaper," Death told him. "The sacrifice is judged by what is given up. And what are resurrections to you, Jason Asano? You, who stand at the threshold of true immortality."

"Oh," he said as realisation struck. "I get it. If you help, we probably win and I turn into an astral king. Then I won't need those resurrections, which means they aren't any sacrifice at all."

"They aren't nothing. But aren't enough."

"What is?" he asked.

"Your path forward is one of power that goes beyond mortality, taking you outside of my authority. But if you commit to respecting my will, even as you move beyond my power, that has value."

Jason narrowed his eyes as he met the gaze of the goddess.

"You don't want a sacrifice," he said. "You want to make some kind of bargain."

"Pacts are how transcendents deal with one another."

"I'm not transcendent yet. Could you please help me out with something so I can understand what we're talking about here? No one has been completely explicit about what half-transcended means. My understanding is that once you max out diamond rank, reaching the maximal stage of mortal power, you're then a half transcendent."

"That is accurate."

"So, if that half is the power requirement, is the other half some way to get you over the line? To cross the threshold of mortality?"

"That's precisely what it is," she confirmed. "Almost all half transcendents have reached the peak of mortal power and search for a means to move past the final limitation. Far less common are those like you, who obtain the other half before reaching the power threshold."

"I haven't obtained either half yet. And I won't, without your help. If you won't accept my sacrifice, why seek a pact with me? Someone who *maybe* has a chance at *potentially* getting halfway to the kind of person you make pacts with? It doesn't sound like a reliable bet."

"Immortality brings patience, Jason Asano. Death knows how to wait. I can gain a concession from you now that you would never accept in the future. The value in that is worth a miracle."

"Obviously, I'm curious about what concession you're looking for, but there's something I have to ask first. When you said that 'death knows how to wait,' were you making a metaphor about the concept of death or were you talking in the third person? On an unrelated note, being in a conversation where that's a genuine question is one of the coolest things that's ever happened to me. And I'm an interdimensional ninja warlock, so epic moments are kind of my thing."

Her only response was to look at him from under raised eyebrows.

"Oh, come on," he said. "I know this is a very serious situation, and this whole thing is a tragedy for the brighthearts where we're trying to salvage what little remains of their people. But some days you have to stop and recognise your life is awesome. I'm negotiating an immortality pact with the goddess of death so I can fight that undead army over there. And the reason I'm doing that is so my friend can use a wizard spell so I can fight over a magic tree inside a warped pocket of reality. This is a top-seven moment for me. Probably. Top-eight, definitely. I once found a taco that looked just like the British actor Brian Blessed. I mean, I think it did; I was pretty drunk."

"I will lay out the concessions I am looking for," she told him, ignoring everything else he said. "I will take your resurrections. Those you have, those you could ever have and those you could bestow upon others. You will agree that whatever your power, whatever your need, you will never bring anyone back from the dead."

"I can accept that."

"It is easy to agree to when you are less than thirty years old. What of when you are thirty thousand? You may come to chafe at the restriction."

"Are you trying to talk me out of giving you what you want?"

"Pacts between immortals can outlast the lifespan of universes. My existence will be relatively short on that scale, but it will be long enough. There is no value in creating an antagonism that will last for millions of years, so a pact must be equitable. It is not a place for short-term thinking."

"It may be short-term thinking, but I've learned that victory and defeat are decided in moments. The right gift in the right moment, however small, is worth more than anything the future has to offer. Where I come from, we say a bird in the hand is worth two in the bush. I'm willing to risk recrimination from my future self."

"So long as you are going into this with understanding, Jason Asano, there can be a compact between us."

"If it is to be a pact, then we need to define terms. Let's start with what you want: no resurrecting people. I can accept that, but I need to know where the line is. Where does drastic emergency healing end and resurrection begin? My understanding is that even magic is blurry on that. Many high-rank healing abilities don't differentiate between healing the near dead and restoring the dead."

"You may use your power to arrest the condition of someone on the border of death, even beyond, if you can. You may keep them until you find someone else that can restore them, so long as you do not do so yourself."

"So, as long as someone isn't too far gone that they can't be brought back with someone else's resurrection magic, I can toss them in my soul space until I find someone who can use that magic? If I'm fast enough that their soul hasn't done a runner, I assume."

"Yes."

"Acceptable. Which means we move on to my terms."

"You will receive a miracle."

"Not enough. You are asking for infinity and offer a moment."

"The right gift in the right moment. Your words. You came to me looking for a miracle."

"At the cost of a sacrifice that you refused. Then you offered a whole other deal. You're the one who asked for a pact for me to enact your will forever. I'm okay with that because, to my surprise, some things really should be left to god. Or gods, as it turns out. Cloning dinosaurs never seems to work out, for example. Not that I'm saying gods should get into dinosaur cloning."

Death gave him a sharp look, and Death's sharp look was very sharp indeed.

"My point is," Jason said, "I don't mind what you're asking for, but it's something I'll be giving you forever. Forever is a long time, even for you. Will you outlast this planet?"

"No. All things have their time, including this planet, its gods and the universe in which it resides. There is even an end for that which lies beyond reality, although such things are not yet for you to know."

"Then, assuming this works out, I'll still be knocking around, respecting your wishes about resurrection, long after you're gone. You said that pacts should be equitable. Should not my benefits be just as eternal as yours?"

"I do not disagree in principle, but do not ask too much if you still want your miracle."

"It occurs to me that if you're asking me to carry out the will of Death, then that's exactly what I should do. If resurrection is anathema to me, shouldn't undeath be as well?"

Death smiled.

"Indeed it should," she said. "Your terms are acceptable."

"We should probably go into specifics."

"You will be satisfied, I give you my word. Are you willing to trust my word, Jason Asano?"

He looked at her for a long, silent moment before nodding.

"I am," he said.

"I would like to point out that I could have offered you only the miracle you need here and nothing else. And I could have asked far more than what I have in return and you would have accepted."

"I would," Jason admitted. "Is that what you're doing?"

"No. But I think my fellow deities would appreciate you gaining an understanding of divine benevolence."

Jason nodded.

"I do understand. I've never denied being a fool, but I'm not a blind fool. I can't deny all the gods have done for me at this point."

"Then perhaps you would have the decency to demonstrate more respect in the future."

"That's fair," Jason said. "I'm self-aware enough to realise that my biases have affected the way I relate to you all. Dominion is still kind of a dick, though."

Death have him a flat look.

"Right, respect. Sorry about that. Personal growth is an ongoing process. Can we move on to the miracle now, please?"

"I must warn you, Jason Asano, that my miracle will not hand you victory. It will give you only a chance that you and your allies must seize with your own hands."

"We don't need you to fight our fight for us. We need a god who helps those who help themselves."

"Then the terms of our pact are set."

Death Pact: The Sanctity of Death

- If you accept the death pact, any ability to resurrect yourself or another will be sealed. This pact will persist through any changes in nature or power that you undergo.
- The power of undeath will be suppressed by your aura. Existing undead will not be impaired but undead will not animate and undeath energy will be purged from the ambient magic.
- The pact will be enacted by the Pallimustus goddess of death guiding your soul to make changes to itself. The deity will not gain access to your soul. Any attempt at instigating changes outside the agreed-upon conditions will be rejected by your soul.
- As an external condition of this pact, the Pallimustus goddess of death shall enact a miracle.

Death held out her hand and Jason did the same, pressing their palms together. He felt the immensity of her power, his own a droplet of water next to an ocean that spanned out forever. That power resonated with his soul, not an attack but a guide, showing him a path to reshape himself.

Jason was well-versed in the offensive methods of soul interaction.

His first and most drastic lesson had been from the Builder, but he had developed those powers for himself, then alongside Amos Pensinata. This was doing the same thing but within an entirely different paradigm, not aggressive but benevolent. Jason watched with his spiritual senses as a new branch of spiritual manipulation was opened up before him.

Concentrating became harder as his soul reshaped itself. It was a relatively small and entirely innocuous change, but it was still his soul reshaping itself. As the process drew to a close, Jason felt the goddess calling out to the power he had taken from all the messengers he had drained. He drew on that power and delivered it to her, as per their agreement. It flowed out of his soul and into her, and then her power withdrew.

- You have accepted a pact with the Pallimustus goddess of death.
- You have accepted the cycle of natural death as an intrinsic element of your soul.

New Title: Keeper of the Cycle

- You may not resurrect yourself or others. This is a change self-applied to your own soul and may not be undone. This effect will carry through any transformation of body or soul. This condition is part of a compact. Should you circumvent this condition, all other aspects of the pact will be negated and you will suffer severe spiritual backlash.
- You have become an exclusion zone for undeath energy. Undeath energy cannot exist in the ambient mana of your soul realm, spirit domains or the area within your aura. Undeath energy of significantly higher rank than your power may fully or partly overcome this exclusion.
- Power bestowed to the undead, such as through divine power, is negated. This has a greater or lesser effect depending on the relative strength of you and the power in question.

- Suppressing the aura of an undead will impede the abilities of
  that undead. Undead able to partially or fully resist your aura
  suppression will resist this effect to an equivalent degree.
  Undead weaker than you may have their animating force
  negated, depending on the nature of the magic animating them.
- Abilities that apply afflictions also apply ghost fire. Abilities
  that drain mana will degrade the animating force of the
  undead. Those with a direct connection to your soul will have
  their abilities enhanced in the same way if they are in relative
  proximity to you.
- While your aura is actively suppressing the undead, allies
  within your aura are affected by ghost fire.

- [Ghost Fire] (affliction, damage-over-time, magic): Ghost fire
  is harmless to the living, calming the mind and shielding them
  from the effects of undead auras and ambient magic infused
  with undeath energy. Ghost fire is extremely harmful to the
  undead, degrading their animating force and inflicting ongoing
  transcendent damage.

Death vanished, but Jason barely noticed as he fell to his knees, his soul
roiling. He struggled to restrain his unstable aura, contain it as best he
could. His insides felt like they were passing through a blender. The gold-
rankers noticed his disrupted aura and Miriam pulled Emir from the
fighting to go check on him.

"Jason, what's happening?" Emir asked as he reached him.

Jason was on his hands and knees, leaning forward as if expecting to
throw up.

"Had a chat with the goddess of death," Jason said, his voice strained
through gritted teeth. "I'm okay."

"Goddess of death?" Emir asked, looking around. "Are you sure?
Death was a god, last I checked, not a goddess."

"I think the gods just pick whatever gender they like on the day. Some
of them, at least. You didn't know that?"

"I've never been especially religious. They just switch it up? I know someone like that. They're still waiting for you to talk to them about your cloud house, by the way. You're making a diamond-ranker very cranky, which is never a great idea."

"Mate, on the seating chart of problems I have to deal with, a cranky diamond-ranker is at the kids' table. Why are you here?"

"I was sent to check if you were okay."

Jason turned from where he'd been staring at the ground to give Emir a pointed look.

"So, uh, are you okay?"

"I've been worse."

"That's what I figured. I checked in with your team healer over voice chat while I was coming over. Neil said you were probably twisting yourself inside out so you could pull some ridiculous power out of your rear end."

"Something like that. I don't suppose you've noticed a miracle going off?"

84
SOMETIMES THEY DO

"A MIRACLE?" EMIR ASKED. "THAT'S WHY YOU MET THE GODDESS OF death?"

"You think we don't need one?" Jason asked.

"No, we definitely need one."

"That's why I thought I'd go supplier direct."

"You know, I used to talk about my fancy diamond-rank connections all the time. Knowing you makes it very hard to be a braggart, Jason."

Jason let out a wheezing laugh that turned into coughing.

"Help me up?" he asked after the fit subsided.

Emir helped Jason unsteadily to his feet.

"Are you really alright?"

"I'll be fine. Spiritual damage is harder to get used to than physical damage, but you can get there. I think I'm building up a tolerance."

"Jason, you may want to re-examine the way you approach life if you're injuring your soul enough to build up a tolerance for it."

"I know, right? You didn't answer me, by the way."

"What was the question?"

"Did you see a miracle happening?"

"I didn't notice one, no."

Jason nodded.

"I told Death I wanted a god who helps those that help themselves. I'd best get on that."

"You're not exactly in fighting shape, Jason."

"It's fine. I just need to get my aura under control. The body will follow. Let's head for the frontline."

Jason took one stumbling step, righting himself before he fell over. Emir grabbed him and slung Jason's arm over his shoulder for support. It was a little awkward as Emir was decently tall while Jason was not, but they got slowly moving. They made their way towards the frontline from the protected position where Jason had communed with Death.

The stonework underfoot was cracked and strewn with sinister, red-veined plants that painted everything with a bloody red glow. Jason could have floated over the uneven floor of the tunnel, but he wasn't using his still-recovering aura. Instead, Emir helped him pick his way through the uneven terrain as he grew stronger and faster by the moment. Moving with care also helped him concentrate on something other than his mind-spike of a headache.

"I can feel your aura starting to calm down," Emir said. "It feels different."

"It does?"

"You can't tell?"

"Right now, my soul feels like a meat smoothie. I guess that's different."

"That's not what I'm talking about."

"I did just make a pact with the goddess of death. Gods don't muck about when cutting deals, as it turns out. Is my aura all deathly now? Bleak and cold with the silent inevitability of the final demise?"

"No," Emir said. "It feels... I'm not sure how to describe it. Natural, but not of nature. It's not plants and trees, it's more like..."

Emir paused to give it some more thought before continuing.

"Jason, your aura has always given off a sense of authority. It's judgemental. Impersonal. Oppressive. It feels like a massive stone slab, engraved with commandments, that will fall over and crush you if you break them."

"That's not the most flattering description I've heard."

"It is what it is, Jason. This change fits into that, another part of that authoritative nature. It's a sense that messing with the laws of life and death around you is a very bad idea. It doesn't feel like something imposed on you from the outside, though. It hasn't changed what you are so much as unveiled something new that still completely fits."

"A new sin for people to commit."

"Yes, but not as harsh as I make that sound. Murder is a transgression too. A rigid authority shielding you from that can be harsh but also comforting in the safety it offers. This is similar, but it also feels natural. Warm. Rather than safety from murder, it's safety from…"

He gestured at the frontline and the undead pushing in on the living.

"…from that," Emir continued. "From the cold, corrupting grip of unlife. It's like your aura went from being a courthouse to being a—"

"Please don't say a church."

"I'm sorry, Jason, but that's what it feels like. Judgemental, but also comforting. Sheltering. An authority that tolerates no transgression but also offers sanctuary."

"I don't want people thinking of my aura like church roaming around. I'm not a tent revival preacher."

"It's a good change, Jason. Your aura needed some softening up."

"Your description doesn't make it sound soft."

"I'll say 'less hard,' then. Freedom is good, and while I know that's a principle you hold, no one seems to have told your aura."

"My aura power is called Hegemony, Emir, not 'let's all have a nice time and talk about scrapbooking.'"

"Yes, but your power is only an aspect of your aura. More important is who you are, at the core."

"So, it's not my power that's a hardcore religious thug, it's me?"

"I'm not saying that. And I'm not saying your aura is bad. It can be hard, yes, but sometimes what you need is hard. Like it or not, Jason, you're our leader here. The ultimate authority in this expedition. Your aura being so authoritative helps when you're giving commands."

"It's mostly Miriam giving commands."

"Jason, most of these adventurers were trained their whole lives. They understand the difference between a field commander and a commander-in-chief. You were a bit uneven at the start of this expedition, it's true. Maybe you let Miriam take the lead a little too much. This kind of leadership is new to you; it's okay to rely on an experienced hand. But when the moment called, you answered. When the dead rose, you took command. You stepped forward and charted our course when what we needed was a strong hand at the tiller. Leadership isn't just about giving commands, Jason. People have to rely on you. An aura that feels like a sanctuary in dangerous times is something people will follow."

"Thank you," Jason said. "You've led a large and successful operation for a long time, and I've seen that your people like and respect you. I admire your leadership ability, so that means a lot coming from you."

"Thank you, although it's mostly Constance, if I'm being honest. Without her, I'd be hopeless. I have ideas, but she's the one who has to figure out how to make them work. She's my Miriam, I guess."

"Then I'd best not learn all my lessons from you. I have no intention of secretly pining after Miriam for a decade before finally growing the balls to propose."

"Do you want to get dropped on the ground?"

Jason chuckled.

"Actually, yes, let me go," he said. "I'm recovering quite quickly, so let's give this another try."

Jason started walking on his own, although Emir kept close in case he stumbled. Jason thought over Emir's words for a while before speaking up, his voice troubled.

"Emir, you said people will follow my aura."

"Yes. Jason, I haven't just been going on and on about this to make small talk. I've been trying to express how your aura feels from the outside because there's something I think you don't understand."

"What's that?"

"The impact your aura has when you stop hiding it. You hide it, most of the time. Not just holding back the strength but masking the more unusual aspects of it. When you take off that mask, the way you have for these battles, people see it in full. You don't realise the impact it has on people."

"I get that my aura is strong and can do some weird stuff, but—"

"It's not about how strong it is, Jason. It's not about how you can use it. I'm talking about the most fundamental thing: how it feels. People of this world are used to potent auras floating around. Adventurers with their well-trained power. Aristocrats stuffed to the gills with monster cores, holding back their auras with magic items so they don't give some old man a heart attack."

He gestured around them.

"Ours is a world of personal power," he said. "My understanding is that yours isn't."

"This is my world now."

"But you weren't raised here. You weren't brought up surrounded by power, but, in this world, we are. Even normal-rankers are exposed to auras they can barely sense, yet wash over them constantly, brushing against their perception their whole lives."

"I'm not sure that I get your point," Jason said.

"The point is that, in this world, we grow up learning what powerful people feel like. And what power that that doesn't come from people feels like. I grew up visiting worship squares and seeing gods. Everyone does. And I'm not saying you feel like a god, Jason, although not entirely unlike one either. I'm saying that your power feels like something different, and the stronger you grow, the closer you get to feeling like other than just a person. You need to understand that this isn't just me talking. Every person you meet in this world who gets a real look at your aura feels that way."

"Are you saying I'm not a person?"

"Of course you're a person, Jason, but your power doesn't feel like it belongs to one. Power like that is something the people of this world grew up learning to venerate. To follow. To worship even."

"Are you trying to get me in trouble with the gods?"

"Jason, you already are. You think just anyone can call up a god to ask for a miracle?"

"Isn't that the whole point of prayer?"

"Most people don't get answers, Jason, let alone a personal visitation. We've been watching gods appear before you as if you were a priest to all of them. We've watched you talk to them as if they're equals, which is one thing, but the way they talk back is very much another. People don't think you're a god, Jason, but we see you standing on the same stage as them. Shining with a power that is maybe closer to theirs than to ours. Everything we've been told about power from when we were children tells us that what you have is something to be followed. And we will follow, believe me. I don't think you get a choice in that."

Jason stopped walking and took a deep breath before letting it out slowly.

"I know I'm the centre of a lot of strangeness, Emir. Some I've chosen and some I haven't. But I'm still just a person in the middle of it all."

"No, you're not. You don't get be 'just' anything anymore. Look at what we're here to do. We're trying to rewrite reality and turn you into what? Some kind of messenger demigod? You're limping along because you just called up the goddess of death to cut a deal."

"I just wanted a miracle. The deal was her idea."

Emir gave him a flat look.

"I'm not exactly refuting your point, am I?" Jason asked.

"Jason, you have a power that goes beyond just being a leader. And we both know it's going to get less normal as the years pass, not more. People feel that and they're going to follow you for it. At some point, you have to decide what you're going to do about that."

"You've been saying my name a lot. It feels aggressive, like a verbal finger poke."

Emir jabbed Jason's forehead with his finger.

"That's because I'm trying to get something through that head. Somewhere in your mind is the idea that you're still that lost kid I met six years ago. That you're a normal person in extraordinary circumstances. You're not. You *are* the extraordinary circumstances, and you're happening to people. Sooner or later, we all need you to take responsibility for that. That's why I'm spending all this time talking about your aura, about how it feels to be around you. That's why I'm talking about leadership."

"I'm looking to be an astral king, Emir, not a regular king."

"Jason, listen to yourself. You're not trying to be a king, you're trying to be a special magic king. But it doesn't matter what label you put on it. Whatever you call it, it's about the responsibility. And you know what I'm talking about, even if you haven't admitted it to yourself. In the Storm Kingdom, you opened a portal that shouldn't have opened. You used it to rescue people it shouldn't have been able to carry. Was that your first miracle, Jason?"

"Doing that almost killed me. Miracles don't kill the people using them."

"Yes, Jason. Sometimes they do."

They resumed their walk in silence while Jason considered Emir's words. His hobble became a walk and his walk became a stride, no longer worried about tripping on vines and uneven ground. Emir was hesitant to go, but the battle lines needed him. It didn't take Jason long to convince him to return to the fray. Jason continued alone and, by the time he reached Miriam, he felt largely intact. He still had a throbbing headache, but his aura had settled enough that he could use it again.

Miriam was unleashing powerful magic while also issuing commands through voice chat. Like Allayeth who had trained her, the plant essence was central to Miriam's power set. She showed visible distaste at using the bizarre plants produced by the messenger tree, but plant specialists were always made stronger by plant-rich environments, especially when those plants had a lot of magic.

"What have you been up to?" she asked Jason when he arrived. She was standing on a large rock for vantage and he employed his now-stable aura to float up next to her.

"You asked for a miracle," he said. "I was praying."

"And how did that go?"

Jason closed his eyes and calmed his mind, readying to push out hard with his aura.

"I think we're about to find out."

They were in a tunnel, wide but easier to hold than open chambers. Miriam surrendered those chambers cheaply, but in the tunnels, the undead had to pay. Jason was floating in the air, not far behind the line where adventurers, cultists and brighthearts held back the unliving tide. The lifeless foes were eerily silent, limitless in number and unconcerned at being mowed down like grass. They had no morale to shake as they climbed over growing mounds of the undead that came before them.

Jason sent his aura flooding down the tunnel to wash over the dead. The effect was immediate as the defenders sensed the pervasive energy of undeath being washed away. The power infused in the undead as a group to devour magic thrown at them vanished; attacks that had landed weakly moments before now slammed home with impact.

Most notably affected were the brighthearts and the messengers. Their elemental powers had been the most severely impeded, fading to little or nothing by the time they struck the undead. Now those attacks were impacting hard. Explosive balls of fire sent charred and dismembered remains flying through the air. Clouds of embers and ash scoured dead flesh from dry bones. Stone spears that had been glancing off undead bodies now tore them apart, creating palisades decorated with helplessly impaled victims.

"This is your miracle?" Miriam asked. "Not bad. You just turned the largest part of our force from all but useless to highly effective."

"The miracle isn't mine and this isn't it," Jason told her. "When it comes, save your thanks for the goddess of death."

"Death is a god."

"Why does no one know about the gender fluid thing?"

"What?"

Jason was saved from giving an explanation, and Miriam from getting it, by the arrival of Death's miracle. Every member of the defending side had ghostly white flames ignite over their bodies, ethereal and pure. It did not burn but had a calming warmth, shoring up morale and forestalling any panic at suddenly catching on fire.

- You have been affected by a miracle of Death.
- You have been affected by [Divine Ghost Fire].
- You may not resurrect while under this effect.
- You are impervious to undeath energy.
- Any undeath-related afflictions have been purged.
- Any undead you contact or affect with your abilities will be affected by [Divine Ghost Fire] which is extremely harmful to them.

- [Divine Ghost Fire] (affliction, damage-over-time, magic): Divine ghost fire is harmless to the living, calming the mind and shielding them from the power of undeath and purging any undeath magic from which they are suffering. Divine ghost fire spreads on contact and is extremely harmful to the undead, degrading their animating force and inflicting ongoing transcendent damage.

Miriam immediately saw a problem. She opened up a voice channel to all the defenders.

"Don't stop and read!" she yelled at them. "Fight!"

85

FIGHTING ALONE

JASON HADN'T YET USED THE GHOST FIRE POWER HE HAD GAINED ON THE undead. Now he was watching the divinely enhanced version engulf the undead like a wildfire, spreading from the defenders as if they were holy arsonists. Any time a weapon, armour or body part touched an undead, flames crawled onto it as if it had been doused in accelerant. The fire passed from one to the other until the entire battlefield was a white, ethereal inferno. Even as they burned, the undead didn't react, continuing to fight in eerie silence, until their bodies were eaten away by the fire.

Jason relaxed his suppression of the undeath energy, unnecessary when all the undead in sight were suffering under the ghostly white flames. Still nursing a divine pact hangover, the chance to let his aura rest was very welcome. Miriam also allowed herself to relax a little, ordering the ranged attackers to take a break. They tended to use the most mana, being heavily made up of spellcasters. They had a chance to recover some of that mana while the flames were pushing the undead back for them.

On the battlefield, even the frontliners were taking a rest. Death's miracle had brought respite to the battlefield, although there were no illusions that the job was done. For now, though, there was peace as the piled bodies of the undead were burned to ash and rainbow smoke. The corpses the undead were animated from had been sustained by death magic, preventing them from dissolving. The ghost flames broke that power.

"This is your miracle," Miriam said.

"Death's miracle," Jason corrected.

"What did you sacrifice for this?"

"Not much. Death was looking for a pretext to step in, so it was just a token, really."

Miriam bowed her head, quietly offering a thankful prayer to the god of death.

"You are welcome, Miriam Vance," Death said, appearing next to her.

Jason looked around and noticed that, once again, Death had restricted who could sense his presence. His new guise was that of a male elf, pale with sharp features and dark eyes. He wore neat grey clothes in the Yaresh style, less flashy than the outfits of tropical Rimaros. His voice was monotone, cold and hollow as an empty tomb.

Miriam knelt before him, on the rock from which she had been observing the defences. Like Jason, Death floated in the air next to her.

"Thank you, Lord Death," Miriam said, head bowed.

"Stand, Miriam Vance," Death told her. "You still command this battle."

"Of course, Lord Death," Miriam said, standing and turning her attention back to the fight. She couldn't help but make side glances at the god, however. She had seen gods her whole life, but this was different. This was no temple or worship square. What she was doing was important enough that a god had appeared. Even if he was mostly here for Asano, he could have hidden from her the way he had from everyone. Instead, he had appeared before her and spoken her name.

"I think you're distracting her a little," Jason told Death.

"She will adapt," Death said. "Her will is strong."

"She has carried a lot on this expedition," Jason said. "Including my noob leadership, most of the time. And now she carries your hopes. I can promise you that they are in good hands."

"I know," Death said.

Miriam drew a sharp, startled breath, not taking her eyes from the battle. She stood rigid between Jason and the god, head spinning as they casually chatted. Like every child, she had been taught how to act during a god's visitation to a worship square or a temple. No one had ever told her what to do now.

"Thanks for the miracle, by the way," Jason said.

"It was an equitable pact, Jason Asano. There is no need for thanks."

"I'll thank you anyway."

"Then I shall thank you again for retrieving my clergy those years ago.

Allowing them to be snatched away and locked in stasis, out of my reach, was a grave failing on my part. Doubly so as they could neither live their lives nor reach their deaths. For faith in me, they were returned to a world where almost everyone they knew was centuries dead. The places they lived were often unrecognisable, if not gone entirely."

"How are they reacclimatising?" Jason asked.

"Some better than others. They were happy to learn of your return from the grave. Despite my admonitions at the sentiment."

Jason noticed the slightest smile tease the corners of Death's mouth, even as his voice remained gravestone flat. He saw curiosity gnawing in Miriam's expression, but she couldn't bring herself to ask in front of the god.

"We gods have asked them to leave you be, for the moment," Death continued. "Many look up to you in a way that we know you are not yet comfortable with. I would advise caution should you encounter the former Purity priests, however. Those who did not find other faiths have suffered. Many are confused and lost. Some have taken their own lives. Others are angry, and some of that rage is directed at you, irrational as that is."

"Anger doesn't have to make sense. And they came by it honestly. Did Purity sanction himself and get replaced by Disguise while they were locked away?"

"Yes."

"That's why he rejected all his priests, then?"

"You are correct," Death said. "Disguise moved slowly and carefully on first adopting the role of Purity. As time passed and the clergy changed with the passage of generations, he moved it painstakingly towards the extreme aspects of Purity's remit."

"But a bunch of people who knew the original recipe wouldn't go for the new spicier flavour."

"It would have been a risk not worth taking, yes."

"Do you not feel even a little bad about not telling everyone that Disguise was faking it for centuries?"

"Jason!" Miriam hissed.

"Worry not, Miriam Vance," Death told her. "I take no offence at Jason Asano's question. It is one being asked of us all around the world, even by our faithful. Especially by our faithful. Have you not asked that question yourself, Miriam Vance? Even in your own mind?"

"I... have," Miriam admitted.

"There is no shame in doubt, child," Death told her, his voice warmer than it had been. "Wisdom comes from knowledge, not ignorance. There is a relationship between gods and mortals, and you were deceived. We were frustrated, as much as our kind can be, but we could do nothing. The hidden gods operate differently from those of us who work in the open. There is a place of worship dedicated to me in every township large enough to support more than one collective temple. My presence exists everywhere in this world where things live and die. My influence has a home in every city and hamlet, and I employ it every day. Gods like Undeath, Destruction and Disguise have only hidden strongholds that are constantly being hunted. They hoard their power, saving it for their attempts at grand works of depravity. Masquerading as Purity was Disguise's greatest triumph, and all we could do was watch and wait."

"For what?" Miriam asked.

"For you to figure out the truth."

"Me?" Miriam asked, eyes wide and voice an octave higher than normal as she turned to stare at Death.

"Mortals," Death clarified.

Jason stifled a chuckle as Miriam turned beet red.

"Eyes on the battle, Miriam Vance," Death reminded her gently.

Miriam let out a whimpering noise as she turned her gaze back to the fight. Her body language was that of a turtle who found itself with no shell to crawl into, despite really, *really* wanting to.

Despite her nervousness, Miriam's mind raced. She was concentrating on the changing state of the battle and the reactions of her forces. The commands she issued through group chat showed no indication of her unease at the presence of the god only Asano could see.

She glanced at Jason, who showed nothing but complete ease in his body language and his aura. It genuinely looked as if he was unfazed by the undead army, the miracle in front of them or the presence of the god responsible for it. He noticed her look and nodded, absently scratching his ear. Whatever he had given up to have Death turn the tide of battle, she was certain it was not so inconsequential as he claimed. If he didn't want to say, then she wouldn't push; she restricted herself to silent gratitude as she turned her attention back to the battle.

Fresh waves of undead were moving in to replace the massive losses they'd suffered from the flames. Many of the elemental messengers hadn't been able to fight at all thus far, for fear of their power being drained. The disappearance of the power devouring their magic and the comforting power of divine ghost fire had emboldened them. Miriam only realised how much when they surged into the attack, flying over the frontline en masse.

"Oh, gods damn it all!" Miriam snarled. "We can barely communicate with these things. How am I meant to get them back into tactical positions?"

"It's good they actually matter now," Jason said.

"They won't matter if they get isolated and cut down. We can't rely on Death's power forever; this is our fight."

Jason smiled at Death's slight nod of approval, although Miriam missed it as she directed the battle lines to adapt to the messengers running wild.

"The tree is the key to the messengers," Jason said. "I don't think it has a mind, but it has a will. Maybe I could try and impart your intentions to it?"

"A multi-stage communication line with an entity that has instincts but maybe not intelligence? No way of issuing clear instructions that it may or may not agree with? In battle, Operations Commander, simplicity is what works. Sometimes. Complexity lasts exactly as long as it takes for one thing to happen and the plan is out the window. I appreciate the offer, but issuing commands to an unreliable ally through a game of whispers with a tree is not something I have time to try."

The actions of the messengers had blown away Miriam's nervousness at the presence of their divine observer as if she'd forgotten his presence. While she'd been explaining to Jason why talking to the tree wouldn't help, she'd also been issuing orders across multiple voice channels. She scanned the field to assess the new situation and look for optimal responses, realigning their forces accordingly. At least the ones that would listen to her.

Jason resumed his aura suppression, using it on the most powerful undead. The gold-rank abominations were too strong for him to entirely suppress, but even partial diminution of their power helped. With their powers diminished and the weaker undead cleared out by fire, the defenders came crashing down on one abomination after another.

"What do you think?" Jason asked once Miriam had stopped barking out constant orders through voice chat. "Is it enough? Will we hold them out of the natural array chamber?"

"Yes. I'm about to order us to push forward and reclaim some of the ground we've given. They'll be back, but it won't be enough. We'll hold."

"Then it's all about the citadel chamber."

"Yes. Fighting back the undead is one thing, but that purple light is another. Once it infests the wall, they're done. Can you push that light back with whatever you're doing to the ambient magic?"

"No. I've felt it growing, and that's not just something in the ambient magic. It's something deeper. The god of undeath is claiming territory, seeping his power into the ground. He's making it his domain. I know that power better than most and it will take more than an aura to stop it."

"Unholy ground?" Miriam asked.

"Yes," Jason said. "I think he's trying to turn this entire underground realm into a massive temple."

"He is," Death confirmed. "Undeath is claiming territory."

"Then what do we do about the wall?" Miriam asked. "Will that fire stop Undeath from expanding his territory over it?"

"No," Death said. "That is why the ghost fire is only half of the miracle I promised."

"What was the other half?" Jason asked.

"Undeath has been liberally spending his influence in this place," Death said.

"Isn't that his whole thing?" Jason asked. "Saving up his 'interfere with the mortal realm' tokens so he can use them all on the big prize? Also, you didn't answer my question."

"Physical reality is a place of limits, even if we gods have none," Death said.

Jason rolled his eyes as his question still went unanswered.

"Those limits," Death continued, "are inescapable if we wish to exert our influence on the physical realm. We gods are in balance—an intricate harmony that works much like the natural world does. We are a part of the natural order, after all. Even gods like Corruption, Destruction and Pain have their place. But Undeath is an exception. Corruption exists within the natural cycle, but the concept of undeath is a corruption of the cycle itself. Its god likewise stands apart, not understanding the balance that exists between the rest of us. He cannot understand it because it is his nature not to. We must, therefore, rein him in from time to time."

"Then why are we even fighting his creepy army?" Jason asked. "Go tell him off. Is that the other part of the miracle? Telling him off?"

"Yes."

"Wait, really?"

"I have reset the territory he has claimed, quashing his domain, but that is as much as I can do. He has already started building it again and I cannot intervene a second time, even as he continues to act. Balance affects me, just as it does him. He has long garnered his power to influence the mortal realm and now he spends it. His domain has started spreading again and his priests conduct a terrible working in the darkness. The conflict between Undeath and myself is a proxy war now, fought between his priests and your adventurers. I hope you do well."

Death was gone as suddenly and silently as he had appeared, without so much as a disturbance of the air.

"Did Death just make us his generals in a holy war?" Miriam asked.

"Yep. I'd say that deserves a sandwich, but the air here is pretty funky. It'd probably taste weird."

"How can you be so casual about this?"

"Nothing's changed," Jason said. "We were always going to fight. If you get worked up every time some diamond-rankers, gods or great astral beings take an interest in you, you'll never get anything done."

"That does not feel even remotely correct."

Jason chuckled.

"I get it," he said. "A god is relying on you and you're feeling that pressure. But I'll say it again: nothing's changed. Put it out of your mind and do what you were already going to do."

Miriam gave a nervous nod. She would not have let that lack of confidence show to any of her subordinates in the expedition, but Jason was her commander. He was the only one she could go to for comfort and he did his best.

"If we can hold long enough to activate the devices here and in the citadel chamber," he said, "then we can face them in the transformation zone. There, Undeath's power won't be able to reach them. The undead will also be divided up into zones, so the priests won't be able to influence them until they conquer those zones one by one. Which means that we can beat them. There is a path to victory, Miriam. We just have to walk it."

She nodded, assuring herself.

"We just have to hold long enough for the devices to activate," she said, glancing down the tunnel behind them. That way led to Clive and the ritualists getting ready in the array chamber.

"Yes," Jason said. "If the citadel doesn't have to deal with their wall turning purple and evil, then the defenders there just have to hold against the undead."

"You're the one who has been speaking to them," Miriam said. "Do you think they can?"

"It doesn't matter what I think; I'm out of things to do about it from here. At this point, all we can do is trust our friends."

"I don't have any friends over there," Miriam said. "I've only just met most of these people."

"Well, I do have friends over there," Jason said. "And believe me, friends are better than allies."

"You're not worried about losing them?"

"Oh, terrified. I've lost people before. But if you try and leave them behind for their own protection, they won't thank you. I lost a brother, a lover and a friend because they decided to fight alongside me. I blamed myself for letting them come along, but I ultimately accepted that they made their own choices. They chose to stand and fight for their world and I had no right to take that from them. We don't get to do that. I've been here before, Miriam. Armies of undead, transformation zones, everything on the line. After I lost those people, I took on the rest of it alone. That helped me realise that what I needed more than anything else was to have the people I trust at my back. This time I do, and I'll take that over fighting alone every time."

86

INSUFFICIENT VESSEL

THE DEATH CHAMBER SIDE OF THE WALL WAS AN UNRECOGNISABLE RUIN from its days as a vertical stack of buildings. The outer walls had been staved in by the invading undead, exposing the insides the defenders had barricaded. Gary stood between the undead and one such barricade, holding them off while the people on the other side reinforced it. It was a large breach, the interior walls smashed apart, and blocking it off effectively was taking time.

After trapping himself on the unpleasant side, Gary hadn't expected to last long. His only intention had been to keep the undead off until his support team finished their work, but then a miracle happened. Just as he was about to be overwhelmed, his body had lit up with flames that burned away the undead dog-piling him.

The white fire and the red glow between the plates of his armour were the only sources of light. The encroaching purple glow of Undeath's domain had vanished with the arrival of the flames, plunging the city into darkness. Now the only light amongst the ruined buildings came from burning undead. As they were tossed off the wall, engulfed in flames, they fell amongst their brethren like sparks in dry brush. The divine ghostly fire swiftly spread from every point they landed.

Jason's interface power had given Gary a message that he had briefly skimmed. After spotting the words 'Death,' 'goddess' and 'miracle,' he decided that was all he needed to know. He closed the window and started swinging his hammer, learning the rest by doing. It was just good to know Jason's interface power was up and running again, punching through the magic interference. Voice chat would have been better, but either the lingering elemental power or the undeath energy was still blocking it.

A zombie messenger loomed over Gary as it lumbered forward, lifting its arms and bringing them back down like twin hammers. They landed on Gary's shield, which budged as much as a windscreen struck by a bug. White flames ran up the zombie's arms as if coated in petrol and Gary sent it stumbling back with a mighty shove. It fell into the undead crammed shoulder-to-shoulder behind it and the flames quickly jumped onto them.

Gary's hammer rose and fell in a mad rush, like a xylophone player on way too much caffeine. Heads were smashed open and limbs torn off by blunt force, every strike delivering more of the ghostly fire. The head of his hammer crashed through the hard shell of an undead beetle the size of a compact car, its insides some kind of fluid. The fluid proved extremely flammable before the ghostly fire. The flames reached it and the beetle immediately detonated, annihilating itself and all the undead around it.

Gary's shield took the bulk of the blast that came his way, but it still hit him like a runaway train. He was hurled back like a thrown rock, bouncing off the barricade to land heavily on the floor. He immediately pushed himself up, turning to the open wall to look for undead. The explosion had cleared it and, thus far, no more were crawling in. Peace wouldn't last with more undead always on the way, but it gave him a brief moment of calm.

He'd dropped his hammer in the blast and pressed his empty weapon hand to the barricade while whispering a spell, his voice hoarse.

"Let integrity be clear in my eyes."

- You have used [Inspector's Eye].
- You are able to perceive the structural integrity of rigid objects, assessing weak and strong points.
- Abilities used by you to weaken or strengthen objects you have inspected are enhanced.
- Non-magical crafting abilities will have enhanced effects when actively used in conjunction with this ability.

The magic allowed Gary to assess the state of the barricade. His support team on the other side of it had made good use of the time he bought them, sealing the breach with a solid barrier, but his spell showed him the weak points left by the rush to get it done. He wanted to use his own powers to fix them, but he had neither the time nor the mana to spare.

The thought made him realise how quiet it was behind him. The undead did not yell or scream in battle, but that only made the sound of them scrambling up half-shattered stairs and climbing through broken walls easier to hear. The absence of that sound meant something unusual, and Gary wasn't having the kind of day where unusual was a good thing.

He looked to the entrance to see a huge leonid standing in the shattered gap of the outer wall. Taller than Gary by a head, he wore simple armour and no weapons. The armour was worn but well-maintained to Gary's trained eye, even as his spell failed to assess it. Gary stared at the leonid for a long time, trying not to look crestfallen.

"Lord Hero," Gary said. He did not kneel, only nodding to the god.

"Well met, Gareth."

The god's voice was quiet for a leonid, soft and gentle like a hand cradling a baby bird.

Gary moved to pick up his dropped hammer. He then rested it on the ground, the handle sticking up ready to be grabbed quickly.

"If you'll forgive me saying, Lord Hero, it isn't well met. Meeting you on a day like this is as grim as it gets."

"I understand. I see people on their darkest days, which is when they are shining brightest."

"That must be nice for you. The wall isn't going to hold, then? Even with that purple filth pushed back?"

"It will not. The fires will slow the dead, but their numbers are too many. You have seen for yourself that this wall was never intended to be a defensive line."

Gary nodded.

"The barricades we put up are stronger than the wall itself," he said. "The brighthearts hollowed it out, leaving just enough strength that the whole thing didn't collapse. To not fall over and little more."

"I am sorry, Gareth."

"Are you?" Gary asked, his voice bitter. "Aren't these the days you live for? The heroic last stands? The blaze of glory that will live in song for a thousand years?"

"Yes," Hero admitted. "These are the days I live for."

Gary hung his head.

"I didn't want to come here, you know," he said in little more than a whisper. "I wanted to put this life behind me. Be a smith. Master my craft and forge the tools that carried my friends to victory. It would have been easier to found another damn city than dig out what's left of the last one and rebuild it."

"Yet, if you and your companions hadn't, the results would have been a disaster on far greater a scale than just one razed city."

"We didn't know that."

"No, you did not. You yourself had the choice not to join, Gareth."

"No, I didn't," Gary growled. "This isn't just some monster hunt I could merrily wait for them to come back from. What kind of man would let his friends go off and do this without him?"

Hero smiled.

"The kind I will never meet."

"Lucky me. Are you holding back the undead?"

"They are avoiding me. Even these mindless creations know to be wary of a god. The echo of Undeath's power in them, perhaps."

"Then go stand in one of the big breaches and leave me alone."

"You know that's not how it works, Gareth."

"Yeah," Gary growled. "I know. But this shouldn't count as a sacrifice anyway. I'm going to live. With this magic fire, the breach behind me closed and the undead on the back foot, I can fight my way to an open breach and get back inside."

"You didn't know about Death's miracle when you came out here, Gareth. You believed that you came here to die. People keep thinking that what the gods want in sacrifice is their lives, but that is not the case. You chose to come out here, believing you would die. Your choice was the sacrifice, not your life."

"For all the good it did me. Might as well get it over with, then. Bring it out."

Hero nodded and stepped forward until he was within arm's reach of Gary. He held out one hand and conjured a large goblet into it. The cup was made of the same dark metal as Gary's armour. Engravings etched into it glowed with the light of molten steel. Hero took his other hand and held a single finger over the goblet.

A rainbow dewdrop appeared on the fingertip, hanging for a moment before falling into the cup. The goblet lit up as it filled with liquid swirling gold, silver and blue, light shining from the top to light up the inside of the building.

"This cup—" Hero began before Gary snatched it from his hand.

"I know what it is," Gary snarled. Not a single drop had splashed from the goblet as he grabbed it, despite the rough treatment.

"Gareth, this choice—"

"Isn't a choice," Gary said, cutting off the god again. Hero made no sign of anger, his expression instead that of a proud but sad father.

"The fact that you see it that way," Hero said, "is what brought us both here."

"How long?" Gary asked as he peered into the cup.

"Around seven hours."

Gary nodded, put the cup to his lips and quaffed it down. None of the liquid spilled from the sides of his mouth, despite crudely chugging it. He tossed the cup aside when he was done and picked up his hammer.

"How long does it take to—"

Gary staggered, dropping his hammer again as power surged through him like a fire-hose enema. Silver light filled his body, glowing under his skin and blazing from his eyes and mouth, open in a silent scream. He dropped to his knees and slumped, head lolled back and motionless as a corpse.

- You have drunk from the Cup of Heroes.
- You have accepted divine power into your soul.
- You have absorbed divine power belonging to the Pallimustus god of heroes. Unless you are isolated from the god's influence, the divine power will naturally work to leave your soul and rejoin the god. Your soul can resist this for another seven hours and forty-one minutes before the power overcomes your ability to contain it.

- Your body is an insufficient vessel to sustain the current spiritual strength of your soul.
- Your divine power is reforging your body into a physical and spiritual gestalt to contain your spiritual strength.

. . .

The light inside Gary shone brighter and brighter. It would be utterly blinding to almost anyone, but the solitary divine witness was unimpeded. He watched through the light as Gary's conjured armour and the clothes beneath dissolved into nothing. Gary's body then did the same. The light vanished, leaving the chamber dark and empty save for Hero and Gary's hammer, still lying on the floor.

Hero felt Gary's soul dragging magic from the astral and using it to forge not just a new body but itself. It began with a golden spark that expanded like a singularity at the birth of a universe. The chamber was flooded with a more blinding light than ever, but this time warm gold instead of cold silver.

Hero watched Gary's new form coalesce, body and soul merging into a single, cohesive state. It came into being kneeling on the floor, head bowed as if he had fallen asleep meditating. Still blazing with light, Gary's new body started moving. He shook his head as if to clear it after waking up. The light faded almost entirely away until all that was left was Gary kneeling naked on the floor. Now the golden light shone only from his eyes.

- Your [Hammer] essence has been replaced with the [Divine Hammer] essence. Your [Divine Hammer] essence abilities have reached [Gold 0].
- Your [Fire] essence has been replaced with the [Divine Fire] essence. Your [Divine Fire] essence abilities have reached [Gold 0].
- Your [Iron] essence has been replaced with the [Divine Iron] essence. Your [Divine Iron] essence abilities have reached [Gold 0].
- Your [Forge] confluence essence has been replaced with the [Demigod] essence.
- Essence ability [Craftsman's Gaze] has been replaced with [All-Seeing Eye]. [All-Seeing Eye] has reached [Gold 0].
- Essence ability [Stoke the Forge] has been replaced with [First Son of the Leonids]. [First Son of the Leonids] has reached [Gold 0].

- Essence ability [Inspector's Eye] has been replaced with [Vessel of the Ancestors]. [Vessel of the Ancestors] has reached [Gold 0].
- Essence ability [Refinement Process] has been replaced with [Divine Forge]. [Divine Forge] has reached [Gold 0].
- Essence ability [Hand that Holds the Hammer] has been replaced with [Hero]. [Hero] has reached [Gold 0].

Gary rose unsteadily to his feet. He looked much the same but with some key differences. He was larger than Hero now, taller and broader of shoulder. His proportions remained identical, however, as if he'd been scaled up from the original. The other major difference was his eyes, a pair of golden orbs that lit up the chamber.

- You have reached [Gold rank].
- Essence ability may advance beyond [Gold 0].
- You have an innate resistance to, and damage reduction against, silver-rank and lower effects.

- Demigod essence ability [Hero] has reached gold [Gold 1].
- Demigod essence ability [Hero] has reached gold [Gold 2].
- Demigod essence ability [Hero] has reached gold [Gold 3].
- Demigod essence ability [Hero] has reached gold [Gold 4].
- Demigod essence ability [Hero] has reached gold [Gold 5].
- Demigod essence ability [Hero] has reached gold [Gold 6].
- Demigod essence ability [Hero] has reached gold [Gold 7].
- Demigod essence ability [Hero] has reached gold [Gold 8].
- Demigod essence ability [Hero] has reached gold [Gold 9].
- Demigod essence ability [Hero] has reached diamond [Diamond 0].

Hero gestured at Gary, whose nakedness was immediately covered in pants and a gambeson of pristine white. Gary made a gesture of his own and a golden fire came into existence, floating in the air before him. It shed enough heat to make the air shimmer.

- You have used [Divine Forge].

Pieces of plated armour started floating out of the fire and attaching themselves to Gary's body. The plates were shining black and etched with gold. As each one settled next to another, the glow of molten steel lit up between them. The final piece was a shield in the same black and gold, molten steel lines running over it, encircling the gold etching. When the armour was complete, it covered Gary neck to toe, leaving only his head revealed. His mane hung wildly behind him, his face a vision of power.

- You have forged [Gary's Divine Armour]. This armour is a divine relic.

There were small hooks set around the waist of the armour. Tiny hammers emerged from the fire and floated to Gary, the loops on their handles settling over the hooks.

- You have forged [Gary's Large Hammer].
- You have forged [Gary's Large Hammer].
- You have forged [Gary's Large Hammer].
- You have forged [Gary's Large Hammer].
- You have forged [Gary's Large Hammer].
- You have forged [Gary's Large Hammer].

Gary knelt to pick up the hammer still lying on the floor. He stood up straight and shoved the hammer and half of his arm into the flames still burning in the air. The fire shrank slowly as it was absorbed into the hammer until the fire was gone entirely, leaving the reforged hammer in Gary's hand.

- You have forged [Gary's Medium Hammer] into [Gary's Last Hammer].

The hammer was not ostentatious or ornately crafted like the armour he now wore. It was a simple thing, made from a single piece of what looked like ordinary steel. It was a sledge with an oversized head and a steel handle wrapped in cloth for grip. It was plain and crude, looking more like a tool than a weapon.

Gary dropped his arm to his side, the hammer resting in his hand so comfortably it was like a part of him.

"You are ready," Hero said. "The fight rages on, Gareth, and it is time for you to rejoin it."

Gary nodded and headed for the open wall leading into the death chamber. He paused at the threshold, half turning his head. When he spoke, his voice was resigned but also resolved.

"Thank you, Hero. For giving me the power to save them."

"No, hero," the god told him. "Thank *you*."

TWIN FLAMES

THE BRIGHTHEART CITY HAD ONCE BEEN A SUBTERRANEAN WONDER.
Sustaining a population in the hundreds of thousands in an enclosed ecology, far from the air and light, was anything but easy. Even with magic, every choice came with compromise, some easier than others.

Gutting the wall between the citadel and main city chambers had seemed like a painless choice. It offered a useful framework and hundreds of tons of raw material, both ideal for stone-shapers. Turning the wall into homes, shops and government administration as the city expanded was an elegant solution. What did the compromised integrity of the wall matter? They hadn't pushed it to dangerous levels, and who would bring war to their deeply buried home?

Now, however, the city chamber was a chamber of death. The building façades were unrecognisable, torn open by the undead crawling inside like ants over a corpse. The barricades set up mid-building were the true defensive line, and were near-impenetrable on the lower levels. That strength waned as the levels went up, time and materials both in limited supply.

The undead were like water, following the path of least resistance. They crawled up exposed stairwells, their exteriors ripped away. They climbed the walls of inactive elevating platform shafts, silver-rank strength gouging grip-holds from the stone. They even climbed over piles of other undead, either slower to move or already inert after encountering defenders.

The fifth floor was the break-even point where the defences were weak enough and the level accessible enough that the undead made their biggest push. Gary had stepped into a major breach on the floor, buying enough time for it to be sealed, but it wasn't enough. He was plugging holes in a boat about to snap in half.

That was when Hero stepped in. Gary was now a vision of divine power, standing taller even than the god's avatar. His armour was ornate, black and gold with heat glowing red between the plates. His hammer was not ornate at all, little more than a block of steel on a metal handle. Gold shot from his eyes like headlights, cutting through the dark.

He stood for a moment at the shattered outer wall, looking down at the flood of undead teeming through the city to the wall. A sea of lesser undead, moving islands of the greater ones interspersed through them. Death's ghostly fire lit up, shrouding his remade body.

Gary launched himself from the wall and into the city of death, trailing a comet-tail of gold and white flames. He crashed to the ground, his feet breaking the flagstone roads in spiderweb fissures. Just the shockwave of his landing destroyed the weakest undead and sent most of the others flying. It was chased by an expanding ring of gold fire that coated everything left in devouring flames.

Lesser undead fell inert as Arabelle drained the magic from them. Streams of dark purple energy extruded from them, snaking through the air for her to collect. She did so in an ethereal jar floating behind her, the purple streams flowing into the top. At the same time, white orbs of purified death magic streaked out of the jar, shooting past the weaker undead.

The gold- and silver-rank undead were too strong to be quickly eliminated by Arabelle draining the power from them. The magic animating them was stronger and greater in quantity, too much to make draining them practical. Instead, Arabelle was refining the undeath magic into the power of natural death it was a corruption of. She was concentrating that refined power into orbs and then firing them off.

The orbs ignored the weaker enemies, seeking out the strongest source of undeath magic. Their power counteracted the animating power of the undead, rarely enough to kill them outright, but enough to slow them down. It worked like a poison, setting them up for her husband Gabriel to deal with.

Gabriel Remore was a more orthodox magic swordsman than his son. While they both employed a mix of mobility, quick spells and powerful special attacks, Gabriel gave up the battle-defining finishers Rufus used for a more conventional approach. His consistent and immediate damage delivery in almost any situation was more in demand than his son's approach. Gabriel was always an in-demand adventurer while Rufus was a better fit for the oddball Team Biscuit.

Gabriel had been showing the value of the orthodox approach by playing clean-up for his wife. She was doing the weird things, throwing the undead's own magic back at them. He did the ordinary but important work of hitting things until they fell down. She defined the battlefield while he made sure nothing slipped through the cracks.

Any of the lesser undead that managed to evade Arabelle's intentions were swiftly and efficiently cleaned up by Gabriel before they got anywhere near his wife. A swift fire bolt spell or the elegant stroke of a flaming scimitar dealt with them quickly. The more powerful undead he jumped on and burned down quickly, weakened as they were by Arabelle's purified death energy.

Gabriel was always where he needed to be. Long experience as an adventurer and fighting alongside his wife made them a well-oiled machine, thorough and efficient. And efficiency was the name of the game when there was always another crisis. They had to carefully balance both time and their mana reserves to last out the battle.

He wielded the twin flames of his own power and the ghost fire as they danced together on his elegant golden scimitar. The ghost fire was invaluable to Gabriel for the simple reason that it cost no mana, allowing him to maintain a healthy reserve. This wasn't just about endurance but also the confidence of having that power available. He knew that if he needed to take a risk in the desperate defence of the wall, he had the power to save himself when something inevitably went wrong.

Even after the retreat of the purple light that marked Undeath's domain, the wall's collapse was an inevitability growing more imminent with every passing moment. They didn't have time to leave the wall and get an update on how close the ritual was to completion, and couldn't have done anything to help if they did. Their role was to buy enough time, and they both had a suspicion they weren't buying enough.

The defenders of the wall included some of the most capable adventurers on the planet and they were already giving their all. Gabriel and Arabelle Remore were certainly counted in this number, but they could not help despair creeping in at the corners of their minds. Then they felt surge a surge of overwhelming power and realised someone had given their all and more.

- You have entered the area of a divine aura.
- You are being affected by the aura ability [Hero].
- All attributes are enhanced.
- All cooldowns are reduced. All abilities have come off cooldown. They will not be reset again if you exit and re-enter the aura.
- You have gained damage reduction.
- You have gained resistance to all negative effects.
- Afflictions will be periodically cleansed from you.
- You have an ongoing healing effect.
- You have an ongoing mana replenishment effect.
- You have an ongoing stamina replenishment effect.
- You have gained divine protection. Hostile divine power will be diminished in effect against you.

Arabelle frowned. Gabriel paused after felling an undead and turned to share a look with his wife.

"Someone drank from the Cup of Heroes," he said grimly.

"Let's not waste it," she told him. "We needed something more and now we have it. Let's hold this wall."

The shockwave of Gary's arrival on the ground wiped out an arena's worth of lesser undead. The stronger of the undead were swayed but not destroyed, for all the good it did them. They moved on Gary even as they burned, and he rushed to meet them. His blows were so powerful that anyone watching would doubt their own aura senses. Silvers were being smashed apart with a strike or two as if they were bronze rank. The golds showed the endurance of silver-rankers instead of the near-indestructibility of their true rank.

Gary was a powerhouse, wielding strength that neared diamond rank and not one but two kinds of divine fire. One was Death's ghostly fire while the other was his own, divine power transforming his fire essence into a weapon of the gods.

In the first minutes after landing amongst the undead, those flames and Gary's might were enough. The lesser undead were soon steering clear of the area at the direction of an undead priestess. Gary's now-divine senses picked her up, channelling her god's power to control more of the undead than she could alone. He could feel her power drawing back the lesser undead and sending more of the greater in his direction.

Greater undead charged at him from all sides. Some were returning from the direction of the wall he had leapt so far from and he grinned savagely. Every major threat that was kept from the wall bought precious moments. Most came from deeper in the city, though, scrambling over broken streets and erupting out of buildings. Clouds of dust sparkled in the light of gold and white flames as whole sections of wall gave way, not even slowing undead too large for doors.

The priestess didn't bother sending even the most powerful silvers. She was gathering the gold-rankers that were the greatest threat to the wall, as Gary was the greatest threat to them. More than a dozen were soon converging on Gary all at once, which was enough for him to start pulling out more powers.

Gary let his hammer drop to the ground, the handle upright as it rested on the square sledge head. He crouched down and plunged both hands into the ground as if the solid stone were a bucket of water. As far as Gary could see, golden chains erupted from the ground to entangle every one of the silver and gold-rank undead.

The undead pulled and thrashed helplessly. The chains were all shrouded in Death's ghostly fire, burning into them. Gary stood up straight, a bundle of chains held in each massive hand as he yanked them from the ground. The chains around the undead tightened, bluntly digging through them to leave burning chunks of flesh resting on the ground.

Gary felt the power of Undeath, the dark god's influence spreading from within his priestess. It touched the remains of the powerful undead, maintaining their animating force as the chunks started rolling together. They reassembled in clumsy replications of their already hideous forms, patchwork flesh abominations now more patchwork than ever.

The undead were again moving on Gary, albeit with less momentum and even more clumsiness. Undeath's power was strong, but had to contend with that of both his nemesis, Death, and Hero, currently with a rich Gary flavour. Gary was a rocket-powered bulldozer as he ploughed into the still-burning undead, his hammer smashing apart what Undeath had stitched back together.

Gary pulled out more divinely enhanced powers, his hammer glowing gold as he threw it. It flew to strike one undead before bouncing to another, each hit triggering a blast of force and the twin fires of Gary and Death. While waiting for it to come back, he cast a Divine Fire Bolt, a golden fire projectile flying off to chain through the enemies like the hammer. When the hammer flew back to his hand, he held it aloft. Golden hammers rained from the sky to smash into the undead.

The power of Undeath was great, but a divinely infused agent also wielding the power of a second god's miracle was too much. A zone that minutes earlier had been a river of undead was now quiet and still. Sizzling spells and crumbling stone were distant sounds coming from the wall behind him. Ahead, the city was dark and eerily quiet for all that a monstrous army lurked within.

The priestess had never come close enough to the battle for Gary to pounce on. He could have chased her down but he was buying time, not hunting priests. The number of gold-rank undead he had just eliminated was a blow even to the seemingly endless horde. The priestess and her god pulled their forces away from Gary entirely, the priestess retreating to the heart of the city while he still fought.

He looked around, deciding his next move. He could chase the priestess to the base of the enemy, tackling the undead at the source. He decided against it; victory was not in how many they killed but in how long they survived. Going after the priests and leaving the undead behind him, free to storm the walls, was a bad idea.

He turned to look at the wall, his new perception ability unhampered by darkness or even solid stone. He could see every undead, every defender, every team working to shore up or replace barricades as the wall grew shakier by the moment. His next move would be to plug some breaches and keep the ship from sinking for a little longer. He would leave a gift for any more of the undead that came this way, though, stalling their reinforcements.

Gary walked in a large circle, a line of golden fire lighting up on the ground in his wake. When the circle was complete, the ground inside it melted, turning to lava. The molten rock then transmuted to metal, gleaming like quicksilver. From the molten metal rose a massive dark figure, white-yellow heat shining from between plates of course dark iron.

The divine forge golem loomed well over twice the height of Gary's own enhanced size. Molten metal dripped from it like water and two holes in the helmet-like head glowed with golden light from within. The metal under its feet cooled into a solid circle and the ring of fire went out. Gary wandered over and tapped the golem companionably on the thigh, then left it to stand sentinel against the next wave of undead.

Looking back to the wall, Gary picked out the spot most in need of help and started running. He gathered speed in a few strides and took a mighty leap, a golden comet streaking through the dark. He crashed into the undead surging into a breach like a meteor and immediately went to work.

88

NAUGHT BUT FAITH

WHILE THE DIVINE GHOST FIRE CONTINUED TO BURN, IT WAS FADING IN strength. What had once annihilated the lesser undead, swiftly burned through the silvers and strongly impeded the golds was now far less efficacious. Miriam adjusted tactics accordingly, bringing forward the adventurers with wide-area attacks that had been taking the chance to recoup their mana.

Jason was finally able to deploy Gordon's butterflies effectively, his aura suppressing the undeath energy in areas where the ghost fire was too weak to do so anymore. He found himself alongside Zara, the former princess of the Storm Kingdom. Her wind and water powers had been suppressed for most of the fight, her elements clashing with the natural array. The undeath energy had suppressed it, but the undead had then started absorbing her elemental powers, along with those of everyone else.

The ghost fire had suppressed the undead's ability to absorb magic, but blowing all her mana on area attacks at that stage would have been redundant. Only now that the fires were weakening could she make a worthwhile contribution. The undead were rallying, but their power to devour magic was still suppressed, partly by the ghost fire and partly by Jason's aura.

Zara found herself shoulder-to-shoulder with Jason. He wasn't deep amidst the enemy the way he usually fought, leaving that to the elemental messengers who had launched themselves into the fray when, like her, their powers were suddenly more effective.

Jason was focused on his roundabout approach to area damage. Using his aura, he'd grabbed a handful of weaker undead, unnerving the melee defenders when he floated them past, despite his warning beforehand. He then afflicted one and let it spread butterflies to the others.

Most of the undead he grabbed were hurled back, deep into the undead lines. The mindless undead failed to recognise the threat and let the butterflies run rampant. Jason, in the meantime, had kept one of the undead. He pulled in more unafflicted for butterflies to spread to before again hurling most of them away. He repeated the process over and over to maximise affliction distribution.

Zara's process was less elaborate: she cast a spell and the undead were destroyed. While Jason was launching undead far into the enemy backline, Zara's spell created a storm of wind and water much closer to the fighting. The storm was much smaller than an actual hurricane, but in a restricted tunnel, it didn't feel like it. Blades of water severed limbs and sliced hideous undead bodies, while others were tossed into the air and pulled apart like rotten fruit.

Some of the elemental messengers were caught up as well, but Zara mentally wrote them off. Their recklessness in the face of danger meant she was far from the only one to pepper them with area powers.

"How are you throwing zombies through my windstorm?" Zara asked Jason, shouting over the wind of her spell.

"You know we have voice chat, right?" he yelled back.

"Oh," she said, too quiet to hear but her sheepish expression said it loud enough.

Jason grinned and opened a private channel.

"How are you getting them through my storm?" she asked again. "It's like they're completely unaffected by the wind."

"I'm using my aura to telekinetically counteract the force of the wind and water your spell is throwing at them."

Her head turned on a swivel to stare at him wide-eyed.

"You're *what*?"

"Your spell isn't that strong at any individual point," he explained. "It's just big. It isn't that hard to sense the individual forces being applied to one object inside the spell's area and apply an equal and opposite force to negate them."

"With your aura?" she exclaimed.

"It's actually great practise. We should do this more."

"I don't know that we'll have regular access to zombies."

Jason laughed, taking his eyes from the battle to give her a side glance. His eyes fell on her copper hair, cropped above her shoulders, shorter than when it had been royal sapphire.

"I owe you an apology," he said.

"What for?"

"Your hair. I had no right to make you do that, however angry I might have been."

"It's just a hairstyle."

"However justified my anger may or may not have been, I don't have the right to tell you what to do with your body. Thinking it's okay to do that may seem harmless when it's hair, but what about when it's not? I'm sorry for that."

"Am I about to get one of your famously questionable moral diatribes?"

"What do you mean, famously questionable?"

She laughed. The sound, like water trickling over rocks, entered Jason's mind through his voice chat, stirring dormant reactions he'd thought long dead. He turned his focus back to the fight, silently admonishing himself.

Jason had been immediately drawn to Zara when they'd met on the other side of the world. She'd still been a teenager and he'd still been an idiot. More of an idiot, he admitted to himself. She was the only woman he'd met whose beauty truly competed with that of Sophie, rank-ups having little improvement to make. The five years before they met again felt like twice that and changed them both, him especially. He had thought those years, followed by events in Rimaros, had completely quashed any lingering affection.

"Do I even have hormones at silver rank?" he muttered.

"What?" she yelled. "I can't hear you without voice chat."

"It's nothing," he said through chat. "I'm just... I shouldn't have told you to do that with your hair."

"You don't like it?"

"What kind of lunatic wouldn't like it? You look amazing."

She blinked, flustered.

"I wasn't expecting that," she admitted.

"We may have our differences, but I've got eyes. I bet you had a trail of people following you around like ducklings in Yaresh. Are there any loose undead left? I think you blew them all away."

Jason panned his gaze, looking for any weak undead he could grab, but Zara and the other area specialists had cleaned them up for the moment.

"I think you're pretty much out of the weak zombies," Zara told him. "There were some people in Yaresh who showed perhaps more interest than I was looking for. I'd appreciate it if you could try to dampen your team spy's enthusiasm."

"You mean Estella?"

"Yes. I'm not as open-minded as she would like."

"She did call dibs."

"What?"

"Nothing."

"I do disagree with something you said, Jason."

"What's that?"

"We don't have differences. You have differences with me, and I understand why. I made some mistakes in Rimaros, and they involved you at a time when you needed space and time to heal from whatever it is you went through on your own world. First, I used your good name when I thought you were dead, then you got caught up with my family. Then, after you finally got away from me, I dropped myself in your path again. After you quite explicitly told me that you didn't want me along. But I'd arranged things so that kicking me out would be more trouble than keeping me. I put you in that position."

"It's a mixed bag," Jason said. "You thought I was dead, in which case I wouldn't care. And as for getting involved with royalty, it turns out Soramir had been watching me from the instant I arrived, so that was inevitable. That last bit, forcing your way onto the expedition, was the only crappy thing I can completely drop on your doorstep. And if we just spend all our time being crappy to one another, we'll both turn into worse people. I'm trying out forgiveness as a philosophy."

"And how is that working out?"

"It's bloody hard. So many people suck, and they're usually the ones you have to forgive. If it was all forgiving beautiful princesses, I'd be all over it."

"I do appreciate it. As I said, while you may have issues with me, I never had any with you."

They both leaned to the side as an undead's severed limb was thrown out of the storm, passing between them to land wetly on the ground behind them.

"Princess, are you hitting on me in the middle of a zombie war?"

"When else am I going to do it? It's always something with you."

Undeath priest Garth Larosse was not happy. His god's nemesis, Death, had no servants in this underground realm, yet had still found pretext to intervene. The territory claimed by Undeath had been driven back to nothing while Death's ghostly fire ravaged their forces. The fires were only truly decisive against the lesser undead, mass-produced from the pits, but that freed the defenders to concentrate on their more powerful forces.

It wasn't an absolute setback; Death's interference could only go so far. The territory could be reclaimed and Death lacked the influence to wipe it clean a second time. The flames would play out, in time, and were already waning, but that time was the critical factor. Undeath had already warned him that they must act with haste to stop what the adventurers were doing, which meant they could not wait for the flames to die out entirely.

Undeath had not told him what the defenders were up to, only that they needed both arrays to accomplish their goal. Garth was certain his side would not be able to claim the natural array chamber in time now, protected as it was by the bulk of the enemy forces and the ghost fire. He would need to refocus his forces on the citadel chamber.

The wall keeping them from the chamber was already hanging by a precarious thread under the weight of their assault. Once breached, they could bring down the citadel and the echo array with it, ending whatever threat had Undeath concerned.

Garth contemplated this inside the city's largest building. It was huge and triangular, with massive crystals in the ceiling that had once bathed everything in yellow light. The elemental power fuelling them had been supplanted, and now their glow was purple. The ground had been covered in firm moss, a triangle playing pitch for some kind of ball sport. The moss was long withered and dead, and most of the space it had occupied now hosted a humungous circular pit.

This was the widest and deepest of the pits that he and his fellow priests had created. Nothing could be seen through the cloud of purple and green miasma within. Nothing, thus far, had emerged from the pit, despite only the best materials going in. The most intact and high-ranking corpse parts, along with most of the power bestowed upon them by their god. This was not a means to conquer the underground realms but the reason why they were doing it.

Garth came to a decision: to move his forces back from attacking the natural array and add them to the assault on the wall. It would cost them, but he would use up Death's miracle by marching bodies into the fires like a tide if that was what it took. He was about to head for the doors to the massive building when they opened to admit the one priestess amongst his servant clergy.

Jameela's long legs carried her quickly as she came striding towards him. For all the power Garth's skeletal body offered, the addition of the tall, beautiful woman to his group had left him almost sad to have given up his flesh. Capable and intelligent, eager and quick to learn, she was the opposite of another priest he had been forced to bring along.

Jameela quickly reached the edge of the pit. She didn't wear robes, like most of the clergy, but the practical leathers of an adventurer. The short, sharp bow she gave Garth was not a matter of disrespect but haste.

"High Priest," she said in greeting. "The defenders of the wall have deployed something or someone new. I'm not certain what, exactly, but it tore through some of our strongest undead, even attacking collectively. It's gold rank, but at a power level like nothing I've ever seen. I withdrew from making more futile attacks and came to report. After our forces stopped assaulting it, it returned to the wall. It's now intervening at our strongest points of attack."

The red lights in the skull sockets that passed for Garth's eyes dimmed as he focused on extending his aura senses. It did not take him long to find what he was looking for. Anger sent the red lights flaring brighter than ever.

"It's a demigod," Garth told her. "Hero has intervened."

"I've never seen anyone who has drunk from the Cup of Heroes," Jameela said. "In retrospect, it's not a startling development. We are pushing them to the brink, which is fertile ground for Hero's miracle."

"The problem isn't the miracle but the timing of it," Garth said. "That wall must come down. I was about to order our forces attacking the natural array to back off and reinforce the wall attack. We can take the array in the aftermath once the threat is dealt with. Redeploy everything to bring down that wall. Collapse it under the sheer weight of bodies if that's what it takes."

"Our resources are many, High Priest, but not infinite. That will deplete us heavily."

"That's the advantage of serving Undeath, Jameela. The harder-fought the battle, the more we have to work with when it's done. This is why everyone is so diligent about suppressing us. They know that unless we are overwhelmingly crushed, every battle makes us stronger and them weaker. The more dangerous our enemies now, the better the servants we will make of them."

A voice filled the air, a deep, harsh rumble that echoed like gravel being dumped into a silo.

"It is not enough," Undeath's voice spoke.

Suddenly, he was standing before them. Garth and Jameela both dropped to their knees, heads down. Undeath looked like a living man in simple black robes, except for his eyes. Like Garth, they were empty sockets containing a crimson spark.

"Death and Hero have both intervened at this critical juncture," Undeath told them. "Hero was not unexpected, as you reasoned, Priestess Jameela. And as you have said, Garth, the issue is the timing. Alone, neither gods' influence would be insurmountable, but both at once requires a response. Death finding a pretext to act was unfortunate."

"I apologise for my failing, Lord," Garth said.

"You have done as I have asked with the resources I have given you," Undeath told him. "If I punish you for following my instructions, I will only end with servants like…"

Undeath turned to the stone door Jameela had come through as it opened again. It was heavy but not unmanageable for a silver-ranker like Priest Jeff, who stepped inside.

"Hey, boss, I think something is going not so great out here…"

Jeff's eyes went wide on spotting Undeath.

"Oh, you're busy. I'll come back."

Jeff backed off and closed the door. Undeath pinched the bridge of his nose.

"If his grandmother wasn't a high priestess of Destruction… I apologise for his presence, Garth. When dealing with other gods, compromises must be made, even by me."

"I have naught but faith in you, Lord," Garth said.

"Thank you, Garth. Stand, both of you."

As the priest and priestess rose to their feet, Undeath moved to the edge of the pit and they followed.

"Unfortunately," Undeath said, "we are forced into another compromise."

Garth looked into the pit and realised what his god was talking about.

"Lord, if we animate it now, it will be too weak a vessel. Without the messenger tree as base material, it will only hold a fraction of the power you intended to bestow."

"As you have correctly just instructed the priestess, Garth, there is always fresh material in the wake of a battle. Beginning again is costly, yes, but we must answer the threat before us now. If we do not react to the demigod, the wall will hold and the adventurers will complete their goal."

"It will take some time to ready it," Garth said. "But if compromise is what you require, there are shortcuts that can be made. The lifespan will be cut short in turn, but that is not the concern here, if I understand correctly."

"You do. Proceed, Garth."

The undead priest of Undeath turned to Jameela.

"Go," he told her. "Order the others to direct everything from the array chamber to the wall, then gather the ritualists and bring them here."

Jameela bowed to Undeath and then to Garth.

"Lord. High Priest."

She strode away and was soon gone.

"If I may ask, Lord," Garth said, "what exactly is the threat these adventurers pose?"

"They are attempting to remake reality in this area. If they complete their ritual, you and all of our forces will be cut off from my power. You will retain any that you have prior to being dragged in, but that is all."

"Remake reality? How is such a thing possible?"

"Cosmic forces, older even than I. Events involved in the very creation of this world. As it stands, we have the numbers while our enemies have the individual power. If we fail and you are brought inside this warped reality, your numbers will be divided as all inside are scattered at random. Your undead will be separated and unguided; you will need to unify them before they are wiped out in isolated pockets."

"If we animate the avatar now, will it be brought with us?"

Undeath nodded.

"It is good that you see, Garth. Even imperfect, it will be a repository of my power that you can use. Finding it will be your first priority, even above reclaiming your forces. The ultimate goal in this warped reality will be to conquer the territories into which it will be divided. Doing so will allow you to collect your forces. But, while conquering territories is one thing, uniting them once you have is another. If you lack the requisite ability, even attempting to do so will end only in disaster. It would serve only Destruction, who has gleefully stepped back to watch events unfold."

"I know not of this power to bend reality to my will, Lord. I assume the other side does?"

"The enemy has one with the power. His name is Jason Asano; kill him if you can. I will give this power to the avatar, so you must find it. Without it, everything else is meaningless."

Undeath looked to the door.

"The ritualists are about to arrive. Be swift, Garth, and do well. Put your faith in me and I shall put my trust in you."

Garth bowed.

"Always, Lord Undeath."

"Two more hours," Clive told Jason. "Maybe an hour and a half. An hour if you can dig up a miracle from the goddess of knowledge that tells us the rest of what we need to do."

"We've already had two miracles," Jason told him. "I think that's more than gracious already."

"What's the other one?" Clive asked.

"I'm talking to Marla, in command of the citadel, through Shade. She said someone drank from something called the Cup of Heroes."

Clive frowned.

"Do we know who?" he asked.

"Not yet. She just said that they're big and gold and have an actual chance of buying the time you need. What is this magic cup thing? Some kind of power boost miracle?"

"Yeah," Clive said grimly. "A power that kills you when it's done. Ask them to find out who used it."

"Asano," Miriam said through voice chat. "We need to talk. The undead are pulling back."

89

THINKING LIKE AN ADVENTURER

MIRIAM AND JASON WATCHED AS THE ELEMENTAL MESSENGERS CHASED the retreating undead.

"Why have they given up on the natural array chamber?" Miriam wondered. "Just consolidating forces, or do they know about the rituals?"

"The latter," Jason said. "Knowledge was the one who put the idea in my head of triggering a transformation zone. Gods exist in balance, so I imagine Undeath warning his own forces was fair game."

"I think we should divert some of our people in response."

"Agreed, but we can't just abandon this position and rush back to the citadel chamber. The undead will just go behind us and move on the array chamber again."

"We can select who we send by who will do the most good there and the least here."

"You're the tactical commander. You make the picks."

"Check in with Marla in the citadel chamber. Get a sense of what they need."

"Sounds good."

Jason wandered off while Miriam looked over the adventurers. They were at something of a loss after the enemy's retreat, Miriam having ordered them not to pursue. The elemental messengers had ignored her once again. Jason moved towards the wall of the tunnel, the closest he could get to a quiet spot.

"Mr Asano," Shade said. "Our forces in the citadel chamber have made a discovery. Marla is going to tell you something, and I hope you can remain calm."

Jason narrowed his eyes in suspicion, but Shade was speaking from Jason's shadow, leaving him nothing to glare at.

"They've found out who used the magic cup thing?"

"Yes."

"Who?"

"Mr Asano, it might be best if—"

"Who?" Jason asked again, his voice an icy blade. "Give me the name."

Rufus had been fighting alongside Taika, Humphrey and Sophie when the undead retreated and they were told to stand down and rest by Miriam. Team Biscuit was not well suited to fixed defensive positions or to being part of a defensive line. Once the fires had come, they had done better, going after the stronger undead while the flames cleared out the rest. The gold-rank undead weren't the equal of an adventurer of the same rank and the team could handle eliminating one of them without gold-rank assistance.

Like the other adventurers, Jason's team was taking the chance to rest. Belinda conjured camp chairs for them, so they didn't have the choice of the stone floor or corrupted plants withered into black filth by undead energy. They didn't relax completely, alert for an undead turnaround. There was also the disconcerting presence of their Builder cult allies.

All the defenders snapped to alert as a sharp sense of danger erupted to fill the space around them. Most of the cultists and brighthearts looked around with tense expressions while the adventurers, with their sharper aura senses, quickly realised the source.

Rufus looked over at Jason, whose wide eyes were glaring at nothing, but with a fury that looked like it would melt stone. Jason's aura receded and Miriam moved to calm their unsettled allies. She threw a glance at Jason, her expression making it clear that there'd damn well better be a good explanation.

Jason's eyes focused as he turned to meet Rufus' gaze and opened a private voice channel. It also brought in Farrah, still working in the natural array chamber.

"What is it?" Farrah asked curtly. "I'm quite busy here."

"Do you know what the Cup of Heroes is?" Jason asked, his voice flat.

"Jason," Farrah said, her voice a warning. "Do not drink from Hero's mug."

"He didn't offer it to me. He offered it…"

Jason drew a sharp breath and let it hiss out through clenched teeth.

"…he offered it to Gary."

Neither Rufus nor Farrah responded immediately, shocked silence reigning on their voice channel until Rufus asked a hesitant question.

"Did he accept?"

"Yes," Jason said, sounding defeated.

"Gods damn it, Gary," Farrah said.

"He's apparently the reason that the citadel chamber wall is still holding," Jason said, doing a poor job of sounding positive. "The time we have for you to complete the ritual is time that Gary bought us. The undead have been pulled from going after your chamber, and he's probably the reason for that too. We're going to send some of our people to buy some more time."

"Rufus," Farrah said. "How bad was Jason when he heard?"

"His aura rattled some people. It wasn't so bad, or you'd have felt it from there."

"Good," Farrah said. "Jason, do not let this make you go off and do something crazy. We need you for what comes next, so no disappearing and wrecking yourself by tapping into your soul realm to do something ridiculous."

"I know."

"You better know. How many times have you had your back to the wall and your solution was calling on some power, whatever the price? You had no intention of accepting the World-Phoenix's blessing, but when you needed to break into an astral space to rescue me, you let your fundamental nature be transformed. When you needed to portal people out of a place you couldn't, you used a reality core to overcharge yourself to the point it took magic we didn't know existed to keep you alive. If Gary has drunk from the Cup of Heroes, he's following your shitty example, and he doesn't come back from the dead. So, if you want to be a hero again—and we could really use some heroes right now—then figure out how to fight smarter instead of yanking yet another fistful of magic out of your ass."

Jason and Rufus stared at each other while Farrah yelled at Jason through voice chat.

"And you'd best believe that Gary is going to get the same…"

Farrah broke off, her second tirade cut off by a sob before it could get started.

"I need to get back to work," she said angrily and left the voice channel.

Jason's fury had been washed away by Farrah's words. He shared a look with Rufus, each feeling the same mix of anger, hopelessness and loss.

"Is this what it feels like?" Jason asked. "Is that what it feels like every time I—"

"Yes," Rufus said.

"I'm sorry."

"You should be. Now, follow Farrah's example and get back to work."

Rufus strode off in Miriam's direction. Jason was about to do the same when he found someone standing in front of him. He looked human, wearing plain armour and carrying no weapon. Jason looked around and saw that no one reacted to the divine presence. Even the people that had been watching him after his aura outburst were suddenly shifting their attention as if they'd forgotten his very existence.

"You're really going to show your face right now?" Jason asked.

"I am sorry about your friend, Jason Asano. But you understand the choices here more than most, I think."

"My friend just gave me an earful for understanding."

"Do you think I like what I do? My name is Hero, yet I will never be one. I have spent my entire existence finding the greatest people on their darkest days, turning their likely deaths into certain ones. I've seen glorious deaths on grand battlefields, immortalised in tapestry and stained glass. I've been the only witness to sacrifices that went completely unnoticed by mortals. Countless lives saved by heroes unremembered and unsung by all but my priests."

"Cool story, bro. I've got a thing, so if you've got some kind of point you're rounding up on, I'd appreciate you getting on with it."

"Each god has a role that defines our mandate to influence the world, determining the nature and degree of our influence."

"So, that's a 'no' to getting on with it?"

"I do have a point to make, Jason Asano, and I do not make it lightly. When a god speaks, it is not without purpose."

Jason opened his mouth to speak, then clamped his mouth shut with a grimace. He'd told Death he would try to be more respectful, and as angry as he was, Hero had been right. He understood sacrifice more than most.

"Alright," he said. "Speak your piece."

"Few gods have as little influence as I, or are so restricted in its use. If heroes are given all they need, then they are not truly heroes. Even my priests gain no miracles from me without doing something very ill-advised. But there are times we can shift the normal limitations. I can act to counterbalance other gods like Coward, Dominion or Despair."

"I get it. You've just got the one miracle, and the one condition to use it."

"You have three times met conditions for my intervention, but I either could or did not intervene for various reasons. The first instance was when you faced a silver-rank monster when you were only iron, to give a village time to evacuate. If you had needed to defeat that monster, rather than simply distract it, I would have offered you the power to do so. For only distraction, I knew that you would refuse."

"No kidding."

"The second time was when you chose to engage the Builder's vessel in personal combat. In this instance, you were in an astral space beyond my area of influence. I only know of this event from stories, and I would not be surprised to learn there are more from your time back in your own world. The final time you opened the door to my intervention was when you overcharged a portal and almost killed yourself in the process."

"People keep bringing that up today."

"I did not intervene there because there was no point once you supplied the power to open the portal yourself. My miracle would only have taken your death from a near certainty to an absolute one."

"Maybe you should expand your miracle repertoire. Add something non-lethal."

"I would very much like that, but there are dangers. My kind do not change with the ease that mortals do, or even other kinds of transcendent. The repercussions of change for us are hard to predict, often indirect and rarely positive. This is especially true for one as specific as myself. Compare me to Purity, whose nature had had many more aspects than I, yet his change was such a debacle. The magnitude of the unintended consequences his act set in motion created so much misery."

"Why did Purity turn himself into an artefact? What did he hope to accomplish?"

"I cannot be certain, only make guesses. The god of purity is one with both very positive and negative aspects. You understand this, I believe. There was a war that engulfed a continent as a human-dominant empire sought to spread a very specific concept of what it meant to be pure. It was a time when Purity was in danger of being seen as one of the dark gods. That empire was where the Order of Redeeming Light was born."

"I thought the order was founded when fake Purity was in charge."

"As do most, but this is not the case. What Disguise made of the order is something else, but the seed had already been planted. I believe that Purity intended to refocus the very concept he embodied, following the fall of that nation."

"He picked a crappy way to do it."

"Indeed he did. Perhaps, then, you can see why I am wary to make changes to my own nature."

"I guess. It feels like maybe you could try something less drastic, though. Now, why are you here? I need to go help my friend you killed."

"I spoke on pushing the limits of my influence. Much of how we use our influence is a matter of pretext, and you have done enough that I can push those limits. Not enough to produce or alter a miracle, but enough to give you a gift, much as Healer did."

Hero held out his hand, which contained an orb filled with blue, gold and silver light. Jason possessed an identical orb, given to him by Healer. He reached out and took this second one.

Item: [Genesis Command: Source] (transcendent rank, legendary)

The authority to link power. (consumable, magic core).

- Effect: Assign or reassign a source of power. Requirements of use vary by the nature of the origin and destination of the power.

- Uses remaining: 1/1

. . .

"It is the best I can do," Hero said, his tone apologetic, and was gone.

Eyes snapped onto Jason as if everyone suddenly remembered that he existed. He put the orb in his inventory as Miriam strode up to him, shaking her head as if shaking off sleep.

"Did you contact Marla?" she asked.

"Sorry, no," Jason said.

"Death again?" Miriam asked. "Hanging around you, I'm starting to recognise the feeling of my perception being divinely pushed aside."

"The gods have done enough," Jason said without answering her question. "It's time Undeath stopped worrying about Death and Hero, and started worrying about us."

Jason, Miriam and Marla discussed the best approach for adventurer reinforcements. Jason and Miriam being in one area and Marla being in the citadel made the conversation logistically awkward. Jason could speak with Miriam in person or to Marla through Shade, but the two women could not speak with each other directly since the latter was out of range. He settled on Shade acting like a translator, relaying to each leader the parts of the conversation they were otherwise not privy to.

"Your friend's intercession has tipped the scales in terms of reacting to wall breaches," Marla said. "As it stands, we won't lose out because of gaps in the wall. That means we can stand as long as the wall itself does. That's time we desperately needed, but it won't last forever. We're waiting for word that the ritual is ready on your side."

"An hour, maybe two," Jason told her. "Somewhere in the middle, most likely. Will the wall last that long?"

"Right now, I'd say yes. But the god's fire dimming means we'll be dealing with raw numbers again soon. Doubly so if the forces attacking you are moving on us. It doesn't matter if they're all weak; they can bring the wall down through sheer weight of numbers."

Jason waited for Shade to finish repeating Marla's words, giving Miriam a chance to respond.

"It sounds like what you need is someone to thin out the numbers on the weaker undead," Miriam said. "None of our gold-rankers are ideally suited to area attacks, but one of our silver-rank teams is."

"Silver-rankers are fine, so long as they can deal with the numbers," Marla said after her own delay. "Oddly enough, we can handle the more powerful threats. Their numbers are low enough that the gold-rankers and our Hero-enhanced warrior are dealing with them. What we need is more clearance of the sheer mass of undead we expect will be coming for us at any moment."

"I'll send you Team Storm Shredder," Miriam said for Shade to pass on. "They come from a kingdom where the adventurers like to specialise, and their specialty is killing a lot of things at once. Good enough?"

"Good enough," came Marla's answer. "I need to get back to commanding the defence, but send them as soon as you can."

Shade retreated into Miriam's shadow as she turned to Jason.

"Will you join them?" she asked. "The rest of your team don't have strong area attacks, but I could attach you to Team Storm Shredder. Your butterflies could be valuable if you can make them work."

"Whether or not I can is definitely a question," Jason said. "My concern is the Undeath priests that are sure to be directing the attack on the wall. Intelligent enemies have a habit of shutting down my butterflies before they reach the critical mass where they can't be stopped."

"You'll stay here, then?" Miriam asked him.

"Actually, I would like to go, and I want to take Emir and Constance Bahadir with me. I had an idea, and I need people who can safely capture some gold-rank undead without destroying them to make it work."

Jason explained his idea to Miriam, who agreed.

"Having some gold-rankers will help you get through the death chamber unscathed," she said. "Gather them up and go immediately."

Jason nodded and got moving, issuing orders through voice chat.

Farrah had been right, Jason realised. His essence abilities had been stalled out since he hit the wall of silver back on Earth and were only starting to crawl forward again. It was his spiritual powers that had grown, and he'd paid the price for that. When faced with dangerous challenges he'd become too reliant on pulling out some crazy power or bullying with his tyrannical aura. He had to fight smarter with the tools he had instead of wrecking himself with reckless improvised power. It was time to stop thinking like an astral king and start thinking like an adventurer again.

DREAD AND CRUSHING DESPAIR

THE REINFORCEMENT GROUP MADE UP OF JASON, EMIR, CONSTANCE AND Team Storm Shredder paused at the massive entrance that led into the former brightheart city. The tunnels and chambers they had passed through to get there had all been abandoned, the undead giving up that territory entirely.

What they had not given up was the city, now a bastion of the undead. They were out there, in the dark, hidden from sight. Far across the chamber, flashing light and faint sound marked the conflict raging several kilometres away.

"There's ten of us," said Kalif, a member of Team Storm Shredder. "How many undead are out there?"

"We can't be certain," Jason said. "There were originally around two hundred thousand brighthearts, most of whom died, plus messengers and Builder cultists that died. There's no telling how many have been turned into undead or stitched together in bigger undead. On the other hand, thousands of them have been destroyed by us, the citadel defenders or Death's ghost fire."

"So, there's more than ten left, then," Kalif said.

"I'd call that a fairly safe assumption, yeah," Jason said.

"Shouldn't we have brought more people?" Kalif asked.

"You say that like you've never fought a hundred thousand undead before," Jason told him.

"And you have?"

"Yep."

"When was this?"

"A couple of years ago."

"Korinne," Kalif said to his team leader. "I think we should find different adventurers to follow around."

Jason chuckled to himself. Indulging in some light banter didn't push Gary's dire predicament out of his mind entirely, but was at least something of a distraction.

The group set out into the airspace of the death chamber, high above the fallen city where the undead were massing. Constance and Emir stood together on a flying cloud conjured up by Emir while the silver-rankers flew in two air skimmers produced by Shade. It wasn't the most secure mode of transport if attacked, but it was fast, convenient and let the group travel in tight formation. It was also low profile to visual and aura perception compared to something like Zara's Pegasus made of sapphires.

The hope was that the mass of powerful clashing auras on the other side of the chamber would distract the undead, letting the group cross the vast cavern unchallenged. The battle for the wall was certainly an attention-grabbing spectacle, visible from the opposite end of the chamber, kilometres away. Spells flared brightly in the dark, Illuminating the sea of undead in brief flashes, like dancers at a rave. Patch remnants of ghost fire were guttering out, taking undead with them as Death's miracle finally petered out. Most arresting was a beacon of gold, exploding in bursts and leaping up and down the wall.

Jason extended his senses to get a closer look at Gary's aura. That wasn't hard as he'd never felt anything short of a diamond-ranker's that compared to what Gary was blasting out. The group had barely started crossing the chamber before Jason's interface gave them all a message about the effects of Gary's aura power, named simply Hero. With dozens of aura powers overlapping, Jason had turned off messages about individual ones, but Gary's power overrode that. Whether due to its divine nature or raw power, Jason's interface decided it was not to be overlooked.

The divinity coursing through Gary was impossible to miss. Jason had discovered his senses were more sensitive to divine power than most, but that wasn't at all necessary here. Gary's golden radiance did everything short of skywriting the word 'demigod' and drawing a giant arrow pointing right at him. Jason's friend was, for the moment, divinity manifested upon the world.

A message notified Jason when he came into communication range of the wall defenders. He resisted the urge to open a channel to Gary, who seemed rather busy, and instead reached out to Marla. He set up command channels for Marla and other leaders like Arabelle to better communicate.

Around halfway across the chamber they finally drew the attention from some of the undead. They were flying in a curve, so as to avoid the heart of undead territory, but some flying monstrosities still noticed them and rose through the air to intercept. There were five gold-rankers amongst them, each a bulbous frankenzombie stitched together from seemingly random parts. They had limbs, none of which matched, affixed in vaguely the right spots. Messenger wings had been stuck on their backs, random in both placement and number. With their bulging bodies and too-small limbs, the elephant-sized nightmare-fuel cherubs were twisted mockeries of not just life but the laws of aerodynamics.

The rest of the flyers were more conventional, a few dozen zombie messengers. Oddly, their normal wings had been removed and replaced with skin stretched over frameworks of segmented bone.

In the absence of Miriam, Jason had designated Emir tactical commander for the group. He was both the most powerful and the most experienced member of the group. Jason waited for him to issue commands, but he didn't. Instead, he conjured a staff of black lacquered wood, etched with gold runes and shod with gold at each end. Holding it vertically, he lifted it slightly and then brought in back down. The small, unhurried movement was sharply contrasted by the result.

Massive pillars, each a dozen metres across and hundreds of metres long came smashing down from above. Each looked identical to Emir's staff, only orders of magnitude bigger. Buildings cracked as the pillars struck heavily and then disappeared.

"We should move instead of fight," Emir said. "That power looks destructive, but mostly, it knocks things around and stuns them for a bit, which undead shake off rather quickly. The ability looks impressive but isn't as powerful as it seems."

"Every power set has a theme," Constance observed.

Emir turned his head to level a flat glare at his wife, who was squeezing her lips pressed tightly together to contain a laugh. At the same time, the cloud and the Shade skimmers were shooting forward, continuing their path to the wall.

The reinforcement group slowed before reaching the point where they would get caught up in the battle for the wall. It was close enough that they could see the state of the battle, the undead piled on top of each other at the base, so many they formed a ramp that the others were climbing over. The real fighting began at the top of the slope, on the third floor. The third through seventh levels saw the most intense fighting as an endless stream of deathless climbers was beaten back by the defenders.

There were now many open breaches in the wall, but the defenders were holding them. As much as Gary's personal intervention helped strained defensive positions, it was his aura that did the most work. His other powers were at the base level of gold rank while his aura power alone had ranked all the way up to diamond. On top of that, it was a wholly unbalanced ability, fuelled by divine power and only made possible by the demigod essence. The raw power of the enhancements it offered were transformative for all of the defenders, even the gold-rank ones.

While his aura was aiding the overall battle, his personal presence arrived like the salvation of a god when he moved to aid the defenders. Every swing of his hammer sent waves of force and fire that devastated even the strongest undead. When he roared, the wall was scoured clean of the enemy, although had to be careful not to blast away sections of the wall itself.

Jason finally couldn't help himself and opened a voice channel to Gary.

"I'm sorry it come to this," Jason said.

"We're adventurers," Gary told him. "We can try and quit all we like, but in the end, someone has to stand up. If that wasn't going to be us, we wouldn't be who we are. I know it. Rufus knows it. You definitely know it; it's been your turn a few too many times already."

"Doesn't mean I have to like it."

Gary laughed.

"You damn well better not. Don't let Rufus get too depressed, alright? I don't want you and him doing the same sad boy tour I did after losing you and Farrah. She's not here, right?"

"She's busy with the ritual."

"Good. I'm pretty sure she'd give me a kicking for this, demigod or not."

Jason laughed.

"Oh, I don't think there's any dodging that, Gary. You can expect her to tear strips off you once we're all in the transformation zone."

"I'm looking forward to it," Gary said, his voice heavy. "Now, I assume you're here to pull out some crazy power to deal with all these undead?"

"No, this is your magic show, Gary. I'm here to play your glamorous assistant Lorena, wearing something sparkly and gesturing prettily when the curtain comes down."

"This wall feels about as flimsy as a curtain."

"You're doing better than anyone thought possible. Have no doubt that without you, we'd have already lost. Clive, Farrah and the others have done a great job of getting the ritual ready as fast as possible, so keep holding and we'll get things done."

"Thanks, Jason."

"No, Gary, thank *you*."

"Hero said almost the exact same thing. You should stop spending time with gods, Jason; they're a bad influence."

Jason laughed as he closed the channel. They were approaching the wall, ranged attacks fending off undead as they headed for a freshly cleared breach to meet Arabelle and Gabriel.

"You'll be under the direct command of Arabelle Remore and the overall command of the brightheart leader, Marla," Jason told Team Storm Shredder. "You'll be operating largely on this side of the wall to thin out the rank and file of the enemy from the relatively safe upper levels. I'll be taking Constance and Emir to hide on the inside of the citadel chamber where it's safe."

Storm Shredder's leader, Korinne, quashed any questions from her own team. They moved into the breach, Jason, Emir and Constance nodding their greetings to Arabelle and Gabriel before getting straight to business.

"I'm going to need you to let through the occasional gold-rank undead," Jason said. As we use them up, we'll need fresh ones, although I'm not sure fresh is the word."

"We won't need to let anything through," Gabriel told him. "Were holding and resealing breaches, but they're still getting in as fresh holes get punched through the wall. The defenders inside are cleaning them up, but you'll have your pick."

"Thanks," Jason said and they moved on, not stopping for small talk.

Korinne and her team were already defending against fresh attempts to enter the breach.

Jason led his gold-rank companions out the citadel side of the wall, still recognisable as something that had once been a building. They were on a balcony looking out at the citadel itself, the massive round construct held in the middle of the chamber by equally massive pillars coming from the floor and ceiling.

The floor pillars were the targets of the undead that had gotten through the breaches. They didn't need to invade the building to stop the ritual ready to take place in the echo array chamber, located in the citadel. If the citadel collapsed entirely, everything inside would naturally be handled.

"How many gold-rank undead can you safely contain at once?" Jason asked.

"It should be a few," Emir said. "They're weak for the rank, and not all of them have special powers. We should prioritise ones that are just big and tough. They don't need arms or legs or anything, right?"

"No," Jason said. "No, they don't."

Jason looked at the limbless undead, held in place by Emir's conjured staves jutting up from the ground to impale it. The monstrosity struggled helpless, the strength and duration of Emir's staves boosted by Constance's support powers.

"This will work," Jason said. "Now let's get to…"

All three turned to look at the wall, even though their senses focused on something far beyond it. Divine power blazed, but this was not Gary. It was not glorious but profane, inspiring nothing but dread and crushing despair.

"What is that?" Constance asked, her voice hollow.

"Gary's job," Jason said. "Undeath is making a clutch play."

"That's not for us to deal with," Emir said. "Hero's miracles are about the greatest of final stands, and Gary is about to make his. We have our own job to do."

"Yes," Jason agreed. "Let's get to work."

AVATAR AND DEMIGOD

THE BATTLE FOR THE WALL WAS BEING FOUGHT IN THE MOUTHS OF THE various breaches. The intercession of Gary and his demigod power had given the defenders breathing room to hold breaches long enough for barricades to be put back in place, but they were duct-taping over holes. Sooner or later, there would be nothing left but duct tape and the wall would crumble.

Deep in the city that was now the territory of the undead, an explosion rocked the darkness. Purple light blasted like a spaceship cannon from the now-missing roof of the largest building in the city. It was a massive triangular building, dwarfing those around it. The defenders fighting on the death chamber side of the breaches couldn't help but stare, wondering what new horror the undead were about to unleash.

Their distraction did not cost them as the undead they were fighting had frozen in place. The aura of Undeath flooded over the city like a tsunami before crashing into the seawall of Gary's divine power. The two auras clashed, reaching a détente that diminished Gary's ability to enhance the entire battlefield, focused as it was on suppressing Undeath's influence.

Standing on the wall next to Gabriel Remore on one of the upper levels, Gary grimaced as he stood in place, pushing back against the god's power. For the first time since drinking from the Cup of Heroes, something was an actual struggle.

The spiritual clash was a wild storm, yet everything else was strangely still. The undead paused, as if frozen and the defenders were reeling from the aura conflict raging around them. There was little movement and, as the rumble of the distant explosion faded, near-silence.

The massive beam of light coming from the building was painting the ceiling of the chamber more than a kilometre in the air. That beam was partially blocked by something moving around inside the building, something that had to be very large. The arm of a giant, pale, sickly and missing chunks of flesh, emerged from the broken roof to grab the wall. A manacle, dangling a broken chain, hung from the wrist. A second arm reached out, grabbing the wall like the first, and a humungous figure pulled itself up and onto the wall.

It was hard to make out, lit from beneath by the purple beam, but it looked like a zombified giant, larger than most of the buildings in the city. Only the one massive structure had been large enough to contain it. The zombie tried climbing the wall, but the wall gave way, crumbling to the ground and dropping the zombie with it. The resulting cloud of stone dust rose to be illuminated by the purple light, like a sunbeam in a dusty room.

The massive zombie pulled itself to its feet, standing amongst the city buildings like a kaiju. Broken chains hung from manacles around its wrists and ankles and started shedding purple light, an echo of the beam still shining behind it.

The zombie rising to its feet was like a starter's gun that set the battle back into motion. The endless horde of the unliving resumed their surge on the wall protecting the citadel chamber and the defenders sent magic blazing out to meet them.

From their high point on the wall, Gabriel and Gary had scant moments before the undead were on them again. Gary's eyes were fixed on the distant zombie as he continued battling its aura. It took an awkward, stumbling step forward, beginning a shambling walk in the direction of the wall.

"That doesn't look stitched together," Gabriel observed. "There was a giant down here for them to animate?"

Gary's divine senses could see things Gabriel could not.

"That's not a thing they animated," he told Gabriel. "It's an avatar of their god, but it's incomplete. They've sent it out unfinished to stop me."

"Will it?"

Gary wasn't even looking at Gabriel, but the grin on his leonine face sent a chill down Gabriel's spine.

"The undead will be climbing back up here soon," Gary said in place of an answer. "Do you want to take them or the big one?"

Gabriel turned to look at him.

"I think I might leave the big one to you."

The undead were on them a moment later and Gabriel went to work, fire blazing down the edge of his golden scimitar. Even without the divine ghost fire, he made short work of anything attempting to enter the breach in the wall. Gary didn't join the fight, staying concentrated on the zombie avatar. After shambling down a ruined boulevard, it stopped and raised its arms, broken chains hanging loosely as it reached for the distant wall as if trying to grab it. The chains grew longer and dug into the ground, piercing through the broken flagstones as if solid stone was loose soil.

From his high vantage, Gary watched the glowing chains dig into the ground with a frown. He suspected the avatar was about to use a power similar to one of his own and did not care for the comparison.

Harpoons the size of school buses erupted from the ground around the zombie avatar, trailing purple chains. A dozen of them rocketed through the air, massive, barbed tips plunging through the wall. The chains then yanked back, pulling taut as the barbs held the harpoons in place.

The air in the citadel chamber was becoming obscured with dust, but it was hard to miss the arrival of the massive harpoons. Jason, Emir and Constance watched as the harpoons were pulled back and their massive tines dug into the wall. Stone around the harpoons cracked as the wall trembled at the strain.

"I'm pretty sure that's bad," Jason said.

"There's not much we can do about it except keep getting ready," Constance said.

"True enough," Jason said, looking at the debilitated gold-rank undead in front of him. "This one's just about done; can you fish me up another?"

On his high platform, the undead kept off him by Gabriel, Gary looked at the chains trying to pull the wall down.

"Nope," he said to himself and took one of the six small hammers hanging from loops around his waist. It lit up with golden flames.

. . .

- You have used [Flame Investiture].
- You have infused [Gary's Large Hammer] with divine fire.

Gary threw the hammer at the closest chain, the hammer growing to the size of a house as it flew. It shattered the chain on contact and immediately deflected towards the next. It did the same thing over and over until every chain had broken, then flew off at the avatar zombie.

The hammer didn't slow down upon hitting the zombie in the torso. They both went crashing into the ground, digging a trough as they slid. The zombie pushed the massive hammer off itself, stood up and moved in the direction of the wall. It was awkward at first, moving with the slow foot-dragging shuffle of the zombie it looked like. With each step, however, the massive light beam behind it dimmed and the zombie grew more coordinated. By the time the beam was gone entirely, the zombie was moving like a living thing. It no longer stumbled over chunks of shattered buildings but navigated them adroitly, approaching the wall with distance-eating strides.

From his high vantage point on the wall, Gary broke into a run, ignoring the undead still fighting Gabriel, between him and the ledge. They bounced off him like bugs hitting a high-voltage fence, not slowing him at all as he reached the edge and leapt off, sailing through the air. His body grew much larger, just as his hammer had, and lit up with a golden radiance that trailed behind him as he soared through the dark.

- You have used [Vessel of the Ancestors].
- Your [Power], [Spirit] and [Speed] attributes are enhanced.
- Your size is increased.
- You have ongoing mana, health and stamina recovery.
- Some of your essence abilities will have altered effects.
- Some of your leonid gifts will have altered effects.

Now as large as the zombie, Gary sailed over its head to land with a thunderous crash. Unused to his new size and power, he hit a building and wound up face down, covered in rubble. He shook it off, pushed himself to his feet and crossed to his giant hammer, still burning with fire where the zombie had left it. It was now a good fit for his giant size and he picked it up before turning to face the avatar, down the rubble-strewn boulevard it had followed towards the wall.

The chains once more hanging loose from the avatar's arms and legs wrapped themselves around its body like armour. It was especially tight around the hands and forearms, like a pair of chain gauntlets.

The avatar turned to face Gary and they stared each other down across the dark and broken city. One was a proud figure of blazing power. The other was a dark figure in chains that glowered with sinister light. Purple and gold beacons in the cold necropolis, undead streamed past their giant feet like water around stones in a shallow creek.

Gary threw his hammer and it flew straight as a well-hung shelf, gravity taking no interest in it. The avatar braced itself, crossing its forearms in front of it like a shield. Chains shot from its body and dug into the ground, anchoring it in place. The hammer struck, this time not smashing the avatar into the ground but pushing it back until its chain anchors pulled tight. The hammer bounced off and fell to the ground, its divine fire dying out. The zombie's arms flopped loosely, broken in various places. They flopped and jerked as the bones snapped back together, sometimes visibly through sections of absent flesh.

Gary pulled his regular hammer from his back where magic had held it in place, ready for convenient grabbing. The chains binding the avatar to the ground were released and the giant zombie held out its arms. A chain snaked out from each of its chain gauntlets and impaled the largest of the gold-rank monsters passing by on the ground. The monsters withered a little, then a dozen glowing purple spikes erupted from them, turning them into the balls on a pair of spiked flails.

The two massive beings stared at each other as they loomed like kaiju amongst the buildings of the broken city. Gary charged at the avatar in a golden blur—they clashed with enough impact to cause shockwaves, divine power against divine power. It was a holy war embodied in two giants so charged with power, their bodies could barely contain it.

Garth had not allowed the Undeath priests to all gather in one place. They were spread out, communicating through animated skeletons linked through magic. He was standing atop a building with a good vantage of both the wall and the battle between the divinely empowered giants.

"Uh, boss?" a nervous voice came through the skeleton next to Garth. "Are you sure you sent me to the right spot?"

"I'm quite certain," Garth said.

"It's just that I'm feeling a bit exposed here."

"Just keep watching, Jeff."

"Well, that's kind of hard because of all the dust. The gold one picked up a building and hit the purple one with it. He used the building that's next to the one I'm standing on. Or, it used to be next to it. It's kind of scattered loosely across the area now."

"The 'purple one,' Jeff, is the avatar of our lord and should be referred to with the appropriate respect."

"Are you sure, boss? It's just that it looks like a regular zombie, but bigger. A bit half-cooked, you know? The magic chains look good, although I'm not sure how that fits with the undeath theme."

"If you can't see through the dust, Jeff, you have my permission to move closer."

"Boss, is this because I said Jameela had nice—"

"That's quite enough, Jeff."

"I didn't know she could hear me. And you have to admit, she does have nice—"

"She can also hear you now," Garth said.

"She's there with you? Are you two…? I just didn't think you could… you're a skeleton, is what I'm saying. I mean, I think you are. You're always wrapped up in that robe thing. Is it a robe, or more like a toga? Or just a complicated cloak? It's hard to tell, especially with the way it drapes. It just looks like it's not a regular person under there, even one made of bones. Not that I'm saying you're not a person."

Garth rapped a knuckle repeatedly against his forehead.

"What's that tapping sound?" Jeff asked. "Anyway, uh, hi, Jamie. You know I'm sorry, right? About saying you had… and that time I tried to… look, I was drunk, to be fair, and a piece of advice: do *not* try fermenting those weird plants the messenger tree makes. The point is, I could apologise properly if we got together and—"

Jameela reached out with one of her long fingers to push the skeleton's jawbone closed, cutting off the communication magic.

"Do you think he'll die?" she asked hopefully.

"No," Garth said with a rueful shake of his skeletal head. "His ability to survive every situation I put him in makes me wonder if he's a test of faith from our lord."

"Would he do that to you?"

"Our lord is neither capricious nor kind, Jameela. It is wise to test those on whom you rely. Their understanding and willingness to endure is a test in itself."

Jameela turned her attention back to the titanic clash.

"Should the avatar let the demigod distract him like this?" she asked. "The goal is to bring down the wall, not kill the demigod. He will die, in time, regardless. And make for excellent raw materials, if we get to them fast enough."

"The demigod was critical in keeping the wall intact," Garth explained. "He can no longer personally defend it and his aura is occupied, pushing back against the avatar's. He can no longer use it to blanket all the defenders, just the closest ones."

"So, when you directed our forces away from the fight between them, it wasn't just to avoid collateral damage but to focus on the weaker parts of the wall defences."

"Precisely. Even if the demigod is not destroyed, so long as it is kept from the defence of the wall, the advantage is ours."

WHAT HE WANTS FOR HIMSELF

GABRIEL SWEPT HIS SWORD IN A HORIZONTAL ARC AND A WAVE OF FLAME washed over the undead. This left the lesser undead falling apart as their flesh turned to ash and their bones to dust, but the greater ones continued unabated. A massive claw from some burrowing monster, grafted to the arm of a messenger, was swung at his head. He vanished, teleporting just a few steps back.

The teleport disorientation was light from a short-range power and he was used to it after years of use, so he didn't lose even half a step. Even so, his wife beat him to the punch as streams of white magic flowed into the patchwork monstrosity. Foul black ichor oozed from the seams where crude stitches had fused flesh and the abomination collapsed, tumbling off the ledge.

"Where have you been?" he asked as Arabelle dropped down from a higher level.

"Setting up some recording crystals," she told him.

"Is this really the time?" he asked.

In response, she pointed at the golden lion and the shackled zombie clashing with such force that shockwaves were visible in how they stirred the dust around them.

"We're seeing a legend play out in front of us," she said. "We may not be able to save Gary, but we can make sure he's remembered for saving us."

More of the lesser undead crawled up to their level and Gabriel cleared them with another flame wave.

"I don't think being remembered as a hero is what Gary wants for himself," Gabriel told his wife.

"No," Arabelle agreed. "But what else can we do?"

"We can remember him as a friend. *That's* what he wants for himself."

———

"Are we done?" Clive asked, sounding surprised at his own question. He stood with Farrah overlooking the formation array of ritual circles set up around the tree.

"Yeah," Farrah said. "This is as far as we can go until the other ritual is active so we can make final calibrations. We need the citadel team to start up the device in the echo array chamber."

"I shall tell them they can begin," Shade said from Farrah's shadow.

"And then how long after we fire this up does everything happen?" Farrah told Clive.

"I've never seen a section of the universe break down into elements based on shortcuts made by the being that created it," Clive said. "Enough time for a sandwich, I think."

"It was thoughtful of Jason to leave us a snack table."

"I've been saving the one with the fire cherry sauce," he said, turning around. "There's nothing as delicious as good food done after hard work... where's my sandwich?"

He looked at the plate now containing only a few crumbs and a note telling no one else to eat it.

"BELINDA!"

———

Zara's windstorm scoured lesser undead from the face of the wall while a lightning arrow from one of her team's strikers chained between the more powerful ones. She couldn't count how many they'd destroyed or at least sent flying, forcing them to return to the wall and start climbing again. Even so, their numbers seemed limitless and the wall ever more fragile. She glanced over at the massive harpoon still buried in it, the broken chain dangling from the back.

Like other groups in the defensive force, they'd been tasked with focusing on an area around one of the dozen harpoons. These were weak points in the wall and there was no telling if the giant zombie would attempt to use them again. Like with the avatar tying up Asano's leonid friend, it served to draw defenders away from the breaches. More and more, the strange explosive undead were getting through and further weakening the wall.

Boris the messenger looked at the now active magical device as the light it shed changed colour again. The rate at which it shifted increased until a second colour at a time was added. More and more colours came with rapidly escalating shifts until it was a blinding kaleidoscope filling the room.

"Well, that's it," he said.

"What now?" Marla asked.

"Now we hope the people in the natural array chamber got something very complicated exactly right."

"Will it work?" she asked, her stern façade cracking to reveal her nervousness.

"I'm not Asano," Boris said. "This is my first time breaking a universe. For all I know, we're all about to die. Which means…"

He turned to look at Marla.

"…we should treat each moment as if it's our last. I know the quiet-yet-undeniable longing between us has gone unspoken—"

Marla strode out the door and Boris shook his head.

"The icy chains she has wrapped around her own heart—"

"She's gay," the brightheart guard on the door said.

"Oh," Boris said. "So that's how she resisted my raw animal magnetism."

"Sure," the guard said. "*That's* how."

It began with a cracking sound. A whole section of wall slid away from the seventh level, turning into an avalanche as the already stressed support structure started giving way. The result wasn't just a breach but the beginning of a slow but unstoppable collapse. Defenders were scrambling to reach safety, rushing back through the breaches to the citadel side. Some were caught on the collapsing side and were forced to get out of the way of falling stone as best they could.

The wall fell in large patches, starting with the façades but taking enough supporting structure with it that whole sections fell away. After the first few moments, it was hard to tell what was happening as clouds of dust obscured everything. The wall, its defenders and the undead attacking it were all obscured, their fates uncertain to anyone looking on.

Garth and Jameela were doing just that. They couldn't see the wall, but the ongoing sounds of collapse dwarfed the thunder of a storm, filling the air more thoroughly than the dust.

"And the final line of defence falls," Garth said with satisfaction, letting out a laugh.

"Listen to this guy," Jason muttered, observing Garth through one of Shade's bodies. "You can't go around laughing like Skeletor when you already look like him. And he needs to learn that the guy inside the explosion cloud is never really dead. Actually, who am I kidding? I would totally go the Skeletor motif."

"What are you mumbling about?" Emir asked. "I can't hear you over all this."

Emir was moving quickly, his staff extending and shrinking as he deflected debris from the collapsing wall away from the living defenders.

"Don't worry about it," Jason told him through voice chat.

Garth and Jameela continued looking on, but it was hard to make anything out. Even the erratic lights of adventurer spells and brightheart powers had died out, leaving the two divine giants as the only sources of light. They hadn't even paused to look as the wall came down, still hitting one another with weapons or even parts of the city, picked up and hurled.

"Now they can't stop us," Garth crowed, audible as the rumbling collapse finally fell away. It still echoed through the chamber, but the cacophonous sound was dying out.

"They barely had the people to hold the breaches," Garth continued gleefully, "let alone an open pile of rubble. They'll have lost defenders too, trapped if not killed outright."

"I doubt they've lost many," Jameela said. "The brighthearts, perhaps, but the adventurers are elites. They're fast and capable whereas our undead have no sense of self-preservation. It's hard to see through the dust, but I imagine we lost far more than the enemy."

"Which we can well afford, while their every loss is a blow."

"But it will cost us time," Jameela pointed out. "If all the undead we had at the wall were crushed, or as many as makes no difference, then we will need our forces to replenish before they can cross the rubble. We still need to breach the chamber and bring down the citadel."

"Yes," Garth agreed. "Thank you, Priestess; getting ahead of myself is unwise. The defenders might not have a lot of time left, but we should take as much of it from them as we can. Signal the priests commanding the undead to have them push on, even if the wall is still in the process of falling. Be clear that only progress matters; losses are irrelevant."

While Jameela used the skeleton standing by them to relay commands to the other priests, Garth continued to look at the wall. Darkness did not impede his vision, the red pinpricks of light in his skull sockets not operating the same way as eyes. They could not see through the dust cloud, however, so when light started appearing within it, he had no idea of the source.

"What is that?"

Jameela turned from the skeleton to follow the priest's gaze. The blue and orange light shining within the dust cloud was easy to spot in the dark. It suffused the cloud, growing brighter and more widespread by the moment. Garth expanded his senses, pushing them through the turbulent magic and roiling auras that pervaded the chamber. The divine auras were the hardest to penetrate, blanketing everything with their vast, clashing power. Garth did manage to sense something floating in the dust cloud, fragile but volatile, and extremely numerous.

As he focused on his senses, Garth noticed something else that had escaped his attention so far, much closer to himself. Even trying to isolate it, he found it hard to pin down, like shadows dancing in the light of a fire. He looked around, attempting to catch it with his senses like trapping a skittering bug.

"What is it?" Jameela asked.

"It's my familiar," came a voice as a dark figure emerged from the shadow of a broken section of wall. It was some manner of shadow entity, made of darkness but with touches of white that made it appear like a neatly dressed humanoid. It gave off the sense of being the ghost of an impeccably attired servant.

"You're Asano," Garth said.

"Your boss told you about me? Probably to make sure you kill me if you get the chance."

"Yes, but that won't be necessary. The citadel will fall shortly. Your demigod has failed."

"Is that so? The way I see it, not only have you failed, but you were always destined to do so."

"What makes you think that?"

"Because the undead are as ugly as it gets. What's your name, bloke?"

"I am Garth Larosse, High Priest of Undeath."

"I'm Jason Asano, man's man, ladies' man, man about town."

"You're a fool."

"Oh yes."

"Why would the undead being ugly have any bearing on victory here?"

"Because it's not about what you do, Garth; it's about how good you look doing it."

"You're just blustering."

"Yeah, but you'll get used to it. The important thing you need to realise is that, as you're about to see for yourself, I make this look *good*."

The shadowy figure turned to look at the dust cloud, now filled to bursting with blue and orange light. Tiny shapes could be made out, flittering within.

"What is that?" Garth asked again.

Like water from a bursting dam, a torrent of tiny glowing butterflies rushed out of the dust cloud. They spilled into the air, a waterfall of light to rival Niagara, pouring down on the undead as they clambered over their own fallen and the rubble that used to be the wall.

"Harbingers of doom?" Garth said.

"You recognise them?" Jason asked, not hiding his surprise.

"They won't be enough to stop all my undead."

"No, but look at that light show. Of secondary importance to the visual spectacle is that they'll slow your creepy army down, which is all we need."

"We'll see."

"We already have, can't you feel it? The universe starting to tear itself apart? Maybe your creepy undead body isn't great at picking up on dimensional phenomena. Still, you're rocking that awesome Skeletor aesthetic, so worth the trade. Way to be a chuuni, bloke."

"You're speaking nonsense."

"Once you get to know me, you'll realise that's how you know you're in trouble."

"He's not bluffing, High Priest," Jameela said. "I can sense something happening around us. The world feels wrong, somehow. Like standing on a frozen lake as the ice starts to crack."

"Yeah," Jason said. "I just got word the ritual was off to the races. I need to go talk to a guy, but we'll probably chat again in the transformation zone. That's what it's called, by the way, the unformed reality we'll be fighting over. See you in there."

Garth reached out to grab the shadow creature, but it dissolved into nothing.

"We've failed," Jameela said.

"Victory may have eluded us for now," Garth said, "but they have not won. They have only avoided defeat. The battlefield is shifting, but the battle continues."

The zombie avatar backed off, retreating rapidly back to the city. Neither Gary nor the avatar had managed to significantly harm the other, the power flowing through them too great to be easily extinguished. Gary released the Vessel of the Ancestors ability, shrinking back to normal size. He was concerned it would accelerate the divine power's passage from his body if he maintained the state too long.

Blue and orange butterflies lit up what passed for a sky in the chamber, seeking out the undead. None came close to Gary as the undead were avoiding him, even after shrinking down. He looked up at the spectacular light display.

"Can't help showing off, can you?"

"What can I say?" Jason asked, stepping out of a shadow. "The difference is presentation."

"It's strange, being able to sense you coming."

"Yeah, I can't hide from divine eyes quite yet. Give me a while and I'll figure it out."

"I don't think I'll have time to wait, sorry."

Jason put a hand on Gary's arm, not just for comfort but to examine his demigod state.

"You're a mess, bloke."

"I'm afraid not even one of your ridiculous stunts can get me out of this one, Jason."

"I can feel the power trying to return to Hero. We're about to go somewhere it can't get away, though. That might buy you some time."

"It will," Gary said. "But that debt will have to be paid eventually."

"Yeah, but I'm pretty sure Hero wants you to live."

"I don't think he gets a choice, Jason."

"I don't think he does, no. But maybe, every now and again, he gets an opportunity."

"What are you saying?"

"That maybe this time, the one who gets the choice is you."

The story will continue in Book Eleven.

THANK YOU FOR READING HE WHO FIGHTS WITH MONSTERS, BOOK TEN.

WE HOPE YOU ENJOYED IT AS MUCH AS WE ENJOYED BRINGING IT TO YOU. We just wanted to take a moment to encourage you to review the book. Follow this link: He Who Fights With Monsters 10 to be directed to the book's Amazon product page to leave your review.

Every review helps further the author's reach and, ultimately, helps them continue writing fantastic books for us all to enjoy.

Want to connect with Shirtaloon?

Discuss He Who Fights With Monsters and more, join Shirtaloon's Discord!

Follow him on www.HeWhoFightsWithMonsters.com where you can find great HWFWM merch and other great content.

HE WHO FIGHTS WITH MONSTERS
BOOK ONE
BOOK TWO

BOOK THREE
BOOK FOUR
BOOK FIVE
BOOK SIX
BOOK SEVEN
BOOK EIGHT
BOOK NINE
BOOK TEN

Check out the entire series! (tap or scan)

Looking for more great books?

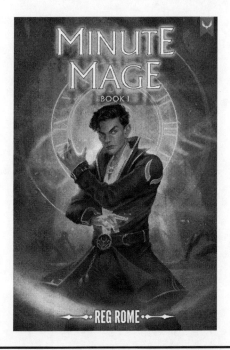

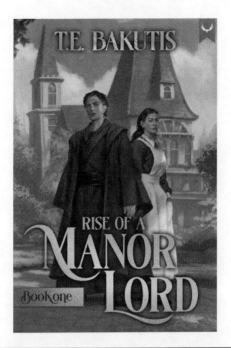

After stabbing an evil demon summoner to death, Drake inherits the old fart's mansion, servants, mountains of gold, and the ability to do magic. Which would be great if it also didn't paint a giant target on his back. With enemies now seeking to kill him for his manor, he must learn to use his powerful magic, win his people's loyalty, thwart his enemies, and fake being powerful until he *actually* becomes so powerful no one dares challenge him.

Get Rise of a Manor Lord Now!

For all our LitRPG books, visit our website.

APPENDIX I: JASON'S ESSENCE ABILITIES

The following is a list of Jason's essence abilities as of silver rank. The list is written for brevity (believe it or not) rather than accuracy or comprehensiveness.

Dark Essence

Midnight Eyes (special ability, perception)

Iron: See through darkness.
Bronze: Sense magic.
Silver: Read auras.

Hand of the Reaper (conjuration)

Iron: Conjure a shadow arm that inflicts **[Creeping Death]**.
Bronze: Also inflicts **[Rigor Mortis]**. A second arm can be conjured.
Silver: Also inflicts **[Weakness of the Flesh]**. Numerous additional arms can be conjured, including at range from shadows.

[Creeping Death] (affliction, disease): Ongoing necrotic damage. Stacking.

[Rigor Mortis] (affliction, unholy): Penalty to [Speed] and [Recovery]. Stacking. Adding to the stack inflicts necrotic damage.

[Weakness of the Flesh] (affliction, magic): Negates immunities to disease and necrotic damage. Cannot be cleansed while the target suffers any disease.

Cloak of Night (conjuration)

Iron: Conjures a cloak that manipulates light and weight.
Bronze: Cloak intercepts projectiles.
Silver: Cloak allows flight and minor space distortion.

Path of Shadows (special ability)

Iron: Teleport through a shadow to anther visible shadow.
Bronze: Create portals across regional distances.
Silver: Create portals across continental distances.

Shadow of the Reaper (familiar, summon, ritual)

Iron: Summon shadow familiar with three bodies.
Bronze: Body count increased to seven. Shades can exert minor physical force and store items in a dimensional space.
Silver: Body count increased to thirty-one. Summoner can share non-combat powers.

Blood Essence

Blood Harvest (spell)

Iron: Drain health, stamina and mana from an enemy corpse. Only affects targets with blood.
Bronze: Affects all enemy corpses in a wide area.
Silver: Gain **[Blood Frenzy]** for each corpse drained, up to a maximum threshold then gain **[Blood of the Immortal]** instead.

[Blood Frenzy] (boon, unholy): Bonus to Speed and Recovery base attributes. Stacking up to a maximum threshold.

[Blood of the Immortal] (boon, unholy, healing): On suffering damage, an instance is consumed to grant a brief, powerful ongoing healing effect. Stacking but does not grow stronger with more stacks.

Leech Bite (special attack, melee)

Iron: Inflicts [Bleeding]. Drains life from bleeding targets.
Bronze: Inflicts [Leech Toxin].
Silver: Inflicts the [Tainted Meridians] condition.

[Bleeding] (affliction, wounding): Ongoing bleed damage and absorbs healing. Cannot be cleansed but is removed after absorbing enough healing.
[Leech Toxin] (affliction, poison stacking): When [Bleeding] is negated, reapplies [Bleeding]. Stacking.
[Tainted Meridians] (affliction, poison): Stamina and mana cost of magical abilities is increased. Bleed effects cause mana loss along with blood loss. Drain attacks are more effective against target.

Haemorrhage (spell)

Iron: Inflicts [Bleeding] and [Sacrificial Victim].
Bronze: Inflicts the [Necrotoxin] condition.
Silver: Inflicts the [Blood From a Stone] condition.

[Sacrificial Victim] (affliction, unholy): Suffer greater effects from drain attacks and blood afflictions.
[Necrotoxin] (affliction, poison): Ongoing necrotic damage. Stacking.
[Blood From a Stone] (affliction, magic): Negates immunity to blood and poison effects. Cannot be cleansed while the target suffers any blood or poison affliction.

Feast of Blood (spell)

Iron: Drain life from bleeding targets.
Bronze: Drains additional life for each poison on the target.

Silver: Gains a variant with additional targets and a longer cooldown.

Sanguine Horror (familiar, summon, ritual)

Iron: Summon a sanguine horror familiar.
Bronze: Gains a worm-that-walks form.
Silver: Can conjure robes for the summoner that enhances drain attacks and regeneration. Can expend own biomass to rapidly heal summoner.

Sin Essence

Punish (special attack, melee)

Iron: Deals necrotic damage and inflicts **[Sin]**.
Bronze: Inflicts **[Price of Absolution]**.
Silver: Inflicts **[Wages of Sin]** on those with **[Sin]**. Does not inflict **[Sin]**, **[Wages of Sin]** or deal necrotic damage on those with **[Penance]**. Instead deals transcendent damage inflicts additional **[Penance]**.

[Sin] (affliction, curse): Necrotic damage taken is increased. Stacking.
[Price of Absolution] (affliction, holy): Suffer transcendent damage for each [Sin] removed.
[Wages of Sin] (affliction, unholy): Deals ongoing necrotic damage. Stacking.
[Penance] (affliction, holy): Ongoing transcendent damage. Stacking. Stacks drop off over time.

Castigate (spell)

Iron: Burns a painful brand into the target, inflicts **[Sin]** and **[Mark of Sin]**.
Bronze: Inflicts the **[Weight of Sin]** and bestows **[Marshal of Judgement]** on the caster.
Silver: Inflicts **[Mortality]**.

[Mark of Sin] (affliction, holy): Turns target's aura into an easily tracked beacon. Cannot be cleansed while the target has [Sin] or [Legacy of Sin].

[Weight of Sin] (affliction, holy): Suffer transcendent damage when subjected to a holy boon, recovery or cleanse effect.

[Marshal of Judgement] (boon, tracking, holy): Track anyone with [Mark of Sin].

[Mortality] (affliction, holy): Negates immunity to curses and reduces resistance to magic afflictions. Cannot be cleansed while any curse is in effect.

Feast of Absolution (spell)

Iron: Remove curses, diseases, poisons and unholy afflictions. Cannot target self.

Bronze: Inflicts [Penance] and [Legacy of Sin] to enemies for each affliction removed.

Silver: Wide area variant.

[Legacy of Sin] (affliction, holy): Execute abilities have a greater effect on the target. Stacking.

Sin Eater (special ability)

Iron: Increased resistance to afflictions. Gain [Resistant] for each affliction resisted or removed.

Bronze: Gain [Integrity] for each affliction resisted or removed.

Silver: Life force, stamina and mana can exceed baseline maximums.

[Resistant] (boon, holy): Resistances are increased. Stacking.

[Integrity] (boon): Ongoing life force and mana recovery. Stacking.

Hegemony (aura)

Iron: Increase ally resistances, reduce enemy resistances.

Bronze: Inflicts [Sin] on enemies attacking allies within the aura.

Silver: Maintain aura strength over a wider area. Incoming transcendent damage is downgraded.

Doom Essence

Inexorable Doom (spell)

Iron: Periodically applies more of existing instances. Cannot be cleansed while other afflictions are in effect.
Bronze: Inflicts/refreshes **[Inescapable]**.
Silver: Inflicts/refreshes **[Persecution]**.

[Inescapable] (affliction, magic): Blocks teleportation.
[Persecution] (affliction): Target gains resistance to cleansing, and positive or ongoing healing boons.

Doom Blade (conjuration)

Iron: Conjures dagger that inflicts **[Vulnerable]** makes wounding effects require more healing to negate.
Bronze: Dagger inflicts **[Ruination of the Spirit]**, **[Ruination of the Blood]** and **[Ruination of the Flesh]**.
Silver: Conjures a sword inflicts **[Price in Blood]** on both wielder and target.

[Vulnerable] (affliction, unholy): Resistances are reduced. Stacking.
[Ruination of the Spirit] (affliction, curse): Ongoing necrotic damage. Stacking.
[Ruination of the Blood] (affliction, poison): Ongoing necrotic damage. Stacking.
[Ruination of the Flesh] (affliction, disease): Ongoing necrotic damage. Stacking.
[Price in Blood] (affliction, holy): Deal additional damage to others with this affliction.

Punition (spell)

Iron: Deal necrotic damage for each affliction on the target.

Bronze: Inflicts **[Penitence]**.
Silver: Damage per affliction can be increased by increasing the mana cost to high, very high, or extreme. This reduces the cooldown to 20 seconds, 10 seconds or none. Consecutive, extreme-cost incantations have truncated incantations.

[Penitence] (affliction, holy): Targets inflicted with **[Penance]** when afflictions are cleansed from them.

Verdict (spell, execute)

Iron: Deals transcendent damage. Sales with injury level of target.
Bronze: Deals additional for instances of **[Penance]**.
Silver: Inflicts/refreshes **[Sanction]**.

[Sanction] (affliction, holy): Healing on target is reduced. Cannot be cleansed while suffering **[Penance]**.

Avatar of Doom (familiar, summon, ritual, {execute}, {holy})

Iron: Summon an Avatar of Doom familiar.
Bronze: Avatar's orbs can be detonated in pairs but take time to replenish.
Silver: Orbs can be consumed to inflict **[Harbinger of Doom]**.

[Harbinger of Doom] (affliction, unholy): Target conjures butterflies that spread all afflictions on the target to other enemies.

APPENDIX II: BOONS & AFFLICTIONS LIST

The following is an alphabetised list of all boons an afflictions produced by Jason's essence abilities. This includes indirectly, such as through conjured items or familiars.

[Bleeding] (affliction, wounding): Ongoing bleed damage and absorbs healing. Cannot be cleansed but is removed after absorbing enough healing.

[Blood Frenzy] (boon, unholy): Bonus to Speed and Recovery base attributes. Stacking up to a maximum threshold.

[Blood From a Stone] (affliction, magic): Negates immunity to blood and poison effects. Cannot be cleansed while the target suffers any blood or poison affliction.

[Blood of the Immortal] (boon, unholy, healing): On suffering damage, an instance is consumed to grant a brief, powerful ongoing healing effect. Stacking but does not grow stronger with more stacks.

[Creeping Death] (affliction, disease): Ongoing necrotic damage. Stacking.

[Harbinger of Doom] (affliction, unholy): Target conjures butterflies that spread all afflictions on the target to other enemies.

[Inescapable] (affliction, magic): Blocks teleportation.

[Integrity] (boon): Ongoing life force and mana recovery. Stacking.

[Leech Toxin] (affliction, poison stacking): When **[Bleeding]** is negated, reapplies **[Bleeding]**. Stacking.

[Legacy of Sin] (affliction, holy): Execute abilities have a greater effect on the target. Stacking.

[Mark of Sin] (affliction, holy): Turns target's aura into an easily tracked beacon. Cannot be cleansed while the target has **[Sin]** or **[Legacy of Sin]**.

[Marshal of Judgement] (boon, tracking, holy): Track anyone with **[Mark of Sin]**.

[Mortality] (affliction, holy): Negates immunity to curses and reduces resistance to magic afflictions. Cannot be cleansed while any curse is in effect.

[Necrotoxin] (affliction, poison): Ongoing necrotic damage. Stacking.

[Penance] (affliction, holy): Ongoing transcendent damage. Stacking. Stacks drop off over time.

[Penitence] (affliction, holy): Targets inflicted with **[Penance]** when afflictions are cleansed from them.

[Persecution] (affliction): Target gains resistance to cleansing, and positive or ongoing healing boons.

[Price in Blood] (affliction, holy): Deal additional damage to those with **[Price in Blood]**.

[Price of Absolution] (affliction, holy): Suffer transcendent damage for each [Sin] removed.

[Rigor Mortis] (affliction, unholy): Penalty to [Speed] and [Recovery]. Stacking. Adding to the stack inflicts necrotic damage.

[Sacrificial Victim] (affliction, unholy): Suffer greater effects from drain attacks and blood afflictions.

[Sin] (affliction, curse): Necrotic damage taken is increased. Stacking.

[Tainted Meridians] (affliction, poison): Cost of abilities is increased. Bleeding adds mana loss to blood loss. Drain attacks are more effective against target.

[Wages of Sin] (affliction, unholy): Deals ongoing necrotic damage. Stacking.

[Weight of Sin] (affliction, holy): Suffer transcendent damage when subjected to a holy boon, recovery or cleanse effect.

[Resistant] (boon, holy): Resistances are increased. Stacking.

[Ruination of the Blood] (affliction, poison): Ongoing necrotic damage. Stacking.

[Ruination of the Spirit] (affliction, curse): Ongoing necrotic damage. Stacking.

[Ruination of the Flesh] (affliction, disease): Ongoing necrotic damage. Stacking.

[Sanction] (affliction, holy): Healing on target is reduced. Cannot be cleansed while suffering **[Penance]**.

[Vulnerable] (affliction, unholy): Resistances are reduced. Stacking.

[Weakness of the Flesh] (affliction, magic): Negates immunities to disease and necrotic damage. Cannot be cleansed while the target suffers any disease.

ABOUT THE AUTHOR

Shirtaloon was working on a very boring academic paper when he realised that writing about an inter-dimensional kung fu wizard would be way more fun.

To discuss He Who Fights With Monsters and more, join Shirtaloon's Discord!

Made in United States
Troutdale, OR
10/31/2024